Publication of *The Complete Works of George Orwell* is a unique bibliographic event as well as a major step in Orwell scholarship. Meticulous textual research by Dr Peter Davison has revealed that all the current editions of Orwell have been mutilated to a greater or lesser extent. This authoritative edition incorporates in Volumes 10-20 all Orwell's known essays, poems, plays, letters, journalism, broadcasts, and diaries, and also letters by his wife, Eileen, and members of his family. In addition there are very many of the letters in newspapers and magazines of readers' reactions to Orwell's articles and reviews. Where the hands of others have intervened, Orwell's original intentions have been restored.

It Is What I Think (1947–48)

Eric Arthur Blair – better known as George Orwell – was born on 25 June 1903 in Bengal. He was educated at Eton and then served with the Indian Imperial Police in Burma. He lived in Paris for two years, and then returned to England where he worked as a private tutor, schoolteacher and bookshop assistant. He fought on the Republican side in the Spanish Civil War and was wounded in the throat. During the Second World War he served as Talks Producer for the Indian Service of the BBC and then joined *Tribune* as its literary editor. He died in London in January 1950.

Dr. Peter Davison is Professor of English and Media at De Montfort University, Leicester. He has written and edited fifteen books as well as the Facsimile Edition of the Manuscript of *Nineteen Eighty-Four* and the twenty volumes of Orwell's *Complete Works*. From 1992 to 1994 he was President of the Bibliographical Society, whose journal he edited for twelve years.

From 1961 Ian Angus was Deputy Librarian and Keeper of the Orwell Archive at University College, London, and from 1975 Librarian of King's College, London. With Sonia Orwell he co-edited the *Collected Essays, Journalism and Letters of George Orwell* (4 vols., 1986). Since early retirement in 1982 he has divided his time equally between assisting in the editing of this edition and growing olives in Italy.

Sheila Davison was a teacher until she retired, for some time teaching the deaf. She checked and proofread all twenty volumes of the complete edition and assisted with the research and indexing.

Down and Out in Paris and London
Burmese Days
A Clergyman's Daughter
Keep the Aspidistra Flying
The Road to Wigan Pier
Homage to Catalonia
Coming Up for Air
Animal Farm
Nineteen Eighty-Four
A Kind of Compulsion (1903-36)
Facing Unpleasant Facts (1937-39)
A Patriot After All (1940-41)
All Propaganda is Lies (1941-42)
Keeping Our Little Corner Clean (1942-43)
Two Wasted Years (1943)
I Have Tried to Tell the Truth (1943-44)
I Belong to the Left (1945)
Smothered Under Journalism (1946)
It is What I Think (1947-48)
Our Job is to Make Life Worth Living (1949-50)

Also by Peter Davison

Books: *Songs of the British Music Hall: A Critical Study; Popular Appeal in English Drama to 1850; Contemporary Drama and the Popular Dramatic Tradition; Hamlet: Text and Performance; Henry V: Masterguide; Othello: The Critical Debate; Orwell: A Literary Life*

Editions: Anonymous: *The Fair Maid of the Exchange* (with Arthur Brown); Shakespeare: *Richard II*; Shakespeare: *The Merchant of Venice*; Shakespeare: *1 Henry IV*; Shakespeare: *2 Henry IV*; Shakespeare: *The First Quarto of King Richard III*; Marston: *The Dutch Courtesan*; Facsimile of the Manuscript of *Nineteen Eighty-Four*; Sheridan: *A Casebook*; *The Book Encompassed: Studies in Twentieth-Century Bibliography*

Series: *Theatrum Redivivum* 17 Volumes (with James Binns); *Literary Taste, Culture, and Mass Communication* 14 Volumes (with Edward Shils and Rolf Meyersohn)

Academic Journals: *ALTA: University of Birmingham Review*, 1966-70; *The Library: Transactions of the Bibliographical Society*, 1971-82

It Is What I Think

1947–48

GEORGE ORWELL

Edited by Peter Davison
Assisted by Ian Angus and Sheila Davison

SECKER & WARBURG

———

LONDON

Revised and updated edition published by Secker & Warburg 2002

2 4 6 8 10 9 7 5 3 1

First published in Great Britain in 1998 by
Secker & Warburg
Random House, 20 Vauxhall Bridge Road,
London SW1V 2SA

Random House Australia (Pty) Limited
20 Alfred Street, Milsons Point, Sydney,
New South Wales 2061, Australia

Random House New Zealand Limited
18 Poland Road, Glenfield,
Auckland 10, New Zealand

Random House (Pty) Limited
Endulini, 5A Jubilee Road, Parktown 2193, South Africa

The Random House Group Limited Reg. No. 954009
www.randomhouse.co.uk

A CIP catalogue record for this book
is available from the British Library

ISBN 0 436 21007 X

Papers used by Random House are natural,
recyclable products made from wood grown in sustainable forests;
the manufacturing processes conform to the environmental
regulations of the country of origin

Typeset in Monophoto Bembo by
Deltatype Limited, Birkenhead, Merseyside
Printed and bound in Great Britain by
Mackays of Chatham PLC

CONTENTS

Titles may be modified and shortened.
Topics discussed in Orwell's column, 'As I Please', are listed in the
Cumulative Index in Volume XX.
Correspondence following Orwell's articles and reviews is not usually listed.

Contents

Contents

Contents

Contents

Contents

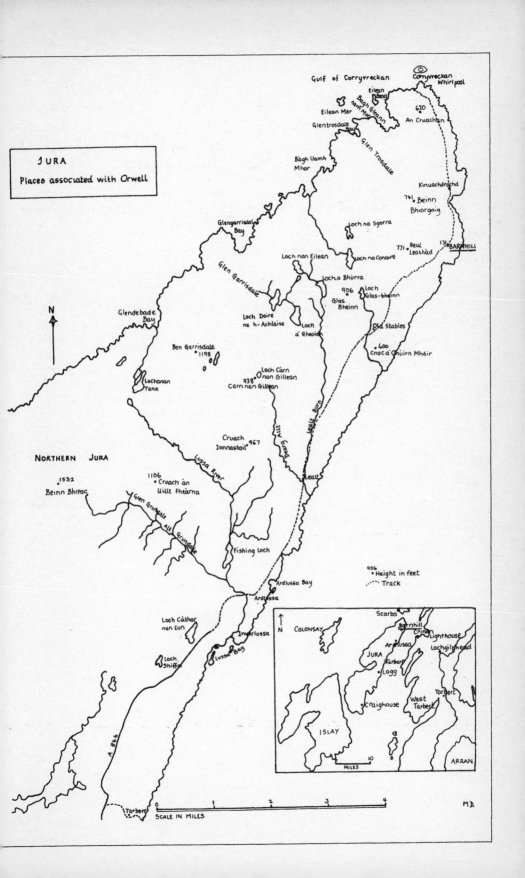

INTRODUCTION to VOLUME XIX

1947–1948: It is What I Think

Much of these years was taken up with Orwell's struggle to complete *Nineteen Eighty-Four* and his fight against illness. He spent the autumn and winter of 1946–47 in London. In that period he wrote 'Lear, Tolstoy and the Fool' (*3181*), and his last contribution to *Tribune*, his eightieth 'As I Please', published on 4 April 1947. He returned to Jura on 11 April 1947 to work on his last novel. He was often ill, and although he did not realise it, he would never return to his flat in Canonbury, London, again. In December 1947 he was admitted to Hairmyres Hospital, Glasgow, and left only at the end of July 1948. The rest of 1948 was spent at Jura where, by a supreme effort, and often in great pain, he managed to complete *Nineteen Eighty-Four*. He left Jura about the 2nd January 1949 and was admitted to Cranham Sanatorium in the Cotswolds; his remaining months were spent there and, later, at University College Hospital, London. Although he relinquished his leases of his cottage at Wallington (September 1947), and his Canonbury flat (December 1948), he lived to the end in the belief that he would continue to be able to write. Thus, he only *suspended* his series of 'As I Please'.

Orwell continued to work on 'Such, Such Were the Joys' (*3409*), even though he knew it could not, for fear of libel, be published in his lifetime, probably completing it about May 1948 when he was in hospital (see *3408* for identification of typewriters used and those involved in the typing). Among the essays he wrote were 'Toward European Unity' (*3244*), 'In Defence of Comrade Zilliacus' (*3254*), which was not published at the time, a Profile of Krishna Menon (with David Astor, *3309*), 'Marx and Russia' (*3346*), 'Writers and Leviathan' (*3364*), 'Britain's Left-Wing Press' (*3366*), 'George Gissing' (*3406*), and 'Britain's Struggle for Survival: The Labour Government after Three Years' (*3462*); most are printed here with Orwell's preparatory notes as adjacent items. He continued to review, though less frequently than in the past. In November 1947 a Ukrainian translation of *Animal Farm* was published for which Orwell wrote a special preface (*3198*). Unfortunately the collaboration of the US Military Government with the USSR led to most of those copies of *Animal Farm* being handed over to the Soviets so ensuring that they could not be read by those for whom they were intended in the Soviet Zone of Germany and points east.

On 17 January 1947, Orwell's adaptation of *Animal Farm* was broadcast in the BBC Third Programme directed by his friend, Rayner Heppenstall. The full script is given in *Collected Works*, VIII, showing changes made in the course of broadcasting. A summary is given at *3152*. The most interesting change was that prompted by Dwight Macdonald's letter of 5 December 1946 (*3128*). Orwell added a few lines of dialogue at a crucial moment in the novel but Heppenstall failed to see the point and cut them out (see *n. 4* to *3128* and VIII, 153, scenes 259–62). For Orwell's response to the broadcast, see *3163*. An extract from *The Road to Wigan Pier* was broadcast in Sweden on 11 September 1947 (*3270*), and the BBC Home Service broadcast 'Shooting an Elephant' on 12 October 1948 (*3472*).

In November 1948, the first volume of *British Pamphleteers*, for which Orwell wrote an introduction, was published (see editorial note, *3487*). He continued to take issue with James Burnham; his 'Burnham's View of the Contemporary World Struggle' was published in March 1947 (*3204*). A few months earlier he had told Philip Rahv that Burnham wouldn't like it: 'However, it is what I think' (XVIII, 232). This characteristic remained constant to the end.

This volume is rich in previously unpublished correspondence, some of which shows how he was pestered—almost hounded—to write for a left-wing journal, the New York *New Leader*, despite his being so ill. Some of Orwell's proposed corrections to *Homage to Catalonia*, which he sent to Yvonne Davet for the French translation, and which he would later send to Roger Senhouse for the English edition, are published in his letter in French to Mme Davet with an English translation. She arranged for these to be made (the translation appeared in 1955) but Senhouse ignored them and it was not until 1986 that Orwell's wishes could be carried out in English in *Complete Works, VI*. The volume includes Fredric Warburg's and David Farrer's reports on *Nineteen Eighty-Four* (*3505* and *3506*). Details are given of Orwell's successful attempts to get justice for those as diverse as Poles threatened with forcible return to Soviet rule, and a railwayman with thirty-nine years of service, sacked without a pension for picking up a few pence worth of coal from the track during an especially bitter winter. This was 'what I think' in practice.

Orwell's Second Literary Notebook is reproduced (*3515*); his third series of notes for his literary executor (*3323*); his Domestic Diary (arranged chronologically); and his sister Avril's briefer record kept from 27 December 1947 to 10 May 1948 whilst her brother was in hospital (*3319* and, as an appendix, *3514*). Orwell's Domestic Diary records, laconically, the near-disaster that struck Orwell and his family in the Corryvreckan whirlpool, north of Jura, on 19 August 1947, and a note explains the circumstances and the confusion over the newspaper reports. On p. xvii is a specially-drawn map of 'Orwell's Jura.'

A full General Introduction will be found in the preliminaries to Volume X

ACKNOWLEDGEMENTS and PROVENANCES

specific to Volume XIX

The editor wishes to express his gratitude to the following institutions and libraries, their trustees, curators, and staffs for their co-operation and valuable help, for making copies of Orwell material available, and for allowing it to be reproduced: BBC Written Archives Centre, Caversham; Yale Collection of American Literature, Beinecke Rare Books and Manuscript Library, Yale University; Henry W. and Albert A. Berg Collection, New York Public Library, Astor, Lenox, and Tilden Foundations; British Library, Department of Manuscripts (for the Orwell papers, Add. Mss 49384 and 73083) and the Evelyn Waugh papers; Penguin UK Archive, Bristol University Library; Arthur Koestler Archive, Special Collections, Edinburgh University Library; Secker & Warburg Archive, Reading University Library; Harry Ransom Humanities Research Center, University of Texas at Austin; Dwight Macdonald papers, Manuscripts and Archives, Yale University Library; and the Library of University College London for material in the Orwell Archive.

Gratitude is expressed to George Allen & Unwin Ltd, Victor Gollancz Ltd, Harcourt, Brace & Company, Penguin UK and Martin Secker & Warburg Ltd for making available their material relating to Orwell.

Thanks are due to Rosemary Davidson, Michael Kennard and G. T. Mandl for making available letters by Orwell or members of his family. I am also deeply indebted to those whose letters by Orwell or members of his family are available because they donated them or presented copies of them to the Orwell Archive; the Hon David Astor (Editor of *The Observer*), Frank Barber, Emilio Cecchi, Humphrey Dakin, Yvonne Davet, Mary and Tosco Fyvel, Celia Goodman, Harcourt Brace and Company, Helmut Klöse, Arthur Koestler and his Literary Executor, Robert L. Morris, Melvin Lasky, S. M. Levitas (Editor of *The New Leader* (New York)), Dwight Macdonald, Sally MacEwan, Michael Meyer, E. W. Orchard, William Phillips and Philip Rahv (Editors of *Partisan Review*), Anthony Powell, Brenda Salkeld, Ihor Ševčenko, Gleb Struve, Julian Symons and George Woodcock; also Rayner Heppenstall for an Orwell letter and Orwell's typescript of his dramatisation of *Animal Farm* for the BBC; and Herbert Read (through Howard Fink) and Vernon Richards for making available to the Orwell Archive copies of the papers of the Freedom Defence Committee.

I am grateful to the following publications for permission to reproduce material which first appeared in their pages: *Freedom*, *The London Magazine*, *The Manchester Evening News*, *The New Leader* (New York), *The New Yorker*, *The Observer*, *Partisan Review* and *Tribune*.

I would like to thank the following for granting me permission to use material whose copyright they own; the Hon David Astor to quote form his letter to Dr Dick; Bill Dunn to publish Avril Blair's Barnhill Diary and two letters by her; Yale University Library to quote from Dwight Macdonald's letters to Orwell; Ihor Ševčenko to quote from his letters to Orwell and the editor; James W. Williamson to publish his reminiscences of Orwell at Hairmyres Hospital; Farrar, Straus & Giroux, Inc. to quote from Edmund Wilson's review of *Dickens, Dali & Others* in *The New Yorker* and a letter by him to Orwell; and Ingeborg Woodcock to quote from George Woodcock's 'George Orwell, Nineteenth Century Liberal' and his 'London Letter' in *Politics*.

For their help and valuable information my thanks are due to the Hon David Astor, Guido Bonsaver, Livia Gollancz, Celia Goodman, Michael Kennard, Janetta Parladé, Ihor Ševčenko, Helen and Telfer Stokes, *The Times Literary Supplement*, James W. Williamson and Miranda Wood.

My thanks are also due to Amrai Ettlinger, Elizabeth Oliver, Janet Percival and Ian Willison for their translations.

A number of individual acknowledgements are made in foot and headnotes to those who have provided information in books or verbally that I have quoted or referred to.

The editor and publishers have made every effort to trace copyright holders of the material published in this volume, but in some cases this has not proved possible. The publishers therefore wish to apologise to the authors or copyright holders of any material which has been reproduced without permission and due acknowledgement.

PROVENANCES

The locations of letters and documents printed in this volume are indicated against their item numbers in the list given below. Where there are letters or documents at an item which come from more than one source, this is indicated, e.g. 3154 Berg, Bristol, OA.

However, letters and documents which are not listed below should be taken as being available for consultation in the Orwell Archive, University College London, either as originals or in the form of copies. Sonia Orwell gave all the Orwell papers then in her possession to the Orwell Archive at its foundation in 1960. Many friends, relations and associates of Orwell have given their Orwell letters or copies of them to the Orwell Archive. There were in Orwell's pamphlet collection that Sonia Orwell gave to the British Museum in 1950 some Orwell papers (now in the British Library. Department of Manuscripts, Add. Mss. 49384 and 73083) and copies of these, at her request, were given by the Director and Principal Librarian of the British Museum to the Orwell Archive in 1965. For simplicity's sake, the British Library Orwell papers are not indicated as such in the location list, but are regarded as being available for consultation in the form of copies in the Orwell Archive.

KEY TO LOCATIONS

A & U	George Allen & Unwin Ltd
BBC	BBC Written Archives Centre, Caversham
Beinecke	Yale Collection of American Literature, Beinecke Rare Book and Manuscript Library, Yale University
Berg	Henry W. and Albert A. Berg Collection, The New York Public Library, Astor, Lenox and Tilden Foundations
BL	Evelyn Waugh papers, Department of Manuscripts, British Library
Bristol	Penguin UK Archive, Bristol University Library
Davidson	Rosemary Davidson
Edinburgh	Arthur Koestler Archive, Special Collections, Edinburgh University Library
Kennard	Michael Kennard
Mandl	G. T. Mandl
OA	Orwell Archive (including the Freedom Defence Committee papers), University College London Library
Reading	Secker & Warburg Archive, Reading University Library
Texas	Harry Ransom Humanities Research Center, University of Texas at Austin
VG	Victor Gollancz Ltd
Yale	Dwight Macdonald papers, Manuscripts and Archives, Yale University Library

Acknowledgements and Provenances

3345 Beinecke
3350 Berg
3353A Davidson
3355 Texas
3358 Berg
3359 Yale
3362 Berg, Reading
3363 Berg
3368 Berg
3371 OA, Reading
3382 Berg
3386 Berg
3389 Berg
3390 Berg
3391 Berg
3392 Yale
3393 OA, Reading

3397 Berg
3398 Berg
3400 Berg
3401 BL
3402A Davidson
3404 Kennard
3405A Davidson
3412 Kennard
3413 Berg
3414 Berg
3415 Berg
3416A Davidson
3420 Berg
3422 Yale
3423 Berg
3424 BBC
3426 Reading

3427 Mandl
3429 Kennard
3433 Berg
3434 Beinecke
3437 Berg
3447 Berg
3456 Berg
3470 Berg
3472 BBC
3474 Berg
3476 Berg
3480 Berg
3481 Berg
3483 Reading
3491 Berg
3501 Berg
3503 Berg

Editorial Note

THE CONTENTS are, in the main, arranged in chronological order of Orwell's writing. Letters arising from his articles or reviews are usually grouped immediately after that item and Orwell's replies to those letters follow thereon. If there is a long delay between when it is known an article or essay was completed and its publication, it is printed at the date of completion. If items are printed much earlier in the chronological sequence than their date of publication, a cross-reference is given at the date of publication. All entries, whether written by Orwell or anyone else, including lengthy notes and cross-references, are given an item number. Because the printing of the edition has taken place over seven years, some letters came to light after the initial editing and the numbering of items had been completed. These items (or those that had in consequence to be repositioned) are given a letter after the number: e.g., *335A*. Some items included after printing and page-proofing had been completed are given in a final appendix to Volume XX and two (received by the editor in mid January 1997) in the Introduction to Volume XV. Numbers preceding item titles are in roman; when referred to in notes they are italicised.

The provenance of items is given in the preliminaries to each volume. Every item that requires explanation about its source or date, or about textual problems it may pose, is provided with such an explanation. Some articles and broadcasts exist in more than one version. The basis upon which they have been edited is explained and lists of variant readings provided. No Procrustean bed has been devised into which such items must be constrained; individual circumstances have been taken into account and editorial practice explained.

Although this is not what is called a 'diplomatic edition'—that is, one that represents the original precisely even in all its deformities to the point of reproducing a letter set upside down—the fundamental approach in presenting these texts has been to interfere with them as little as possible consistent with the removal of deformities and typographic errors. Orwell took great pains over the writing of his books: the facsimile edition of *Nineteen Eighty-Four*[1] shows that, but in order to meet the demands of broadcasting and publication schedules he often wrote fast and under great pressure. The speed with which he sometimes wrote meant that what he produced was not always what he would have wished to have published had he had time to revise. And, of course, as with any printing, errors can be introduced by those setting the type. It would be easy in places to surmise what Orwell would have done but I have only made changes where there would otherwise have been confusion. Obvious spelling mistakes, which could well be the compositor's or typist's (and the typist might be Orwell), have been corrected silently, but if there is any doubt, a footnote has drawn attention to the problem.

In brief, therefore, I have tried to present what Orwell wrote in his manuscripts and typescripts, not what I thought he should have written; and what he was represented as having written and not what I think should have been typed or printed on his behalf. This is not a 'warts and all' approach because gross errors are amended, significant changes noted, and textual complexities are discussed in preliminary notes. The aim is to bring Orwell, not the editor's version of Orwell, to the fore. Although textual issues are given due weight, an attempt has been made to produce an attractive, readable text.

The setting of this edition has been directly from xeroxes of original letters (if typed), typed copies of manuscript (prepared by one or other of the editors), surviving scripts for broadcasts, and xeroxes of essays, articles, and reviews as originally published (unless a headnote states otherwise). For *The Collected Essays, Journalism and Letters of George Orwell* a 1968 house style was adopted but for this edition, no attempt has been made to impose a late twentieth-century house style on the very different styles used by journals and editors of fifty to eighty years ago. Texts are therefore reproduced in the style given them in the journals from which they are reprinted. To 'correct' might well cause even more confusion as to what was and was not Orwell's: see below regarding paragraphing. Nevertheless, although it is not possible *to know*, one may sometimes hazard a guess at what underlies a printed text. Thus, I believe that most often when 'address' and 'aggression' are printed, Orwell typed or wrote 'adress' (especially until about the outbreak of World War II) and 'agression.' Although American spellings (such as 'Labor') have been retained in articles published in the United States, on very rare occasions, if I could be certain that a form of a word had been printed that Orwell would not have used—such as the American 'accommodations'—I have changed it to the form he would have used: 'accommodation'. Some variations, especially of proper names, have been accepted even if they look incongruous; so, 'Chiang Kai-Shek' as part of a book title but 'Chiang Kai-shek' throughout the text that follows.

Hyphenation presents tricky problems, especially when the first part of a word appears at the end of a line. Examples can be found in the originals of, for example, 'the middle-class,' 'the middle class', and 'the middleclass.' What should one do when a line ends with 'middle-'? Is it 'fore-deck' or 'foredeck'? If 'fore-' appears at the end of a line of the copy being reproduced, should the word be hyphenated or not? *OED* 1991 still hyphenates; Chambers in 1972 spelt it as one word. Where it would help (and it does not include every problem word), the ninth edition of F. Howard Collins, *Authors' & Printers' Dictionary*, Oxford University Press, 1946 (an edition appropriate to the mature Orwell) has been drawn upon. But Collins does not include fore-deck/foredeck. On a number of occasions Orwell's letters, or the text itself, is either obscure or wrong. In order to avoid the irritating repetition of *sic*, a small degree sign has been placed above the line at the doubtful point (°). It is hoped that this will be clear but inconspicuous. It is not usually repeated to mark a repetition of that characteristic in the same item. Orwell was sparing in his use of the question-mark in his letters; his practice has in the main been followed.

Paragraphing presents intractable problems. Orwell tended to write in long paragraphs. Indeed, it is possible to show from the use of many short paragraphs that News Review scripts so written are not by Orwell. The key example is News Review, 30, 11 July 1942 (*1267*), for which there is also external evidence that this is not by Orwell. This has twenty-one paragraphs as compared to eight in the script for the following week. It so happens that we know that Orwell was not at the BBC for two weeks before the 11 July nor on that day: he was on holiday, fishing at Callow End, Worcestershire (and on that day caught a single dace). But though paragraph length is helpful in such instances in identifying Orwell's work, that is not always so. It is of no use when considering his articles published in Paris in 1928–29 nor those he wrote for the *Manchester Evening News*. These tend to have extremely short paragraphs—sometimes paragraphs of only a line or two, splitting the sense illogically. A good example is the series of reviews published on 2 November 1944 (*2572*) where a two-line paragraph about Trollope's *The Small House at Allington* should clearly be part of the preceding four-line paragraph, both relating the books discussed to Barchester; see also *2463*, n. *2* and *2608*, n. *4*. There is no question but that this is the work of sub-editors. It would often be possible to make a reasonable stab at paragraphing more intelligently, but, as with verbal clarification, the result might be the more confusing as to what really was Orwell's work and what this editor's. It has been thought better to leave the house-styles as they are, even if it is plain that it is not Orwell's style, rather than pass off changes as if the edited concoction represented Orwell's work.

Usually it is fairly certain that titles of essays are Orwell's but it is not always possible to know whether titles of articles are his. Reviews were also frequently given titles. Orwell's own typescript for his review of Harold Laski's *Faith, Reason and Civilisation* (*2309*), which survived because rejected by the *Manchester Evening News*, has neither heading (other than the name of the author and title of the book being reviewed), nor sub-headings. That would seem to be his style. In nearly every case titles of reviews and groups of letters, and cross-heads inserted by sub-editors, have been cut out. Occasionally such a title is kept if it is an aid to clarity but it is never placed within quotation marks. Other than for his BBC broadcasts (where Orwell's authorship is clear unless stated otherwise), titles are placed within single quotation marks if it is fairly certain that they are Orwell's.

Telegrams and cables are printed in small capitals. Quite often articles and reviews have passages in capitals. These look unsightly and, in the main, they have been reduced to small capitals. The exceptions are where the typography makes a point, as in the sound of an explosion: BOOM! Orwell sometimes abbreviated words. He always wrote an ampersand for 'and' and there are various abbreviated forms for such words as 'about'. It is not always plain just what letters make up abbreviations (and this sometimes applies to his signatures) and these have regularly been spelt out with the exception of the ampersand for 'and'. This serves as a reminder that the original is handwritten. Orwell often shortened some words and abbreviations in his own way, e.g., Gov.t, Sup.ts (Superintendents), NB. and N.W (each with a single stop), and ie.; these forms have been retained. In order that the diaries should readily be apparent for what they are, they have been set in sloped roman (rather than italic, long passages of which can be tiring to the eye), with roman for textual variations. Square and half square brackets are used to differentiate sources for the diaries (see, for example, the headnote to War-Time Diary II, *1025*) and for what was written and actually broadcast (see, for example, Orwell's adaptation of Ignazio Silone's *The Fox*, *2270*). Particular usages are explained in headnotes to broadcasts etc., and before the first entries of diaries and notebooks.

Orwell usually dated his letters but there are exceptions and sometimes he (and Eileen) give only the day of the week. Where a date has to be guessed it is placed within square brackets and a justification for the dating is given. If Orwell simply signs a letter, the name he used is given without comment. If he signs over a typed version of his name, or initials a copy of a letter, what he signed or initialled is given over the typed version. There has been some slight regularisation of his initialling of letters. If he omitted the final stop after 'E. A. B', no stop is added (and, as here, editorial punctuation *follows* the final quotation mark instead of being inside it). Sometimes Orwell placed the stops midway up the letters: 'E·A·B'; this has been regularised to 'E. A. B'.

Wherever changes are made in a text that can be deemed to be even slightly significant the alteration is either placed within square brackets (for example, an obviously missing word) or the alteration is footnoted. Attention should be drawn to one particular category of change. Orwell had a remarkably good memory. He quoted not only poetry but prose from memory. Mulk Raj Anand has said that, at the BBC, Orwell could, and would, quote lengthy passages from the Book of Common Prayer.[2] As so often with people with this gift, the quotation is not always exact. If what Orwell argues depends precisely upon what he is quoting, the quotation is not corrected if it is inaccurate but a footnote gives the correct reading. If his argument does not depend upon the words actually quoted, the quotation is corrected and a footnote records that.

So far as possible, I have endeavoured to footnote everything that might puzzle a reader at the risk of annoying some readers by seeming to annotate too readily and too frequently what is known to them. I have, therefore, tried to identify all references to people, events, books, and institutions. However, I have not been so presumptuous as to attempt to rewrite the history of this century and, in the main, have relied upon a small number of easily accessible histories. Thus, for the Spanish Civil War I have referred in the main to *The Spanish Civil War* by Hugh Thomas; and for the Second World War, to Winston Churchill's and Liddell Hart's histories. The former has useful and conveniently available documents, and the latter was by a historian with whom Orwell corresponded. They were both his contemporaries and he reviewed the work of both men. These have been checked for factual information from more recent sources, one by Continental historians deliberately chosen as an aid to objectivity in an edition that will have world-wide circulation. It is assumed that readers with a particular interest in World War II will draw on their own knowledge and sources and the annotation is relatively light in providing such background information. Similarly, biographical details are, paradoxically, relatively modest for people as well known as T. S. Eliot and E. M. Forster, but far fuller for those who are significant to Orwell but less well known and about whom information is harder to track down, for example, George(s) Kopp, Joseph Czapski, and Victor Serge. It is tricky judging how often biographical and explicatory information should be reproduced. I have assumed most people will not want more than one volume at a time before them and so have repeated myself (often in shortened form with cross-references to fuller notes) more, perhaps, than is strictly necessary. Whilst I would claim that I have made every attempt not to mislead, it is important that historical and biographical information be checked if a detail is significant to a scholar's argument. History, as Orwell was quick to show, is not a matter of simple, indisputable fact. In annotating I have tried not to be contentious nor to direct the reader unfairly, but annotation cannot be wholly impartial.[3]

Each opening is dated. These dates, though drawn from the printed matter, are not necessarily those of the text reproduced on the page on which a date appears. The dates, known or calculated of letters, articles, broadcasts, diaries, etc., will correspond with the running-head date, but, for example, when correspondence (which may have run on for several weeks) springs from an article and follows directly on that article, the date of the article is continued *within square brackets*. Sometimes an item is printed out of chronological order (the reason for which is always given) and the running-head date will again be set within square brackets. Wherever practicable, the running-head date is that of the first item of the opening; if an opening has no date, the last date of a preceding opening is carried forward. Articles published in journals dated by month are considered for the purpose to be published on the first of the month. Inevitably some dates are more specific than is wholly justified, e.g., that for 'British Cookery' (*1954*). However, it is hoped that if readers always treat dates within square brackets with circumspection, the dates will give a clear indication of 'where they are' in Orwell's life.

Great efforts have been made to ensure the accuracy of these volumes. The three editors and Roberta Leighton (in New York) have read and re-read them a total of six times but it is obvious that errors will, as it used to be put so charmingly in the sixteenth century, have 'escaped in the printing.' I offer one plea for understanding. Much of the copy-preparation and proof-reading has been of type set during and after the war when newsprint was in short supply and mere literary articles would be set in microscopic-sized type. Many of the BBC scripts were blown up from microfilm and extremely difficult to puzzle out. When one proof-reads against xeroxes of dim printing on creased paper, the possibilities for error are increased and the eyes so run with tears that vision is impaired. We hope we have corrected most errors, but we know we shall not have caught them all.

P.D.

A slightly fuller version of this note is printed in the preliminaries to Volume X.

1. *George Orwell, Nineteen Eighty-Four: The Facsimile of the Extant Manuscript*, edited by Peter Davison, London, New York, and Weston, Mass., 1984.
2. Information from W. J. West, 22 July 1994.
3. The problems of presenting acceptable history even for the professional historian are well outlined by Norman Davies in *Europe: A History*, Oxford University Press, Oxford and New York, 1996, 2–7. I am obviously attempting nothing so grand, yet even 'simple' historical explication is not always quite so simple.

REFERENCES

References to Orwell's books are to the editions in Vols I to IX of the *Complete Works* (edited P. Davison, published by Secker & Warburg, 1986–87). The pagination is almost always identical with that in the Penguin Twentieth-Century Classics edition, 1989–90. The volumes are numbered in chronological order and references are by volume number (in roman), page, and, if necessary (after a diagonal) line, so: II.37/5 means line five of page 37 of *Burmese Days*. Secker editions have Textual Notes and apparatus. Penguin editions have A Note on the Text; these are not identical with the Secker Textual Notes and Penguin editions do not list variants. There is a 32-page introduction to the Secker *Down and Out in Paris and London*. Items in Volumes X to XX are numbered individually; they (and their notes) are referred to by italicised numerals, e.g. *2736* and *2736 n. 3*.

REFERENCE WORKS: These are the principal reference works frequently consulted:

The Oxford English Dictionary, second edition (Compact Version, Oxford 1991): (*OED*).

The Dictionary of National Biography (Oxford 1885–1900, with supplements and *The Twentieth-Century*, 1901–): (*DNB*).

Dictionary of American Biography (New York, 1946, with supplements).

Dictionnaire biographique du mouvement ouvrier français, publié sous la direction de Jean Maitron, 4ᵉ ptie 1914–1939: De la Première à la Seconde Guerre mondiale (t. 16–43, Paris, Les Éditions Ouvrières, 1981–93).

Who's Who; Who Was Who; Who's Who in the Theatre; Who Was Who in Literature 1906–1934 (2 vols., Detroit, 1979); *Who Was Who Among English and European Authors 1931–1949* (3 vols., Detroit 1978); *Contemporary Authors* and its *Cumulative Index* (Detroit, 1993); *Who's Who In Filmland*, edited and compiled by Langford Reed and Hetty Spiers (1928); Roy Busby, *British Music Hall: An Illustrated Who's Who from 1850 to the Present Day* (London and New Hampshire, USA, 1976).

The Feminist Companion to Literature in English, edited by Virginia Blain, Patricia Clements, and Isobel Grundy, Batsford 1990.

The New Cambridge Bibliography of English Literature, edited by George Watson and Ian Willison, 4 vols., Cambridge, 1974–79.

Martin Seymour-Smith, *Guide to Modern World Literature*, 3rd revised edition, Macmillan 1985.

The War Papers, co-ordinating editor, Richard Widdows, 75 Parts, Marshall Cavendish, 1976–78.

The following are referred to by abbreviations:

CEJL: *The Collected Essays, Journalism and Letters of George Orwell*, ed. Sonia Orwell

References

and Ian Angus, 4 volumes, Secker & Warburg 1968; Penguin Books, 1970; references are by volume and page number of the more conveniently available Penguin edition.

Crick: Bernard Crick, *George Orwell: A Life*, 1980; 3rd edition, Penguin Books, Harmondsworth, 1992 edition. References are to the 1992 edition.

Eric & Us: Jacintha Buddicom, *Eric and Us: A Remembrance of George Orwell*, Leslie Frewin, 1974.

Lewis: Peter Lewis, *George Orwell: The Road to 1984*, Heinemann, 1981.

Liddell Hart: B. H. Liddell Hart, *History of the Second World War*, Cassell, 1970; 8th Printing, Pan, 1983.

Orwell Remembered: Audrey Coppard and Bernard Crick, eds., *Orwell Remembered*, Ariel Books, BBC, 1984.

Remembering Orwell: Stephen Wadhams, *Remembering Orwell*, Penguin Books Canada, Markham, Ontario; Penguin Books, Harmondsworth, 1984.

Shelden: Michael Shelden, *Orwell: The Authorised Biography*, Heinemann, London; Harper Collins, New York; 1991. The American pagination differs from that of the English edition; both are given in references, the English first.

Stansky and Abrahams I: Peter Stansky and William Abrahams, *The Unknown Orwell*, Constable 1972; edition referred to here, Granada, St Albans, 1981.

Stansky and Abrahams II: Peter Stansky and William Abrahams, *The Transformation*, Constable 1979; edition referred to here, Granada, St Albans, 1981.

Thomas: Hugh Thomas, *The Spanish Civil War*, 3rd edition; Hamish Hamilton and Penguin Books, Harmondsworth, 1977.

Thompson: John Thompson, *Orwell's London*, Fourth Estate 1984.

West: *Broadcasts*: W. J. West, *Orwell: The War Broadcasts*, Duckworth/BBC 1985.

West: *Commentaries*: W. J. West, *Orwell: The War Commentaries*, Duckworth/BBC, 1985.

Willison: I. R. Willison, 'George Orwell: Some Materials for a Bibliography,' Librarianship Diploma Thesis, University College London, 1953. A copy is held by the Orwell Archive, UCL.

2194 Days of War: *2194 Days of War*, compiled by Cesare Salmaggi and Alfredo Pallavisini, translated by Hugh Young, Arnoldo Mondadori, Milan 1977; rev. edn Galley Press, Leicester 1988.

A Bibliography of works, books, memoirs and essays found helpful in preparing Volumes X to XX of *The Complete Works of George Orwell* will be found in the preliminaries to Volume X.

CHRONOLOGY

In the main, Orwell's publications, except books, are not listed

25 June 1903 Eric Arthur Blair born in Motihari, Bengal, India.

---

14 January 1947 Orwell's radio adaptation of *Animal Farm* broadcast by BBC Third Programme.

4 April 1947 Eightieth, and last, 'As I Please', published in *Tribune*.

11 April–20 Dec 1947 At Barnhill, Jura, writing *Nineteen Eighty-Four* and often ill.

31 May 1947 Sends Fredric Warburg version of 'Such, Such Were the Joys'; final version probably completed about May 1948.

August 1947 *The English People* published by Collins in the series, *Britain in Pictures*; as *Diet engelske Folk*, Copenhagen, February, 1948; *Die Engländer*, Braunschweig, December 1948.

September 1947 Gives up lease of The Stores, Wallington.

31 October 1947 So ill has to work in bed.

7 Nov 1947 First draft of *Nineteen Eighty-Four* completed.

20 Dec 1947–28 Jul 1948 Patient in Hairmyres Hospital, East Kilbride (near Glasgow), with tuberculosis of the left lung.

March 1948 Writes 'Writers and Leviathan' for *Politics and Letters*, No. 4, Summer 1948; also published in *New Leader*, New York, 19 June 1948.

May 1948 Starts second draft of *Nineteen Eighty-Four*. Writes 'Britain's Left-Wing Press' for *The Progressive*, and 'George Gissing' for *Politics and Letters*.

13 May 1948 *Coming Up for Air* published as first volume in Secker's Uniform Edition.

28 Jul 1948–*c*. Jan 1949 At Barnhill, Jura.

Early Nov 1948 Finishes writing *Nineteen Eighty-Four*.

15 Nov 1948 *British Pamphleteers*, Vol 1 published by Alan Wingate, with Introduction by Orwell (written spring 1947).

4 Dec 1948 Completes typing fair copy of *Nineteen Eighty-Four* and posts copies to Moore and Warburg. Has serious relapse.

December 1948 Gives up lease of flat in Canonbury Square, Islington.

24 Dec 1948 Makes final entry in his last Domestic Diary.

c. 2 Jan 1949 Leaves Jura.

---

21 January 1950 Orwell dies of pulmonary tuberculosis, aged 46.

THE COMPLETE WORKS OF
GEORGE ORWELL · NINETEEN

IT IS WHAT I THINK

1947

3144. Freedom Defence Committee Appeal

1947

Issues 5 and 6 of the *Freedom Defence Committee Bulletin*, July–August 1947 and Spring 1948, gives lists of those who responded to the appeal for funds in 1947. Some 200 people or groups contributed sums varying between 2s. 8d and £10.10s (in the main, around £1). There were five who contributed more: one, £50; one, £25; two £20, and Orwell, £30 (£20 in the first six months of the year and £10 in the second six months). The £50 was contributed by V. G., almost certainly Victor Gollancz; the £25 came from E. M. F., Cambridge, and must be E. M. Forster. The other two sets of initials, C. I., Stockport, and M. B., Tyldesley, have not been identified. See also *2783*.

3145. Orwell at Jura

January 1947

Orwell arrived at Barnhill, Jura, on 2 January 1947. He should have arrived on 31 December 1946, but he missed the boat and had to spend two nights in Glasgow; see Domestic Diary, *3147, 4.1.47*. He had returned to Canonbury Square, London, by 9 January.

3146. 'As I Please,' 68

Tribune, 3 January 1947[1]

Nearly a quarter of a century ago I was travelling on a liner to Burma. Though not a big ship, it was a comfortable and even a luxurious one, and when one was not asleep or playing deck games one usually seemed to be eating. The meals were of that stupendous kind that steamship companies used to vie with one another in producing, and in between times there were snacks such as apples, ices, biscuits and cups of soup, lest anyone should find himself fainting from hunger. Moreover, the bars opened at ten in the morning, and, since we were at sea, alcohol was relatively cheap.

The ships of this line were mostly manned by Indians, but apart from the officers and the stewards they carried four European quartermasters whose job was to take the wheel. One of these quartermasters, though I suppose he was only aged forty or so, was one of those old sailors on whose back you almost expect to see barnacles growing. He was a short, powerful, rather ape-like man, with enormous forearms covered by a mat of golden hair. A blond moustache which might have belonged to Charlemagne completely hid his mouth. I was only twenty years old[2] and very conscious of my parasitic status as a mere passenger, and I looked up to the quartermasters, especially the fair-haired one, as godlike beings on a par with the officers. It would not have occurred to me to speak to one of them without being spoken to first.

One day, for some reason, I came up from lunch early. The deck was empty except for the fair-haired quartermaster, who was scurrying like a rat along the side of the deck-houses, with something partially concealed between his monstrous hands. I had just time to see what it was before he shot past me and vanished into a doorway. It was a pie dish containing a half-eaten baked custard pudding.

At one glance I took in the situation—indeed, the man's air of guilt made it unmistakable. The pudding was a left-over from one of the passengers' tables. It had been illicitly given to him by a steward, and he was carrying it off to the seamen's quarters to devour it at leisure. Across more than twenty years I can still faintly feel the shock of astonishment that I felt at that moment. It took me some time to see the incident in all its bearings: but do I seem to exaggerate when I say that this sudden revelation of the gap between function and reward—the revelation that a highly-skilled craftsman, who might literally hold all our lives in his hands, was glad to steal scraps of food from our table—taught me more than I could have learned from half a dozen Socialist pamphlets?

A news item to the effect that Yugoslavia is now engaged on a purge of writers and artists led me to look once again at the reports of the recent literary purge in the U.S.S.R., when Zoschenko, Akhmatova[3] and others were expelled from the Writers' Union.

In England this kind of thing is not happening to us as yet, so that we can view it with a certain detachment, and, curiously enough, as I look again at the accounts of what happened, I feel somewhat more sorry for the persecutors than for their victims. Chief among the persecutors is Andrei Zhdanov, considered by some to be Stalin's probable successor.[4] Zhdanov, though he has conducted literary purges before, is a full-time politician with—to judge from his speeches—about as much knowledge of literature as I have of aerodynamics. He does not give the impression of being, according to his own lights, a wicked or dishonest man. He is truly shocked by the defection of certain Soviet writers, which appears to him as an incomprehensible piece of treachery, like a military mutiny in the middle of a battle. The purpose of literature is to glorify the Soviet Union; surely that must be obvious to everyone? But instead of carrying out their plain duty, these misguided writers keep straying away from the paths of propaganda, producing non-political works, and even, in the case of Zoschenko, allowing a satirical note to creep into their writings. It is all very painful and bewildering. It is as though you set a man to work in an excellent, up-to-date, air-conditioned factory, gave him high wages, short hours, good canteens and playing-grounds, a comfortable flat, a nursery-school for his children, all-round social insurance and music while you work—only to find the ungrateful fellow throwing spanners into the machinery on his very first day.

What makes the whole thing somewhat pathetic is the general admission—an honest admission, seeing that Soviet publicists are not in the habit of decrying their own country—that Russian literature as a whole is not what it ought to be. Since the U.S.S.R. represents the highest existing form of civilisation, it is obvious that it ought to lead the world in literature as in everything else. "Surely," says Zhdanov, "our new Socialist system, embodying all that is best in the history of human civilisation and culture, is capable of creating the most advanced literature, which will leave far behind the best creations of olden times." *Izvestia* (as quoted by the New York paper, *Politics*), goes further: "Our culture stands on an immeasurably higher level than bourgeois culture. . . . Is it not clear that our culture has the right not to act as pupil and imitator but, on the contrary, to teach others the general human morals?" And yet somehow the expected thing never happens. Directives are issued, resolutions are passed unanimously, recalcitrant writers are silenced: and yet for some reason a vigorous and original literature, unmistakably superior to that of capitalist countries, fails to emerge.

All this has happened before, and more than once. Freedom of expression has had its ups and downs in the U.S.S.R., but the general tendency has been towards tighter censorship. The thing that politicians are seemingly unable to understand is that you cannot produce a vigorous literature by terrorising everyone into conformity. A writer's inventive faculties will not work unless he is allowed to say approximately what he feels. You can destroy spontaneity and produce a literature which is orthodox but feeble, or you can let people say what they choose and take the risk that some of them will utter heresies. There is no way out of that dilemma so long as books have to be written by individuals.

That is why, in a way, I feel sorrier for the persecutors than for the victims. It is probable that Zoschenko and the others at least have the satisfaction of understanding what is happening to them: the politicians who harry them are merely attempting the impossible. For Zhdanov and his kind to say, "The Soviet Union can exist without literature," would be reasonable. But that is just what they can't say. They don't know what literature is, but they know that it is important, that it has prestige value, and that it is necessary for propaganda purposes, and they would like to encourage it, if only they knew how. So they continue with their purges and directives, like a fish bashing its nose against the wall of an aquarium again and again, too dim-witted to realise that glass and water are not the same thing.

From *The Thoughts of the Emperor Marcus Aurelius*:

In the morning when thou risest unwillingly, let this thought be present—I am rising to the work of a human being. Why then am I dissatisfied if I am going to do the things for which I exist and for which I was brought into the world? Or have I been made for this, to lie in the bed-clothes and keep myself warm?—But this is more pleasant—Dost thou exist then to take thy pleasure, and not at all for action or exertion? Dost thou not see the little plants, the little birds, the ants, the spiders, the bees working together to put in order their several parts of the universe? And art thou unwilling to do the work of a human being, and dost thou not make haste to do that which is according to thy nature?

It is a good plan to print this well-known exhortation in large letters and hang it on the wall opposite your bed. And if that fails, as I am told it sometimes does, another good plan is to buy the loudest alarm clock you can get and place it in such a position that you have to get out of bed and go round several pieces of furniture in order to silence it.

1. Following Orwell's death, on Saturday, 21 January 1950, this example of 'As I Please' was chosen to be reprinted in tribute to him in *Tribune* for 27 January 1950.
2. He was only nineteen, though his passport showed he was twenty; see *3103, headnote.*
3. Anna Akhmatova (1888–1966) was a poet whose works were condemned in 1920 and again in 1946. She was rehabilitated in the 1950s and officially recognised at her death. Mikhail Zoschenko (1895–1957 or 1958), Soviet satirist, particularly in short-story and sketch form, who in the 1930s and 1940s suffered severely from critics of the socialist-realist persuasion. He was vilified for such satirical anecdotes and reminiscences as those intended to be published in instalments under the title 'Before Sunrise' in the journal *Oktyabr* in 1943. Their publication was suspended after the second had been published. He was criticised for, among other things, malicious distortions of popular speech. His expulsion from the Union of Soviet Writers in 1946 virtually brought to an end his creative-writing career.
4. Andrei Aleksandrovich Zhdanov (1896–1948), Secretary of the Central Committee in charge of ideology and a close associate of Stalin, was an advocate of socialist realism in the 1930s. He was largely responsible for initiating a resolution adopted by the Central Committee of the Communist Party on 14 August 1946 directed against the literary journals *Zvezda* and *Leningrad* and the writings of Mikhail Zoschenko, Anna Akhmatova, and Boris Pasternak in particular. As a result, Zoschenko, Akhmatova, and others were expelled from the Union of Soviet Writers. This oppressive cultural policy was given the name 'Zhdanovshchina.' Zhdanov did not succeed Stalin; Stalin survived him.

3147. Domestic Diary

<u>4.1.47.</u> *Have been here since 2.1.47. Was to arrive two days earlier, but missed boat on 30th & had to hang about for 2 days in Glasgow. Rough crossing from Tarbert, & was very sick. Did not take tablets until on the point of being sick—on the return journey shall take them before embarking. It took the boat about half an hour to tie up at Craighouse pier, as with the sea that was running she could not get in close. After tying up she could only keep in position for a minute or two, in spite of the cables, & the passengers had only just time to nip across the gangway.*

The day I arrived here was a beautiful sunny day, like April. Yesterday raining most of the time & the wind so violent that it was difficult to stay on one's feet. Today somewhat better—cold & overcast, but not much wind.

All the small plants I put in—pansies, lupins, cheddar pinks & cabbages— have completely disappeared, evidently owing to rabbits. The rabbits had also grubbed up & eaten the few turnips that were still in the ground, but had not touched the carrots. What is worse is that they have destroyed most of the strawberries. A few are all right, but most of them have disappeared— however, if the crowns are still there they may revive in the spring. The wire round the flower bed was not pegged down & the rabbits have got under it. Am setting traps before leaving. Round the vegetable patch it is sunk a few inches & there was no sign that they had got under it, so they must have climbed over (3 ft. wire), which they are said to be able to do.

Today planted 1 doz fruit trees, 1 doz red currants, 1 doz black currants, 1 doz gooseberries, 1 doz rhubarb, 1 doz roses (6 ramblers & climbers). Shall plant raspberries tomorrow.

On the verso page facing the entry for 4 January 1947, Orwell drew a plan to show the layout of his fruit trees; see p. 10. To the left of the house on the plan: two morello cherry trees. Ten trees are shown on the plan below the outline of the house, five in each of two columns. Against the first tree of the left-hand column is a question mark; the three below are Allington Pippin, Ribston Pippin, and Lord Derby; the fifth is unnamed. The right-hand column lists Golden Spire, Ellison's Orange, one unnamed, James Grieve, and Lady Sudeley.

5.1.47. *Much wind in night. This morning wind still strong, & sea rough. Sunny but cold.*
Planted raspberries (2 dozen, not very good plants).
Set 2 traps
Tulips fairly well up.
NB. That when returning we have in store:
About 30 galls paraffin (about 8 weeks supply).
2 cylinders Calor Gas (about 9 weeks supply).
2 tons coal (at Ardlussa) (about 2 months supply).

This completed the entries to Volume III of Orwell's Domestic Diary. Volume IV begins 12 April 1947. At the end of the Domestic Diary III notebook are Orwell's notes for his essay 'Politics and the English Language;' see 2816.

3148. To Leonard Moore

9 January 1947   Typewritten

27B Canonbury Square,
Islington, N.1.

Dear Moore,
Many thanks for several letters. I got them all together today, as I have been away in Scotland for 10 days and it was impossible to forward letters.
I note that you have paid in another £3433–14–11 on behalf of further royalties on A.F. Have Harrison & Hill been informed about this? I would like them to do the income tax business as before, ie. let me know what sum must be laid aside for income tax purposes. I don't know whether Harrison is

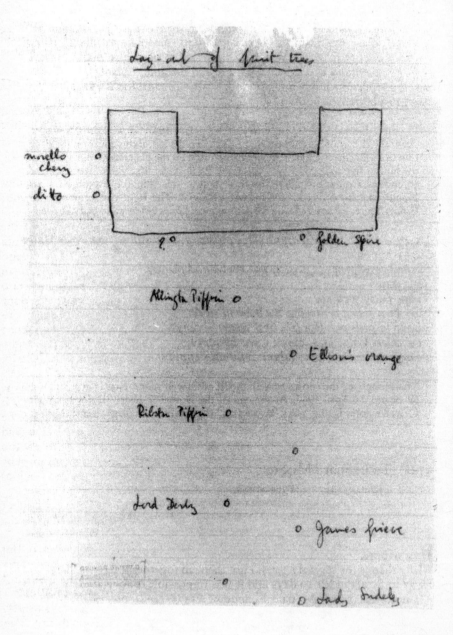

back from the US—at any rate I haven't heard so. I understood from him that it was possible to pay only US income tax on sums which one left in that country, *if* one made oneself into a limited liability company for that purpose. I did not wish to leave *all* American earnings there, but I thought I might do so with certain sums, eg. anything I get from the New Yorker, because I might have occasion to go to the US some time. In that case it would be useful to have a few hundred dollars lying there, and one might as well pay as little tax as possible.

As to the Dutch publication of A.F.[1] I enclose a rather alarming letter from the publishers, which you might perhaps deal with. I am sure I don't know what arrangements we made about serialisation, but if anything irregular is happening, do please try and put a stop to it. As to the paper which is serialising it being "reactionary," I don't know that we can help that. Obviously a book of that type is liable to be made use of by Conservatives, Catholics etc.

As to a Serbian translation of A.F.[2] I think it is [a] waste of time to attempt doing it in Jugoslavia, but did that Mr Amakumovic communicate with you? He came here recently and saw me, and was then going to see Warburg and find out whether it would be possible to make arrangements about the printing of a Serbian edition in this country. He said that if the book could actually be produced—the difficulty would chiefly be paper, and also composition in a foreign language, though he says they can use Roman script—he thought that about 5000 copies might be smuggled into Jugoslavia. I *believe* also that a clandestine Ukrainian translation is being done in the American Zone in Germany.[3] I had some correspondence about it with a Ukrainian D.P., who said that so many of his countrymen were marooned there that the book could have quite a wide circulation. He seemed to know English very well. I don't know whether this translation has actually appeared, but I gathered from him that the work of translating it had been done. Of course I can't officially know anything about that, nor about the Serbian translation, and the less said about either of them the better. But if it ever became possible to make such translations legally, they would not be prejudiced by a previous clandestine appearance, because the latter would only involve a few thousand copies at most. It is important not to say too much about this, because I suppose all printing in the American zone must be controlled by AMG,[4] and I don't suppose they would encourage a book of this type. For that reason I didn't say anything to you about this earlier.

I presume the printing of 15 pages from "Burmese Days" wouldn't prejudice any later re-issue of the book in the US, so could you tell the University of Chicago to go ahead.[5]

I am arranging about copies of the script of the radio version of A.F. But it's possible that I shall only be able to secure one copy. I haven't a copy of my own script and shall have to send you one of the BBC's° ones—which, I suppose, will as usual be very different from the version I sent to them.[6]

Yours sincerely
[Signed] Eric Blair
Eric Blair

1. *Animal Farm* was published in the Netherlands as *De Boerderij der Dieren: een sprockje voor groote menschen* by Uigeverij Phoenix Gebr. E & M Cohen, Bussum, October 1947. It was translated by Anthony Ross and fully illustrated by Karel Thole 'in mock imitation of those in modern children's books (for example, *The House at Pooh Corner*)' (Willison).
2. A Serbian translation was not made in Orwell's lifetime.
3. The Ukrainian translation of *Animal Farm*, *Kolhosp Tvaryn*, was published by Prometheus, Münich, November 1947, and printed in Belgium. The translator is named as Ivan Cherniatync'kyī (Ihor Szewczenko). It was distributed through a displaced-persons organisation in Germany. In Orwell's 'Notes on Translations' he stated that 'MB authorities seized about half of the edition of 5000 and handed them over to the Soviet repatriation commission (1947) but the others said to have been distributed successfully' (see *3728*). For some details of the problems of publishing the Ukrainian translation and the request for a special preface, see correspondence with Ihor Szewczenko, *3188*; for the English version of that preface, see *3198*.
4. Allied Military Government [of Germany].
5. In the University of Chicago's *University Observer*, Vol. 1, No. 2, Summer 1947, Orwell's essay on James Burnham (originally published in *Polemic*, May 1946; see *2989*) was reprinted. There is nothing from *Burmese Days* in that issue or the earlier one, apparently the only two published, so presumably this was a proposal for the inclusion of an extract from the novel to be included in an anthology which the University of Chicago Press wished to publish.
6. A portion of Orwell's typescript has survived. It is, verbally, almost identical with the BBC script as originally prepared, but it does include one or two short passages that were cut from the latter and pasted over so that the lines originally written by Orwell were lost. See *3152*.

3149. To Helmut Klöse

10 January 1947   Typewritten

27B Canonbury Square,
Islington, N.1.

Dear Klose,°
Did I not write to you forwarding Gollancz's suggestions?[1] He did reply to my letter, and suggested several sources, one of which was, I think, Chatham House,[2] but I now cannot find his letter and don't remember at all well what he said in it. At need we shall have to make further enquiries, but at any rate don't let your friend get the impression that Gollancz took no interest.

Yours,
[Signed] Geo. Orwell
George Orwell

1. If Orwell forwarded Gollancz's suggestions, that letter has not been traced.
2. Chatham House, St James's Square, London, housed the Royal Institute of International Affairs.

3150. To Gleb Struve

    10 January 1947   Typewritten

27B Canonbury Square,
Islington, N. 1.

Dear Struve,
I have just received a letter from your wife, who told me that she had forwarded my previous letter to you but thought it would be better if I wrote to you again in America.

What I wanted to know was whether that proposed English edition of Zamyatin's "We" has come to anything. Because if it hasn't, and if we could get hold of a copy of the American edition or even of the French edition, I think that Warburg might be interested. Mrs. Struve said that you had been in communication with Zamyatin's widow, and that she had sent you some other books of his. The one that you refer to in your "History of Soviet Literature", the satire on England,[1] always sounded to me the sort of book that ought to be translated.

I hope to see you again when you get back.

Yours sincerely,
[Signed] Geo. Orwell
George Orwell

1. *Islanders* and *The Fisher of Men* are both satires of English life. The former was written by Zamyatin in 1917 whilst he was working in England and the latter the following year on his return to Russia. Both were published in Russian in 1918. An English translation by Sophie Fuller and Julian Sacchi was published in 1984 and as a Flamingo (Fontana) paperback the following year.

3151. To Yvonne Davet

    13 January 1947   Typewritten

27B Canonbury Square,
Islington, N. 1.

Chère Madame Davet,
Je n'ai reçu votre lettre qu'il-y-a deux jours, parce que je viens de passer quinze jours[1] en Ecosse.

Quant à CRITICAL ESSAYS, j'ai une idée qu'un autre éditeur français est déjà en train de faire une traduction. Je n'en suis pas sûr, mais je vais demander de mon agent. Quant à HOMAGE TO CATALONIA, il y a quelques fautes typographiques etc. qu'il faut corriger et dont je vous donne une liste ci-dessous:—

Pp. 3–4. "Tipping was forbidden . . . a lift boy." Il serait peut-être meilleur de supprimer[2] cette phrase, vu qu'en réalité les pourboires avaient étés supprimés depuis le temps de Primo de Rivera.

P. 7. (et peut-être ailleurs.) "Puron." Doit être "Poron."

P. 29.[3] "but occasionally . . . (red-yellow-purple.)" Je ne suis pas complètement sûr que les Fascistes se servaient du drapeau republicain, mais je crois qu'ils l'employaient quelquefois avec un swastika surimposé. Il y a aussi une allusion au même sujet aux pages 193–4. C'est une question qu'on pourrait peut-être vérifier.

P. 156. "26 mm." Doit être ".26 inch."

P. 159 (deux fois.) "Roldan." Doit être "Roldan Cortada."

P. 272. "Wallowed." Doit être "walloped."

P. 298. "El colonel." Doit être "el coronel."

En addition j'ai déjà fait suggestion qu'il serait meilleur de soulever deux chapitres et les mettre à la fin du livre, en forme d'appendice. Ces deux chapitres sont V et XI. Ils traitent de la politique intérieure de la révolution espagnole et il me semble que le lecteur ordinaire les trouverait ennuyeux. Mais au même temps ils ont un valeur historique, surtout le chapitre XI, et il serait dommage de les supprimer. En écrivant le livre j'ai tâché de concentrer mes réflections politiques dans ces deux chapitres, et on les peut mettre à la fin sans interrompre le récit.[4]

Il me semble aussi que le livre a besoin d'une introduction écrite par quelqu'un qui comprend bien les affaires espagnoles.

Je resterai à Londres jusqu'à Avril, et puis nous allons passer l'été en Ecosse. Au moment je suis assez occupé avec le journalisme, mais en février ou mars j'espère retourner au roman que j'ai commencé le dernier année. J'espère le finir avant la fin de 1947, mais ça est le meilleur que je peux promettre. Je demanderai de mon agent ce qu'il a fait avec CRITICAL ESSAYS—c'est à dire, si il l'a déjà offert à un éditeur français—et je vous signalerai sa reponse.

Très amicalement

[Signed] Geo. Orwell

George Orwell

Translation

I only received your letter two days ago, because I have just spent a fortnight[1] in Scotland.

As for *Critical Essays*, I have the feeling that another French publisher is already having a translation done. I'm not sure, but I'll ask my agent. As for *Homage to Catalonia*, there are a few typographical errors etc. that need correcting. Here is a list of them.

Pp. 3–4. "Tipping was forbidden . . . a lift boy." It would probably be better to take out[2] this sentence, as in actual fact tipping had been forbidden since the time of Primo de Rivera.

P. 7. (and perhaps elsewhere.) "Puron." Should be "Poron."

P. 29.[3] "but occasionally . . . (red-yellow-purple.)" I'm not quite sure whether the Fascists used the Republican flag, but I think they sometimes used it with a swastika superimposed on it. There is also an allusion to the same subject on pages 193–4. That's something that could perhaps be checked.

P. 156. "26 mm." Should be ".26 inch."

P. 159 (twice.) "Roldan." Should be "Roldan Cortada."
P. 272. "Wallowed." Should be "walloped."
P. 298. "El colonel." Should be "el coronel."
Besides this, I've already suggested that it would be better to take out two chapters and put them at the end of the book in the form of an appendix. These are chapters V and XI. They deal with the internal politics of the Spanish revolution and I feel the ordinary reader would find them tedious. But at the same time they do have historical value, especially chapter XI, and it would be a pity to cut them out altogether. In writing the book I tried to concentrate my political remarks in these two chapters, and they can go at the end without interrupting the narrative.[4]

I also think that the book needs an introduction written by someone with a good understanding of Spanish affairs.

I am staying in London till April, then we shall spend the summer in Scotland. At the moment I'm fairly busy with journalism, but in February or March I hope to come back to the novel I started last year. I hope to finish it before the end of 1947, but that's the best I can promise. I'll ask my agent what he did with *Critical Essays*—that is, whether he has already offered it to a French publisher—and I'll tell you what he says.

1. There is no conflict between the 'ten days' in the letter to Moore, 9 January, and 'quinze jours' here. Both are generalised periods; the equivalent to 'fortnight' in French is 'quinze jours.'
2. Orwell typed 'soulever' (to lift, to revolt), crossed it through, and wrote in the margin, 'supprimer.' Orwell's typewriter did not have accents, and he added them later. One or two were missed, and these (as usually in this edition) have been added. Two spelling errors, 'espagnolles' (twice) and 'étée,' have been corrected.
3. In the margin below 'supprimer' are written a number of page references in a hand other than Orwell's. These are preceded by a word that appears to be 'dactyl': that is, an instruction to the dactylographe (typist). Opposite this line is written 'p. 31'; opposite, and linked by a line to 193–4, is written 'p. 204'; opposite p. 156 is written 'p. 164'; and opposite p. 272 is written '286.'
4. For some account of these alterations and others requested by Orwell, see Textual Note to *Homage to Catalonia*, *CW*, VI, 251–61.

3152. Radio Adaptation of *Animal Farm*

14 January 1947

Orwell's own adaptation of *Animal Farm* was broadcast by the BBC Third Programme on 14 January 1947; it was repeated live the following evening, and a recording of the first broadcast was transmitted on 2 February 1947. Orwell's script, with production amendments and a short editorial introduction, is reproduced as Appendix III to *CW*, VIII.

It was thought that the typescript Orwell had submitted to the BBC (see his letter of 9 January 1947 to Leonard Moore, *3148*) had not survived, but thirty-three pages, erroneously marked 'Part of Adaptation by Peter Duval Smith, transmitted 3/3/1952' have been identified by Guido Bonsaver as part of the version submitted to the BBC. The editor is grateful to Mr. Bonsaver for drawing this to his attention. This typescript is held in the Orwell Archive, University College London (G.15899). The surviving pages are 29–46, 50–54, and 56–65: scenes 281–456, end of 475 to 503, and the latter part of 506 to 561. This numbering is derived from the script as prepared for production by the BBC; the original typescript submitted was not numbered.

Despite the fears Orwell expressed to Moore that the BBC's production script would be very different from the version he sent them, the dialogue, and even many of the directions, are almost the same in both versions. As would be expected, what Orwell submitted was modified in the course of production and all those changes are shown in the version reproduced in *CW*, VIII. The chief differences between what Orwell submitted and what was typed up as a production script by the BBC (based on amendments written into Orwell's script, almost certainly by Rayner Heppenstall, the producer) are as follows.

Orwell's script has been worked over to clarify which of several undifferentiated voices would speak which lines—thus, for 'A Pig,' 'The Pig,' or 'Voices,' Heppenstall specified 'Pig 1,' or 'Pig 2', etc. Directions have been further developed and effects have been indicated, and these, and all speeches, numbered. (These numbers, used also in *CW*, VIII, are given for reference here, but it should be understood that they do not appear in the script submitted by Orwell.) The most important differences are a few single lines or words cut from the script he submitted (by scoring through); two typing errors, one of which, though not its cause, is noted in *CW*, VIII; and short passages which, it was suggested in the introduction to the version printed in *CW*, VIII, had been pasted over in the BBC script. These can now be recovered. There are some insignificant typing errors in the typescript submitted by Orwell which the BBC production script silently corrects (e.g., 'riles' is corrected to 'tiles' in 397); these are not noted here.

Orwell's adaptation was shortened considerably in the course of production. Of the 2,200 lines of the script as typed by the BBC, some 490 lines were cut. (See *CW*, VIII, 119–20 for full details.) It can be seen from the typescript submitted to the BBC that Orwell originally wrote a very much longer version. The script has been typed on at least two machines. These were not the ones used for correspondence about this time (and that which he had used for typing the first section of *Nineteen Eighty-Four* reproduced in the Facsimile edition). These machines have a different 'j' from that which appears in correspondence about this time and they do not feature the slightly offset dot over the main body of the 'i' to be found in the script for *Animal Farm*. Thirty-one of the surviving pages are typed on one or possibly two machines of the same make; these are from the final version of Orwell's adaptation. Two pages, typed in a larger fount, were orginally numbered 73 and 74, but these numbers have been x-ed out and page numbers in the new sequence, 58 and 59, have been typed on a machine of the kind which produced the majority of the surviving pages. Three more of the surviving pages, all typed in the smaller fount (though not necessarily on the same machines), have also been renumbered: 56 has become 45; 57 has become 45; and a renumbered page 46 appears to have originally been 60. the '6' and '0' are incorrectly aligned (the '0' is higher than the '6'). Precisely the same misalignment is found in the regularly numbered page 60 and is probably the result of a less-than-professional typist operating the key shift before striking the o/O key. It rather looks as if, in order to get the script to Heppenstall in some haste, more than one person typed up the fair copy and that, when he could, Orwell incorporated pages from an earlier draft. However, there can be no doubt that these surviving pages are from the text which Orwell submitted to the BBC.

Below, in three groups, are listed differences in dialogue between the text Orwell submitted and that typed as the production script upon which the broadcast was based. Changes in speech headings (that is, the subdivision and identification of undifferentiated speeches) and directions are not listed. TS = Orwell's version submitted to the BBC.

1. Passages pasted over in production script
Some sections of the text were obliterated by pasting new copy over them (see *CW*, VIII, 119). These can now be recovered:
348: Before 'Even Boxer was vaguely troubled' Orwell originally had 'The animals were taken aback. Some of them might have protested if they could have thought of the right arguments.' See footnote to *CW*, VIII, 160.
445 and 445a: Where the BBC script has Napoleon says, in a 'terrible voice,' 'Has any other animal anything to confess?' and the Narrator begins, 'Three hens came forward . . .', TS has the Narrator say: 'The dogs promptly tore out the throats of the four pigs, and in a terrible voice Napoleon demanded whether any other animal had anything to confess. / At this three hens came forward. . . '. The line 'They, too, were immediately slaughtered. Then . . .' which precedes 'a goose came forward and confessed . . .' in TS was pasted over in the BBC script and 'a' was capitalised.
Where the BBC script has 'Two sheep confessed . . .' TS had 'Then two sheep confessed. . . .'
At the end of 445a, after 'the smell of blood,' which concludes the production script version, TS had 'the smell of blood, which had been unknown there since the expulsion of Jones. / When it was all over, the remaining animals, except the pigs and the dogs, crept away in a body, frightened and miserable. They did not know which to think more dreadful—the treachery of the animals who had leagued themselves with Snowball, or the cruel retribution they had just witnessed.' See footnotes to *CW*, VIII, 173.

2. Omitted in error by BBC typist
495: At the end of this speech, as found in the BBC script, TS goes on, 'Those were his very last words—"Napoleon is always right." ' The last three words are repeated immediately below one another in TS, so the BBC copy-typist's eyes have almost certainly skipped and caused her to omit this final sentence.
507: 'It may happen in the lifetime . . .' is given correctly in TS as 'It may not happen in the lifetime. . . .' The omission of 'not' is almost certainly a typing error; 'not' appears in the novel, and see first footnote, *CW*, VIII, 185.

3. Passages scored through in typescript submitted to BBC
This is probably Heppenstall's work, but it is just possible that one or two omissions (such as 395 and the first of those in 397) were made by Orwell.
318: In TS, 318–36 were typed as a single 'speech' with the speech-heading 'VOICES.' This, presumably, Heppenstall divided among the characters available. It was probably not until this stage of the production that it was known how many actors and actresses would be engaged. The 'speech' began with 'Look! Dogs! Dogs! Huge dogs!', which was scored through in TS and thus not copied by the BBC copy-typist.
336: 'Look out!' was 'But look out!' in TS.
395: After 'The animals were tired but happy,' TS has 'They had had a hard year, and so much of their time had been spent in carting loads of stones that' and 'some' begins the next sentence as 'Some.'
397: After 'Towards morning' TS has 'there was a tremendous crash that woke all the animals simultaneously.' After the 'Sound of masonry falling' TS has the

Narrator say, 'All the animals rushed out of their stalls together. And—'
Between 414 and 415: TS has 'NARRATOR: The animals were stupefied. This was a wickedness far outdoing Snowball's destruction of the windmill. But—'.
422: For 'I remember' TS has 'I do remember'.
431: After 'to Napoleon's feet,' TS has 'The tumult died down, and.'
438: After Pig 4's 'And I,' TS has another pig repeat 'And I.'
513: After 513, TS has 'NARRATOR: The animals all rushed into the yard in a body. And—.'
523: For 'The sheep kept this up for several minutes,' TS has 'The sheep kept up their bleating of "Four legs good, two legs *better*" for several minutes.'

According to Programmes as Broadcast, the 'orchestra' (so described) which played the music specially composed by Anthony Hopkins comprised one flute doubling piccolo, one trumpet and percussion. Hopkins himself played tubular bells for ten seconds. The singing was by sixteen members of the BBC Variety Chorus.

3153. 'As I Please,' 69

Tribune, 17 January 1947

The *Daily Herald* for January 1, 1947, has a headline MEN WHO SPOKE FOR HITLER HERE, and underneath this a photograph of two Indians who are declared to be Brijlal Mukerjee and Anjit Singh, and are described as having come "from Berlin." The news column below the photograph goes on to say that "four Indians who might have been shot as traitors" are staying at a London hotel, and further describes the group of Indians who broadcast over the German radio during the war as "collaborators." It is worth looking a bit more closely at these various statements.

To begin with, there are at least two errors of fact, one of them a very serious one. Anjit Singh did not broadcast on the Nazi radio, but only from Italian stations, while the man described as "Brijlal Mukerjee" is an Indian who has been in England throughout the war and is well known to myself and many other people in London.[1] But these inaccuracies are really the symptom of an attitude of mind which comes out more clearly in the phraseology of the report.

What right have we to describe the Indians who broadcast on the German radio as "collaborators"? They were citizens of an occupied country, hitting back at the occupying power in the way that seemed to them best. I am not suggesting that the way they chose was the right one. Even from the narrow point of view which would assume that Indian independence is the only cause that matters, I think they were gravely wrong, because if the Axis had won the war—and their efforts must have aided the Axis to some extent—India would merely have had a new and worse master. But the line they took was one that could perfectly well be taken in good faith, and cannot with fairness or even with accuracy be termed "collaboration." The word "collaboration" is associated with people like Quisling and Laval. It implies, first of all, treachery to one's own country, secondly, full co-operation with the conqueror, and thirdly, ideological agreement, or at least partial agreement. But how does this apply to the Indians who sided with the Axis? They were not being traitors to their own country—on the contrary, they were working for its independence, as they believed—and they recognised no obligation to Britain. Nor did they co-operate in the same manner as Quisling, etc. The Germans allowed them a separate broadcasting unit on which they said what they liked and followed, in many cases, a political line quite different from the Axis one. In my opinion they were mistaken and mischievous, but in moral attitude, and probably in the effects of what they did, they were quite different from ordinary renegades.

Meanwhile one has to consider the effect of this kind of thing in India. Rightly or wrongly, these men will be welcomed as heroes when they get home, and the fact that British newspapers insult them will not go unnoticed. Nor will the slovenly handling of the photographs. The caption "Brijlal Mukerjee" appears under the face of a totally different person. No doubt the photograph was taken at the reception which the repatriated Indians were given by their fellow-countrymen in London, and the photographer snapped the wrong man by mistake. But suppose the person in question had been William Joyce. In that case, don't you think the *Daily Herald* would have taken good care that it *was* photographing William Joyce and not somebody else? But since it's only an Indian, a mistake of this kind doesn't matter—so runs the unspoken thought. And this happens not in the *Daily Graphic*, but in Britain's sole Labour newspaper.

I hope everyone who can get access to a copy will take at least a glance at Victor Gollancz's recently published book, *In Darkest Germany* (Gollancz, 8/6). It is not a literary book, but a piece of brilliant journalism intended to shock the public of this country into some kind of consciousness of the hunger, disease, chaos and lunatic mismanagement prevailing in the British zone. This business of making people *conscious* of what is happening outside their own small circle is one of the major problems of our time, and a new literary technique will have to be evolved to meet it. Considering that the people of this country are not having a very comfortable time, you can't, perhaps, blame them for being somewhat callous about suffering elsewhere, but the remarkable thing is the extent to which they manage to remain unaware of it. Tales of starvation, ruined cities, concentration camps, mass deportations, homeless refugees, persecuted Jews—all this is received with a sort of incurious surprise, as though such things had never been heard of before but at the same time were not particularly interesting. The now-familiar photographs of skeleton-like children make very little impression. As time goes on and the horrors pile up, the mind seems to secrete a sort of self-protecting ignorance which needs a harder and harder shock to pierce it, just as the body will become immunised to a drug and require bigger and bigger doses.

Half of Victor Gollancz's book consists of photographs, and he has taken the wise precaution of including himself in a good many of them. This at least proves that the photographs are genuine and cuts out the routine charge that they have been obtained from an agency and are "all propaganda." But I think the best device in the book, after innumerable descriptions of people living on "biscuit soup," potatoes and cabbage, skim milk and ersatz coffee, was to include some menus of dinners in the messes provided for the Control Commission. Mr. Gollancz says that he slipped a menu card into his pocket whenever he could do so unobserved, and he prints half a dozen of them. Here is the first on the list:

Consommé in cups

———

Fried Soles in Butter
Fresh potatoes

———

Dutch Steak
Mashed Potatoes
Cauliflower

———

Raspberry Cream

———

Cheese

———

Coffee.[2]

These accounts of starvation in Europe seem to link up with a paragraph, headed "This Week's Hint for Dog-lovers," which I cut out of the *Evening Standard* just before Christmas:

> Your dog may also have that "after Christmas hangover" feeling if you have been indulging him with too many titbits. Many owners like to give their pets "a taste of everything," regardless of the fact that many of the items of Christmas fare are unsuitable for dogs.
>
> No permanent harm may be done, but if the dog seems dull, the tongue loses colour and the breath becomes offensive, a dose of castor oil is indicated.
>
> Twelve hours rest from food, followed by a light diet for a few days, usually effects a speedy cure—and from eight to twelve grains of carbonate of bismuth may be given three times a day. The dog should be encouraged to drink barley water rather than plain water.

Signed by a Fellow of the Zoological Society.

Looking through what I have written above, I notice that I have used the phrase "a totally different person." For the first time it occurs to me what a stupid expression this is. As though there could be such a thing as a partially different person! I shall try to cut this phrase (and also "a very different person" and "a different person altogether") out of my vocabulary from now onwards.

But there are other words and phrases which obviously deserve to go on the scrapheap, but which continue to be used because there seems to be no convenient substitute. An example is the word "certain." We say, for instance, "After a certain age one's hair turns grey," or "There will probably be a certain amount of snow in February." In all such sentences, "certain" means *uncertain*. Why do we have to use this word in two opposite meanings? And yet, unless one pedantically says "after an uncertain age," etc., there appears to be no other word which will exactly cover the required meaning.

1. For some details and examples of Axis propaganda directed to India, see W. J. West, *Orwell: The War Commentaries*, Appendix, 220–39, and *Orwell: The War Broadcasts*, Appendix C, 'The principles of Axis and Allied propaganda,' 289–93. Orwell included a propaganda talk by Subhas Chandra Bose (1897–1945), who led the Indian National Army (supported by the Japanese), in *Talking to India*, November 1943, 157–61. For Subhas Chandra Bose and Ras Bihari Bose, see *1119* and *1119, n. 5* and *1081, n. 4* respectively.
2. A letter to *Tribune* from Tom Agar, 7 February 1947, commented on *In Darkest Germany* and Orwell's article. It was fashionable, he said, inside and outside Parliament, to 'slam at the Control Commission without ever giving credit where it is due.' People were always delighted to hear the worst and nebulous generalisations became accepted as facts. The menu quoted was not typical. He had met Gollancz in Hamburg when he was staying at the mess for senior officers of the Food and Agriculture branch, one of the best messes in Germany; 'I could have shown him officers' messes where the food and accommodation was° very bad indeed.' There were 'hundreds of psychological misfits occupying controlling posts in the Control Commission but there were many who were conscientious.' He thought the political branch was doing particularly good work, and 'its officers from top to bottom are Socialist in outlook. Indeed, this is the reason for its success.' Even 'the best-intentioned delegation or visitor simply cannot give a complete picture of the difficulties, whilst too many people are apt to forget that we are not a law unto ourselves. There are three other powers with which to contend. . . .'

3154. To Leonard Moore

17 January 1947   Typewritten

27B Canonbury Square,
Islington, N.1.

Dear Moore,
Many thanks for your letter of the 15th.[1] Yes, a Penguin edition of "Burmese Days" will do perfectly well for the uniform edition, as the Penguin version was taken from the American edition which was the right one.

Do you think that Lane's[2] would give us another copy of "Down and Out"? They must have one, and the book doesn't seem to be procurable any other way. As for "Coming up° for Air", this is the one that Warburg especially wants because he himself has not read it. I thought that my sister had a copy, but it turns out that she has not. As it was never in a cheap edition it will be a very difficult book to get hold of, but I am going to get Simmonds to advertise for it.

I enclose herewith four copies of the script of the radio version of "Animal Farm". This was the script as I wrote it, but I need not say that it was very much altered before it got on to the air. In particular, it was cut down considerably as it was too long. However, if you succeed in selling it anywhere I suppose they can do their own cutting.

Yours sincerely,
[Signed] Geo. Orwell
George Orwell

1. Moore's letter to Orwell has not been traced, but on the same day he wrote to Mr. A. S. B. Glover, of the Editorial Department of Penguin Books, in reply to Glover's (lost) letter to him of 18 December. Penguin had only a small stock left of *Burmese Days*, and Moore suggested that unless Penguin intended reprinting, rights should revert to Orwell. Glover replied on 24 January saying that Penguin Books had about 500 copies in stock and they would allow the rights to revert provided they could sell these books. Moore acknowledged Glover's letter on 29 January and accepted this arrangement. Moore also wrote to Warburg on 15 January explaining that Penguin Books had about 500 copies of the paperback edition in stock; he assumed that Warburg would not object to Penguin selling off those copies 'any more than Penguin Books would object to that volume appearing in the uniform set. The one does not affect the other in any way.' For the relationship of the U.S., Gollancz, and Penguin editions of *Burmese Days*, see *CW*, II, Textual Note, 302–22.
2. Presumably Allen Lane, director and progenitor of Penguin Books.

3155. To Fredric Warburg

17 January 1947   Typewritten

27B Canonbury Square,
Islington, N.1.

Dear Fred,
Thanks so much for your letter.[1] It is very awkward about copies of these books. I made sure that I had a copy of "Coming Up for Air" at my sister's flat, but when we got there there doesn't appear to be one. I know that Moore sent off his last copy for the French translation, and it is most unlikely that Gollancz has one. I think the only thing to do will be to try an advertisement. I am going to get Simmonds of Fleet Street to insert an advertisement in the "Clique", and I suppose we shall get a copy that way. "Down and Out" and "Burmese Days" should be more easily procurable because of having been in the Penguins. I am writing to Moore to ask if he can get Penguin editions of them.

I have not yet paid you for those shoes, and I can't now remember what it was. Could you just let me know and I will send you a cheque. I also owed your Miss Bullock° something for that typing she did for me.[2]

Yours,
[Signed] Geo. Orwell
George Orwell

1. On 16 January 1947, Fredric Warburg wrote to Orwell to say that Secker & Warburg was anxious 'to get on here with the negotiation of contracts for BURMESE DAYS, DOWN AND OUT IN LONDON AND PARIS° and COMING UP FOR AIR.' Specimen copies of all three were needed urgently, but especially of the last named. He asked Orwell 'to make a big effort to get them to us as soon as possible.'

2. The letter has been annotated in Warburg's office: '*I think I can borrow a copy of this from Kensington Public Library. Would that be any good to you? PM.' 'PM' was Miss Murtough, whom Warburg asked on 20 January to obtain a copy so that he could read the book. On the same day he wrote to Orwell telling him he was obtaining a copy in this way and that the shoes had cost £4.12.6. Orwell's account would be debited for the typing Miss Plummer—not Miss Bullock—had done (the radio script of *Animal Farm*; see *3133*). Warburg's letter was typed by Miss Plummer.

3156. To and from Konni Zilliacus

17, 24, 31 January and 7 February 1947

Konni Zilliacus belatedly read Orwell's London Letter in *Partisan Review* for Summer 1946; see *2990*. He wrote to *Tribune* to complain about Orwell's reference to him, and Orwell responded. Their letters were published on 17, 24, 31 January and 7 February 1947. They are reproduced following *2990*.

3157. Central Office of Information to Secker & Warburg

23 January 1947

On 23 January 1947, Katherine Clutton, Copyright Section, Publications Division of the Central Office of Information, wrote to Fredric Warburg asking for his comments on a proposal for the publication of *Animal Farm* 'in a cheap English edition in Hungary.' He advised her the following day to write to Leonard Moore. No further correspondence has been traced, and there does not seem to have been a Hungarian edition published in English or Hungarian in Orwell's lifetime. Ian Willison records that an English version of *Animal Farm* was broadcast by the European Service of the BBC in 1948–49; he was not able to find a script.

3158. 'As I Please,' 70

Tribune, 24 January 1947

Recently I was listening to a conversation between two small business-men in a Scottish hotel.[1] One of them, an alert-looking, well-dressed man of about forty-five, was something to do with the Federation of Master Builders. The other, a good deal older, with white hair and a broad Scottish accent, was some kind of wholesale tradesman. He said grace before his meals, a thing I had not seen anyone do for many a year. They belonged, I should say, in the £2,000-a-year and the £1,000-a-year income groups respectively.[2]

We were sitting round a rather inadequate peat fire, and the conversation started off with the coal shortage. There was no coal, it appeared, because the British miners refused to dig it out, but on the other hand it was important not to let Poles work in the pits because this would lead to unemployment. There was severe unemployment in Scotland already. The older man then remarked with quiet satisfaction that he was very glad—"varra glad indeed"—that Labour had won the general election. Any government that had to clean up after the war was in for a bad time, and as a result of five years of rationing, housing shortage, unofficial strikes and so forth, the general public would see through the promises of the Socialists and vote Conservative next time.

They began talking about the housing problem, and almost immediately they were back to the congenial subject of the Poles. The younger man had just sold his flat in Edinburgh at a good profit and was trying to buy a house. He was willing to pay £2,700. The other was trying to sell his house for £1,500 and buy a smaller one. But it seemed that it was impossible to buy houses or flats nowadays. The Poles were buying them all up, and "where they get the money from is a mystery." The Poles were also invading the medical profession. They even had their own medical school in Edinburgh or Glasgow (I forget which) and were turning out doctors in great numbers while "our lads" found it impossible to buy practices. Didn't everyone know that Britain had more doctors than it could use? Let the Poles go back to their own country. There were too many people in this country already. What was needed was emigration.

The younger man remarked that he belonged to several business and civic associations, and that on all of them he made a point of putting forward resolutions that the Poles should be sent back to their own country. The older one added that the Poles were "very degraded in their morals." They were responsible for much of the immorality that was prevalent nowadays. "Their ways are not our ways," he concluded piously. It was not mentioned that the Poles pushed their way to the head of queues, wore bright-coloured clothes and displayed cowardice during air raids, but if I had put forward a suggestion to this effect I am sure it would have been accepted.

One cannot, of course, do very much about this kind of thing. It is the contemporary equivalent of anti-semitism. By 1947, people of the kind I am describing would have caught up with the fact that anti-semitism is discreditable, and so the scapegoat is sought elsewhere. But the race hatred and mass delusions which are part of the pattern of our time might be somewhat less bad in their effects if they were not reinforced by ignorance. If in the years before the war, for instance, the facts about the persecution of Jews in Germany had been better known, the subjective popular feeling against Jews would probably not have been less, but the actual treatment of Jewish refugees might have been better. The refusal to allow refugees in significant numbers into this country would have been branded as disgraceful. The average man would still have felt a grudge against the refugees, but in practice more lives would have been saved.

So also with the Poles. The thing that most depressed me in the abovementioned conversation was the recurrent phrase, "let them go back to their own country." If I had said to those two business-men, "Most of these people have no country to go back to," they would have gaped. Not one of the relevant facts would have been known to them. They would never have heard of the various things that have happened to Poland since 1939, any more than they would have known that the over-population of Britain is a fallacy or that local unemployment can co-exist with a general shortage of labour. I think it is a mistake to give such people the excuse of ignorance. You can't actually change their feelings, but you can make them understand what they are saying when they demand that homeless refugees shall be driven from our shores, and the knowledge may make them a little less actively malignant.[3]

The other week, in the *Spectator*, Mr. Harold Nicolson[4] was consoling himself as best he could for having reached the age of sixty. As he perceived, the only positive satisfaction in growing older is that after a certain point you can begin boasting of having seen things that no one will ever have the chance to see again. It set me wondering what boasts I could make myself, at forty-four, or nearly. Mr. Nicolson had seen the Czar, surrounded by his bodyguard of enormous Cossacks, blessing the Neva. I never saw that, but I did see Marie Lloyd[5] already almost a legendary figure, and I saw Little Tich[6]—who, I think, did not die till about 1928, but who must have retired at about the same time as Marie Lloyd—and I have seen a whole string of crowned heads and other celebrities from Edward VII onwards. But on only two occasions did I feel, at the time, that I was seeing something significant, and on one of those occasions it was the circumstances and not the person concerned that made me feel this.

One of these celebrities was Pétain.[7] It was at Foch's[8] funeral in 1929. Pétain's personal prestige in France was very great. He was honoured as the defender of Verdun, and the phrase "They shall not pass" was popularly supposed to have been coined by him. He was given a place to himself in the procession, with a gap of several yards in front of and behind him. As he stalked past—a tall, lean, very erect figure, though he must have been seventy years old or thereabouts, with great sweeping white moustaches like the wings of a gull—a whisper of "*Voilà Pétain!*" went rippling through the vast crowd. His appearance impressed me so much that I dimly felt, in spite of his considerable age, that he might still have some kind of distinguished future ahead of him.

The other celebrity was Queen Mary.[9] One day I was walking past Windsor Castle when a sort of electric shock seemed to go through the street. People were taking their hats off, soldiers springing to attention. And then, clattering over the cobbles, there came a huge, plum-coloured open carriage drawn by four horses with postillions. I believe it was the first and last time in my life that I have seen a postillion. On the rear seat, with his back to the carriage, another groom sat stiffly upright, with his arms folded. The groom who sat at the back used to be called the tiger. I hardly noticed the Queen, my eyes were fixed on that strange, archaic figure at the back, immobile as a waxwork, with his white breeches that looked as though he had been poured into them, and the cockade on his top hat. Even at that date (1920 or thereabouts) it gave me a wonderful feeling of looking backwards through a window into the nineteenth century.

Some scraps of literary intelligence:—

A few weeks ago I quoted an Indian proverb in this column,[10] and erroneously said that it had been translated by a friend of mine. Actually the verse I quoted comes from Kipling. This illustrates something I have pointed out elsewhere—that Kipling is one of those writers whom one quotes unconsciously.

The *Partisan Review*, one of the best of the American highbrow magazines—rather like a synthesis of *Horizon* and *Polemic*—is to be published in London from February onwards.

Zamyatin's novel *We*, about which I wrote an article in *Tribune* a year or so ago,[11] is to be reissued in this country. A fresh translation is being made from the Russian. Look out for this book.

1. Presumably this conversation took place on either 30 or 31 December 1946, when Orwell 'had to hang about for 2 days in Glasgow'; see *3147*.
2. The average wage in 1946 was about £350 a year.
3. Orwell took considerable interest in the fate of Poles living in Scotland; see 'As I Please,' 73, 14 February 1947, *3171*. This may have stemmed from his time as a war correspondent in Germany in 1945. It was probably prompted by the debate on this issue when he was in Jura in 1946. For example, from 30 August to 11 October 1946 a fairly vituperative correspondence attacking the presence of Poles in Scotland was published by *John O'Groat Journal*. This, on the Scottish side, sought to require their return to Poland; the semi-official responses from a Polish organisation (much more temperately expressed) pointed out the part played by Poles in the Allied forces and stressed the danger they faced if they returned home to a Soviet-dominated society. Orwell seemed to have played no part in this correspondence but amongst his papers at his death was a long letter from John M. Sutherland of Bonar Bridge, Sutherland, dated 16 September 1946. This opens 'Dear Sir' and refers to 'your letter' in the *Journal* of 13 September. The only letter on this subject in that issue was from Z. Nagórski of the Polish Press Agency, 43 Charlotte Square, Edinburgh, which set out the three chief reasons for hostility to the Poles: a minority were Communists; extreme Protestants in Scotland feared an influx of Roman Catholic Poles; and 'Scots of all parties but mainly nationalists . . . see in Polish resettlement an attempt by England to pay her debt to Poland at the expense of Scotland . . . in accord with the historic English tradition of paying her debts out of someone else's pocket.' He believed 'few Scots have any real hostility to the Poles' and if they were at loggerheads it would serve English interests by keeping their minds off more serious problems. Two sections of the letter have been marked. These are particularly anti-English and are quoted and discussed by Orwell in 'As I Please,' 73, 14 February 1947, *3171*. It is clear that this letter was sent to Orwell by Nagórski because in a postscript to a letter Nagórski sent Orwell on 25 February regarding help being sought of the Freedom Defence Committee for a Polish soldier, he says that 'the writer of the letter you quoted in your column' (in 'As I Please,' 73) 'wrote to me asking in strong words how did you get hold of this letter to me. Of course I wrote back to him explaining how it happened.' *John O'Groat Journal* seems to have made no comment about this correspondence and it has no leaders on the subject. For the main burden of Nagórski's correspondence with Orwell—the fate of Polish soldiers repatriated from Scotland to Poland, see *3180, n. 1*.
4. Hon. Harold George Nicolson (1886–1968; Kt., 1953), diplomat and author. Before 1929 he held a number of posts in the diplomatic service in Madrid, Istanbul, Teheran, and Berlin. He was National Labour M.P., 1935–45. His first book, *Sweet Waters* (1921), was a novel but thereafter he concentrated (though not exclusively) on biography and criticism; among his books were *Paul Verlaine* (1921); *Tennyson* (1923); *Byron: The Last Journey* (1924); *Swinburne* (1926); *Curzon: The Last Phase* (1934); *Diplomacy* (1939); *Why Britain is at War* (1939; a Penguin Special); *The Congress of Vienna* (1946); *King George the Fifth* (1952); *Sainte-Beuve* (1957); *The Age of Reason 1700–1789* (1960); *Monarchy* (1962); *Diaries and Letters*, 3 vols, (1966–68). He married Victoria Sackville-West in 1913.
5. Marie Lloyd (pseudonym of Matilda Alice Victoria Wood; 1870–1922), an outstanding star of the music hall and a greatly loved personality. She was dubbed 'The Bernhardt of the

Music Halls' by Sarah Bernhardt. She collapsed in the wings as she left the stage on 4 October 1922 and died three days later.

6. Little Tich (pseudonym of Harry Relph, 1867–1928), a music-hall performer of genius. He worked in pantomime with Marie Lloyd and was at home in English and French music halls. In 1910 he was made an officer of the Académie Française in recognition of his service to French variety. Although Orwell had his date of death right, Little Tich retired only three months earlier, on 13 November 1927.

7. Henri Pétain (1856–1951), Marshal of France; see *644, n. 1*.

8. Ferdinand Foch (1851–1929), Marshal of France, outstanding as a soldier and for the warmth of his character. A small piece of land upon which his statue stands outside Victoria Station, London (from which so many British soldiers left to fight in France) is French soil. The plinth bears his words: 'I am conscious of serving Britain as I served my own country.' He was buried at Les Invalides on 26 March 1929. Orwell therefore witnessed his funeral just four days after being discharged from the Hôpital Cochin; see *3104, n. 1*.

9. Queen Mary (Princess Mary of Teck; 1867–1953), consort of King George V (reigned 1910–36) and grandmother of Queen Elizabeth II.

10. See 'As I Please,' 63, 29 November 1946, *3126, n. 1*.

11. See 'Freedom and Happiness,' *Tribune*, 4 January 1946, *2841*.

3159. To Mamaine Koestler

24 January 1947   Typewritten

27B Canonbury Square,
Islington, N.1.

Dear Mamaine,

I can't thank you enough for the tea.[1] We always seem to drink more than we can legally get, and are always slightly inclined to go round cadging it, but I don't want to give you the impression that the shortage is calamitous.

As to books, I have only got a very little way with a novel which I hope to finish about the end of 1947, if too many things don't intervene. I don't really know how I stand about contracts with French publishers. Several books of mine are now being translated or have recently been translated, and I don't know whether I have exclusive agreements with any of the publishers. In any case, I don't like making arrangements before a book is written because I think it puts a hoodoo on it.

I have just read "Thieves in the Night",[2] which I could not get hold of before. I enjoyed reading it, but you know my views, or at any rate Arthur knows my views about this terrorism business. You might just tell Arthur from me that his ideas about the prevalence of circumcision are quite incorrect. So far from stamping anyone as Jewish, this practice used at any rate to be so common, especially among the richer classes, that a boy at a public school felt embarrassed at swimming pools and so forth if he was not circumcised. I believe it is getting less common now, but is also commoner among the working classes. I have a good mind to put a piece about this in my column some time.

I am glad you liked the radio version of "Animal Farm." Most people seemed to, and it got quite a good press. I had the feeling that they had spoilt it, but one nearly always does with anything one writes for the air.

Richard is very well, and is talking distinctly more.

With love,
George

1. The tea ration had been increased in July 1945 from 2 ounces a week to 2½, but it was still a meagre amount, especially for someone who drank as much strong tea as Orwell did. The Koestlers preferred coffee to tea, hence their being able to spare some of their ration for him. For fuller details of rationing, see *3017, n. 3* and *3044, n. 3.*
2. A novel, about the Zionist struggle to set up an independent Jewish state in Palestine, by Mamaine's husband, Arthur Koestler, published in 1946.

3160. To Dwight Macdonald

24 January 1947   Typewritten

27B Canonbury Square,
Islington, N.1.

Dear Dwight,

Thanks so much for your letter of the 18th.[1] I am sorry you have not had the money for the shoes. I thought I had asked my agent to get it transferred to you, but anyway I have written to him again to do so.

As to the Tolstoy article, I have no objection to its being cut so long as there is some indication that there has been a cut. I think there is something in what you say about Tolstoy's denunciation of Shakespeare not being worth answering, but I had in any case to make an exposition of it because it is now a very rare pamphlet which few people have read. I know this because some years ago when I wanted a copy I had the greatest difficulty in procuring it.

As to the stuff from "Tribune", the position is a bit awkward. Some months ago the New Republic, which occasionally reprints my stuff—they have some kind of reciprocal arrangement with Tribune—wrote and asked me, when I re-started the "As I Please" column, to send them carbons so that when they wished they could print the stuff almost as soon as it appeared in Tribune. I agreed to do this, and I did send them the carbons for the first week or so, but I then stopped because it seemed to me that this column would largely be topical British stuff which could not interest them. But as I did give the undertaking, I suppose they might feel they still had a prior claim here, and might be annoyed if you reprinted a piece of it in Politics. For all I know, they have from time to time reprinted items from the column.[2] I know they did in one case, but I would not necessarily know in every case until they paid me, because they don't usually send copies of the paper. Do you by any chance know anyone on the staff in a friendly way? If so, we could get this thrashed out. I'd really much rather be printed by you than by them, and there is the added difficulty that I am politically even less in their camp than yours, so that what they picked out would probably be mostly trivialities.

I enclose a short list of possible subscribers for Politics. Of course, for all I know some of them may be on your list already. If you are circularising any of them I should send a copy of the paper if possible. It is very difficult to buy here.

I followed your controversy with the Editors of P.R. closely. I thought that in polemical terms you had the better of it, but on the whole I agree with them because I think it is about time to get the wider public conscious of the meaning of fellow-travellerism and quislingism generally. Where you reproach them for not saying plainly that they would be willing to make war if necessary, I think you are right. It seems to me that if one expresses oneself as being against appeasement, one is saying that in certain circumstances one is willing to go to war and one ought to admit this quite plainly. Before the war, for example, all the talk about a United Front of the peace-loving nations and so forth was humbug. The issue was between having a war and letting Germany dominate Europe up to the Urals. On the other hand, if one expresses oneself as being against war in all circumstances, I think one ought to realise that one means appeasement and say that at need one is willing to give away anything rather than shed blood. Just in passing, I may say that I don't think war will be averted, though it probably won't happen within ten or twenty years.

I think Woodcock's article[3] was extremely good—much the most serious criticism I have had. His book on Godwin[4] seems to be doing quite well here. At any rate, it has had very good reviews everywhere.

Yours,
Geo. Orwell

1. Macdonald wrote to tell Orwell that he had posted him a pair of shoes five days earlier, declaring them as clothes. He had not put them into two parcels because 'there might be as much chance of *your* only getting one as of some pilferer only getting one if I sent them singly.' He thought Orwell's explanation of his intention in writing *Animal Farm* first rate (see *3128*), effectively answering the left-wing critics to whom Macdonald had referred. He thought Orwell particularly shrewd in his point that critics who can see no alternative except capitalism or dictatorship were the people who were pessimistic. He promised to send Orwell an argument he had had in *Politics* some years earlier with a defender of the Communist Party who was more optimistic than Macdonald about the USSR, whereas Macdonald claimed to be more optimistic in that he thought human beings could solve their political problems without lies and slavery. He thought the essay 'Lear, Tolstoy and the Fool' 'somewhat uneven.' The opening and close could be taken for granted but the middle section—the bulk of the article—was very good. He sought permission to reprint 'roughly, pages 8 to 22' of the typescript. (The paragraph beginning 'At this point one is obliged to start guessing' begins two-thirds down page 8 of the extant typescript, a copy of which Macdonald presumably had before him; page 22 is wholly taken up with the paragraph beginning 'We do not know a great deal about Shakespeare's religious beliefs,' a paragraph that runs nearly to the end of 23.) However, Macdonald did not print this in *Politics*. He thought Orwell's 'revived column' in *Tribune* 'absolutely first-class.' He particularly enjoyed the first and last items of 'As I Please,' 68, 3 January 1947 (see *3146*) and had 'read them aloud to Nancy and to friends.' (It was this contribution that *Tribune* chose to reprint following Orwell's death; see *3146, n. 1*). Macdonald wanted to reprint selections from the past four columns each month in *Politics* under the title 'As I Please.' Orwell was saying in these columns 'a lot of things that should be said on *this* side of the Atlantic as well.'
2. The first section of 'As I Please,' 60, 8 November 1946, *3108*, was reprinted, slightly abridged, as 'It Looks Different from Abroad,' in *The New Republic*, 2 December 1946.
3. 'George Orwell, Nineteenth Century Liberal,' *Politics*, December 1946. This formed chapter 7 of Woodcock's *The Writer and Politics* (1948). (See also his book-length study of Orwell, *The*

Crystal Spirit, 1967.) The essay, in its concentrated form, gives a fine insight into Orwell and his work. He sees Orwell, with Herbert Read and Graham Greene, as one of the few writers of the thirties who has not worn badly. They were not, in their different ways, tarnished by their political records. He praises Orwell for the 'economy, clarity, fluency, [and] descriptive vividness' of his writing, but those, he says, 'are all *superficial* virtues,' and he goes on to analyse what he finds lacking in Orwell. For example: 'His description of the Eastern landscape and of the attitude of Europeans towards Orientals may be the best of its kind; nevertheless, one fails to find understanding of the mentality and peculiar problems of Oriental people.' He finds his 'political writing rarely satisfying' and his 'social writings rarely justify completely our expectations.' At times, he says, Orwell condemns people or groups sincerely but unjustly, because he does not understand their real motives: 'Orwell has never really understood *why* pacifists act as they do,' for example. He describes Orwell as 'essentially the iconoclast. The fact that his blows sometimes hit wide of the mark is not important. The great thing about Orwell is that when he exposes a lie he is usually *substantially* right, and that he will always pursue his attacks without fear or favour.' He is, he concludes, an 'old-style liberal' and the liberal 'is a rare survivor in the atomic age' and one like Orwell 'who has developed the necessary vigour of attack is even less common. His old-fashioned pragmatism, his nineteenth-century radical honesty and frankness, his respect for such excellent bourgeois mottoes as "Fair Play" and "Don't kick a man when he's down," which have been too much vitiated by the sneers of Marxist amoralism, his consideration for the freedom of speech and writing, are all essentially liberal virtues.' Orwell is closely akin to his own portrait of Dickens: 'He is laughing, with a touch of anger in his laughter, but no triumph, no malignity. It is the face of a man who is always fighting against something, but who fights in the open and is not frightened, the face of a man who is *generously angry*—in other words, of a nineteenth-century liberal, a free intelligence—a type hated with equal hatred by all the smelly little orthodoxies which are now contending for our soul' (384, 386, 387–88).

4. *Godwin: A Biographical Study* (1946).

3161. To Leonard Moore

24 January 1947   Typewritten

27B Canonbury Square,
Islington, N. 1.

Dear Moore,

Many thanks for your letter of the 23rd. I am so glad that you managed to get so good a price for the article from the "Atlantic Monthly." I have no objection to their cutting it. I assume that they will do so in a manner that doesn't deform it.

I have just heard from my friend Dwight Macdonald that he has sent me the pair of shoes I asked him to get, so do you think you could arrange for whoever it is to transfer ten dollars to him? In case I did not give it to you before, his address is "Politics", 45 Astor Place, New York, 3, N.Y.[1]

Yours sincerely,
[Signed] Geo. Orwell
George Orwell

P.S. By the way, Mme. Davet said something about having procured a copy of Critical Essays from Warburg, and taking it round to French publishers. I had the impression that someone was translating it already. I gave her a caveat, and said I would find out from you how matters stood. If somebody is translating it, do you think you could send her a line to that effect?[2]

1. An annotation in the left-hand margin made in Moore's office reads: 'Wrote H Brace 11/12/46.'
2. An annotation in the left-hand margin, written in Moore's office, states: 'We sent Madame Davet a copy on 7.10.46 telling her French rights were free.' The only translation of *Critical Essays* made in Orwell's lifetime was that published by Sur, Buenos Aires, July 1948, translated into Spanish by B. R. Hopenhaym.

3162. To Fredric Warburg

24 January 1947   Typewritten

27B Canonbury Square,
Islington, N.1.

Dear Fred,

I enclose a cheque for £4–12–6d. I am sorry about the delay in sending this, but I kept forgetting it. You won't forget to pay Miss Plummer (I don't know why I remembered her name wrong) and debit it to me, will you?

I have advertised for a copy of "Coming Up for Air" but whether that will come to anything, Lord knows. I suppose at the worst we might pinch one from a library or something. I have just secured a copy of "Burmese Days", but that edition is now very rare and Moore says that he has a Penguin copy, which is the same so far as the text goes, so if possible I would prefer this copy not to be broken up.[1]

Yours sincerely,
[Signed] George
George Orwell

1. Warburg replied on 28 January. He said that he had now read *Coming Up for Air* and had 'formed a considerable admiration for it.' He thought it would reprint very successfully, and had made a tentative offer to Moore covering the reprinting of that, *Burmese Days*, and *Down and Out in Paris and London*. He said that he and Roger Senhouse had discussed the order in which the three should be reprinted in the Uniform Edition. He favoured reprinting *Coming Up for Air* first because it had not been reprinted since 1939 and was less 'available'; *Burmese Days* would follow next. Senhouse preferred to reprint *Coming Up for Air* last. Warburg asked Orwell for his opinion.

3163. To Rayner Heppenstall

25 January 1947   Typewritten

27B Canonbury Square,
Islington, N.1.

Dear Rayner,

Thanks for your letter. Re. Animal Farm.[1] I had a number of people here to listen to it on the first day, and they all seemed to think it was good, and Porteous,[2] who had not read the book, grasped what was happening after a few minutes. I also had one or two fan letters and the press notices were good except on my native ground, ie. Tribune. As to what I thought myself, it's hard to get a detached view, because whenever I write anything for the air I have the impression it has been spoiled, owing to its inevitably coming out different to one's conception of it. I must say I don't agree about there being too much narrator. If anything I thought there should have been more explanation. People are always yearning to get rid of the narrator, but it seems to me that until certain problems have been overcome you only get rid of the narrator at the expense of having to play a lot of stupid tricks in order to let people know what is happening. The thing is to make the narrator a good turn in himself. But that means writing serious prose, which people don't, and making the actors stick to it instead of gagging and trying to make everything homey and naturalistic.

I can't write or promise to write anything more at present, I am too busy. I've still got ideas about fairy stories. I wish they would dig up and re-b'cast my adaptation of the Emperor's New Clothes. It was done on the Eastern and African services, but in those days I wasn't well-connected enough to crash the Home. I expect the discs would have been scrap[p]ed, however. I had them illicitly re-recorded at a commercial studio, but that lot of discs got lost. I've often pondered over Cinderella, which of course is the tops so far as fairy stories go but on the face of it is too visual to be suitable for the air. But don't you think one could make the godmother turn her into a wonderful singer who could sing a higher note than anyone else, or something of that kind? The best way would be if she had a wonderful voice but could not sing in tune, like Trilby, and the godmother cured this. One could make it quite comic with the wicked sisters singing in screeching voices. It might be worth talking over some time. Give my love to Margaret.[3]

Yours
Eric

1. Heppenstall had written on 24 January 1947 asking for Orwell's conclusions about the broadcast of *Animal Farm*. He said that the opinion at the BBC, with which he agreed, was that 'there were too many lengthy pieces of narration—that in fact the adaptation was not sufficiently ruthless and complete.' He asked also whether Orwell had further ideas for the Third Programme, for instance, 'any Imaginary Conversation' and whether he wanted more scripts of *Animal Farm*.
2. Hugh Gordon Porteous (1906–1993), literary and art critic and sinologist. In 1933 he remarked, 'Verse will be worn longer this season and rather red,' blaming Auden for being the reddening agent (Valentine Cunningham, *British Writers of the Thirties*, 1988, 27). He reviewed

extensively, especially for T. S. Eliot in *The Criterion* in the thirties and in *The Listener* in the sixties.
3. Mrs. Rayner Heppenstall. Heppenstall replied on 29 January 1947. He was anxious to convince Orwell 'about this business of narration.' He did not agree that narration could be avoided only by resorting to 'a lot of stupid tricks.' Narration involved 'a very marked change of pace . . . straight reading and . . . dramatic presentation don't mix.' He said he would never allow an actor to gag (ad lib). He thought the fairy stories should 'follow Red Riding Hood to Children's Hour' unless Orwell had something more sophisticated in mind. His wife hoped Orwell would 'presently come to supper.' He had seen Richard Rees for the first time since the outbreak of the war and remarked how greatly he had aged. The second page of this letter has not been traced.

3164. To Dudley Cloud

27 January 1947   Typewritten

Orwell's letter to Dudley Cloud, managing editor of *The Atlantic Monthly*, in which he explains his use of the term 'modern physics,' is reproduced as *2791*. The article to which it refers, 'The Prevention of Literature,' which was reprinted in *The Atlantic Monthly*, in an abridged form, in March 1947, is *2792*.

3165. Freedom Defence Committee to the Public

Freedom, Peace News, Tribune, and *Forward* 29 January 1947

The Freedom Defence Committee was founded in 1945 to deal with cases of the infringement of the civil liberties of any citizens within the British Empire, and since its foundation it has intervened successfully in a considerable number of cases, which have been duly reported in its Bulletin. The impression that the need for such a committee has ceased with the advent of peace is an illusion: on the contrary, new cases are brought to our attention almost daily. But this impression has been responsible for a crippling decrease in our resources and, unless immediate support is forthcoming, we must close down.

At the end of 1946 we had a deficit of about £50. We need an immediate sum of £250 if we are to maintain an office and a typist-organiser, and in order to carry on efficiently we need a regular income of at least £500 per annum. This sum is ridiculously small in relation to the value of the work we are doing. You have not space for a recitation of all the cases of unjust imprisonment, excessive sentences, racial discrimination and other infringements of elementary civil liberties which we have handled in the past, but we would be glad to supply any of your readers who may be willing to support us, with such information.

We need five hundred regular subscribers at a guinea a year: even more urgently we need the lump sum already mentioned (£250) to enable us to pay our debts and keep our office open.

Subscriptions should be sent to The Treasurer, Freedom Defence Committee, 8, Endsleigh Gardens, London, W.C.1.

Herbert Read, Chairman
George Orwell, Vice-Chairman
George Woodcock, Secretary
H. B. Gibson, Treasurer

The letter was typed in two paragraphs, the second comprising the last three lines. *Tribune* (7 February) re-paragraphed the letter as printed here (and also capitalised 'committee" in the second sentence); *Forward* (15 February) split the letter into two paragraphs, the second beginning, 'You have not space . . .'; *Freedom* (1 February) printed the letter as a single paragraph; and *Peace News* (7 February) arranged it in six paragraphs.

An original of the letter, dated 29 January 1947 and signed by Read, Orwell, Woodcock, and Gibson, sent to *Politics*, is in Yale University Library. Among the forty-three members of the Committee were Mulk Raj Anand, Arthur Ballard, Vera Brittain, Benjamin Britten, Fenner Brockway, Alex Comfort, Cyril Connolly, Michael Foot, E. M. Forster, B. H. Liddell Hart, Julian Huxley, Augustus John, Ethel Mannin, Henry Moore, J. Middleton Murry, Peter Pears, Bertrand Russell, Osbert Sitwell, Graham Sutherland, and Michael Tippett. *Politics* did not publish the letter, but in George Woodcock's 'London Letter,' *Politics*, March–April 1947, he devoted a long paragraph to the plight of pacifist, socialist, libertarian, anarchist, and 'protective' organisations (such as the Freedom Defence Committee). He gave a number of reasons for the lack of financial and individual support. People had less money, the cost of living had risen, the sense of solidarity during the war had died away leaving only a core of those supporting each movement, many thought the advent of a Labour government would do away with the need for many such organisations (though not the anarchists), and many organisations had compromised or left uncertain their stance during the war. He also thought that, generally speaking, 'none of the minority groups has any longer a reliable basis among the workers.'

3166. To Fredric Warburg

30 January 1947   Typewritten

27B Canonbury Square,
Islington, N.1.

Dear Fred,

Many thanks for your letter of the 28th. I am still in pursuit of a copy of COMING UP FOR AIR, but have not come upon one yet. As to the order in which these books are reprinted, in my opinion it would be better to start off with COMING UP FOR AIR because that is the least available of the lot, and the other two I should say have definitely appeared too recently in the Penguin edition.[1] I suppose it is not impossible that the Penguins might re-issue those two, as they only did wartime editions of about 35,000 and those were sold out. I believe they do make fresh printings of back numbers occasionally.[2] I suppose we should have to make sure how the matter stands, so that their appearance as Penguins might not cut across your uniform edition. If I remember rightly, there are one or two misprints in COMING UP FOR AIR which I would like to put right before it is reprinted.[3]

Signature cut off and sent to Allen Lane, Penguin Books, 23 July 1951.

1. *Coming Up for Air* was printed first in the Uniform Edition in May 1948; *Burmese Days* appeared in January 1949 and *Down and Out in Paris and London* in September 1949. All three were published by Harcourt, Brace, New York, in January 1950 (the month that Orwell died), *Coming Up for Air* for the first time in the United States.
2. Penguin Books published 55,000 copies of *Down and Out in Paris and London* in December 1940, and 60,000 copies of *Burmese Days* in May 1944. No reprinting followed. A. S. B. Glover told Moore that Penguin Books had only some 500 copies of *Burmese Days* in stock at the beginning of 1947; see *3154, n. 1.*
3. For details of misprints, see Textual Note to *Coming Up for Air, CW*, VII.

3167. 'As I Pleased,'° 71

Tribune, 31 January 1947

One's relations with a newspaper or a magazine are more variable and intermittent than they can be with a human being. From time to time a human being may dye his hair or become converted to Roman Catholicism, but he cannot change himself fundamentally, whereas a periodical will go through a whole series of different existences under the same name. *Tribune* in its short life has been two distinct papers, if not three, and my own contacts with it have varied sharply, starting off, if I remember rightly, with a rap on the knuckles.

I did not learn of the existence of *Tribune* till some time in 1939. It had started early in 1937, but of the thirty months that intervened before the outbreak of war I spent five in hospital and thirteen abroad. What first drew my attention to it, I believe, was a none too friendly review of a novel of mine. During the period 1939–42 I produced three or four books and reprints, and I think it is true that I never had what is called a "good" review in *Tribune* until after I became a member of the staff. (The two events were unconnected, needless to say.) Somewhat later, in the cold winter of 1939, I started writing for *Tribune*, though at first, curiously enough, without seeing it regularly or getting a clear idea of what kind of paper it was.

Raymond Postgate,[1] who was then editor, had asked me to do the novel reviews from time to time. I was not paid (until recently it was unusual for contributors to left-wing papers to be paid), and I only saw the paper on the somewhat rare occasions when I went up to London and visited Postgate in a bare and dusty office near London Wall. *Tribune* (until a good deal later everyone called it "the" *Tribune*) was at that time in difficulties. It was still a threepenny paper aimed primarily at the industrial workers and following more or less the Popular Front line which had been associated with the Left Book Club and the Socialist League. With the outbreak of war its circulation had taken a severe knock, because the Communists and near-Communists who had been among its warmest supporters now refused to help in distributing it. Some of them went on writing for it, however, and the futile controversy between "supporters" and "opposers" of the war continued to rumble in its columns while the German armies gathered for the spring offensives.

Early in 1940 there was a large meeting in a public hall, the purpose of which was to discuss both the future of *Tribune* and the policy of the left wing of the Labour Party. As is usual on such occasions nothing very definite was said, and what I chiefly remember is a political tip which I received from an inside source. The Norway campaign was ending in disaster, and I had walked to the hall past gloomy posters. Two M.P.s, whom I will not name, had just arrived from the House.

"What chance is there," I asked them, "of this business getting rid of Chamberlain?"

"Not a hope," they both said. "He's solid."

I don't remember dates, but I think it can only have been a week or two before Chamberlain was out of the Premiership.

After that *Tribune* passed out of my consciousness for nearly two years. I was very busy trying to earn a living and write a book amid the bombs and the general disorganisation, and any spare time I had was taken up by the Home Guard, which was still an amateur force and demanded an immense amount of work from its members. When I became aware of *Tribune* again I was working in the Eastern Service of the B.B.C. It was now an almost completely different paper. It had a different make-up, cost sixpence, was orientated chiefly towards foreign policy, and was rapidly acquiring a new public which mostly belonged, I should say, to the out-at-elbow middle class. Its prestige among the B.B.C. personnel was very striking. In the libraries where commentators went to prime themselves it was one of the most sought-after periodicals, not only because it was largely written by people who knew something at first hand about Europe, but because it was then the only paper of any standing which criticised the Government. Perhaps "criticised" is an over-mild word. Sir Stafford Cripps had gone into the Government, and the fiery personality of Aneurin Bevan gave the paper its tone. On one occasion there were some surprisingly violent attacks on Churchill by someone who called himself Thomas Rainsboro'.[2] This was obviously a pseudonym, and I spent a whole afternoon trying to determine the authorship by stylistic evidence, as the literary critics employed by the Gestapo were said to do with anonymous pamphlets. Finally I decided that "Thomas Rainsboro'" was a certain W——. A day or two later I met Victor Gollancz, who said to me:

"Do you know who wrote those Thomas Rainsboro' articles in *Tribune*? I've just heard. It was W——."

This made me feel very acute, but a day or two later I heard that we were both wrong.[3]

During this period I occasionally wrote articles for *Tribune*, but only at long intervals, because I had little time or energy. However, towards the end of 1943 I decided to give up my job in the B.B.C., and I was asked to take over the literary editorship of *Tribune*, in place of John Atkins,[4] who was expecting call-up. I went on being literary editor, as well as writing the "As I Please" column, until the beginning of 1945. It was interesting, but it is not a period that I look back on with pride. The fact is that I am no good at editing. I hate planning ahead, and I have a psychical or even physical inability to answer letters.[5] My most essential memory of that time is of pulling out a drawer here and a drawer there, finding it in each case to be stuffed with letters and manuscripts which ought to have been dealt with weeks earlier, and hurriedly shutting it up again. Also, I have a fatal tendency to accept manuscripts which I know very well are too bad to be printed. It is questionable whether anyone who has had long experience as a freelance journalist ought to become an editor. It is too like taking a convict out of his cell and making him governor of the prison. Still, it was "all experience," as they say, and I have friendly memories of my cramped little office looking out on a back yard, and the three of us who shared it huddling in the corner as the doodle-bugs came zooming over, and the peaceful click-click of the typewriters starting up again as soon as the bomb had crashed.

Early in 1945 I went to Paris as correspondent for the *Observer*. In Paris *Tribune* had a prestige which was somewhat astonishing and which dated from before the liberation. It was impossible to buy it, and the ten copies which the British Embassy received weekly did not, I believe, get outside the walls of the building. Yet all the French journalists I met seemed to have heard of it and to know that it was the one paper in England which had neither supported the Government uncritically, nor opposed the war, nor swallowed the Russian myth. At that time there was—I should like to be sure that it still exists—a weekly paper named *Libertés*, which was roughly speaking the opposite number of *Tribune* and which during the occupation had been clandestinely produced on the same machines as printed the *Pariser Zeitung*.

Libertés, which was opposed to the Gaullists on one side and the Communists on the other, had almost no money and was distributed by groups of volunteers on bicycles. On some weeks it was mangled out of recognition by the censorship; often nothing would be left of an article except some such title as "The Truth About Indo-China" and a completely blank column beneath it. A day or two after I reached Paris I was taken to a semi-public meeting of the supporters of *Libertés*, and was amazed to find that about half of them knew all about me and about *Tribune*. A large working-man in black corduroy breeches came up to me, exclaimed "Ah, vous êtes Georges Orrvell!" and crushed the bones of my hand almost to pulp. He had heard of me because *Libertés* made a practice of translating extracts from *Tribune*. I believe one of the editors used to go to the British Embassy every week and demand to see a copy. It seemed to me somehow touching that one could have acquired, without knowing it, a public among people like this: whereas among the huge tribe of American journalists at the Hotel Scribe, with their glittering uniforms and their stupendous salaries, I never encountered one who had heard of *Tribune*.

For six months during the summer of 1946 I gave up being a writer in *Tribune* and became merely a reader, and no doubt from time to time I shall do the same again; but I hope that my association with it may long continue, and I hope that in 1957 I shall be writing another anniversary article. I do not even hope that by that time *Tribune* will have slaughtered all its rivals. It takes all sorts to make a world, and if one could work these things out one might discover that even the——[6] serves a useful purpose. Nor is *Tribune* itself perfect, as I should know, having seen it from the inside. But I do think that it is the only existing weekly paper that makes a genuine effort to be both progressive and humane—that is, to combine a radical Socialist policy with a respect for freedom of speech and a civilised attitude towards literature and the arts: and I think that its relative popularity, and even its survival in its present form for five years or more, is a hopeful symptom.

A '*Tribune* Who's Who?' was printed in a ruled-off section of Orwell's article.

TRIBUNE
Who's Who?

Sir Stafford Cripps, M.P., President of the Board of Trade: Founder of *Tribune*, Chairman Board of Directors and Editorial Board, 1937–1940. Resigned when appointed British Ambassador to Moscow.

Aneurin Bevan, M.P., Minister of Health: Founder of *Tribune*, Director and Editorial Board, 1937–1945. Resigned on appointment as Minister of Health.

Ellen Wilkinson, M.P., Minister of Education: Founder of *Tribune*, Director until May, 1940. Resigned on appointment as Under-Secretary, Ministry of Pensions.

G. R. Strauss, M.P., Under-Secretary, Ministry of Transport: Founder of *Tribune*, Director, 1937–1945; Editorial Board, 1937–1942. Resigned from Editorial Board on appointment as P.P.S. to Sir Stafford Cripps in 1942; resigned as Director on appointment to present office in 1945.

William Mellor: Editor and Founder of *Tribune*. Died 1942.

Raymond Postgate: Editor, 1940–1941.

Victor Gollancz: Director and Editorial Board, 1938–1942.

Mrs. Patricia Strauss, L.C.C.: Director, 1945—

Jennie Lee, M.P.: Director, 1945—

Michael Foot, M.P.: Editorial Staff *Tribune*, 1937–1938; Director, 1945—

1. Raymond William Postgate (1896–1971) edited several Socialist periodicals, including *Tribune*, and wrote extensively on food and wine; see 497, n. 2.
2. Thomas Rainsborough or Rainborow (d. 1648), commanded the *Swallow* in the Parliament's navy in 1643, and a regiment in the New Model Army in 1645, fighting at Naseby and elsewhere. He was elected M.P. for Droitwich in 1646 and was a leading republican in the debates which divided the Parliamentarians in 1647. He was reconciled with Cromwell, however, and was appointed to command the siege of Pontefract. He was wounded and died at Doncaster. He succinctly expressed the stand of the Levellers in his statement, 'The poorest hee that is in England hath a life to live as the greatest hee.' Ideas expressed in the Agreement of the People, which was largely shaped by Leveller arguments, were reflected in the Constitution of the United States.
3. The pseudonym was adopted by Frank Owen (1905–1979), Liberal M.P., 1929–31; editor of the *Daily Express*, 1931–37, and the *Evening Standard*, 1938–41 (both right-wing, Beaverbrook

newspapers); see *1141, n. 4*. In 1943 he was editor of a newspaper for South East Asia Command (which reprinted several of Orwell essays from the *Evening Standard*).
4. John Atkins (1916–) worked for *Tribune* from 1941 to 1943. His *George Orwell: A Literary Study* was published in 1954.
5. Although there is no doubt that Orwell's feelings of guilt were genuine and that he found it difficult to reject prospective contributions, as he showed at the BBC and in answering inquiries from those he did not know, he was remarkably punctilious in dealing with correspondence.
6. The long dash appears in the original; it is left to the reader to make a choice of the journal's name he or she thinks appropriate.

3168. 'Help Poles in Germany' Memorandum

February 1947

Tadeusz Katelbach, Secretary General of the 'Help Poles in Germany' Polish Social Committee (35, Cambridge Gardens, London, W 10) sent Orwell (among others) a lengthy memorandum about the pressures being placed on Poles in Germany to accept repatriation against their will. In the British, American, and French zones of Germany, it was claimed that there remained about 400,000 Poles who were refusing to return to Poland. Of this number, about 15,000 were former political prisoners who had been incarcerated in German concentration camps; about 80,000 were former prisoners of war; over 200,000 were former forced labourers who had been taken to Germany to serve the German war machine; and many were Poles who had escaped from Poland as a result of political persecution by the current Warsaw government. It was claimed that the United Nations Relief and Rehabilitation Administration was attempting by 'perfidious methods' to force these Poles back to Poland. In particular, UNRRA, it was claimed, accused the Poles of being unwilling to work and simultaneously did its utmost to prevent their finding work in Germany or emigrating overseas. The report had been sent to Trygve Lie, Secretary-General of the United Nations. This document was still among Orwell's papers at his death.

3169. 'As I Please,' 72

Tribune, 7 February 1947

Recently I have been looking through Mr. Peter Hunot's *Man About the House*, published a month or two back by the Pilot Press. Books telling you how to do household repairs are fairly numerous, but I think this is about the best I have seen. The author gathered his experience the hard way, by taking over a nearly derelict house and making it habitable with his own hands. He thus concentrates on the sort of difficulties that do actually arise in real life, and does not, like the author of another book in my possession, tell you how to mend Venetian blinds while ignoring electrical fittings. I looked up all the domestic calamities that I have had to deal with during the past year, and found all of them mentioned, except mice, which perhaps hardly come under the heading of decorations and repairs. The book is also simply written and well illustrated, and takes account of the difficulty nowadays of getting hold of tools and materials.

But I still think that there is room for a very large, comprehensive book of this type, a sort of dictionary or encyclopedia with every conceivable household job tabulated under alphabetical headings. You would then be able to look up *Tap, how to stop a dripping*, or *Floorboards, causes of squeaking in*, with the same certainty of getting the right answer as when you look up madeira cake or Welsh rarebit in Mrs. Beeton's cookery book. The time was when the amateur handyman, with his tack hammer and his pocketful of rawlplugs, was looked on as a mere eccentric, a joke to his friends and a nuisance to his women-folk. Nowadays, however, you either do your repairs yourself or they don't get done, and most of us are still remarkably helpless. How many people even know how to replace a broken sash cord, for instance?

As Mr. Hunot points out, much of the tinkering that now goes on would be unnecessary, or would be much easier, if our houses were sensibly built. Even so simple a precaution as putting fuse boxes in get-at-able places would save a lot of nuisance, and the miserable business of putting up shelves could be greatly simplified without any extra materials or radical change in methods. I hear rumours that the new houses now being built will have the pipes so placed that they will not freeze, but surely this cannot be true. There will be a snag somewhere, and the annual freeze-up will happen as usual. Burst water-pipes are a part of the English winter, no less than muffins or roasted chestnuts, and doubtless Shakespeare would have mentioned them in the song at the end of *Love's Labour's Lost*, if there had been water-pipes in those days.

It is too early to cheer, but I must say that up to date the phenomena of the freeze-up have been less unpleasant than those of 1940.[1] On that occasion the village where I lived was not only so completely snowed up that for a week or more it was impossible to get out of it, or for any food vans to get in, but every tap and pump in the village froze so hard that for several days we had no water except melted snow. The disagreeable thing about this is that snow is always dirty, except just after it has fallen. I have noticed this even in the high peaks of the Atlas mountains,[2] miles from human habitation. The everlasting snow which looks so virginal, is in fact distinctly grimy when you get close to it.

About the time when Sir Stafford Cripps came back from India, I heard it remarked that the Cripps offer had not been extended to Burma because the Burmese would have accepted it. I don't know whether any such calculation really entered into the minds of Churchill and the rest. It is perfectly possible: at any rate, I think that responsible Burmese politicians would have accepted such an offer, although at that moment Burma was in process of being over-run by the Japanese. I also believe that an offer of Dominion Status would have been gladly accepted if we had made it in 1944 and had named a definite date. As it is, the suspicions of the Burmese have been well roused, and it will probably end by our simply getting out of Burma on the terms least advantageous to both countries.

If that happens, I should like to think that the position of the racial minorities could be safeguarded by something better than promises. They number ten to twenty per cent. of the population, and they present several different kinds of problem. The biggest group, the Karens, are a racial enclave living largely within Burma proper. The Kachins and other frontier tribes are a good deal more backward and more different from the Burmese in customs and appearance. They have never been under Burmese rule—indeed, their territories were only very sketchily occupied even by the British. In the past they were well able to maintain their independence, but probably would not be able to do so in the face of modern weapons. The other big group, the Shans, who are racially akin to the Siamese, enjoyed some faint traces of autonomy under British rule. The minority who are in the most difficult position of all are the Indians. There were over a million of them in Burma before the war. Two hundred thousand of them fled to India at the time of the Japanese invasion—an act which demonstrated better than any words could have done their real position in the country.

I remember twenty years ago a Karen remarking to me, "I hope the British will stay in Burma for two hundred years."—"Why?"—"Because we do not wish to be ruled by Burmese." Even at the time it struck me that sooner or later this would become a problem. The fact is that the question of minorities is literally insoluble so long as nationalism remains a real force. The desire of some of the peoples of Burma for autonomy is genuine, but it cannot be satisfied in any secure way unless the sovereignty of Burma as a whole is interfered with. The same problem comes up in a hundred other places. Ought the Sudan to be independent of Egypt? Ought Ulster to be independent of Eire? Ought Eire to be independent of Britain? And so on. Whenever A is oppressing B, it is clear to people of good will that B ought to be independent, but then it always turns out that there is another group, C, which is anxious to be independent of B. The question is always *how large* must a minority be before it deserves autonomy. At best, each case can only be treated on its merits in a rough and ready way: in practice, no one is consistent in his thinking on this subject, and the minorities which win the most sympathy are those that have the best means of publicity. Who is there who champions equally the Jews, the Balts, the Indonesians, the expelled Germans, the Sudanese, the Indian Untouchables and the South African Kaffirs? Sympathy for one group almost invariably entails callousness towards another.

When H. G. Wells's *The Island of Doctor Moreau* was reprinted in the Penguin Library, I looked to see whether the slips and misprints which I remembered in earlier editions had been repeated in it. Sure enough, they were still there.[3] One of them is a particularly stupid misprint, of a kind to make most writers squirm. In 1941 I pointed this out to H. G. Wells, and asked him why he did not remove it. It had persisted through edition after edition ever since 1896. Rather to my surprise, he said that he remembered the misprint, but could not be bothered to do anything about it. He no longer took the faintest interest in his early books: they had been written so long ago that he no longer felt them to be part of himself. I have never been quite sure whether to admire this attitude or not. It is magnificent to be so free from literary vanity. And yet, what writer of Wells's gifts, if he had had any power of self-criticism or regard for his own reputation, would have poured out in fifty years a total of ninety-five books, quite two-thirds of which have already ceased to be readable?

1. It *was* too early to cheer. It proved to be a very bitter winter; see letter to Dwight Macdonald, 26 February 1947, *3175*.
2. After finishing the first draft of *Coming Up for Air*, in January 1939, Orwell and his wife spent a week's holiday at Taddert in the Atlas Mountains.
3. Penguin Books reacted to Orwell's comment. See his letter to A. S. B. Glover, 19 March 1947, *3192*.

3170. To Leonard Moore

11 February 1947   Typewritten

27B Canonbury Square,
Islington, N.1.

Dear Moore,
I am writing to you on behalf of my friend Paul Potts,[1] whom I think you might be able to help in your capacity as literary agent. A year or two ago he received a contract from Nicholson & Watson to write a book for them, and the manuscript was accepted for publication in October 1946. It appears that within the last week or two it has been sent to the printer. He has now received a letter from them saying that owing to the paper shortage they are obliged to cut down their lists, and that his book cannot be published. He has had some money from them in advance on the manuscript, but not the full amount mentioned in the contract.

There is a complicating factor in the fact that the book was to have been published by "Poetry London," which is a sort of offshoot of Nicholson and Watson, but the contract was signed by the latter, and the letter announcing the scrapping of the book also comes from them. It appears to me that at the least he should receive the balance not yet paid in the form of an advance, and it would be at any rate equitable, though I don't know how the legal position stands, if he also received something to recompense him for the delay. I don't imagine it is any use trying to force N. and W. to publish the book against their will, and what is needed is to get the manuscript back from them, and, if possible, some money with it. You could also perhaps handle the book for him and advise him about another publisher.

He will send you the relevant documents and give you his address, and you can perhaps ask him for any further information you need.

Yours sincerely
[Signed] Eric Blair
Eric Blair

1. See *1971, n. 1* and *2620, n. 1*.

3171. 'As I Please,' 73

Tribune, 14 February 1947

Here are some excerpts from a letter from a Scottish Nationalist.[1] I have cut out anything likely to reveal the writer's identity. The frequent references to Poland are there because the letter is primarily concerned with the presence of exiled Poles in Scotland:

> The Polish forces have now discovered how untrue it is to say "An Englishman's word is his bond." We could have told you so hundreds of years ago. The invasion of Poland was only an excuse for these brigands in bowler hats to beat up their rivals the Germans and the Japs, with the help of Americans, Poles, Scots, Frenchmen, etc., etc. Surely no Pole believes any longer in English promises. Now that the war is over you are to be cast aside and dumped in Scotland. If this leads to friction between the Poles and Scots so much the better. Let them slit each other's throats and two problems would be thereupon "solved." Dear, kind little England! It is time for all Poles to shed any ideas they may have about England as a champion of freedom. Look at her record in Scotland, for instance. And please don't refer to us as "Britons." There is *no* such race. We are Scots and that's good enough for us. The English changed their name to British; but even if a criminal changes his name he can be known by his fingerprints. . . . Please disregard any anti-Polish statement in the John O'Groat Journal.[2] It is a boot-licking pro-English (pro-Moscow you would call it) rag. Scotland experienced her Yalta in 1707 when English gold achieved what English guns could not do. But we will never accept defeat. After more than two hundred years we are still fighting for our country and will never acknowledge defeat whatever the odds.

There is a good deal more in the letter, but this should be enough. It will be noted that the writer is not attacking England from what is called a "left" standpoint, but on the ground that Scotland and England are enemies *as nations*. I don't know whether it would be fair to read race-theory into this letter, but certainly the writer hates us as bitterly as a devout Nazi would hate a Jew. It is not a hatred of the capitalist class, or anything like that, but *of England*. And though the fact is not sufficiently realised, there is an appreciable amount of this kind of thing knocking about. I have seen almost equally violent statements in print.

Up to date the Scottish Nationalist movement seems to have gone almost unnoticed in England. To take the nearest example to hand, I don't remember having seen it mentioned in *Tribune*, except occasionally in book reviews. It is true that it is a small movement, but it could grow, because there is a basis for it. In this country I don't think it is enough realised—I myself had no idea of it until a few years ago—that Scotland has a case against England. On economic grounds it may not be a very strong case. In the past, certainly, we have plundered Scotland shamefully, but whether it is *now* true that England as a whole exploits Scotland as a whole, and that Scotland would be better off if fully autonomous, is another question. The point is that many Scottish people, often quite moderate in outlook, are beginning to think about autonomy and to feel that they are pushed into an inferior position. They have a good deal of reason. In some areas, at any rate, Scotland is almost an occupied country. You have an English or Anglicised upper-class, and a Scottish working-class which speaks with a markedly different accent, or even, part of the time, in a different language. This is a more dangerous kind of class division than any now existing in England. Given favourable circumstances it might develop in an ugly way, and the fact that there was a progressive Labour Government in London might not make much difference.

No doubt Scotland's major ills will have to be cured along with those of England. But meanwhile there are things that could be done to ease the cultural situation. One small but not negligible point is the language. In the Gaelic-speaking areas, Gaelic is not taught in the schools. I am speaking from limited experience, but I should say that this is beginning to cause resentment. Also, the B.B.C. only broadcasts two or three half-hour Gaelic programmes a week, and they give the impression of being rather amateurish programmes. Even so they are eagerly listened to. How easy it would be to buy a little goodwill by putting on a Gaelic programme at least once daily.

At one time I would have said that it is absurd to keep alive an archaic language like Gaelic, spoken by only a few hundred thousand people. Now I am not so sure. To begin with, if people feel that they have a special culture which ought to be preserved, and that the language is part of it, difficulties should not be put in their way when they want their children to learn it properly. Secondly, it is probable that the effort of being bi-lingual is a valuable education in itself. The Scottish Gaelic-speaking peasants speak beautiful English, partly, I think, because English is an almost foreign language which they sometimes do not use for days together. Probably they benefit intellectually by having to be aware of dictionaries and grammatical rules, as their English opposite numbers would not be.

At any rate, I think we should pay more attention to the small but violent separatist movements which exist within our own island. They may look very unimportant now, but, after all, the Communist Manifesto was once a very obscure document, and the Nazi Party only had six members when Hitler joined it.[3]

To change the subject a bit, here is an excerpt from another letter. It is from a whisky distiller:

> We regret we are reluctantly compelled to return your cheque as owing to Mr. Strachey's failure to fulfil his promise to release barley for distilling in Scotland we dare not take on any new business. . . . When you have difficulty in obtaining a drink it will be some consolation to you to know that Mr. Strachey has sent 35,000 tons of barley to NEUTRAL Eire for brewing purposes.

People must be feeling very warmed-up when they put that kind of thing into a business letter which, by the look of it, is almost a circular letter. It doesn't matter very much, because whisky distillers and even their customers don't add up to many votes. But I wish I could feel sure that the people who make remarks like the one I overheard in the greengrocer's queue yesterday—"Government! They couldn't govern a sausage-shop, this lot couldn't!"—were equally few in numbers.

Skelton is not an easy poet to get hold of, and I have never yet possessed a complete edition of his works. Recently, in a selection I had picked up, I looked for and failed to find a poem which I remember reading years ago. It was what is called a macaronic poem—part English, part Latin—and was an elegy on the death of somebody or other. The only passage I can recall runs:

> Sepultus est among the weeds,
> God forgive him his misdeeds,
> With hey ho, rumbelo,
> Rumpopulorum,
> Per omnia saecula,
> Saecula saeculorum.[4]

It has stuck in my mind because it expresses an outlook totally impossible in our own age. Today there is literally no one who could write of death in that light-hearted manner. Since the decay of the belief in personal immortality, death has never seemed funny, and it will be a long time before it does so again. Hence the disappearance of the facetious epitaph, once a common feature of country churchyards. I should be astonished to see a comic epitaph dated later than 1850. There is one in Kew, if I remember rightly, which might be about that date. About half the tombstone is covered with a long panegyric on his dead wife by a bereaved husband: at the bottom of the stone is a later inscription which reads, "Now he's gone, too."

One of the best epitaphs in English is Landor's epitaph on "Dirce," a pseudonym for I do not know whom. It is not exactly comic, but it is essentially profane. If I were a woman it would be my favourite epitaph—that is to say, it would be the one I should like to have for myself. It runs:

> Stand close around, ye Stygian set,
> With Dirce in the boat conveyed,
> Lest Charon, seeing her, forget
> That he is old and she a shade.

It would almost be worth being dead to have that written about you.

1. This letter, from John M. Sutherland, dated 16 September 1946, was sent to Orwell by Z. Nagórski of the Polish Press Agency, Edinburgh, in connection with the case of a Polish soldier which Orwell raised with the Freedom Defence Committee; see *3180*. See also 'As I Please,' 70, 24 January 1947, *3158*, *n. 3*.
2. The name of the journal is left as a blank in 'As I Please,' but it appears in the original letter, of course. It has been restored here.
3. Orwell's comments on nationalism drew a long letter from Cyril Hughes of 3 March 1947 in which he explained that as he understood nationalism from a Welsh standpoint, Orwell's 'underlining of economic causes' in defence of nationalism was not the most important issue. What mattered in Wales, he argued, was that 'The tribe, or gwely . . . founded on a limited

consanguinity, had evolved a sense of mutual social responsibility superior to any comparable modern practice.' Though he conceded that one could not return to tribalism, which had been 'bloodily rooted out, and an alien [social system] planted in the wound,' it was important to recognise that nations had not learned the social lessons exemplified by tribes. 'The Nationalist believes that nationhood, far from being finished as a structural experiment, has never yet begun' and that it was folly to offer the concept of a World State as a panacea without considering who would dominate it—America, Russia, England? 'It is true that we must be glad at the sight of England in economic difficulty and at logger-heads° with Russia, but we should not gloat morbidly over the spectacle. From the destruction of England as a power our own emancipation will come . . .' He concluded by making plain that he did not purport to speak with the 'Voice of Wales' and he appreciated that he had had so to compress his argument that its presentation was unfair. The argument about tribalism may be sound but the Welsh is not. The Welsh for 'tribe' is *llwyth*. Mr Hughes may have confused *gwely* and *gwehelyth*. The latter means 'lineage'; *gwely* means 'bed'.

The final paragraph of this opening section served as an epigraph for two articles in *English Digest*, July 1947, under the heading 'Britain's Occupied Territory.' These were a condensation entitled 'New Deal for Wales?' by Harold A. Albert, which had first appeared in *Star Weekly*, Toronto; and 'Now's the Time and Now's the Hour?' (on Scottish demands) by Neil McCallum, which had first appeared in *The New Statesman and Nation*.

4. Orwell may be quoting from a corrupt version of Skelton's poem, but, since he had a facility for remembering verse, sometimes with slight inaccuracies, the errors reproduced are more probably the result of lines being recalled from memory. They do not form a continuous passage, and the last two lines he quotes should be the single line '*Per omnia secula seculorum.*'Skelton (c. 1460–1529) was tutor to Henry VIII when Prince Henry and held the rectorship of Diss in his native Norfolk in the early years of the sixteenth century. These lines come from an epitaph: a 'treatise devised . . . Of two knaves sometime of Diss,' John Jayberd (to whom these lines refer) and Adam Addersall, a bailiff. Sixty-two lines, mainly in Latin, separate the first two and the last four lines Orwell quotes, in Philip Henderson's edition of the *Complete Poems*, 1931 (revised 1948, 1959, 1964). Skelton uses 'in secula seculorum' elsewhere (e.g., in 'Colin Clout'), and Henderson translates that as 'to secular pursuits' rather than 'from one generation to another' for 'saecula saeculorum.' (See Henderson's edition, 454–56 and 293.)

3172. 'As I Please,' 74

Manchester Evening News, for *Tribune*, 21 February 1947

For the third and fourth weeks of February 1947, the national weekend reviews and many trade papers were suspended from publication by government order because of the severe shortage of fuel and the consequent power cuts. To help out during the crisis, *The Observer*, the *Manchester Evening News*, and the *Daily Herald* offered *Tribune* the hospitality of their columns. Orwell refers to the suspension and the loss of revenue for *Tribune* in his letter to Dwight Macdonald of 26 February 1947; see *3175*. See also 'As I Please,' 78, *3196*.

The following is an extract from George Orwell's page, "As I Please," included each week in "Tribune."

The news that, for the second time in the last few months, a play banned from the stage is to be broadcast by the B.B.C. (which will probably enable it to reach a much bigger public than it would if it were acted) brings out once again the absurdity of the rules governing literary censorship in Britain.

It is only stage plays and films that have to be submitted for censorship before they appear. So far as books go you can print what you like and take the risk of prosecution. Thus, banned plays like Granville Barker's "Waste"[1] and Bernard Shaw's "Mrs. Warren's Profession" could immediately appear in book form with no danger of prosecution, and no doubt sell all the better for the scandal that had happened beforehand. It is fair to say that, if they are any good, banned plays usually see the light sooner or later. Even "Waste," which brought in politics as well as sex, was finally allowed to appear thirty years after it was written, when the topicality which gave it a good deal of its force had vanished.

The trouble with the Lord Chamberlain's censorship of plays is not that it happens, but that it is barbarous and stupid—being, apparently, done by bureaucrats with no literary training. If there is to be censorship, it is better that it should happen beforehand, so that the author may know where he stands. Books are only very rarely banned in Britain, but the bannings that do happen are usually quite arbitrary. "The Well of Loneliness,"[2] for example, was suppressed, while other books on the same theme, appearing round about the same time, went unnoticed.

The book that gets dropped on is the one that happens to have been brought to the attention of some illiterate official. Perhaps half the novels now published might suffer this fate if they happened to get into the right hands. Indeed—though the dead are always respectable—I doubt whether Petronius, or Chaucer, or Rabelais, or Shakespeare would remain un-bowdlerised if our magistrates and police were greater readers.

1. *Waste* by Harley Granville-Barker (1877–1946) was banned by the Lord Chamberlain in 1907 because the play, a tragedy, included an abortion. It was publicly presented in 1936.
2. (Marguerite) Radclyffe Hall (1880–1943), novelist and poet. She published several volumes of poetry, 1906–15, and then novels and stories, including *Adam's Breed* (1926), *The Well of Loneliness* (1928), and *The Master of the House* (1932). *Adam's Breed* won the James Tait Black Memorial Prize, Femina Vie Heureuse Prize, and the Eichelberger Gold Humane Award. *The Well of Loneliness* was withdrawn in England on 28 August 1928 following the scandal aroused because of its depiction of lesbianism. It was immediately reissued in Paris and it was also published in New York, in 1928, with a commentary by Havelock Ellis. The novel was republished in London (without commentary) in 1949. Miss Hall's companion, Lady Una Vicenzo Troubridge, wrote *The Life and Death of Radclyffe Hall* (1961).

3173. To Leonard Moore

21 February 1947   Typewritten

27B Canonbury Square,
Islington, N.1.

Dear Moore,

With reference to your two letters of the 18th and the 19th.

I don't think the offer to dramatise "Animal Farm" sounds very promising, in fact I don't see what we get out of it except that there would then be a dramatic version existing, which I suppose would make it slightly more likely to reach the stage. But we would also be tied down to that particular adaptor, at least for a year, and somebody else might make a more inviting offer in the mean time, though I am bound to say I do not think it is a suitable book to adapt for stage production. One doesn't, of course, know what sort of version he and his collaborator would make, but from the fact of his referring to the book as "The" Animal Farm I assume he has not read it very attentively. I don't think I should close with him.[1]

I have meanwhile received a cable from some people in New York enquiring about film rights. I hope I shall have got you on the phone before this letter reaches you, but if not I will send the cable on with another letter.

As to Warburg. I want Warburg to become my regular publisher, because, although he may not sell the books so largely, I can trust him to publish whatever I write. At the same time we must settle this business about the uniform edition, as I don't see much point in simply re-issuing, in different formats, various books which have already appeared and therefore can't be expected to sell large numbers straight off. I had understood that what was intended was to produce all the books involved as paper became available in a uniform binding and at rather a low price—though I suppose not always the same price as some are much longer than others. But as to the variation in length, it is in most cases only between about 80,000 and about 50,000. The exception is Animal Farm (30,000), but I suppose he wouldn't work round to this till last, and one might put something else with it to bring it up to the right length. As to your query about cheap editions, I am not quite sure what is involved there. Is it a question of whether Warburg has all rights for cheap editions as well? I imagine the only reprint firm likely to do any of my books is the Penguin Library, which has already done two. I presume Warburg wouldn't object to a book being Penguinised, as I shouldn't think this cuts across ordinary sales much.

Do you think you could get this fixed up with Warburg as soon as possible[?] Tell him that I am fully ready for him to be my regular publisher, but that I want the following conditions:

(i) That though he may, if he wishes, issue ordinary editions of any books, he will also undertake to do a uniform edition which will include the six books we have agreed on and any suitable future books.

(ii) That though I will give him first refusal of all full-length books, I can if I choose do odd jobs for other publishers, such as introductions, contributions to miscellanies, etc.

Even if we can't draw up a full agreement immediately, I would like some settlement to be made as soon as possible about "Coming Up for Air." Warburg proposed to do this as the first of the re-issues, and he says that if the matter can be settled quickly he might get it onto his March paper quota. I would like this to happen, because I shall not have anything ready to be published before 1948 and it would not be a bad idea to have something appearing this year. Also I think that book was rather sunk by appearing just before the outbreak of war, and it is now very completely out of print.

Yours sincerely
[Signed] Eric Blair
Eric Blair

Moore wrote to Warburg on 27 February 1947 quoting much of this letter. The sections quoted began with 'I want Warburg . . .' to '. . . it up to the right length'; and 'Tell him' to the end of condition ii. The rest of Orwell's letter is summarised with the slightly surprising omission of Orwell's statement that he could trust Warburg to publish whatever he wrote. Moore's letter concludes with a reminder that Gollancz has an option on Orwell's next two novels: 'It may be, however, we can make some arrangement regarding this.' This was eventually agreed. See letters to Warburg, 28 February 1947, *3179*, and to Gollancz, 14 March 1947, *3191*.

1. Details of this proposal have not been traced. A dramatized version, with music and lyrics, directed by Peter Hall, was given with great success at the National Theatre on 25 April 1984. In 1985 it toured nine cities.

3174. To Leonard Moore

23 February 1947   Handwritten

> 27B Canonbury Square,
> Islington, N.1.

Dear Moore,
Here is that cable I mentioned in my previous letter.[1] I have cabled back asking them to get in touch with you.

> Yours sincerely
> E. A. Blair

1. The cable was from New York and concerned the film rights of *Animal Farm*; see *3173*.

3175. To Dwight Macdonald

26 February 1947   Typewritten

> 27B Canonbury Square,
> Islington, N.1.

Dear Dwight,
Thanks awfully for sending the shoes which arrived today. I trust they have sent you the money for them—I wrote to my agent to remind him to do this and he said he had done so. I am sorry to say they were too small after all,[1] however it doesn't matter because I recently managed to get another pair owing to somebody who takes the same size ordering a pair about a year ago and not wanting them when done. I shall send this pair on to Germany where doubtless they will be appreciated.

I wanted to ask, when you print the excerpt from the Tolstoy article,[2] if you're paying for it, could you pay the money to my American agents, McIntosh & Otis. I'm trying to let any money I earn in the USA pile up over there in case I ever make a visit there. I don't know whether I shall do so, but even if I don't, I'm not short of money at present and might as well let it lie there as pay British income tax on it.

It's been a lousy winter here what with the fuel breakdown and this unheard-of weather. I suppose conditions here are now what would be normal postwar winter conditions in, say, Paris. "Polemic" were very pleased with the long note you gave them in "Politics." I think the paper is now taking shape a bit, and it is doing fairly well from the point of view of circulation, though hampered by the usual organisational difficulties. I have now joined the editorial board, but I probably shan't do much on it as I am going back to Scotland in April and shall go on with a novel which I am doing and hope to finish by the end of 1947. While in London I have been snowed up with hackwork as usual. This two-weeks' closure of the weeklies[3] has meant an awful lot of nuisance and incidentally lost Tribune a lot of money it can ill afford.

Yours
George

1. The error arose because Orwell took a twelve in English sizes, which is equivalent to an American 12½. See headnote to Orwell's letter to Macdonald, 5 December 1946, 3128 and 3128, n. 3.
2. Macdonald did not print an excerpt from 'Lear, Tolstoy and the Fool'; see 3160, n. 1.
3. Because of large-scale electricity power cuts.

3176. 'As I Please,' 75A

Daily Herald for Tribune, 27 February 1947

The extracts from Tribune were preceded by this statement: 'The Daily Herald has again allotted space to "Tribune", the Socialist weekly, which has had to suspend publication because of the power cuts.' The space allotted on 20 February was not devoted to anything by Orwell, nor does anything of his appear on any other day during this period. A different section of 'As I Please,' 75, was published by the Manchester Evening News on 28 February; see 3177.

Recently I was looking through a child's illustrated alphabet, published this year. It is what is called a "travel alphabet." Here are the rhymes accompanying three of the letters, J, N and U:

J for the Junk which the Chinaman finds
Is useful for carrying goods of all kinds.

N for the Native from Africa's land.
He looks very fierce with his spear in his hand.

U for the Union Jacks Pam and John carry
While out for a hike with their nice Uncle Harry.

The "native" in the picture is a Zulu dressed only in some bracelets and a fragment of leopard skin. As for the Junk, the detail of the picture is very small, but the "Chinamen" portrayed in it appear to be wearing pigtails.

Perhaps there is not much to object to in the presence of the Union Jack. This is an age of competing nationalisms, and who shall blame us if we flourish our own emblems along with all the rest? But is it really necessary, in 1947, to teach children to use expressions like "native" and "Chinaman"?

The last-named word has been regarded as offensive by the Chinese for at least a dozen years. As for "native," it was being officially discountenanced even in India as long as twenty years ago.

It is no use answering that it is childish for an Indian or an African to feel insulted when he is called a "native." We all have these feelings in one form or another. If a Chinese wants to be called a Chinese and not a Chinaman, if a Scotsman objects to being called a Scotchman, or if a Negro demands his capital N, it is only the most ordinary politeness to do what is asked of one.[1]

The sad thing about this alphabet-book is that the writer obviously has no intention of insulting the "lower" races. He is merely not quite aware that they are human beings like ourselves. A "native" is a comic black man with very few clothes on; a "Chinaman" wears a pigtail and travels in a junk— which is about as true as saying that an Englishman wears a top hat and travels in a hansom cab.

This unconsciously patronising attitude is learned in childhood and then, as here, passed on to a new generation of children. And sometimes it pops up in quite enlightened people, with disconcerting results; as for instance at the end of 1941, when China officially became our Ally, and at the first important anniversary the B.B.C. celebrated the occasion by flying the Chinese flag over Broadcasting House, and flying it upside-down.

1. Orwell's attitude to racial descriptions and the policy he advocated is outlined in the Textual Note to *Burmese Days*, *CW*, II, 309–10; see also 'As I Please,' 2, 10 December 1943, *2391*, regarding Negro with a capital 'N,' Chinese for Chinaman (and Moslem for Mahomedan). Orwell's advocacy of politeness towards people from Scotland had changed since he wrote to Anthony Powell, 8 June 1936: 'I am glad to see you make a point of calling them "Scotchmen", not "Scotsmen" as they like to be called. I find this a good easy way of annoying them'; see *314*.

3177. 'As I Please,' 75B

Manchester Evening News for *Tribune*, 28 February 1947[1]

One thing one notices in these days when typewriters have become so scarce is the astonishing badness of nearly everyone's handwriting.

A handwriting which is both pleasant to look at and easy to read is now a very rare thing. To bring about an improvement we should probably have to evolve a generally accepted "style" of writing such as we possessed in the past and have now lost.

For several centuries[2] in the Middle Ages the professional scribes wrote an exquisite script, or rather a series of scripts, which no one now living could equal. Then handwriting declined, reviving in the nineteenth century after the invention of the steel pen. The style then favoured was "copperplate." It was neat and legible, but it was full of unnecessary lines and did not fit in with the modern tendency to get rid of ornament wherever possible. Then it became the fashion to teach children script, usually with disastrous results. To write script with real neatness one practically has to learn to draw, and it is impossible to write it as rapidly as a cursive hand. Many young or youngish people now make use of an uneasy compromise between script and copperplate, and indeed there are many adult and fully literate people whose handwriting has never properly "formed."

It would be interesting to know whether there is any connection between neat handwriting and literary ability. I must say that the modern examples I am able to think of do not seem to prove much. Miss Rebecca West has an exquisite handwriting, and so has Mr. Middleton Murry. Sir Osbert Sitwell, Mr. Stephen Spender, and Mr. Evelyn Waugh all have handwritings which, to put it as politely as possible, are not good. Professor Laski writes a hand which is attractive to look at but difficult to read. Arnold Bennett wrote a beautiful tiny hand over which he took immense pains. H. G. Wells had an attractive but untidy writing. Carlyle's writing was so bad that one compositor is said to have left Edinburgh in order to get away from the job of setting it up. Mr. Bernard Shaw writes a small, clear but not very elegant hand. And as for the most famous and respected of living English novelists, his writing is such that when I was at the B.B.C. and had the honour of putting him on the air once a month there was only one secretary in the whole department who could decipher his manuscripts.[3]

1. See headnote to 'As I Please,' 74 (*3172*) for publication of Orwell's column in the *Manchester Evening News*. Another section, numbered here 75A, appeared the preceding day in the *Daily Herald*. One of the trade papers to which the *Manchester Evening News* gave hospitality during the crisis was *The Shoe and Leather Record*. In a report from that journal printed immediately below Orwell's column was a statement that the fuel crisis had caused a loss in production of 10,000,000 shoes, giving added point to Orwell's difficulty in finding footwear.
2. centuries] *printed as* countries
3. The reference is to E. M. Forster's handwriting.

3178. To Emilio Cecchi

28 February 1947   Typewritten

27B Canonbury Square,
Islington, N.1.

Dear Mr. Cecchi,[1]
Very many thanks for the cutting from the "Corriere della Sera". It was very kind of you to give me such a long review.[2] I hope we shall meet again some time.[3]

Yours sincerely,
[Signed] Geo. Orwell
George Orwell

1. Emilio Cecchi (1884–1966), Italian journalist, art and literary critic, and translator. He served in World War I and then went to London as a newspaper correspondent. Back in Italy, and from 1927 until his death, he wrote for *Corriere della Sera*. He taught Italian culture at the University of California at Berkeley, 1930–31; wrote on English and American literature and culture (including an essay on Kipling, 1911, and *America amara*, 1939); and translated Shakespeare, Shelley, and Chesterton into Italian.
2. This review of *Animal Farm* appeared in *Il Nuovo Corriere della Sera* (as it was then called), 16 February 1947, and was twenty-four column inches long.
3. Cecchi annotated Orwell's letter to say that he had replied on 4 March 1947. On 20 March Orwell invited him to Canonbury Square, 'as you did before'; see *3194*.

3179. To Fredric Warburg

28 February 1947   Typewritten

27B Canonbury Square,
Islington, N.1.

Dear Fred,

I said I would write to you following on our telephone conversation. I wrote to Moore some days back, asking him to expedite the business of COMING UP FOR AIR and if possible to get the whole contract settled. I told him that I wanted you to be my regular publisher and to have first refusal of all my books, but there were some conditions, none of which I imagine are of a kind you would object to. One was that you should publish a uniform edition. The second was that I should have the right to do odd jobs for other publishers such as, for instance, introductions or contributions to miscellaneous publications, and the other was that you would not object to certain classes of cheap editions being done elsewhere, for instance, Penguins. Some of my books have been done as Penguins, and I suppose this might arise again.

Moore has just written again raising the point about my previous contract with Gollancz. Gollancz is still supposed to have an option on two works of fiction, though in my opinion it should be only one as he refused ANIMAL FARM and then claimed that it was not a work of fiction of standard length. Moore is anxious to get this settled. I must say I was inclined to leave it hanging, because actually I can think of ways to evade the contract with Gollancz. However, if it must be settled it would probably be better if I saw Gollancz personally.[1] But meanwhile, need we let this hold up the re-publication of COMING UP FOR AIR, the copyright of which is, I suppose, my own?[2]

Your sincerely,
[Signed] Geo. Orwell
George Orwell

1. This sentence had been annotated in the left-hand margin in Warburg's office: 'Go & see VG.'
2. The rights reverted to Orwell because the book had been allowed to go out of print for a period of time as laid out in the original contract. Gollancz's records state that the rights had reverted to Orwell on 22 November 1946. See letter to Moore, 7 March 1947, *3183*.

3180. To the Secretary, Freedom Defence Committee (George Woodcock)

28 February 1947   Typewritten

27B Canonbury Square,
Islington, N.1.

Dear Sir,

This letter follows on the previous one I had about the Polish fugitive in the British zone.[1] It clears up the point about his position, i.e. he is not in custody but is wandering about, presumably living with civilians.

Yours sincerely,
[Signed] Geo. Orwell
George Orwell

1. Franciszek Kilański had been repatriated from Scotland to Poland. In a report dated 15 January 1947 it was stated that he, with twenty-five other former Polish soldiers, had been arrested east of Poznań, and twenty-three had been charged with being spies, one of whom was Kilański. His identification papers had been taken from him, but he managed to escape and found his way into the British Zone of Germany, where he could not gain admission to any displaced persons' camp and was wandering about. (The implication would be that he would have no ration book and so would have great difficulty getting food.) He reported that the Americans were handing over Polish refugees who had reached their zone to the Soviets. Two, whom he knew, had documents proving that their parents lived in Belgium; nevertheless, to his surprise, they had been handed back to the Russians. 'Their fate is already sealed,' he said. Another four were shot trying to cross from the Soviet Zone. Orwell marked this report, 'Not to be made public.' On 21 February Orwell wrote to Mr. Z. Nagórski, of the Polish Press Agency, Edinburgh. This letter has not been traced. Nagórski replied on 25 February; he thanked Orwell for that letter but was sorry that the Freedom Defence Committee was 'unable to do much for the soldier in question.' He restated the situation in which these repatriated soldiers found themselves and said that 'American authorities seem to forget the right of asylum which is generally granted freely to political refugees.' Orwell forwarded Nagórski's letter to Woodcock with the covering note printed above. Woodcock, as Secretary of the FDC, wrote to the Secretary of the Refugees' Defence Committee, 5 Victoria Street, London, on 13 March 1947, Orwell having provided him with the address (see his letter of 7 March, 3185). Woodcock summarised the 'political persecution' faced by these repatriated soldiers and asked what their status was if they managed to get to the British or American zones of Germany. On 14 April the Control Office for Germany and Austria advised Woodcock that such Polish nationals would be given the status of German nationals, entitling them to German ration cards. For the argument in Scotland about the presence of Poles in that country, and Orwell's response, see 'As I Please,' 70, 24 January 1947, and 73, 14 February 1947, 3158 and its n. 3, and 3171, and n. 1.

3181. 'Lear, Tolstoy and the Fool'

Polemic, 7.   March 1947

Tolstoy's pamphlets are the least-known part of his work, and his attack on Shakespeare* is not even an easy document to get hold of, at any rate in an

* *Shakespeare and the Drama*. Written about 1903 as an introduction to another pamphlet, *Shakespeare and the Working Classes*, by Ernest Crosby. [Orwell's footnote.]

English translation. Perhaps, therefore, it will be useful if I give a summary of the pamphlet before trying to discuss it.

Tolstoy begins by saying that throughout life Shakespeare has aroused in him 'an irresistible repulsion and tedium'. Conscious that the opinion of the civilized world is against him, he has made one attempt after another on Shakespeare's works, reading and re-reading them in Russian, English and German; but 'I invariably underwent the same feelings; repulsion, weariness and bewilderment'. Now, at the age of seventy-five, he has once again re-read the entire works of Shakespeare, including the historical plays, and

> I have felt with even greater force, the same feelings—this time, however, not of bewilderment, but of firm, indubitable conviction that the unquestionable glory of a great genius which Shakespeare enjoys, and which compels writers of our time to imitate him and readers and spectators to discover in him non-existent merits—thereby distorting their aesthetic and ethical understanding—is a great evil, as is every untruth.

Shakespeare, Tolstoy adds, is not merely no genius, but is not even 'an average author', and in order to demonstrate this fact he will examine *King Lear*, which, as he is able to show by quotations from Hazlitt, Brandes and others, has been extravagantly praised and can be taken as an example of Shakespeare's best work.

Tolstoy then makes a sort of exposition of the plot of *King Lear*, finding it at every step to be stupid, verbose, unnatural, unintelligible, bombastic, vulgar, tedious and full of incredible events, 'wild ravings', 'mirthless jokes', anachronisms, irrelevancies, obscenities, worn-out stage conventions and other faults both moral and aesthetic. *Lear* is, in any case, a plagiarism of an earlier and much better play, *King Leir*, by an unknown author, which Shakespeare stole and then ruined. It is worth quoting a specimen paragraph to illustrate the manner in which Tolstoy goes to work. Act III, Scene 2 (in which Lear, Kent and the Fool are together in the storm) is summarized thus:

> Lear walks about the heath and says words which are meant to express his despair: he desires that the winds should blow so hard that they (the winds) should crack their cheeks and that the rain should flood everything, that lightning should singe his white head, and the thunder flatten the world and destroy all germs 'that make ungrateful man'! The fool keeps uttering still more senseless words. Enter Kent: Lear says that for some reason during this storm all criminals shall be found out and convicted. Kent, still unrecognized by Lear, endeavours to persuade him to take refuge in a hovel. At this point the fool utters a prophecy in no wise related to the situation and they all depart.

Tolstoy's final verdict on *Lear* is that no unhypnotized observer, if such an observer existed, could read it to the end with any feeling except 'aversion and weariness'. And exactly the same is true of 'all the other extolled dramas of Shakespeare, not to mention the senseless dramatized tales, *Pericles, Twelfth Night, The Tempest, Cymbeline, Troilus and Cressida*'.

Having dealt with *Lear* Tolstoy draws up a more general indictment against Shakespeare. He finds that Shakespeare has a certain technical skill which is partly traceable to his having been an actor, but otherwise no merits whatever. He has no power of delineating character or of making words and actions spring naturally out of situations, his language is uniformly exaggerated and ridiculous, he constantly thrusts his own random thoughts into the mouth of any character who happens to be handy, he displays a 'complete absence of aesthetic feeling', and his words 'have nothing whatever in common with art and poetry'. 'Shakespeare might have been whatever you like,' Tolstoy concludes, 'but he was not an artist.' Moreover, his opinions are not original or interesting, and his tendency is 'of the lowest and most immoral'. Curiously enough, Tolstoy does not base this last judgment on Shakespeare's own utterances, but on the statements of two critics, Gervinus and Brandes. According to Gervinus (or at any rate Tolstoy's reading of Gervinus) 'Shakespeare taught . . . that one *may be too good*', while according to Brandes 'Shakespeare's fundamental principle . . . is that *the end justifies the means*'. Tolstoy adds on his own account that Shakespeare was a jingo patriot of the worst type, but apart from this he considers that Gervinus and Brandes have given a true and adequate description of Shakespeare's view of life.

Tolstoy then recapitulates in a few paragraphs the theory of art which he had expressed at greater length elsewhere. Put still more shortly, it amounts to a demand for dignity of subject matter, sincerity, and good craftsmanship. A great work of art must deal with some subject which is 'important to the life of mankind', it must express something which the author genuinely feels, and it must use such technical methods as will produce the desired effect. As Shakespeare is debased in outlook, slipshod in execution and incapable of being sincere even for a moment, he obviously stands condemned.

But here there arises a difficult question. If Shakespeare is all that Tolstoy has shown him to be, how did he ever come to be so generally admired? Evidently the answer can only lie in a sort of mass hypnosis, or 'epidemic suggestion'. The whole civilized world has somehow been deluded into thinking Shakespeare a good writer, and even the plainest demonstration to the contrary makes no impression, because one is not dealing with a reasoned opinion but with something akin to religious faith. Throughout history, says Tolstoy, there has been an endless series of these 'epidemic suggestions'—for example, the Crusades, the search for the Philosopher's Stone, the craze for tulip-growing which once swept over Holland,[1] and so on and so forth. As a contemporary instance he cites, rather significantly, the Dreyfus case, over which the whole world grew violently excited for no sufficient reason. There are also sudden shortlived crazes for new political and philosophical theories, or for this or that writer, artist or scientist—for example, Darwin, who (in 1903) is 'beginning to be forgotten'. And in some cases a quite worthless popular idol may remain in favour for centuries, for 'it also happens that such crazes, having arisen in consequence of special reasons accidentally favouring their establishment, correspond in such a degree to the views of life spread in society, and especially in literary circles, that they are maintained for a long time'. Shakespeare's plays have continued to be admired over a long period because 'they corresponded to the irreligious and immoral frame of mind of the upper classes of his time and ours'.

As to the manner in which Shakespeare's fame *started*, Tolstoy explains it as having been 'got up' by German professors towards the end of the eighteenth century. His reputation 'originated in Germany, and thence was transferred to England'. The Germans chose to elevate Shakespeare because, at a time when there was no German drama worth speaking about and French classical literature was beginning to seem frigid and artificial, they were captivated by Shakespeare's 'clever development of scenes' and also found in him a good expression of their own attitude towards life. Goethe pronounced Shakespeare a great poet, whereupon all the other critics flocked after him like a troop of parrots, and the general infatuation has lasted ever since. The result has been a further debasement of the drama—Tolstoy is careful to include his own plays when condemning the contemporary stage—and a further corruption of the prevailing moral outlook. It follows that 'the false glorification of Shakespeare' is an important evil which Tolstoy feels it his duty to combat.

This, then, is the substance of Tolstoy's pamphlet. One's first feeling is that in describing Shakespeare as a bad writer he is saying something demonstrably untrue. But this is not the case. In reality there is no kind of evidence or argument by which one can show that Shakespeare, or any other writer, is 'good'. Nor is there any way of definitely proving that—for instance—Warwick Deeping is 'bad'.[3] Ultimately there is no test of literary merit except survival, which is itself merely an index to majority opinion. Artistic theories such as Tolstoy's are quite worthless, because they not only start out with arbitrary assumptions, but depend on vague terms ('sincere', 'important' and so forth) which can be interpreted in any way one chooses. Properly speaking one cannot *answer* Tolstoy's attack. The interesting question is: why did he make it? But it should be noticed in passing that he uses many weak or dishonest arguments. Some of these are worth pointing out, not because they invalidate his main charge but because they are, so to speak, evidence of malice.

To begin with, his examination of *King Lear* is not 'impartial', as he twice claims. On the contrary, it is a prolonged exercise in misrepresentation. It is obvious that when you are summarizing *King Lear* for the benefit of someone who has not read it, you are not really being impartial if you introduce an important speech (Lear's speech when Cordelia is dead in his arms) in this manner: 'Again begin Lear's awful ravings, at which one feels ashamed, as at unsuccessful jokes.' And in a long series of instances Tolstoy slightly alters or colours the passages he is criticizing, always in such a way as to make the plot appear a little more complicated and improbable, or the language a little more exaggerated. For example, we are told that Lear 'has no necessity or motive for his abdication', although his reason for abdicating (that he is old and wishes to retire from the cares of State) has been clearly indicated in the first scene. It will be seen that even in the passage which I quoted earlier, Tolstoy has wilfully misunderstood one phrase and slightly changed the meaning of another, making nonsense of a remark which is reasonable enough in its context. None of these mis-readings° is very gross in itself, but their cumulative effect is to exaggerate the psychological incoherence of the play. Again, Tolstoy is not able to explain why Shakespeare's plays were still in print, and still on the stage, two hundred years after his death (*before* the 'epidemic suggestion' started, that is); and his whole account of Shakespeare's rise to fame is guesswork punctuated by outright mis-statements.° And again, various of his accusations contradict one another: for example, Shakespeare is a mere entertainer and 'not in earnest', but on the other hand he is constantly putting his own thoughts into the mouths of his characters. On the whole it is difficult to feel that Tolstoy's criticisms are uttered in good faith. In any case it is impossible that he should fully have believed in his main thesis—believed, that is to say, that for a century or more the entire civilized world had been taken in by a huge and palpable lie which he alone was able to see through. Certainly his dislike of Shakespeare is real enough, but the reasons for it may be different, or partly different, from what he avows; and therein lies the interest of his pamphlet.

At this point one is obliged to start guessing. However, there is one possible clue, or at least there is a question which may point the way to a clue. It is: why did Tolstoy, with thirty or more plays to choose from, pick out *King Lear* as his especial target? True, *Lear* is so well known and has been so much praised that it could justly be taken as representative of Shakespeare's best work; still, for the purpose of a hostile analysis Tolstoy would probably choose the play he disliked most. Is it not possible that he bore an especial enmity towards this particular play because he was aware, consciously or unconsciously, of the resemblance between Lear's story and his own? But it is better to approach this clue from the opposite direction—that is, by examining *Lear* itself, and the qualities in it that Tolstoy fails to mention.

One of the first things an English reader would notice in Tolstoy's pamphlet is that it hardly deals with Shakespeare as a poet. Shakespeare is treated as a dramatist, and in so far as his popularity is not spurious, it is held to be due to tricks of stagecraft which give good opportunities to clever actors. Now, so far as the English-speaking countries go, this is not true. Several of the plays which are most valued by lovers of Shakespeare (for instance, *Timon of Athens*) are seldom or never acted, while some of the most actable, such as *A Midsummer Night's Dream*, are the least admired. Those who care most for Shakespeare value him in the first place for his use of language, the 'verbal music' which even Bernard Shaw, another hostile critic, admits to be 'irresistible'. Tolstoy ignores this, and does not seem to realize that a poem may have a special value for those who speak the language in which it was written. However, even if one puts oneself in Tolstoy's place and tries to think of Shakespeare as a foreign poet it is still clear that there is something that Tolstoy has left out. Poetry, it seems, is *not* solely a matter of sound and association, and valueless outside its own language-group: otherwise, how is it that some poems, including poems written in dead languages, succeed in crossing frontiers? Clearly a lyric like 'Tomorrow is Saint Valentine's Day' could not be satisfactorily translated, but in Shakespeare's major work there is something describable as poetry that can be separated from the words. Tolstoy is right in saying that *Lear* is not a very good play, as a play. It is too drawn-out and has too many characters and sub-plots. One wicked daughter would have been quite enough, and Edgar is a superfluous character: indeed it would probably be a better play if Gloucester and both his sons were eliminated. Nevertheless, something, a kind of pattern, or perhaps only an atmosphere, survives the complications and the *longueurs*. *Lear* can be imagined as a puppet show, a mime, a ballet, a series of pictures. Part of its poetry, perhaps the most essential part,is inherent in the story and is dependent neither on any particular set of words, nor on flesh-and-blood presentation.

Shut your eyes and think of *King Lear*, if possible without calling to mind any of the dialogue. What do you see? Here at any rate is what I see: a majestic old man in a long black robe, with flowing white hair and beard, a figure out of Blake's drawings (but also, curiously enough, rather like Tolstoy), wandering through a storm and cursing the heavens, in company with a Fool and a lunatic. Presently the scene shifts, and the old man, still cursing, still understanding nothing, is holding a dead girl in his arms while the Fool dangles on a gallows somewhere in the background. This is the bare skeleton of the play, and even here Tolstoy wants to cut out most of what is essential. He objects to the storm, as being unnecessary, to the Fool, who in his eyes is simply a tedious nuisance and an excuse for making bad jokes, and to the death of Cordelia, which, as he sees it, robs the play of its moral. According to Tolstoy, the earlier play, *King Leir*, which Shakespeare adapted

> terminates more naturally and more in accordance with the moral demands of the spectator than does Shakespeare's: namely, by the King of the Gauls conquering the husbands of the elder sisters, and by Cordelia, instead of being killed, restoring Leir to his former position.

In other words the tragedy ought to have been a comedy, or perhaps a melodrama. It is doubtful whether the sense of tragedy is compatible with belief in God: at any rate, it is not compatible with disbelief in human dignity and with the kind of 'moral demand' which feels cheated when virtue fails to triumph. A tragic situation exists precisely when virtue does *not* triumph but when it is still felt that man is nobler than the forces which destroy him. It is perhaps more significant that Tolstoy sees no justification for the presence of the Fool. The Fool is integral to the play. He acts not only as a sort of chorus, making the central situation clearer by commenting on it more intelligently than the other characters, but as a foil to Lear's frenzies. His jokes, riddles and scraps of rhyme, and his endless digs at Lear's high-minded folly, ranging from mere derision to a sort of melancholy poetry ('All thy other titles thou hast given away; that thou wast born with'), are like a trickle of sanity running through the play, a reminder that somewhere or other, in spite of the injustices, cruelties, intrigues, deceptions and misunderstandings that are being enacted here, life if going on much as usual. In Tolstoy's impatience with the Fool one gets a glimpse of his deeper quarrel with Shakespeare. He objects, with some justification, to the raggedness of Shakespeare's plays, the irrelevancies, the incredible plots, the exaggerated language: but what at

59

bottom he probably most dislikes is a sort of exuberance, a tendency to take—not so much a pleasure, as simply an interest in the actual process of life. It is a mistake to write Tolstoy off as a moralist attacking an artist. He never said that art, as such, is wicked or meaningless, nor did he even say that technical virtuosity is unimportant. But his main aim, in his later years, was to narrow the range of human consciousness. One's interests, one's points of attachment to the physical world and the day-to-day struggle, must be as few and not as many as possible. Literature must consist of parables, stripped of detail and almost independent of language. The parables—this is where Tolstoy differs from the average vulgar puritan—must themselves be works of art, but pleasure and curiosity must be excluded from them. Science, also, must be divorced from curiosity. The business of science, he says, is not to discover what happens, but to teach men how they ought to live. So also with history and politics. Many problems (for example, the Dreyfus case) are simply not worth solving, and he is willing to leave them as loose ends. Indeed his whole theory of 'crazes ' or 'epidemic suggestions', in which he lumps together such things as the Crusades and the Dutch passion of tulip-growing, shows a willingness to regard many human activities as mere ant-like rushings to and fro, inexplicable and uninteresting. Clearly he could have no patience with a chaotic, detailed, discursive writer like Shakespeare. His reaction is that of an irritable old man who is being pestered by a noisy child. 'Why do you keep jumping up and down like that? Why can't you sit still like I do?' In a way the old man is in the right, but the trouble is that the child has a feeling in its limbs which the old man has lost. And if the old man knows of the existence of this feeling, the effect is merely to increase his irritation: he would make children senile, if he could. Tolstoy does not know, perhaps, just *what* he misses in Shakespeare, but he is aware that he misses something, and he is determined that others shall be deprived of it as well. By nature he was imperious as well as egotistical. Well after he was grown up he would still occasionally strike his servant in moments of anger, and somewhat later, according to his English biographer, Derrick Leon, he felt 'a frequent desire upon the slenderest provocation to slap the faces of those with whom he disagreed'. One does not necessarily get rid of that kind of temperament by undergoing religious conversion, and indeed it is obvious that the illusion of having been reborn may allow one's native vices to flourish more freely than ever, though perhaps in subtler forms. Tolstoy was capable of abjuring physical violence and of seeing what this implies, but he was not capable of tolerance or humility, and even if one knew nothing of his other writings, one could deduce his tendency towards spiritual bullying from this single pamphlet.

However, Tolstoy is not simply trying to rob others of a pleasure he does not share. He is doing that, but his quarrel with Shakespeare goes further. It is the quarrel between the religious and the humanist attitudes towards life. Here one comes back to the central theme of *King Lear*, which Tolstoy does not mention, although he sets forth the plot in some detail.

Lear is one of the minority of Shakespeare's plays that are unmistakably *about* something. As Tolstoy justly complains, much rubbish has been written about Shakespeare as a philosopher, as a psychologist, as a 'great moral teacher', and what-not. Shakespeare was not a systematic thinker, his most serious thoughts are uttered irrelevantly or indirectly, and we do not know to what extent he wrote with a 'purpose' or even how much of the work attributed to him was actually written by him. In the Sonnets he never even refers to the plays as part of his achievement, though he does make what seems to be a half-ashamed allusion to his career as an actor. It is perfectly possible that he looked on at least half of his plays as mere pot-boilers and hardly bothered about purpose or probability so long as he could patch up something, usually from stolen material, which would more or less hang together on the stage. However, that is not the whole story. To begin with, as Tolstoy himself points out, Shakespeare has a habit of thrusting uncalled-for general reflections into the mouths of his characters. This is a serious fault in a dramatist, but it does not fit in with Tolstoy's picture of Shakespeare as a vulgar hack who has no opinions of his own and merely wishes to produce the greatest effect with the least trouble. And more than this, about a dozen of his plays, written for the most part later than 1600, do unquestionably have a meaning and even a moral. They revolve round a central subject which in some cases can be reduced to a single word. For example, *Macbeth* is about ambition, *Othello* is about jealousy, and *Timon of Athens* is about money. The subject of *Lear* is renunciation, and it is only by being wilfully blind that one can fail to understand what Shakespeare is saying.

Lear renounces his throne but expects everyone to continue treating him as a king. He does not see that if he surrenders power, other people will take advantage of his weakness: also that those who flatter him the most grossly, i.e. Regan and Goneril, are exactly the ones who will turn against him. The moment he finds that he can no longer make people obey him as he did before, he falls into a rage which Tolstoy describes as 'strange and unnatural', but which in fact is perfectly in character. In his madness and despair, he passes through two moods which again are natural enough in his circumstances, though in one of them it is probable that he is being used partly as a mouthpiece for Shakespeare's own opinions. One is the mood of disgust in which Lear repents, as it were, for having been a king, and grasps for the first time the rottenness of formal justice and vulgar morality. The other is a mood of impotent fury in which he wreaks imaginary revenges upon those who have wronged him. 'To have a thousand with red burning spits Come hissing in upon 'em!', and:

> 'It were a delicate stratagem to shoe
> A troop of horse with felt: I'll put't in proof;
> And when I have stol'n upon these sons-in-law,
> Then kill, kill, kill, kill, kill!'

Only at the end does he realize, as a sane man, that power, revenge and victory are not worth while:

> 'No, no, no, no! Come, let's away to prison . . .
> . . . . and we'll wear out

> In a wall'd prison, packs and sects of great ones
> That ebb and flow by the moon.'

But by the time he makes this discovery it is too late, for his death and Cordelia's are already decided on. That is the story, and, allowing for some clumsiness in the telling, it is a very good story.

But is it not also curiously similar to the history of Tolstoy himself? There is a general resemblance which one can hardly avoid seeing, because the most impressive event in Tolstoy's life, as in Lear's, was a huge gratuitous act of renunciation. In his old age he renounced his estate, his title and his copyrights, and made an attempt—a sincere attempt, though it was not successful—to escape from his privileged position and live the life of a peasant. But the deeper resemblance lies in the fact that Tolstoy, like Lear, acted on mistaken motives and failed to get the results he had hoped for. According to Tolstoy, the aim of every human being is happiness, and happiness can only be attained by doing the will of God. But doing the will of God means casting off all earthly pleasures and ambitions, and living only for others. Ultimately, therefore, Tolstoy renounced the world under the expectation that this would make him happier. But if there is one thing certain about his later years, it is that he was *not* happy. On the contrary, he was driven almost to the edge of madness by the behaviour of the people about him, who persecuted him precisely *because* of his renunciation. Like Lear, Tolstoy was not humble and not a good judge of character. He was inclined at moments to revert to the attitudes of an aristocrat, in spite of his peasant's blouse, and he even had two children whom he had believed in and who ultimately turned against him—though, of course, in a less sensational manner than Regan and Goneril. His exaggerated revulsion from sexuality was also distinctly similar to Lear's. Tolstoy's remark that marriage is 'slavery, satiety, repulsion' and means putting up with the proximity of 'ugliness, dirtiness, smell, sores', is matched by Lear's well-known outburst:

> 'But to the girdle do the gods inherit,
> Beneath is all the fiends';
> There's hell, there's darkness, there's the sulphurous pit,
> Burning, scalding, stench, consumption', etc., etc.

And though Tolstoy could not foresee it when he wrote his essay on Shakespeare, even the ending of his life—the sudden unplanned flight across country, accompanied only by a faithful daughter, the death in a cottage in a strange village—seems to have in it a sort of phantom reminiscence of *Lear*.

Of course, one cannot assume that Tolstoy was aware of this resemblance, or would have admitted it if it had been pointed out to him. But his attitude towards the play must have been influenced by its theme. Renouncing power, giving away your lands, was a subject on which he had reason to feel deeply. Probably, therefore, he would be more angered and disturbed by the moral that Shakespeare draws than he would be in the case of some other play—*Macbeth*, for example—which did not touch so closely on his own life.

But what exactly *is* the moral of *Lear*? Evidently there are two morals, one explicit, the other implied in the story.

Shakespeare starts by assuming that to make yourself powerless is to invite an attack. This does not mean that *everyone* will turn against you (Kent and the Fool stand by Lear from first to last), but in all probability *someone* will. If you throw away your weapons, some less scrupulous person will pick them up. If you turn the other cheek, you will get a harder blow on it than you got on the first one. This does not always happen, but it is to be expected, and you ought not to complain if it does happen. The second blow is, so to speak, part of the act of turning the other cheek. First of all, therefore, there is the vulgar, commonsense moral drawn by the Fool: 'Don't relinquish power, don't give away your lands.' But there is also another moral. Shakespeare never utters it in so many words, and it does not very much matter whether he was fully aware of it. It is contained in the story, which, after all, he made up, or altered to suit his purposes. It is: 'Give away your lands if you want to, but don't expect to gain happiness by doing so. Probably you won't gain happiness. If you live for others, you must live *for others*, and not as a roundabout way of getting an advantage for yourself.'

Obviously neither of these conclusions could have been pleasing to Tolstoy. The first of them expresses the ordinary, belly-to-earth selfishness from which he was genuinely trying to escape. The other conflicts with his desire to eat his cake and have it—that is, to destroy his own egoism and by so doing to gain eternal life. Of course, *Lear* is not a sermon in favour of altruism. It merely points out the results of practising self-denial for selfish reasons. Shakespeare had a considerable streak of worldliness in him, and if he had been forced to take sides in his own play, his sympathies would probably have lain with the Fool. But at least he could see the whole issue and treat it at the level of tragedy. Vice is punished, but virtue is not rewarded. The morality of Shakespeare's later tragedies is not religious in the ordinary sense, and certainly is not Christian. Only two of them, *Hamlet* and *Othello*, are supposedly occurring inside the Christian era, and even in those, apart from the antics of the ghost in *Hamlet*, there is no indication of a 'next world' where everything is to be put right. All of these tragedies start out with the humanist assumption that life, although full of sorrow, is worth living, and that Man is a noble animal—a belief which Tolstoy in his old age did not share.

Tolstoy was not a saint, but he tried very hard to make himself into a saint, and the standards he applied to literature were other-worldly ones. It is important to realize that the difference between a saint and an ordinary human being is a difference of kind and not of degree. That is, the one is not to be regarded as an imperfect form of the other. The saint, at any rate Tolstoy's kind of saint, is not trying to work an improvement in earthly life: he is trying to bring it to an end and put something different in its place. One obvious expression of this is the claim that celibacy is 'higher' than marriage. If only, Tolstoy says in effect, we would stop breeding, fighting, struggling and enjoying, if we could get rid not only of our sins but of everything else that binds us to the surface of the earth—including love, in the ordinary sense of caring more for one human being than another—then the whole painful process would be over and the Kingdom of Heaven would arrive. But a normal human being does not want the Kingdom of Heaven: he wants life on earth to continue. This is not solely because he is 'weak', 'sinful' and anxious for a 'good time'. Most people get a fair amount of fun out of their lives, but on balance life is suffering, and only the very young or the very foolish imagine otherwise. Ultimately it is the Christian attitude which is self-interested and hedonistic, since the aim is always to get away from the painful struggle of earthly life and find eternal peace in some kind of Heaven or Nirvana. The humanist attitude is that the struggle must continue and that death is the price of life. 'Men must endure. Their going hence, even as their coming hither: Ripeness is all'—which is an un-Christian sentiment. Often there is a seeming truce between the humanist and the religious believer, but in fact their attitudes cannot be reconciled: one must choose between this world and the next. And the enormous majority of human beings, if they understood the issue, would choose this world. They do make that choice when they continue working, breeding and dying instead of crippling their faculties in the hope of obtaining a new lease of existence elsewhere.

We do not know a great deal about Shakespeare's religious beliefs, and from the evidence of his writings it would be difficult to prove that he had any. But at any rate he was not a saint or a would-be saint: he was a human being, and in some ways not a very good one. It is clear, for instance, that he liked to stand well with the rich and powerful, and was capable of flattering them in the most servile way. He is also noticeably cautious, not to say cowardly, in his manner of uttering unpopular opinions. Almost never does he put a subversive or sceptical remark into the mouth of a character likely to be identified with himself. Throughout his plays the acute social critics, the people who are not taken in by accepted fallacies, are buffoons, villains, lunatics or persons who are shamming insanity or are in a state of violent hysteria. *Lear* is a play in which this tendency is particularly well-marked. It contains a great deal of veiled social criticism—a point Tolstoy misses—but it is all uttered either by the Fool, by Edgar when he is pretending to be mad, or by Lear during his bouts of madness. In his sane moments Lear hardly ever makes an intelligent remark. And yet the very fact that Shakespeare had to use these subterfuges shows how widely his thoughts ranged. He could not restrain himself from commenting on almost everything, although he put on a series of masks in order to do so. If one has once read Shakespeare with attention, it is not easy to go a day without quoting him, because there are not many subjects of major importance that he does not discuss or at least mention somewhere or other, in his unsystematic but illuminating way. Even the irrelevancies that litter every one of his plays—the puns and riddles, the lists of names, the scraps of *reportage* like the conversation of the carriers in *Henry IV*, the bawdy jokes, the rescued fragments of forgotten ballads—are merely the products of excessive vitality. Shakespeare was not a philosopher or a scientist, but he did have curiosity: he loved the surface of the earth and the process of life—which, it should be repeated, is *not* the same thing as wanting to have a good time and stay alive as long as possible. Of course, it is not because of the quality of his thought that Shakespeare has survived, and he might not even be remembered as a dramatist if he had not also been a poet. His main hold on us is through language. How deeply Shakespeare himself was fascinated by the music of words can probably be inferred from the speeches of Pistol. What Pistol says is largely meaningless, but if one considers his lines singly they are magnificent rhetorical verse. Evidently, pieces of resounding nonsense ('Let floods o'erswell, and fiends for food howl on', etc.) were constantly appearing in Shakespeare's mind of their own accord, and a half-lunatic character had to be invented to use them up. Tolstoy's native tongue was not English, and one cannot blame him for being unmoved by Shakespeare's verse, nor even, perhaps, for refusing to believe that Shakespeare's skill with words was something out of the ordinary. But he would also have rejected the whole notion of valuing poetry for its texture—valuing it, that is to say, as a kind of music. If it could somehow have been proved to him that his whole explanation of Shakespeare's rise to fame is mistaken, that inside the English-speaking world, at any rate, Shakespeare's popularity is genuine, that his mere skill in placing one syllable beside another has given acute pleasure to generation after generation of English-speaking people—all this would not have been counted as a merit to Shakespeare, but rather the contrary. It would simply have been one more proof of the irreligious, earthbound nature of Shakespeare and his admirers. Tolstoy would have said that poetry is to be judged by its meaning, and that seductive sounds merely cause false meanings to go unnoticed. At every level it is the same issue—this world against the next: and certainly the music of words is something that belongs to this world.

A sort of doubt has always hung round the character of Tolstoy, as round the character of Gandhi. He was not a vulgar hypocrite, as some people declared him to be, and he would probably have imposed even greater sacrifices on himself than he did, if he had not been interfered with at every step by the people surrounding him, especially his wife. But on the other hand it is dangerous to take such men as Tolstoy at their disciples' valuation. There is always the possibility—the probability, indeed—that they have done no more than exchange one form of egoism for another. Tolstoy renounced wealth, fame and privilege; he abjured violence in all its forms and was ready to suffer for doing so; but it is not so easy to believe that he abjured the principle of coercion, or at least the *desire* to coerce others. There are families in which the father will say to his child, 'You'll get a thick ear if you do that again,' while the mother, her eyes brimming over with tears, will take the child in her arms and murmur lovingly, 'Now, darling, *is* it kind to Mummy to do that?' And who would maintain that the second method is less tyrannous than the first? The distinction that really matters is not between violence and non-violence, but between having and not having the appetite for power. There are people who are convinced of the wickedness both of armies and of police forces, but who are nevertheless much more intolerant and inquisitorial in outlook than the normal person who believes that it is necessary to use violence in certain circumstances. They will not say to somebody else, 'Do this, that and the other or you will go to prison,' but they will, if they can, get inside his brain and dictate his thoughts for him in the minutest particulars. Creeds like pacifism and anarchism, which seem on the surface to imply a complete renunciation of power, rather encourage this habit of mind. For if you have embraced a creed which appears to be free from the ordinary dirtiness of politics—a creed from which you yourself cannot expect to draw any material advantage—surely that proves that you are in the right? And the more you are in the right, the more natural that everyone else should be bullied into thinking likewise.

If we are to believe what he says in his pamphlet, Tolstoy had never been able to see any merit in Shakespeare, and was always astonished to find that his fellow-writers, Turgenev, Fet and others, thought differently. We may be sure that in his unregenerate days Tolstoy's conclusion would have been: 'You like Shakespeare—I don't. Let's leave it at that.' Later, when his perception that it takes all sorts to make a world had deserted him, he came to think of Shakespeare's writings as something dangerous to himself. The more pleasure people took in Shakespeare, the less they would listen to Tolstoy. Therefore nobody must be *allowed* to enjoy Shakespeare, just as nobody must be allowed to drink alcohol or smoke tobacco. True, Tolstoy would not prevent them by force. He is not demanding that the police shall impound every copy of Shakespeare's works. But he will do dirt on Shakespeare, if he can. He will try to get inside the mind of every lover of Shakespeare and kill his enjoyment by every trick he can think of, including—as I have shown in my summary of his pamphlet—arguments which are self-contradictory or even doubtfully honest.

But finally the most striking thing is how little difference it all makes. As I said earlier, one cannot *answer* Tolstoy's pamphlet, at least on its main counts. There is no argument by which one can defend a poem. It defends itself by surviving, or it is indefensible. And if this test is valid, I think the verdict in Shakespeare's case must be 'not guilty'. Like every other writer, Shakespeare will be forgotten sooner or later, but it is unlikely that a heavier indictment will ever be brought against him. Tolstoy was perhaps the most admired literary man of his age, and he was certainly not its least able pamphleteer. He turned all his powers of denunciation against Shakespeare, like all the guns of a battleship roaring simultaneously. And with what result? Forty years later, Shakespeare is still there, completely unaffected, and of the attempt to demolish him nothing remains except the yellowing pages of a pamphlet which hardly anyone has read, and which would be forgotten altogether if Tolstoy had not also been the author of *War and Peace* and *Anna Karenina*.

A neatly prepared typescript of this article has survived. The typing does not appear to be Orwell's and though decently done is not to the highest professional standard. There are no verbal and only two punctuation differences between the typed and printed versions. Twice (paragraph 2, line 5, after 'feelings,' and paragraph 10, line 6) a colon is substituted in print for the semi-colon in the typescript; the semi-colon has been restored (with more conviction on the second occasion than the first). The printed text uses caps and small caps for proper names; the typescript (which is followed here) uses upper and lower case. One verbal error in the typescript has been corrected by hand: in the passage quoted in the second paragraph the typist typed 'their aesthetic and ethical understanding.'

On 18 January 1947, Dwight Macdonald wrote to Orwell to say that he would like to use a shortened form of this article; see *3160, n. 1*. A copy was sent to him with this undated handwritten covering note: 'Herewith the essay I spoke to you of in case you can use it—its° fearfully long (abt 6000 words). G.O.' Macdonald wrote to Orwell on 9 April 1947 explaining that he would not be able to use it until at least the 'next fall'; see *3215*. In the event, Macdonald did not use it.

Tolstoy's essay was published in 1906 in *The Fortnightly Review* and then in *Tolstoy on Shakespeare*, translated by V. Tchertkoff (New York, 1907). It is included in *Shakespeare in Europe*, edited by Oswald LeWinter (Cleveland, Ohio, 1963; Harmondsworth, 1970).

1. Tulips seem to have originated in Turkey. A mania for them struck Holland in the seventeenth century with devastating financial results. In Alkmaar, in 1639, 120 tulip bulbs were sold for 90,000 florins; a single bulb, the Viceroy, fetched 4,203 guilders. In the eighteenth century, such was the economic damage being caused, the government stopped the tulip traffic. Orwell may have known the novel, *La Tulipe Noire* (1850) by Alexandre Dumas. An abridged version was often set for schoolboys to read (in French).
3. Warwick Deeping (1877–1950), prolific and popular novelist. Perhaps his best-known work is *Sorrell and Son* (1925; New York, 1926). In *Keep the Aspidistra Flying* it looks as if Orwell originally intended to have Gordon Comstock call the novels of Warwick Deeping and of Ethel M. Dell 'garbage.' This was, however, suppressed on legal advice. See *CW*, IV, Textual Note, 7/34 (282). Despite that, Deeping (but not Dell) rated well enough to be included in *The New Cambridge Bibliography of English Literature*, iv (1972).

3182. 'As I Please,' 76

Tribune, 7 March 1947

One of the great faults of the present Government is its failure to tell the people what is happening and why. That is so generally agreed that in itself it is hardly worth saying over again. However, with the wartime machinery of propaganda largely scrapped, and the Press under control of private owners, some of whom are none too friendly, it is not easy for the Government to publicise itself. Posters—at any rate, posters like the present ones—will not achieve much, films are expensive, pamphlets and White Papers are not read by the big public. The most obvious means of publicity is the radio, and we are up against the difficulty that politicians in this country are seldom radio-conscious.

During the recent crisis,ᵃ people were to be heard remarking that the Minister of this or that ought to "come to the microphone" more frequently. But it is not much use coming to the microphone unless what you say is listened to. When I worked in the B.B.C., and frequently had to put eminent people on the air, I was struck by the fact that few professional politicians seemed to realise that broadcasting is an art that has to be learned, and that it is quite different from platform speaking. A first-rate performer in one medium may be hopeless in the other, unless re-trained. Ernest Bevin, for instance, is a good platform speaker but a poor broadcaster. Attlee is better, so far as his voice goes, but does not seem to have a gift for the telling phrase. Churchill's wartime broadcasts were good of their Corinthian kind, but Churchill, unlike most of the others, gives the impression of having studied microphone technique.

When a speaker is invisible, he not only cannot make use of his personal charm, if any, he also cannot make gestures to emphasise his points. He cannot act with his body, and therefore has to act much more elaborately with his larynx. A good exercise for anyone trying to improve his microphone delivery is to have one of his speeches recorded, and then listen to it. This is an astonishing and even shocking experience. Not only does one's voice, heard externally, sound completely different from what it sounds like inside one's skull, but it always sounds much less emphatic. To sound natural on the air one has to have the impression, internally, that one is overacting. If one speaks as one would in everyday life, or on a platform, one always sounds bored. That, indeed, is the impression that the majority of untrained broadcasters do give, especially when they speak from scripts: and when the speaker sounds bored, the audience is apt to follow suit.

Some time ago a foreign visitor[1] asked me if I could recommend a good, representative anthology of English verse. When I thought it over I found that I could not name a single one that seemed to me satisfactory. Of course there are innumerable period anthologies, but nothing, so far as I know, that attempts to cover the whole of English literature except Palgrave's *Golden Treasury* and, more comprehensive and more up-to-date, the *Oxford Book of English Verse*.

Now, I do not deny that the *Oxford Book* is useful, that there is a great deal of good stuff in it, and that every schoolchild ought to have a copy, in default of something better. Still, when you look at the last 50 pages, you think twice about recommending such a book to a foreigner who may imagine that it is really representative of English verse. Indeed, the whole of this part of the book is a lamentable illustration of what happens to professors of literature when they have to exercise independent judgement. Up to 1850, or thereabouts, one could not go very wrong in compiling an anthology, because, after all, it is on the whole the best poems that have survived. But as soon as Sir Arthur Quiller-Couch reached his contemporaries, all semblance of taste deserted him.

The *Oxford Book* stops at 1900, and it is true that the last decades of the nineteenth century were a poor period for verse. Still, there were poets even in the 'nineties. There was Ernest Dowson[2]—*Cynara* is not my idea of a good poem, but I would sooner have it than Henley's "England, My England"— there was Hardy, who published his first poems in 1898, and there was Housman, who published *A Shropshire Lad* in 1896. There was also Hopkins, who was not in print or barely in print, but whom Sir Arthur Quiller-Couch must have known about. None of these appears in the *Oxford Book*. Yeats, who had already published a great deal at that date, does appear shortly, but he is not represented by his best poems: neither is Kipling, who, I think, did write one or two poems (for instance, "How far is St. Helena")[3] which deserve to be included in a serious anthology. And on the other hand, just look at the stuff that *has* been included! Sir Henry Newbolt's Old Cliftonian keeping a stiff upper lip on the North-West Frontier;[4] other patriotic pieces by Henley and Kipling; and page after page of weak, sickly, imitative verse by Andrew Lang, Sir William Watson, A. C. Benson, Alice Meynell[5] and others now forgotten. What is one to think of an anthologist who puts Newbolt and Edmund Gosse in the same volume with Shakespeare, Wordsworth and Blake?

Perhaps I am just being ignorant and there does already exist a comprehensive anthology running all the way from Chaucer to Dylan Thomas and including no tripe. But if not, I think it is time to compile one, or at least to bring the *Oxford Book* up to date by making a completely new selection of poets from Tennyson onwards.[6]

Looking through what I have written above, I see that I have spoken rather snootily of Dowson's *Cynara*. I know it is a bad poem, but it is bad in a good way, or good in a bad way, and I do not wish to pretend that I never admired it. Indeed, it was one of the favourites of my boyhood. I am quoting from memory:

I have forgot much, Cynara, gone with the wind,
Flung roses, roses riotously with the throng
Dancing, to put thy pale lost lilies out of mind;
But I was desolate and sick of an old passion—
Yea, all the time, because the dance was long—
I have been faithful to thee, Cynara, in my fashion.

Surely those lines possess, if not actual merit, at least the same kind of charm as belongs to a pink geranium or a soft-centre chocolate.

a. A widespread transport strike and a shortage of coal, followed by non-stop blizzards, led to a serious food and fuel crisis.

1. Presumably Helmut Klöse; see Orwell's letter to him, 18 November 1946, *3118*.

2. Ernest Dowson (1867–1900), from 'Non Sum Qualis Eram.' In the original, Dowson's name was given as Dawson. Orwell explained that this was a misprint at the end of 'As I Please,' 77, 14 March 1947; see *3190*. Orwell remembered the poem verbally with accuracy. He omitted a few punctuation marks—notably the exclamation points after Cynara—but his version has not been amended.

3. 'How far is St. Helena' was printed in *Rewards and Fairies* (1910).

4. 'Vitaï Lampada, with its refrain, 'Play up! play up! and play the game!', to which Orwell refers several times, for example, see *688*, n. 3 and *694*, n. 5.

5. On 6 July 1932 Orwell, wrote to Leonard Moore about a proposed title for his first book. He suggested 'putting at the start the quotation The Lady Poverty was fair, / But she hath lost her looks of late' and calling what was to be *Down and Out in Paris and London* 'The Lady Poverty' or 'Lady Poverty' (see *133*). These lines, as Orwell notes in his letter, are by Alice Meynell.

6. In 1972 *The New Oxford Book of English Verse 1250–1950*, chosen and edited by Helen Gardner, was published. Hardy, Housman, Hopkins, and Dylan Thomas were included; Newbolt, Lang, Watson, Gosse, and Benson were deleted. Poems by Henley and Kipling were not patriotic, and 'England, My England' was dropped; 'Cynara' was retained. The following year, Philip Larkin's *The Oxford Book of Twentieth-Century English Verse* was published. This included Orwell's 'As One Non-Combatant to Another'; see *2138*.

3183. To Leonard Moore

7 March 1947   Typewritten

27B Canonbury Square,
Islington, N.1.

Dear Moore,
I enclose the contract for "Homage to Catalonia," duly signed. I am so glad you managed to bring this off. I suppose the publishers know about the minor alteration I suggested—at any rate I think Madame Davet knows about it.[1]

Could you let me have a copy of the contract for "Coming Up for Air." I think I had better see Gollancz before I go away, and I want to know just where I stand with him, in particular with regard to this particular book. So far as I remember the rights in it reverted to me after two years. If avoidable I don't want the re-issue of this book held up, because I shall not have anything else coming out this year, ie. in book form.[2]

I have just rung up the Anglo-French Literary Agency about "Animal Farm." They say the French edition is not coming out till the middle of the year (which I suppose means later)[3] but that the hold-up was not political but was genuinely because Mlle. Pathé was dissatisfied with the translation.

Yours sincerely
Eric Blair

1. The French translation, by Madame Yvonne Davet, was not brought out by Gallimard, Paris, until 1955, five years after Orwell's death. For changes he required, see Textual Note to *CW*, VI.
2. The Uniform Edition of *Coming Up for Air* was not published until May 1948.
3. 'Later' proved correct: the French translation of *Animal Farm, Les Animaux Partout!* was published in October 1947.

3184. To Leonard Moore

7 March 1947   Typewritten

27B Canonbury Square,
Islington, N.1.

Dear Moore,
I forgot in the other letter to give you the biographical details asked for by Charlot.[1]

Born 1903 in India.
Educated Eton (King's Scholar) 1917–21.
Served in Indian Imperial Police (Burma) 1922–27.
Lived in Paris 1928–29.
School-teacher from 1930–33.
Worked in a bookshop 1934–35.
Fought in Spanish civil war (POUM militia) 1937.

Visited French Morocco 1938–39.
Worked in BBC (Eastern Service) 1941–43.
Literary editor of Tribune 1943–44.
"Observer" correspondent in Paris and Germany 1945.
Widower with one son aged nearly 3.

If they want a photograph I have plenty now.

Yours sincerely
[Signed] Eric Blair
Eric Blair

1. Charlot was seeing *Homage to Catalonia* through the press; see *3036* and *3216, n. 2.*

3185. To·George Woodcock (as Secretary, Freedom Defence Committee)

7 March 1947   Typewritten

27B Canonbury Square,
Islington, N.1.

Dear George,
Following on our telephone conversation, here is that address.

The Refuges' Defence Committee
5 Victoria Street.[1]

What I am not certain is whether it is actually in being yet. I read about it in a magazine called the Baltic Review which said that Lord Beveridge "has accepted an invitation to become chairman" of it. Other people associated are Michael Foot, Vernon Bartlett and Sir Arthur Salter,[2] so I suppose it is all right. Any way they are people to establish contact with.

Yours
George

1. This presumably refers to the case of the Polish soldier, Franciszek Kilański; see Orwell's letter to Woodcock, 28 February 1947, *3180, n. 1.* The address has been ringed and annotated 'see letter 13/3/47' but no letter of that date has been traced.
2. Sir Arthur Salter (1881–1975; Baron Salter, 1953) was a professor of political theory and Independent MP for Oxford University, 1937–50. He made a study of the Depression of the inter-war years. For Vernon Bartlett, see *654, n. 2.*

3186. To *The New Leader* (New York)

12 March 1947

HAVE AIRMAILED ARTICLE FIVE THOUSAND

ORWELL

The cable refers to 'Burnham's View of the Contemporary World Struggle,' a review of Burnham's book *The Struggle for the World.* The review was published by *The New Leader* on 29 March 1947; see *3204*. With the typescript Orwell sent a covering note:

I hope this was the kind of thing you wanted. It should be a little under 5000 words. Could you be kind enough to make payment to my literary agents—

McIntosh & Otis Inc.
18 East 41st Street
New York 17 N.Y.

G. O.

On 19 March. S. M. Levitas, executive editor of *The New Leader*, wrote acknowledging the receipt of Orwell's article. He was convinced, he said, that 'we see eye to eye on all important problems' and he hoped this review would be the beginning of closer relations with each other. He hoped also that Orwell would find time to write more often for *The New Leader*. (Orwell made two further contributions, 19 June 1948 and 14 May 1949; the former was reprinted from *Politics and Letters*.) Levitas told Orwell that 'The Communists have already opened up their guns against Jimmie [Burnham] and a battle royal is in prospect.' He also explained that *The New Leader* had been in existence for twenty-two years and had 'constantly devoted its pages to combatting totalitarian forces.'

On the same day, Levitas sent a cheque for $25.00 in payment for the article to McIntosh & Otis, as Orwell had requested. In a letter to *The New Leader*, also of 19 March, Elizabeth R. Otis explained that this firm was handling Orwell's magazine work in the United States.

3187. From Ihor Szewczenko to Orwell

On 7 March 1947, Ihor Szewczenko[1] wrote to Orwell under some pressure from the publisher of the Ukrainian translation of *Animal Farm* (see *2969*) for a preface by Orwell. The Ukrainian translation had been given to the publisher in the early autumn of 1946. Now, in a letter of 19 February 1947, the publisher had requested a preface for this version, regarding it as absolutely essential to the satisfactory reception of *Animal Farm* in Ukrainian. Szewczenko explained that delays had arisen because he had moved from Münich to Belgium (where the book was being printed), although he still worked in Germany, and because of difficulties in sending letters to Germany. Although the printer and publisher of *Animal Farm* had been licensed by the occupying powers, Szewczenko did not know whether a licence to publish *Animal Farm* had been applied for by them. If Orwell could not send a preface, he was asked to provide biographical notes.

Szewczenko then set out the political background of the publishers of the Ukrainian version of *Animal Farm*, who were, he said, 'genuinely interested' in the story. They were, in the main, Soviet Ukrainians, many of them former members of the Bolshevik Party, but afterwards inmates of Siberian camps. They were the nucleus of a political group. They 'stand on the "Soviet" platform and defend the "acquisitions of the October revolution", but they turn against the "counter-revolutionary Bonapartism" [of] Stalin and the Russian nationalistic exploitation of the Ukrainian people; their conviction is, that the revolution will contribute to the full national development. Britain's socialistic effort (which they take literally) is of foremost interest and importance, they say. Their situation and past, causes them to sympathise with trotskyites, although there are several differences between them. Their theoretical weapon is marxism, unfortunately in a somewhat vulgarised (Soviet) edition. But it could not be otherwise. These are men formed within the Soviet regime.' He concluded his first letter by saying that to 'unveil' them as dissatisfied, regional, party elements would be a quarter-truth—'AF is not being published by Ukrainian Joneses.'

1. Ihor Szewczenko, a Soviet Ukrainian who had grown up in Poland, was, when he first wrote to Orwell (see 2969, *n. 1*), commuting from Münich, where he then lived, to Quackenbrück, where he worked on a newspaper published by the 2nd Polish Division. His move to join his family in Belgium had complicated his life, the translation of *Animal Farm* (which he did at lunch-times and back at home late at night), and its publication. He later emigrated to the United States, where, as Ihor Ševčenko, he became professor of Byzantine literature at Harvard.

3188. To Ihor Szewczenko

13 March 1947   Typewritten

27B Canonbury Square,
Islington, N.1.

Dear Mr Szewczenko,
Many thanks for your letter of the 7th, which I received today.

I am frightfully busy, but I will try to send you a short introduction to A.F. and to despatch it not more than a week from hence. I gather that you want it to contain some biographical material, and also, I suppose, an account of how the book came to be written. I assume that the book will be produced in a very simple style with no illustrations on the cover, but just in case it should be wanted I will send a photograph as well.

I was very interested to hear about the people responsible for translating A.F.,[1] and encouraged to learn that that type of opposition exists in the USSR. I do hope it will not all end by the Displaced persons° being shipped back to the USSR or else mostly absorbed by Argentina. I think our desperate labour shortage may compel us to encourage a good many D.Ps to settle in this country, but at present the government is only talking of letting them in as servants etc., because there is still working-class resistance against letting in foreign workers, owing to fear of unemployment, and the Communists and "sympathisers" are able to play on this.

I have noted your new address and presume you will be there till further notice. I shall be at the above address until April 10th, and after that at the Scottish address. I think you have this, but in case you have not I will give it you:

Barnhill
Isle of Jura
Argyllshire, SCOTLAND.

Yours sincerely
[Signed] Geo. Orwell
George Orwell

1. This seems to be a slight misunderstanding by Orwell of Szewczenko's letter. Szewczenko was undertaking the translation (it appeared under his name as Ivan Cherniatync'kyi). In his letter of 7 March 1947 (see *3187*), he states clearly that the 'publisher' or 'publishers'—he puts both words within single quotation marks—'are for the greater part Soviet Ukrainians,' many of them onetime members of the Bolshevik Party and later 'inmates of the Siberian camps.' He describes them as 'the nucleus of a political group' opposed to 'Stalin's and the Russian nationalistic exploitation of the Ukrainian people.'

3189. Freedom Defence Committee and Driver Stowe

13 March 1947

Orwell appears to have been involved in correspondence connected with the case of Driver Stowe, which the Freedom Defence Committee took up, though none of his letters has been traced. Driver Stowe had had thirty-nine years of service with the London & North Eastern Railway and its antecedents before the grouping of the railways in 1923. He had been dismissed after picking up coal which had dropped onto the track, valued at 1s 10d, with the loss of all pension rights, despite the case being thrown out by the magistrates. A mitigating circumstance was the exceptionally cold weather and shortage of fuel. He was, however, reinstated on appeal, though that might have been due, largely or in part, to reports in the press. One of the documents (dated 13 March 1947) is marked 'Orwell informed.'[1]

1. Such harsh management has continued to 1992. A railwayman and three colleagues were dismissed for having half-a-pint of lager at lunch-time to celebrate his retirement. With that dismissal went the loss of £20,000 in pension entitlement. Public reaction led to their reinstatement with the loss of a week's wages each.

3190. 'As I Please,' 77

Tribune, 14 March 1947

I have not yet read more than a newspaper paragraph about Nu Speling,[1] in connection with which somebody is introducing a Bill in Parliament, but if it is like most other schemes for rationalising our spelling, I am against it in advance, as I imagine most people will be.

Probably the strongest reason for resisting rationalised spelling is laziness. We have all learned to read and write already, and we don't want to have to do it over again. But there are other more respectable objections. To begin with, unless the scheme were rigidly enforced, the resulting chaos, with some newspapers and publishing houses accepting it, others refusing it, and others adopting it in patches, would be fearful. Then again, anyone who had learned only the new system would find it very difficult to read books printed in the old one, so that the huge labour of re-spelling the entire literature of the past would have to be undertaken.[2] And again, you can only fully rationalise spelling if you give a fixed value to each letter. But this means standardising pronunciation, which could not be done in this country without an unholy row. What do you do, for instance, about words like "butter" or "glass," which are pronounced in different ways in London and Newcastle? Other words, such as "were," are pronounced in two different ways according to individual inclination, or according to context.

However, I do not want to pre-judge the inventors of Nu Speling. Perhaps they have already thought of a way round these difficulties. And certainly our existing spelling system is preposterous and must be a torment to foreign students. This is a pity, because English is well fitted to be the universal second language, if there ever is such a thing. It has a large start over any natural language and an enormous start over any manufactured one, and apart from the spelling it is very easy to learn. Would it not be possible to rationalise it by little and little, a few words every year? Already some of the more ridiculous spellings do tend to get killed off unofficially. For instance, how many people now spell "hiccup" as "hiccough?"

Another thing I am against in advance—for it is bound to be suggested sooner or later—is the complete scrapping of our present system of weights and measures.[3]

Obviously you have got to have the metric system for certain purposes. For scientific work it has long been in use, and it is also needed for tools and machinery, especially if you want to export them. But there is a strong case for keeping on the old measurements for use in everyday life. One reason is that the metric system does not possess, or has not succeeded in establishing, a large number of units that can be visualised. There is, for instance, effectively no unit between the metre, which is more than a yard, and the centimetre, which is less than half an inch. In English you can describe someone as being five feet three inches high, or five feet nine inches, or six feet one inch, and your hearer will know fairly accurately what you mean. But I have never heard a Frenchman say, "He is a hundred and forty-two centimetres high"; it would not convey any visual image. So also with the various other measurements. Rods and acres, pints, quarts and gallons, pounds, stones and hundredweights, are all of them units with which we are intimately familiar, and we should be slightly poorer without them. Actually, in countries where the metric system is in force a few of the old measurements tend to linger on for everyday purposes, although officially discouraged.

There is also the literary consideration, which cannot be left quite out of account. The names of the units in the old system are short homely words which lend themselves to vigorous speech. Putting a quart into a pint pot is a good image, which could hardly be expressed in the metric system. Also, the literature of the past deals only in the old measurements, and many passages would become an irritation if one had to do a sum in arthmetic when one read them, as one does with those tiresome versts[4] in a Russian novel.

The emmet's inch[5] and eagle's mile
Make lame philosophy to smile:

fancy having to turn that into millimetres!

I have just been reading about a party of German teachers, journalists, trade union delegates and others who have been on a visit to this country. It appears that while here they were given food parcels by trade unions and other organisations, only to have them taken away again by the Customs officials at Harwich. They were not even allowed to take out of the country the 15 lb. of food which is permitted to a returning prisoner of war. The newspaper reporting this adds without apparent irony that the Germans in question had been here "on a six weeks' course in democracy."

I wonder whether it would be possible, before the next bout of cold weather comes along, to do something about the racket in firewood? Last week I paid fifteen shillings for a hundred logs. They were very small logs, weighing I should say a pound to a pound and a half each, so that weight for weight they will have been twice or three times as expensive as coal. A day or two later I heard of logs being sold at a pound or thirty shillings a hundred. In any case, much of the wood that is hawked round the streets in cold weather is full of sap and almost unburnable.

Incidentally, does not the weather we have just been through reinforce my earlier plea for better use of our peat resources? At the time various people said to me: "Ah, but you see, English people aren't used to peat. You'd never get them to use it." During the last two weeks, most of the people known to me have used anything, not despising the furniture as a last resort. I kept going for a day myself on a blitzed bedstead, and wrote an article by its grateful warmth.

The other day I had occasion to write something about the teaching of history in private schools,[6] and the following scene, which was only rather loosely connected with what I was writing, floated into my memory. It was less than fifteen years ago that I witnessed it.[7]
"Jones!"
"Yessir!"
"Causes of the French Revolution."
"Please, sir, the French Revolution was due to three causes, the teachings of Voltaire and Rousseau, the oppression of the nobles by the people and—"
At this moment a faint chill, like the first premonitory symptom of an illness, falls upon Jones. Is it possible that he has gone wrong somewhere? The master's face is inscrutable. Swiftly Jones casts his mind back to the unappetising little book, with the gritty brown cover, a page of which is memorised daily. He could have sworn he had the whole thing right. But at this moment Jones discovers for the first time the deceptiveness of visual memory. The whole page is clear in his mind, the shape of every paragraph

accurately recorded, but the trouble is that there is no saying which way round the words go. He had made sure it was the oppression of the nobles by the people; but then it might have been the oppression of the people by the nobles. It is a toss-up. Desperately he takes his decision—better to stick to his first version. He gabbles on:

"The oppression of the nobles by the people and—"

"JONES!"

Is that kind of thing still going on, I wonder?

To forestall a flood of letters:—

(a) As I have found out since writing my column last week, there are already several inclusive anthologies which deal with modern verse more satisfactorily than the *Oxford Book*; and

(b) "Ernest Dawson" (for "Dowson") was a misprint.[8]

1. 'Nu Speling' was presented to Parliament (as New Spelling) in 1949. It was to be introduced in three stages: 1. for five years in primary schools, after which old spelling would not be taught; 2. for five years in advertising and public announcements; and 3. thereafter in all legal documents and records; new literature would not be copyrighted unless in new spelling. The bill was rejected by 87 votes to 84. (David Crystal, *The Cambridge Encyclopedia of Language* (1987), which calls it Nue Spelling, 215; an example of what Crystal calls New Spelling is given on 216.)
2. Compare the rewriting of earlier texts, for example, Shakespeare, in Newspeak in *Nineteen Eighty-Four*; see *CW*, IX, 325.
3. European Community Directive 89/617 phases out British imperial measures. Parliament's Units of Measurement Regulations, 1995, makes it a criminal offence to sell, for example, fruit or vegetables by the pound, requiring that 'the old measurements' be replaced by metric measures. Selling by imperial measure will render people liable to a fine of up to £5,000. According to a schedule attached to these Regulations, an ounce must be referred to in public documents as 28·349523125 grams; one horsepower as 0·74569987158227022 kilowatts, and so on. (*Sunday Telegraph*, 22 July and 6 August; *Daily Telegraph*, 8 August 1995).
4. versts] *set as* verses. A verst is about two-thirds of a mile or approximately one kilometre.
5. An emmet is an ant.
6. Possibly a reference to 'Such, Such Were the Joys,' and particularly to the 'unrelated, unintelligible facts' that had to be learned for the Harrow History Prize, referred to therein; see *3409*.
7. Less than fifteen years before March 1947 would be after that month in 1932. In April 1932 Orwell started teaching at The Hawthorns, Hayes, Middlesex.
8. See 'As I Please,' 76, 7 March 1947, *3182, n. 2.*

3191. To Victor Gollancz

14 March 1947   Typewritten

> 27B Canonbury Square,
> Islington, N.1.

Dear Gollancz,

I believe Leonard Moore has already spoken to you about the contract which I still have with you and about my wish to be released from it.[1] I believe that the contract that still subsists between us is the one made for KEEP THE ASPIDISTRA FLYING in 1937, which provided that I would give you the first refusal of my next three novels. COMING UP FOR AIR worked off one of these, but you did not accept ANIMAL FARM, which you saw and refused in 1944, as working off another. So that by the terms of the contract I still owe you the refusal of two other novels.

I know that I am asking you a very great favour in asking that you should cancel the contract, but various circumstances have changed in the ten years since it was made, and I believe that it might be to your advantage, as it certainly would be to mine, to bring it to an end. The position is that since then you have published three books of mine[2] but you have also refused two others on political grounds,[3] and there was also another which you did not refuse but which it seemed natural to take to another publisher.[4] The crucial case was ANIMAL FARM. At the time when this book was finished, it was very hard indeed to get it published, and I determined then that if possible I would take all my future output to the publishers who would produce it, because I knew that anyone who would risk this book would risk anything. Secker & Warburg were not only ready to publish ANIMAL FARM but are willing, when paper becomes available, to do a uniform edition of such of my books as I think worth reprinting, including some which are at present very completely out of print. They are also anxious to reprint my novel COMING UP FOR AIR in an ordinary edition this year, but, not unnaturally, they are only willing to do all this if they can have a comprehensive contract giving them control of anything I write.

From my own point of view it is clearly very unsatisfactory to have to take my novels to one publisher and at the same time to be obliged, at any rate in some cases, to take non-fiction books elsewhere. I recognise, of course, that your political position is not now exactly what it was when you refused ANIMAL FARM, and in any case I respect your unwillingness to publish books which go directly counter to your political principles. But it seems to me that this difficulty is likely to arise again in some form or other, and that it would be better if you are willing to bring the whole thing to an end.

If you wish to see me personally about this, I am at your disposal. I shall be at this address until about April 10th.

Yours sincerely,
[Signed] Geo. Orwell
George Orwell

1. See Orwell's letter to Moore, 21 February 1947, *3173*.
2. The contract was not actually made 'for' *Keep the Aspidistra Flying* (which had been published on 20 April 1936), but it referred to it. The first clause of the draft contract (all that survives) states 'EB grants to G exclusive right to publish in English next 3 "new and original full-length novels" after Keep the A.' This was signed on Orwell's behalf—he was in Spain—by Eileen, who was empowered so to do. She returned the contract to Gollancz on 31 January 1937, expressing her delight at its terms and certain that her husband would be as pleased as she was. The three books published since then were *The Road to Wigan Pier*, *Coming Up for Air*, and *Inside the Whale*. Only the second is a novel, of course. Orwell could, perhaps, have mentioned that he had also collaborated with Gollancz on *The Betrayal of the Left*.
3. The two refused on political grounds were *Homage to Catalonia* and *Animal Farm*. Although there was no doubt that *Animal Farm* was refused on political grounds, Gollancz had a point that—whatever Orwell may have felt (as expressed in his letter to Warburg, 28 February 1947;

see *3179*)—it was hardly 'a work of fiction of standard length.' The contract—if it repeated the wording of the draft—did specifically refer to 'full-length novels.'
4. Presumably either *The Lion and the Unicorn* or *Critical Essays*, both published by Secker & Warburg.

3192. To A. S. B. Glover, Penguin Books

19 March 1947   Typewritten

27B Canonbury Square,
Islington, N.1.

Dear Sir,

Many thanks for your letter of the 14th. I have the impression that I came across two or three misprints in the Penguin edition of THE ISLAND OF DR. MOREAU, but there is only one which I can track down straight off, and I have not time to search right through the book again.[1] This one is:

Penguin edition, p. 84, paragraph 2, line 9, "Beast flash" (should be "flesh"). This is the misprint which I pointed out to Wells. It is a very stupid one and should be put right.

As to slips, the one that struck me in re-reading the book is this. Dr. Moreau says that the yacht in which he and his assistant came to the island was stolen and lost. The assistant is nevertheless shown as travelling to the mainland on a steamer, to pick up new supplies of animals. Obviously, if they were on an island away from the shipping lanes and had no boat of their own, they would have had no way of arranging for any ship to pick them up. I have no doubt that this was a slip on Wells's part, but it is hardly the kind of thing that one could put right without the author's agreement.

Yours truly,
[Signed] Geo. Orwell
George Orwell

1. Orwell mentioned errors in the reprinting in 'As I Please,' 72, 7 February 1947; see *3169*.

3193. To Leonard Moore

19 March 1947   Typewritten

27B Canonbury Square,
Islington, N.1.

Dear Moore,

I am today airmailing the article, 1500 words, to the New Yorker.[1]

I have written to Gollancz asking him to release me from the contract and explaining the reasons, but have not yet had an answer.

Yours sincerely,
[Signed] Geo. Orwell
George Orwell

1. 'The Final Years of Lady Gregory,' a review of *Lady Gregory's Journals*, edited by Lennox Robinson, published 19 April 1947; see *3218*. It was the first of his two contributions to *The New Yorker*.

3194. To Emilio Cecchi

20 March 1947   Typewritten

> 27B Canonbury Square,
> Islington, N.1.

Dear Mr Cecchi,[1]
Many thanks for your letter of the 19th.

Would it be possible for you to come round here after dinner, as you did before, on Sunday evening (23rd)? Perhaps you could come here about 8 to half past? You know the way here now. You might ring me some time before then and confirm this.

> Yours sincerely
> [Signed] Geo. Orwell
> George Orwell

1. See *3178, n. 1*.

3195. To Brenda Salkeld

20 March 1947   Typewritten

> 27B Canonbury Square,
> Islington, N.1.

Dearest Brenda,[1]
I tried to phone you last night but couldn't get any sense out of the phone.

In case this reaches you in time on Friday morning. I'm afraid Friday is hopeless for me. I'm going out to lunch, and, little as I want to, I believe I have got to go out to dinner as well. I shall be at home during the morning up to about 12.30, and during the afternoon. So ring if you get the chance.

I have now literally no fuel whatever. However it isn't quite so stinkingly cold, in fact we've distinctly seen the sun on more than one occasion, and I heard some birds trying to sing the other morning. I've been frantically busy but have now cleared off the more urgent stuff. I've only one more job to do and hope to get that out of the way before we leave for Barnhill, as I do so want not to have to take any bits and pieces of work with me. We have arranged to leave on April 10th, and if I can fix the tickets are going to fly from Glasgow to Islay, which ought to cut out about 6 hours of that dismal journey. Richard has had a nasty feverish cold and he had a temperature two days, but I think he's all right now. *Do* make sure to see me before we go, and try and fix up about coming to stay at Barnhill. I think after this stinking winter the weather ought to be better this year.

Take care of yourself and try and give me a ring tomorrow. Perhaps you could look in for a cup of tea, say about 3 or 4 in the afternoon?

Much love
Eric

1. Brenda Salkeld (1900–1999) and Orwell had first met in 1928 at Southwold, where she worked as gym mistress at St Felix School for Girls. They remained friends throughout Orwell's life. See her reminiscences in *Orwell Remembered*, 67–68, and in *Remembering Orwell*, 39–41.

3196. 'As I Please,' 78

Tribune, 21 March 1947

The atomic bomb is frightening, but to anyone who wants to counteract it by a different kind of fright I recommend Mr. Mark Abrams's book, *The Population of Great Britain*, published in 1945. This can be read in conjunction with the Mass Observation survey, *Britain and Her Birth-rate*, published about the same time, and other recent books on the same subject. They all tell more or less the same story, and it has very unpleasant implications for anyone who expects to be alive in 1970.

At present, as Mr. Abrams's figures show, the age composition of our population is favourable, if one thinks in terms of labour units. We still have the benefit of the relatively high birth-rate just before and just after the 1914–18 war, so that well over half our population is of working age. But the trouble is that we can't freeze the figures at this point. The working population grows older all the time, and sufficient children are not being born. In 1881, when our total population was only about two-thirds of what it is now, the number of babies (under four) was actually larger by about half a million, while the number of old people (over 65) was less by something over three millions. In 1881 more than a third of the population was under 14: today the corresponding figure is less than a quarter. If there had been an Old Age Pension in 1881, less than 5 per cent. of the population would have been eligible for it: today more than 10 per cent. are eligible for it. To see the full significance of this one has to look forward a bit.

By 1970, Mr. Abrams calculates, the number of people over 55 may well be 14 millions—this in a population which may be smaller than the present one. That is to say that about one person in three will be almost past work: or, to put it differently, that every two able-bodied people will be supporting one old person between them! When Mr. Abrams produced his book, the birth-rate had been rising during the later war years, and I believe it has again risen during 1946, but not to anywhere near replacement level: in any case the sudden jump in births may have happened merely because, owing to the war, people have been marrying earlier. The downward trend has been happening for more than half a century, and some of its effects cannot be escaped from, but the worst would be avoided if the birth-rate reached and stayed at the point where the average family was four children, and not, as at present, a little over two. But this must happen within the next decade; otherwise there will not be enough women of child-bearing age to restore the situation.

It is curious how little dismay the dropping birth-rate caused until very recently. Even now, as the Mass Observation report brings out, most people merely think that it means a smaller population and do not realise that it also means an ageing population. Thirty years ago, even ten or fifteen years ago, to advocate smaller families was a mark of enlightenment. The key phrases were "surplus population" and "the multiplication of the unfit." Even now there is strong social pressure against large families, not to mention the crude economic consideration. All writers on this subject seem to agree that the causes of the decline are complex and that it may not be possible to reverse the trend merely by family allowances, day nurseries, etc. But clearly there must be *some* financial inducement, because, in an industrialised society which is also socially competitive, a large family is an unbearable economic burden. At the best it means making sure that your children will start off with a poorer chance in life than you had yourself.

Over the past twenty-five years, what innumerable people must have kept their families down from directly economic motives! It is a queer kind of prudence if you consider the community and not the individual. In another twenty-five years the parents of today will be past work, and the children they have not had will not be there to support them. I wonder if the Old Age Pension will stay at the equivalent of £1 a week when one person in three is in receipt of it?

I wonder if there exists—indeed I am sure something of the kind must exist— a short and simple textbook from which the ordinary citizen can get a working knowledge of the laws he lives under? Recently I had occasion to refer in this column to the rules governing the selection of juries. No doubt it was very ignorant on my part not to know that juries are picked out on a system that tends to exclude the working class; but evidently thousands of other people did not know it either, and the discovery came as a shock. Every now and again this kind of thing happens. By some chance or other—for instance, by reading the reports of a murder case—one finds out how the law stands on a certain subject, and it is frequently so stupid or so unfair that one would not have believed it if one had not seen it in black and white.

For instance, I have just been reading the Government White Paper dealing with the confession made by David Ware in the Manchester murder case. Walter Rowland, since hanged, had been convicted of the murder, and Ware afterwards made a confession which Rowland's counsel attempted to use as evidence at the appeal. After reading the White Paper I have not the slightest doubt that the confession was spurious and that it was right to disregard it. But that is not the point. It came out in the appeal proceedings that the judges had no power to hear evidence of that kind. True or false, the confession could not be admitted as evidence. An innocent man might be convicted, the real criminal might make an unmistakeably genuine confession, and the innocent man might still be hanged, unless the Home Secretary chose to intervene. Did you know that that is how the law stands? I certainly didn't, and the incident shows how rash it is to try to infer what the law would be on any given subject, using common sense as a starting-point.

Here is another instance, but in this case my ignorance is probably less excusable. In a recent *cause célèbre*, in which the accused was acquitted, it came out that the very heavy costs of the defence were paid by a Sunday paper. I confess that I had not realised until then that when you are found not guilty on a criminal charge, you still have to pay your own costs. I had vaguely imagined that when the Crown is discovered to be in the wrong, it pays up, like the unsuccessful claimant in a civil suit. However, it seems that if you are actually indigent, the Crown will provide you with counsel, but it takes care not to be seriously out of pocket by doing so. In this case, it is stated, the leading counsel briefed by the Sunday paper received about £500, whereas if briefed by the Crown he would have received less than £20. Apply that to an ordinary burglary or embezzlement case, where there is not much notoriety to be won, and see what it means to an indigent person's chance of getting the best possible defence.

What an outcry there has been over the suspension of the weekly papers![1] Even the *Smallholder* protested, and there was a very sharp editorial comment in *Practical Engineering*. The *Universe*, if I remember rightly, said that this was the prelude to the imposition of Press censorship. And in general the idea seems to have seeped round that there was some kind of political motive for the suspension—the motive, presumably, being to prevent comment on the Government's mistakes.

A well-known writer said to me that the banning of weekly papers was much the same kind of thing as the "co-ordination" of the Press in totalitarian countries. This seems to me the point at which suspicion turns into folly. Obviously there was no idea of silencing criticism, since the daily papers were left alone. The Beaverbrook Press, for instance, is far more hostile to the Government than any weekly paper of standing, besides having an enormously larger circulation. How much ignorant abuse Shinwell[2] might have escaped, if during the crisis he had made even one public appearance to explain what he was doing!

1. See 'As I Please,' 74, 21 February 1947, 3172.
2. When Labour came to power in 1945, Emmanuel Shinwell (1884–1986; life peer, 1970), a bellicose Labour M.P. from 1922, was appointed Minister of Fuel and Power. He was responsible for the nationalisation of the mines on 1 January 1947, but this coincided with massive absenteeism from the pits, the arrival of the bitterest winter for many years, a cut in the fresh-meat ration, a road haulage strike, and extensive power cuts. Conditions were so bad that the army had to use flame-throwers to cut through drifts to rescue stranded people. He was responsible, too, for the suspension of the weekly papers. Later in 1947, Shinwell was appointed Secretary of State for War, and in 1950–51, in the second post-war Labour government, he was Minister of Defence.

3196A. Arthur Koestler

21 March 1947   Typewritten

27B Canonbury Square,
Islington, N.1.

Dear Arthur,

Thanks for your letter. Ref. the Freedom Defence Committee. It is a very small organisation which does the best it can with inadequate funds. The sum they were appealing for on this occasion was £250, and they got somewhat more than that. Naturally they want an assured income to pay for premises and staff, and regular legal assistance. What they actually have at present is some small premises and one secretary, and the (I imagine) rather precarious aid of one lawyer who does not demand much in the way of fees. Of course one can do very little on such a tiny establishment, but they can hardly make it larger unless people do give them money. I think up to date they have done a certain amount of good. They have certainly taken up quite a few cases and bombarded secretaries of state etc. with letters, which is usually about all one can do. The point is that the N.C.C.L. became a Stalinist organisation, and since then there has been no organisation aiming chiefly at the defence of civil liberties. Even a tiny nucleus like this is better than nothing, and if it became better known it could get more money, and so become larger. I think sooner or later there may be a row about the larger aims of the Committee, because at present the moving spirits in it are anarchists and there is a tendency to use it for anarchist propaganda. However, that might correct itself if the organisation became larger, because most of the new supporters would presumably be people of ordinary liberal views. I certainly think the Committee is worth £5 a year. If 9 other people have guaranteed the same sum, £50 a year assured is quite a consideration. It would cover stationary, for example.

I am going back to Jura in April and hope then to get back to the novel I started last year. While in London I've been swamped with footling jobs as usual. The weather and the fuel shortage have been unbearable. For about a month one did nothing except try to keep warm. Richard is well and is talking rather more – in all other ways he seems fairly forward. Please give my love to Mamaine.

Yours
George

3197. To Ihor Szewczenko

21 March 1947   Typewritten

27B Canonbury Square,
Islington, N. 1.

Dear Mr Szewczenko,
I enclose the preface herewith, and I hope it is the kind of thing you wanted.
You are at liberty to cut out as much as you wish, and to add any notes you
think necessary. I also enclose a photograph in case it should be wanted.

Yours sincerely
[Signed] Geo. Orwell
George Orwell

On 25 March 1947, Szewczenko acknowledged receipt of the preface and
photograph. He thanked Orwell warmly: the preface was just what was wanted
to 'dissipate possible misunderstandings as to your standpoint.' Although a
reader ought, he admitted, to be able to understand the book without a preface,
many of its prospective readers were former inmates of displaced persons
camps, peasants or workers, or half-educated nationalists, 'but they all read
eagerly. In such circumstances it is better to say things twice.' It was hoped to
smuggle some copies to Soviet soldiers occupying Germany, but that involved
risks for both sides.

Szewczenko, making 'usage of the liberty you have granted me,' proposed to
omit all the first page and the first two lines of the second. This he identifies as 'I
have never visited USSR . . . with a citizen of the USSR'; or only, 'When
Stuttgart was captured . . . with a citizen of the USSR.' Although 'I have never
visited Russia' appears in the translation back into English of the Ukrainian as
printed (see *CW*, VIII, 111, line 32), it seems that the second omission was made
and that sentence transferred to later in the preface. Szewczenko explained: First,
about half the prospective readers were Western Ukrainians who were Polish
citizens until 1939; second, the others were 'extremely self-conscious and
sensitive, especially as far as the contacts with the West or Westerners are
concerned. . . . They often are poor people with strained nerves.' Szewczenko
was grateful for the photograph, but did not know if it would be practical to
reproduce it.

He also suggested that Orwell discuss the fate of the Socialist anthem, the
'Internationale,' in 'As I Please.' He wondered if it was still sung at meetings in
Britain.[1] He explained that the song 'had for me a great emotional appeal,
increased 1939–45 by fear etc. After the armistice I no sooner realised that it was
no longer forbidden, than it occurred to me that it no longer had "much sense."'
This was a reaction of many of those he knew, and in the preceding two and a
half years he had never heard it sung.

Orwell's original English version of this preface has not been found; the
English version reproduced here (see *3198*) was translated from the Ukrainian
text by Amrai Ettlinger and Ian Willison. In a letter to the editor of 13 August
1992, Professor Ševčenko says he cut some sentences from Orwell's preface and
so committed 'an unpardonable sin against literature,' but he was then only
twenty-five and could not know 'what the future had in store for Orwell.' He
also said that he had deposited in the Houghton Library, at Harvard, a corrected
copy of his translation of *Animal Farm*.

1. The 'Internationale' was written by Eugène Pottier (1816–1887) in 1871, the year that the Second Commune was proclaimed in France. Following the dissolution of the Comintern (the Communist International) by Stalin on 15 May 1943, as a gesture to his Allies (see Orwell's News Commentary for Malaya, 35, 28 May 1943, *2102*), it was announced that the 'Internationale' would no longer be sung as the official anthem of the Soviet Union.

3198. Preface to the Ukrainian Edition of *Animal Farm*

[March 1947][1]

I have been asked to write a preface to the Ukrainian translation of *Animal Farm*. I am aware that I write for readers about whom I know nothing, but also that they too have probably never had the slightest opportunity to know anything about me.

In this preface they will most likely expect me to say something of how *Animal Farm* originated but first I would like to say something about myself and the experiences by which I arrived at my political position.

I was born in India in 1903. My father was an official in the English administration there, and my family was one of those ordinary middle-class families of soldiers, clergymen, government officials, teachers, lawyers, doctors, etc. I was educated at Eton, the most costly and snobbish of the English Public Schools.* But I had only got in there by means of a scholarship; otherwise my father could not have afforded to send me to a school of this type.

Shortly after I left school (I wasn't quite twenty years old then) I went to Burma and joined the Indian Imperial Police. This was an armed police, a sort of *gendarmerie* very similar to the Spanish *Guardia Civil* or the *Garde Mobile* in France. I stayed five years in the service. It did not suit me and made me hate imperialism, although at that time nationalist feelings in Burma were not very marked, and relations between the English and the Burmese were not particularly unfriendly. When on leave in England in 1927, I resigned from the service and decided to become a writer: at first without any especial success. In 1928–9 I lived in Paris and wrote short stories and novels that nobody would print (I have since destroyed them all). In the following years I lived mostly from hand to mouth, and went hungry on several occasions. It was only from 1934 onwards that I was able to live on what I earned from my writing. In the meantime I sometimes lived for months on end amongst the poor and half-criminal elements who inhabit the worst parts of the poorer

---

* These are not public 'national schools', but something quite the opposite: exclusive and expensive residential secondary schools, scattered far apart. Until recently they admitted almost no one but the sons of rich aristocratic families. It was the dream of *nouveau riche* bankers of the nineteenth century to push their sons into a Public School. At such schools the greatest stress is laid on sport, which forms, so to speak, a lordly, tough and gentlemanly outlook. Among these schools, Eton is particularly famous. Wellington is reported to have said that the victory of Waterloo was decided on the playing fields of Eton. It is not so very long ago that an overwhelming majority of the people who in one way or another ruled England came from the Public School. [Orwell's footnote.]

quarters, or take to the streets, begging and stealing. At that time I associated with them through lack of money, but later their way of life interested me very much for its own sake. I spent many months (more systematically this time) studying the conditions of the miners in the north of England. Up to 1930 I did not on the whole look upon myself as a Socialist. In fact I had as yet no clearly defined political views. I became pro-Socialist more out of disgust with the way the poorer section of the industrial workers were oppressed and neglected than out of any theoretical admiration for a planned society.

In 1936 I got married. In almost the same week the civil war broke out in Spain. My wife and I both wanted to go to Spain and fight for the Spanish Government. We were ready in six months, as soon as I had finished the book I was writing. In Spain I spent almost six months on the Aragon front until, at Huesca, a Fascist sniper shot me through the throat.

In the early stages of the war foreigners were on the whole unaware of the inner struggles between the various political parties supporting the Government. Through a series of accidents I joined not the International Brigade like the majority of foreigners, but the POUM militia—i.e. the Spanish Trotskyists.

So in the middle of 1937, when the Communists gained control (or partial control) of the Spanish Government and began to hunt down the Trotskyists, we both found ourselves amongst the victims. We were very lucky to get out of Spain alive, and not even to have been arrested once. Many of our friends were shot, and others spent a long time in prison or simply disappeared.

These man-hunts in Spain went on at the same time as the great purges in the USSR and were a sort of supplement to them. In Spain as well as in Russia the nature of the accusations (namely, conspiracy with the Fascists) was the same and as far as Spain was concerned I had every reason to believe that the accusations were false. To experience all this was a valuable object lesson: it taught me how easily totalitarian propaganda can control the opinion of enlightened people in democratic countries.

My wife and I both saw innocent people being thrown into prison merely because they were suspected of unorthodoxy. Yet on our return to England we found numerous sensible and well-informed observers believing the most fantastic accounts of conspiracy, treachery and sabotage which the press reported from the Moscow trials.

And so I understood, more clearly than ever, the negative influence of the Soviet myth upon the western Socialist movement.

And here I must pause to describe my attitude to the Soviet régime.

I have never visited Russia and my knowledge of it consists only of what can be learned by reading books and newspapers. Even if I had the power, I would not wish to interfere in Soviet domestic affairs: I would not condemn Stalin and his associates merely for their barbaric and undemocratic methods. It is quite possible that, even with the best intentions, they could not have acted otherwise under the conditions prevailing there.

But on the other hand it was of the utmost importance to me that people in western Europe should see the Soviet régime for what it really was. Since 1930 I had seen little evidence that the USSR was progressing towards anything that one could truly call Socialism. On the contrary, I was struck by clear signs of its transformation into a hierarchical society, in which the rulers have no more reason to give up their power than any other ruling class. Moreover, the workers and intelligentsia in a country like England cannot understand that the USSR of today is altogether different from what it was in 1917. It is partly that they do not want to understand (i.e. they want to believe that, somewhere, a really Socialist country does actually exist), and partly that, being accustomed to comparative freedom and moderation in public life, totalitarianism is completely incomprehensible to them.

Yet one must remember that England is not completely democratic. It is also a capitalist country with great class privileges and (even now, after a war that has tended to equalise everybody) with great differences in wealth. But nevertheless it is a country in which people have lived together for several hundred years without major conflict, in which the laws are relatively just and official news and statistics can almost invariably be believed, and, last but not least, in which to hold and to voice minority views does not involve any mortal danger. In such an atmosphere the man in the street has no real understanding of things like concentration camps, mass deportations, arrests without trial, press censorship, etc. Everything he reads about a country like the USSR is automatically translated into English terms, and he quite innocently accepts the lies of totalitarian propaganda. Up to 1939, and even later, the majority of English people were incapable of assessing the true nature of the Nazi régime in Germany, and now, with the Soviet régime, they are still to a large extent under the same sort of illusion.

This has caused great harm to the Socialist movement in England, and had serious consequences for English foreign policy. Indeed, in my opinion, nothing has contributed so much to the corruption of the original idea of Socialism as the belief that Russia is a Socialist country and that every act of its rulers must be excused, if not imitated.

And so for the past ten years I have been convinced that the destruction of the Soviet myth was essential if we wanted a revival of the Socialist movement.

On my return from Spain I thought of exposing the Soviet myth in a story that could be easily understood by almost anyone and which could be easily translated into other languages. However, the actual details of the story did not come to me for some time until one day (I was then living in a small village) I saw a little boy, perhaps ten years old, driving a huge cart-horse along a narrow path, whipping it whenever it tried to turn. It struck me that if only such animals became aware of their strength we should have no power over them, and that men exploit animals in much the same way as the rich exploit the proletariat.

I proceeded to analyse Marx's theory from the animals' point of view. To them it was clear that the concept of a class struggle between humans was pure illusion, since whenever it was necessary to exploit animals, all humans united against them: the true struggle is between animals and humans. From this point of departure, it was not difficult to elaborate the story. I did not write it out till 1943, for I was always engaged on other work which gave me no time; and in the end I included some events, for example the Teheran Conference, which were taking place while I was writing. Thus the main outlines of the story were in my mind over a period of six years before it was actually written.

I do not wish to comment on the work; if it does not speak for itself, it is a failure. But I should like to emphasise two points: first, that although the various episodes are taken from the actual history of the Russian Revolution, they are dealt with schematically and their chronological order is changed; this was necessary for the symmetry of the story. The second point has been missed by most critics, possibly because I did not emphasise it sufficiently. A number of readers may finish the book with the impression that it ends in the complete reconciliation of the pigs and the humans. That was not my intention; on the contrary I meant it to end on a loud note of discord, for I wrote it immediately after the Teheran Conference which everybody thought had established the best possible relations between the USSR and the West. I personally did not believe that such good relations would last long; and as events have shown, I wasn't far wrong.

I don't know what more I need add. If anyone is interested in personal details, I should add that I am a widower with a son almost three years old, that by profession I am a writer, and that since the beginning of the war I have worked mainly as a journalist.

The periodical to which I contribute most regularly is *Tribune*, a socio-political weekly which represents, generally speaking, the left wing of the Labour Party. The following of my books might most interest the ordinary reader (should any reader of this translation find copies of them): *Burmese Days* (a story about Burma), *Homage to Catalonia* (arising from my experiences in the Spanish Civil War), and *Critical Essays* (essays mainly about contemporary popular English literature and instructive more from the sociological than from the literary point of view).

1. For the origins of this Preface, see *2969*; for the dating, see *3197*.

3199. To Leonard Moore

25 March 1947   Typewritten

27 B Canonbury Square
Islington
London   N 1[1]

Dear Moore,
I wrote a week or two ago to Gollancz asking him to cancel our contract, and have had a reply from him saying he is not anxious to do so but does not absolutely refuse. I am going to write again telling him that I would much rather terminate the contract. I know this trouble will come up again, and it is better to sever the connection if he can be got to agree.

Could you please fix up the contract for Warburg's reprinting of "Coming

Up for Air" as soon as possible. I would like it if the book could re-appear this year, as I shan't have anything new coming out.

I am going back to Jura about April 10th, but will let you have the exact date later.

Yours sincerely
[Signed] Eric Blair
Eric Blair

1. From this letter onwards, Orwell seems to have used up his stock of headed paper for Canonbury Square. This letter is placed out of alphabetical sequence for this day because it clearly precedes that sent to Gollancz (*3200*).

3200. To Victor Gollancz

25 March 1947   Typewritten

27 B Canonbury Square
Islington
London N 1

Dear Gollancz,

I must thank you for your kind and considerate letter, and I have thought it over with some care. I nevertheless still think, if you are willing to agree, that it would be better to terminate our contract. It is not that anything in the book I am now writing is likely to lead to trouble, but I have to think of the over-all position. Neither Warburg nor anyone else can regard me as a good proposition unless he can have an option on my whole output, which is never very large in any case. It is obviously better if I can be with one publisher altogether, and, as I don't suppose I shall cease writing about politics from time to time, I am afraid of further differences arising, as in the past. You know what the difficulty is, ie., Russia. For quite 15 years I have regarded that regime with plain horror, and though, of course, I would change my opinion if I saw reason, I don't think my feelings are likely to change so long as the Communist party remains in power. I know that your position in recent years has been not very far from mine, but I don't know what it would be if, for instance, there is another seeming raprochement° between Russia and the West, which is a possible development in the next few years. Or again in an actual war situation. I don't, God knows, want a war to break out, but if one were compelled to choose between Russia and America—and I suppose that is the choice one might have to make—I would always choose America. I know Warburg and his opinions well enough to know that he is very unlikely ever to refuse anything of mine on political grounds. As you say, no publisher can sign blind an undertaking to print anything a writer produces, but I think Warbug is less likely to jib than most.

I know that I am asking a great deal of you, since after all we have a contract which I signed freely and by which I am still bound. If you decide that the contract must stand, of course I shall not violate it. But so far as my own feelings go I would rather terminate it. Please forgive me for what must seem like ungraciousness, and for causing you all this trouble.

Yours sincerely
Geo. Orwell

3201. 'As I Please,' 79

Tribune, 28 March 1947

I have been reading with interest the February–March bulletin of Mass-Observation, which appears just ten years after this organisation first came into being. It is curious to remember with what hostility it was greeted at the beginning. It was violently attacked in the *New Statesman*, for instance, where Mr. Stonier[1] declared that the typical Mass-Observer would have "elephant ears, a loping walk and a permanent sore eye from looking through keyholes," or words to that effect. Another attacker was Mr. Stephen Spender.[2] But on the whole the opposition to this or any other kind of social survey comes from people of Conservative opinions, who often seem to be genuinely indignant at the idea of finding out what the big public is thinking.

If asked why, they generally answer that what is discovered is of no interest, and that in any case any intelligent person always knows already what are the main trends of public opinion. Another argument is that social surveys are an interference with individual liberty and a first step towards totalitarianism. The *Daily Express* ran this line for several years and tried to laugh the small social survey unit instituted by the Ministry of Information out of existence by nicknaming it Cooper's Snoopers.[3] Of course, behind much of this opposition there lies a well-justified fear of finding that mass sentiment on many subjects is not Conservative.

But some people do seem sincerely to feel that it is a bad thing for the Government to know too much about what people are thinking, just as others feel that it is a kind of presumption when the Government tries to educate public opinion. Actually you can't have democracy unless both processes are at work. Democracy is only possible when the law-makers and administrators know what the masses want, and what they can be counted on to understand. If the present Government paid more attention to this last point, they would word some of their publicity differently. Mass-Observation issued a report last week on the White Paper on the economic situation. They found, as usual, that the abstract words and phrases which are flung to and fro in official announcements mean nothing to countless ordinary citizens. Many people are even flummoxed by the word "assets," which is thought to have something to do with "assist"!

The Mass-Observation bulletin gives some account of the methods its investigators use, but does not touch on a very important point, and that is the manner in which social surveys are financed. Mass-Observation itself appears to keep going in a hand-to-mouth way by publishing books and by undertaking specific jobs for the Government or for commercial organisations. Some of its best surveys, such as that dealing with the birth-rate, were carried out for the Advertising Service Guild. The trouble with this method is that a subject only gets investigated if some large, wealthy organisation happens to be interested in it. An obvious example is anti-semitism, which I believe has never been looked into, or only in a very sketchy way. But anti-semitism is only one variant of the great modern disease of nationalism. We know very little about the real causes of nationalism, and we might conceivably be on the way towards curing it if we knew more. But who is sufficiently interested to put up the thousands of pounds that an exhaustive survey would cost?

For some weeks there has been correspondence in the *Observer* about the persistence of "spit and polish" in the Armed Forces. The last issue had a good letter from someone who signed himself "Conscript," describing how he and his comrades were forced to waste their time in polishing brass, blacking the rubber hoses on stirrup pumps with boot polish, scraping broom handles with razor blades, and so on. But "Conscript" then goes on to say:

> When an officer (a major) carried out routine reading of King's Regulations regarding venereal disease, he did not hesitate to add: "There is nothing to be ashamed of if you have the disease—it is quite natural. But make sure that you report for treatment at once."

I must say that it seems to me strange, amid the other idiocies mentioned, to object to one of the few sensible things in the army system, i.e., its straightforward attitude towards venereal disease. We shall never be able to stamp out syphilis and gonorrhea until the stigma of sinfulness is removed from them. When full conscription was introduced in the 1914–1918 war it was discovered, if I remember rightly, that nearly half the population suffered or had suffered from some form of venereal disease, and this frightened the authorities into taking a few precautions. During the inter-war years the struggle against venereal disease languished, so far as the civilian population went. There was provision for treatment of those already infected, but the proposal to set up "early treatment centres," as in the Army, was quelled by the puritans. Then came another war, with the increase in venereal disease that war necessarily causes, and another attempt to deal with the problem. The Ministry of Health posters are timid enough, but even these would have provoked an outcry from the pious ones if military necessity had not called them into being.

You can't deal with these diseases so long as they are thought of as visitations of God, in a totally different category from all other diseases. The inevitable result of that is concealment and quack remedies. And it is humbug to say that "clean living is the only real remedy." You are bound to have promiscuity and prostitution in a society like ours, where people mature sexually at about fifteen and are discouraged from marrying till they are in their twenties, where conscription and the need for mobility of labour break up family life, and where young people living in big towns have no regular way of forming acquaintanceships. It is impossible to solve the problem by making people more moral, because they won't, within any foreseeable time, become as moral as all that. Besides, many of the victims of venereal disease are husbands or wives who have not themselves committed any so-called immoral act. The only sensible course is to recognise that syphilis and gonorrhea are merely *diseases*, more preventable if not more curable than most, and that to suffer from them is not disgraceful. No doubt the pious ones would squeal. But in doing so they might avow their real motives, and then we should be a little nearer to wiping out this evil.

For the last five minutes I have been gazing out of the window into the square, keeping a sharp look-out for signs of spring. There is a thinnish patch in the clouds with a faint hint of blue behind it, and on a sycamore tree there are some things that look as if they might be buds. Otherwise it is still winter. But don't worry! Two days ago, after a careful search in Hyde Park, I came on a hawthorn bush that was definitely in bud, and some birds, though not actually singing, were making noises like an orchestra tuning up. Spring is coming after all, and recent rumours that this was the beginning of another Ice Age were unfounded. In only three weeks' time we shall be listening to the cuckoo, which usually gives tongue about the fourteenth of April. Another three weeks after that, and we shall be basking under blue skies, eating ices off barrows and neglecting to lay up fuel for next winter.

How appropriate the ancient poems in praise of spring have seemed these last few years! They have a meaning that they did not have in the days when there was no fuel shortage and you could get almost anything at any time of year. Of all passages celebrating spring, I think I like best those two stanzas from the beginning of one of the Robin Hood ballads. I modernise the spelling:

When shaws be sheen and swards full fair,
And leaves both large and long,
It is merry walking in the fair forest
To hear the small birds' song.

The woodwele sang and would not cease,
Sitting upon the spray,
So loud he wakened Robin Hood
In the greenwood where he lay.

But what exactly was the woodwele? The Oxford Dictionary seems to suggest that it was the woodpecker, which is not a notable songster, and I should be interested to know whether it can be identified with some more probable bird.

In *Tribune*, 18 April 1947, on behalf of Mass Observation, Tom Harrisson and H. D. Willcock took up points made in earlier issues by Orwell and R. C. Churchill. One of Orwell's 'sympathetic remarks,' they said,

included one about the difficulty of financing solid long-term social research. This difficulty is very real. Social research of a virile and realistic nature is not always or entirely suitable for the university atmosphere; Government departments and commercial organisations generally want research of an *ad hoc* nature and do not want it published. It has been a constant struggle for ten years to maintain the independence of M.-O. and only to do work on which we preserve the copyright. We hope we have done some useful stuff. But we could have done much more had we had a reasonable annual grant, without any strings attached.

The whole present system for supporting the social sciences is hopelessly inadequate.

In the issue for 4 April 1947, R. H. Geare answered Orwell's question, 'what exactly was the woodwele?'

In answer to George Orwell's question, as to what exactly was the woodwele, the following remarks may be of interest.

In Chaucer's *Romance of the Rose* we read:

"And he (Cupid) was all with birds covered,
With popinjay, with nightingale,
With chalaundrye, and with wodewale."

where Skeat explains *Wodewale* by "green woodpecker." Mayhew and Skeat, in their *Concise Dictionary of Middle English*, give under *Wodewale* "the name of a bird also called *Witwall*."

In *British Nesting Birds*, Westell gives the following local names still in use: Great Spotted Woodpecker: *Witwall*, *Woodall*. Green Woodpecker: *Witwall*, *Woodwall*, *Popinjay*.

Now Chaucer's popinjay and *Wodewale* are obviously different birds. If the popinjay is the Green Woodpecker, his *Wodewale* must be another bird; otherwise it could be either woodpecker. But the *Woodwele*, which wakened Robin Hood, was apparently a small bird which sang sitting upon the spray. The woodpeckers in question are neither small birds nor songsters, nor do they sit upon the spray.

It is at least interesting to note that the Woodlark, only six and a half inches in length, and famous as a songster, has the local name *Woodwell*, and fulfils all the conditions.

Another possibility is suggested from the thirteenth century poem, *The Owl and the Nightingale*, where the *Wudewale* accompanies Thrush and Throstle. Professor Morris derives *Wudewale* from the Anglo-Saxon *Wudu* and *Wealh* with the meaning "woodstranger."

The Wood Warbler is a summer migrant to the British Isles, where it especially favours beech woods. This small bird might well have been the stranger whose loud and persistent song wakened Robin Hood.

R. H. Geare wrote from Wallington, the name of the village in Hertfordshire where Orwell had lived just before the war. However, there is a Wallington in Hampshire and another in Northumberland.

1. George Walter Stonier (1903–1985), Australian-born journalist who was assistant literary editor of *The New Statesman and Nation*, 1928–45. In *When I Was* (1989) Desmond Hawkins

says Kingsley Martin 'seemed content to let Stonier run the literary section more or less as he pleased: this he did with the pleasantly wry humour that is enshrined in the title of his book, *Shaving through the Blitz*' (1943), (161–62). Stonier wrote a number of plays for the BBC.
2. Stephen Spender (1909–1995), poet, dramatist, and critic; he and Orwell first met before the war. See *411, n. 2.*
3. Alfred Duff Cooper (1890–1954) politician and author; see *628, n. 6.* When Churchill succeeded Chamberlain as prime minister in May 1940, Duff Cooper was made Minister of Information, a post he did not enjoy. It was in this period that the MOI social survey unit, 'Cooper's Snoopers,' was set up. He became Chancellor of the Duchy of Lancaster in July 1941. From January 1944 he served as the British representative with the French Committee of National Liberation established under General de Gaulle in North Africa, and became British ambassador in Paris November 1944, a post he held for three years. Among his books were biographies of Talleyrand (1932) and Earl Haig (two vols., 1935–36); *Sergeant Shakespeare* (1949); and an important autobiography, *Old Men Forget* (1953).

3202. To Leonard Moore

28 March 1947   Typewritten

27b Canonbury Square
N.1

Dear Moore,

I enclose the contract herewith. I have again written to Gollancz saying that I would much rather be released from the contract, but that if he holds me to it I shall, of course, not violate it. I had previously seen Warburg and talked it over, and I imagine that so far as COMING UP FOR AIR goes, they will get that swinging fairly soon. At the same time, I have no doubt they would very much rather get this other business settled first, as there is not very much point in wasting paper on a reprint unless it is part of a larger programme.

Yours sincerely,
[Signed] Geo. Orwell
George Orwell

3203. To Secker & Warburg

28 March 1947   Typewritten postcard

From George Orwell.

As from April 8th my address will be:

Barn Hill,
Isle of Jura,
Argyllshire,
Scotland.[1]

[Unsigned]

1. The postcard has been marked for the attention of SPO, PLU, and MUR. These are

probably not initials, but the first three letters of surnames: Miss Plummer (Warburg's secretary), Miss Murtough (who offered to borrow a copy of *Coming Up for Air*; see *3155, n. 1*), and an unidentified person. The card has been annotated 'Noted' and initialled by Miss M. C. Plummer. The card has been dated from its postmark.

3204. 'Burnham's View of the Contemporary World Struggle'

The New Leader (New York), 29 March 1947

One fallacy left over from the nineteenth century and still influencing our thoughts is the notion that two major wars cannot happen within a few years of one another. The American Civil War and the Franco-Prussian War, it is true, occurred almost simultaneously, but they were fought in different continents and by different people. Otherwise the rule seemed to hold good that you can only get people to fight when everyone who remembers what the last war was like is beyond military age. Even the gap between the two World Wars—twenty-one years—was large enough to ensure that very few men took part in both of them as common soldiers. Hence the widespread vague belief, or hope, that a third world war could not break out before about 1970, by which time, it is hopefully argued, "all sorts of things may have happened."

As James Burnham points out,* the atomic bomb has altered all that. His book is, in effect, a product of atomic weapons: it is a revision, almost an abandonment of his earlier world-picture, in the light of the fact that great nations are now in a position actually to annihilate one another. When weapons have reached this level of deadliness, one cannot take the risk of letting the enemy get his blow in first, so that as soon as two hostile nations possess atomic bombs, the explosion will follow almost immediately. In Burnham's opinion, we have perhaps ten years, but more probably only five, before the third world war, which has been raging unofficially ever since 1944, enters its open phase.

No doubt it is not necessary to say what powers this war will be between. Burnham's main aim in writing his book is to urge the United States to seize the initiative and establish what amounts to a world empire now, before Communism swallows the whole of Eurasia. The actual continuity of civilisation, he says, is threatened by the existence of atomic weapons, and there is no safeguard except to make sure that only one nation possesses them. Ideally, atomic energy would be controlled by an international authority, but no such thing exists or is likely to exist for a long time to come, and meanwhile the only serious competitors for world power are the United States and the USSR. However, the struggle is not merely between Western democracy and Communism. Burnham's definition of Communism is central to the book, and it is worth stopping to examine it.

---

* *The Struggle for the World*, by James Burnham.

He does not accept the now widely-spread belief that Communism is simply Russian imperialism. In its way, it is a genuinely international movement, and the USSR is merely the base, or nucleus, from which it expands, sucking one territory after another into its system. Even if the system covered the whole earth, the real center of power and government would no doubt continue to be the Eurasian "heartland"; but world Communism does not so much mean conquest by Russia as conquest by a special form of social organization. Communism is not in the ordinary sense a political movement: it is a world-wide conspiratorial movement for the capture of power. Its aim is to establish everywhere a system similar to that which prevails in Soviet Russia—that is, a system which is technically collectivist, but which concentrates all power in a very few hands, is based on forced labor, and eliminates all real or imaginary opponents by means of terrorism. It can expand even outside the striking range of the Red Army, because in every country there are a few people who are its devoted adherents, others, more numerous, who are in some degree deceived, and yet others who will more or less accept Communism so long as it seems to be winning and they are offered no alternative. In every country which they are unable to dominate, the Communists act as a Fifth Column, working through cover organizations of every kind, playing on working-class aspirations and the ignorance of well-meaning liberals, always with the object of sowing demoralization against the day when war breaks out. All Communist activities are really directed towards this war. Unless Communism can be forced back upon the defensive, there is no chance of the war being averted, since the inevitability of a "final struggle" is part of the Leninist mythology and is believed in as an article of faith.

After discussing the nature of Communism and of Soviet foreign policy, Burnham examines the strategic situation. "Communism"—that is to say, the USSR with its satellite nations and Fifth Columns—has enormous advantages in manpower, in natural resources, in the inaccessibility of the Eurasian "heartland," in the quasi-religious appeal of the Communist myth, and above all, perhaps, in the quality of its leadership. The supreme commanders of the Communist movement are men who have no aim in life except to capture power and who are not troubled by scruples nor obliged to take much account of public opinion. They are both experts and fanatics, whereas their opponents are bungling, half-hearted amateurs. On the other hand, "Communism" is technologically backward and suffers from the disadvantage that its mythology is most easily swallowed by people who have not seen Russian rule at close quarters. The United States is relatively weak in manpower and its geographical position is none too strong, but in industrial output and technique it is far ahead of all rivals, and it has potential allies all over the world, especially in western Europe. The greatest handicap of the United States, therefore, is the lack of any definite world-view: if the American people understood their own strength, and also the danger that threatens them, the situation would be retrievable.

Burnham discusses what ought to be done, what could be done, and what probably will be done. He writes off pacifism as a practical remedy. In principle it could solve the world's ills, but since significant numbers of people cannot be induced to adopt it, it can only provide salvation for scattered individuals, not for societies. The real alternatives before the world are domination by Communism and domination by the United States. Obviously the latter is preferable, and the United States must act swiftly and make its purpose unmistakably clear. It must start off by proposing a union— not an alliance, but a complete fusion—with Britain and the British Dominions, and strive to draw the whole of Western Europe into its orbit. It must ruthlessly extirpate Communism within its own borders. It must frankly set itself up as the world's champion against Communism, and conduct unremitting propaganda to the people of the Russian-occupied countries, and still more to the Russian people themselves, making clear to them that not they but their rulers are regarded as the enemy. It must take up the firmest possible attitude towards the USSR, always understanding that a threat or gesture not backed by military force is useless. It must stick by its friends and not make gifts of food and machinery to its enemies. And above all, the United States must have a clear policy. Unless it has a definite, intelligible plan for world organization it cannot seize the initiative from Communism. It is on this point that Burnham is most pessimistic. At present, the American people as a whole have no grasp of the world situation, and American foreign policy is weak, unstable and contradictory. It must be so, because—quite apart from the sabotage of "fellow-travelers" and the intrusion of home politics—there is no general, over-riding purpose. In outlining a policy for the United States, Burnham says, he is only pointing out what *could* be done. What probably *will* happen is yet more confusion and vacillation, leading in five or ten years to a war which the United States will enter at grave disadvantage.

That is the general outline of Burnham's argument, though I have slightly re-arranged the order in which he presents it. It will be seen that he is demanding, or all but demanding, an immediate preventive war against Russia. True, he does not *want* the war to happen, and he thinks that it may possibly be prevented if sufficient firmness is shown. Still, the main point of his plan is that only one country should be allowed to possess the atomic bombs: and the Russians, unless crippled in war, are bound to get hold of them sooner or later. It will also be seen that Burnham is largely scrapping his earlier world-picture, and not merely the geographical aspect of it. In *The Managerial Revolution*, Burnham foretold the rise of three super-states which would be unable to conquer one another and would divide the world between them. Now the super-states have dwindled to two, and, thanks to atomic weapons, neither of them is invincible. But more has changed than that. In *The Managerial Revolution* it was implied that all three super-states would be very much alike. They would all be totalitarian in structure: that is, they would be collectivist but not democratic, and would be ruled over by a caste of managers, scientists and bureaucrats who would destroy old-style capitalism and keep the working class permanently in subjection. In other words, something rather like "Communism" would prevail everywhere. In *The Machiavellians*, Burnham somewhat toned down his theory, but

98

continued to insist that politics is only the struggle for power, and that government has to be based on force and fraud. Democracy is unworkable, and in any case the masses do not want it and will not make sacrifices in defense of it. In his present book, however, Burnham is in effect the champion of old-style democracy. There is, he now decides, a great deal in Western society that is worth preserving. Managerialism, with its forced labor, deportation, massacres and frame-up trials, is not really the unavoidable next stage in human development, and we must all get together and quell it before it is too late. All the available forces must rally immediately under the banner of anti-Communism. It is essentially a conservative program, making its appeal to the love of liberty and ordinary decency, but not to international sentiment.

Before criticizing Burnham's thesis, there is one thing that must be said. This is that Burnham has intellectual courage, and writes about real issues. He is certain to be denounced as a warmonger for writing this book. Yet if the danger is as acute as he believes, the course he suggests would probably be the right one: and more than this, he avoids the usual hypocritical attitude of "condemning" Russian policy while denying that it could be right in any circumstances to go to war. In international politics, as he realizes, you must either be ready to practice appeasement indefinitely, or at some point you must be ready to fight. He also sees that appeasement is an unreal policy, since a great nation, conscious of its own strength, never really carries it through. All that happens is that sooner or later some demand is felt to be intolerable, and one flounders into a war that might have been avoided by taking a firm attitude earlier. It is not fashionable to say such things nowadays, and Burnham deserves credit for saying them. However, it does not follow that he is right in his main argument. The important thing is the time factor. How much time have we got before the moment of crisis? Burnham, as usual, sees everything in the darkest colors and allows us only five years, or at most ten. If that were right, an American world empire would probably be the only hope. On the other hand, if we have twenty years in which to maneuver, there are other and better possibilities which ought not to be abandoned.

Unless the signs are very deceiving, the USSR is preparing for war against the Western democracies. Indeed, as Burnham rightly says, the war is already happening in a desultory way. How soon it could break out into full-scale conflict is a difficult question, bringing in all kinds of military, economic and scientific problems on which the ordinary journalist or political observer has no data. But there is one point, very important to Burnham's argument, which can be profitably discussed, and that is the position of the Communist parties and the "fellow-travelers" and the reliance placed on them by Russian strategy.

Burnham lays great stress on the Communist tactic of "infiltration." The Communists and their associates, open and secret, and the liberals who play their game unknowingly, are everywhere. They are in the trade unions, in the armed forces, in the State Department, in the press, in the churches, in cultural organizations, in every kind of league or union or committee with ostensibly progressive aims, seeping into everything like a filter-passing virus. For the moment they spread confusion and disaffection, and presently, when the crisis comes, they will hit out with all their strength. Moreover, a Communist is psychologically quite different from an ordinary human being. According to Burnham:

> The true Communist . . . is a "dedicated man." He has no life apart from his organization and his rigidly systematic set of ideas. Everything that he does, everything that he has, family, job, money, belief, friends, talents, life, everything is subordinated to his Communism. He is not a Communist just on election day or at Party headquarters. He is a Communist always. He eats, reads, makes love, thinks, goes to parties, changes residence, laughs, insults, always as a Communist. For him, the world is divided into just two classes of human beings: the Communists, and all the rest.

And again:

> The Moscow Show Trials revealed what has always been true of the Communist morality: that it is not merely the material possessions or the life of the individual which must be subordinated, but his reputation, his conscience, his honor, his dignity. He must lie and grovel, cheat and inform and betray, for Communism, as well as die. There is no restraint, no limit.

There are many similar passages. They all sound true enough until one begins applying them to the Communists whom one actually knows. No doubt, Burnham's description of the "true Communist" holds good for a few hundred thousand or a few million fanatical, dehumanized people, mostly inside the USSR, who are the nucleus of the movement. It holds good for Stalin, Molotov, Zhdanov, etc., and the more faithful of their agents abroad. But if there is one well-attested fact about the Communist parties of almost all countries, it is the rapid turnover in membership. People drift in, sometimes by scores of thousands at a time, and presently drift out again. In a country like the United States or Britain, a Communist Party consists essentially of an inner ring of completely subservient long-term members, some of whom have salaried jobs; a larger group of industrial workers who are faithful to the party but do not necessarily grasp its real aims; and a shifting mass of people who are full of zeal to start with, but rapidly cool off. Certainly every effort is made to induce in Communist Party members the totalitarian mentality that Burnham describes. In a few cases this succeeds permanently, in many others temporarily: still, it is possible to meet thinking people who have remained Communists for as much as ten years before resigning or being expelled, and who have not been intellectually crippled by the experience. In principle, the Communist parties all over the world are Quisling organizations, existing for the purpose of espionage and disruption, but they are not necessarily so efficient and dangerous as Burnham makes out. One ought not to think of the Soviet Government as controlling in every country a huge secret army of fanatical warriors, completely devoid of fear or scruples and having no thought except to live and die for the Workers'

Fatherland. Indeed, if Stalin really disposed of such a weapon as that, one would be wasting one's time in trying to resist him.

Also, it is not altogether an advantage to a political party to sail under false colors. There is always the danger that its followers may desert it at some moment of crisis when its actions are plainly against the general interest. Let me take an example near at hand. The British Communist Party appears to have given up, at any rate for the time being, the attempt to become a mass party, and to have concentrated instead on capturing key positions, especially in the trade unions. So long as they are not obviously acting as a sectional group, this gives the Communists an influence out of proportion of their numbers. Thus, owing to having won the leadership of several important unions, a handful of Communist delegates can swing several million votes at a Labor Party conference. But this results from the undemocratic inner working of the Labor Party, which allows a delegate to speak on behalf of millions of people who have barely heard of him and may be in complete disagreement with him. In a parliamentary election, where the individual votes on his own behalf, a Communist candidate can as a rule get almost no support. In the 1945 general election, the Communist Party won only 100,000 votes in the country as a whole, although in theory it controls several million votes merely inside the trade unions. When public opinion is dormant, a great deal can be achieved by groups of wire-pullers, but in moments of emergency, a political party must have a mass following as well. An obvious illustration of this was the failure of the British Communist Party, in spite of much trying, to disrupt the war effort during the period 1939–41. Certainly the Communists are everywhere a serious force, above all in Asia, where they have, or can plausibly present themselves as having, something to offer to the colonial populations. But one should not assume, as Burnham seems to do, that they can draw their followers after them, whatever policy they choose to adopt.

There is also the question of the "fellow-travelers," "cryptos" and sympathizers of various shades who further the aims of the Communists without having any official connection with them. Burnham does not claim that these people are all crooks or conscious traitors, but he does seem to believe that they will always continue in the same strain, even if the world situation deteriorates into open warfare. But after all, the disillusioned "fellow-traveler" is a common figure, like the disillusioned Communist. The important thing to do with these people—and it is extremely difficult since one has only inferential evidence—is to sort them out and determine which of them is honest and which is not. There is, for instance, a whole group of MP's in the British Parliament (Pritt, Zilliacus, etc.) who are commonly nicknamed "the cryptos." They have undoubtedly done a great deal of mischief, especially in confusing public opinion about the nature of the puppet regimes in Eastern Europe; but one ought not hurriedly to assume that they are all equally dishonest or even that they all hold the same opinions. Probably some of them are actuated by nothing worse than stupidity. After all, such things have happened before.

There was also the pro-Fascist bias of British Tories and corresponding strata in the United States in the years before 1939. When one saw British Conservative MP's cheering the news that British ships had been bombed by Italian aeroplanes in the service of Franco, it was tempting to believe that these people were actually treacherous to their own country. But when the pinch came, it was found that they were subjectively quite as patriotic as anyone else. They had merely based their opinions on a syllogism which lacked a middle term: Fascism is opposed to Communism; therefore it is on our side. In left-wing circles there is the corresponding syllogism: Communism is opposed to capitalism; therefore it is progressive and democratic. This is stupid, but it can be accepted in good faith by people who will be capable of seeing through it sooner or later. The question is not whether the "cryptos" and "fellow-travelers" advance the interests of the USSR against those of the democracies. Obviously they do so. The real question is, how many of them would continue on the same lines if war were really imminent? For a major war—unless it is a war waged by a few specialists, a Pearl Harbor with atomic bombs—is not possible until the issues have become fairly clear.

I have dwelt on this question of the Communist fifth columns inside the democratic countries, because it is more nearly verifiable than the other questions raised by Burnham's book. About the USSR itself we are reduced to guesswork. We do not know how strong the Russians are, how badly they have been crippled by the war, to what extent their recovery will depend on American aid, how much internal disaffection they have to contend with, or how soon they will get hold of atomic weapons. All we know with certainty is that at present no great country except the United States is physically able to make war, and the United States is not psychologically prepared to do so. At the one point where some kind of evidence is available, Burnham seems to me to overstate his case. After all, that is his besetting sin. He is too fond of apocalyptic visions, too ready to believe that the muddled processes of history will happen suddenly and logically. But suppose he is wrong. Suppose the ship is not sinking, only leaking. Suppose that Communism is not yet strong enough to swallow the world and that the danger of war can be staved off for twenty years or more: then we don't have to accept Burnham's remedy—or, at least, we don't have to accept it immediately and without question.

Burnham's thesis, if accepted, demands certain immediate actions. One thing that it *appears* to demand is a preventive war in the very near future, while the Americans have atomic bombs and the Russians have not. Even if this inference is unjustified, there can be no doubt about the reactionary nature of other points in Burnham's program. For instance, writing in 1946, Burnham considers that, for strategic reasons, full independence ought not to be granted to India. This is the kind of decision that sometimes has to be taken under pressure of military necessity, but which is indefensible in any normal circumstances. And again, Burnham is in favor of suppressing the American Communist Party, and of doing the job thoroughly, which would probably mean using the same methods as the Communists, when in power, use against *their* opponents. Now, there are times when it is justifiable to suppress a political party. If you are fighting for your life, and if there is some organization which is plainly acting on behalf of the enemy, and is strong enough to do harm, then you have got to crush it. But to suppress the Communist Party *now*, or at any time when it did not unmistakably endanger national survival, would be calamitous. One has only to think of the people who would approve! Burnham claims perhaps rightly, that when once the American empire had been established, it might be possible to pass on to some more satisfactory kind of world organization. But the first appeal of his program must be to conservatives, and if such an empire came into being, the strongest intellectual influence in it would probably be that of the Catholic Church.

Meanwhile there is one other solution which is at any rate thinkable, and which Burnham dismisses almost unmentioned. That is, somewhere or other—not in Norway or New Zealand, but over a large area—[how] to make democratic Socialism work. If one could somewhere present the spectacle of economic security without concentration camps, the pretext for the Russian dictatorship would disappear and Communism would lose much of its appeal. But the only feasible area is western Europe plus Africa. The idea of forming this vast territory into a Socialist United States has as yet hardly gained any ground, and the practical and psychological difficulties in the way are enormous. Still, it is a *possible* project if people really wanted it, and if there were ten or twenty years of assured peace in which to bring it about. And since the initiative would have to come in the first place from Britain, the important thing is that this idea should take root among British Socialists. At present, so far as the idea of a unified Europe has any currency at all, it is associated with Churchill. Here one comes back to one of the main points in Burnham's program—the fusion of Britain with the United States.

Burnham assumes that the main difficulty in the way of this would be national pride, since Britain would be very much the junior partner. Actually there is not much pride of that kind left, and has not been for many years past. On the whole, anti-American feeling is strongest among those who are also anti-imperialist and anti-military. This is true not only of Communists and "fellow-travelers" who are anxious to make mischief, but of people of good will who see that to be tied to America probably means preserving capitalism in Britain. I have several times overheard or taken part in conversations something like this:

"How I hate the Americans! Sometimes they make me feel almost pro-Russian."

"Yes, but they're not actually our enemies. They helped us in 1940, when the Russians were selling oil to the Germans. We can't stand on our own feet much longer, and in the end we may have to choose between knuckling under to Russia or going in with America."

"I refuse to choose. They're just a pair of gangsters."

"Yes, but supposing you *had* to choose. Suppose there was no other way out, and you had to live under one system or the other. Which would you choose, Russia or America?"

"Oh, well, of course, if one *had* to choose, there's no question about it—America."

Fusion with the United States is widely realized to be one way out of our difficulties. Indeed, we have been almost a dependency of the United States ever since 1940, and our desperate economic plight drives us in this direction all the faster. The union desired by Burnham may happen almost of its own accord, without formal arrangement and with no plan or idea behind it. A noisy but, I believe, very small minority would like Britain to be integrated into the Soviet system. The mass of the British people would never accept this, but the thinking ones among them do not regard the probable alternative—absorption by America—with enthusiasm. Most English left-wingers at present favor a niggling policy of "getting along with Russia" by being strong enough to prevent an attack and weak enough to disarm suspicion. Under this lies the hope that when the Russians become more prosperous, they may become more friendly. The other way out for Britain, the Socialist United States of Europe, has not as yet much magnetism. And the more the pessimistic world-view of Burnham and others like him prevails, the harder it is for such ideas to take hold.

Burnham offers a plan which would probably work, but which is a *pis aller* and should not be accepted willingly. In the end, the European peoples may have to accept American domination as a way of avoiding domination by Russia, but they ought to realize, while there is yet time, that there are other possibilities. In rather the same way, English Socialists of almost all colors accepted the leadership of Churchill during the war. Granted that they did not want Britain to be defeated, they could hardly help themselves, because effectively there was no one else, and Churchill was preferable to Hitler. But the situation might have been different if the European peoples could have grasped the nature of Fascism about five years earlier. In that case the war, if it happened at all, might have been a different kind of war, fought under different leaders for different ends.

The tendency of writers like Burnham, whose key concept is "realism", is to overrate the part played in human affairs by sheer force. I do not say that he is wrong all the time. He is quite right to insist that gratitude is not a factor in international politics; that even the most high-minded policy is no use unless you can show a practical way of putting it into effect, and that in the affairs of nations and societies, as opposed to individuals, one cannot hope for more than temporary and imperfect solutions. And he is probably right in arguing from this that one cannot apply to politics the same moral code that one practices or tries to practice in private life. But somehow his picture of the world is always slightly distorted. *The Managerial Revolution*, for instance, seemed to me a good description of what is actually happening in various parts of the world, i.e., the growth of societies neither capitalist nor socialist, and organized more or less on the lines of a caste system. But Burnham went on to argue that because this *was* happening, nothing else *could* happen, and the new, tightly-knit totalitarian state *must* be stronger than the chaotic democracies. Therefore, among other things, Germany had to win the war. Yet in the event Germany collapsed at least partly because of her totalitarian structure. A more democratic, less efficient country would not have made such errors in politics and strategy, nor would it have aroused such a volume of hatred throughout the world.

Of course, there is more in Burnham's book than the mere proposal for the setting-up of an American empire, and in detail there is much with which one can agree. I think he is mainly right in his account of the way in which Communist propaganda works, and the difficulty of countering it, and he is certainly right in saying that one of the most important problems at this moment is to find a way of speaking to the Russian people over the heads of their rulers. But the central subject of this book, as of almost everything that Burnham writes, is power. Burnham is always fascinated by power, whether he is for it or against it, and he always sees it a little larger than life. First it was Germany that was to swallow the world, then Russia, now perhaps America. When *The Managerial Revolution* was published, I for one derived the impression that Burnham's sympathies were on the whole with Germany, and at any rate that he was anxious that the United States should not throw good money after bad by coming to the rescue of Britain. The much-discussed essay, *Lenin's Heir*, which was a dissertation—a rhapsody, rather—on the strength, cunning and cruelty of Stalin, could be interpreted as expressing either approval or disapproval. I myself took it to be an expression of approval, though of a rather horrified kind.

It now appears that this was wrong. Burnham is not in favor of Stalin or Stalinism, and he has begun to find virtues in the capitalist democracy which he once considered moribund. But the note of fascination is still there. Communism may be wicked, but at any rate it is *big*: it is a terrible, all-devouring monster which one fights against but which one cannot help admiring. Burnham thinks always in terms of monsters and cataclysms. Hence he does not even mention, or barely mentions, two possibilities which should at least have been discussed in a book of this scope. One is that the Russian regime may become more liberal and less dangerous a generation hence, if war has not broken out in the meantime. Of course, this would not happen with the consent of the ruling clique, but it is thinkable that the mechanics of the situation may bring it about. The other possibility is that the great powers will be simply too frightened of the effects of atomic weapons ever to make use of them. But that would be much too dull for Burnham. Everything must happen suddenly and completely, and the choice must be all or nothing, glory or bust:

> It may be that the darkness of great tragedy will bring to a quick end the short, bright history of the United States—for there is enough truth in the dream of the New World to make the action tragic. The United States is called before the rehearsals are completed. Its strength and promise have not been matured by the wisdom of time and suffering. And the summons is for nothing less than the leadership of the world, for that or nothing. If it is reasonable to expect failure, that is only a measure of how great the triumph could be.

It may be that modern weapons have speeded things up to the point at which Burnham would be right. But if one can judge from the past, even from such huge calamities as the fall of the Roman Empire, history never happens quite so melodramatically as that.

3205. To Leonard Moore

29 March 1947   Typewritten

> 27 B Canonbury Square
> Islington
> London N 1

Dear Moore,

Many thanks for the royalty statement on "Dickens, Dali & Others." I enclose Reynall° & Hitchcock's account.

Looking through my books, I cannot find any record of their earlier payment to me. I remember they paid me an advance, which must have been some time in 1946, but I cannot remember the amount and therefore cannot work out how many copies the book has sold. If you have a record of it I should be obliged if you would let me know. This last sale has been something over 1100 copies, and if the advance they paid me was £100 I suppose the total sales would be something between 2000 and 3000.

> Yours sincerely
> [Signed] Eric Blair
> Eric Blair

1. Reynal & Hitchcock had 5,000 copies printed; the publication date was 29 April 1946. Type was distributed in June 1948. All the copies had not been sold by 1 January 1952, when the price was then raised from $2.50 to $2.75 (Willison).

3206. Introduction to *British Pamphleteers*, Volume I, edited by George Orwell and Reginald Reynolds[1]

Written Spring 1947?; published 15 November 1948

The present collection of pamphlets contains twenty-five specimens, reproduced either in whole or in part. They have been chosen for their representativeness as well as for their literary merit, and between them they cover the two centuries between the Reformation, with which English pamphleteering may be said to have started, and the War of American Independence. Later it is planned to issue a second series which will carry the history of the pamphlet down to our own times.

Mr. Reginald Reynolds, who has compiled and arranged this book, had to make his selection from a vast amount of material, as can be seen from the fact that 22,000 pamphlets and tracts of various kinds circulated in London merely between 1640 and 1661. The difficulty in a job like this is not merely to pick out the best pieces, but also to decide what is and what is not a pamphlet. To ask 'What is a pamphlet?' is rather like asking 'What is a dog?' We all know a dog when we see one, or at least we think we do, but it is not easy to give a clear verbal definition, nor even to distinguish at sight between a dog and some kindred creature such as a wolf or a jackal. The pamphlet is habitually confused with other things that are quite different from it, such as leaflets, manifestoes, memorials, religious tracts, circular letters, instructional manuals and indeed almost any kind of booklet published cheaply in paper covers. The true pamphlet, however, is a special literary form which has persisted without radical change for hundreds of years, though it has had its good periods and its bad ones. It is worth defining it carefully, even at the risk of seeming pedantic.

A pamphlet is a short piece of polemical writing, printed in the form of a booklet and aimed at a large public. One cannot lay down rigid rules about length, but evidently a leaflet containing nothing but the words DOWN WITH MUSSOLINI would not be a pamphlet, and neither would a book of the length of *Candide* or *The Tale of a Tub*. Probably a true pamphlet will always be somewhere between five hundred and ten thousand words, and it will always be unbound and obtainable for a few pence. A pamphlet is never written primarily to give entertainment or to make money. It is written because there is something that one wants to say *now*, and because one believes there is no other way of getting a hearing. Pamphlets may turn on points of ethics or theology, but they always have a clear political implication. A pamphlet may be written either 'for' or 'against' somebody or something, but in essence it is always a protest.

As Mr. Reynolds points out, pamphleteering can only flourish when it is fairly easy to get one's writings printed, legally or illegally. Probably a slight flavour of illegality is rather beneficial to the pamphlet. When there is genuine freedom of speech and all points of view are represented in the press, part of the reason for pamphleteering disappears, and on the other hand, if one is obliged to break the law in order to write at all, one is less afraid of uttering libels. Violence and scurrility are part of the pamphlet tradition, and up to a point press censorship favours them. It will be seen that a number of the pamphlets in this collection are anonymous, or were printed abroad and then smuggled into England. This was normal in the sixteenth and seventeenth centuries, when almost all governments were both oppressive and inefficient. No one, when in power, would allow his adversaries a fair hearing, but at the same time there was no police force worth bothering about, and illegal literature could circulate freely. In a modern totalitarian state, pamphleteering after the seventeenth-century manner would be impossible. Clandestine printing, if it can be practised at all, is so desperately dangerous that no one who undertakes it has much time for literary graces. The baroque English of the seventeenth-century pamphlets does not give the impression of coming from people who were frightened for their skins. Here are a couple of sentences from the anonymous *Tyranipocrit*. Notice the profusion of adjectives:

> But tell me thou propesturous impious world, if thou canst, who hath taught thee to punish the transgressors of the second Table of God's Commandments more than the first? Who hath taught thee to hang poore artlesse theeves and to maintain tyrants, and rich artificiall, proud, hypocritical, partial theeves, in their impious practices?

And here is the Digger Gerrard Winstanley, who was bankrupted by the Civil War and meanly persecuted under the Commonwealth:

> And you zealous preachers and professors of the City of London, and you great officers and soldiery of the army, where are all your victories over the Cavaliers, that you made such a blaze in your land, in giving God thanks for, and which you begged in your fasting days and morning exercises? Are they all sunk into the Norman power again and must the old prerogative laws stand? . . . Oh, thou City, thou hypocritical City! Thou blindfold, drowsy England, that sleeps and snorts in the bed of covetousness, awake, awake! The enemy is upon thy back, he is ready to scale the walls and enter possession, and wilt thou not look out?

Who would bother to use language like that when political controversy has to be carried on by means of stickybacks and chalkings on pavements?

Good pamphlets are likely to be written by men who passionately want to say something and who feel that the truth is being obscured but that the public would support them if only it knew the facts. If one had not a certain faith in democracy, one would not write pamphlets, one would try to gain one's ends by intriguing among influential people. This is another way of saying that pamphleteering will flourish when there is some great struggle in which honest and gifted men are to be found on both sides. The pamphlets in this collection have been chosen to cover the period as completely as possible, but it will be noticed that only four of them belong to the years between 1714 and 1789: and of those only one (Paine's *Common Sense*) deals with English internal affairs. Mr. Reynolds remarks on this 'interval' in political controversy, and points out the reason. During that period—after the Protestant Succession had been secured and before the outbreak of revolution in France—there was no clash of ideologies. The political struggle had ended with the complete victory of one faction, the wars against France were not wars for survival, and the controversies over Negro slavery or the exploits of the East India Company only touched minorities. In the two preceding centuries it had been different. Issues were being fought out which affected every thinking person, and in which each side genuinely felt the other to be sinning against the light. In its broad outlines the intellectual situation was curiously similar to that of our own day.

All the pamphlets in Mr. Reynolds's collection, up to and including Swift's, are really volleys in a single great battle. It is the battle of Catholic against Protestant, Feudalism against Capitalism. At the beginning the struggle is between England and Spain, then between King and Parliament, then between Whig and Tory: and mixed up with this—growing out of it, one should perhaps say—is the struggle of the victorious Parliamentary party against its own left wing. Looking back at the main encounter, it is easy to see that the forces represented by Cromwell deserved to win, since they at least offered a hope for the future, whereas their adversaries did not. But, as some observers realised at the time, their victory brought no actual benefit, but merely the promise of one. Its outcome was the rise of modern capitalism, which can only be regarded as a progressive event in so much that it has made possible another change which has not yet happened. If one judges capitalism by what it has actually achieved—the horrors of the Industrial Revolution, the destruction of one culture after another, the piling-up of millions of human beings in hideous ant-heaps of cities, and, above all, the enslavement of the coloured races—it is difficult to feel that in itself it is superior to feudalism. At the time of the Civil War, the long-term effects of a Parliamentary victory could not be foreseen, but the war was hardly over before it became clear that the causes for which the rank and file had believed themselves to be fighting were largely lost. The old tyranny had been overthrown, but neither liberty of opinion nor social equality had been brought much nearer.

To-day the whole process seems familiar, like one of the classic openings at chess. It is as though history, while not actually repeating itself, were in the habit of moving in spirals, so that events of hundreds of years ago can appear to be happening at one's elbow. Certain figures, arguments and habits of mind always recur. There is always the visionary, like Winstanley, who is equally persecuted by both parties. There is always the argument that one must go forward or go back, and the counter-argument that the first necessity is to consolidate the position that has been won. There is always the charge that the revolutionary extremist is really an agent of the reactionaries. And once the struggle is well over, there is always the conservative who is more progressive than the radicals who have triumphed. It is fitting that the last pamphlet in the series dealing with the Catholic-Protestant struggle should be *A Modest Proposal*, in which Swift—not a Catholic and not a Jacobite, but certainly an adherent of the losing side—puts in a word for the downtrodden Irish.

The most encouraging fact about revolutionary activity is that, although it always fails, it always continues. The vision of a world of free and equal human beings, living together in a state of brotherhood—in one age it is called the Kingdom of Heaven, in another the classless society—never materialises, but the belief in it never seems to die out. The English Diggers and Levellers, represented by three pamphlets in this series, are links in a chain of thought which stretches from the slave revolts of antiquity, through various peasant risings and heretical sects of the Middle Ages, down to the Socialists of the nineteenth century and the Trotskyists and Anarchists of our own day. One thing that can be detected here and there in these pamphlets is a half-belief that the ideal society has existed at some time in the past, so that a true revolution would really be a return. In Winstanley's pamphlets the word 'Norman' recurs over and over again. Everything that is oppressive and unjust—the King, the laws, the Church, the aristocracy—is 'Norman': by which Winstanley implies that the common people of England were once free and that the bondage in which they live is a foreign thing which has been forced upon them comparatively recently. In less crude forms, this belief still survives in our own time. Living before the machine age, Winstanley and his associates necessarily thought in terms of primitive peasant communes, and did not foresee that man might be freed from brute labour as well as from inequality. Their programme, unless one thinks a low standard of living desirable in itself, is out of date. But their essential predicament is that of any intelligent democratic Socialist to-day.

One ought not to press the analogy between the seventeenth and the twentieth centuries too hard, because the factors now involved are more complicated and the mental atmosphere has been altered by the coming of the machine and the decay of religious belief. Still, the general similarity is striking, and therefore the question arises: why has our own age not been to the same extent an age of pamphleteering?

It should be noticed that this *is* a pamphleteering age, so far as mere bulk of output goes. Pamphlets are published in such a haphazard way that it would be impossible to discover how many are appearing at any given moment, but during the fifteen years or so since Hitler came to power, the number has certainly been enormous. All through those years, however bad the paper situation might be, Conservatives, Socialists, Communists, Anarchists, Pacifists, Trotskyists, currency reformers, vegetarians, opponents of vivisection, trade unions, employers' associations, minor political parties or fractions within parties, religious bodies ranging from the Catholic Church to the British Israelites, miscellaneous research groups and, of course, official and semi-official organisations of all kinds were pouring forth pamphlets in an unending stream. The figure mentioned by Mr. Reynolds, of 22,000 pamphlets circulating in London between 1640 and 1661, is impressive, but the contemporary rate of output is probably faster. I know no way of checking this, but it seems likely that between 1935 and 1945 (the flood appears to have slackened in the past year or two) pamphlets were being issued in Britain at the rate of several thousands a year. And yet in all those acres of print there has been very little that was either worth reading for its own sake or had any noticeable effect. There have been short books, such as *Guilty Men*,[2] which have had a wide circulation and have influenced public opinion, but these are hardly pamphlets, if one accepts the definition I have given above. As for pamphlets possessing any literary merit, they are no longer to be found. The pamphlet survives, it even flourishes if one judges merely by numbers, but something has happened to it, and it is worth enquiring the reason.

One thing one must take notice of first of all is the decay of the English language. This is all the more important because pamphlets are intended as propaganda and are not normally produced by people who are writers first and foremost. In any age one can write fairly good prose if one takes the trouble, but a purely political kind of literature is likely to be better when the language which lies ready to hand is uncorrupted. As an illustration, here are a couple of extracts, one from Mr. Victor Gollancz's recent pamphlet, *Leaving them to their Fate*, the other from John Aylmer's *Harborowe for Faithfull and Trewe Subjectes*. They are similar enough in subject-matter to allow of a comparison. Both writers are engaged (though not from the same motives) in pointing out that the people of England are better off than those of Germany. *Leaving them to their Fate* is more simply and vigorously written than the majority of modern pamphlets, so that the comparison is not an unfair one. Here is the twentieth century:

So that is the situation at the moment of writing on March 30th. The people of Germany are eating seed potatoes, and policemen, I am informed, are falling at their posts. The ration is to be maintained at about 1000 calories for the month of April. This is being achieved partly by raiding the very last reserves, and partly by the diversion of small shipments on their way to Britain, against a guarantee of very early replacement from supplies that would otherwise go to Germany. What will happen in May is anybody's guess . . . During the whole period of which I have been writing the average daily calories of the British people, according to repeated official statements, have been 2850, as against the 2650 stipulated by UNRRA as necessary for full health and working efficiency. On March 11th, after the cut in fats and dried egg, the figure was actually given by Dr. Summerskill as 2900. And the stocks of food and feeding stuffs in this country owned and controlled by the Minister of Food, exclusive of stocks on farms or held by secondary wholesalers and certain manufacturers, were estimated to total on the last day of March this year no less than a round four million tons.

Here is the sixteenth century (I am modernising the spelling):

Now compare (the Germans) with thee: and thou shalt see how happy thou art. They eat herbs: and thou beef and mutton. They roots: and thou butter, cheese and eggs. They drink commonly water: and thou good ale and beer. They go from the market with a salad: and thou with good flesh fill thy wallet. They likely never see any sea fish: and thou hast thy belly full of it. They pay till their bones rattle in their skin: and thou layest up for thy son and heir. Thou art twice or thrice in thy lifetime called upon to help thy country, with a subsidy or contribution: and they pay daily and never cease. Thou livest like a Lord, and they like Dogs. God defend us from the feeling of their misery.

I am not claiming that the second extract is in all ways better than the first. The modern way of writing has its virtues, which are due partly to the spread of the scientific outlook. Evidently the sixteenth-century writer, even if he had heard of such things as calories, would never bother with the kind of precise statement that is attempted in the first extract. One thing that strikes one all through the earlier pamphlets in this collection is the lack of any reasoned argument: very seldom is there anything more than assertion backed up by doubtful authority. In the last century or two we have grown to have a better idea of what is meant by evidence and proof, and language itself has grown more precise and capable of a wider range of meaning. Still, who could read those two passages one after the other and not feel that an enormous deterioration has happened? What has fallen is the *average* level of prose, the phraseology that one uses when one is not picking one's words for aesthetic reasons. 'Thou hast thy belly full of it'—'pay till their bones rattle in their skin'—'God defend us from the feeling of their misery'—that is not the kind of language that would come naturally to the compilers of White Papers or the publicists of the Fabian Society. So much the less chance that any purely political writing will be art as well as propaganda.

But the modern pamphlet suffers another serious disadvantage in the fact that the public is not, so to speak, pamphlet-conscious. Unlike a novel or a book of verse, a pamphlet has no assured channel by which it can reach the readers most likely to appreciate it. The pamphlets of Milton, Swift, Defoe, Junius and others were literary events, and they were also a recognised part of the political life of the period. Nowadays this would probably not be the case, even if pamphlets of comparable power were appearing. Indeed, because of the manner in which pamphlets are distributed, it would be possible for a first-rate piece of work to pass almost unnoticed, even if the author of it were already known as a writer of books or newspaper articles.

Pamphlets are not only produced in great numbers, but some of them sell tens or scores of thousands of copies. However, their circulation is as a rule largely spurious. The majority of them are produced by political parties or groups, which make use of them, along with posters, leaflets, processions, pavement-chalking and what-not, as part of their general propaganda drive. At public meetings they are forced on members of the audience, who buy them as a way of paying for their seats; or they are circulated to party branches and zealous individuals who give a standing order for all the literature of the party they support; or they are given away free or sent through the post to M.P.s and other public men. In all cases many or most of the copies disposed of simply lie about unread, or go straight into the waste-paper basket. Moreover, even if one is interested in getting hold of a particular pamphlet, it is often very difficult to do so. Pamphlets are issued by a multitude of different organisations, including many which disappear or change their names soon after they have come into being. No bookseller stocks or even attempts to stock all of them, they are nowhere listed in any comprehensive way, and only a small proportion of them are ever noticed in the press. Even the keenest collector of pamphlets could not hope to keep track of anywhere near the whole output. It can be seen that a pamphlet is always liable to miss its potential public, and, although appearing as a separate booklet, to have less effect and receive less attention than it would if it were published as an article in a monthly magazine.

Of course, most pamphlets do not deserve attention. Most of them are rubbish. This must have been true at all times, but there are reasons, apart from those I have mentioned already, that work against even the occasional appearance of good pamphlets in our own day. Pamphlet literature has come to be thought of not only as propaganda, but essentially as party propaganda. It expresses not the outlook of an individual but the 'line' of some organised movement, or group, or committee, and even the actual writing is not necessarily done in its entirety by any one person. Pamphleteering after the old style, when some independent writer with a grievance to air, or a plan to propose, or a rival to attack, would take his manuscript to the printer, perhaps a clandestine printer, and then hawk the product round the streets at a few pence a time, is almost unheard of. Few people would know how to set about doing it, and the very occasional pamphleteer who does publish at his own expense is usually some uninteresting kind of crank or outright lunatic. On the other hand commercial publishers seldom interest themselves in pamphlets, i.e., political pamphlets. If one wants to write in this particular form one is practically obliged to do it under the wing of some organised body, with all the sacrifices of spontaneity and even of honesty that that implies.

There are five anonymous pamphlets in Mr. Reynolds's collection. Of the other twenty, nineteen—and, in Mr. Reynolds's opinion, probably the twentieth as well—are the work of individual persons. And in a less definable way they all, when compared with modern political writing, give an impression of individuality, which comes out in their language and in a certain exuberance of argument. Until quite recently there was no accepted political jargon. Even a venal writer, hired like a lawyer to turn black into white, chose his diction for himself, and probably also chose the line that he would take in building up his case. Look for instance at the extract from *Royal Religion*, in which Daniel Defoe has been commissioned to 'write up' William III as a model of piety. We may assume that Defoe's motives were not very lofty ones and that he did not undertake this pamphlet because he was burning with zeal to say just that particular thing. And yet how lively he manages to make it! It is like a volley of custard pies, every one of them bang on the target. A modern political hack, boosting some doubtful cause, would be very unlikely to show the same humour and ingenuity, because he could never allow his imagination to range so freely. Party orthodoxy would not only take all the colour out of his vocabulary, but would dictate the main lines of his argument in advance.

In *Some Cautions for Choice of Members of Parliament* the Marquis of Halifax attacks the party system, which was beginning to govern political life by the end of the seventeenth century. Since then, various of the evils he mentions have swollen vastly, and fresh ones have appeared. If one thinks out what is involved, it is difficult to see how the growth of the party system could have been avoided in England, but there can be no doubt about the deadening effect that it has had on political thought and writing. It must be so, because collective action demands a sort of gregarious thinking, while literature has to be produced by individuals. It follows that, except by some kind of accident, good pamphlets cannot appear when this class of literature is under the control of closely organised groups. The typical modern pamphlet is either a predigested version of some longer work on sociology or economics, or it is a handbook intended to provide speakers with talking-points and quotable figures, or it is simply an extended slogan. Good pamphlets will begin to appear again when the pamphlet is looked upon as a means of getting a hearing for individual opinions, and when it seems normal, if you have something that you urgently want to say, to print and distribute it yourself without much expectation of profit.

Whether a literary form survives or perishes may be determined by mechanical factors which have nothing to do with its intrinsic merits. The three-volume novel, for instance, went out partly because the lending libraries decided against it, and it is probably for economic reasons that the 'long-short' story, called in French a *nouvelle* (the story of from fifteen to thirty thousand words, say), has not flourished in England. The pamphlet, I have suggested, has decayed partly because it has been captured by professional politicians, and hence has ceased to be taken seriously or to attract gifted writers. It is hard to imagine Swift or Milton, or even Defoe or Tom Paine, bothering to write pamphlets if they were alive now. The sort of public that they would aim at would have to be reached in some other way. The pity is that in a pamphlet one can do things that are possible in no other medium. The pamphlet is a one-man show. One has complete freedom of expression, including, if one chooses, the freedom to be scurrilous, abusive and seditious; or, on the other hand, to be more detailed, serious and 'highbrow' than is ever possible in a newspaper or in most kinds of periodical. At the same time, since the pamphlet is always short and unbound, it can be produced much more quickly than a book, and in principle, at any rate, can reach a bigger public. Above all, the pamphlet does not have to follow any prescribed pattern. It can be in prose or in verse, it can consist largely of maps or statistics or quotations, it can take the form of a story, a fable, a letter, an essay, a dialogue or a piece of 'reportage'. All that is required of it is that it shall be topical, polemical and short. How great a variation is possible can be seen even in the twenty-five specimens assembled here, ranging as they do from earnest argument through satire and rhetoric to sheer abuse.

The great function of the pamphlet is to act as a sort of foot-note or marginal comment on official history. It not only keeps unpopular viewpoints alive, but supplies documentation on events that the authorities of the day have reason to falsify. A good example in this collection is the description of the trial of Penn the Quaker, *The People's Ancient and Just Liberties Asserted*, which has the appearance of being truthful and gives an interesting picture of nascent totalitarianism. Outrages of this kind, and indeed all minor controversial events, such as plots, real or imaginary, riots, massacres and assassinations are likely to be documented in pamphlet form or not at all. It is a job that needs doing in all ages, and surely never more than in the present one.

Introducing Anthony Benezet's *Caution and Warning*, Mr. Reynolds remarks that in the middle years of the eighteenth century such issues as Negro slavery 'at least gave the pamphleteers something to write about'. In our century, dearth of subject-matter is not one of the things that a pamphleteer suffers from. Probably there never was an age that so cried out for his activities. Not only are the ideological hatreds bitterer than ever, but minorities are suppressed and truth perverted in a way never before dreamed of. Wherever one looks one sees fiercer struggles than the Crusades, worse tyrannies than the Inquisition, and bigger lies than the Popish Plot. It might be argued that in England, with its free and reasonably varied press, there is not much scope for the pamphleteer; but this will not be endorsed by anyone who has ever tried to get a hearing for a genuinely unpopular cause. Certainly the British press has juridical freedom, which is not a sham but a very real blessing, and in the modern world an increasingly rare one. But it is not true that the British press adequately represents all shades of opinion. Nearly always it is safe to put one's political opinions on paper, but to get them into print, and still more to get them to a big public, is not so easy. Because of the way in which newspapers are owned and operated, not only can minority opinions—and even majority opinions, when they are not backed by some influential group—go almost unheard, but events of the utmost importance can pass unnoticed or can reach the public only in some shrunken and distorted form. At any given moment there is a sort of all-prevailing orthodoxy, a general tacit agreement not to discuss some large and uncomfortable fact. Take one recent example out of the scores that could easily be assembled: the expulsion of some twelve million Germans from their homes in East Prussia, the Sudetenland, etc. How much mention has this deed, for which Britain must be held at least partly responsible, received in the British press? How strongly has the British public reacted to it? Indeed, if the necessary enquiries could be made, would it be surprising to find that a majority of adult British citizens have not even heard of it?

It is true, of course, that events of this kind do not go altogether undocumented in pamphlet form. As I have said, the actual number of modern pamphlets is very large. But they are poor things, not much read and seldom deserving to be read—mere fragments of party orthodoxy describing a short parabola from printing-press to waste-paper basket. In general they are not written by people who are primarily writers, because no one who feels deeply about literature, or even prefers good English to bad, can accept the discipline of a political party. It would be difficult to name a single eminent English writer who has produced a pamphlet during the last fifteen years. There is no Swift or Defoe living to-day, but even those who are nearest to them never bother to write pamphlets. In order that they should begin doing so, it is necessary that people should once again become aware of the possibilities of the pamphlet as a method of influencing opinion, and as a literary form: in other words, that the prestige of the pamphlet should be restored. It is hoped that this collection and the one that will follow it, quite apart from being worth reading for their own sakes, will contribute towards that end.

1. Despite the title-page attribution to Orwell as joint editor, Orwell makes plain in the second paragraph of his introduction that it was Reginald Reynolds who had 'compiled and arranged this book.' Later he refers to 'Mr. Reynolds's collection.' The first volume was devoted to pamphlets from the sixteenth century to the French Revolution. The second volume, comprising pamphlets from the French Revolution to the 1930s, was published in 1951. This was edited by W. J. Reynolds and had an introduction by A. J. P. Taylor. (The dust-jacket erroneously stated that it was 'by A. J. P. Taylor and Reginald Reynolds.') In his introduction, Taylor referred several times to Orwell: that he 'wrote the admirable introduction to the first volume of this work'; that he 'wanted to be a rebel all his life; when he died, tragically young, he was a best-seller in two continents'; that 'the expression of unpopular or unusual views is becoming more difficult' (Taylor doubted that – rather that such views had become more difficult to find); and the anxiety Orwell felt at the end of his life: dare we risk intellectual freedom in the face of Communism? The placing of this introduction within spring 1947 is arbitrary; it was when Orwell left London for Jura, and he probably finished this task before leaving for Scotland. The original was printed in italic.
2. *Guilty Men* (1940) by Michael Foot (see *2725, n. 5*) Frank Owen (see *1141, n. 4*), and Peter Howard.

3207. To Leonard Moore

        2 April 1947   Typewritten

                                        27 B Canonbury Square
                                               Islington
                                      London N 1

Dear Moore,
Some people in Holland have written asking for leave to broadcast a Dutch version of "Animal Farm." They are called Vereniging Van Arbeiders Radio Amateurs and write from Hilversum. I have given them your address and asked them to get in touch with you.[1]

                                             Yours sincerely
                                    [Signed] Eric Blair
                                         Eric Blair

1. Annotated in Moore's office: '£20 *paid*. for° each subsequent b'cast £10.'

3208. 'As I Please,' 80

        Tribune, 4 April 1947

The Royal Commission on the Press is now getting to work, after mysterious delays. Presumably it will be a long time before it reaches any definite conclusions, and still longer before its findings are acted upon. Nevertheless, it seems to me that now is the time to start discussing the problem of preserving a free Press in a socialised economy. Because, unless we become aware of the difficulties before they are actually upon us, the ultimate condition of the Press in this country will be worse than it need be.

    During the fuel crisis I remarked to several people on the badness of Government publicity, to be met each time with the answer that the present Government has hardly any organs of expression under its control. That, of course, is true. I then said, "Why not take over the *Daily* —— and run it as a Government organ?" This suggestion was always greeted with horror. Apparently to nationalise the Press would be "Fascism," while "freedom of the Press" consists in allowing a few millionaires to coerce hundreds of journalists into falsifying their opinions. But I pass over the question of how free the British Press is at present. The point is, what will finally happen if the present trend towards nationalisation continues?

    Sooner or later, it seems to me, the Press is certain to be nationalised, so far as its major organs go. It could hardly continue to exist as a huge patch of private enterprise, like a sort of game reserve, in the middle of a collectivised economy. But does that mean that *all* channels of expression will ultimately be under the control of bureaucrats? Some such thing could quite easily happen if the people most concerned are indifferent to their fate. One can quite well imagine newspapers, periodicals, magazines, books, films, radio, music and the drama all being lumped together and "co-ordinated" under the guidance of some enormous Ministry of Fine Arts (or whatever its name might be). It is not a pleasant prospect, but I believe it can be averted if the danger is realised in advance.

What is meant by freedom of the Press? The Press is free, I should say, when it is easy and not illegal to get minority opinions into print and distribute them to the public. Britain is luckier in this respect than most countries, and it is fair to say that this is partly due to the variations that exist in the big commercial Press. The leading daily papers, few though they are, contain more shades of difference than a Government-controlled Press would be likely to do. Still, the main guardians of minority opinion are the small independent weekly and monthly papers, and the book-publishing houses. It is only through those channels that you can make sure of getting a hearing for *any* opinion that does not express a libel or an incitement to violence. Therefore, if the big Press is certain to be nationalised any way, could not this principle be laid down in advance: that nationalisation shall only apply to so much of the Press as comes under the heading of "big business," while small concerns will be left alone?

Obviously the proprietor of a chain of a hundred newspapers is a capitalist. So is a small publisher or the owner-editor of a monthly magazine, strictly speaking. But you are not obliged to treat them both alike, just as in abolishing large-scale ownership of land you are not obliged to rob the smallholder or market gardener of his few acres. So long as a minority Press can exist, and count on continued existence, even in a hole and corner way, the essential freedom will be safeguarded. But the first step is to realise that nationalisation is inevitable, and lay our plans accordingly. Otherwise the people specially concerned, the journalists, artists, actors, etc., may have no bargaining power when the time comes, and that unappetising Ministry of Fine Arts may engulf the whole lot of them.

Recently I was talking to the editor of a newspaper with a very large circulation,[1] who told me that it was now quite easy for his paper to live on its sales alone. This would probably continue to be true, he said, until the paper situation improved, which would mean reverting to pre-war bulk, at enormously greater expense. Until then, advertisements would be of only secondary importance as a source of revenue.

If that is so—and I believe many papers could now exist without advertisements—is not this just the moment for an all-out drive against patent medicines? Before the war it was never possible to attack patent medicines in a big way, because the Press, which would have had to make the exposure, lived partly off advertisements for them. As a start, some enterprising publisher might track down and reprint the two volumes of that rare and very entertaining book, *Secret Remedies*. This was issued, if I remember rightly, by the British Medical Association—at any rate, by some association of doctors—the first volume appearing about 1912 and the second during the nineteen-twenties. It consisted simply of a list of existing proprietary medicines, with a statement of their claims, an analysis of their contents, and an estimate of their cost. There was very little comment, which in most cases was hardly necesary. I distinctly remember that one "consumption cure" sold to the public at thirty-five shillings a bottle was estimated to cost a halfpenny.

Neither volume made much impact on the public. The Press, for reasons indicated above, practically ignored both issues, and they are now so rare that I have not seen a copy for years. (Incidentally, if any reader has a copy I would gladly buy it—especially the second volume, which I think is the rarer.) If reissued, the book would need bringing up to date, for the claim to cure certain diseases is now forbidden by law, while many new kinds of rubbish have come on to the market. But many of the old ones are still there—that is the significant point. Is it not possible that the consumption of patent medicines might decrease if people were given a clearer idea of the nature and the real cost of the stuff they are pouring down their throats?[2]

A few weeks back a correspondent in *Tribune* asked why we are not allowed to grow and cure tobacco for our own use,[3] In practice, I think, you can do so. There is a law against it, but it is not strictly enforced—at any rate, I have certainly known people who grew their own tobacco, and even prepared it in cakes like the commercial article. I tried some once, and thought it the perfect tobacco for a non-smoker. The trouble with English tobacco is that it is so mild that you can hardly taste it. This is not, I believe, due to the lack of sun but to some deficiency in the soil. However, any tobacco is better than none, and a few thousand acres laid down to it in the south of England might help us through the cigarette shortage which is likely to happen this year, without using up any dollars or robbing the State of any revenue.

I have just been reading about the pidgin English (or "bêche-la-mar"[9]) used in the Solomon and New Hebrides Islands in the South Pacific. It is the lingua franca between many islands whose inhabitants speak different languages or dialects. As it has only a tiny vocabulary and is lacking in many necessary parts of speech, it has to make use of astonishing circumlocutions. An aeroplane, for instance, is called "lanich (launch) belong fly allsame pigeon." A violin is described thus: "One small bokkis (box) belong whiteman all he scratch him belly belong him sing out good fella." Here is a passage in what seems, judging by the other extracts given, to be very high-class pidgin. It announces the Coronation of King George VI:

> King George, he dead. Number one son, Edward, he no want him clothes. Number two son he like. Bishop he make plenty talk along new King. He say: "You look out good along all the people?" King he talk: "Yes." Then bishop and plenty Government official and storekeeper and soldier and bank manager and policeman, all he stand up and sing and blow him trumpet. Finish.

There are similar pidgins, most of them not quite so bad, in other parts of the world. In some cases the people who first formed them were probably influenced by the feeling that a subject race ought to talk comically. But there are areas where a lingua franca of some kind is indispensable, and the perversions actually in use make one see what a lot there is to be said for Basic.[4]

Orwell left for Jura on 10 April. He 'dropped the Tribune° column,' as he put it in his letter of 15 April 1947 to Frank D. Barber (see *3214*), in order to get on with writing *Nineteen Eighty-Four*. It proved to be his last contribution to *Tribune*.

1. Unidentified. Orwell had lunched with Lord Beaverbrook in mid-January 1946 (see *2852* and *2870, n. 7*), but that was hardly recent, and Beaverbrook was a proprietor, not an editor. Tom Hopkinson was editor of *Picture Post*—hardly to be described as a newspaper—but *Picture Post* was capable of such a crusade, and Orwell saw Hopkinson on 10 January 1946 (see *2852*). David Astor, whom Orwell saw often, did not become editor of *The Observer* until 1948, and *The Observer* hardly had 'a very large circulation' in comparison with the mass-circulation newspapers.
2. On 25 April 1947, *Tribune* published a long letter from A. Stephens supporting Orwell on the subject of patent medicines. He had been trying, without success, to buy a copy of the second edition of *Secret Remedies* for a long time. Members of the Labour Party, had long tried to 'end this scandal' and now that Labour was in power it should do so. On 29 April 1947, the publishers George Allen & Unwin wrote to Orwell of their attempts to republish *Secret Remedies*. They had written to the British Medical Association (the publishers of the first two volumes, in 1908 and 1912). Dr. Charles Hill (1904–1989; Lord Hill of Luton, 1963), widely known as 'The Radio Doctor,' a populariser of healthy living, but also a distinguished medical administrator and an M.P., 1950–63, explained that as a result of the publication of these books, the Association had been involved in a costly libel action. Though they won the case, they never received the costs awarded. In addition to the risk of further libel actions, extensive revision would now be necessary, and there seemed no prospect of the British Medical Association undertaking this task. George Allen & Unwin did not think, in these circumstances, that they could follow Orwell's suggestion for a reissue. See Orwell's letter to Stanley Unwin, 8 September 1947, *3266*.
3. The letter calling for the right to grow and cure tobacco (and also the right to sell home-made wines and to 'make our own stills' in order to produce spirits) was from Oswell Blakeston and was published on 7 March 1947.
4. Basic English; a simplified form of standard English with a vocabulary of 850 words designed especially for non-English-speakers. Orwell referred to it on several occasions: see, for example, 'As I Please,' 9, 28 January 1944, *2412*; 'As I Please,' 38, 18 August 1944, *2534*; and *The English People*, where he describes it as a 'very simple pidgin dialect' like bêche-de-mer, *2475, n. 4*.

3209. To Yvonne Davet

7 April 1947   Typewritten

27 B Canonbury Square
Islington
London N 1

Chère Madame Davet,
J'ai reçu votre lettre il y a une sémaine,° mais je viens de passer quelques jours au lit (la grippe). Au jour d'hui° ça va un peu mieux. Nous avons eu un hiver complètement insupportable, et même maintenant il fait froid comme on ne pourrait pas imaginer. Nous partons en Ecosse le 10 avril, et j'espère y trouver du meilleur temps. En tous cas en obtient le charbon et le bois plus facilement là qu'ici.
    Je crois que j'ai déjà signé le contrat avec Charlot pour la traduction de "Homage to Catalonia." Quant au titre, comme je vous ai déjà dit, il me

semble impossible de choisir un titre dans une langue étrangère, mais "Dignité de l'homme" me semble très bon. Naturellement je serais très content si Malraux voudrait écrire une préface, mais, même si il a assez de loisir à present, il le trouverait peut-être un peu embarassant de point de vue politique.[1] Il se souviendra peut-être du livre, car je lui ai donné un exemplaire il y a deux ans. Je ne peux pas dire que je le connais, mais je l'ai rencontré une fois chez un ami.

Quant au drapeau républicain (pages 29 et 293–4 du texte anglais). Vu que je ne suis pas sûr, il serait meilleur de supprimer ces deux allusions, ce qu'on peut facilement faire en corrigeant les épreuves.

Reste une petite chose. J'ai deux ou trois fois écrit le mot espagnol *poron* (sorte de vaisseau à boire) comme *puron*. Je ne suis pas sûr si je vous ai déjà signalé cet erreur.

Je resterai six mois en Ecosse. J'espère finir mon roman avant la fin de 1947, mais on tous cas je le pourrai continuer, ce qui semble impossible à Londres, où je ne peux jamais échapper d'un tas de journalisme. Mon petit garçon va très bien. Il aura trois ans en mai. Vous avez, je crois, mon adresse écossaise. Je vais adresser ceci à Nice.

Très amicalement
Geo. Orwell

Translation

I received your letter a week ago, but I have been in bed for several days (influenza). Today I'm a bit better. We have had a quite unendurable winter, and even now it is colder than you could imagine. We are going to Scotland on April 10th, and I hope to find better weather there. At least we can get coal and wood more easily there than here.

I think I have already signed the contract with Charlot for *Homage to Catalonia*. As for the title, as I said before, I don't think I can possibly choose a title in a foreign language, but *Dignité de l'Homme* [Dignity of Man] sounds very good. Of course I should be very pleased if Malraux wanted to write a preface, but even if he had time just now, he would perhaps find it politically rather embarrassing.[1] He will perhaps remember the book, as I gave him a copy two years ago. I can't say I know him, but I met him once at a friend's house.

As for the Republican flag (pages 29 and 293–4 of the English text), because I am not sure, it would be better to take out these two allusions. This can easily be done when the proofs are corrected.

There is one more thing. I wrote the Spanish word *poron* (a kind of drinking vessel) two or three times as *puron*. I am not sure if I have already told you about this mistake.

I shall stay in Scotland for six months. I hope to finish my novel before the end of 1947, but in any case I shall be able to get on with it, which seems impossible in London, where I can never escape from a mountain of journalism. My little boy is very well. He will be three in May. I think you've got my Scottish address. I am sending this to Nice.

1. Georges Kopp, Orwell's commander in Spain, had written an introduction for the French translation of *Homage to Catalonia* made in 1938–9. On 19 June 1939, Orwell told Yvonne Davet, that he liked Kopp's introduction very much; see *550*. In his letter to Leonard Moore of 15 April 1947 (see *3216*), Orwell confirms that Kopp wrote an introduction but that it was not now suitable. Kopp's introduction has not been traced. André Malraux (1901–1976), author and politician, had been active in various left-wing causes before the war. Though not himself a pilot, he had rapidly helped organise air support for the Republicans in the Spanish civil war and was appointed a colonel (see Hugh Thomas, *The Spanish Civil War*, 364, n. 4). He fought in the French Resistance during World War II and then became closely associated with General de Gaulle, serving as his Minister of Information, November 1945–January 1946. When de Gaulle retired temporarily, Malraux advocated the aims of de Gaulle's Rassemblement du Peuple Français. De Gaulle appointed him Minister of Cultural Affairs, 1958–68. Orwell evidently sensed the change in direction of Malraux's political convictions—hence his letter to Moore, 7 July 1947; see *3246*.

3210. To George Woodcock

9 April 1947   Typewritten

27B Canonbury Square
Islington, N. 1

Dear George,
As I think you know, I am going away to Scotland tomorrow, 10th. I had wanted to get in touch with you, but I have been ill in bed for a week. I have just had a letter about the Annual General Meeting on May 16th.[1] I cannot possibly come down for it, because to get there and back would mean something like a week's journey. Do you think that would be all right, and that I could see the Agenda beforehand?

I think you know my Scottish address, but in case not it is Barn Hill,° Isle of Jura, Argyllshire. If you and Ingie would like to come up any time, I shall be there continuously till October, and I think it is safe to say there would always be beds, but just let me know about a week beforehand because the posts are infrequent and one has to make arrangements about the journey.

Yours,
George

1. Of the Freedom Defence Committee, reported in its *Bulletin*, 5, July–August 1947, 4, 5, 8.

3211. To Victor Gollancz

9 April 1947   Typewritten; copy

27B Canonbury Square
Islington, N.1

Dear Gollancz,
I should have written several days earlier, but I have been ill in bed. Very many thanks for your generous action.[1]

Yours sincerely,
George Orwell

1. Gollancz's generous action was to relinquish his right to publish Orwell's next two novels—in effect, *Nineteen Eighty-Four*. The contract was for the next three novels after *Keep the Aspidistra Flying*; *Coming Up for Air* was the first of the three.

3212. To Sonia Brownell

12 April 1947   Handwritten

Barnhill
Isle of Jura
Argyllshire

Dearest Sonia,[1]
I am handwriting this because my typewriter is downstairs. We arrived O.K. & without incident yesterday. Richard was as good as gold & rather enjoyed having a sleeper to himself after he had got over the first strangeness, & as soon as we got into the plane at Glasgow he went to sleep, probably because of the noise. I hadn't been by plane before & I think it's really better. It costs £2 or £3 more, but it saves about 5 hours & the boredom of going on boats, & even if one was sick its° only three quarters of an hour whereas if one goes by sea one is sick for five or six hours, ie. if it is bad weather. Everything up here is just as backward as in England, hardly a bud showing & I saw quite a lot of snow yesterday. However it's beautiful spring weather now & the plants I put in at the new year seem to be mostly alive. There are daffodils all over the place, the only flower out. I'm still wrestling with more or less virgin meadow, but I think by next year I'll have quite a nice garden here. Of course we've had a nightmare all today getting things straight, with Richard only too ready to help, but it's more or less right now & the house is beginning to look quite civilized. It will be some weeks before we've got the transport problem fully solved, but otherwise we are fairly well appointed. I'm going to send for some hens as soon as we have put the hen house up, & this year I have been also able to arrange for alcohol so that we have just a little, a sort of rum ration, each day. Last year we had to be practically T.T. I think in a week everything will be straight & the essential work in the garden done, & then I can get down to some work.
    I wrote to Genetta[2] asking her to come whenever she liked & giving

instructions about the journey. So long as she's bringing the child, not just sending it, it should be simple enough. I want to give you the complete details about the journey, which isn't so formidable as it looks on paper. The facts are these:

There are boats to Jura on *Mondays, Wednesdays & Fridays.* You have to catch the boat train at Glasgow at 8 am, which means that it's safer to sleep the preceding night at Glasgow, because the all-night trains have a nasty way of coming in an hour or two hours late, & then one misses the boat train. The times & so on are as follows:

8 am leave Glasgow Central for GOUROCK.

Join boat for Tarbert (TARBERT) at Gourock.

About 12 noon arrive East Tarbert.

Travel by bus to West Tarbert (bus runs in conjunction with the boats).

Join boat for CRAIGHOUSE (Jura) at West Tarbert.

About 3.30 pm arrive Craighouse.

Take hired car to LEALT, where we meet you.

If you want to go by plane, the planes run daily (except Sundays I think), & they nearly always take off unless it's very misty. The itinerary then is:

10.30 arrive at Scottish Airways office at St. Enoch Station, Glasgow (the air office is in the railway station).

10.40 leave by bus for RENFREW.

11.15 leave by plane for ISLAY. (Pronounced EYELY).

12 noon arrive Islay.

Hire a car (or take bus) to the ferry which leads to Jura.

About 1 pm cross ferry.

Hired car to LEALT.

It's important to let us know in advance when you are coming, because of the hired car. There are only 2 posts a week here, & only 2 occasions on which I can send down to Craighouse to order the car. If you come by boat, you could probably get a car all right by asking on the quay, but if you come by air there wouldn't be a car at the ferry (which is several miles from Craighouse) unless ordered beforehand. Therefore if you proposed coming on, say, June 15th, it would be as well to write about June 5th because, according to the day of the week, it may be 4 or 5 days before your letter reaches me, & another 3 or 4 days before I can send a message. It's no use wiring because the telegrams come by the postman.

You want a raincoat & if possible stout boots or shoes—gum boots if you have them. We may have some spare gum boots, I'm not sure—we are fairly well off for spare oilskins & things like that. It would help if you brought that week's rations, because they're not quick at getting any newcomer's rations here, & a little flour & tea.

I am afraid I am making this all sound very intimidating, but really it's easy enough & the house is quite comfortable. The room you would have is rather small, but it looks out on the sea. I do so want to have you here. By that time I hope we'll have got hold of an engine for the boat, & if we get decent weather we can go round to the completely uninhabited bays on the west side of the island, where there is beautiful white sand & clear water with seals swimming about in it. At one of them there is a cave where we can take shelter when it rains, & at another there is a shepherd's hut which is disused but quite livable where one could even picnic for a day or two. Anyway do come, & come whenever you like for as long as you like, only try to let me know beforehand. And meanwhile take care of yourself & be happy.

I've just remembered I never paid you for that brandy you got for me, so enclose £3. I think it was about that wasn't it? The brandy was very nice & was much appreciated on the journey up because they can't get alcohol here at all easily. The next island, Islay, distills whisky but it all goes to America. I gave the lorry driver a large wallop, more than a double, & it disappeared so promptly that it seemed to hit the bottom of his belly with a click.

With much love
George

1. Sonia Brownell (1918–1980), whom Orwell met in the early nineteen forties (see *3693, n. 1*) and married in 1949, some three months before his death, was one of two editoral assistants on *Horizon*, for which she worked from 1945 to 1950; the other was Lys Lubbock (see Michael Shelden, *Friends of Promise: Cyril Connolly and the World of 'Horizon,'* 1989). For a picture of them, see Crick, plate 27; Shelden, *Orwell*, following 372, and Shelden, *Friends of Promise*, following 146. Orwell's friend, Tosco Fyvel, wrote in *George Orwell: A Personal Memoir*, 'after Eileen's death in 1945 [Orwell] had . . . a brief (and unsatisfactory) affair with Sonia Brownell' (151).
2. Janetta Woolley (now Parladé) was a friend of those who ran *Horizon* and *Polemic*. She may have met Orwell through her former husband, Humphrey Slater (see *2955, n. 4*), but it seems more likely it was through Cyril Connolly. At this time she had changed her name by deed-poll to Sinclair-Loutit, whilst living with Kenneth Sinclair-Loutit: their daughter, Nicolette, then nearly four years old, is the child mentioned in this letter. Sonia Brownell had suggested to Orwell that Nicolette would be a suitable same-age companion for young Richard, hence Orwell's invitation, but in the event Janetta and Nicolette did not go to Jura. Kenneth Sinclair-Loutit also knew Orwell, having been in the Spanish civil war as a doctor in the International Brigade and had first met him in Spain. Janetta and David Astor were witnesses to the marriage of George Orwell and Sonia Brownell; see *3702*.

3213. Domestic Diary

12 April–11 September 1947

Volume IV of Orwell's Domestic Diary is written in ink on ninety-five recto pages and six verso pages of a notebook measuring 7½ × 6½ inches with twenty-two ruled lines to a page. Before the first entry, Orwell has written 'VOL. IV' and below that, 'Diary (cont. from previous volume).' Volume V continues from 12 September 1947 in a different notebook. Most of the people mentioned are noted in annotations to Orwell's 1946 Diary, and the headnote to it (see *2996*) gives a brief description of Jura and the relative positions of the places mentioned. Therefore only brief personal and topographical cross-references are given here. Although this diary is so much taken up with the frustrations and pleasures of what had become for Orwell something akin to his 'golden country,' where he intended making his main home, he was during all this time writing *Nineteen Eighty-Four*. Orwell underlines in his manuscript totals of gallons of petrol used. These amounts are given in roman type here.

12.4.47. *Barnhill. Arrived yesterday evening. Fine yesterday & today, but coldish. Everything extremely backward. Grass has not started to grow, ditto rushes, birds on trees hardly visible. Daffodils just coming out, snowdrops barely over—a few still in bloom. Flying from Glasgow saw many streaks of snow still on high ground. There was about 6 weeks frost on Jura, then rain, & ground is still very sodden. Many lambs & calves lost during the winter. Reason given, the sheep & cows had not enough milk.*

The trees & bushes I planted all seem to be alive. The two cordon trees against the south wall budding well. Onions etc. that I saved & which were well up in January have practically all disappeared in the frost. Most of the stawberries seem to have survived, but are very tiny. Rhubarb is coming up well. Tulips well up.

They have caught no sea fish yet. Rabbits said to be scarce this year.

Beautiful day all day, striking chilly about 5 pm. Saw one primrose blooming in a sheltered spot, otherwise no wild flowers. Stone crop just beginning to sprout, wild irises & bluebells coming up. Grass still completely wintry in appearance. Saw a few rabbits. Pigeons towering up with a loud rattle of wings—their courting flight, I think. Sea very calm. No seals about.

Sowed dwarf peas. NB. to sow a second batch about 25.4.47. Pruned roses drastically. Several have no buds showing at all, so cannot yet tell whether they are alive. Ground in bad state & impossible to sow small seeds. Covered rhubarb with manure. D.[1] has ploughed roughly the patch I asked him to do. Shall hoe it over enough to get some sort of tilth & then sow potatoes when I can get some. It ought to be properly dug over, but[,] after all[,] this much cultivation is all that a field crop gets.

Compost put in pit last autumn has not properly rotted down yet.

13.4.47. *Fine all day, but colder than yesterday. A good deal of wind, from west & south. Sea rougher.*

Put up sectional henhouse. Wretched workmanship, & will need a lot of strengthening & weighting down to make it stay in place. Two of the wheels arrived broken. Before the war these were easily obtainable, but probably not now. Planted 4 dozen gladiolus bulbs (pink & yellow). Soil somewhat better after the wind, so it may be possible to sow small seeds tomorrow.

14.4.47. *Much rain in the night. Today fine, with fair sun, but again cold & windy. Sea moderate. Raven in the distance dancing about, evidently courting.*

Put up stakes for wire round hen-run. Sowed marigolds. Could not do much outside as R. fell this morning & gashed his forehead extremely badly. Hope to get him to the doctor tomorrow—impossible today, as no conveyance.

Opened bottle of brandy. With a small ration each daily, we[2] hope to make one bottle last a week.

DBST[3] started yesterday. Three different times are observed on this island.

1. Donald Darroch; see *3003, n. 2.*
2. Orwell and his sister Avril.
3. Double British Summer Time. To aid daylight saving, clocks are advanced one hour from late

spring to early autumn; during the war and in the years immediately after, clocks were advanced for one hour throughout the year and for a second hour during the 'summer' period. The measure was particularly unpopular with farmers. By three different times, Orwell probably means DBST, a time advanced by only one hour, and 'natural time,' that which regulated farm and stock management.

3214. To Frank D. Barber

15 April 1947   Typewritten

Barnhill
Isle of Jura
Argyllshire

Dear Barber,[1]

Many thanks for your letter of the 9th. I am up here for 6 months trying to get on with a novel, which is why I have dropped the Tribune column. I didn't see the Daily Graphic's effort, but I suppose I shall get the press cutting.[2] The whole Kemsley press is a disgusting phenomenon, but it is comforting to think that the Graphic has by far the lowest circulation of the gutter papers, and I think less than some of the serious papers. I think I am also right in saying that it has dropped heavily in the last few years.

The weather here is as disgusting as in England, but it isn't quite so cold and a little easier to get fuel. I don't know if you have ever been in these parts. I spent last summer here and intend to spend all my summers here as far as possible. These islands are one of the most beautiful parts of the British Isles and largely uninhabited. This island, which is as large as a small county, only has 300 people on it. Of course it rains all the time, but if one takes that for granted it doesn't seem to matter.

Yours sincerely
[Signed] Geo. Orwell
George Orwell

1. Frank D. Barber (1917–1999), journalist. Orwell had corresponded with him in 1944 and 1945. He was assistant editor of the *Leeds Weekly Citizen* when he first wrote to Orwell.
2. Untraced; there is nothing in the period 12 March 1947 to 14 April 1947 that refers to Orwell.

3215. To Dwight Macdonald

15 April 1947   Typewritten

Orwell's letter is in reply to one from Macdonald of 9 April 1947. Macdonald said that since his last letter to Orwell he had decided to devote the May–June issue of *Politics* to the USSR and the issue after that to France. There would therefore be no room for even an abridged version of Orwell's 'Lear, Tolstoy and the Fool' until September–October at the earliest. He would hold on to the article but would give it to someone else if Orwell wished. It was not published in *Politics*. He asked Orwell for help in compiling a reading list of 50–60 books and articles 'which might be called the basic ones for the layman if he wants to understand Russia today.' Had Orwell any 'pet discoveries'? What ten books would he recommend to a friend ignorant of Russia but seeking enlightenment? He also wanted another 50–60 titles of more specialized books on the best in Soviet art, movies, literature. He said he had no friendly contacts with the higher editors of *The New Republic*. His friends were being 'weeded out at a great rate,' and he guessed that Orwell's column 'As I Please' would not be published now that 'the mag has become well-vulgarized by the Wallace crowd.' He suggested Orwell ask his agents to approach *The Nation*. Macdonald had airmailed his profile of Henry Wallace,[1] because, since Wallace was now in England, Orwell might care to tell his readers about it. He confirmed that he had received payment for the shoes he had obtained for Orwell (but which, unfortunately, proved too small).

Barnhill
Isle of Jura
Argyllshire

Dear Dwight,

Many thanks for your very interesting and informative article on Wallace, which reached me yesterday—unfortunately a few days after I'd left London for the summer. I've sent it on to Tribune, as I should think they could well use parts of it, at least as background material. I left London the day before W. had his big public meeting at the Albert Hall, but I heard him say a few words of welcome on arrival and got the impression that he meant to be very conciliatory and not make the sort of remarks about "British imperialism" which he has been making in the USA. His visit here has been timed to do the maximum of mischief, and I was somewhat surprised by the respectful welcome given to him by nearly everyone, incidentally including Tribune, which has given him some raps over the knuckles in the past.

It doesn't matter about the Tolstoy article. If you feel you do want to use a piece of it sooner or later, hang on to it until then. Otherwise, could you be kind enough to send it on to my agents, McIntosh & Otis, explaining the circumstances. It's possible they might be able to do something with it, though as they failed with another Polemic article (one on Swift), perhaps this one is no good for the American market either.

As to books on the USSR. It's very hard to think of a good list, and looking back, it seems to me that whatever I have learned, or rather guessed, about that country has come from reading between the lines of newspaper reports. I tried to think of "pro" books, but couldn't think of any good ones except very early ones such as Ten Days that Shook the World[2] (which I haven't read through but have read *in*, of course.) The Webbs' Soviet Communism,[3] which I have not read, no doubt contains a lot of facts, but Michael Polanyi's little essay[4] on it certainly convicted the W.s of misrepresentation on some points. A nephew of Beatrice Webb[5] whom I know told me she admitted privately that there were things about the USSR that it was better not to put on paper. For the period round about the Revolution, Krupskaya's Memories of Lenin has some interesting facts. So does Angelica Balabanov's My Life as a Rebel.[6] The later editions of Krupskaya's book have been tampered with a little, at any rate in England. Of the same period, Bertrand Russell's Theory and Practice of Bolshevism (a very rare book which he will not bother to reprint) is interesting because he not only met all the tops but was able to foretell in general terms a good deal that happened later. Rosenberg's History of Bolshevism is said to be good and unprejudiced, but I haven't read it and his book on the German Republic seemed to me rather dry and cagey. A book that taught me more than any other about the general course of the Revolution was Franz Borkenau's The Communist International. This of course is only partly concerned with the USSR itself, and it is perhaps too much written round a thesis, but it is stuffed with facts which I believe have not been successfully disputed. As for books of "revelations," I must say I was doubtful of the authenticity of Valtin's book, but I thought Krivitsky's book[7] genuine although written in a cheap sensational style. In one place where it crossed with my own experiences it seemed to me substantially true. Kravchenko's book[8] is not out in England yet. For the concentration camps, Anton Ciliga's The Russian Enigma[9] is good, and more recently The Dark Side of the Moon[10] (now I think published in the USA) which is compiled from the experiences of many exiled Poles. A little book by a Polish woman, Liberation, Russian Style,[11] which appeared during the war and fell flat, overlaps with The Dark Side and is more detailed. I think the most important of very recent books is the Blue Book on the Canadian spy trials,[12] which is fascinating psychologically. As for literature, Gleb Struve's Twenty-five Years of Soviet Russian Literature is an invaluable handbook and I am told very accurate. Mirsky's Russian Literature 1881–1927 (I think that is the title) takes in the earlier part of post-revolutionary literature. There is also Max Eastman's Artists in Uniform. You've probably read everything I have mentioned except perhaps the Blue Book. If you haven't read the latter, don't miss it—it's a real thriller.

I am up here for 6 months. Last year I was just taking a holiday after six years of non-stop journalism, but this year I am going to get on with a novel. I shan't finish it in six months but I ought to break its back and might finish it at the end of the year. It is very hard to get back to quiet continuous work after living in a lunatic asylum for years. Not that conditions are now any better than during the war—worse in many ways. This last winter has been quite unendurable, and even now the weather is appalling, but one is a little better off up here where it is a bit easier to get food and fuel than in London.

Yours
George

1. Henry Agard Wallace (1888–1965), U.S. Secretary of Agriculture, 1933–41; Vice-President, 1941–45. He was replaced, for his very liberal views, by Harry S. Truman as vice-presidential candidate for President Franklin Roosevelt's third and final term of office, but served as Secretary of Commerce until, because of his opposition to Truman's policy towards Russia, he was forced to resign. He was editor of The New Republic, 1946–47 (see 3218). In 1948, he became the presidential candidate of the Progressive Party, which, among its policies, advocated closer cooperation with the Soviet Union; he received more than one million votes, though none in the Electoral College. He was the author of several books.
2. John Reed, Ten Days That Shook the World (1919). Reed (1887–1920) was involved in setting

up the Communist Party in the United States. He died of typhus and was buried in the Kremlin wall; see *2880, n. 1*.

3. Sidney James Webb (1859–1947) and Beatrice Webb (1858–1943), *Soviet Communism: A New Civilisation?* (2 vols, London, 1935; New York, 1936). Republished in London in 1937, but without the question mark, and in 1941 with a new introduction by Beatrice Webb.
4. Michael Polanyi (1891–1976), *The Contempt of Freedom: The Russian Experiment and After* (1940). Includes his 'Soviet Economics—Fact and Theory' (1935), 'Truth and Propaganda' (1936), 'Collectivist Planning' (1940).
5. Malcolm Muggeridge (see *2860, n. 1*); the section of this letter from 'A nephew' to 'on paper' was marked in the margin, in Orwell's hand, 'Off the record.'
6. Nadezhda Krupskaya (1869–1939), wife of Lenin and active in his revolutionary programme. Her *Memories of Lenin* is quoted more than once by Orwell; for example, at the opening of his introduction to Jack London's *Love of Life and Other Stories*; see *2781*. Martin Lawrence published the first English translation, by Eric Verney, in two volumes (1930, 1932), based on the second Russian edition (Moscow, 1930). Lawrence & Wishart published an abridged version in 1942 in its Workers' Library series. Angelica Balabanov (1878–1965), associate editor with Mussolini of *Avanti*, worked with Lenin and Trotsky during the Russian Revolution and was the first secretary of the Third International. Her memoir was published in 1937.
7. Jan Valtin (pseudonym of Richard Krebs, 1904–1951), *Out of the Night* (New York, 1940; London and Toronto, 1941). He later became a war correspondent with the American forces in the Pacific. Walter G. Krivitsky (d. 1941), *In Stalin's Secret Service* (New York, 1939; *I Was Stalin's Agent*, London, 1963). He was head of the western division of the NKVD, but defected.
8. Victor Kravchenko (1905–1966), *I Chose Freedom: The Personal and Political Life of a Soviet Official* (New York, 1946; London, 1947). During the Spanish civil war, Kravchenko served as an aide to General Dimitri Pavlov (who was shot on Stalin's orders in 1941); see Thomas, 588, n. 1. See also *3577, n. 3*.
9. See *2988, n. 3*; *The Russian Enigma* was published in English in 1940 (in French, Paris, 1938). It is concerned chiefly with Russian economic policy, 1928–1932, and with its prisons.
10. Anonymous, *The Dark Side of the Moon* (London, 1946; New York, 1947), deals with Soviet-Polish relations. It has a preface by T. S. Eliot, a director of the book's English publishers, Faber & Faber.
11. Ada Halpern, *Liberation—Russian Style* (1945); it is listed by Whitaker as August 1945 and so published not during but just as the war was ending.
12. In the left-hand margin, against one or both of *Liberation—Russian Style* and the Canadian Government Blue Book, is a marker arrow, presumably added by Macdonald. The Blue Book referred to reported on a Canadian Royal Commission which investigated Soviet espionage in Canada, 1946 and 1947. This found that a spy ring had been built up by the Soviet Military Attaché, Colonel Zabotin. Amongst those sentenced to terms of imprisonment were Fred Rose, the only Canadian Communist M.P.

3216. To Leonard Moore

15 April 1947   Typewritten

Barnhill
Isle of Jura
Argyllshire

Dear Moore,
I am sorry if I did wrong in asking Miss Otis to collect that money for me.[1] I thought it was the natural way of going to work—ie. that the papers concerned would not be bothered to keep it for me.

As to the introduction for the French translation of "Homage to Catalonia," I think there is a slight mistake. The English edition had no introduction. When Madame Davet first translated it, on spec, she got my old friend Georges Kopp to write an introduction as she was then in touch with him and he and I had been in Spain together. It was not a very suitable one and in any case would have no point now, as she herself recognizes. But evidently she has sent it along to the publisher along with the body of the book, and he has assumed that it was present in the English edition. I have no objection at all to the book having an introduction by someone especially acquainted with Spain—in fact I suggested this to Madame Davet. She thought it possible that André Malraux might do one. If he would, of course it would be splendid, and it's just thinkable, as he may have read the book—at any rate I gave him a copy a couple of years ago.[2]

I heard from Gollancz that he was willing to terminate the contract, so I suppose everything can be fixed up with Warburg. I suppose there will be long delays before they can produce "Coming Up for Air," but when it does go to press I should like to be sure of seeing a proof. I definitely remember one misprint in the original edition, of a kind that would probably be copied, and I suppose there may be new ones when they re-set it.

Yours sincerely
[Signed] Eric Blair
Eric Blair

1. See *3186*.
2. Against this paragraph are annotations written in Moore's office: 'K.A.L.,' in large letters, and 'told Charlot 23/4/47.' K.A.L. was K.A.G.S. Lane, a director of Christy & Moore; see *3081, n. 1*. Charlot was involved in the production of the French version of *Homage to Catalonia* (see *3036, n. 1*) and what he was told is marked off in the letter above: from 'But evidently' to 'the English edition.' For Kopp's proposed introduction, see *550*.

3217. Domestic Diary

<u>15.4.47.</u> *Raining almost all day, very windy & rather cold. Did nothing in garden etc., as was taking R. to be treated by the doctor. Two stitches put in. NB. to be removed about a week hence (not more than 10 days.)*

<u>16.4.47.</u> *Cold, overcast & rather windy. Somewhat finer in late evening, & sea calmer.*

Impossible to sow seeds. Spread lime (not very well slaked), put roofing felt on hen-house.

Saw one of the whitish rabbits this evening (in the distance, but seemingly a full-grown one).

<u>17.4.47.</u> *Much better day. Some wind, but sunny & fairly warm. Began digging the ploughed patch. Not bad—will do for potatoes. Sowed turnips, carrots, cress, lettuces (NB. next sowing about the 27th), clarkias, godetias. Also sowed a few of the potatoes we bought for eating, no seed potatoes having turned up yet. They all had eyes so should come up all right.*

Tried the RAF rubber dinghy. Very buoyant, & seemingly has no tendency to turn over, but hardly navigable at all. Evidently it will only be useful for getting out to the other boat.

A dead deer down by our bay. Rather unpleasant as it is too heavy to drag away.

A few more primroses out, & one or two celandine. Brought home a root or two of primroses. It is remarkable what a difference it makes when there is no bracken—ie. the relative easiness of walking everywhere. No midges yet. Cormorants swimming in the bay, so presumably there are some fish about. 18.4.47. *Cold, blowy & overcast. A little sun during the afternoon, then light rain. Sea moderate.*

Dug a little more of the ploughed patch, put in posts for gate of hen-run.

While digging the ploughed patch, dug up a nest of 3 young rabbits—about 10 day's° old, I should say. One appeared to be dead already, the other two I killed. The nest was only a few inches below the surface. It was evidently reached by a hole outside the garden, about 10 yards away.

Saw a number of ordinary green plovers. I do not think I remember seeing these birds here before. Brought in some frog spawn in a jar. Should be hatched out in a week or 10 days.

3218. Review of Lady Gregory's Journals, edited by Lennox Robinson

The New Yorker, 19 April 1947

Lady Gregory is one of the central figures in the Irish literary revival. It would be difficult to think of her without also thinking of Yeats and the Abbey Theatre, just as one could hardly hear the phrase "the nineties" without having at least a fleeting vision of Beardsley and the *Yellow Book*. But the associations that her name calls up are not all of them pleasant ones. She is also the subject of a memorable sneer, in "Ulysses," which is worth quoting because, cruel and probably unfair though it is, it does help to bring this unfortunate, good-hearted old woman into truer perspective. In "Ulysses," Joyce has Buck Mulligan say, "Longworth is awfully sick . . . after what you wrote about that old hake Gregory. O you inquisitional drunken jew jesuit! She gets you a job on the paper and then you go and slate her drivel to Jaysus. Couldn't you do the Yeats touch?"

Was that really how Yeats and the rest of them thought of her? Was she simply an old fool to be blarneyed and made use of? Evidently, it was not so crude as that; besides, in her old age—always at her wits' end for rent and taxes, riding to and fro in buses, lunching off tea and bread and butter—she was hardly worth sponging on. But Joyce's words are perhaps true at the level of caricature. Something of that kind is always partly true of the enlightened aristocrat, the person who wants to be an artist as well as a patron, especially when, as in this case, there is a difference of race and religion and culture on top of the simple class distinction.

Augusta Gregory (her maiden name was Persse) was born into the landed gentry of Ireland—the people who lived in tumbledown mansions with hordes of servants, streamed across the countryside in pink coats, and, partly because of poverty and remoteness, kept up a claret-drinking, Horace-quoting eighteenth-century refinement that their English counterparts had lost. They called themselves Irish, and politically they were often the worst enemies that England had, but they were generally Protestants and, as their names show, largely English in extraction. "Lady Gregory's Journals," which has been edited by Lennox Robinson and published by Macmillan, covers the fourteen years from 1916 to 1930, and rambles across a multitude of subjects, some of them very trivial ones. Mr. Robinson has rearranged the journals by what is probably the best system; that is, he has taken half a dozen dominant themes and grouped the entries around them, so one passes the same dates over and over again. The most important of these themes are Coole Park (the country place, celebrated by Yeats, that Lady Gregory inherited from her husband), the Abbey Theatre, the Terror and the Civil War, and the long, complicated battle over Sir Hugh Lane's collection of pictures. In most of these contexts, Lady Gregory was fighting against the British government, but in all of them, in a less direct, less conscious way, she was fighting against the native Irish, whom she loved and championed but by no means resembled.

The ambiguity of Lady Gregory's position comes out particularly in the period of the "troubles." She was in sympathy with the agrarian revolution, she planned to sell her land to the government and remain in Coole Park only as a tenant, and in any case she and her husband had had a good record as landlords, but none of this stopped the peasants from constantly prowling around her dwindled demesne, cutting down the young trees in the plantations, stealing the fruit that she was always ready to give away, and making blackmailing demands for "subscriptions." She was on their side, but they were not altogether on hers, and it is queer to watch her torn one way politically and the other way emotionally, approving the breakup of the great estates and yet yearning to keep the beloved house and gardens for her grandchildren. Even her horror of the Black and Tans,[1] the banditti let loose by the British government in 1919, was colored by class feeling. On hearing that fifteen officers of the Guards had volunteered to join this force, Lady Gregory remarked, "I say . . . it would be an improvement to have at least gentlemen." She wrote articles in the British press denouncing the Black and Tans, but—once again with an eye on her grandchildren—left the articles unsigned, because she wanted to preserve Coole unburned.

Lady Gregory's son, Robert, had been killed in Italy in the first World War, fighting for the British government.[2] Even after the Easter Rising, it still seemed natural to her to send her grandson to Harrow and to defend the English public-school system against Bernard Shaw. Politically, she was always for Ireland against England—even, to some extent, for the Republicans against the Free State government—but instinct and training pulled her in the other direction. So far as the Abbey Theatre went, it was chiefly the puritanism and hypocrisy of the Catholic Irish that had to be fought against. When O'Casey's "The Plough and the Stars" was first performed, the audience stormed the stage because members of the Citizen Army were shown carrying their flag into a public house. There were also objections to the inclusion of a prostitute among the characters, on the ground that there were no prostitutes in Dublin. How ready Lady Gregory was to put her own feelings aside, and how close her ties were with the fashionable English world, is revealed in the struggle over the Lane pictures. Her nephew, Sir Hugh Lane, had amassed an extremely valuable collection of paintings, which he left in his will to the National Gallery, in London. Later, shortly before being drowned in the sinking of the Lusitania, he added a codicil leaving them to the city of Dublin instead. It was evident that he meant them to go to Dublin, but the codicil, not having been witnessed, was not legal, and the incident ended with the British government's keeping the pictures, or most of them. Intermittently for years, right through every kind of public and private disaster, Lady Gregory was pulling wires in London—a shabby old figure with dripping umbrella, but able because of her family connections to get the ear of a surprising variety of influential people. She did not care what their political color might be if there was any chance that they would help her to recover the Lane pictures. She even contemplated trying the Royal Family, and was told that "the King would be no use . . . the Queen might possibly do something." Oddly enough, the British politician who backed her up most strongly was the vicious reactionary and Unionist Sir Edward Carson, who had armed the Ulster Volunteers in 1912 and prosecuted Casement in 1916.

There was almost no English or Irish literary man of her day, nor were there many people distinguished in other fields, whom Lady Gregory did not know or at least meet, and her diaries contain a considerable amount of informative gossip about Shaw, Yeats, Kipling, Cosgrave, De Valera, Michael Collins, and many another. She herself almost never makes a witty or illuminating remark, but she gives the impression of being a good observer and a truthful reporter, and her account, for instance, of John Dillon's comments on the Easter Rising probably has real historical value. These diaries cover only the fag end of her enormous life. She was born in 1852 and married in 1880 a man much older than herself. At the date when the diaries start, her husband had been dead a quarter of a century, her son had only two years to live, the hardest part of the struggle for the Abbey Theatre was over, and the chance of a decent settlement between England and Ireland had passed away. It was certainly a heroic life, and probably it was a useful one. Without her, Yeats might have written less, and it is conceivable that O'Casey would never have been heard of. In 1930, aged seventy-eight, with cancer of the breast and with not much money, she could be on the whole contented: "I used long ago to say I should like, I thought, to live until Richard's 21st birthday. And it comes tomorrow. . . . It is a contrast to Robert's coming-of-age, with the gathering of cousins and the big feast and dance for the tenants—Coole no longer ours. But the days of landed property have passed. It is better so. Yet I wish someone of our blood would after my death care enough for what has been a home so long, to keep it open."

However, no one could keep Coole open, for it was demolished after Lady Gregory's death. Roxboro', the house where she was born, had been burned down years earlier, during the "troubles." Since then, the Anglo-Irish gentry have vanished or turned into fossils, the priests have tightened their grip, and the Irish literary movement has not lived up to its promise. The tensions that produced it have been resolved and the special type represented by Lady Gregory—the conqueror who identifies himself with the subject race—has no longer much function.

1. Special constables, known as Black and Tans from their uniforms, were enrolled in England with the intention of restoring order in Ireland. Eight hundred arrived on 26 March 1920. They were recruited from among the unemployed who had recently been demobilised from the army. They were armed and, even in such violent times, achieved particular notoriety.
2. His death was the motive for two of Yeats's best-known poems: 'In Memory of Major Robert Gregory' ('Now that we're almost settled in our house / I'll name the friends that cannot sup with us') and 'An Irish Airman Foresees his Death.' He was Lady Gregory's only son.

3219. To George Woodcock

19 April 1947   Typewritten

> Barnhill
> Isle of Jura
> Argyllshire

Dear George,

Thanks for your letter which I got yesterday.

Certainly the University Observer can reprint the article if they want to.[1]

We are here till early October, so if you feel like coming drop in any time before then. But try and give me good notice (it's best to write quite 10 days ahead because of slowness of posts), because of arranging about meeting you. There are boats to Jura on Mondays, Wed.s and Fridays, so one can travel up to Glasgow by the night train, but it's safer to sleep the preceding night in Glasgow because sometimes the night trains are late and then you miss the boat train. The itinerary is:

8 am leave Glasgow Central for Gourock. Join boat at Gourock.
About 1 pm reach East Tarbert.
Travel to West Tarbert by bus (runs in conjunction with boat). Join boat at West Tarbert.
Reach Craighouse (Jura) about 3.30 pm.
Hired car to Lealt, where we meet you.

They have had an awful winter here and everything is very backward. The weather is still cold now, but it's been a bit better the last day or two and I've managed to get a few seeds in. Richard had a bad accident a few days ago—he feel off a chair on to a jug which broke under him and cut his forehead very badly. However we got him to the doctor and it was stitched up neatly, so I don't think there will be a very bad scar. There have been no after-effects, and he didn't seem worried by it after the first few minutes.

David Martin has just sent me a copy of his book on the Tito–Mihailovich business (publishers Prentice-Hall.)[2] You ought to notice it in "Freedom" if you can—I don't suppose it will get much publicity in the British press. Love to Ingie.[3]

Yours
George

1. *The University Observer: A Journal of Politics,* University of Chicago, reprinted 'Second Thoughts on James Burnham' (under the title 'James Burnham') in its Vol. 1, No. 2, Summer 1947.
2. *Ally Betrayed: The Uncensored Story of Tito and Mihailovich,* Foreword by Rebecca West (New York and London, 1946). For David Martin see *2839, n. 3.*
3. In 1949 Inge became Mrs. George Woodcock.

3220. Domestic Diary

<u>19.4.47.</u> *A better day. Sunny & not much wind, though not very warm. Evening blowy & cold, with some rain. Sea roughish outside the bay.*

Dug some more of patch, weeded & limed strawberries. These do not now look so bad, & there are fewer gaps than I thought. Unlikely to give much fruit this year, however.

Only one of the roses is still showing no buds (an American pillar[1]). One by the gate (Alberic Barbier[2]), which I thought dead, has a tiny bud down near the root, so I cut it down to just above the end. Made 2 cement blocks, about 1 ft. square & 2″ deep (or even less), reinforced with wire netting. Will do as part of path. NB. for 2 square feet of cement block, 5 fire shovels of sand & one of cement needed—more if it is to be at least 2″ thick, as it should be.

<u>20.4.47.</u> *Very violent gale all last night, & much rain. Today till about 5 pm blowing hard, mostly from south, cold & usually raining. Sea very rough, breaking right over the point. This evening calmer, some interludes of sunshine, but still far from warm.*

Could not do much out of doors. Shot a rabbit, the first this year. I notice that when rabbits are shy the ones one succeeds in shooting are almost invariably gravid females. I never fancy eating these. I suppose it is partly because the pregnant ones are less in a hurry about running away, but last year females preponderated so greatly among the rabbits I shot as to make me wonder whether they are actually more numerous than the males.

Alastair & the D.s[3] in a great state with the sheep. They are lambing in such a state of weakness that they have no milk, sometimes actually refuse to take their lambs, & even now that the grass is coming on, some of them are too weak to graze. The D.s say the gulls & hoodies attack weak sheep, & yesterday took the eye out of one of them.

<u>21.4.47.</u> *Awful weather. Violent gale all last night, & still more so this morning, at times so strong that one could hardly stay on one's feet.*

Chicken-house blown off its base—fortunately not damaged. Shall have to fix it down with guy ropes. Rain most of day. About 4 pm finer & some sun, but wind not abating. Sea rough.

Bottle of brandy lasts A. & me 1 week, with a fairly good peg each (a bit less than a double) once a day.

Did nothing out of doors.

22.4.47. *A better day. Wind still high, but not much rain, some interludes of sun, & somewhat warmer. Sea calming down a little.*

Still not feeling well enough to do much out of doors. A. finished digging the first plot in the ploughed patch. Room there for 4 rows of potatoes (about 10 lb. of seed). Am going to use some of D.D's seed—Great Scott I think.

Took down the corrugated iron at the side of the house. Will be enough to cover hen-house, & the frame it was on will make a gate for the run. Impossible to finish this job till the wind drops. Cut sticks for dwarf peas. Began cutting bean sticks. The lone sheep in the field has lambed. Does not take much notice of the lamb, & walks on whenever the latter begins to suck. Nevertheless she made a demonstration when I picked the lamb up with the idea of taking it indoors. Lamb fairly strong, though it only seemed to me to weigh a pound or two.

Many more birds round the house owing to chaff in the yard. Still no sparrows, but flocks of chaffinches almost as numerous as sparrows. Qy. whether these also attack peas & beetroots.

Fruit bushes now mostly budding fairly well.

D.D. says the cuckoo is usually heard here earlier than this. Swallows, on the other hand, do not usually appear till about May 12th.

Cannot be sure, but I think we are using quite 4 galls of paraffin a week—if so, the current barrel will give out about the end of May (have another in stock). The reason is the cold weather & consequent use of Valor stoves. One of these uses quite ½ gall a day if burning all the time.

Some rain after about 7 pm.

To be ordered for next year (better order early this time.)

3 cooking apple trees
4 plums
1 damson
1 greengage
1 quince
6 cherries (eating)
2 doz. bush roses
1 doz° peony roots (red & pink)
200 tulip bulbs
Strawberries? [crossed through]   3 loganberries [written in lighter ink]
[On facing page]
NB. Order also:
6 roses (2 climbing, 4 bush)
6 gooseberries.

23.4.47. *Dreadful weather till about 4 pm. Violent wind, continuous rain, & very cold. After that somewhat better, mostly raining but a few intervals of* sun. *In the evening very still, rain still falling. Sea calms down with surprising speed.*

The lamb born yesterday died this morning. A. found it in a moribund condition & brought it in. It was oozing blood from the mouth, & according to Alastair had been attacked by gulls or hoodies. The mother seems quite strong & well, but she more or less ignored the lamb from the start, so presumably she has no milk.

R. very poorly with feverish cold & cough, which started last night. However his forehead is making a good job of healing. The doctor took the stitches out today, & there were no complications & does not look as if there would be much of a scar. Seed potatoes (Great Scott) arrived yesterday. Can sow as soon as ground dries a little.

Some more primroses out. Gorse well out. Otherwise no wild flowers except a very occasional celandine.

Wind today strong enough to blow off some sticks of young rhubarb. Tulips not damaged, but they are more sheltered. All roses now budding except one.

24.4.47. Morning fine, windy & cold. In the afternoon rainstorms & showers alternating with sun. Some hail about 5.30 pm. Cold all day, & wind strong until evening. Fined up the new patch with hoe & cultivator, but it will have to dry a bit before it is even possible to put potatoes in it. Began cutting bean sticks.

R. slightly better, but feverish again this evening.

Have ordered trees etc. for next year.

All apple trees now budding except the James Grieve, which looks rather as if it were dead. No buds on raspberries yet. I think all the other fruit bushes are budding. NB. the Jas. Grieve was the one with the broken root.

25.4.47. Vile weather. Very cold, rain almost continuous, & strong wind from about midday onwards. Mud worse than ever. Did nothing out of doors. R's cough still bad, & temperature high during most of day.

Saw in the distance a bird which might have been a martin.

Violent, driving rainstorms during the evening.

26.4.47. A much better day. Fine, windy & less cold. Ground drying up nicely, but still not quite fit for the potatoes. Dug a little more of the ploughed patch, sowed spring onions (White Lisbon), began cutting grass between fruit trees. Patches of this can be cut with the mower, but one has to take the clumps of old grass off with the scythe or sheers.° The second cutting could be done with the mower.

R. seems better—hardly any temperature at 6 pm, & the rash, which was over most of him including his legs a few hours earlier, had temporarily disappeared.

A. heard the cuckoo this morning.

They have now finished ploughing the field in front of the house. About 4½ acres, & yesterday & today I should say they were on it about 8 hours in all, including two occasions when the tractor was bogged. They have taken in a bit more than last year, which will mean fewer rushes.

A. saw a mountain hare, still almost white! Presumably when they change colour is determined simply by the temperature.

It is now definitely established that R. has measles. He will have to be in bed another week & stay indoors for a week after that.

27.4.47.   Violent rain all night, or almost all night. Huge pools everywhere this morning.

Morning rainy & cold. Afternoon mostly sunny & windy, with some rainstorms. Net effect of day has probably been to dry the ground slightly.

Did nothing out of doors. Made frame for gate of hen-run. Very heavy, & it will be difficult to hinge it, as I not only have no hinges of that size, but the piece it will hang on is not straight. The gate will have to rest on the ground, in which case the best way to hinge it is probably with ropes or wires. Ideally one would put wheels at the bottom of the gate, but I think skids (bottom of barrel) will do if I level the ground.

R. better. Tried to make jigsaw puzzle for him, but can only cut pieces with straight edges as my only coping-saw blade is broken.

A. yesterday saw unidentified duck-like birds—probably some kind of diver.

Saw a swallow (or martin—only a glimpse.)

28.4.47.   Rain in the night (& hail, according to K.D.) Most of today blowy & overcast, with rain showers & fair patches alternating. Evening still & fine. Cold all day. This evening is about the first time the wind has dropped in a week or more. I do not think it has shifted away from the west all that time.

Set up gate on its skid, which seems fairly satisfactory.

Heard the cuckoo (first time). Primroses now comparatively numerous, buds getting fairly thick on the hazels, wild irises about 6" to 1' high. No sign of bracken growing yet.

29.4.47.   Seemingly no rain during last night. Rain began about 10 am & fell almost continuously (not very heavy) till about 8 pm, when it cleared somewhat.

Everything is again a morass. There has been much less wind than yesterday.

Could not do anything out of doors. Cemented crack in larder wall.

We are using up oil very fast, owing to having two Valor stoves going all day. Impossible to get hold of dry firewood in this weather. Even in the barn, which is quite watertight, it stays damp, & I notice that cement takes days to get dry.

1. American Pillar (which Orwell spells with small 'p') is a carmine pink climbing rose with a white eye and golden stamens.
2. Albéric Barbier is a vigorous climbing rose with a creamy white flower with a yellow centre. It was introduced by the same raiser as Albertine, the rose Orwell grew so successfully at his cottage at Wallington before the war. Orwell omitted the accent.
3. Alastair M'Kechnie and the Darrochs, the brother and sister Donald and Katie, often given as D. or D.D and K.D.

3221. To Janamañci Rāmakrisna

30 April 1947   Copy; reproduced from Telugu edition[1]

Barnhill, Isle of Jura
Argyllshire,
Scotland

Dear Mr. Ramakrishna,°
Many thanks for your letter of March 22nd, which only got to me last week.
I should be delighted for "Animal Farm" to be translated into Telugu.[2]
The copyright is mine, so you can deal with me directly. I do not want any
payment, but I should be obliged if you could send me two or three copies of
the translation when it is published.

Yours truly,
(Sd.) George Orwell

1. This letter is printed (as reproduced here) on page 2 of the Telugu edition, perhaps as a licence
to publish the translation.
2. *Animal Farm* was translated into Telugu by Janamañci Rāmakrisna. He arranged for its
publication by the Lodrha Press, Madras, in September 1949, as *Pasuvuladivānam: Uhākalpita-
maina peddakatha*. The title includes Orwell's sub-title, 'A Fairy Tale.' The edition has a
number of illustrations, in a Disneyish style, signed Bāpu (Willison).

3222. To Miss Sunday Wilshin

30 April 1947   Typewritten

Barnhill
Isle of Jura
Argyllshire

Dear Miss Wilshin,[1]
Many thanks for your letter of the 23rd.
I am afraid I cannot undertake any talks at present. I am trying to write a
book and do not want to do anything else, and in any case I shall be up here
until October. Please forgive me.

Yours sincerely
[Signed] Geo. Orwell
George Orwell

1. Sunday Wilshin wrote to Orwell on 23 April 1947 asking him to cooperate in a new series of
BBC programmes for India in which those with experience of, or special interest in, India
recounted their experiences or stated their current views: 'we want to avoid dealing with the
major political and communal issues in India, and of course above all else, we do not want to
give listeners the impression that they are being "lectured."' The talks were to last 13½
minutes (about 1,800 words). Sunday Wilshin (1905–) made her debut on the London stage in
1915 in *Where the Rainbow Ends*; between the outbreak of war and taking over from Orwell in
the Eastern Service, she acted and produced for the BBC. See also *2600, n. 1*.

3223. Domestic Diary

<u>30.4.47.</u>   A much better day, though very cold. No rain, sun shining all day, & a raging wind from the north which has dried things up considerably.

Peas, lettuces & turnips have all just appeared, but the chaffinches have pulled up, I think, all the lettuce seedlings, & at any rate many of the turnips. They were also starting on the peas. Re-sowed lettuces & covered seeds with wire, which I should have done at the beginning. Three gooseberry bushes still not budding. Some of the raspberries budding down near the roots—I should probably have cut the canes off short when I put them in. Jas. Grieve still has no signs of buds. Weeds are now getting started.

Dug a little more, finished cutting the grass between fruit trees, staked the peas. Next time this grass can be cut entirely with the machine, & the holes where I dug out rushes can be filled & re-sown or turfed. Started new cylinder of Calor Gas today (nb. to order 2 more). Should last till first week in June. There is less paraffin than I thought (1–2 weeks supply, I should say). However we have a barrel in hand.

<u>1.5.47.</u>   Fine day. No rain, though it looked threatening for about half an hour in the afternoon. Otherwise sunny all day. Less wind than yesterday, but still cold.

Sowed potatoes (Great Scott), 5 rows, about 15 lb. of seed, or perhaps nearer 20 lb. Rooted up old gooseberry bushes. With help of Neal McArthur & Duggie Clark,[1] got hen house on to base. Trust it will not be blown down again before I can fix bolts.

Killed a mouse in the larder. A. came out to tell me there was one there behaving in a very bold way. Went in & found it eating something on the floor & paying no attention to either of us. Hit it with a barrel stave & killed it. It is curious how the tameness of animals varies from one day to another.

Gooseberries & currants forming on the old plants—however there are very few of these, & I can hardly expect my own bushes to fruit this year.

<u>2.5.47.</u>   Fine all day. Warmer than yesterday & very little wind. Overcast for a while in the afternoon & literally a few drops of rain.

Put corrugated iron on chicken house. Should stay on, I think, but it still remains to anchor the house down. I cannot bolt it to the floor because I have no bolts long enough. Examined how DD's henhouse is wired down. Huge rocks are placed at either side of the house & a piece of fence wire wound round them double. Then a double strand of wire passed round the wire on the stones, & over the roof. This wire is then tightened up by twisting. I think this is the normal method here.

For the first time this year, saw one or two youngish rabbits. Chaffinches etc. still flocking to roost, so they cannot have nests yet. The chaffinches have evidently destroyed all the turnips, so I shall have to re-sow.

Paraffin barrel feels as if it will only last a few more days—ie. about 1 month instead of 2 as I anticipated. However there may have been less in it than I thought when we left last year.

R. came downstairs for first time today. Also had his bandage off for the first time. Scar has healed beautifully & is not very conspicuous.

3.5.47. *Cold & overcast nearly all day. Light rain during much of afternoon. Evening somewhat finer, but cold. Sea rough.*

Could not do much out of doors. Dug a little more, made seed-protector, re-sowed turnips. NB. that even with wire netting over them the chaffinches still go for the seeds. They are not afraid to go under the netting.

The last rose has a bud, so there are no dead ones. Some of the new currant bushes which are in fairly full leaf have currants on them, though of course not very many.

4.5.47. *Fine all day, except for a very few spots of rain for a few minutes in the evening. Not very sunny, but warmer than yesterday. Sea still rough in the morning, calming down in the evening.*

Dug a little more, finished cutting grass between beds of fruit bushes, sowed clarkia, marigolds, Shirley poppies, candytuft.

Frogspawn failed to hatch out, probably owing to not adding fresh water, which I did not think to be necessary before the tadpoles hatched.

A few strawberries showing flower buds.

Chaffinches still going for the turnip seed, in spite of wire & cottons. Shot one & left its body on the bed. Probably the effect of this will only last for a day or two.

Looking down towards the sea, over the wood, hardly a green leaf to be seen anywhere.

Drum of paraffin almost at an end—almost 5 weeks less than I thought. But there may have been less in it than I imagined to start with.

Sending for 2 cylinders of calor gas. (Have sent empties).

5.5.47. *Mostly overcast, with a few sunny intervals & some wind. A few short showers.*

Dug a little more, cut bean sticks, staked cherry trees, pegged down henhouse—very amateurish job, but probably enough for the summer winds.

Many primroses now out. Stonecrop barely visible & has not started growing. They have not heard the cuckoo at Ardlussa yet.

They sowed & harrowed the field in front of the house today. The seed was sown first on to the raw ploughed soil (broadcasting about 4½ acres only seemed to take about 2 hours), then the field was harrowed twice over afterwards. Did not know it was possible to do it this way round, & would have thought it meant burying the corn at very uneven depths & for the most part much too deeply, as where raw sods have been turned up you get a furrow quite 8" deep. It has the advantage that the seed all rolls down into the furrows & thus comes up in rows, but it tends to do this anyway, as even after harrowing a trace of the furrows remains.

Drum of paraffin gave out today.

D's trap killed an enormous rat in the byre.

6.5.47. *Some rain in the morning, sunny & windy in the afternoon. Somewhat warmer.*

Dug a little more, retrained cherry trees & one of the espalier apples. These last have masses of blossom coming, but not much of it is likely to stay on, also it may not get fertilised if the other apples do not blossom.

Bracken fronds now coming up.

<u>7.5.47.</u>   *Very still all day, & mostly overcast. A little very light rain in the morning. Sea calm.*

Sowed peas (Daisy, 2nd early, 1½ ft) & lettuces. A few of the first lot of lettuces seem to have survived the chaffinches.

Several of the rhubarb plants have died—reason, probably, that they were young tender plants & I put too much cow manure on top of them. Raspberries are now mostly budding round the roots. Three gooseberries still not budding & I am afraid they are dead.

Began new drum of paraffin today. Should last to end of July at least, but NB. <u>to start agitating for a new drum some time in June</u>.

One or two of the primroses I transferred beginning to flower.

<u>8.5.47.</u>   *Morning still & overcast. Some rain during afternoon. Fairly warm.*

Began putting wire round hen-run.

<u>9.5.47.</u>   *Beautiful, warm, still day, sunny till evening. The first day since we have been here when it was pleasant to sit about out of doors. Sea very calm.*

Not well enough to do much. Cut grass in front of house (a lot of ragwort etc., but this can be easily kept down by frequent cutting). Inspected peat beds. Peat now dry enough to cut. Made tousling fork. Lit rubbish fire.

Gladioli (planted 13.4.47) showing here & there.

Saw violets in bloom (first I have seen this year, but A. had seen them earlier.)

Another dead deer up not far from the ruined hut. They say a lot have died this winter.

Saw a swallow sitting on the ground, which I think is unusual.

An hour or two's rain in late evening.

<u>12.5.47.</u>   *In bed last 3 days. 8 tablets M & B.[2] on 10.5.47. Very sick until this morning. Got up for some hours this afternoon. Still shaky.*

A thunderstorm & heavy rain for an hour or two on the evening of 10.5.47, otherwise all these days warm & still. Vegetation jumping remarkably.

Wild cherries covered with blossom. One or two tulips out. Shirley poppies sown 4.5.47 are up. A good many gladioli now showing.

<u>13.5.47.</u>   *Better. Went out a little, but did not do anything.*

Beautiful day. Vegetation all jumping.

They sowed the field with rye-grass today. This comes up later than the oats & is not much affected by the reaping of the latter. The following year it can be harvested as hay, but in this case will be left as pasture at least the first year. The seed is sown with a "spinner," which shoots it out in all directions—being so light, it would be difficult to broadcast in the ordinary way. By operating a small lever, some of the seed comes out of the bag onto a tin disc divided into sections, which can rotate rapidly. The sower walks along slowly, with the apparatus hanging round his neck, & rotates the disk by working a bow to & fro. One sack did whole field (4½ acres.)

Outboard has arrived at Ardlussa. Can fetch boat next week, when car is running.

Have ordered hens—8 28 week old pullets, preferably R.I.R. × W.L.[3] crosses. They have to come from Yorkshire, a long journey.

14.5.47. *Blowy & overcast in morning, but fairly warm. Rain a good deal of afternoon.*

Somewhat better. Put some more of the wire round the hen run. Will need a good deal of pegging down.

Cast a plug for bathroom basin out of lead. There is something in this operation that I do wrong. Although it lies quite smooth in the melting pot, the lead always boils & splutters when poured into the mould, & one does not seem to be able to get a cast free from flaws. Q. because of differences of temperature. In that case ought one to heat the mould?

R. is 3 years old today.

Cylinder of Calor gas gave out, after only a fortnight! Gas from new cylinder difficult to light because pressure appears too strong. Perhaps the filling of these things is irregular.

15.5.47. *Morning blowy & rather cold. Some showers in afternoon, then fine & warm. Evening pleasant & still. Sea calm.*

Went on with wire netting. Nearly finished, apart from pegging down etc. Cut sticks for gladioli (first bed are now all up.)

Went over to Kinuachdrach for first time in about 10 days. A few bluebells out. Some blackthorn just budding (I remember that we did not find any sloes last year.) Hazels barely leafing. Saw the brown flies one finds on cowdung for the first time this year. Bluebottles getting fairly common.

K.D. says last night's wireless announced no poultry were to be sent from England to Scotland, to prevent spread of some disease or other. There is certainly some order about not importing poultry into the U.K. from abroad. Shall perhaps hear next mail from the dealer to whom I wrote.

Lettuces sown 7.5.46° are up, but not the onions sown a few days earlier.

16.5.47. *Fine & sunny all day, but wind rather chilly at times.*

Finished putting wire up (still needs pegging down.)

Cleaned strawberry bed & trimmed edges, cut down raspberries. Weeds now getting very rampant.

Onions coming up.

17.5.47. *Overcast, but not very cold. Rain or drizzle all afternoon & evening.*

Sowed parsley, cut more gladiolus sticks (now have enough.) Slugs getting more numerous. Trying tobacco powder round lettuces.

A. saw some kind of whale crossing the bay this morning. Perhaps a grampus,[4] like last year.

Saw one of the white-collared rabbits, in the same place as usual. First time this year.

Stonecrop at last starting to grow on the rocks. Wild irises a foot or eighteen inches high.

18.5.47. *Evidently a good deal of rain in the night. This morning blowy & overcast, with some rain. Afternoon sunny, but coldish all day.*

Dug a little more (still cannot dig much), cut out place for marrow bed, pegged down wire (one or two corners still a bit sketchy.)

Tulips we bought as mixed are nearly all yellow.

1. Duggie (Dougie?) Clark worked on the Astors' estate at Tarbert, as, probably, did Neal (Neil?) McArthur.
2. May and Baker, makers of sulphonamides, and the drug sulphapyridine, used to treat pneumonia, and commonly known by the manufacturer's initials.
3. A cross of Rhode Island Reds with White Leghorns.
4. Properly Risso's dolphin, but used generally of whales of different kinds.

3224. To Secker & Warburg

19 May 1947

Only a record that this letter existed in the files of Secker & Warburg has been traced. It was addressed to David Farrar, Publicity Manager.

3225. Domestic Diary

<u>19.5.47.</u> *Beautiful sunny day. Sea calm.*
Sowed marrows (bush) out of doors under pots, ie tins with hole in the bottom. NB. to look in about a week & see if they have germinated. Sticked gladioli, hoed turnips, began thinning second bed. Pruned roses some more, as they seem to need it.
One or two other apple trees now budding. Those on the cordon trees are now opening & probably will not get fertilised. One or two blossoms coming on the cherry trees.
<u>20.5.47.</u> *Beautiful, hot, still day.*
Prepared ground for beetroots. Cut bean sticks. Some strawberries setting fruits. A good many apple blossoms open. Corn in field in front of house well up. Large king-cups in marshy places. Primroses out everywhere.
Reflections of the lighthouses on the islands visible today, which is said locally to be a sign that rain is coming.
If weather is fine, we intend bringing the boat home on Sunday (25th).

3226. To Leonard Moore

21 May 1947   Typewritten

Barnhill
Isle of Jura
Argyllshire

Dear Moore,
Many thanks for your letter, and the account.
    I am glad "Animal Farm" is to be broadcast in New Zealand and South

Africa. As you say, it would be better to see the proposed alterations, but it doesn't matter so much if it is only cuts.

As to the Swiss magazine. At another time I would like to take up their offer but I don't want to do so now. I am struggling with this book[1] which I *may* finish by the end of the year—at any rate I shall have broken its back by then so long as I can keep well and keep off journalistic work until the autumn. I am therefore trying to make no commitments before then. You could perhaps be kind enough to explain this in replying to them?

I have never written anything you could properly call a short story. I have written sketches. Of course I have no copies here at all, but I could tell you some suitable ones in case you can get hold of copies, which is never easy now:

"Shooting an Elephant" ("New Writing" 1936, and reprinted a number of times.)

"A Hanging" (the "Adelphi" 1931, reprinted in the "Savoy" 1947.)

"Looking Back on the Spanish War" ("New Road", published by the Grey Walls Press, 1943 or 1944—1943 I think.)[2]

"How the Poor Die" ("Now" 1947.)[3]

Yours sincerely
Eric Blair

1. *Nineteen Eighty-Four.*
2. It was written in the autumn of 1942 and published in 1943, probably in June. See *1421.*
3. Published November 1946; see *3104.* The sentence, 'it doesn't matter so much if it is only cuts' has been underlined in Moore's office and marked in the margin. Heavy quotation marks have been written before the first title and after the last in Moore's office. The name Paul Potts has been written at the lower right of the letter, also perhaps in Moore's office.

3227. Domestic Diary

<u>21.5.47.</u> *Still day, overcast in morning, sunny most of afternoon. Sea very calm, rather misty.*

Began cutting peat. Cut 200 blocks, which takes 2 people 2 hours, including stripping off the turf beforehand. Slung a rope round them, which I hope may keep the deer & cattle off. We hope to cut not less than 1000 blocks in all.

Put tobacco dust on apple trees. NB. to wash off tomorrow. Four of the trees, ie. of those in the grass, have quite a lot of blossom coming, but it will probably not coincide with the espalier trees.

Thrift flowering.

So many cormorants always in the bay that I think there must be a colony of nests down there, as at this time of year they could not be constantly at a long distance from their nesting places.

<u>22.5.47.</u> *Overcast, but not cold. Very little wind. Light rain most of afternoon. Sea calm.*

Sowed beetroots & turnips.

Hens have arrived, ie. at Ardlussa. Will presumably get here on Saturday.

Don't yet know what kind (ordered crosses if possible, failing that pure R.I.Rs.)

23.5.47. *Beautiful warm day. Sea calm.*

Moved wire from round fruit patch, cut grass in front of house, began cutting among fruit trees. Applied sodium chlorate to some of the rushes & nettles.

Some of the leaves of apple trees still do not look too good.

Cow bogged last night. When dragged out, she was too weak to stand, & had to be given gruel which A. made.

24.5.47. *Not so warm as yesterday, & more blowy. Wind changing round to all quarters. Sea rather rough.*

Brought in bits of stonecrop which I want to attempt acclimatising. Thrift stuck in last year has taken pretty well.

Hens have arrived (Rhodes). They have been waiting at Ardlussa since the 21st, during which time they laid 6 eggs. By the look of them all or most are coming into lay.

The F.s[1] yesterday got a lot of gulls eggs, of which however a good many were already sat-on, so it is evidently now too late. Mem. that about the 15th–20th must be the proper date. But they also got a lot of good ones & gave us 16. Surprisingly large eggs, as large as hens' eggs. Perhaps of the black-backed gull or herring gull. These could not be sold as counterfeit for plovers eggs, as I think used to be done with some gulls' eggs.

Slugs are eating marigolds. Trying tobacco powder.

25.5.47. *Fine, but windier than yesterday. Went over to Ardlussa with the idea of bringing the boat back, but the sea seemed too rough.*

Everything at Ardlussa more forward than here.

Hens laid no eggs.

1. The Fletchers, Margaret and Robin: see *2638, n. 13* and *3025, n. 2* respectively.

3228. To George Woodcock

26 May 1947   Typewritten; handwritten postscript

> Barnhill
> Isle of Jura
> Argyllshire

Dear George,

Thanks for your letter of the 18th.

I don't know if anything has transpired about the French edition of "Animal Farm." The edition which Pathé are doing ought to be out by now. Do you think it would be possible for M. Prunier to write to my agents who have all the dope. Their address is: Christy & Moore, The Ride Annexe, Dukes Wood Avenue, Gerrards Cross, Bucks.

I can't write anything now. I've read, or read in, David Martin's book on Mihailovich, but it's a subject on which I am far from being an expert, and in any case I am struggling with this book of mine and trying not to do any journalism. I shan't finish the book by the end of the year, but I hope to break its back, which I shan't do if I undertake other jobs.

It's just possible the Observer would give Inge some kind of nominal assignment for Germany. They'd at any rate be glad to consider anything she wrote while there, and if she seemed to them a promising correspondent I suppose they could give her some kind of status. It's a pity I'm not in London, but what I would advise is, ring up the Observer and ask to see Mr Tomlinson,[1] the news editor. About Tuesday or Wednesday is the best day. When Inge sees him she should mention my name and say I thought the proposition would interest them. Rub it in that she speaks German and can get some secure news from the Russian zone. Or I suppose Tribune might do. You probably know either Fyvel or Evelyn Anderson.[2] In their case you can say more plainly that what she really wants is the status of a correspondent.

The weather has cheered up after being filthy for weeks, and things are growing at last. Richard is blooming after all his calamities. The place on his forehead has healed up nicely, though of course it has left a scar. We have just started cutting peat, which I think is really less work than cutting wood. We hope to see you both here some time.

Yours
George

P.S. Do you know if Kravchenko's book[3] (the American title was "I chose Freedom") has come out yet? If so, do you think the Freedom Bookshop could get & send me a copy? I asked Simmonds to get me one but he hasn't done so.

1. See Orwell's letter to Frederick Tomlinson, 24 November 1947, *3307*, and *3307*, *n. 1*.
2. Evelyn Anderson was deputy editor of *Tribune* in 1945 when Orwell was anxious to give up the literary editorship. He and she arranged for Tosco Fyvel to take it over. See T. R. Fyvel, *George Orwell, A Personal Memoir* (1982), 139.
3. See *3215, n. 8*.

3229. Domestic Diary

<u>26.5.47.</u> *Fine & very blowy. Sea rough, calming somewhat towards evening.*

Cut more peat (150 blocks), continued cutting grass between trees.

1 potato showing, from second lot. The others (sown 17.4.47) still not up, but they are germinating, as I uncovered one or two to see.

Some showers in late evening.

No eggs.

<u>27.5.47.</u> *Still & fairly warm. Overcast a good deal of the time. Sea fairly calm.*

Cut peat (150 blocks) & put the first lot into threes. Thinned clarkia (slugs have eaten some of them), put sodium chlorate on docks in back yard.

With A. & myself working together, cutting peat seems to work out pretty regularly at 100 blocks an hour. If one doubles this, to allow for the time taken up in turning, stacking & carting, it would take about 40 hours work (for 2 people) to bring in a ton of peat. No doubt practiced diggers can do it immensely faster, & also it would be easier if there were 3 or 4 people, which saves changing from one operation to another.
<u>28.5.47.</u> *Fine day, mostly windy. Sea roughish till evening, when it calmed down.*

Did nothing out of doors, as I was busy making a post-box.

Turnips sown 22.5.47 are up.

Still no eggs. Janet McK.[1] said the hens they got from England went off lay for a week after arriving.

1. Janet M'Kechnie; Orwell uses the forms M'Kechnie and McKechnie.

3230. To Leonard Moore

      29 May 1947   Typewritten

                                 Barnhill
                              Isle of Jura
                           Argyllshire

Dear Moore,
I see from the enclosed account that Penguin Books still seem to be selling copies of "Burmese Days." In that case do you think it would be possible to get a few copies from them? Last time I asked they said they had none left, and I have only one copy of the book in the world.[1]

                            Yours sincerely
                       [Signed] Eric Blair
                              Eric Blair

1. Annotated in Moore's office: 'Can K.A.L. spare one?' which is ticked through. K.A.L. was K. A. G. S. Lane, a director of Christy & Moore; see *3081, n. 1.*

3231. Domestic Diary

<u>29.5.47.</u> *Some rain in night. Light rain & rolling mists a good deal of the day. Sea calmer.*

Sowed alyssum (annual), thinned first lot of turnips. The Jas. Grieve apple is evidently not dead. The deaths therefore—from about 90 plants excluding the strawberries—are 3 gooseberries, 1 blackcurrant, 3 roots of rhubarb, about ½ dozen raspberries. Not bad considering late planting & very bad weather conditions.

2 eggs (the first we have had).

A good many potatoes up from first lot.

30. 5.47.   Still & warm.
Ian[1] *brought boat round last night, as they were going round to Glengarrisdale to collect drift. Took her round to Kinuachdrach. Some trouble in starting (plug not very good.)*
This afternoon landed on island at mouth of harbour to see if the terns are nesting yet. Had not started, but found one gull's egg.
A. saw some more fawn-coloured rabbits.
Bluebells about in full swing.
No eggs.

1. Ian M'Kechnie. Glengarrisdale Bay is on the western side of Jura, almost directly opposite Barnhill.

3232. To Fredric Warburg

  31 May 1947 Typewritten

                 Barnhill
                Isle of Jura
               Argyllshire

Dear Fred,
Many thanks for your letter. I have made a fairly good start on the book and I think I must have written nearly a third of the rough draft. I have not got as far as I had hoped to do by this time, because I have really been in most wretched health this year ever since about January (my chest as usual) and can't quite shake it off. However I keep pegging away, and I hope that when I leave here in October I shall either have finished the rough draft or at any rate broken its back. Of course the rough draft is always a ghastly mess having very little relation to the finished result, but all the same it is the main part of the job. So if I do finish the rough draft by October I might get the book done fairly early in 1948, barring illnesses. I don't like talking about books before they are written, but I will tell you now that this is a novel about the future— that is, it is in a sense a fantasy, but in the form of a naturalistic novel. That is what makes it a difficult job—of course as a book of anticipations it would be comparatively simple to write.
 I am sending you separately a long autobiographical sketch[1] which I originally undertook as a sort of pendant to Cyril Connolly's "Enemies of Promise," he having asked me to write a reminiscence of the preparatory school we were at together. I haven't actually sent it to Connolly or Horizon, because apart from being too long for a periodical I think it is really too libellous to print, and I am not disposed to change it, except perhaps the names. But I think it should be printed sooner or later when the people most concerned are dead, and maybe sooner or later I might do a book of collected sketches. I must apologise for the typescript. It is not only the carbon copy, but is very bad commercial typing which I have had to correct considerably— however, I think I have got most of the actual errors out.

Richard is very well in spite of various calamities. First he fell down and cut his forehead and had to have two stitches put in, and after that he had measles. He is talking a good deal more now (he was three a week or two ago.) The weather has cheered up after being absolutely stinking, and the garden we are creating out of virgin jungle is getting quite nice. Please remember me to Pamela and Roger.[2]

Yours
George

1. In the margin there is a handwritten annotation (in Warburg's hand?): "Such, Such were the Joys." For the development of this essay and for the nature of the 'commercial typing,' see headnote to the essay, *3408*. Cyril Connolly's *Enemies of Promise* was published in 1938. Warburg wrote to Orwell on 6 June saying, 'I have read the autobiographical sketch about your prep. school and passed it to Roger.'
2. Fredric Warburg's second wife, formerly Pamela de Bayou (they married in 1933); and Roger Senhouse.

3233. Domestic Diary

<u>31.5.47.</u> *Evidently a good deal of rain last night. Today still & warm, mostly not very sunny. Sea calm.*

Finished cutting grass between trees, thinned clarkia & poppies. Beetroots (sown 22.5.47) are up. One marrow just poking through the earth.

2 eggs. Have started the hens on Karswood.[1]

We have started on the 50 gallon drum of petrol (which has to last till end of August). A. took out 9 galls.

<u>1.6.47.</u> *Thunder & heavy rain during the night. Today mostly fine & warm, but misty, after a sharp shower in the morning.*

Went over to Scarba.[2] *About ½ hour's run in the boat (3–4 miles). When we returned the engine would not start (probably defective plug) & we were obliged to row. A stiff job, taking about 2 hours. Scarba much barer than Jura. Almost no trees, good grass. While there killed a very large snake.*

Sowed lettuces.

1 egg.

1. A proprietary brand of poultry feed.
2. Scarba lies to the north of Jura; the islands are separated by the Gulf of Corryvreckan.

3234. To John Gawsworth, Editor of *The Literary Digest*

2 June 1947   Typewritten

Barnhill
Isle of Jura
Argyllshire

Dear Sir,[1]
Many thanks for your letter of May 20th, which was forwarded to me here.
You may reprint the article on nonsense poetry from "Tribune."[2]

Yours faithfully
[Signed] Geo. Orwell
George Orwell

1. For John Gawsworth, see *3138, n. 1*.
2. Published 21 December 1945; see *2823*. It was reprinted in an abridged form in the Autumn 1948 issue of *The Literary Digest* as 'Lear and Nonsense Poetry.'

3235. Domestic Diary

2.6.47. *Beautiful warm, still day, with some mist. Sea very calm.*
Cut peat (200 blocks). Applied more sodium chlorate.
2 eggs (a third hen is now in lay.)
2 roses now have buds. All except two apple trees have now blossomed. Second lot of gladioli have not come up well (only about half have appeared).
D.D. gave me a load of manure.
Cuckoos all over the place. Qy. whether they really change their note in June or merely become more irritating as they cease to be a novelty.
3.6.47. *Still, cloudy & warm. No rain, though it looked like rain several times. Sea very smooth. Milk sours quickly this weather.*
Finished preparing ground for beans. Greased outboard motor, cut petrol feed as I. M'K.[1] suggested, & put in new plug. This was taken from the Austin & appeared to me as bad as the old one—however, have sent for new ones. Could not try engine as the boat was out of reach. Shall take the RAF dinghy round to Kinuachdrach as soon as the engine is running.
A. & B.D.[2] went fishing last night—again nothing. Apparently there are only tiddlers about.
Blossom on the old pear tree in the hedge. However, when I arrived here last year (& everything was weeks earlier), I had the impression it had blossomed, but it gave no fruit. Alyssum is coming up. Rowan trees coming into blossom. Oaks in full leaf.
3 eggs. (10)
4.6.47. *A good deal of rain in the night. Rain & "Scotch mist" almost all day. Ground very sodden.*
Impossible to sow beans. Began sticking peas, fixed bolt on barn door, trimmed lamps.

Found a columbine in the garden (the old-fashioned purple kind). It must have survived here from the time when the house was last inhabited, about 12 years ago. The other flowers to survive are daffodils, snowdrops (both of these in great numbers), red hot pokers, monkshood.

Paraffin consumption at present only 1–2 gallons a week.

4 eggs (I think 5 hens are laying.) (14).

1. Ian M'Kechnie.
2. Avril and Bill Dunn. William Dunn (1921–1992) had been an officer in the army, but after the loss of a leg had been invalided out. He came to Jura to farm in 1947. After five months he moved down from his farm above Barnhill and joined Orwell and his sister, Avril; see 3277. He later entered into a partnership with Richard Rees to farm Barnhill. He married Avril in 1951 and they brought up Richard, Orwell's adopted son. See transcript of his interview by Nigel Williams in *Orwell Remembered*, 231–35; also *Remembering Orwell*, 182–85.

3236. Sir Edward Marsh: Talk on George Orwell

BBC French Service, 5 June 1947

On 5 June 1947, Sir Edward Marsh[1] gave a talk in the French Service of the BBC on George Orwell. This included 1,230 words of Orwell's 'Politics and the English Language,' for which a royalty of £2.2.0 was paid.

1. Sir Edward Howard Marsh (1872–1953), civil servant, patron of the arts. He is particularly associated with the editing of *Georgian Poetry* (1912–22), the first volume of which he prepared in association with Rupert Brooke. A distinguished civil servant, he served, amongst others, Winston Churchill, and was instrumental in securing a pension from the Civil List for James Joyce. He published several volumes of translations, including the Fables of La Fontaine and Proust's *Oriane* (1952). After his retirement in 1937, he undertook the scrupulous correction of proofs for friends, including Churchill and Somerset Maugham.

3237. Domestic Diary

5.6.47. *Overcast, coldish, & raining lightly most of day. Clearing somewhat in evening. Sea calm.*

Sowed beans (dibbed them, as the ground was very sticky) & sticked them. Made another attempt to get the engine started—no use. Cannot be sure till the new plugs arrive, but I am afraid the trouble may be the magneto, which I do not understand.

While with D.D. in the boat he landed on the island.

No terns' eggs yet, but they appear to be making their nests (ie. scooping hollows). D.D. found a nest with two fledged chicks, dark & striped, about the size of a day-old chick. Probably oyster-catchers, as two of these are always round there.

A lot of water in the boat—however, this was probably mostly rainwater. No eggs.

6.6.47. *Windy, mostly fine but some intervals of mist & light rain.*

Cut more grass. B.D. & D.D. caught one fish (small saythe) last night.

4 eggs (18).

<u>7.6.47.</u> *Blowy, mostly fine. Coldish in morning. Sea rougher.*

Last night shot a very young rabbit in the garden. Threw the corpse into the trench, whence it had disappeared this morning—presumably cats. NB. to put up the rest of the wire soon.

Put new plug in the motor-boat engine and, on the advice of Ian M'K. increased the proportion of petrol in the tank. The boat was high & dry, so I fitted the engine on the stern to try it, the propellor being clear of the ground. It started almost at once, & then would not stop, probably owing to throttle wire sticking. So it was running for about 5 minutes without water, & by the time the petrol in the carburettor gave out the grease in the gear box was sizzling. Trust no harm done. Tap of petrol barrel tends to drip.

Took out about a gallon, making 10 gallons.

3 eggs (21).

Received cwt. of maize yesterday from the F.s.

<u>8.6.47.</u> *Blowy, coldish, raining on & off throughout the day. Wind mostly from west. Sea rough.*

Another rabbit in the garden last night. Shot at him but missed him.

Sowed sweet peas (a few) & anchusas. Took up tulips & the 3 dead gooseberry bushes. From the look of the roots of one of these I thought it possible that it was not dead.

Drip from petrol drum seems to be about a pint in the 24 hours. If one lost one-tenth of this by evaporation, the loss would be about 1 gallon in 2½ months, whch I suppose is not excessive.

2 eggs (23).

3238. To Leonard Moore

9 June 1947   Typewritten

Barnhill
Isle of Jura
Argyllshire

Dear Moore,

Many thanks for sending the two copies of "Burmese Days." I wonder if you could arrange for copies of the following books to be sent with the author's compliments. I have been asked for copies and have none here.

To M. J. Arquer,[1] 4 Rue de l'Ancienne Comedie, Paris 6eme.
"Homage to Catalonia"
"Animal Farm."

To Benedetto Croce.
"Animal Farm."[2]

I suppose there are copies available. I have no idea of Croce's address, except that he is in Italy, but as he is more or less a public figure (he was in the Italian government but I don't think he is now) it should not be difficult to find it out.

I enclose the exemption certificates duly signed.

Yours sincerely
[Signed] Eric Blair
Eric Blair

P.S. A friend writes to say that the Italian publishing house Casa Editrice A. Mondadori, Via Corridoni 39, Milan, is anxious to buy the rights of all my books. I really don't know how we stand about Italian translations and am asking them to communicate with you.[3]

1. Jordi Arquer; the 'M' is not an initial but stands for Monsieur, because Arquer, a Catalan, was living in Paris. He published *Las Interpretacinoes del Marxismo* (Barcelona, 1937); *El Futur de Catalunya i els Deures Politics de l'Emigració Catalana* (Mexic, D.F., 1943); he also wrote the introduction for *Diari d'un Refugiat Català* by the pseudonymously named R. d'Almenara (Mexic, D.F., 1943). Arquer was one of the accused in the 'POUM Trial' of October–November 1938; see Orwell's draft letter to Raymond Postgate, 21 October 1938, *497*. He was initially charged with espionage and desertion but the accusations collapsed because of the transparent absurdity of the evidence. Nevertheless, Arquer was found guilty of having organised a meeting in Lérida in preparation for the May Events in Barcelona; though he maintained he was preparing reinforcements for the front, he was sentenced to eleven years' imprisonment. (See *The New Leader*, 21 October, 4 and 11 November 1938). At his trial, Arquer caused difficulties by insisting on testifying in Catalan (Thomas, 866). In evidence it was stated that the officer commanding the army of Aragon had commended the POUM troops for their part in operations round Huesca, and *The New Leader*, 11 November 1938, notes that it was in this campaign that 'our comrades, George Orwell and Roger Williams, were wounded.' Orwell's letter has been annotated in Moore's office to indicate that a copy of *Animal Farm* was sent on 12 June 1947 but that no copies of *Homage to Catalonia* were available (though it was still in print). On 22 June 1949, Orwell asked Moore to arrange to send Arquer a copy of the Italian translation of *Homage to Catalonia*.
2. An annotation indicates that a copy was sent on 13 June 1947. Benedetto Croce (1866–1952) was one of the most important Italian philosophers of the twentieth century. Initially he did not regard Mussolini's rise to power as significant, but later he stood in the forefront of those opposed to Fascism. After Italy's defeat in World War II, he gave his country moral leadership. In his last years he established the Italian Institute for Historical Studies.
3. In Orwell's lifetime, Mondadori published *Animal Farm* (October 1947) and *Homage to Catalonia* (December 1948); in the year of his death the firm published *Nineteen Eighty-Four* (November 1950). Another Italian publishing house, Longanesi, published *Burmese Days* (November 1948). In giving the address, Orwell spelled 'Casa' as 'Case.'

3239. To George Woodcock

9 June 1947   Typewritten

Barnhill
Isle of Jura
Argyllshire

Dear George,

I enclose cheque for £5–13–0, 13/– for a subscription to "Now" and £5 for the fund.[1]

All goes well here. My book is getting on very slowly but still it is getting on. I hope to finish it fairly early in 1948. The weather was wonderful for some weeks but has now turned rather nasty again. Richard is very well. We haven't started catching any fish yet, but we have got a few hens and managed to wangle a bit of corn for them, so the food situation is fairly good. Please give my love to Inge. I hope it came to something about her visit to Germany.

Yours
George

1. *Now* was first published in 1940–41 (7 numbers); it was relaunched by George Woodcock in 1943; nine numbers were published at various intervals until the last, for July/August 1947. Orwell's 'How the Poor Die' appeared in No. 6, November 1946; see *3104*. It is not clear whether the £5 was for *Now* or the Freedom Defence Committee. *Now* did not make a specific appeal. Orwell is credited with donating £20 to the FDC in its *Bulletin*, 5, July–August 1947, and the £5 might be included in that.

3240. Domestic Diary

<u>9.6.47.</u> *Fine warm day. Sea calm. Little wind.*

Put up rest of wire netting (only gate uncovered now), cleared raspberry & rhubarb beds. Shot another young rabbit trying to get into garden.

In the evening tried to take the RAF dinghy round to Kinuachdrach, towing it behind the boat. Fearful job as the engine stopped half way (probably over-oiling) & we had to row, leaving the dinghy at old Kinuachdrach harbour until we can pick it up.

Saw an owl (first I have seen this year). It appeared to be definitely black & white.[1]

3 eggs (26).

<u>10.6.47.</u> *Overcast all day, light rain most of the time. Little wind. Sea calm.*

Cut grass in front. Made hens' drinking trough. 5 roses now budding. No ramblers budding yet.

4 eggs (30).

NB. Petrol drip. This is put in a bottle & poured into car[2] *from time to time. Must keep note of amount used up in this way. To date, 3 pints.*

<u>11.6.47.</u> *Beautiful, still, hot day, about the best day we have had this year. Sea like glass.*

Thinned carrots.

Took dinghy to Kinuachdrach. One cannot satisfactorily propel oneself by poling, so the best method will be to use a rope to pull oneself out by. Tried engine with more petrol in the mixture. It started at once, so over-oiling must have been the trouble.

Parsley (sown 17.5.47) just showing.

Petrol drip 4 pints.

4 eggs (34).

<u>12.6.47.</u> *Beautiful still day, more misty than yesterday, but about equally hot in the afternoon. Sea very calm.*

Cut peat (150 blocks) & put the rest into "threes." The deer have been on it, but not seriously. Sowed parsnips.

Cotton grass out all over the place. Rowans in full bloom. Their flowers

have the same smell as hawthorn or elder, but even more oppresive.°
Cherries forming on the wild cherry trees (also on the little morello trees, but
most of these will probably drop off.) All but 2 or 3 potatoes now through.

Saw the buzzard carrying a rat or something about that size in its claws.
The first time I have seen one of these birds with prey.

Five rats (2 young ones, 2 enormous) caught in the byre during about the
last fortnight. These rats seem to let themselves be caught very easily. The
traps are simply set in the runs, unbaited & almost unconcealed. Also no
precautions taken about handling them. I hear that recently two children at
Ardlussa were bitten by rats (in the face, as usual.)

Petrol drip 5 pints.

5 eggs (39).

13.6.47.   Evidently a good deal of rain in the night. Overcast all day, light
drizzle a good deal of the time. Very still. Sea calm. Everything very sodden.

Foxgloves budding (in garden). Last year they were full out long before
this.

Think hens have lice, applied DDT. Found what appeared to be the white
of an egg in one nest, but no signs of shell. Possibly some kind of accident &
not egg-eating.

Petrol drip 6 pints.

5 eggs (44).

14.6.47.   Fine & still, but not so warm as the day before yesterday. Sea
somewhat less calm.

Hoed potatoes, thinned turnips, gave strawberries liquid manure.

This evening two rabbits not only in the garden, but actually taking refuge
under the house. There is a drain or something of the kind behind one of the
apple trees, which D.D. warned me they went into during winter. The
trouble is it probably leads out into the back yard, so that they have a way of
circumventing the wire netting. Probably it is they & not slugs which have
been eating down the clarkia. Closed hole with a slate jammed in place by a
stone. NB. to put wire on gate.

A. & B.D. caught 16 fish last night (smallish).

Petrol drip 7 pints. To be on safe side better call it a gallon, making 11
gallons.

Fuchsia nearly in flower (last year in flower at end of May).

3 eggs (47).

15.6.47.   Some rain in the night. Today sunny & windy, not very warm.
Sea fresher. No breakers.

Got both the rabbits that were sheltering in the hole under the house, by
pushing a trap inside the hole & then re-blocking it. Both young ones. As
they both tried to get out this way, there cannot be any outlet the other end.
D.D. says the hole is only a ventilator.

Put a long rope from the shore to the anchor buoy, so that when the boat is
out of reach one can get to her with the dinghy.

Took out 3 galls of petrol, making 14 galls.

Big drip, 1½ pints (drip worse after using tap.)

5 eggs (52).

Several raspberries I thought dead are sprouting.
Earthed up first lot of potatoes.
A. & B.D. caught 31 fish last night.
<u>16.6.47.</u> *There may perhaps have been a little rain in the night. Most of day overcast, blowy & coldish. In the late afternoon strong wind from south, & a little rain. Sea rough, with heavy breakers outside. Seemed all right in Kinuachdrach harbour, the wind being in the south.*
Sowed peas (last lot).
Having reset the trap in the hole under the house, caught a rat in it, (small one). So there may be a way through to the back for rats, though there evidently is not for rabbits.
Some wild irises out. D.D is sowing turnips, 2 acres. It will be a ghastly job thinning this quantity by hand.
Petrol drip, 3 pints.
6 eggs (58).
<u>17.6.47.</u> *Pelting rain late last evening & some rain in night. This morning overcast, then clearing up for a few hours. More rain & wind this evening. Sea rough.*
Baled out boat, which was full of water. Put wire over gate. Ditto round gooseberry bushes, to prevent R. getting at them.
Eggs & bacon[3] just coming out. Some strawberries about the size of acorns.
A. starts waterglassing eggs today.[4]
Petrol drip 4 pints (not quite so bad now.)
5 eggs (63).

1. That is, in its summer plumage.
2. This could be 'can' but 'car' is clear at *3245, 3.7.47.*
3. Toad flax or field snapdragon.
4. In order to preserve them for use in the winter. Eggs preserved in waterglass could not be used as boiled eggs; they had to be used for cooking or, perhaps, scrambled.

3241. To George Woodcock

18 June 1947   Typewritten

Barnhill, Isle of Jura, Argyllshire[1]

Dear George,
Yes, certainly the people in Munich may reprint the piece from "Now."[2]
I'm glad you are managing to do some work, and that you contemplate writing something on Wilde. I've always been very pro-Wilde. I particularly like "Dorian Gray," absurd as it is in a way. I just recently read Hesketh Pearson's life of him—only the ordinary hack biography, but I found bits of it quite interesting, especially the part about Wilde's time in prison. I don't think I'd read a life of Wilde before, though years ago I read some reminiscences by Frank Harris,[3] obviously untruthful, and part of a book by Sherard,[4] answering Harris's biography. I should like to read a more detailed

account of the two trials. I was amused by that woman's remarks in the American magazine you sent me.[5] What an ass! The weather here has turned filthy again after being nice for a week or two.

Yours
George

1. This is the first letter sent from Barnhill to be written on headed paper. The address, in large italic type, is written in a single line, centred on the page. It can be distinguished from typed or written addresses because it is punctuated and in one line; and distinguished from a later printed heading (see *3513, n. 1*) by 'Argyllshire' instead of 'Argyll.'
2. 'How the Poor Die,' *3104*; the journal has not been identified.
3. Presumably *The Life & Loves* (4 volumes, Paris, 1922–27; as one volume, including a fifth, previously unpublished, New York, 1963; London, 1964). See especially Vol. 2, chap 17; and Vol. 3, chaps. 9 and 12. Frank Harris (1856–1931) (see *165, n. 3*) published *Oscar Wilde: His Life and Confessions*, together with *Memories of Oscar Wilde* by Bernard Shaw (New York, 1918).
4. Robert Harborough Sherard (1861–1943), awarded the French Cross of the Legion of Honour for service to French literature. His books on Wilde include *Oscar Wilde: The Story of an Unhappy Friendship* (1902), *The Life of Oscar Wilde* (1906), supplemented by *The Real Wilde* (1937), *Oscar Wilde, Twice Defended from André Gide's Wicked Lies and Frank Harris' Cruel Libel* (Chicago, 1934), and *Bernard Shaw, Frank Harris and Oscar Wilde* (1937). Sherard might have proved a particularly interesting author for Orwell because he wrote a number of books on the theme of 'how the poor live,' among them *The White Slaves of England* (1897), *The Cry of the Poor* (1901), *At the Closed Door*, 'an experiment *in propria persona*' on the treatment of pauper immigrants arriving at New York (1902), and *Paris: Some Sidelights on Its Inner Life* (1911).
5. Not identified.

3242. Domestic Diary

<u>18.6.47.</u> *Evidently a good deal of rain in the night. Dense mists this morning, clearing off about 2 pm. Afternoon sunny & moderately warm, with little wind.*

Earthed up second lot of potatoes. Thinned beetroots. Began turfing up holes in grass among fruit trees. A. applied sodium chlorate to rushes in side garden. Thinned marrows.

One rambler roses° has flower buds coming. The trees have set quite a lot of apples between them, but of course not many will stay on.

Big petrol drip (better today) 3½ pints.

No. of eggs now in waterglass, 9.

4 eggs (67).

<u>19.6.47.</u> *A little rain in the night. Today a few brief showers, but mostly fine & still, moderately warm. Sea calm.*

Tried outboard engine again. Ran perfectly at first, then, after stopping, refused to re-start. Landed on island. Found 3 terns' eggs (not worth taking). Found dead tern. Struck by brilliant scarlet colour of its beak & legs. Oyster catchers which frequent the island evidently live almost exclusively on limpets. Struck by luxuriance of grass & wildflowers (thrift & stonecrop) on the island, which is about 40 yards long by 5–10 wide. Some deer living there. Apparently a deer swam out to it when being chased.

Saw two sheld-duck in the nearer bay. Eyebright in flower. Killed a green wasp (A. killed one some time ago.) D.D. rolled the oats in front of the house today. They are about 6″ high, which I suppose is the right height to roll them at. Young wagtail being fed on the ground by parents. Afraid one hen is already broody.

Big petrol drip, 4 pints.

5 eggs (72).

20.6.47. (filling this in on 21.6.47).

Dense mist most of day, & a few light showers. Very still till evening, wind springing up about 6 pm & veering about. Sea calm. Went to Ardlussa by boat, car being punctured. Each way the journey Barnhill–Ardlussa took about 1¼ hours, with wind & sea against us. Hugged shore as close as possible. Engine runs all right if the mixture is exact, but still difficult starting.

Saw an eagle, sitting on ground, later taking to the wing, near the shore about half way between the new stable & the old stable.

Big petrol drip 5½ pints (worse when it is opened up). Took out a gallon, making 15 gallons.

4 eggs (76).

Cylinder of Calor Gas giving out. It was started on 15.5.47, so has run 5 weeks as scheduled. The previous cylinder must have been defective.

Some stonecrop beginning to flower on the rocks. Sea pinks past their best.

21.6.47. Dry, sunny & windy, not very warm. Wind in north in morning, later changing to west. Sea calm inshore, breakers in strait part of day.

Cut peat (150 blocks) & set up last lot. Cows had been over it, but not much damage. That completes the 1000 blocks. If dry weather should continue, it could be put into small piles in about a week, & into a single pile about a fortnight after that.

Weeded & hoed small seedlings, which get droopy in the dry wind. Slugs have eaten one of the two marrow plants—may possibly recover.

Shot a gull (kittiwake) for the tail feathers. Not very large or stiff. A goose's wing feathers are definitely the best.

Caught another rat under the house (young one).

Started new cylinder of Calor Gas. Should run to nearly end of July.

Big petrol drip, 6 pints.

5 eggs (81).

22.6.47. Dry, warm & still. Sea calm.

A good many runner beans showing. Some sweet peas showing. Fuchsia almost out (last year out towards end of May), mallow out. A lot of roses coming on one or two of the plants.

Last night a deer (hind) in the corn. Don't know where it got in, as gate was shut.

Forgot to mention yesterday killed a very large snake in the yard. It was lying on the coal-heap.

Big petrol drip 6½ pints.

6 eggs (87).

23.6.47. Overcast all day & raining most of the time. Clearing up a little in the evening. Sea variable, but part of the day roughish in the bay.

First peas have a flower or two. Gave them liquid manure. Slugs have destroyed one of the two marrow plants. Ought not to have thinned them out so early. Last lot of peas just showing.

Big petrol drip, 7 pints.

Eggs now in water glass, 12.

6 eggs (93).

Amount of paraffin in drum now about 20 galls (probably). NB. to order new drum soon.

24.6.47. Rain almost continuous all day. Coldish & blowy, wind mostly from SW. Sea rough.

Began clearing strawberry bed. It is time they were strawed up. There seem to be a fair number of strawberries coming, but very small.

Herd of cows came down from Lealt & have been on the peat, but hitherto not very badly.

Big petrol drip, 7¼ pints, say 1 gall, making 16 gallons.

Eggs now in waterglass, 17.

5 eggs (98). It is a month today since hens arrived, in which time they have averaged about 2 doz. a week.

25.6.47. Sunny & windy in the morning, looking like rain but not actually raining—Afternoon drier & a great deal warmer. Evening clouding over again.

Strawed strawberries (not enough straw.)

Two hens now broody, & 6 laying.

5 eggs (103).

26.6.47. Blowy & cold. A little sun in the afternoon, but not warm. No rain, but a damp feeling in the air. Evening overcast & looking like rain. Sea rough.

Sowed carrots & a few radishes.

A. & B.D. fished last night—nothing. It was decidedly rough, & last year when it was rough we generally did not catch anything except a few pollock. However, we never had an actually blank day in the Barnhill bay.

An eagle flew over the house yesterday.

Big petrol drip (including yesterday) ½ pint.

Eggs now in waterglass, 20.

3 eggs (106).

27.6.47. Overcast, warm & close. Strongish wind during part of afternoon, but most of day still. Once or twice it looked like rain, but no rain fell.

Set out to take boat down to the beach near Lealt & collect drift. As usual, boat started well at the beginning, then would not re-start after stopping at Barnhill to take A. & R. aboard. It took half an hour to get her started again, so ran back to Kinuachdrach. A. landed on island. About a dozen terns' eggs—not worth taking as they are very tiny. 3 gulls' eggs, which we took.★

Spotted orchis out in great numbers & very fine. Really well worth

---

★ All bad, with chicks quite far developed inside. [Orwell's note on facing page.]

acclimatising if we could identify the bulbs in autumn. A. found one butterfly orchis. A good many wild irises now out.

Big petrol drip, 1 pint.

Took out ½ gall., making 16½ galls.

Parsnips still not up—perhaps bad seed.

5 eggs (111).

<u>28.6.47.</u> *Close, warm & still. Overcast most of time, but some sun. Sea calm.*

Set remaining peat up into "threes." Cows had been on it, but not very badly. Some of what is undisturbed is very dry. Could be built up into small piles if we had two or three dry days running.

A few parsnips showing, but not very good.

Balancer meal arrived today, evidently 12 lb., 1 month's ration.

An egg had been eaten in one of the boxes—no doubt accidently broken. In addition to this, 4 eggs (115).

<u>29.6.47.</u> *Some rain in the night. This morning close & warm, afternoon somewhat colder, with a little more wind. Overcast all day. A few drops of rain occasionally. Sea roughish in morning, calming somewhat by evening.*

Cut front grass. Transplanted a few lettuces. Slugs have had the last marrow—it may survive, but they have eaten the growing point out. Found a monstrous slug at it last night, in spite of a ring of soot & sand.

Went fishing last night, —nothing, though we did see one fish jump.

5 eggs (120).

<u>30.6.47.</u> *Very still, overcast & damp all day. Rather close, getting cooler in evening. Light drizzling rain & dense mist all afternoon. Everything very sodden. Sea like glass.*

Impossible to do much out of doors. Netted strawberries. Last night tried putting out bran mixed with Meta[1] for slugs. A good many dead this morning—not certain, however, whether the net effect of this is not to attract slugs to the neighbourhood of plants one wants to protect.

Sweet peas well up, but there are only a very few of them—about 1 doz. seeds from each packet.

4 eggs (124).

1. Metaldehyde, used in solid block form as a fuel from 1924, and as a slug-killer from 1938.

3243. Background to 'Toward European Unity'

Partisan Review had invited a number of well-known authors to contribute to a series to be called 'The Future of Socialism.' Orwell's essay was the fourth (see 3070). Orwell's title was probably 'Towards European Unity.' The U.S. text of *Nineteen Eighty-Four* changes his every use of 'towards' to 'toward'; in that novel he wrote 'toward' only once. See *CW*, IX, 329. The series was translated into French, Italian, Dutch, and German and published under these titles:

'L'avenir du socialisme,' *Echo*, Tome 3, numero 15, November 1947;

'L'avvenire del socialismo,' *Eco del Mondo*, Volume 3, numero 15, November 1947;

'De toekomst van het socialisme,' *Internationale Echo*, 3e Deel, Nummer 15, Nov/Dec 1947;
'Ein sozialistisches Europa,' *Stuttgarter Rundschau*, Volume 2, 1947.

The translations into French, Italian, and Dutch were commissioned by the Central Office of Information and were preceded by a short editorial introduction. That in French is reproduced at the end of this headnote; the other two were very similar.

The introduction explains that the editors of *Partisan Review* had sent an explanatory note to each of the contributors (also printed as a preface to the first of the series) which drew attention to the uncertain foundation of socialism after the war, the confusion that existed in many minds between socialism and communism, and the fact that several countries of Western Europe which had adopted a socialist policy had not succeeded in freeing themselves from a narrow nationalism nor realising a fresh, authentic, and creative political approach. Contributors were asked to consider whether socialism had suffered a temporary setback or a more permanent check to its progress and to consider what was the way forward. Readers were reminded that Orwell's 'Notes on Nationalism' (*Polemic*, 1, October 1945; see *2668*) had been published in the first volume of *Écho*. (Unlike that essay, which had been abridged, this was given in full.) Orwell's approach was described as typically pessimistic and provocative.

Il y a quelques mois, la *Partisan Review* invita plusieurs écrivains célèbres à apporter leur contribution à une série d'articles sur l'avenir du socialisme. Dans une note adressée à chacun des collaborateurs et ultérieurement imprimée en guise de préface au premier article de la série, la rédaction attirait l'attention sur les bases incertaines du socialisme d'après guerre, sur la confusion qui règne dans beaucoup d'esprits entre le socialisme et le communisme, sur le fait que plusieurs pays d'Europe occidentale, bien qu'ayant adopté une politique socialiste, n'ont pas réussi à se libérer des idées nationalistes, ni à manifester des tendances politiques authentiquement nouvelles et créatrices. La rédaction demandait à ses collaborateurs s'il convenait de considérer la position actuelle du socialisme comme marquant un recul temporaire ou comme indiquant au contraire un échec définitif—s'il fallait remplacer par d'autres certains principes socialistes dont la valeur est contestée—et enfin par quels moyens le véritable socialisme pourrait devenir une réalité.

Parmi les divers articles de cette série, nous avons choisi celui de George Orwell, dont les *Réflexions sur le chauvinisme*, publiées dans le premier numéro d'ÉCHO, ont soulevé un vif intérêt. Dans cet article, George Orwell traite de l'avenir du socialisme, du point de vue de la politique internationale, à sa manière typiquement pessimiste et provocante, et exprime sans ménagements les opinions et conclusions auxquelles il est personnellement parvenu. Bien des lecteurs seront en désaccord avec lui sur bien des points; mais, comme les *Réflexions sur le chauvinisme*, les pages qu'on va lire pourront amorcer la discussion.

3244. 'Toward European Unity'
Partisan Review, July–August 1947

A socialist today is in the position of a doctor treating an all but hopeless case. As a doctor, it is his duty to keep the patient alive, and therefore to assume that the patient has at least a chance of recovery. As a scientist, it is his duty to face the facts, and therefore to admit that the patient will probably die. Our activities as socialists only have meaning if we assume that socialism *can* be established, but if we stop to consider what probably *will* happen, then we must admit, I think, that the chances are against us. If I were a bookmaker, simply calculating the probabilities and leaving my own wishes out of account, I would give odds against the survival of civilization within the next few hundred years. As far as I can see, there are three possibilities ahead of us:

1. That the Americans will decide to use the atomic bomb while they have it and the Russians haven't. This would solve nothing. It would do away with the particular danger that is now presented by the USSR, but would lead to the rise of new empires, fresh rivalries, more wars, more atomic bombs, etc. In any case this is, I think, the least likely outcome of the three, because a preventive war is a crime not easily committed by a country that retains any traces of democracy.

2. That the present "cold war" will continue until the USSR, and several other countries, have atomic bombs as well. Then there will only be a short breathing-space before whizz! go the rockets, wallop! go the bombs, and the industrial centers of the world are wiped out, probably beyond repair. Even if any one state, or group of states, emerges from such a war as technical victor, it will probably be unable to build up the machine civilization anew. The world, therefore, will once again be inhabited by a few million, or a few hundred million human beings living by subsistence agriculture, and probably, after a couple of generations, retaining no more of the culture of the past than a knowledge of how to smelt metals. Conceivably this is a desirable outcome, but obviously it has nothing to do with socialism.

3. That the fear inspired by the atomic bomb and other weapons yet to come will be so great that everyone will refrain from using them. This seems to me the worst possibility of all. It would mean the division of the world among two or three vast superstates, unable to conquer one another and unable to be overthrown by any internal rebellion. In all probability their structure would be hierarchic, with a semidivine caste at the top and outright slavery at the bottom, and the crushing out of liberty would exceed anything that the world has yet seen. Within each state the necessary psychological atmosphere would be kept up by complete severance from the outer world, and by a continuous phony war against rival states. Civilizations of this type might remain static for thousands of years.

Most of the dangers that I have outlined existed and were forseeable long before the atomic bomb was invented. The only way of avoiding them that I can imagine is to present somewhere or other, on a large scale, the spectacle of a community where people are relatively free and happy and where the main motive in life is not the pursuit of money or power. In other words, democratic socialism must be made to work throughout some large area. But the only area in which it could conceivably be made to work, in any near future, is western Europe. Apart from Australia and New Zealand, the tradition of democratic socialism can only be said to exist—and even there it only exists precariously—in Scandinavia, Germany, Austria, Czecho-Slovakia, Switzerland, the Low Countries, France, Britain, Spain, and Italy. Only in those countries are there still large numbers of people to whom the word "socialism" has some appeal and for whom it is bound up with liberty, equality, and internationalism. Elsewhere it either has no foothold or it means something different. In North America the masses are contented with capitalism, and one cannot tell what turn they will take when capitalism begins to collapse. In the USSR there prevails a sort of oligarchical collectivism which could only develop into democratic socialism against the will of the ruling minority. Into Asia even the word "socialism" has barely penetrated. The Asiatic nationalist movements are either fascist in character, or look toward Moscow, or manage to combine both attitudes: and at present all movements among the colored peoples are tinged by racial mysticism. In most of South America the position is essentially similar, so is it in Africa and the Middle East. Socialism does not exist anywhere, but even as an idea it is at present valid only in Europe. Of course, socialism cannot properly be said to be established until it is world-wide, but the process must begin somewhere, and I cannot imagine it beginning except through the federation of the western European states, transformed into socialist republics without colonial dependencies. Therefore a socialist United States of Europe seems to me the only worth-while political objective today. Such a federation would contain about 250 million people, including perhaps half the skilled industrial workers of the world. I do not need to be told that the difficulties of bringing any such thing into being are enormous and terrifying, and I will list some of them in a moment. But we ought not to feel that it is of its nature impossible, or that countries so different from one another would not voluntarily unite. A western European union is in itself a less improbable concatenation than the Soviet Union or the British Empire.

Now as to the difficulties. The greatest difficulty of all is the apathy and conservatism of people everywhere, their unawareness of danger, their inability to imagine anything new—in general, as Bertrand Russell put it recently, the unwillingness of the human race to acquiesce in its own survival. But there are also active malignant forces working against European unity, and there are existing economic relationships on which the European peoples depend for their standard of life and which are not compatible with true socialism. I list what seem to me to be the four main obstacles, explaining each of them as shortly as I can manage:

1. Russian hostility. The Russians cannot but be hostile to any European union not under their own control. The reasons, both the pretended and the real ones, are obvious. One has to count, therefore, with the danger of a preventive war, with the systematic terrorizing of the smaller nations, and with the sabotage of the Communist parties everywhere. Above all there is

the danger that the European masses will continue to believe in the Russian myth. As long as they believe it, the idea of a socialist Europe will not be sufficiently magnetic to call forth the necessary effort.

2. American hostility. If the United States remains capitalist, and especially if it needs markets for exports, it cannot regard a socialist Europe with a friendly eye. No doubt it is less likely than the USSR to intervene with brute force, but American pressure is an important factor because it can be exerted most easily on Britain, the one country in Europe which is outside the Russian orbit. Since 1940 Britain has kept its feet against the European dictators at the expense of becoming almost a dependency of the USA. Indeed, Britain can only get free of America by dropping the attempt to be an extra-European power. The English-speaking Dominions, the colonial dependencies, except perhaps in Africa, and even Britain's supplies of oil, are all hostages in American hands. Therefore there is always the danger that the United States will break up any European coalition by drawing Britain out of it.

3. Imperialism. The European peoples, and especially the British, have long owed their high standard of life to direct or indirect exploitation of the colored peoples. This relationship has never been made clear by official socialist propaganda, and the British worker, instead of being told that, by world standards, he is living above his income, has been taught to think of himself as an overworked, down-trodden slave. To the masses everywhere "socialism" means, or at least is associated with, higher wages, shorter hours, better houses, all-round social insurance, etc., etc. But it is by no means certain that we can afford these things if we throw away the advantages we derive from colonial exploitation. However evenly the national income is divided up, if the income as a whole falls, the working-class standard of living must fall with it. At best there is liable to be a long and uncomfortable reconstruction period for which public opinion has nowhere been prepared. But at the same time the European nations *must* stop being exploiters abroad if they are to build true socialism at home. The first step toward a European socialist federation is for the British to get out of India. But this entails something else. If the United States of Europe is to be self-sufficient and able to hold its own against Russia and America, it must include Africa and the Middle East. But that means that the position of the indigenous peoples in those countries must be changed out of recognition— that Morocco or Nigeria or Abyssinia must cease to be colonies or semicolonies and become autonomous republics on a complete equality with the European peoples. This entails a vast change of outlook and a bitter, complex struggle which is not likely to be settled without bloodshed. When the pinch comes the forces of imperialism will turn out to be extremely strong, and the British worker, if he has been taught to think of socialism in materialistic terms, may ultimately decide that it is better to remain an imperial power at the expense of playing second fiddle to America. In varying degrees all the European peoples, at any rate those who are to form part of the proposed union, will be faced with the same choice.

4. The Catholic Church. As the struggle between East and West becomes

more naked, there is danger that democratic socialists and mere reactionaries will be driven into combining in a sort of Popular Front. The Church is the likeliest bridge between them. In any case the Church will make every effort to capture and sterilize any movement aiming at European unity. The dangerous thing about the Church is that it is *not* reactionary in the ordinary sense. It is not tied to laissez-faire capitalism or to the existing class system, and will not necessarily perish with them. It is perfectly capable of coming to terms with socialism, or appearing to do so, provided that its own position is safeguarded. But if it is allowed to survive as a powerful organization, it will make the establishment of true socialism impossible, because its influence is and always must be against freedom of thought and speech, against human equality, and against any form of society tending to promote earthly happiness.

When I think of these and other difficulties, when I think of the enormous mental readjustment that would have to be made, the appearance of a socialist United States of Europe seems to me a very unlikely event. I don't mean that the bulk of the people are not prepared for it, in a passive way. I mean that I see no person or group of persons with the slightest chance of attaining power and at the same time with the imaginative grasp to see what is needed and to demand the necessary sacrifices from their followers. But I also can't at present see any other hopeful objective. At one time I believed that it might be possible to form the British Empire into a federation of socialist republics, but if that chance ever existed, we lost it by failing to liberate India, and by our attitude toward the colored peoples generally. It may be that Europe is finished and that in the long run some better form of society will arise in India or China. But I believe that it is only in Europe, if anywhere, that democratic socialism could be made a reality in short enough time to prevent the dropping of the atom bombs.

Of course, there are reasons, if not for optimism, at least for suspending judgment on certain points. One thing in our favor is that a major war is not likely to happen immediately. We could, I suppose, have the kind of war that consists in shooting rockets, but not a war involving the mobilization of tens of millions of men. At present any large army would simply melt away, and that may remain true for ten or even twenty years. Within that time some unexpected things might happen. For example, a powerful socialist movement might for the first time arise in the United States. In England it is now the fashion to talk of the United States as "capitalistic," with the implication that this is something unalterable, a sort of racial characteristic like the color of eyes or hair. But in fact it cannot be unalterable, since capitalism itself has manifestly no future, and we cannot be sure in advance that the next change in the United States will not be a change for the better.

Then, again, we do not know what changes will take place in the USSR if war can be staved off for the next generation or so. In a society of that type, a radical change of outlook always seems unlikely, not only because there can be no open opposition but because the regime, with its complete hold over education, news, etc., deliberately aims at preventing the pendulum swing between generations which seems to occur naturally in liberal societies. But for all we know the tendency of one generation to reject the ideas of the last is an abiding human characteristic which even the NKVD will be unable to eradicate. In that case there may by 1960 be millions of young Russians who are bored by dictatorship and loyalty parades, eager for more freedom, and friendly in their attitude toward the West.

Or again, it is even possible that if the world falls apart into three unconquerable superstates, the liberal tradition will be strong enough within the Anglo-American section of the world to make life tolerable and even offer some hope of progress. But all this is speculation. The actual outlook, so far as I can calculate the probabilities, is very dark, and any serious thought should start out from that fact.

3245. Domestic Diary

<u>1.7.47.</u> *Morning very still, with dense mists which cleared up later. Rather close. Evening cooler, with a little more wind & some light drizzling rain from about 6 pm onwards. Sea very calm.*

Went down to the bay I noticed on the way to Ardlussa, & collected about 4 cwt. of drift. A lot more still there, including pit props & large planks. Coming back, dropped A. & R. & the wood at Barnhill, then petrol ran out about half way to Kinuachdrach, so had to come back after a hard row. We had started out with about ¾ gall., evidently not enough for this journey, which would be about half the run to Ardlussa, ie. as a return journey about 8 miles. One must allow quite 1½ galls. for the run to Ardlussa. NB. that the engine stops when there is still about ½" of petrol in the tank. Starting now much better.

Gave liquid manure to one or two roses about to come into flower.

Young cormorants swimming in the sea with their mother—behaviour very similar to families of ducks. Four wild ducks (mallard) flying together—qy. whether two of them this year's birds. Two small birds I could not identify in the garden, one of them quite impressive, with reddish-brown rump, black head & a white spot on top of this.* The others seemed very interested in the strawberries, in spite of the pea-guards over them— Wild rose (white, but qy. whether not ordinary briar) in bloom. A good many of first peas in bloom.

Took out ½ gall petrol, making 17 galls. Drip is now negligible.

2 eggs (126).

<u>2.7.47.</u> *Dense mist in the morning, clearing somewhat in afternoon. Rain at about 5 pm. Fairly warm & very still. Sea very calm.*

Some turnips (sown 17.4.47.) almost ready to pull.

Wild roses out. Took out 2 galls. petrol, making 19 galls.

A. & B.D. fished last night—2 fish.

R.R.,[1] crossing from Tarbert today, saw a large shark in the strait.

3 eggs (129).

* Redstart? [Orwell's note on facing page.]

3.7.47. *Filthy day till about 8 pm. Mist & rain, sometimes only a drizzle, sometimes fairly heavy. Evening clearer. Sea calm.*

A few strawberries reddening.

Afraid we have an egg-eater among the hens. If so & I can detect her, shall kill her.

Petrol dripped about ¾ gall. owing to my leaving the tap pointing downwards. Put this into the car. Call it one gallon, making 20 galls.

3 eggs (132).

4.7.47. *Filthy day. Blowy, overcast, coldish & raining on & off, quite heavily at times. Sea choppy.*

Lealt herd have been down again (the reason for their coming here is no doubt the Highland bull) & trampled the peat, but not badly. Set up what they had knocked over. A lot of it is fairly dry. If there were about 3 good days it could be set up into small piles.

Could not do much out of doors. Gave liquid manure to some more roses. All except 3 roses now have flower buds coming.

Wild duck with young ones (could not see what kind, but did not look like sheld-duck) swimming in bay near Kinuachdrach.

A. & B.D. fished last night—again nothing. The lobster fishermen from Luing[2] say it is possible to catch some fish about 1 am.

2 eggs. Afraid there must be an egg-eater at work. (134).

5.7.47. *Better day. Blowy & windy all day (wind in west), & mostly sunny though coldish. No rain except for a short shower about 2 pm. Sea choppy, with breakers in the sound.*

Went over to Ardlussa to return the pony. Walked most of way, as it was too tiring sitting on the pony with no saddle, D.D. riding Prince. Had pony shod, then borrowed saddle & rode on to Tarbert. Only 6 miles, but somewhat sore after being on a horse for the first time in many years.

Saw a mountain hare near Tarbert. Definitely smaller than the brown hare, long legs, a lot of white round the rump. Saw several lots of skuas—the first time I have seen them, though I believe they are common here.

Roses full out at Ardlussa, some lupins already seeding, a red hot poker already in bloom.

Planted out 25 broccoli* seedlings which arrived yesterday by post. Not good weather for planting, especially after they have been out of the ground for several days.

2 eggs (136).

Took out 1 gall petrol making 21 galls.

6.7.47. *Fine, blowy, not very warm. Some black clouds occasionally, but no rain.*

A. fell & dislocated her shoulder. R.R. has taken her down to Craighouse to the doctor.[3]

Put new ropes on creels. Tacked down loose rib on boat & put on a small patch of paint. Thinned runner beans. Put net over "wild" red currants.

---

* cabbage [Orwell's note on facing page.]

Some strawberries reddening. One rose showing colour (pink). A little honeysuckle out, including some growing on the rocks almost in the sea.

Took out 4 galls petrol, making 25 gallons. Provided we have recorded takings-out correctly, & there has been no appreciable wastage, there should be 25 galls left, which has to last till the end of August. That is, our consumption from now on should not average more than 3 galls a week. The run to Ardlussa, by either boat or car, takes about 1½ galls for the return journey, so we should manage.

5 eggs (141).

1. Sir Richard Rees (1900–1970), editor, painter, and critic; he and Orwell became friends through *The Adelphi* (see headnote to *95*), and Rees was to be Orwell's literary executor. He came to Jura to paint and stayed with Orwell until September. In his *George Orwell: Fugitive from the Camp of Victory* he gives a good account of Orwell's life on Jura; and see passages reprinted in *Orwell Remembered* (115–23). One passage epitomises Orwell on Jura: 'Life on the isle of Jura revealed clearly another not unexpected characteristic, namely, his enthusiasm for heroic and desperate remedies. The district was supposed to be infested by adders [see, for example, *3242, 22.6.47*] and Orwell greatly relished the idea—though I can imagine no one who would be more reluctant to apply it—of the cigar cure for snake bites. This consisted, according to him, in lighting a cigar and then stubbing it out against the wound' (152; *Orwell Remembered*, 122).
2. Orwell writes this as 'Ling' but he must mean the island of Luing, rather than its adjacent islet of Lunga or a place on the mainland also called Lunga; all three are within about half-a-dozen miles of the northern tip of Jura. What tilts the likelihood towards Luing is the report of Orwell's escape from the whirlpool of Corryvreckan in the *Glasgow Herald*, 30 August 1947. This states that two fishermen came to the aid of Orwell's party and that they came from 'Toberonochy, island of Luing.' See *3257, 19.8.47, n. 3*.
3. Rees recalls this incident in his book: 'his sister dislocated her arm in jumping over a wall. Orwell rushed back to the house and called to me: "You've done first aid, haven't you? [Rees served with an ambulance unit on the Madrid front in the Spanish civil war.] Avril's put her arm out. You'll be able to get it back? You just have to jerk it sharply upwards, isn't that it?" The remedy did not work, perhaps because I didn't summon up enough sharpness (Orwell made no attempt to summon up any) and we had to drive the twenty-five miles to the doctor, who was also unsuccessful' (*George Orwell*, 152; *Orwell Remembered*, 122). See also *3247, 7.7.47*.

3246. To Leonard Moore

7 July 1947   Typewritten

Barnhill, Isle of Jura, Argyllshire

Dear Moore,

Many thanks for your letter of the 30th. I don't know M. David Rousset,[1] but I assume the publishers know who is a suitable person to write the introduction for "Homage to Catalonia," and I am quite happy to accept their choice. Actually in the present situation I don't think it would have been very wise to get Malraux to do it, even if he had been willing.[2]

Yours sincerely
[Signed] Eric Blair
Eric Blair

1. David Rousset wrote *L'Univers Concentrationnaire*, which Roger Senhouse translated into English in 1948, and *Les Jours de Notre Mort*. Orwell read Senhouse's translation of the first book against the original whilst in Hairmyres Hospital and had a copy of the second, but by early May 1948 had not then read it; see his letters to Senhouse, 3 May and 13 (or 20) May 1948, *3393* and *3399*.
2. Letter annotated in Moore's office: 'Wrote Charlot 10/7/47' (see *3184, n. 1*). For the proposal that Malraux write an introduction and for a note on Malraux, see *3209* and *3209, n. 1*.

3247. Domestic Diary

<u>7.7.47.</u> *Coldish, blowy, overcast, some rain. Sea roughish.*

As the doctor could not set A's arm, D.D., R.R. & B.D. took her across to Crinan in the boat. They returned on the tide about 11 pm. Evidently a nasty trip. A's arm was set at Lochgilphead & is evidently now all right.[1]

Too busy with R. etc. to do anything out of doors.[2]

Took out 1¾ galls. petrol, say 2 galls, making, 27 gallons.

2 eggs (143).

<u>8.7.47.</u> *Most of day rather cold & overcast, with showers. Some rain during last night. This evening fine & pleasant. Sea calm.*

Picked literally a handful of strawberries, the first fruits of the garden, barring gooseberries. Carrots sown 26.6.47 are up.

Many lettuces coming up among the oats in the field. This was over-sown with rye-grass, which would come up after the corn has been cut & form hay next year. Qy. whether wrong seed was used (rye-grass is very small seed) or merely impure seed.*

Deer in the field again—Must stop up hole.

4 eggs (147).

<u>9.7.47.</u> *Fine, sunny & blowy. Not very warm. Sea calm. Everything has dried up a great deal.*

Stacked peat into small piles. A good deal of it is pretty dry, especially the small blocks (NB. to cut thinner blocks next year.) Took up tulip bulbs.

2 eggs (149).

<u>10.7.47.</u> *Overcast nearly all day, but no rain. Not very warm. Sea calm, & this evening glassy.*

Pulled first turnips.

A. went fishing last night—6 saythe, 2 lithe.

Set creels (first time this year). The netting is old & may give, but they have new ropes on, so the frame-work should not be lost.

Paraffin getting very low. Another drum is ready for us, but it is questionable when it will arrive.

Drink gave out today—just 3 months for 12 bottles.[3] *No more has arrived yet.*

2 eggs (151).

---

* Chicory. Mixed in seed intentionally as it is supposed to improve the soil. [Orwell's note on facing page.]

<u>11.7.47.</u>   *Finer. A little rain during last night. Very faint drizzle for a few minutes during the day. Not much wind. Sea calm.*

Took up creels—nothing. One, I now notice, is damaged near the bottom, & a lobster could have crawled out. Put meta° round strawberries, which slugs are eating badly.

Several roses have buds opening—no white ones, I am glad to say. Picked a bunch of wild roses this afternoon. Three definitely different kinds of rose. One pink, apparently the ordinary briar, except that it had a smell, which I thought the briar did not. One a little rather frail white rose which I think is the "white rose of Scotland." Another also white, with more robust growth &—I think—blunter leaves. Both these last have something like the sweet briar smell.

Took out 1 gall petrol, making 28 galls. Managed to get the air-hole at the top open & measured the petrol. Cask seems almost half full, so my records have probably been about correct.

2 eggs (153).

<u>12.7.47.</u>   *Overcast most of day, with a few sunny intervals. In the evening a very few spots of rain, & stronger wind. Sea calm till evening, then roughening somewhat.*

R. has trampled on two of the cauliflowers. The others appear to have rooted all right. The first rose is out (salmon pink).

7 eggs (5 laid out) (160).

<u>13.7.47.</u>   *Some rain in the night, I think. Drizzle in the morning, clearing up to a beautiful, still, sunny afternoon & evening. Sea calm.*

Had to put prop for bough of one apple tree, because already weighted down with fruit. Got a small picking of strawberries, less than ½ lb. More coming. Many runners. Evidently they do well here, so shall try to put in some more this autumn if I can get the ground ready.

2 eggs (162).

1. Because the doctor at Craighouse could not set Avril's dislocated arm (see *3245, n. 3*), Donald Darroch, Bill Dunn, and Richard Rees took her across the Sound of Jura (about six miles, direct sailing—but see *3257, 16.8.47*) to the little port of Crinan on the mainland and then a further six miles by road to Lochgilphead, which lies on the shore of Loch Fyne. By the time she had her arm set, Avril had been driven some fifty miles on Jura's rough roads, sailed six miles, and then been driven a further six, before making the return trip of a dozen miles.
2. Rees, in his *George Orwell*, says that Orwell was 'certainly happy' on Jura, 'working in the garden, fishing for mackerel from a boat, being bullied by his adopted son' (149; *Orwell Remembered*, 120).
3. Brandy, presumably; see *3213, 14.4.47*.

3248. To Leonard Moore

14 July 1947   Typewritten

Barnhill, Isle of Jura, Argyllshire

Dear Moore,

I wonder if you could get in touch with the "Britain in Pictures" people and find out what they are doing about a booklet, "The British People," which I wrote for them 3 or 4 years ago. The history of it was this.[1]

In 1943 W. J. Turner,[2] who was editing the series, told me that they had had books on British scenery, British railways, etc., but none on the British people, and that they would like me to do one. I was not very keen on the idea, but as it was to be a short book (15,000) and Turner promised me I should have a free hand, I agreed. Before going to work I submitted a detailed synopsis, which was approved. I then wrote the book, and it was no sooner sent in than the reader for Collins's, who were publishing the series, raised a long series of objections which amounted, in effect, to a demand that I should turn the book into a much cruder kind of propaganda. I pointed out that I had closely followed the agreed synopsis, and said I was not going to change anything. Turner backed me up, and the matter seemed to be settled. About a year later, nothing having happened, I met Turner in the street and told him I thought I ought to have some money for the book, on which I had been promised an advance of £50. He said he could get me £25, and did so. About this time he told me it had been decided to get someone else to do a companion volume to mine, on the same subject, so as to give as it were two sides to the picture. They first got Edmund Blunden,[3] who made such a mess of it that his copy was unprintable, so there was another delay. They afterwards got someone else, I forget whom, to do the companion volume. Turner and his assistant, Miss Shannon, several times told me that the objections to my book had been over-ruled and that it would appear in due course. About a year ago I was sent the proofs and corrected them. I was told then, or shortly afterwards, that they were choosing the illustrations, and if I remember rightly Miss Shannon told me what the illustrations would be. During last winter Turner died suddenly, and Miss Shannon wrote to say that this would impose another short delay, but that the book would appear shortly. Since then nothing has happened. I think it must be more than 4 years since I submitted the manuscript.

I haven't the faintest interest in the book nor any desire that it should appear in print. It was simply a wartime book, part of a series designed to "sell" Britain in the USA. At the same time I obviously ought to have some more money out of them, at least the other half of the £50 advance. £50 was incidentally rather a small advance, since these books, when once on the market, usually sold largely. Unfortunately I have not my copy of the contract, as this was one of the documents that were destroyed when my flat was bombed in 1944.[4] However, I suppose that wouldn't matter, and I am sure Miss Shannon, if she is still helping to run the series, would be co-operative.

Yours sincerely
[Signed] Eric Blair
Eric Blair

Orwell's report of Blunden's failure in the Britain in Pictures series is surprising, for Blunden had already written *English Villages* for the series and it was published in 1941. Listed on the dust-jacket of Rose Macaulay's *Life Among the English* were two forthcoming books, both entitled *The British People*, one by George Orwell, the other by Edmund Blunden. Her volume was published in 1942 (the British Library copy is date-stamped 23 October 1942). Two other books dated 1942, John Piper's *British Romantic Artists* (reviewed in *TLS*, December 1942) and the Bishop of Chichester's *The English Church* (reviewed in *TLS*, August 1942) advertise *The British People* by Sir John Squire—no mention of Orwell or Blunden. Squire's book is advertised in 1943 on Noel Sabine's *The British Colonial Empire*. On Neville Cardus's *English Cricket* (1945), Orwell's and Blunden's books are said to be in preparation, but in 1946 and 1947 only Orwell's book is advertised—still as *The British People*—on a number of jackets. Orwell refers to the book as 'Britain in Pictures' (the title of the series) in his Payments Book. Two things are clear: the title must have been changed to *The English People* just before publication; and the publisher made three tries at getting two different books published, but only Orwell's appeared. Orwell's book was included in the section devoted to 'Social Life and Character.' See Peter Eads, 'Britain in Pictures,' *The Private Library*, 3rd Series, Vol. 9, No. 3 (Autumn 1986), 119–31; *The English People* is volume 100 of 132 issued.

1. *The English People* was commissioned for the Britain in Pictures series in September 1943. In his Payments Book Orwell recorded the work against the date 22 May 1944, with a note that payment was to be made later; that date would indicate when the typescript had been handed in to Collins. Against the date 14 July 1945 Orwell recorded the receipt of £20 towards payment for that book, so in recording in this letter the receipt of £25 his memory has played him slightly false. Though he did not realise it when he wrote to Moore, *The English People* was about to be published, in August 1947: Collins had not bothered to inform the author. The text is reproduced at *2475*. See also Orwell's letter to Moore, 8 September 1947 (*3265*), in which he seeks more copies than the single volume supplied by Collins, and 9 October 1947 (*3284*) for his letter to Julian Symons, thanking him for his review.
2. W. J. Turner (1889–1946), poet, novelist, and music critic who did a variety of publishing and journalistic work, including acting as general editor of the Britain in Pictures series for Collins. See *1743, n. 1*.
2. Edmund Charles Blunden (1896–1974), poet, critic, and teacher; see *1401, n. 1*.
4. Orwell and his wife were bombed out on 14 July 1944.

3249. Domestic Diary

<u>14.7.47.</u> *Warm, some wind from south, overcast part of the time, but no rain. Sea calm.*

Went down to collect drift. Boat ran well. Great difficulty in getting her afloat again on a stony beach, the tide having gone down a little while we were collecting drift. NB. with a boat as heavy as this one should always leave her anchored in fairly deep water.

Another rose out (dark red polyantha). Thinned apples.

Petrol drip, 2 pints.

4 eggs (166).

<u>15.7.47.</u> *Beautiful sunny day, one of the best we have had. Hardly any wind. Sea very calm.*

Stacked up peat. It makes a stack 4' by 5'. Most of it now pretty dry.

.*A. went fishing last night—nothing. Apparently they are catching hardly anything at Ardlussa either.*

Picked a very few strawberries.

3 eggs (169).

<u>16.7.47.</u> *A filthy day. Rain almost continuous until about 7 pm. Evidently some rain during last night as well. Sea calm.*

Thinned first carrots (final thinning).

3 eggs (172).

<u>17.7.47.</u> *Warm, rather close, overcast some of the time but no rain. Sea calm.*

Thinned radishes, put netting round third° peas (no more sticks).[1] *Another rose coming out. Candytuft budding, ditto poppies.*

Petrol drip ¾ gall. (owing to changing taps), plus, 1 quart previously, 1 gall, making 29 galls.

2 eggs, (174).

<u>18.7.47.</u> *Close, still day, overcast much of the time but not actually raining till 6 pm, when there was a heavy shower. Sea like glass. This morning so still that when a cormorant rose from the sea I could hear its wings flapping from my room (distance about 400 yards).*

Sowed perennial alyssum. Cut front grass & scattered sand on it.

Took out 1 gall. petrol, making 30 galls. This leaves 20 galls to last us to end of August, ie. about 3 galls a week, but we have the prospect of another 7 galls.

3 eggs (177).

<u>19.7.47.</u> *Some fairly heavy rain during last night. Today very warm & close, overcast a good deal of the time, but no rain. Sea less calm. Horseflies ("cligs") very bad.*

Dug a few of the first lot of potatoes (3 months in the ground)—much too small, must be left another 3 weeks or so. Picked a few strawberries, less than ½ lb.

Began making path.

Currants changing colour. Perhaps about 1 lb. in all in this garden. The third rose to come out is apparently the same as the first one. Of the dozen roses I had last year, only about 3 are bushes, the rest all polyantha, ramblers or climbers. May get some better ones this time as they are getting less scarce.

3 eggs (180).

Cylinder of Calor gas gave out today. Only 4 weeks this time. Put on the last one. NB. to send for more as soon as possible.

<u>20.7.47.</u> *Some rain in the night. Today warm & overcast, no rain till about*

7 pm when there was a light shower. Sea not very calm.

Started removing elder trees from place where gate will come.

Another rose out (dark red polyantha, like the other).

Petrol drip 1 quart.

3 eggs (183).

<u>21.7.47.</u> *Rain almost continuous till about 5 pm, after which it cleared & a strong wind began blowing from S. or SE. Sea rough all day, increasingly so in the evening.*

Could not do much out of doors. Thinned parsnips.

Some hens moulting. Today a double egg, supposed to be a bad sign, as it is said to be the last of the clutch so far as that particular hen is concerned.

4 eggs (187).

An eagle over the field today, soaring high up. It is always in windy weather that one sees them here.

<u>22.7.47.</u> *A very few drops of rain about 10 am, otherwise dry & windy, quite warm in afternoon. Sea rough.*

Finished path but could not sow it as it was too windy.

Eagle over field again today. Crows mobbing him appeared to succeed in forcing him down to the ground. Peat pretty dry in spite of yesterday's rain. Two or three more windy days, & it would be dry enough to bring in, after which a couple of weeks in the barn would finish it.

Petrol drip ½ gall (put this into car).

3 eggs (190).

<u>23.7.47.</u> *Rain almost continuous all day. Some mist in the morning. Strongish wind, mostly from south, in afternoon. Sea calm.*

Tried to set creels, but impossible to get boat out, as the tide was very low. Have set one buoy nearer to the anchor.

A. & B.D. caught 11 fish last night.

D.D. has started to mow the field behind the house, but impossible to continue in the rain.

Picked the last of the strawberries. In all about 1 to 2 lb.—perhaps not bad for first year.

3 eggs (193).

<u>24.7.47.</u> *Rain most of morning. Afternoon fairly fine, but not much sun. Some wind most of day, dropping in the evening. Sea calm.*

Sowed path (rather thin one end as there was not quite enough seed.)

A. now picking second lot of turnips (sown 22.5.47). First peas ready to pick in about a week.

Mended lobster box. Transferred the wood R.R. has cut to the stable. NB. to see whether it stays drier there.

I note one hen is steadily laying a pullet-sized egg. I think it must be a hen that was broody & has come off. Two hens went broody almost at once, when they can only have laid a very small clutch. One may have gone broody before she had finished her pullet eggs, & therefore is still laying the small ones.

Candytuft flowering. Two more polyantha roses almost out (lighter red than the others).

4 eggs (197.)

<u>25.7.47.</u> *Beautiful day. Morning overcast, warm & still, afternoon sunny. Hardly a breath of wind. Sea very calm.*

Removed straw from strawberry bed. Pegged down one or two runners to fill up gaps.

Hay cut in the field behind the house already in the small heaps. Not good hay, half of it rushes.

A. fished last night—nothing.

Some carrots ready to pull. Currants nearly ripe.

Today saw a pair of bullfinches. The cock very striking. Only the second time I have seen them here.

Petrol drip ¾ gall.

4 eggs (201). This makes almost exactly 200 in 2 months, or 2 doz. a week. If this was an average for 8 hens it will be all right, but of course they will go off when they begin to moult.

<u>26.7.47.</u> *Warm, very still day, but not very sunny. Sea calm.*

Part of the field behind the house has hay already in the small stacks, called here ricks, about 8 ft. high. Each of these appears to use up the hay of 400 or 500 square yards, ie. where the hay is poor, as here. Apparently, given good weather, the procedure is as follows. Soon after the hay is cut, perhaps 24 hours after, it is raked up into lines. These are then raked up into heaps about 2 ft. high. Next day these are scattered again. The hay is again raked into lines. Then it is raked together into a circle containing enough hay for a rick. Two people with pitchforks stand inside the circle & build the rick, which is tapered off when it has reached 5 or 6 feet. The sides are combed with the rake to get out the loose bits. Then a rope is strained over the top & tied to a thick twist of hay at the bottom on both sides (more usually 2 ropes, & some people weight them with stones). Given good weather, this whole process need only take about 3 days, but the hay has to dry in the rick for some days more before being stacked.

Pulled first carrots today.

Killed very large snake. As soon as it saw us it showed fight, turning round & hissing. I have not seen them do this before.

4 eggs (205).

<u>27.7.47.</u> *Beautiful hot day. No wind. Sea like glass.*

Planted 3 lupins—not very suitable weather or time of year for doing so.

Took up creels. 1 lobster, 1 crab. First lobster of the year. Lobster box is unsatisfactory, as it has too many apertures in it & therefore does not submerge properly. Could not reset creels, as we had no bait.

3 eggs (208).

---

1. After 'sticks,' Orwell wrote: 'thinned carrots (trimmings just large enough to eat)' but then crossed it through, presumably because he realised that the 'final thinning' had been done the preceding day.

3250. To Lydia Jackson

28 July 1947   Typewritten; copy

Barnhill, Isle of Jura, Argyllshire

Dear Lydia,

I have just received notice to quit the Wallington Cottage.[1] It was bound to happen sooner or later, and of course as it is only a weekly tenancy they can do it on very short notice. However the date given on the notice is August 4th, so that in theory your furniture ought to be removed by that date. I wrote off at once to the Solicitors explaining that you could hardly be expected to get out at such short notice, as you must find somewhere to put your furniture. If you want to write to them direct they are Balderston Warren & Co, Solicitors, Baldock, Herts. I have no doubt you could get more time, but of course if ordered to get out we have to do so, especially as I, the theoretical tenant, am not using the cottage at all, and you are only using it for week ends. I believe actually on a weekly tenancy they are supposed to give six week° notice. I am very sorry this should have happened.

If you'd like to come and stay any time, please do,[2] I shall be here till October, and there are always beds here. Just give me good notice, so that I can arrange about meeting you. The weather has been filthy but has lately turned nice again. Love to Pat.

Yours,
George

1. The Stores, Wallington; Orwell moved there on 2 April 1936, and it was his home until May 1940. He seems to have used it rarely thereafter (most often for a few days in 1940 and 1941, and perhaps a Bank Holiday weekend in 1942). Lydia Jackson (1899–1983; pen-name, 'Elisaveta Fen'; see *534A*) had met Eileen Blair in 1934, when they were graduate students at University College London, and they became close friends. (See *Remembering Orwell*, 66–68, where she says, 'I was always sorry that Eileen married George.') She and her flatmate, Patricia Donahue, used the cottage during and after the war. On 11 May 1945 Orwell wrote to her from Paris about their shared use of the cottage. He did not then want to give it up entirely, so Richard could 'get a few days of country air now and then.' His taking over Barnhill in the spring of 1946 ended any dependence he might feel on The Stores.
2. Lydia Jackson visited Barnhill 26 March to 2 April 1948. She might have retyped the final version of 'Such, Such Were the Joys' while she was there; see *3408*.

3251. To Leonard Moore

28 July 1947   Typewritten

Barnhill, Isle of Jura, Argyllshire

Dear Moore,

Herewith the proofs.[1] It seems quite a good translation, so far as I am able to judge. I have made a few corrections, but mostly of punctuation etc.

Many thanks for your offices in connection with the Britain in Pictures book.

I am getting on fairly well with the novel, and expect to finish the rough draft by October. I dare say it will need another six months° work on it after that, but I can't say yet when it is likely to be finished because I am not sure of my movements. I have to come back to London in October and shall probably stay at any rate a month, but we are thinking of spending most of the winter up here because I think it is not quite so cold here and fuel is a bit easier to get. If I do stay here I shall no doubt get on with the rewriting of the novel faster than if I am in London and involved in journalism. At any rate I have some hopes of finishing it fairly early next year.

Yours sincerely
[Signed] Eric Blair
Eric Blair

1. Presumably proofs of the French translation of *Animal Farm*, published in October 1947.

3252. Domestic Diary

<u>28.7.47.</u> *A dreadful day. About 8 am a violent thunderstorm & extremely heavy rain, going on for some hours. The burns immediately turned into large torrents & flowed across the fields. Surface of the road washed away in some places. Wooden bridge near Kinuachdrach washed away. Two drills of D.D's turnips destroyed. In the middle of the day it cleared up slightly, but there was more thunder & heavy rain during most of the afternoon. Dense "Scotch mist" in the evening. Everything in the garden looks battered & splashed with mud.*

In the afternoon tried fishing in the Lealt,[1] as we had to go to meet J.[2] Only 1 very small trout. There were more there, but without a boat it was impossible to get to the place where they were rising.

5 eggs (213).

<u>29.7.47.</u> *Fine sunny day, with some wind from the west. Sea calm.*

Made 1 lobster box. There will have to be two, as I have no box big enough to divide into compartments.

D.D. turning hay over again, but what was lying out is too wet to be built up into ricks. Picked a few roses—the first picking. Afraid grass-seed has been washed away from the path, but it is difficult to make sure.

3 eggs (216).

1. Lealt Burn runs from two small lochs a little south and to the west of Barnhill down to the Sound of Jura about five miles south of Barnhill; the small hamlet of Lealt stands where the road from Barnhill to Ardlussa crosses Lealt Burn.
2. Orwell's niece, Jane Dakin. Crick notes: 'That summer Humphrey Dakin, now a widower, sent his daughters, teenage Lucy and her sister Jane, just leaving the Women's Land Army, to stay with their aunt and uncle for a longer holiday. Their elder brother Henry also turned up, then a second lieutenant in the Army on leave. They liked their uncle Eric, though for days on end they hardly saw him, just like at Leeds [their home town] when they were small children, except at mealtimes since he worked almost without interruption' (527). See also Shelden, 461; U.S.: 422.

3253. Publication of *The English People*

August 1947

The English People was commissioned by Collins for its Britain in Pictures series. For a summary of the history of its writing and publication, see *3248*. The text is reproduced at 22 May 1944 (see *2475*), the date it was handed in to the publisher. According to Michael Carney, Collins printed 23,118 copies; 18,275 were sold, 316 remaindered, and the rest unsold (*Britain in Pictures: A History and Bibliography* (1995), 107). The plates were possibly scrapped in 1952. A Danish translation, *Det engelske Folk*, was published by Hasselbalch, 11 February 1948 (2,350 copies) and a German translation, *Die Engländer*, by Schlösser, December 1948 (5,000 copies). Mondadori bought the Italian rights, but these were cancelled in 1952 (Willison).

W. J. Turner, the series editor, chose the illustrations, and these are of a high order. Eight are in colour and seventeen in black-and-white. Among the artists are Walter Sickert, Lucien Pissarro, Graham Bell, Henry Lamb, Henry Moore, Laura Knight, John Minton, Edward Ardizzone, L. S. Lowry, and Feliks Topolski.

Although in its day it was only the sixty-first most popular of the 126 volumes published (James Fisher's *The Birds of Britain* was the most popular selling 84,218 copies), it is currently the mostly costly volume secondhand (Carney, 37, 65, and 121–23).

3254. 'In Defence of Comrade Zilliacus'

August–September? 1947; intended for *Tribune* but not published[1]

George Orwell
Barnhill
Isle of Jura, Argyll

Some weeks ago Mr K. Zilliacus[2] addressed a long and, as usual, abusive letter to *Tribune*, in which he accused it of having no definite and viable foreign policy, but of being in effect an anti-Russian paper while keeping up a show of hostility to Ernest Bevin. Bevin, he said, was far more realistic than *Tribune*, since he grasped that to oppose Russia it was necessary to rely on America and "bolster up Fascism," while *Tribune* was merely sitting on the fence, uttering contradictory slogans and getting nowhere.

I am not often in agreement with Mr Zilliacus, and it is therefore all the more of a pleasure to record my agreement with him on this occasion. Granting him his own special terminology, I think his accusation is fully justified. One must remember, of course, that in the mouths of Mr Zilliacus and his associates, words like democracy, Fascism or totalitarianism do not bear quite their normal meanings. In general they tend to turn into their opposites, Fascism meaning unfaked elections, democracy meaning minority rule, and so on. But this does not alter the fact that he is dwelling on real issues—issues on which *Tribune* has consistently, over a period of years, failed to make its position clear. He knows that the only big political questions in the world today are: for Russia—against Russia, for America—against America, for democracy—against democracy. And though he may describe his own activities in different words from what most of us would use, at least we can see at a glance where he stands.

But where does *Tribune* stand? I know, or think I know, what foreign policy *Tribune* favours, but I know it by inference and from private contacts. Casual readers can, and to my knowledge do, draw very different impressions. If one had to sum up *Tribune's apparent* policy in a single word, the name one would have to coin for it would be anti-Bevinism. The first rule of this "ism" is that when Bevin[3] says or does something, a way must be found of showing that it is wrong, even if it happens to be what *Tribune* was advocating in the previous week. The second rule is that though Russian policy may be criticised, extenuating circumstances must always be found. The third rule is that when the United States can be insulted, it must be insulted. The effect of framing a policy on these principles is that one cannot even find out what solution *Tribune* offers for the specific problems it most discusses. To take some examples. Is *Tribune* in favour of clearing out of Greece unconditionally? Does *Tribune* think the USSR should have the Dardanelles? Is *Tribune* in favour of unrestricted Jewish immigration into Palestine? Does *Tribune* think Egypt should be allowed to annex the Sudan? In some cases I know the answers, but I think it would be very difficult to discover them simply by reading the paper.

Part of the trouble, I believe, is that after building Bevin up into Public Enemy Number One, *Tribune* has found out that it is not genuinely in disagreement with him. Certainly there are real differences over Palestine, Spain and perhaps Greece, but broadly, I think, he and *Tribune* stand for the same kind of policy. There are, it is generally agreed, only three possible foreign policies for Great Britain. One is to do as Mr Zilliacus would have us do, ie., to become part of the Russian system, with a government perhaps less servile than that of Poland or Czechoslovakia, but essentially similar. Another is to move definitely into the orbit of the United States. And another is to become part of a federation of western European Socialist republics, including if possible Africa, and again if possible (though this is less likely) the British dominions. *Tribune*, I infer—for it has never been clearly stated—favours the third policy, and so I believe does Bevin, that is to say, the Government. But *Tribune* is not only involved in its personal feud with Bevin; it is also unwilling to face two facts—very unpopular facts at the moment—which must be faced if one is to discuss a Western union seriously. One is that such a union could hardly succeed without a friendly America behind it, and the other is that however peaceful its intentions might be, it would be bound to incur Russian hostility. It is exactly here that *Tribune* has failed as an organ of opinion. All its other equivocations, I believe, spring from a dread of flouting fashionable opinion on the subject of Russia and America.

One very noticeable thing in *Tribune* is the pretence that Bevin's policy is exclusively his own. Apparently he is a sort of runaway horse dragging an unwilling Cabinet behind him, and our policy would have been quite different—above all, our relations with the USSR would have been better—if only we had had a more enlightened foreign secretary. Now it is obvious that this cannot be so. A minister who is really thwarting the will of the rest of the government does not stay in office for two years. Why then the attempt to put all the blame on one person? Was it not because otherwise it would have been necessary to say a very unpopular thing: namely that a Labour Government, as such, is almost bound to be on bad terms with the government of the USSR? With a government headed by Pritt and Zilliacus we could no doubt have excellent relations, of a kind, with Russia, and with a government headed by Churchill and Beaverbrook we could probably patch up some kind of arrangement: but any government genuinely representative of the Labour movement *must* be regarded with hostility. From the point of view of the Russians and the Communists, Social Democracy is a deadly enemy, and to do them justice they have frequently admitted it. Even such controversial questions as the formation of a Western union are irrelevant here. Even if we had no influence in Europe and made no attempt to interfere there, it would still be to the interest of the Russian government to bring about the failure of the British Labour government, if possible. The reason is clear enough. Social Democracy, unlike capitalism, offers an alternative to Communism, and if somewhere or other it can be made to work on a big scale—if it turns out that after all it *is* possible to introduce Socialism without secret police forces, mass deportations and so forth—then the excuse for dictatorship vanishes. With a Labour government in office, relations with Russia, bad already, were bound to deteriorate. Various observers pointed this out at the time of the General Election, but I do not remember *Tribune* doing so, then or since. Was it not because it was easier, more popular, to encourage the widespread delusion that "a government of the Left can get on better with Russia" and that Communism is much the same thing as Socialism, only more so—and then, when things didn't turn out that way, to register pained surprise and look round for a scapegoat?

And what, I wonder, is behind *Tribune's* persistent anti-Americanism? In *Tribune* over the past year I can recall three polite references to America (one of those was a reference to Henry Wallace) and a whole string of petty insults. I have just received a letter from some students at an American university. They ask me if I can explain why *Tribune* thinks it necessary to boo at America. What am I to say to these people? I shall tell them what I believe to be the truth—namely that *Tribune's* anti-Americanism is not sincere but is an attempt to keep in with fashionable opinion. To be anti-American nowadays is to shout with the mob. Of course it is only a minor mob, but it is a vocal one. Although there was probably some growth of ill-feeling as a result of the presence of the American troops, I do not believe the mass of the people in this country are anti-American politically, and certainly they are not so culturally. But politico-literary intellectuals are not usually frightened of mass opinion. What they are frightened of is the prevailing opinion within their own group. At any given moment there is always an orthodoxy, a parrot cry which must be repeated, and in the more active section of the Left the orthodoxy of the moment is anti-Americanism. I believe part of the reason (I am thinking of some remarks in Mr G. D. H. Cole's last 1143-page compilation[4]) is the idea that if we can cut our links with the United States we might succeed in staying neutral in the case of Russia and America going to war. How anyone can believe this, after looking at the map and remembering what happened to neutrals in the late war, I do not know. There is also the rather mean consideration that the Americans are *not* really our enemies, that they are unlikely to start dropping atomic bombs on us or even to let us starve to death, and therefore that we can safely take liberties with them if it pays to do so. But at any rate the orthodoxy is there. To speak favourably of America, to recall that the Americans helped us in 1940 when the Russians were supplying the Germans with oil and setting on their Communist parties to sabotage the war effort, is to be branded as a "reactionary." And I suspect that when *Tribune* joins in the chorus it is more from fear of this label than from genuine conviction.

Surely, if one is going to write about foreign policy at all, there is one question that should be answered plainly. It is: "If you *had* to choose between Russia and America, which would you choose?" It will not do to give the usual quibbling answer, "I refuse to choose." In the end the choice may be forced upon us. We are no longer strong enough to stand alone, and if we fail to bring a western European union into being, we shall be obliged, in the long run, to subordinate our policy to that of one Great Power or the other. And in spite of all the fashionable chatter of the moment, everyone knows in his heart that we should choose America. The great mass of people in this country would, I believe, make this choice almost instinctively. Certainly there is a small minority that would choose the other way. Mr Zilliacus, for instance, is one of them. I think he is wrong, but at least he makes his position clear. I also know perfectly well what *Tribune's* position is. But has *Tribune* ever made it clear?

How subject we are in this country to the intellectual tyranny of minorities can be seen from the composition of the press. A foreign observer who judged Britain solely by its press would assume that the Conservative party was out and away the strongest party, with the Liberals second, the Communists third and the Labour party nowhere. The one genuine mass party has no daily paper that is undisputedly its own, and among the political weeklies it has no reliable supporter. Suppose *Tribune* came out with a plain statement of the principles that are implicit in some of its individual decisions—in its support of conscription, for instance. Would it be going against the main body of Labour party opinion? I doubt it. But it would be going against the fashionable minority who can make things unpleasant for a political journalist. These people have a regular technique of smears and ridicule—a whole specialised vocabulary designed to show that anyone who will not repeat the accepted catchwords is a rather laughable kind of lunatic. Mr Zilliacus, for instance, accuses *Tribune* of being "rabidly anti-Russian" (or "rabidly anti-Communist"—it was one or the other.) The key-word here is rabid. Other words used in this context are insensate, demented, "sick with hatred" (the *New Republic's* phrase) and maniacal. The upshot is that if from time to time you express a mild distaste for slave-labour camps or one-candidate elections, you are either insane or actuated by the worst motives. In the same way, when Henry Wallace is asked by a newspaper interviewer why he issues falsified versions of his speeches to the press, he replies: "So you are one of these people who are clamouring for war with Russia?" It doesn't answer the question, but it would frighten most people into silence. Or there is the milder kind of ridicule that consists in pretending that a reasoned opinion is indistinguishable from an absurd out-of-date prejudice. If you do not like Communism you are a red-baiter, a believer in Bolshevik atrocities, the nationalisation of women, Moscow Gold, and so on. Similarly, when Catholicism was almost as fashionable among the English intelligentsia as Communism is now, anyone who said that the Catholic Church was a sinister organisation and no friend to democracy, was promptly accused of swallowing the worst follies of the No-Popery organisations, of looking under his bed lest jesuits should be concealed there, of believing stories about babies' skeletons dug up from the floors of nunneries, and all the rest of it. But a few people stuck to their opinion, and I think it is safe to say that the Catholic Church is less fashionable now than it was then.

After all, what does it matter to be laughed at? The big public, in any case, usually doesn't see the joke, and if you state your principles clearly and stick to them, it is wonderful how people come round to you in the end. There is no doubt about whom *Tribune* is frightened of. It is frightened of the Communists, the fellow-travellers and the fellow-travellers of fellow-travellers. Hence its endless equivocations: a paragraph of protest when this of our friends is shot—silence when that one is shot, denunciation of this one faked election—qualified approval of that one, and so on. The result is that in American papers I have more than once seen the phrase "the Foot-Zilliacus group" (or words to that effect.) Of course Foot[5] and Zilliacus are not allies, but they can appear so from the outside. Meanwhile, does this kind of thing even conciliate the people it is aimed at? Does it conciliate Mr Zilliacus, for instance? He has been treated with remarkable tenderness by *Tribune*. He has been allowed to infest its correspondence columns like a perennial weed, and when a little while ago *Tribune* reviewed a book of his, I looked in vain in that review[6] for any plain statement of what he is or whose interests he is serving. Instead there was only a mild disagreement, a suggestion that he was perhaps a little over-zealous, a little given to special pleading—all this balanced by praise wherever possible, and headed by the friendly title, "The Fighting Propagandist." But is Mr Zilliacus grateful? On the contrary, only a few weeks later he turns round and without any provocation delivers a good hard boot on the shins.

It is hard to blame him, since he knows very well that *Tribune* is not on his side and does not really like him. But whereas he is willing to make this clear, *Tribune*, in spite of occasional side-thrusts, is not. I do not claim for Mr Zilliacus that he is honest, but at least he is sincere. We know where he stands, and he prefers to hit his enemies rather than his friends. Of course it is true that he is saying what is safe and fashionable at this moment, but I imagine he would stick to his opinions if the tide turned.

1. Although Orwell's proposed open letter to *Tribune* cannot be dated precisely, that it was written before he became ill in the autumn of 1947 is stated by him in his letter to Julian Symons, 2 January 1948; see *3325*. Several letters that autumn refer to his being in 'wretched health a lot of the year' (for example, see *3275, 3277, 3290, 3296, 3298*). He made a last entry in his Domestic Diary on 29 October (see *3299*), and on 31 October he wrote to Moore whilst ill in bed with inflammation of the lungs (see *3300*); that was the first of a handwritten sequence of letters—a clear indication of how sick he was. On 29 November he wrote to Anthony Powell saying that, though still on his back, he was 'getting better after many relapses'; see *3308*. Although he writes of being ill for much of the year, it is only on 20 September (of letters extant) that he first mentions illness. By 31 October he was incapacitated enough to be able to correspond only by hand. The text of his letter to *Tribune* is reproduced here from Orwell's typescript. His address at Barnhill is at the top of the first page. Page numbers 3–6 have been altered in blue-black Biro from the originally typed 4–7. The change does not indicate a cut, but, by the looks of the typescript, simple misnumbering. Orwell found a Biro particularly useful when writing in bed; see his letter to Symons, 2 January 1948, *3325*. However, this does not imply that the correction was made whilst Orwell was in bed.
2. For Konni Zilliacus and the correspondence in *Tribune* with Orwell in January 1947, see *2990*; and Orwell's London Letter to *Partisan Review*, Summer 1946, *2990*, from which it arose. Zilliacus (1894–1967) was at the time a left-wing Labour M.P. He was expelled from the Party in 1949 for persistent criticism of its foreign policy and lost his seat in the 1950 General Election when standing as an Independent Labour candidate. He re-entered Parliament in 1955 as a Labour M.P. See also *2990, n. 2.*
3. Ernest Bevin (1881–1951), a self-taught orphan who developed as one of the, if not *the*, most powerful and forceful trade-union leaders in Britain; see *763, n. 22*. He won a momentous court case for his union in 1929 against a leading barrister so earning the soubriquet, 'the dockers' KC' [King's Counsel]. From 1921 to 1940 he was General Secretary of the Transport and General Workers' Union, which he built up into a powerful organisation. In 1940 he became an MP and Churchill appointed him to the War Cabinet as Minister of Labour and National Service. From 1945–51 he was Foreign Secretary in Attlee's administration. Despite their political differences, he and Churchill shared certain 'bulldog characteristics.' The background to the animosity Bevin could arouse among readers of *Tribune* can be gauged from this passage from Tosco Fyvel's *George Orwell: A Personal Memoir*: 'Ernest Bevin, rather like a wooden man-of-war camouflaged as steel, became neurotically obsessed with trying against American opposition at all costs to prevent Jewish refugees from reaching Palestine, to prevent them indeed from leaving Europe. Ugly clashes and incidents took place. Within the Labour Party, the fight against Bevin was led by my wartime colleague, Richard Crossman [1907–1974, see *639, n. 7*]. In the columns of *Tribune*, I wrote pieces highly critical of Bevin's policies. As I knew well, the Palestine Arabs had a case, but Bevin's policy was not that. It was an attempt made at the expense of the Palestine Jews to sustain British strategic military and political control over the Middle East. . . . I knew Orwell completely disagreed with me: to him the Palestine Arabs were coloured Asians, the Palestine Jews the equivalent of the white rulers in India and Burma, an over-simplification from which he would not be budged, but then it did contain one sliver of truth' (142). See also Orwell's letter to Fyvel, 31 December 1947, *3322*, penultimate paragraph.
4. *The Intelligent Man's Guide to the Post-War World* (1947).
5. Michael Foot, left-wing Labour M.P. and a director of *Tribune* at this time. See also *1241, n. 2* and *2955, n. 2*.
6. The review was by T. R. Fyvel, of *Mirror of the Present* by Konni Zilliacus, *Tribune*, 6 June 1947. Fyvel had reviewed *Animal Farm* in *Tribune* on 24 August 1945. The review was short and bland, doing little more than recount 'the story'. It seems to avoid being percipient – hardly what might be expected of *Tribune*. *Animal Farm* was described as a 'gentle satire', 'a sad and gentle tale', and 'one of the best and most simply written books for the child of today.'

3255. Domestic Diary

<u>1.8.47.</u>   *Last 3 days at Glengarrisdale.*[1] *Marvellous weather all the time. Sea very calm. Journey either way 2 hours or a little under, or somewhat less than 1 gall. petrol. Going, we timed it so as to pass Kinuachdrach ½ hour before high tide, & coming back so as to leave Glengarrisdale about an hour before low tide.*

Fished yesterday in Loch nan Eilean.[2] *Six good-sized trout & some tiddlers. The two biggest fish were about ½ lb, the rest 5 or 6 ounces. Mostly taken on a claret-coloured fly. Lost about as many as I caught, owing to difficulty of using the landing net when single-handed.*

Enormous quantities of puffins on the west side of the island—seldom seen round this side.

A small patch of the garden appears to have been struck by lightning in the storm on Monday. The day after it happened I noticed that the potatoes seemed to be withering up. Now, over a patch about 5 yards square, nearly all the potatoes, most of the runner beans, some turnips & radishes, some young peas, & even some weeds, are frizzled up & dying, as though a flame had passed over them. It must be something to do with the storm, & I do not think the rush of water can have washed any bad substance into the bed. What is impressive is that all the damaged plants are in one patch, the rest of the garden being untouched. It is true, however, that within this patch there is one row of peas that does not seem affected.

Eggs from 30th onwards (3 days) 7 (223).

<u>2.8.47.</u>   *Warm & overcast. A few drops of rain about midday, light drizzle in the evening. Sea calm.*

Picked some peas (first picking, sown 12.4.47).

Forgot to mention, took out 3 galls. petrol before the trip to Glengarrisdale, making 33 galls. Think I have forgotten to enter some, so say 35 galls. Have secured a slightly larger allocation as from September. Hayfield now largely cut. About a dozen of the "ricks" now up. Today what was spread out had to be put in small heaps in expectation of rain.

2 eggs (225).

<u>3.8.47.</u>   *Evidently a good deal of rain in the night. This morning misty & drizzling. Afternoon warm, still & sunny. Sea calm.*

Took up creels—nothing. Prepared the two new creels & took over the new lobster boxes. The lobster in the store box was dead, probably owing to the fresh water washed down by the storm. The crab all right. Thinned carrots.

The blasted patch in the garden cannot actually have been struck by lightning, but I suppose that it is imaginable that a flash of lightning may pass through a sheet of rain on its way down, so that it reaches the ground heavily charged with electricity. At any rate, as the withering-up effect appeared the day after the storm, & has affected only one patch of the garden, it must be in some way connected with the storm.

Forgot to mention A. took out 1 gall. of petrol day before yesterday, making 36 galls.

Killed a small snake in the hayfield yesterday. D.D. killed one there the day before.

Another egg eaten today.

3 eggs. (228).

4.8.47. *Beautiful sunny day till evening. A fair amount of wind. Mist coming off the hill in the evening. Sea calm.*

The hayfield behind the house now cut, & about half of it in "ricks." It appears there will be 28 or 30 of these, which will make up into 3 stacks. So presumably a stack equals about 10 ricks. To build a rick, once the hay is more or less gathered together, takes 3 people about 20 minutes. One stands on top & builds up, while the others fork the hay to him.

Marigolds out. Ditto the pink flower (don't know name) which M. F.[3] gave us.

4 eggs (232).

5.8.47. *Scotch mist till about 4 pm. After that somewhat clearer, but no sun. Very close & still most of the day. Sea calm.*

Put out creels (all 4). Although it was almost low tide, nearly lost one of them, as there is evidently a hole about 200 yards along to the left from the harbour.

Some young seagulls (brown plumage) flying about.

R.R. began bringing in the peat, which is fairly dry but will have to dry off in the barn for some weeks.

3 eggs (235).

6.8.47. *Overcast all day, but no rain, & quite warm most of day. A fair amount of wind from west & north. Sea calm.*

Made nursery bed & pricked out wallflowers, sweet williams, lupins, canterbury bells & a few other flowers, which A. had sown. Started clearing one of the beds. Garden now in a bad state after being almost untouched for a week.

Another rose out (pale pink). Rambler by gate just coming out (crimson).

2 eggs (237).

1. Camping on the Atlantic side of Jura, in a shepherd's hut more or less opposite Barnhill.
2. Loch nan Eilean is about one mile inland from the west coast at Glengarrisdale and some 2½ to 3 miles as the crow flies from Barnhill.
3. Margaret Fletcher; see *2638, n. 13.*

3255A. To Lydia Jackson

7 August 1947   Typewritten

Barnhill Isle of Jura, Argyllshire

Dear Lydia,

I have received letters from various solicitors about the Wallington cottage. Your solicitor says you have told him you are my regular tenant and therefore cannot be evicted by Dearman. Dearman's solicitor threatens me with court proceedings – for what, I am not certain, but presumably because I ought not to have sublet unfurnished without getting Dearman's permission. I have written to both telling them that so far as my intentions went the arrangement between you and me was certainly not a regular tenancy. There was no kind of lease or written agreement between us. It was simply a friendly arrangement which incidentally left me slightly out of pocket, as over a period of years I was paying the rates as well as the rent, and merely recouping the rent from you. It is possible, however, that Dearman has latterly been paying the rates, as I do not remember getting a rates demand during the past year.

Obviously you ought to leave the cottage if Dearman wants it. You merely use it for weekends, whereas he wants to live in it. It would also be extremely unpleasant to have court proceedings which either you or I, whoever is the defendant, is bound to lose, as we have no sort of standing in the matter if the owner wants the house for himself.

Yours
[Signed] George

3255B. Domestic Diary

<u>7.8.47.</u> *Beautiful, sunny, warm day. Little wind. Sea calm & very blue.*

Took up creels. All 4 completely empty. Tried anchoring the boat in a new place. Not sure whether we can get to her there at high tide, but if so will save the misery of dragging her up & down.

Cut grass in front. Scythed down ragwort in hen-run.

4 eggs. 2 of these laid out, including one which looked as if it had been laid some days. Also another which had got broken in the house, perhaps owing to insufficient chaff in the nesting boxes. (241).

<u>8.8.47.</u> *Beautiful sunny day. A good deal of wind from south. Sea slightly less calm.*

Set creels. Place where we tried anchoring the boat is not good as one cannot get to it at high tide. Tried anchoring in front of slip, but about 5 yards further out, with a long shore rope, along which one could work the dinghy at high tide.

Took runners off strawberries, except two which I have allowed to root to fill up gaps.

A., J. & B.D. caught 39 fish last night, including 8 mackerel (first this year.)

One or two clarkia beginning to flower.

3 eggs, also another Richard broke. Shells are very thin—NB. to get more shell grit. (244).

3256. To George Woodcock

9 August 1947   Typewritten

Barnhill, Isle of Jura, Argyllshire

Dear George,

I at last get round to answering your letter of 25th July. I am, as you,° say in principle prepared to do an article in the series you mention, but "in principle" is about right, because I am busy and don't want to undertake any more work in the near future. I am struggling with this novel which I hope to finish early in 1948. I don't even expect to finish the rough draft before about October, then I must come to London for about a month to see to various things and do one or two articles I have promised, then I shall get down to the rewriting of the book which will probably take me 4 or 5 months. It always takes me a hell of a time to write a book even if I am doing nothing else, and I can't help doing an occasional article, usually for some American magazine, because one must earn some money occasionally.

I think probably I shall come back in November and we shall spend the winter here. I can work here with fewer interruptions, and I think we shall be less cold here. The climate, although wet, is not quite so cold as England, and it is much easier to get fuel. We are saving our coal as much as possible and hope to start the winter with a reserve of 3 tons, and you can get oil by the 40 gallon drum here, whereas last winter in London you had to go down on your knees to get a gallon once a fortnight. There are also wood and peat, which are a fag to collect but help out the coal. Part of the winter may be pretty bleak and one is sometimes cut off from the mainland for a week or two, but it doesn't matter so long as you have flour in hand to make scones. Latterly the weather has been quite incredible, and I am afraid we shall be paying for it soon. Last week we went round in the boat and spent a couple of days on the completely uninhabited Atlantic side of the island in an empty shepherd's hut—no beds, but otherwise quite comfortable. There are beautiful white beaches round that side, and if you do about an hour's climb into the hills you come to lochs which are full of trout but never fished because too unget-atable. This last week of course we've all been breaking our backs helping to get the hay in, including Richard, who likes to roll about in the hay stark naked. If you want to come here any time, of course do, only just give me a week's notice because of meeting. After September the weather gets pretty wild, though I know there are very warm days even in mid winter.

I got two copies of the FDC[1] bulletin. I am not too happy about following up the Nunn May case, ie, building him up as a well-meaning man who has been victimised. I think the Home Secretary can make hay of this claim if he wants to. I signed the first petition, not without misgivings, simply because I thought 10 years too stiff a sentence (assuming that *any* prison sentence is ever justified.) If I had had to argue the case, I should have pointed out that if he had communicated the information to the USA he would probably have got off with 2 years at most. But the fact is that he was an ordinary spy—I don't mean that he was doing it for money—and went out to Canada as part of a spy ring. I suppose you read the Blue Book[2] on the subject. It also seems to me a weak argument to say that he felt information was being withheld from an ally, because in his position he must have known that the Russians never communicated military information to anybody. However, in so far as the object is simply to get him out of jail somewhat earlier, I am not against it.

Yours
George

1. This was *Freedom Defence Committee Bulletin*, 5, July–August 1947. This issue outlines action taken to have Nunn May's sentence reduced, achieving, if possible, 'early release.' For details of the case, see Orwell's letter to Vernon Richards, 6 August 1946, *3042, n. 3.*
2. Issued by the Canadian government; see Orwell's letter to Dwight Macdonald, 15 April 1947, *3215.*

3257. Domestic Diary

<u>9.8.47.</u> *Dry, warm, windy day. Wind veering about, mostly south & east. Breakers on the sea in the morning, calm in afternoon & evening.*

Weeded raspberries. Burnt some of the grass in the side patch.

Two snakes killed in the hayfield yesterday. Large slowworm (about 1 ft. long) in the garden today.

Took out 2½ galls petrol, making 38½ galls (ie. about 10–12 galls left till end of August, but we have some supplementary coupons.[1])

3 eggs (247).

<u>10.8.47.</u> *Dry & warm, somewhat less sunny, very little wind. Sea very calm.*

Went down to the near bay, next beyond Barnhill, to collect driftwood. A good deal there, including a large block which would do for a small anvil.

Everything in garden very dried up. Seedlings in nursery bed have to be watered every evening, & even so I think some of the wallflowers have died. A few runner beans trying to flower (sown 5.6.47). Dug some more of the first lot of potatoes, sown nearly 4 months ago. Now quite good, but of course not good as "new" potatoes as they are not an early kind. The others will I am afraid come to nothing after their blasting.

Took out ½ gall petrol, making 39 galls.

2 eggs (249).

<u>11.8.47.</u> *Mostly overcast, less warm than yesterday. Sea calm. Sowed turnips & a few swedes (probably not too late as a last sowing.) Gave liquid manure to runner beans, which, even apart from the blasted ones, are not very good.*

Another rambler coming out (pink).

Berries on rowan trees getting red. Hazel nuts pretty large.

4 eggs (253).

<u>12.8.47.</u> *Warm, dry, fairly sunny, some wind. Sea calm. Earth now very dried up.*

A. & the others fishing last night—about 30 fish, including 1 mackerel.
Brought home oar to make mast for boat.
2 eggs (255).
<u>13.8.47.</u> *Blazing hot day. Sea calm.*
Made mast for boat (6½ feet high, ie. six & a half after clearing the
gunwhale.)
New drum of paraffin arrived.
4 eggs (259).
<u>14.8.47.</u> *Blazing hot day, about the hottest we have had. Sea like glass.*
Tried to raise creels—no use as the tide was not low enough. After this
fished, but only 2 saithe.
One or two godetias coming out.
Took out 1½ galls. petrol, making 40½ galls.
5 eggs (264).
Rats in byre very bad. Reset traps, caught one rat.
<u>15.8.47.</u> *Similar day to yesterday.*
Everything very dried up. Water in tank very low—about 2 days' supply, I
should say, unless it rains.
New barrel of oil arrived yesterday, but the old one is not quite finished
yet. It was started on 6.5.47. Supposing it to last 2 weeks more, as I should
think it would by the weight of it, our average summer consumption (40 galls
in about 14–15 weeks) is less than 3 galls a week.
Started cylinder of Calor Gas today. The last, which gave out yesterday,
was started on 19.7.47, so has run less than 4 weeks.
4 eggs (268).
<u>16.8.47.</u> *Fine hot day, little wind. Sea very calm.*
Went over to Crinan to buy oatmeal. About 1 hour 10 minutes going
(probably about 8 miles), more coming back, owing to aiming too far south
& being swept down the sound by the tide.
Took out ¾ gall petrol, making about 41½ galls.
Last night saw the northern lights for the first time. Long streaks of white
stuff, like cloud, forming an arc[2] in the sky, & every now & then an
extraordinary flickering passing over them, as though a searchlight were
playing upon them.
3 eggs (271).
<u>19.8.47.</u> *Since 17.8.47. at Glengarrisdale. Fine weather all the time. Sea*
calm. Water supply has dried up & will not begin again until it rains. Well in
field fairly good water.
Time to Glengarrisdale about 1 hour 45 minutes. On return journey today
ran into the whirlpool[3] & were all nearly drowned. Engine sucked off by the
sea & went to the bottom. Just managed to keep the boat steady with the oars,
& after going through the whirlpool twice, ran into smooth water & found
ourselves only about 100 yards from Eilean Mór,[4] so ran in quickly &
managed to clamber ashore. H.D.[5] jumped ashore first with the rope, then
the boat overturned spilling L.D.,[6] R. & myself into the sea. R. trapped under
the boat for a moment, but we managed to get him out. Most of the stuff in
the boat lost including the oars. Eilean Mór is larger than it looks—I should

say 2 acres at least. The whole surface completely undermined by puffins' nests. Countless wild birds, including many young cormorants learning to fly. Curiously enough it has a considerable pool of what appears to be fresh water, so there must be a spring. No wood whatever on the island, as there is no place where drift could fetch up. However we managed to get my cigarette lighter dry & made a fire of dead grass & lumps of dry peat, prised off the surface, at which we dried our clothes. We were taken off about 3 hours later by the Ling° fishermen who happened to be bringing picknickers round. We left Glengarrisdale at about 10.30, which was about 2 hours after high tide, & must have struck Corryvreckan at about 11.30, ie. when the tide had been ebbing about 3 hours. It appears this was the very worst time, & one should time it so as to pass Corryvreckan on slack water. The boat is all right. Only serious loss, the engine & 12 blankets.

Yesterday fished Loch nan Eilean & a Bhùrra.[7] 12 trout, mostly small. There are a lot of fish in a Bhùrra but I could not catch anything over about 5 ounces. It is very shallow, with a sandy or shingly bottom.

Took out 1½ galls. petrol making 43 galls.

Eggs for last 3 days 15 (286).

20.8.47.   Weather as before. Sea very calm. The house has now had no water for about 4 days.

Caulked boat as best I could, not having either tar or proper caulking twine, & being very short of plasticine. She was not much damaged, merely a grating & one seat gone, & a little sprung near the bows, which I think I have tightened up.

Godetias now well in flower. All except one rose have now flowered. Marrow has a good many fruits coming but no flowers out yet.

Yesterday put in an L.T. battery in the wireless. They are supposed to last 2 months, the H.T. batteries 4 months, so we shall need one of each about 20th October. NB. to write about 10th October.

5 eggs (291).

21.8.47.   Weather as before. Sea a little less calm.

Cleared strawberry bed. Runners still growing very fast. Some gladioli now have flower buds. One or two raspberries fruiting (only one or two berries).

5 eggs (296).

22.8.47.   More overcast than yesterday, still very hot. Sea less calm.

Started trying to make new back seat for boat.

Some red hot pokers have buds. Turnips sown 11.8.47 are up in places. Honeysuckle almost over. Dead shrew on the path. Corn ripening in places. Candytuft almost over. Seedlings in nursery bed still alive in spite of drought.

8 eggs (4 laid out) (304).

Old drum of paraffin about at an end. Begun 7.5.47. Ie. 40 galls. has lasted 14–15 weeks, so that summer expenditure averages less than 3 galls. a week.

23.8.47.   Warm & dry, a good deal of wind (W.) at times, no sign of rain. Sea calm.

Planted 25 sprouting broccoli on place where I had taken the peas up. Not

*very good weather for planting, & they had been several days in the post as
well.*

5 eggs (309).

<u>24.8.47.</u>   *Weather much as before. Heavy low mist late last night & early
this morning, but no sign of rain. Sea very calm.*

*Cut grass in front. Took up the potatoes, as they had withered up—would
not make any more growth. Slightly better than I had expected, as they had
only been planted 3 months when blasted. About 100 lb. from 5 rows (about
25 lb. of seed), & perhaps 10–20 pounds had been dug before. The seed was
Great Scott, & with normal growth I think one might expect 2¾ cwt. from
this amount of seed.*

4 eggs (313).

1. Fuel was strictly rationed, but sometimes supplementary supplies were allowed against specially issued coupons.
2. 'an arc' makes sense, but the writing looks more like 'a one,' which makes no sense.
3. The whirlpool in the Gulf of Corryvreckan, between Jura and Scarba, was—and still is—extremely dangerous. Orwell makes light of this escapade, but they were singularly fortunate not to be drowned. Crick reproduces Henry Dakin's graphic account (527–29) and Orwell's statement that the story was reported to the *Daily Express* (see Orwell's letter to Anthony Powell, 8 September 1947, *3267*). It has not been traced in the London editions of the *Daily Express* held by the British Library; a search of the *Scottish Daily Express* made on the editor's behalf by Mrs. Helen Stokes in the National Library of Scotland, Edinburgh, and by Mr. Telfer Stokes in the Mitchell Library, Glasgow, proved fruitless. No copies were held in Edinburgh; in Glasgow there were no copies of a Scottish edition for August; no mention was made in the September issues (from the second number of which the masthead name changed from *Daily Express* to *Scottish Daily Express*). It *was* reported by the *Glasgow Herald*, 30 August 1947. This stated: 'They had gone to see the whirlpool when their motor-boat was drawn into one of the smaller whirlpools and overturned. Fortunately, with Mr Blair's help, they all reached a small islet from which, after several hours, they were rescued by two fishermen from Toberonochy, island of Luing.' Luing is north of Scarba, and Toberonochy is six or seven miles from the north tip of Jura and a little further from Eilean Mór, the islet referred to. Both Donald Darroch and Ian McKechnie stoutly defended Orwell: Orwell knew well what he was doing, even though he might have taken more advice: he had simply misread the tide tables which was 'easy enough to do' (Crick, 529). Shelden gives a briefer account, 461–62; U.S.: 422–23.
4. Eilean Mór is a little island some five hundred yards off the northwest tip of Jura. Orwell omits the accent.
5. Henry Dakin; see *3252, n. 2.*
6. Lucy Dakin; see *3252, n. 2.*
7. Loch a Bhùrra lies a little to the southeast of Loch nan Eilean and is midway between the east and west coasts of Jura. Orwell spells it 'Bura.'

3258. To Leonard Moore

25 August 1947   Typewritten

Barnhill, Isle of Jura, Argyllshire

Dear Moore,

I don't think it is worth doing an article I don't especially want to do, for thirty-five dollars. Could you be kind enough to tell the Saturday Review people that I can't do reviews at these rates.[1]

Yours sincerely
[Signed] Eric Blair
Eric Blair

1. Annotated in Moore's office: 'Wrote Saturday Review 28/8/47' (the '8' of '28' is unclearly drawn). Orwell's letter is date-stamped as having been received on the 28th. In another hand is written 'letter'—presumably Moore's instruction to his secretary to write to *The Saturday Review of Literature*. The topic of the review has not been traced. In 1947 $35 was less than £8.14s.

3259. To William Phillips, *Partisan Review*

25 August 1947   Typewritten

Barnhill, Isle of Jura, Argyllshire

Dear Phillips,
Many thanks for your letter of July 16th (only just reached me.) I'll write something for you when I can,[1] but I'm struggling with a novel which I don't expect to get finished till some time next spring. I am trying not to do anything else, which is partly why I am staying in Scotland and not going back to London. All this time you have very kindly kept me on your free list, but please don't do so any more as I am taking out a subscription to the English edition.

I expect to be in London for a little while in November, otherwise the above address will find me.

Yours
[Signed] Geo. Orwell
George Orwell

1. Orwell's next contribution to *Partisan Review* was to be 'Reflections on Gandhi,' published in January 1949. This was included in two *Partisan Review* anthologies edited by Phillips and Philip Rahv (1953 and 1962).

3260. Domestic Diary

25.8.47.   *Weather as before. Sea less calm this morning, but glassy again in the afternoon.*
Finished mending boat. Seat not good. Very difficult job putting it in unless one has good timber & a vice to shape it in.
One or two gladioli out (pink). A few rowan berries ripe.
Started new drum of paraffin. Should last at least to middle of November.
7 eggs (320).

26.8.47.   *Weather as before. Sea very calm.*

Dug over patch where potatoes had been. Ground very dry & lumpy. Perpetual spinach to go here. Should have been sown 2–3 weeks ago. Sowed grass seed in bare patches on path.

A. tried the boat last night—still letting in water badly. More caulking needed near bows.

R.R. saw a grampus (or something of the kind) in the sound today.

3 eggs (323).

27.8.47.   *As before. A little less warm. Sea calm.*

Caulked boat some more & applied a little tar. Difficult to apply as I had no brush.

Cylinder of Calor Gas gave out today. Put on new one. The last has gone only for 12 days. However we have used nothing else for cooking & heating water for over a week, as until there is water in the tanks it is dangerous to light the fire.

Runner beans & late peas very poor, no doubt owing to drought.

5 eggs (328).

28.8.47.   *As before. Very warm in afternoon.*

Sowed perpetual spinach. Should have been sown about 3 weeks ago, but I had not the ground ready.

D.D. started cutting corn. Seemingly much better than last year, with more & better straw.

Honeysuckle over, most rowan berries ripe, loosestrife about over, some blackberries red, a good many hazel nuts, but not ripe yet. A good many corn marigolds about—A. says she did not see any last year. Dews now very heavy, which is the salvation of turnips in the garden.

4 eggs (332).

29.8.47.   *As before. Very hot in afternoon. Sea glassy.*

Tried boat on water. Does not seem to take in quite as badly. Watered sprouting broccoli, which look very sorry for themselves.

Have sent for Calor Gas.

4 eggs (336).

30.8.47.   *As before. A little less warm. Sea calm.*

Tried fishing in the Lealt again. It is dried up into a series of disconnected shallow pools in which actually there are a good many fish, but all very small. Could not catch anything even as large as ¼ lb. Also when the water is so shrunken the fish can see you & will not rise unless you hide yourself while casting.

Yellow gladioli out. One or two sweet peas beginning to flower.

4 eggs (346).

31.8.47.   *Somewhat less warm. Overcast & sometimes misty. Sea calm.*

Most of afternoon trying to mend typewriter. Removed more strawberry runners. Started on new balancer meal.

1 egg (341).

3261. To Leonard Moore

1 September 1947   Typewritten

Barnhill, Isle of Jura, Argyllshire

Dear Moore,

Many thanks for your letter of the 26th August.

I have signed the book and sent it on to the Sino-Internationale people. I shouldn't have thought it was necessary to write to them, beyond sending the book.[1]

A friend of mine in Paris has just written to tell me that someone called Jean Texcier, whom I had not heard of, has been engaged to write a foreword to the French edition of "Animal Farm."[2] Texcier wants some biographical details, which I will send him, and he also wants copies of "Down & Out" and "Wigan Pier." I don't know whether any of these are available (I suppose a Left Book Club copy of W.P. would be), but if you have any, and there is no mistake about the matter, I should be obliged if you would send him them. The only thing is that I have the impression that you told me they had engaged someone else to do the preface. Perhaps you could confirm this with Odile Pathé.

We have had wonderful weather here for 6 weeks or more, in fact we are now suffering from a severe drought, which is not a common complaint in these parts. I expect to be in London during November and then return here for the winter.

Yours sincerely
Eric Blair

1. Probably a copy of *Animal Farm*.
2. "Animal Farm" is underlined and in the margin someone in Moore's office has written "Homage to Catalonia." Below that is written: 'No copies.' After Kopp (whose introduction was not used), and the proposals that Malraux and David Rousset should write an introduction, Jean Texcier actually did so. He was a former member of the Resistance and Texcier was a pseudonym.

3262. To Brenda Salkeld

1 September 1947   Typed and handwritten

Barnhill, Isle of Jura, Argyllshire

Dearest Brenda,

At last I get round to answering your letter. We have had unheard-of weather here for the last six weeks, one blazing day after another, and in fact at present we're suffering from a severe drought, which is not a usual complaint in these parts. There has been no water in the taps for nearly a fortnight, and everyone has had to stagger to and fro with buckets from a well about 200 yards away. However there have been plenty of people to do it as the house was very full with people staying. We made several expeditions round to Glengarrisdale and slept a couple of nights in the shepherd's cottage—no beds, only blankets and piles of bracken, but otherwise quite comfortable. Unfortunately on the last expedition we had a bad boat accident on the way back and 4 of us including Richard were nearly drowned. We got into the whirlpool, owing to trying to go through the gulf at the wrong state of the tide, and the outboard motor was sucked off the boat. We managed to get out of it with the oars and then got to one of the little islands, just rocks covered with sea birds, which are dotted about there. The sea was pretty bad and the boat turned over as we were getting ashore, so that we lost everything we had including the oars and including 12 blankets. We might normally have expected to be there till next day, but luckily a boat came past some hours later and took us off. Luckily, also, it was a hot day and we managed to get a fire going and dry our clothes. Richard loved every moment of it except when he went into the water. The boat which picked us up put us off at the bay we used to call the W bay,[1] and then we had to walk home over the hill, barefooted because most of our boots had gone with the other wreckage.[2] Our boat luckily wasn't damaged apart from the loss of the engine, but I'm trying to get hold of a bigger one as these trips are really a bit too unsafe in a little rowing boat. I went fishing in the lochs near Glengarrisdale both times (I've got to continue in pen because the wire of the typewriter has slipped) & caught quite a lot of trout. Several of these lochs are full of trout but never fished because however you approach them it's a day's expedition to get there.

We're going to spend the winter up here, but I shall be in London roughly for November—I haven't fixed a date because it partly depends on when I finish the rough draft of my novel. I'll let you know later just when I am coming up.

Love
Eric

1. Presumably the adjacent bays of Glentrosdale and Gleann nam Muc at the northwestern tip of Jura. Eilean Mór lies opposite the centre point of the 'W.'
2. This would involve a walk of at least three miles over rough country.

3263. To Fredric Warburg

1 September 1947   Typewritten

Barnhill, Isle of Jura, Argyllshire

Dear Fred,

Many thanks for your letter of the 27th August.

I expect to be in London roughly for November. I am not at any rate coming up before then, unless something unexpected happens. I have to come then, because there are one or two things to be seen to, and also I stupidly let myself in for giving a lecture early in November.[1] I hope to finish the rough draft of the novel some time in October, and I should think the rewriting would take quite four or five months. It is an awful mess at present, but I think has possibilities. I can work quietly here, and I think we shall be more comfortable for the winter here than in London, as the fuel situation is decidedly better. We have had quite incredible weather for the last six weeks or so, one blazing day after another. We are even suffering from a severe drought, which is not a common complaint in these parts, and have had no water in our taps for 10 days. Richard is very well, growing enormous and talking a good deal more. If you are coming back in October I expect I shall see you when I come up.

I suppose everyone is loading you with commissions to execute in the USA, but if you do happen to have about 20 dollars loose I wish you would buy me a pair of shoes. You could send them by post and I can repay you at this end. Some time back I got a friend in New York to send me a pair size 12, but it appears the American sizes are different and they were too small. But I know that shoes that fit you fit me. Don't do it if it puts you out at all, just if it crosses your mind and you see a pair of stout walking shoes that would fit.

Please give my love to Pamela.

Yours
George

1. The lecture was to be at the Working Men's College, Crowndale Road, London NW1, on 12 November 1947; see *3271, n. 4.*

3264. Domestic Diary

1.9.47. *Much as before. Sea calm.*
They have started cutting D.D.'s field with the reaper & binder. This makes much larger sheaves, which I think are somewhat easier to build into stooks. Saw a grampus[1] momentarily.
1 egg & 1 laid out (343).
2.9.47. *Cooler, & distinctly chilly in evening. Wind from W. & heavy low cloud a good deal of the time, but still no rain. Sea calm. Fire in sitting room for first time today.*
Weeded between blackcurrants etc. with help of G.,[2] & lit a bonfire in hopes of getting some ash to spread. All that patch of ground is obviously very sour & I think needs potash as well as lime. Shall try to get some Kainit.[3]
D.D.'s corn now all cut & stooked (binder was here today.)
2 eggs (345).
3.9.47. *Cold & overcast, with low clouds. A very few spots of rain, not enough to wet the ground. More rain coming, by appearances. Wind from S. Sea rougher.*
Felt unwell, did nothing out of doors. The field in front cut & stooked today, in spite of various mishaps to binder (string breaking etc.) About half a dozen rabbits killed. Three hens now broody.
Finished up cask of petrol.
1 egg (346).
4.9.47. *Evidently a very little rain in the night. Fairly persistent but very*

thin drizzle most of day. Stream to tank still dry, soil only wetted about 1″ deep.

Sea less calm.

New wheelbarrow arrived (rather too small.) Began manuring patch for spring cabbages. Retied one or two apple trees. At least 3 hens now broody.

1 egg (347).

5.9.47.[4] *Somewhat more rain, but clearing up again this afternoon. Stream to tank still not affected. This evening very clear, with some sun. Sea fairly calm.*

Unwell (chest), hardly went outside. Turnips sown 11.8.47 want thinning.

1 egg (348).

6.9.47. *Some rain, including one or two heavyish showers. Tomorrow we intend taking the top off the tank to get some water direct if it rains. Ought to have done this earlier. Little rain & midges awful. Sea calm.*

Thinned carrots & turnips, weeded between gooseberries, transplanted alyssum to nursery bed, ditto one or two rooted strawberry runners. Gooseberries very poor & have hardly made any growth this year. Presumably sour soil, though it had a fairly good liming this spring. If obtainable shall apply Kainit to make up the potash, then more lime in spring. Dug in 1 lb. of Epsom salts under the apple tree which I think has magnesium deficiency.

1 egg (349).

7.9.47. *Drizzle most of day. A few patches of sun. Water in taps now, but none in hot tank. Sea calm. Ground still very dry a few inches down.*

Started making pen for ducklings. Am ordering 6. (3 weeks).

Cylinder of Calor Gas gave out. Cannot light kitchen fire till water in hot tank.

Ate first cabbage today (planted 5.7.47).

1 egg (350).

1. Orwell spells this 'granpus.'
2. Probably Gwen O'Shaughnessy, Eileen's sister-in-law, who came up to Jura with her children (Crick, 527).
3. Kainit is the German name for hydrous magnesium sulphate with potassium chloride (found in salt deposits); it was used as a fertiliser.
4. The dates 5.9.47 and 6.9.47 are dated as 1945.

3265. To Leonard Moore

8 September 1947   Typewritten

> Barnhill
> Isle of Jura
> Argyllshire

Dear Moore,

The contracts are herewith, duly signed.

The Britain in Pictures people[1] only sent me one copy of "The English People." I forget how the contract stood, but I suppose the usual six copies were allowed. If not, I wonder if you could procure me two or three extra copies. I should like some to give away.

> Yours sincerely
> [Signed] Eric Blair
> Eric Blair

1. Collins; see *3248*. Annotations made to this letter in Moore's office indicate that the contract did not allow for six copies for the author; and that Moore asked Collins to provide two or three copies on 12 September.

3266. To Stanley Unwin

8 September 1947   Typewritten

> Barnhill, Isle of Jura, Argyllshire

Dear Sir Stanley,

Many thanks for your letter of September 2nd.[1]

I am very flattered that you should think me a suitable person to write the book on "How Democracy works," but I am afraid I simply cannot undertake it, because I have not the time. I am struggling with a novel which I hope to finish by the spring, and I am trying to do nothing else meanwhile. I hope you will forgive me.

By the way, I rather think I neglected to answer a letter from your firm, giving me some information about the rare book "Secret Remedies", and the reason why it was not reprinted.[2] I was glad to get some more facts on the subject, and am sorry that I should have failed to answer, but I have no secretary here and often get behind with my correspondence.

> Yours sincerely
> [Signed] Geo. Orwell
> George Orwell

1. Stanley Unwin wrote in connection with his work on the British Council. He said suggestions had been received from overseas that 'a good popular, illustrated book should be written by a British subject, with an impressive name, under some such title as HOW DEMOCRACY WORKS. . . .' It should deal with all the leading countries, including Russia. It should not be argued that the British form of democracy was best, but that democratic institutions, adapted to the needs of different countries—agricultural as distinct from

industrial, rich as distinct from poor—was the best means of ensuring happiness for the peoples concerned. 'If this job were well done' (and Sir Stanley was quoting from suggestions received), 'it is probable that our real thesis that the British form is best would emerge, without it being necessary to point the moral.' The phrase 'our real thesis' sounds as if Sir Stanley was not quoting directly from suggestions from overseas but from a summary of those suggestions made by the British Council. He thought Orwell 'undoubtedly the best person' to write such a book; it should not conflict with his recent book 'on the British people,' *The English People*.

2. See *3208, n. 2.*

3267. To Anthony Powell

8 September 1947   Typewritten

Barnhill, Isle of Jura, Argyllshire

Dear Tony,[1]

Thanks so much for your postcard which I think was rather lucky to get here—at any rate I think the crofter who brings the post the last seven miles might have suppressed it if he had seen it.[2] I am coming down to London about the beginning of November, but probably only for about a month. We are planning to spend the winter here, because I can get on with my work without constantly getting bogged down in journalism, and also I think it will be a bit more comfortable here in spite of the mud and isolation. One is better off for fuel here, and on the whole better off for food. The worst privation really is bread rationing, and the new petrol cut, as we unavoidably have to make a car journey once a week to fetch groceries etc. We have got the house quite comfortable now, except that of course we are still using oil lamps for lighting, and I have got a bit of garden round. We have had incredible weather, indeed a severe drought, with the result that there was no water in the taps for about a fortnight, during which time nobody had a bath. Theoretically one can bathe in the sea, but I find it much too cold at my time of life and have never been in it except once or twice involuntarily. Recently four of us including Richard were all but drowned in the famous whirlpool of Corrievrechan° which came into a film called "I know where I'm going."[3] There was a very incorrect account of the disaster in the Daily Express.[4] It was very unpleasant while it lasted, and it ended by our being literally wrecked on a desert island where we might have been stranded for a day or two, but very luckily some lobster fishermen saw the fire we lit for a signal and got us off. Richard loved every moment of it except when he was actually in the water. He is getting enormous and talking a good deal more. He had a bad fall earlier in the year and scarred his forehead, but I imagine the scar will disappear after a year or two. I am getting on with my novel and hope to finish it in the spring if I don't do anything else. I know that if I return to London and get caught up in weekly articles I shall never get on with anything longer. One just seems to have a limited capacity for work nowadays and one has to husband it. Mrs Christen[5] says you sent me a book—I think a reprint of some Victorian novels to which you wrote an introduction[6]—but she hasn't sent it on yet. Many thanks any way. I'll ring you up as soon as I return to London. Please give my love to Violet.[7]

Yours
George

1. Anthony Powell (1905–2000), novelist and editor; see *2656, ns. 1* and *3*.
2. The postcard was of the Donald McGill type: 'Male Customer: "Do you keep stationery, miss?" Young Lady Assistant: "Sometimes I wriggle a little." '
3. *I Know Where I'm Going* was a British film, starring Wendy Hiller and Roger Livesey, released in 1946.
4. No news item in the *Daily Express* has been traced; see *3257, 19.8.47* and *n. 3*.
5. Mrs. Christen (now Mrs. Miranda Wood) was staying in Orwell's flat in London. There she typed a draft of *Nineteen Eighty-Four* and a fair copy of 'Such, Such Were the Joys'; see *3308, n. 3*. See also her Memoir, *3735*.
6. *Novels of High Society from the Victorian Age*, edited and with an introduction, by Anthony Powell (1947). This includes Disraeli's *Henrietta Temple*; *Guy Livingstone*, by G. A. Lawrence; and *Moths*, by 'Ouida.'
7. The Lady Violet Powell, Anthony Powell's wife.

3268. To George Woodcock

8 September 1947   Typewritten

Barnhill, Isle of Jura, Argyllshire

Dear George,

Thanks ever so for the tea, which was most welcome. I hope you could really spare it.[1] I am coming up to London for November, but shall probably only stay about a month. I think the winter here will be a bit more bearable than in London, in spite of the mud and the isolation, so we are going to try wintering here. I am getting on fairly well with the novel, which I hope to finish by the spring if I don't do anything else. We have had incredible weather, six weeks without rain, resulting in a severe drought which is almost unheard of in these parts. We had no water in our taps for more than a fortnight, during which nobody had a bath, but they're beginning to trickle again after the recent rain. Thanks to the good weather they got the hay and oats in quickly. Some years the harvest is an absolute nightmare here, and you have to go round the stooks feeling the sheaves and taking them in hastily as soon as they are dry. I hope you have a nice time in Switzerland. No doubt there is plenty to eat there, anyway. All the best to Inge.

Yours
George

1. Woodcock and his wife did not drink tea and supplemented Orwell's meagre ration from time to time by sending him theirs.

3269. Domestic Diary

8.9.47.   *Raining on & off through the day, with sunny patches. Rain at times fairly heavy. Little wind. Sea calm. Put up place for ducklings. Sweet peas fairly well out. Soil still extremely dry.*
   No eggs. (350).
9.9.47.   *Raining all or most of last night. Violent rain during much of the day, & very violent wind from S. & W. Sea very rough till evening, when it calmed somewhat. Water in taps now normal. Spinach germinating.*
   1 egg (351).
10.9.47.   *Rain a good deal of the day. Little wind till evening. Sea fairly calm.*
   No eggs (351).

3270. BBC Contract for Excerpt from *The Road to Wigan Pier*
Broadcast 11 September 1947

On 3 September 1947, T. Jungstedt, a Swedish Programme Assistant in the BBC Overseas Service, wrote to Miss B. H. Alexander of the BBC Copyright Department asking her to clear his use of some 130 lines of the Swedish translation of *The Road to Wigan Pier* ('reading time about 10 minutes') for use in a broadcast to be transmitted on 11 September. Miss Alexander wrote to Orwell (at Canonbury Square) on 4 September, sending him a contract. Part of this document is missing, including the area where Orwell would have signed. The contract bears a date stamp, 15 September 1947, indicating it was returned.

3271. Domestic Diary

11.9.47.   *Light rain most of the morning, clearing up in evening. Little wind. Sea fairly calm.*
   Picked the first bunch of sweet peas. Everything very flattened out by the wind & rain. Clarkia & godetias about over.
   No eggs. (351).

The last double opening of Domestic Diary IV was used by Orwell for various notes. The question marks and ticks reproduced are as in the manuscript.
   On verso:

   Before going away.

   Take up all crops.
   Weed all patches.
   Spread manure.
   Put wire across gap.
   Get in stakes.

Put barbed wire round cherry trees.
Cut grass.
Dig patch for spring vegetables.
Mark places for fruit trees etc.
Plant tulip bulbs & peonies (?)
Plant perennial flowers (if any).
Make bottom of gate rabbit-proof.
Weight down hen-house.
Drag up & cover boat.
Prune bush roses (?)
Make sure fruit trees properly tied.
Make sure wood etc. is in dry place.
Oil / calor gas.
Engine?[1]
Grease tools.
Manure fruit trees & bushes √

   Wanted
Fence wire
Barbed wire
Wire netting[2]
Staples (large)
Stakes (for barbed wire)
Angle irons.
Wheelbarrow √
Tarpaulins.

On recto:

"Coming Up"	*not later than*	*30.4.48*
"Burmese Days"	..	*31.10.48*
"Down & Out"	..	*30.4.49[3]*
"Homage to Catalonia"		
"Critical Essays"		*when original edit.s*
"Animal Farm"		*out of print*

12.11.47 —*lecture, Working Men's College, Crowndale Rd. NW.1.*
   time? (lecture 45–60 mins.)[4]
November —*introduction (Borough Librarian. St. Pancras.*
   Town Hall, Euston Rd.
   TER 7070)

£7,826–8–7 (19–6.47)
   (£250)
   (£150)[5]

1. Crossed through.
2. Crossed through; 'Barbed wire' is probably a substitution.
3. These are presumably the dates when Orwell expected his books to be published in the

Uniform Edition. *Coming Up for Air* was published in May 1948; *Burmese Days*, January 1949; *Down and Out in Paris and London*, September 1949; *Homage to Catalonia*, February 1951; *Critical Essays*, 22 February 1951. *Animal Farm* appeared in a cheap edition, similar in appearance to the Uniform Edition, in June 1949, but was not re-set until October 1965 for the Collected Edition.

4. Orwell was too ill to leave Jura to give this lecture. The St Pancras Borough Librarian, Frederick Sinclair, was keen to develop cultural activities and would almost certainly have introduced Orwell.

5. Presumably money received by Orwell, although whether £7,826 8s 7d was the amount received on 19 June 1947 or up until that date is not known. After the publication of *Animal Farm*, he certainly received much larger royalties and fees than those recorded for earlier years in his Payments Book.

3272. Domestic Diary

Volume V of Orwell's Domestic Diary (as he described and numbered it) runs on immediately from Volume IV. It continues, with two major breaks and a period entered by Orwell's sister, Avril, until 24 December 1948. The first part of the Diary—to 10 May 1948—is written on thirty-three recto and three verso pages of a notebook measuring $9\frac{3}{4} \times 7\frac{3}{4}$ in., with twenty-six printed lines to a page. Orwell broke off entries at 29 October 1947, and Avril continued from 27 December 1947 to 10 May 1948. Orwell re-opened the diary after seven months' absence in hospital (as he put it) on 31 July 1948 and continued until 24 December 1948, when he had just completed *Nineteen Eighty-Four*. This second part of the diary is written on a further twenty-five pages of the notebook, on fifteen of which are written notes (usually brief) on the versos. Orwell's entries are reproduced chronologically. Avril's entries are reproduced by kind permission of her husband, William Dunn. The four for 27–30 December 1947 are placed together, chronologically; those from 1 January to 10 May 1948 have been gathered together as an Appendix to 1948.

12.9.47. *Raining a good deal of the day. Strong wind, mostly from S. till evening. Sea rough.*
Applied chicken manure to the place for the new black currants.° Had to stake some of the raspberries, which were being loosened at the root. NB. to put wires next year.
9 eggs (laid out.) (360).
13.9.47. *Fine but overcast most of day. Little wind. A few spots of rain in the evening. Not very warm. Breakers on sea most of day.*
Planted about 50 spring cabbage.
Put on new cylinder of Calor Gas.
9 eggs (laid out.) (369.)
14.9.47. *Driving rain most of day till evening, when it cleared up somewhat. Violent wind from SW, dropping a little in the evening. Sea very rough most of day.*
No eggs (369).
15.9.47. *Rain part of day. Violent wind from S. in afternoon. Sea rough.*
Took the 3 broodies out of the henhouse & let them loose in the back yard, in hopes this may cure them.

Most of afternoon opening up drain from kitchen sink, which was blocked.

15 galls petrol arrived (supposed to last to end of October.) About 2 tons of coal delivered.

1 egg (370).

<u>16.9.47.</u> *Raining till about 5 pm.*

Gave the grass path its first cut, chiefly to keep down dandelions etc.

9 eggs (laid out). (379).

<u>17.9.47.</u> *Finer. Only a few drops of rain. Sunny most of day, but not very warm. Little wind. Sea fairly calm.*

Put broodies back. Re-covered drain, provisionally. Edged off path, which now looks fairly good.

6 eggs (4 laid out). (385).

<u>18.9.47.</u> *Only a drop or two of rain, about 5 pm. Otherwise fine autumnal weather, sunny but not very warm. Little wind sea calm.*

Tarred bottom of boat, ie. as thoroughly as I could, as there was only a little tar left.

D.D. is building a stack in the field behind the house. Some of his own hay already stowed away in the barn.

Picked about ½ lb. of nuts, more or less ripe. A. picked about 1 lb. blackberries (the first this year). R. R. found some mushrooms, not very many but large & good.

2 eggs (387).

3273. To Helmut Klöse

19 September 1947   Typewritten

Barnhill, Isle of Jura, Argyllshire

Dear Klose,

I am sure it was you who sent us a box of beautiful apples last week. I can't thank you enough—we are always so glad to get hold of fruit here, where there isn't much to be had except blackberries. I have got a few apples° trees of my own now, which I put in during the winter, but of course they are very tiny trees and I can't hope for much off them for another year or two.

I wonder how you are getting on. I am assuming that you are still at the same place. We have made ourselves quite comfortable here now and have got a bit of garden broken in, and we intend spending the winter here, though I shall be in London during November. Although it doesn't seem as though it would be so if you look at the map, I think the winters here are less cold, and one is certainly better off as regards fuel. On the whole one is also better off for food, as one can keep hens and so forth. The croft on which this house stands has been derelict, but it is beginning to be cultivated again, and I rather want if it can be arranged to share a tractor with the man who intends to take it over. I was going to write asking your advice any way, because I remember that it was you who first told me about a very light tractor, about 6 hp., called

205

an Iron Horse. Do you know whether a machine of this type is powerful enough to [be] used in the field, and at the same time manoeuvrable enough to use in the garden. For my own use I want something with which one could plough up small patches between fruit trees etc, but also I would like to know whether a thing of this type will take attachments such as a harrow or hay-cutter, and whether it would have a pulley-wheel off which one could run an electric light plant or a small saw. Also whether any of these small tractors run off paraffin or whether they are all petrol. I would be much obliged if you could give me some advice about this.

We had a marvellous summer, so much so that there was quite a severe drought for several weeks. My little boy is now nearly three and a half and is getting enormous. I am busy on a novel which I hope to finish about May, which is part of the reason for staying the winter here, as I don't want to get involved in journalism at present. With many thanks again for the apples.

Yours
Geo. Orwell

3274. Domestic Diary

<u>19.9.47.</u> *Weather much as yesterday. No rain. Little or no wind. Sea fairly calm.*
Applied wood ash (& peat ash) to gooseberries.
B.D. bought 22 lambs, presumably about 6 months old, price 43/6^d each.
Took out 2 galls petrol. 2 galls.
3 eggs (390).

3275. To Arthur Koestler

20 September 1947   Typewritten

Barnhill, Isle of Jura, Argyllshire

Dear Arthur,
I think a Ukrainian refugee named Ihor Sevcenko[1] may have written to you—he told me that he had written and that you had not yet answered.

What he wanted to know was whether they could translate some of your stuff into Ukrainian, without payment of course, for distribution among the Ukrainian D.Ps, who now seem to have printing outfits of their own going in the American Zone and in Belgium. I told him I thought you would be delighted to have your stuff disseminated among Soviet citizens and would not press for payment, which in any case these people could not make. They made a Ukrainian translation of "Animal Farm" which appeared recently, reasonably well printed and got up, and, so far as I could judge by my correspondence with Sevcenko, well translated. I have just heard from them that the American authorities in Munich have siezed° 1500 copies of it and handed them over to the Soviet repatriation people, but it appears about 2000 copies got distributed among the D.Ps first. If you decide to let them have some of your stuff, I think it is well to treat it as a matter of confidence and not tell too many people this end, as the whole thing is more or less illicit. Sevcenko asked me simultaneously whether he thought Laski[2] would agree to let them have some of his stuff (they are apparently trying to get hold of representative samples of Western thought.) I told him to have nothing to do with Laski and by no means let a person of that type know that illicit printing in Soviet languages is going on in the allied zones, but I told him you were a person to be trusted. I am sure we ought to help these people all we can, and I have been saying ever since 1945 that the DPs were a godsent opportunity for breaking down the wall between Russia and the west. If our government won't see this, one must do what one can privately.

I shall be in London during November but am going to spend the winter up here because I think it will be easier to keep warm (more coal etc.) and because I want to get on with the novel I am doing. I hope to finish it about next spring, and I am not doing much else in the meantime. I have been in wretched health a lot of the year—my chest as usual—starting with last winter. But we are quite comfortable here and better off for food than in London. Richard is getting enormous. Love to Mamaine.

Yours
George

1. Ihor Szewczenko; see *3187* and *3188*.
2. Harold J. Laski (1893–1950), political theorist, Marxist, author, and journalist, was connected with the London School of Economics from 1920 and Professor of Political Science in the University of London from 1926, member of the Fabian Executive, 1922 and 1936, member of the Executive Committee of the Labour Party, 1936–49. See *1241, n. 4*. Although critical of Laski, Orwell had appealed for support for him after Laski lost an action for libel; see 'As I Please,' 67, 27 December 1946, *3140*.

3275A. To Christy & Moore

20 September 1947   Typewritten

Barnhill, Isle of Jura, Argyllshire

Dear Sir,

Many thanks for your letter of the 15th.

1. I have no objection to the date of writing being omitted from the French version of "Animal Farm." (Incidentally the date given was 1943–44, not 1941–42, but I do not suppose this would make any difference.)

2. I would be much obliged if copies could be sent to the following:

Andre Gide, Malraux, Mauriac, Jean-paul° Sartre, Albert Camus, Paul Mounier ("Esprit,") Simone de Beauvoir, Julian Green, Jules Romains.[1]

Yours faithfully
[Signed] Eric Blair
Eric Blair

1. Annotated in Moore's office: 'Told W G Corp 25/9/47.'

3276. Domestic Diary

<u>20.9.47.</u> *Fairly heavy rain in the morning. Rest of day overcast, still, fairly warm. Sea calm. Little wind till evening.*

Took up last lot of peas.

Took out 1 gall petrol. 3 galls.

It is now pretty dark at 8 pm.

3 eggs (393).

<u>21.9.47.</u> *Beautiful clear day, not very warm. A very few light drops of rain. Sea calm.*

2 eggs (395).

<u>22.9.47.</u> *Violent rain & wind almost continuous all day, clearing slightly in the evening. Wind mostly from S. Sea very rough.*

2 eggs (397).

<u>23.9.47.</u> *Squally, with some sun & fairly sharp showers of rain. Sea roughish.*

Went fishing in Lussa river.[1] Hooked a salmon (3–4 lb. by his appearance) but lost him almost immediately. Cast did not break so presumably he was only lightly hooked.

Took out 2½ galls petrol. 5½ galls.

4 eggs (401).

<u>24.9.47.</u> *Raining lightly most of morning, clearing in afternoon. Wind mostly from N. or N.W. Sea roughish in morning, calming in afternoon.*

R.R. picked a considerable quantity of mushrooms.

Took runners off strawberries (this must be the 4th or 5th time).

2 eggs (403).

<u>25.9.47.</u> *Beautiful clear day, sunny most of the time. Sea calm.*

Picked first marrow (the only one & very poor.)

Apples came from Rankin.[2] About 15–20 lb. of eating apples, ditto of cookers, & some pears.

3 eggs (406).

<u>26.9.47.</u> *Beautiful clear day till late evening, when a little rain. Fairly warm. Sea calm.*

Field in front "hutted," ie. put up into small stacks, today.

2 eggs (408).

<u>27.9.47.</u> *Horrible day. Thin driving rain all day, wind from W. Sea variable, sometimes quite rough.*

Worked out area of Barnhill croft as accurately as I could from the 6" map. Exclusive of the garden & the marshy field it appears to me to be just over 16 acres.

Started sack of wheat (140 lb) today. Three hens now moulting. One broody.

3 eggs (411).

<u>28.9.47.</u> *Alternative rain & sun all day. Rather cold. Sea fairly calm.*

Bracken mostly going brown.

Took out 2 galls petrol. 7½ galls.

1 egg (412).

1. The Lussa River runs southeast across Jura into the sea via Ardlussa and Inverlussa.
2. Rankin was a greengrocer on the mainland.

3277. To David Astor

29 September 1947   Typewritten

Barnhill, Isle of Jura, Argyllshire

Dear David,

I wonder how things are going with you and the family. I am going to be in London for November to see to some odds and ends of business, but after that we intend spending the winter here. I think it will be easier to keep warm here, as we are better off for coal etc., also I am struggling with this novel and can work more quietly here. I hope to finish it some time in the spring. I have got on fairly well but not so fast as I could have wished because I have been in wretched health a lot of the year, starting with last winter. We have got the house a lot more in order and some more garden broken in, and I am going to send up some more furniture this winter. I think the Barnhill croft is going to be farmed after all, which eases my conscience about living here. A chap I don't think you have met named Bill Dunn, who lost a foot in the war, has been living with the Darrochs all the summer as a pupil, and in the spring he is going to take over the Barnhill croft and live with us. Apart from the land getting cultivated again, it is very convenient for us because we can then share implements such as a small tractor which it [is] not worth getting for the garden alone, and also have various animals which I have hitherto hesitated to get for fear a moment should come when nobody was here. We have had a marvellous summer here, in fact there was a severe drought and no bath water for ten days. Four of us including Richard were nearly drowned in Corrievrechan,° an event which got into the newspapers even as far away as Glasgow.[1] Richard is getting enormous and unbelievably destructive, and is now talking a good deal more. I expect your baby will have grown out of recognition by this time. I don't know if you're going to be up here any time in the winter but if so do look in here. There's always a bed and food of sorts, and the road is I think slightly better as it's being drained in places. Your friend Donovan came over riding on Bob and bearing incredible quantities of food, evidently sure he would find us starving. Actually we do very well for food here except bread, because we buy huge hunks of venison off the Fletchers whenever they break up a deer, also lobsters, and we have a few hens and can get plenty of milk.

Please remember me to your wife.

Yours
George

P.S. Do you want Bob wintered again by any chance? I got hay for him last year and he seemed to me in pretty good condition when I took him back, though I'm no judge. Till the day I took him back I had never mounted him, because the Darrochs had built up a picture of him as a sort of raging unicorn, and I was in such poor health I felt I was getting past that sort of thing. Actually he was as good as gold even when ridden bareback.

1. No reference has been traced; some issues of Glasgow newspapers could not be found.

3278. Domestic Diary

29.9.47   *A nasty day. Patches of sun, but mostly thin driving rain, & decidedly cold. Wind from W. & N. Sea fairly calm in daytime.*
  1 egg (413).
30.9.47   *Somewhat better day. Some light showers. Sea fairly calm.*
  3 eggs (416).

3279. What Is the English Character?
World Digest, October 1947

Except for its last paragraph, this extract draws from all but paragraphs 1, 2, and 13 of the first section of *The English People*, 'England at First Glance.' The last paragraph reads, 'But ... the outstanding and, by contemporary standards, highly original quality of the English is their habit *of not killing one another.*' This is drawn from the first word and second sentence of the third paragraph of the book's final section, 'The Future of the English People,' italics included.

3280. Proposal to Re-issue *Down and Out in Paris and London* in the United States

On 1 October 1947, 'June,' on behalf of Barrows Mussey, wrote to Frank S. MacGregor of Harper & Brothers inquiring whether, following the success of *Animal Farm*, consideration had been given to re-issuing *Down and Out in Paris and London*. Harper had published 1,750 copies in June 1933; 383 copies were remaindered; the type was distributed, 13 February 1934 (Willison). It may have, the letter said, 'dated in a way that would kill it. Then again, it may not. It was a very good book.' Macgregor replied to Mr. Barrows Mussey on 21 October 1947, but addressing the letter to June, that this had been considered but it had seemed that the chances of its being worthwhile were not good enough for Harper to undertake it.

On 20 August 1947, Leonard Moore had written to Harper & Brothers asking them to confirm that the copyrights of *Down and Out in Paris and London* and *Burmese Days* were legally vested in the author. Dorothy B. Fiske, of Harper's Copyright Department, replied on 8 September 1947 that *Down and Out in Paris and London* was copyrighted in the name of Eric Blair on 30 June 1933, Registration Number A–63479; and *Burmese Days* similarly on 25 October 1934, Registration Number A–75972.

3281. Domestic Diary

1.10.47. *Overcast. Only a few drops of rain. Sea calm.*
A few godetias & shirley poppies, & a good many marigolds still blooming, ditto red-hot pokers. Picked the first parsnips today—very poor.
 1 egg (417).
2.10.47. *Beautiful still day. Overcast part of time, but sunny & quite hot in the afternoon. Sea like glass.*
 D.D. now has all his corn stacked.
 Picked a few blackberries. Still not a great number ripe.
 2 eggs (419).
3.10.47. *Beautiful still day. Not very warm. Sea calm.*
 3 eggs (422).

3282. To Leonard Moore

4 October 1947   Typewritten

Barnhill, Isle of Jura, Argyllshire

Dear Moore,
The "Books for Germany" people, of which I am a sponsor, have issued a list of the books they want immediately, and of my own they want "Animal Farm"[1] and "Coming Up for Air." I imagine the latter is completely unobtainable, but could you please send them a copy of A.F. I suppose you have some of the American edition. *If* you have a copy of the German translation to spare, perhaps you could send that as well. The address is:

> A.I.R.G.
> Foreign Office
> German Section
> 48 Princes Gardens
> LONDON SW 7.

Yours sincerely
[Signed] Eric Blair
Eric Blair

1. Annotated in Moore's office, against *Animal Farm*: 'done'; also, below the text is written: 'noted on card.'

3283. Domestic Diary

4.10.47. *Beautiful day. Mist from about 4 pm, thickening from then onwards. Not very warm. Sea calm.*
 Took up bean sticks. Cleared parsnips (very poor).

Took out about 2 galls petrol. 9½ galls. There seems to be hardly any left in the cask (supposed to be 15 gallons.)

3 eggs (425).

<u>5.10.47.</u> *Thick mist last night. Still, overcast day with occasional sun. Not very warm. Sea calm.*

Removed dandelions from grass path (already very numerous).

A. picked considerable quantities of blackberries. Saw two eagles over the house.

3 eggs (428).

<u>6.10.47.</u> *Still day, mostly overcast, but no rain. Not very warm. Sea calm.*

Manured all fruit bushes (NB. I think the black currant° bushes could do with a bit more.)

Still some runners on strawberries, which I removed. One or two recently-ripened raspberries, so I think these must be an autumn kind.

3 eggs (431).

<u>7.10.47.</u> *Still, overcast, light rain during much of the afternoon. Sea rougher.*

The corn in the front field brought into the byre today (very damp). Window of stable mended. Sent for Calor Gas.

4 eggs (435).

<u>8.10.47.</u> *Rough night. Sea very rough this morning, calming by evening. This morning windy & rainy, this afternoon better, with sunny intervals & drizzle.*

Started clearing out shrubs for tulip bed.

4 eggs (439).

3284. To Julian Symons

9 October 1947   Typewritten

Barnhill, Isle of Jura, Argyllshire

Dear Julian,[1]

I'm going to be in London for November, arriving about the 5th I think, and hope we can meet. I'll ring or write nearer the time.

You gave me much too kind a review of that silly little "English People" book in the M. E. News.[2] The only real excuse for it was that I was almost physically bullied into writing it by Turner.[3] It was written about the beginning of 1944, but this didn't appear from the text, as last year the proof-reader hurriedly went through it shoving in a remark here and there to show the general election had happened in the mean time.

I am very busy with a novel which I hope to finish some time next year. I have to do various bits of business in town, but we are going to spend the winter up here because I can be quieter and also it's a bit easier to get food and fuel up here, and actually the climate is a bit warmer. We've got this house quite comfortable now, except that we haven't electric light, and got a bit of a garden going and a few hens—cow and pigs later when we can wangle food for them. We have also been able to make an arrangement by which the derelict croft on which this house stands is to be farmed after all, so I shan't have bad conscience about keeping someone else off cultivable land. Richard is getting enormous and talking a lot more. He has had quite an eventful summer including having measles and cutting an enormous chunk out of his forehead on a broken jug, also being wrecked on a desert island and nearly drowned. The weather on the whole has been marvellous. We had six consecutive weeks without rain, in fact even no water in the taps for a week or two. Later it has rained a good deal, but they got the harvest in with less agony than last year.

Please remember me to your wife.

Yours
Geo. Orwell

1. Julian Symons (1912–1994), poet, novelist, biographer, and crime writer (see *913, n. 5* and *3111, n. 1*). He took over from Orwell as guest critic in the *Manchester Evening News* feature 'Life, People and Books,' 28 November 1946. He and Orwell first met in 1944 and remained friends until Orwell's death.
2. *Manchester Evening News*, 7 August 1947.
3. For W. J. Turner, see *1743, n. 1*.

3285. Domestic Diary

9.10.47.   *Nasty morning & sea rough. Clearer in afternoon, with occasional sun, & sea calmer.*

Cleared out fuchsia stump.

Started new cylinder of Calor Gas. Last cylinder has gone less than a month, but has been used a good deal.

2 eggs (441).

10.10.47.   *Mostly fine, though overcast. A short light shower about 1 pm. Sea fairly calm.*

Began preparing tulip bed.

3 eggs (444).

11.10.47.   *Filthy day, raining most of time, with nasty driving wind from S. in the afternoon. Sea roughish.*

4 eggs (445).[1]

1. The 4 eggs added to the 444 of 10.10.47 should, of course, give a total of 448. Totals hereafter are 3 short.

3286. To D. F. Boyd, BBC Talks Department

12 October 1947   Typewritten

Barnhill, Isle of Jura, Argyllshire

Dear Mr Boyd,

Many thanks for your letter of the 7th.

I'm afraid I cannot possibly undertake a talk on November 12th. I shall probably be in London by that date, but shall be travelling just beforehand. I am in any case very much occupied at present and don't want to undertake any more work. Please forgive me.

Yours sincerely
[Signed] Geo. Orwell
George Orwell

D. F. Boyd, Chief Producer, Talks Department, BBC Home Service, had written to Orwell on 7 October to tell him that in November the BBC was celebrating its jubilee and the anniversary of the Third Programme. A number of important talks were to be transmitted on the theme of broadcasting. Orwell was asked to make one of the 'chief contributions,' a half-hour talk on 'broadcast speech and its effect.' Boyd said that Orwell had perhaps already had a message from Andrew Stewart about this proposal [not traced]. The broadcast was to be given on 12 November, originally at 8:00 P.M., changed on 9 October to 7:00 P.M.

3287. Domestic Diary

12.10.47.   *Very stormy last night & sea rough this morning. Raining a good deal of the day, but wind dropping by afternoon. Sea fairly calm by evening.*

Slight cold, did not go out of doors.

4 eggs (449).

13.10.47.   *Beautiful clear day. Sun quite hot for part of the morning. Sea calm.*

Unwell, did not go out.

2 eggs (451).

14.10.47.   *Mostly fine, some showers. Sea calm. Began digging tulip bed.*

3 eggs (454).[1]

15.10.47.   *Nasty day. Overcast & rather cold, with mist & thin driving rain most of time. Wind from W. Sea calm inshore, roughish outside.*

4 eggs (458).

16.10.47.   *Beautiful clear day, sunny but not very warm. No wind. Sea calm.*

Finished tulip bed (will take about 150 bulbs), began clearing bed under window.

Two Golden Spire apples ripe, which we ate. Quite good crisp apples, lemony flavour.

Stags roaring all night. Have only been hearing them for about the last 10 days.

D.D. taking in the last of his hay today (from the field behind the house). B.D. put his sheep up on the hill as they should be there before the frosts begin.

4 eggs, but I think 1 other had been broken & eaten. (462).

<u>17.10.47.</u>   *Nasty damp day, but not actually much rain, & no wind. Sea calm.*

Paraffin running rather low (started about 6 weeks ago). Have ordered another drum.

Took out 1 gall petrol. 10½ galls. Only a little left in cask.

2 eggs (464).

<u>18.10.47.</u>   *Dull, still day. Hardly any rain. Sea calm.*

Began clearing flower bed.

3 eggs (467).

<u>19.10.47.</u>   *Dull, overcast day, no rain, not cold. Some wind in afternoon. Sea roughish, especially in morning.*

Went on clearing flower bed, spread a little manure (very short of this.) New oil cooker used for first time today (Valor).

The swallows I think have gone. The last time I saw one was a week or 10 days ago. Chaffinches flocking.

4 eggs (471).

<u>20.10.47.</u>   *Fine, sunny, windy day. Chilly in morning & evening. Sea roughish.*

Planted tulips (the new bulbs, about 100–150). Gave them a very little potassium sulphate. Finished clearing flower bed.

New oil cooker seems to use about 1 pint an hour for each burner (one burner works oven).

One hen still almost naked from moulting, & the others persecuting her a bit. Qy. whether to segregate her as she is probably not getting enough to eat.

3 eggs (474).

1. An entry has been crossed through between 14 and 15 October. The day of the month cannot be deciphered, but the entry reads: 'Very stormy last night & sea rough this morning. Raining a good deal of the day, but wind dropping by afternoon. Sea fairly calm by evening.' This suggests that entries were not always made at the end of the day to which they refer or, at the latest, on the following day; Orwell would otherwise have remembered what the weather was like on what must have been 15 October, especially because it was so very different from that of the fourteenth.

3288. S. M. Levitas to Orwell

21 October 1947

Mr. Levitas, the editor of *The New Leader* (New York), wrote to say how 'very uncomfortable' he was to learn that Orwell had asked his agents, McIntosh & Otis, New York, to take out a year's subscription to *The New Leader* because Orwell felt 'uneasy' about being on the free list. Levitas could not understand why Orwell had asked for this to be done. He was eager to have Orwell read *The New Leader* regularly and to contribute frequently: 'three or four articles from you during the year would be very important for all concerned.' He enclosed proofs of an article by James Burnham on the rebirth of the Comintern, and asked Orwell for 1,000 to 1,500 words on it. Levitas's letter arrived when Orwell had become seriously ill and he did not reply until 4 June 1948, after Levitas had written again on 25 May; see *3410*.

3288A. To Arthur Koestler, 21 October 1947: see Vol xx, last appendix.

3289. Domestic Diary

<u>21.10.47.</u> *Fine day, sunny with some mist, rather cold. Sea fairly calm. Planted Madonna lilies (6 I think).*
3 eggs (477).

3290. To Roger Senhouse

22 October 1947   Typewritten

Barnhill, Isle of Jura, Argyllshire

Dear Roger,
I'm returning the proofs of "Coming Up for Air."
There are not many corrections. In just one or two cases I've altered something that had been correctly transcribed, including one or two misprints that existed in the original text. I note that on p. 46 the compositor has twice altered "Boars" to "Boers," evidently taking it for a misprint. "Boars" was intentional, however (a lot of people used to pronounce it like that.)[1]
What about dates? On the title page it says "1947," but it isn't going to be published in 1947. And should there not somewhere be a mention of the fact that the book was first published in 1939?
Did you know by the way that this book hasn't got a semicolon in it? I had decided about that time that the semicolon is an unnecessary stop and that I would write my next book without one.[2]
I'm coming up to London on November 7th and shall be there for about a month. I have various time-wasting things to do, lectures and so on. I *hope* before I arrive to have finished the rough draft of my novel, which I'm on the last lap of now. But its° a most dreadful mess and about two-thirds of it will have to be rewritten entirely besides the usual touching up. I don't know how long that will take—I hope only 4 or 5 months but it might well be longer. I've been in such wretched health all this year that I never seem to have much spare energy. I wonder if Fred will be back by November.[3] I hope to see you both then.

Yours
George

1. See Textual Note to *Coming Up for Air*, *CW*, VII, 249. In the event, the Uniform Edition printed 'Boars' thrice against the original Gollancz edition, which correctly spelt the word this way twice. It would appear that one 'Boer' was incorrectly marked as 'Boar.'
2. See Textual Note to *Coming Up for Air*, *CW*, VII, 249–50. Despite Orwell's clearly expressed wishes, the proofs and Uniform Edition include three semi-colons. Whether Orwell missed these (and they do make for easier reading than do the commas he wished to have used) or whether his instructions were ignored is not clear.
3. Warburg had gone on his first of a dozen visits to the United States. Orwell had written to him on 1 September 1947 (see *3263*) asking him, if he had time, to buy him a pair of shoes. Warburg describes what he calls 'The American Goldfields,' and in particular that first visit, in chapter 8 of his *All Authors Are Equal*. He does not give specific dates for his departure or return.

3291. Domestic Diary

<u>22.10.47.</u> *Fine, clear, coldish day till about 8 pm, when it began raining. Sea fairly calm.*
Planted more tulips (about 120) & transplanted one or two sweet williams.
3 eggs (480).

3292. To Anthony Powell

23 October 1947   Typewritten

Barnhill, Isle of Jura, Argyllshire

Dear Tony,
Re. the Gissing book[1]—I'd love to do it, but I'm really afraid I must say no. The thing is I'm not only struggling with this book of mine but shall also be pretty busy while in London. I've got all manner of time-wasting things to do, and in addition I've been landed with another long article which I can't dodge out of.[2] I hope to at any rate break the back of it while in London, but that means not undertaking anything else. I'm sorry—I'd much rather have done the Gissing article.

I'm coming up on the 7th and will ring you up. Winter is setting in here, rather dark and gloomy. Already we light the lamps at about half past five. However, we've got a lot more coal here than we should have in London, and this house is a lot more weather proof than my flat, where the water was coming through the roof in twelve places last winter. Please give my love to Violet.

Yours
George

1. Anthony Powell had asked him to review *A Life's Morning* by George Gissing for the middle page of the *Times Literary Supplement*.
2. This has not been identified with certainty, but it may be a reference to the Profile of Krishna Menon published in *The Observer*, 30 November 1947; see *3309*. However, it is likely that Orwell did not write the article, probably because he was taken ill; see letter to Leonard

Moore, 31 October 1947, *3300*. Although he wrote seven reviews which were published between February and June 1948 (two of them lengthy), his next articles did not appear until mid-1948 ('Writers and Leviathan,' *3364*, and 'Britain's Left-Wing Press,' *3366*), and it looks as if they were not required (according to his Second Literary Notebook) until 20 June 1948. For a summary of the position regarding the articles published in 1948, see Orwell's letter to Julian Symons, 21 March 1948, *3363, n. 1*. Orwell did write an essay on Gissing in 1948; see *3406*. That began as a review for *Politics and Letters* of two reprinted books, *In the Year of the Jubilee* and *The Whirlpool* but the journal ceased publication before it could be published.

3293. Domestic Diary

<u>23.10.47.</u> *Evidently fairly heavy rain in the night. Today dull, overcast, still, with occasional rain & mist. Sea very calm.*

Planted crocuses, supposed to be 200 but I think not so many. Very poor bulbs, & not enough of them. Must order about 100 more. NB. to order some scillas as well.

4 eggs (484).

On the facing page against *23.10.47* Orwell has written and ticked, implying he had placed the following order:

Order crocuses.

<u>24.10.47.</u> *Clear, fine day, quite warm in the morning. Sea roughish.*

Today a burst water pipe, a great nuisance but fortunately in the scullery & not upstairs. Nobody knows where the main cock is, as it is somewhere underground, near the door of the byre probably. The only way of cutting off the water is to disconnect the pipe from the tank, at the point where it crosses the stream. This soon empties the cistern & thus stops the water running, but of course while one is doing the mend the water is running out of the tank, & in dry weather it might not be easy to get it full again. NB. that one cannot disconnect the pipe without a large monkey wrench which we have not got.

3 eggs (487).

On the facing page against this date Orwell has written:

Order monkey wrench.

3294. To Leonard Moore

25 October 1947   Typewritten

Barnhill, Isle of Jura, Argyllshire

Dear Moore,

Fenner Brockway,[1] who is helping to edit a new magazine called "World Opinion",[2] wrote asking me whether they could reprint in it an excerpt of about 1500 words from "The English People." He says they have approached the editorial committee of Britain in Pictures, who refused them leave to reprint. Do you know what the position is and whose the copyright is? I really don't mind one way or the other, but so far as it lies with me I have no objection to their reprinting.[3]

My friend George Woodcock is looking for a literary agent and asked me to ask you whether you would care to handle his work. I think he will also write to you himself. He recently published a book on William Godwin, and I think has published others, and is now at work on some commissioned books. He says he wants an agent because the business side of his work is getting rather beyond him, and also because he expects to be in Ireland part of next year. His address is 24 Highgate West Hill, N. 6.[4]

Yours sincerely
[Signed] Eric Blair
Eric Blair

1. (Archibald) Fenner Brockway (1888–1988; Lord Brockway, 1964), writer and politician, campaigned for many causes. He was Secretary of the No Conscription Fellowship, 1917; worked especially in the cause of Indian independence; was jailed on several occasions, for two years with hard labour in July 1917 as a conscientious objector; and was prominent in the affairs of the Independent Labour Party from 1922 to 1946, when he joined the Labour Party and was an M.P., 1950–64. His association with Orwell went back to Orwell's bookshop days (they met when Orwell worked for Francis Westrope; Crick 254), and was strengthened when Orwell fought in the ILP contingent in the Spanish civil war and attended ILP Summer Schools. Brockway had suggested that Warburg, who had published Brockway's *The Workers' Front* (1938), might publish *Homage to Catalonia*. Brockway wrote some thirty books and a number of pamphlets. He died shortly after reaching the age of one hundred.
2. No such journal has been traced.
3. Annotated in Moore's office: 'wrote Adprint 31/10/47'; Adprint is given in the preliminaries of *The English People* as having produced the book, though it was published by Collins and printed by Jarrold and Sons Ltd. Against Brockway's name is noted, in a different hand: 'wrote 13.11.47.'
4. Annotated in Moore's office, in the first of the hands noted above: 'Wrote George Woodcock 31/10/47.'

3295. To Julian Symons

25 October 1947   Typewritten

Barnhill, Isle of Jura, Argyllshire

Dear Julian,

I can't resist taking up a point of pedantry. Kid Lewis *may* have been a welter-weight, but I think he was a light-weight.[1] At any rate he wasn't a heavy or a light-heavy, and I'll tell you how I remember. He fought Carpentier, a sort of grudge battle, Lewis having challenged Carpentier, whom he declared to be overrated. At first Carpentier (a light-heavy weight) said that he refused to fight someone who was below his own weight. In the end they fought and Lewis was knocked out, his supporters claiming that he had been fouled. This was about 1922. (Perhaps later).

He was a supporter of Mosley[2] in the New Party, and stood for Whitechapel in the election—I suppose it was 1931—in which the New Party had its fiasco. I think he must have stuck to Mosley a bit longer and after M. started calling himself a Fascist, because I remember Boothroyd ("Yaffle" of Reynolds's)[3] telling me about an affray at a public meeting, about 1932, in which Lewis was involved. I believe Mosley at the beginning had a regular bodyguard of Jewish prizefighters. Fascism was not then thought of as antisemitic, and Mosley did not take up anti-semitism until about 1933 or 1934.

Looking forward to seeing you.

Yours
George

1. Orwell had referred to Kid Lewis's boxing and political career in *The English People*, which Symons had reviewed in the *Manchester Evening News*. Lewis's world title fights against Jack Britton (USA) in 1921 and George Carpentier (France) in 1922 were both at light heavyweight (though in the fight against Carpentier, the latter's heavyweight title was also at stake).
2. Sir Oswald Mosley, (1896–1980), politician, successively Conservative, Independent, and Labour M.P. In 1931 he broke away from the Labour Party to form the New Party. He became fanatically pro-Hitler and his party became the British Union of Fascists.
3. John Basil Boothroyd (1910–1988), writer, humorist, broadcaster; served in the RAF Police, 1941–45 (as Personal Assistant to the Provost-Marshal from 1943). He wrote for a number of periodicals but in later years was particularly associated with *Punch*, as contributor from 1938, and as an assistant editor, 1952–70. Most of his books were humorous, but he also wrote *Philip* (1971), the approved biography of HRH the Duke of Edinburgh. Orwell described *Reynold's News*, with the *News Chronicle* and *The New Statesman*, as a mouthpiece of the left-wing intelligentsia clamouring for a Popular Front in a letter to the *New English Weekly*, 26 May 1938; see 446. It was a Sunday paper that appealed to a mass readership. It ceased publication (then as the *Sunday Citizen*) on 18 June 1967. The headnote to 446 gives some details of Boothroyd's involvement in Orwell's concern at that time.

3296. To George Woodcock

25 October 1947   Typewritten

Barnhill, Isle of Jura, Argyllshire.

Dear George,

I am writing to my agent, and will tell him you would like to deal with him. You might also care to communicate with him yourself. The address is:

> Christy & Moore
> Literary Agents
> The Ride Annexe
> Dukes Wood Avenue
> Gerrards Cross, Bucks.

I don't know whether they are actually the best agents (I believe Watt's are supposed to be good), but I have always dealt with them. They are partly lecturing agents, and somewhat lowbrow in tendency, but do a certain amount of high-class business, and have good connections here and in the USA. I think you will find Moore (he is the active partner) will want you to sign a contract engaging to do all your business through him. Of course this inevitably means that one is often paying the agent his 10 percent commission when one has in fact done all the negotiations oneself, but it is worth it, because an agent with his connections can fix up translations, American editions and so forth which one could never do for oneself. For instance Moore fixed up 15 or more translations of "Animal Farm" whereas I don't suppose I could have arranged more than two or three myself, as I would not have known how to go about it. Also an agent will screw better terms out of publishers and take all the misery of contracts and so forth off one's back. But when signing any agreement with Moore I would make sure that it refers only to books and not journalism. It is most tiresome if one has to handle magazine and newspaper articles through an agent. At the same time, even if one has a clause of that kind in the agreement, they'll be quite ready to negotiate individual articles, eg. ones that you think might be saleable in America.

I'm coming up to London on November 7th and shall stay for a few weeks. I've about finished the rough draft of my novel, so should get it done by about next summer. I haven't got on as fast as I should because I've been in such wretched health this year. Yes, we did nearly get drowned, and ended up by managing to scramble ashore on a tiny islet after losing both the engine and the oars from the boat, so that we couldn't get off again. Very luckily some lobster fishermen happened to pass and saw the fire we had lit, so we got away after only a few hours. Richard enjoyed every minute of it except when he was in the water. Please give my love to Inge. I look forward to seeing you both.

Yours
George

3297. Domestic Diary

<u>25.10.47.</u> *Beautiful, clear, windless day. Sea somewhat calmer.*
Pruned gooseberry bushes (old ones). Applied sulphate of potash to fruit bushes & strawberries, & the two espalier apple trees.
Put new batteries in radio. NB. we shall need H.T. battery about 25.2.48 & L.T. battery about 25.12.47. Order 10 days beforehand.
Saw a piece of honeysuckle in bloom yesterday, in a bush that had ripe berries. One or two flowers on the thrift, must be second blooming. Forgot to mention, saw some starlings about a week ago.
3 eggs (490).

Against this date on the facing page Orwell has written:

Order H.T. battery 15.2.48.
Order L.T. battery 15.12.47.

<u>26.10.47.</u> *Still day, more overcast than yesterday, but no rain. Sea calm.*
Gave manure to apple trees. The scion of the James Grieve appeared to have rooted. Cut the rootlets through—not certain whether this is the right thing to do.
5 eggs (495).

3298. To Celia Kirwan

27 October 1947   Typewritten

Barnhill, Isle of Jura, Argyllshire

Dearest Celia,[1]
How nice to get your letter (dated 14th but didn't get here till about 3 days ago.)

I can't possibly write anything at present. I am smothered under work. I am struggling with this[2] novel which I am supposed to finish some time in the spring, and shortly I have to go up to London and waste the better part of a month doing all kinds of time-wasting things. I have been in lousy health most of this year, my chest as usual, so I haven't got on with the novel so fast as I should have. Richard is getting enormous and is full of vigour in spite of having measles and now, I am afraid, sickening for whooping cough, as he spent some time with some children who developed whooping cough immediately afterwards. He talks a good deal more but is still rather backward that way. Early in the spring he fell down and cut his forehead very badly, but it healed up nicely and I don't think the scar will show after a year or two. We had a marvellous summer, six weeks without a drop of rain, and we went for some wonderful picnics on the other side of the island, which is quite uninhabited but where there is an empty shepherd's cottage one can sleep in. It is a beautiful coast, green water and white sand, and a few miles inland lochs full of trout which never get fished because they're too far from anywhere. We had intended to go back to London for the winter, but we decided to stay here because I think it will be a little easier to keep warm. There is rather more fuel, and also the winter is not quite so cold as in the south of England, though it is very wet.

I will write for you when I can. I certainly would like some French francs. I have translations of various books coming out, but my books never sell in France, and in one case recently I must say I didn't wonder when I saw what the translation was like.

I haven't heard from Inez[3] for some months, but of course I shall look her up as soon as I am in town. I had hoped she was going to come and stay up here in the autumn but it fell through for some reason.

With love
George

P.S. Do you know the inner story of what happened to Polemic?[4] I merely had a line from Humphrey saying they were packing up. Did Rodney Phillips get sick of spending money on it, or was there a quarrel? I'm going to send this to "Occident" as you didn't give the arrondissement of your address.

1. Celia Kirwan (see *2836, n. 3*) had worked as an editorial assistant on *Polemic*. When *Polemic* collapsed, she moved to Paris and worked as an editorial assistant on a tri-lingual magazine, *Occident*. One of her duties was to seek out new material, and it was for this reason that she wrote to Orwell (and also to Arthur Koestler, her brother-in-law, who did contribute an article).
2. Orwell typed 'the this.'
3. Inez Holden (1906–1974), author and journalist; cousin to Celia Kirwan; see *1326, n. 1*.
4. *Polemic* ran for seven numbers from September 1945 to 1947. It was edited by Humphrey Slater (see *2955, n. 4*) and financed by Rodney Phillips. When Phillips tired of giving it financial support, it folded. Slater then moved to Spain. There was no quarrel at its closure.

3299. Domestic Diary

<u>27.10.47.</u> *Fine still day, not much sun, no wind. Sea fairly calm.*
New gate & tomato house have arrived. Also ½ ton hay, barrel of paraffin, calor gas. Gateposts 8½ long, must be cut down, as in this soil it would be almost impossible to sink them deep enough.
1 egg. (496).
<u>28.10.47.</u> *Fine still day, not much sun, little wind, coldish. Sea calm.*
Started clearing stable. NB. order large stiff broom.
Began new drum of paraffin. Allowing that we use 5 galls a week, this should last to 28.12.47. Important not to run out at Xmas time. Order another drum at beginning of December.
3 eggs (499).

Against this date on the facing page Orwell has written:

Order yard broom.
Order paraffin about 1.12.47.

29.10.47. *Fine clear day, not very warm, with some sun. Sea roughish.*
A. & B.D. continued clearing stable. Mowed lawn (last time this year).
3 eggs (& 1 I think eaten). 502.

After this entry, Orwell ceased to write his diary, owing to becoming seriously
ill. His letters from here on and well into 1948 were handwritten from bed.

3300. To Leonard Moore

31 October 1947   Handwritten

Barnhill, Isle of Jura, Argyllshire

Dear Moore,
I am writing this in bed (inflammation of the lungs), so I shan't be coming up
to London in early November as planned. I shall try to come up later in the
month, but certainly it will be several weeks before I can travel. Harcourt
Brace have just written expressing interest in the novel I am now writing & in
the idea of reprinting various earlier ones, ie. those Warburg is reprinting.
Warburgs has° sent them proofs of "Coming up for Air," apparently.

I am not sure how we stand with Harcourt & Brace on the one hand, &
Reynall° & Hitchcock on the other? Is it not the latter who have the first
refusal of *new* work? But how about reprints? I would certainly like to see
"Burmese Days" (which H.B mention) reprinted in the U S A.[1]

If writing to H.B. could you ask them to forgive me for not writing—
explain I am ill—particularly sorry not writing as they exerted themselves
about getting a pair of shoes for me. Might also tell Secker & Warburg & Miss
Otis[2] that I am ill.

Yours sincerely
Eric Blair

1. Harcourt, Brace published a new edition of *Burmese Days* in New York in January 1950.
2. Of McIntosh & Otis, Orwell's American agent for magazine publishing.

3301. Ukrainian Translation of *Animal Farm*

November 1947

According to Willison, the Ukrainian translation of *Animal Farm* was published
by Prometheus in Munich, in November 1947. It was translated by Ivan
Cherniatync'kyi (Ihor Szewczenko) and printed in Belgium. It was distributed
through a displaced persons organisation in Munich. A large number of the
5,000 copies printed were handed to the Soviets by the American occupying
power in Germany. See *2969, 3187, 3188, 3197, 3198* and especially *3304* for the
possible effect of a change of American policy in Germany.

3302. Subscription to International P.E.N. English Centre
1947–48

Early in September 1947, members of the International P.E.N. English Centre were advised of an increase in the subscription. Among Orwell's papers was a reminder, perhaps dating from November 1947, that he had not signed a revised banker's order for the payment of his subscription at the new rate of £2.2.0 (instead of £1.6.0). He was asked to pay the difference (16s. 0d) and arrange for his bank to pay £2.2.0 from 1 October 1948. See *3355*.

3303. To Leonard Moore
7 November 1947   Handwritten

Barnhill, Isle of Jura, Argyllshire

Dear Moore,
Thanks for your letter of the 30th October. I shall be very pleased to have "Burmese Days" translated into Hungarian.

With ref. to your other letter—no, I only did one review for the New Yorker.[1] They have not sent me any more books.

I have been very unwell & intend to stay in bed for some weeks & try & get right again, so I probably shan't be coming up to London, unless for a very short business trip. I have finished the rough draft of my novel, so I ought to get the book done by about May or June unless this illness drags out. I can't work in my present state—constant high temperature etc.

Yours sincerely
Eric Blair

1. The review was given the title 'The Final Years of Lady Gregory,' 19 April 1947; see *3218*.

3304. To Leonard Moore
8 November 1947   Handwritten

Barnhill, Isle of Jura, Argyllshire

Dear Moore,
Many thanks for your letter of the 3rd. I would be very glad to see a German translation of A.F. circulating in Germany & don't mind if the financial return is small. I think this is the right moment, as the USA is altering its policy in Germany & doing more vigorous anti-Russian propaganda, but it wouldn't surprise me to see them drop that line again quite soon. No doubt Amstutz[1] appreciates that point.

Yours sincerely
Eric Blair

1. Verlag Amstutz, Herdeg & Co, Zürich, published *Animal Farm* in German, as *Farm der Tiere*, in October 1946. It was translated by N. O. Scarpi (Fritz Bondy). It was then serialised as 'Der Hofstaat der Tiere: Eine satirische Fabel' (in the same translation) by the American-sponsored *Der Monat* in West Berlin, February–April 1949, nos. 5, 6, and 7. Scarpi's translation was published under a third title, and in a third country, Austria, in October 1951, as *Die Republik der Tiere: Eine Zeitsatire*. This was distributed free by the Viennese newspaper *Die Presse* (Willison).

3305. To Roger Senhouse
14 November 1947   Handwritten

Barnhill, Isle of Jura, Argyllshire

Dear Roger,
I enclose the draft blurb, with slight emendations. I must say I don't think the tone of it is quite right, but I suppose it's in the blurb tradition.

As to your other corrections, I'm keeping the list, but I can't give any opinion on the doubtful ones without a copy of the proofs.[1]

I think I sent a message saying I am ill. I'm still in bed & very weak. I don't suppose I'll be in London much before the end of the month.

Yours
George

1. Presumably proofs of *Coming Up for Air*, then in production as the first in the Uniform Edition.

3306. To Arthur Koestler
24 November 1947   Handwritten

Barnhill, Isle of Jura, Argyllshire

Dear Arthur,
I'm very ill in bed (chest as usual) & trying to get well enough to travel up to London & see a specialist. I dare say I'll have to spend a month or so in a nursing home then. I've really been very bad for several months tho' I didn't take to my bed till about 3 weeks ago.

I can't take part in any committees etc. I quite agree about French translations, they are sometimes quite shameful. They entirely ruined one book of mine in translation.[1] But I think it's because French publishers won't pay decent fees for translations. I should have said English translations of French books were generally fairly good.

Thanks for offer of house, but I don't think we could, ie. as a family, come away, & as a matter of fact we're fairly comfortable here—good sound house, hot water & plenty of food, tho' no electric light certainly. Love to you both.

George

1. In his notes for his literary executor, mid-June 1949, Orwell annotated the French translation of *Burmese Days*, published by Nagel in 1946, 'VERY BAD translation'; see *3728*, 'Notes on Translations.' For Koestler's scheme for improving translations into French, see *3288A*, Vol xx, last appendix.

3307. To Frederick Tomlinson, *The Observer*

24 November 1947   Handwritten

Barnhill, Isle of Jura, Argyllshire

Dear Tomlinson,[1]
Many thanks for your letter of the 18th.[2] I can't really give you any answer now, because I have been seriously ill for some weeks & am still merely trying to get well enough to make the journey to London & see a specialist. It is my chest as usual, & even if I don't need any special treatment I think I shall have to stay in a nursing home for a month or so in order to be nursed. I can't tell how long it will all take, & therefore I don't really know about my movements. I am just half way through a book which I am supposed to finish in the spring or early summer, but which of course I can't touch till I'm well again. I'll let you know later how I go on.

Yours
George Orwell

1. Frederick Tomlinson was news editor of *The Observer* and a great admirer of Orwell. He was always keen to get material from Orwell into the paper, according to David Astor (1 September 1992).
2. Tomlinson had suggested to Orwell that he spend three months in Africa—unless he had retired from journalism for ever—on assignment to cover the first results of the groundnut scheme in East Africa and the South African elections for *The Observer*. It would enable Orwell to write on problems of colonial development, the British government's responsibilities to Africans, to its people at home greatly in need of the food Africa could produce, and the social, economic, and political scene in South Africa as the Nationalists sought power. He had made no arrangements and was writing informally in David Astor's absence in America. In all, Orwell would be away for about four months in the spring of 1948—provided he was well enough. The attempt to grow groundnuts in East Africa proved a disastrous failure and was subjected to much (often unfair) ridicule. In the South African elections, May 1948, the Nationalists won, Daniel Malan (1874–1959) taking over as prime minister from Field Marshal Jan Smuts, who had held that office since 1939 and who suffered the indignity of losing his seat in Parliament. See also *1116, n. 15.*

3308. To Anthony Powell

29 November 1947   Handwritten

Barnhill, Isle of Jura, Argyllshire

Dear Tony,
Thanks so much for your letter. I'm still on my back, but I think really getting better after many relapses. I'd probably be all right by this time if I could have got to my usual chest specialist, but I dare not make the journey to

the mainland while I have a temperature. It's really a foul journey in winter even if one flies part of the way. However I've arranged for a man to come from Glasgow & give me the once-over, & then maybe I'll get up to London later, or perhaps only as far as Glasgow. I think I'll have to go into hospital for a bit, because apart from treatment there's the X-raying etc., & after that I might have a stab at going abroad for a couple of months if I can get a newspaper assignment to some where° warm. Of course I've done no work for weeks—have only done the rough draft of my novel, which I always consider as the halfway mark. I was supposed to finish it by May—now, God knows when. I'm glad the Aubrey book[1] is coming along at last. I think in these days besides putting the date of publication in books one also ought to put the date of writing. In the spring I'm reprinting a novel which came out in 1939[2] & was rather killed by the war, so that makes up a little for being late with my new one.

Apparently Mrs Christen[3] has just sailed. What I partly wrote about was this: have you got, or do you know anyone who has got, a saddle for sale? Good condition doesn't matter very much so long as it has a sound girth & stirrups. It's for a horse only about 14 h. but on the stout side, so very likely a saddle belonging to a big horse would do. It's the sort of thing someone might have kicking round, & you can't buy them for love or money. The farm pony we have here is ridden for certain errands to save petrol, & it's so tiring riding bareback. I am ready to pay a reasonable price.

Richard is *offensively* well & full of violence. He went through whooping cough without noticing that he had it. My love to everyone. I hope to see you all some day.

Yours
George

1. Powell published *John Aubrey and His Friends* in 1948, and *Brief Lives and Other Selected Writings of John Aubrey* in 1949.
2. *Coming Up for Air.*
3. Mrs. Miranda Christen (now Mrs. Wood; 1914–), had stayed in Orwell's London flat during the summers of 1946 and 1947. She had returned from the Far East early in 1946 after 3½ years in Japanese-occupied territory. Whilst pursuing the lengthy procedures of a divorce, naturalisation (she was technically of German nationality), and a passage to Singapore, she was glad to have the use of Orwell's flat in his absence. Anthony Powell had introduced her to Orwell. Early in her second summer there, Orwell wrote from Jura asking if she knew anyone willing to type a draft of work he had in progress. Since she had had experience in working in two publishers' offices before the war, she was glad to undertake this task. An appropriate reduction was made in the rent she paid, and about every two weeks a batch of material would arrive in the post and she would make a fair and a carbon copy on the portable typewriter she found in the flat. These she posted back to Orwell. Mrs. Wood described the material, in an unpublished memoir, as 'presumably the initial draft'; it was 'partly self-typed, partly handwritten.' She was provided with a glossary of Newspeak, but that, alas, has not survived. She also typed a fair copy of 'a bleary typescript of the essay "Such, Such Were the Joys." ' . . . It looked as if it had been lying around for a considerable time.' She had left for Singapore by 20 November 1947; the final batch of *Nineteen Eighty-Four* sent to her 'stopped a few hundred words short of the end. The Appendix was not included.' The only part of Mrs. Wood's typing to survive is page 239; that she identified for the editor in November 1983. For how her work fitted into the genesis of *Nineteen Eighty-Four*, see Introduction to the *Facsimile*, especially xvii–xx; for 'Such, Such Were the Joys,' see *3408* and *3409*. For her memoir of her time in Orwell's Canonbury flat whilst he was at Barnhill in 1946 and 1947, see *3735*.

3309. Profile of Krishna Menon. By David Astor in consultation with Orwell[1]

The Observer, 30 November 1947

One man to whom the Exhibition of Indian Art, just open at Burlington House, will bring quiet pride is Mr. V. K. Krishna Menon,[2] High Commissioner in London for the Dominion of India. His new post and the Exhibition are both tokens of a sympathetic intercourse between Britain and India which in earlier life he can scarcely have expected. People here used to think of Mr. Menon as the arch-rebel, working in their midst against the British Raj. For years they watched him conducting his political activities from 165 Strand, the old office of the India League.

Menon came to this country in 1924, a young man of twenty-six. From Mrs. Annie Besant,[3] his political guru, he had heard much about Britain; his study of Burke, Mill, and Shakespeare had given him a great wish to see the strange land which had such titles to fame and could yet keep millions of his own people in subjugation. His intention, then, was to return to India in six months. Instead, he stayed on and has been here ever since, rarely visiting India and then only for short periods.

This tall, severe-looking man with classical features is by nature an ascetic: he neither drinks nor smokes, has never married, and is a strict vegetarian. Before moving a few months ago into that magnificent edifice in Aldwych called India House, he used to live in a small bed-and-breakfast room in one of the side-streets of Camden Town. From 1934 up to his recent appointment he sat for Labour on the St. Pancras Borough Council. He had been active in the Labour movement even earlier, working closely with Ellen Wilkinson[4] in the grim "hunger-march" days.

In 1939 he was chosen as parliamentary Labour candidate for Dundee, but resigned from the party over its India policy during the war years. Then, as always with him, India came first. He rejoined in 1945, after the Labour Party conference had passed its famous "Independence for India" resolution against the advice of the executive.

Even as a boy, wandering in the streets of Calicut, the land of black pepper and coco-nuts where trains pass through gardens and gardens touch the sea, Menon dreamt of freedom for India. Defiance runs in his family. His father, a lawyer, had little respect for British-made laws; his eldest sister fought her way against sex discrimination into a secondary school hitherto reserved for boys.

Soon after graduating from the Presidency College, Madras, Menon was drawn into Mrs. Besant's "Home Rule" agitation, and she promptly chose him as one of her young volunteers. For five years he lived and worked in the Besant community, leaving only to come to England.

His first job here was teaching history at St. Christopher's School, Letchworth. At the same time he took evening classes at the London

School of Economics, graduating with first-class honours and also gaining the London University Diploma in Education. After a period of research in the psychological laboratory of University College, which brought him his M.A., he returned to the L.S.E., where he became one of Professor Laski's favourite pupils and added the M.Sc (Economics) to his remarkable bag of academic distinctions.

His inclination, however, was towards an independent profession rather than a teaching post; his next step was to qualify as a barrister of the Inner Temple. He practised at the Bar, but was not a great success; perhaps because law is a jealous mistress, and his first love has always been politics. A fluent speaker, he soon became known in Labour circles as an authority on India. In 1929 he was elected General Secretary of the India League, then not much more than a club where Left-wing sympathisers such as Lansbury, Lee Smith, and Pethick-Lawrence met to discuss Indian problems with earnest young Indians. Menon made the League a political force; before long the Congress leaders recognised it as their chief mouthpiece in Europe.

In 1935 Pandit Nehru came to London; he was impressed by Menon's work, and the friendship then formed between the two men has never waned. It was certain that as Nehru's star rose Menon's would rise with it. When last year Nehru became Vice-President of the Indian Interim Government he at once made Menon his personal envoy in Europe, and later sent him to the United Nations General Assembly as a member of the Indian delegation. Finally, when Nehru became Prime Minister, Menon was appointed to represent his country at the Court of St. James's.°

However, it would be quite wrong to think of Menon as merely a client of Nehru. He is a self-made man with an arresting personality who would in any event have carved out a notable career for himself, very possibly in Parliament. He writes English as well as he speaks it, is the author of several books and innumerable pamphlets, and was the first editor of the Pelican Series and the Twentieth Century Library, a most unusual distinction for an Indian.

In personal life Menon is difficult to know. He has an immense range of acquaintances, but not many friends. People either admire or condemn him; they rarely get an opportunity to break through his armour of reserve. He is sensitive to the reactions of others and tries to take them into his confidence, but he is seldom able to lower his guard. Only with children does he find it easy to unbend.

To his subordinates Menon often seems a hard taskmaster; he has an almost Curzonian passion for detail and likes to keep the strings of authority in his own hands. Tireless himself, he is often at his desk by 8 a.m., and is apt to work eighteen hours a day. But he has seen enough of the ups and downs of life to appreciate the difficulties of others; his judgments are more generous than his manner usually allows him to show. Very few have ever suffered at his hands, though more than a few have tried to damage his reputation.

Because of his critical role in the past many people imagine that Menon does not like the British. Nothing could be further from truth. In fact, it is inconceivable that he would ever feel at home now in any other country. He has lived with the British so long and has known them so well that he has grown genuinely fond of them. With Lord and Lady Mountbatten he has established lately a firm friendship: for his character and integrity they have a high regard. We can be sure that the former rebel will do his utmost to strengthen the new alliance—the free alliance he has always wanted—between his country and ours.

1. In letters to the editor of 1 and 8 September 1992, David Astor expressed uncertainty about his and Orwell's shares in the composition of this profile. He did not think Orwell did the actual writing but he 'certainly . . . contributed quite a lot of information' and advice on how to handle a difficult subject. 'I remember him wondering what a London policeman who might have recently had to watch him as a rabble-rousing orator would make of him suddenly reappearing as the Indian High Commissioner.' In his letter to Anthony Powell, 23 October 1947 (see *3292*), Orwell says he has been 'landed with another long article which I can't dodge out of.' It looks as if this must have been the profile of Menon, and that, because Orwell was taken ill within a few days of writing to Powell and was unable to write or complete the article, Astor took it over. See *3292, n. 2* for an analysis of the circumstances.
2. (Vengalil Krishnan) Krishna Menon (1897–1974), Indian politician and diplomat; see *1080, n. 5*.
3. Annie Besant (1847–1933), social reformer and, following her association with Madame Blavatsky in 1889, a theosophist. She was President of the Theosophical Society, 1907–33. In 1916 she founded the Indian Home Rule League and spent much of her time promoting Indian nationalism and education. She died in India.
4. Ellen Wilkinson (1891–1947), prominent Labour leader, was closely associated with the Jarrow Crusade, which set out to draw attention to the unemployment in that area, which she represented in Parliament. She visited the International Brigade in Spain in 1937 and was appointed Minister of Education in the Labour Government of 1945.

3310. To Leonard Moore

30 November 1947   Handwritten

Barnhill, Isle of Jura, Argyllshire

Dear Moore,

Many thanks for your letters. I enclose the Hungarian contract, duly signed.[1]

I am still on my back but I think I am now really getting better. I have got a chest specialist coming from Glasgow to see me next week, & I dare say in a little while I'll be able to make the journey to either London or Glasgow. But I am bound to be incapacitated for some time, & I dare say after that they will tell me to go to a hot climate for a month or two, if I can get a newspaper assignment to somewhere hot.[2] Of course I've done no work for weeks. I had done the rough draft of my novel, after which I usually consider there is 4–5 months' work to do—now, I can't say when I'll get back to it. I must get well first, & then get strong again.

Settle it between Harcourt Brace & Reynal & Hitchcock as you think fit,[3] &, if you will, apologise on my behalf for not writing, & impress on them that I am & have been seriously ill. If R. & H.—who, so far as I remember, really had the right to my next book—are generously willing to withdraw, I think it would be better to stick to H.B. But do make them understand that thanks to this illness I am bound to be late with the new book. H.B. speak in their letter about reprinting "Burmese Days" etc. I am of course most anxious that this should happen, but—though they would know best—I should think it would be better to reprint any of these books *after* the new novel has appeared, not before. The time to reprint "Burmese Days" was immediately after "Animal Farm". I urged Harper's to do it then, but they wouldn't.

I'll tell you how I go on after I've seen the doctors. If they tell me that I've got to go into a sanatorium for a year,[4] or something like that, I suppose I'll be able to arrange it so that I can do some work there.

Yours sincerely
Eric Blair

1. For a translation of *Burmese Days*; see *3303*. No translation into Hungarian was published in Orwell's lifetime.
2. See suggestion by Frederick Tomlinson, of *The Observer*, *3307, n. 2*.
3. On 12 November 1947, Eugene Reynal, of Reynal & Hitchcock, wrote to Leonard Moore expressing the hope that they would be able to publish Orwell's work in America. However, he made it plain that he would not do anything that would stand in the way of Orwell's work being handled as he wished in America: 'I think it is of primary importance that he shall decide with what house he will receive the most sympathetic and interested treatment in this country.' If he chose Harcourt, Brace, Reynal & Hitchcock would release him from the options they had under the contract entered into with them. On 18 November 1947, Chester Kerr, of Reynal & Hitchcock, wrote to Fredric Warburg, reviewing the future publishing plans of a number of authors; 'Of the first importance to us is the future of George Orwell's work in this country.' They were prepared to go ahead with *Coming Up for Air*, in step with Warburg's plans for reprinting, and Moore had offered them 'the Adprint book' (*The English People*) 'as fulfilment of our option,' but their feelings about that were, he hoped, 'disguised' in their reply to Moore, two copies of which they had enclosed for Warburg to see. They did not 'view such an idea with any real pleasure.' The second copy of Eugene Reynal's reply to Moore was enclosed should Warburg wish to send it on to Orwell with any comment he might consider suitable. They fully appreciated Warburg's neutral position. Harcourt, Brace and Company took over the publication of Orwell's work in the United States. They became Harcourt Brace Jovanovich on 2 June 1970 and Harcourt Brace & Company in January 1993. Reynal & Hitchcock closed in 1947 and were then absorbed by Harcourt, Brace.
4. This was a common treatment for those with tuberculosis at the time.

3311. Questionnaire: The Three Best Books of 1947

Horizon, December 1947

Horizon asked a number of people—those whose responses were published on the same page as Orwell's were Kingsley Martin, Raymond Mortimer, Harold Nicolson, William Plomer, and Alan Pryce-Jones—to give the titles of three books published in 1947 (if possible, not reprints) which they had read with great interest and enjoyment. Orwell replied:

Writing this in bed—very unwell. Have read a lot this year but nothing of any value except old books, mostly in cheap reprints. I enjoyed especially, i.e. among books I had not read before:

Under Western Eyes. Joseph Conrad
The Aspern Papers. Henry James
Framley Parsonage. Anthony Trollope
No new English books of any value published in 1947, so far as I know. Quite willing to be convinced I am wrong in this, but shall need evidence.

3312. To Celia Kirwan

7 December 1947   Handwritten

Barnhill, Isle of Jura, Argyllshire

Dearest Celia,
How nice it was to get your letter. Unfortunately I can't reply at any length, because I'm really very ill. As to your query about Inez.[1] I haven't actually heard from her, but when I found I couldn't go up to London (because of this illness) I wrote asking her to ring up & inform various friends, which she did, so she's about, anyway.

I've been in bed 6 weeks, & was feeling unwell some time before that. I kept trying to get just well enough to make the journey to London—finally I brought a chest specialist here. He says I have got to go into a sanatorium, probably for about 4 months. It's an awful bore, however perhaps it's all for the best if they can cure me. I don't think living in Jura has had a bad effect on my health—in any case the sanatorium I'm going to is near Glasgow, which is the same climate. Actually we've had marvellous weather this year & very dry. Even now I'm looking out on what might be a spring day if the bracken was green.

Richard is ever so well & getting very solid & heavy. I'll let you know the address of the sanatorium when I get there, & I'll also try to write you a better letter, that is if they let you sit up there. I would love to see you some time—but heaven knows when that will happen.

With much love
George

1. Inez Holden; see *3298, n. 3.*

3313. To Leonard Moore

7 December 1947   Handwritten

Barnhill, Isle of Jura, Argyllshire

Dear Moore,
Thanks for your letter of the 1st. I have of course no objection to the arrangement with the F.O.[1] about "A.F." I had already written to the U.S. Information Service to tell them they could broadcast it free of charge.

I have seen a chest specialist, &, as I feared, I am seriously ill. As soon as there is a bed vacant, I think in about 10 days, I shall have to go into a sanatorium—for how long I don't know of course, but I gather probably something like 4 months. It's T.B., as I suspected. They think they can cure it all right, but I am bound to be hors de combat for a good while. Could you inform all the publishers etc. concerned. Could you also thank very kindly Harcourt Brace for getting & sending me a pair of shoes (just arrived) & find out from Fred Warburg who paid for them, ie. whom I should repay. I believe Warburg paid.

Yours sincerely
Eric Blair

P.S. I'll send you the address of the hospital as soon as I'm there, but any way this address will find me.

1. The Foreign Office.

3314. To Leonard Moore

17 December 1947   Handwritten

Barnhill, Isle of Jura, Argyllshire

Dear Moore,

Thank you for your two letters. I expect to move into hospital at the end of this week,[1] & so far as I know the address is: Hairmyres Hospital, East Killbride,° near Glasgow. But if this is incorrect I can give you the exact address later.

I'm not surprised about the Czech version of A.F. What did surprise me was anyone accepting it in that country.[2] If they question you again, please say that A.F. is intended as a satire on dictatorship in general, but *of course* the Russian Revolution is the chief target. It is humbug to pretend anything else. It doesn't any way make much odds because I don't think the book could be openly published in any iron curtain country until the map changes a good deal. Do you know what's happened to the French version?[3] It's well over a year since I was shown the translation.

The German publisher could have "Inside the whale"° if he likes. You might explain to him the other two essays are also in the other book. With the Dickens & Koestler essays it should make about 35,000 words, & if he liked he could have two from "Polemic," "Politics vs. Literature" (on Swift), & "Lear, Tolstoy & the Fool." Unfortunately "Polemic" has wound up & I haven't a copy of the second essay here. I have one of the Swift essay, I think.

I shan't be able to see "Coming up° for Air" through the press. You will see to it, won't you, that they don't bring it out as a new book but definitely as the first in a uniform series, in some sort of modest cover which can be reproduced in others of the series.[4]

Yours sincerely
Eric Blair

1. Orwell entered Hairmyres Hospital, East Kilbride, near Glasgow, on 21 December 1947. See Shelden, 463–65; U.S.: 424–25.
2. A Czech version of *Animal Farm*, prepared by J. Salae & Co, Prague, was banned by the Czech authorities (Willison).
3. The French version of *Animal Farm* was published on 15 October 1947. An annotation against this sentence in Orwell's letter reads 'copy sent when' (though 'sent' looks very like 'set'). A copy was sent to Orwell, which he acknowledged on 26 December 1947; see *3317*.
4. The last sentence has been heavily underlined in Moore's office, and the whole paragraph bracketed and placed in quotes; beneath is written: 'Wrote Warburg 22 12 47.'

3315. To Frederick Tomlinson, *The Observer*

23 December 1947   Handwritten

Ward 3
Hairmyres Hospital
East Kilbride
Nr. Glasgow
[Telephone] East Kilbride 325

Dear Tomlinson,
I'm afraid it's all off about Africa so far as I'm concerned, much as I'd like to have done the trip. As you see I'm in hospital & I think likely to remain here 3–4 months. After being really very ill for about 2 months I got a chest specialist to come from the mainland, & sure enough it was T.B. as I feared. I've had it before, but not so badly. This time it's what they call "extensive" but they seem confident they can patch me up in a few months. For some time I've been far too ill even to attempt any work, but I'm beginning to feel somewhat better, & I was wondering whether the Obs. would like to start letting me have some books to review again. I suppose this isn't your department, but perhaps you could be kind enough to shove the suggestion along to Ivor Brown.[1]
I haven't heard from David[2] so don't know if he's back yet. Please give all the best to everybody from me.

Yours
Geo. Orwell

1. Ivor Brown (1891–1974), author of fiction and nonfiction, critic, and drama critic for *The Observer*, 1929–54, and its editor, 1942–48. See *1480, n. 2*.
2. David Astor.

3316. BBC Copyright Department to Orwell

23 December 1947

The Copyright Department of the BBC (in the person of Miss B. H. Alexander, from the reference) wrote to Orwell at his London address on 23 December 1947 apologising that Christopher Marsden, Producer of 'London Calling Europe' had overlooked obtaining permission to broadcast extracts from *The English People* 'totalling 3/4 minutes.' They hoped Orwell would give retrospective authority and offered a fee of £3. No reply has been traced.

3317. To Leonard Moore
26 December 1947   Handwritten

Ward 3
Hairmyres Hospital
East Kilbride
Nr. Glasgow

Dear Moore,
Many thanks for the copy of the French version of "Animal Farm." When the others come, would you keep them for me, as if sent on here they'll only get lost or something.

The above is my correct address & I gather I'll be here for some months. The treatment is to put the affected lung out of action so that it can heal, which is presumably a slow process. I can't do any serious work in bed, but I've felt slightly better in the last week or two, so I may start doing some book-reviewing soon, just to keep my hand in.

Yours sincerely
Eric Blair

3318. To Julian Symons
26 December 1947   Handwritten

Ward 3
Hairmyres Hospital
East Kilbride
Nr. Glasgow

Dear Julian,
I wonder if you'd do me a great favour & buy me a Biro pen. Mine is just coming to an end—I can have it refilled but meanwhile I should have nothing to write with. I forget what they cost, but enclose £3.[1]

As you see, I've landed up in hospital & am likely to be here some months. It is T.B., as I had feared. I've had this before, but not so badly. I think this bout really started in the cold of last winter. I thought early in the year I was seriously ill but rather foolishly decided to stave it off for a year as I'd just started writing a book. Of course what happened was that I half finished the book, which is much the same as not starting it, & then was so ill I had to take to my bed. For 2–3 months I've really been very sick indeed & have lost 1½ stone in weight, & have of course not done a stroke of work. However since getting to hospital I've felt better & don't have quite so much temperature &

sickness, so I am planning soon to start some book reviewing, as I might as well earn some money while on my back. With luck I'll be all right by the summer. They seem confident of being able to patch me up. It's a good hospital, & everyone is extraordinarily nice to me. I think all the same I'll spend next winter in a warm climate if possible.

Please remember me to your wife. Richard is getting enormous. It was a calamity "Polemic" stopping, wasn't it, & I think "Tribune" gets worse & worse.

Yours
George

1. A Biro pen cost £2.15.0 in November 1946. See headnote to 2375 for Orwell's first use of such a pen.

3319. Avril Blair's Barnhill Diary

Whilst Orwell was away from Barnhill, Avril kept up his Domestic Diary, from 27 December 1947 to 10 May 1948. Orwell re-opened the Diary on 31 July 1948. Except for the five consecutive entries below (all those from 1947), Avril's entries form Appendix 1 to 1948, 3514. See headnote to 3272.

27.12.47. *Very high wind & rough sea. Occasional showers of rain & sleet. Brilliant moonlit night.*
Hens started to lay again. One egg, the first since last entry in diary. (503).
28.12.47. *Beautiful morning with light sun & no wind. Overcast in afternoon turning to heavy showers of rain. Wind rising in the evening.*
2 eggs (505).
29.12.47. *Very slight fall of snow in the night. Melted by 10 am & followed by sleet showers on & off all day.*
2 eggs (507)
30.12.47. *Occasional sleet showers. Cat ice on the puddles in the early morning, quickly melting. No snow on surrounding hills. Mt Scarba[1] heavily covered. Not very cold.*
1 egg (508). Bill[2] sowing fertilizer on front field.
Dougie Clark brought up the hay from Craighouse.[3]
31.12.47. *Light powdering of snow in the morning, gone in the afternoon. Not much wind. Sea calm. cold.°*
1 egg (509). Bill finished the field.

1. Mt. Scarba dominated the island of Scarba, just to the north of Jura; its peak, 1,474 feet, is about five or six miles from Barnhill.
2. Bill Dunn.
3. Craighouse lies some twenty-five miles south of Barnhill; see 3025, n. 3. Dougie Clark worked on the Astors' estate at Tarbert, some seventeen miles south of Barnhill on the east coast of Jura. (There was also a Tarbert on the mainland opposite Jura.)

3320. To David Astor

31 December 1947   Handwritten

Ward 3
Hairmyres Hospital
East Kilbride
Lanarkshire

Dear David,

I have to continue this in pencil as my Biro pen is giving out. I was so glad to get your letter and know you were back. I'd love it if you did come and see me some time—don't put yourself out of course, but if you had to visit these parts anyway. I came by car, so I'm not certain how far out of Glasgow this is, but I think about 20 minutes drive. They don't seem to be very lavish with visiting hours. The official hours are: Sundays, Weds. & Sats., 2.30 to 3.30 pm, Tuesdays 6–7 pm.

As to what you say about Richard, he's in Jura with my sister at present, but later in the year I might be very glad to take advantage of your offer and dump him on you for a few weeks. The thing is that I don't know about my movements. The treatment they are giving me is one that must take a long time, and even if I get well enough to get out of bed and even leave the hospital, I imagine I should have to stay for some months in London or Glasgow or somewhere and go once a week for a "refill", which means having air pumped into one's diaphragm. My sister is going up to London for a short while in January or Feb. to do shopping etc., and she will leave R. with friends in Edinburgh. I am going to have him X-rayed then, though I must say of his appearance he doesn't look very T.B. I kept him away from me as best we could after I knew what was wrong with me, and we are getting a T.T. cow so as to make sure of his milk. We boil all his milk, but of course one can forget sometimes. Although he is still backward about talking, he is getting very big and rowdy, and loves working round the farm. I think he much prefers machinery to animals. One has to keep him off anything that can be taken to pieces. He even succeeded in uncoupling the trailer from the Fletchers' tractor. This is the first Christmas that he has more or less understood what it is all about, so I was very glad to get away just beforehand and not be a skeleton at the Christmas dinner. There were 4 of them there so I dare say they had quite a good time.

I'm writing to I.B.[1] suggesting that I should do an article once a fortnight, as I did before. I think I'll try and fix another article with somebody else, as I think I'm probably up to doing one a week now, and I might as well earn some money while I'm on my back. Of course I've done no work at all for 2–3 months, and indeed haven't been out of bed during that time. I've lost a stone and a half of weight, and still feel deadly sick and so forth all the time, but I think I've been better the last week or two. The treatment they are giving me is to put the affected lung out of action, which is supposed to give it a better chance to heal. I suppose this takes a long time, but they say it generally works. It is a nice hospital and everyone is extraordinarily kind to me.

Hoping to see you some time,   Yours, George.

P.S. You don't want to sell Bob,[2] I suppose? You know we have been wintering him again. He seems very good and tractable, and McIntyre seemed glad to get rid of him for the winter, as he said they had "plenty to winter already" Bill Dunn rides him when he goes to round up the sheep, but we did plan also to use him in the trap when the car goes to be overhauled, also for dragging wood etc.

1. Ivor Brown; see *3315, n. 1*.
2. In notes Avril made for Ian Angus elucidating references in the diaries, she wrote that 'David Astor was so concerned that Eric had no transport that he lent him Bob the pony.'

3321. To Ivor Brown

31 December 1947   Handwritten

Ward 3
Hairmyres Hospital
East Kilbride
Nr. Glasgow

Dear Ivor Brown[1]
Many thanks for your letter, & please excuse pencil.

If it were convenient to you, could I do you a review once a fortnight, as I used to do before? I'd be very happy to do them sometimes for the leader page, as you suggest. As to type of books, I prefer the sociological ones, or else literary criticism.

I'm afraid I shall have to send in my stuff in handwriting, but I'll try to make it legible & won't use pencil. It is just that my pen has given out at present.

I expect to be here some months. The treatment takes a long time, but in any case I don't think I'll be strong enough to get out of bed for a couple of months or two.°

Yours sincerely
Geo. Orwell

1. Brown had written to Orwell on 27 December saying how sorry he was to hear of his illness and offering to find some of the 'pitifully small' space available for book reviews. It would help, he wrote, if he could contribute some reviews in the form of short leader-page articles when that was appropriate to the subject matter.

3322. To Tosco Fyvel

31 December 1947   Handwritten

Ward 3
Hairmyres Hospital
East Kilbride
Lanarkshire

Dear Tosco,[1]

Thanks so much for your letter. I'd love it if you did come & see me some time. Don't put yourself out, of course, but if it was convenient. They don't seem very lavish with their visiting hours, though. The official hours are: Sundays, Weds. & Sats., 2.30–3.30 pm, Tuesdays 6–7 pm. This is a long way to come. I came by car, so I'm not sure how far out of Glasgow it is, but I think about 20 minutes drive.

I've only been in the hospital about 10 days, but I've been deadly sick for about 2–3 months & not very well the whole year. Of course I've had this disease before, but not so seriously. I was very well last year, & I think this show really started in that beastly cold of last winter. I was conscious early this year of being seriously ill & thought I'd probably got T.B. but like a fool I decided not to go to a doctor as I knew I'd be stuck in bed & I wanted to get on with the book I was writing. All that happened is that I've half written the book, which in my case is much the same as not starting it. However, they seem pretty confident they can patch me up, so I might be able to get back to some serious work some time in 1948. I am going shortly to start a little book-reviewing for the Observer. I might as well earn a bit of money while on my back, & I've felt somewhat better the last week or so. The treatment is to put the affected lung out of action, which is supposed to give it a better chance to heal. It is a slow job, I suppose, but meanwhile it does one good to have proper nursing here. It is a nice hospital & everyone is very kind to me. The next thing is to prevent Richard getting this disease, though I must say of his physique he doesn't look much like it at present. He is developing into a regular tough & loves working on the farm & messing about with machinery. I kept him away from me as best I could after I knew what was wrong with me, & we are getting a T.T. cow so as to feel a bit surer about his milk. We have been boiling his milk, but of course one can forget sometimes. Early in the year when my sister goes up to London for shopping, etc., I am going to have him X-rayed just to make sure.

I should think it would be quite nice living at Amersham. It's beautiful country round there. I remember we went on Home Guard[2] manoeuvres on Berkhampstead common,° and everywhere there were wild cherry trees weighted down with fruit. That night we were billeted in a barn, and early in the morning I woke up and was seriously alarmed to hear a lion roaring. Of course we were near Whipsnade,[3] which I didn't know.

Please give my love to Mary[4] and all the others. I don't know if it is much use now worrying about Palestine or anything else.[5] This stupid war is coming off in about 10–20 years, and this country will be blown off the map whatever else happens. The only hope is to have a home with a few animals in some place not worth a bomb.

Hoping to see you some time.

Yours,
George

1. T. R. (Tosco) Fyvel (1907–1985), author, journalist, broadcaster, and sociologist; see *2654*, *n. 1*.
2. The Home Guard, of which Orwell had been an early advocate and an active member; see his letter to *Time & Tide*, 22 June 1940, *642*, and a section of his London Letter, *Partisan Review*, November–December 1941, *843*.
3. Whipsnade Zoo, which is some three miles to the north of Berkhampstead Common (a favourite area in the 1930s and '40s for cadet force and similar exercises).
4. Mrs. T. R. Fyvel, of whom Orwell was very fond.
5. Fyvel, in his letter to Orwell, had presumably referred to the unsettled state of Palestine and the incipient violence of the situation. On 29 November 1947, the General Assembly of the United Nations had voted to partition Palestine, setting up separate Arab and Jewish states with a special status for Jerusalem. There was rejoicing by Jews, but an Arab spokesman, Dr. Hussein Khalidi, called for a crusade against the Jews. The UN made no provision for giving effect to its resolution. On 11 December 1947 the British government announced it would terminate its responsibility for Palestine under its mandate on 15 May 1948, and British troops then withdrew. See *3254, n. 3*, and for fuller discussion, Conor Cruise O'Brien, *The Siege: The Saga of Israel and Zionism* (1986).

APPENDIX

3323. List of Reprintable and Not Reprintable Works
   1947?

Orwell prepared four sets of notes, each marked specifically for his literary executor or listing his writings that he thought were reprintable. The first two sets date, in the main, from early 1945 (one is signed 31 March 1945); see *2648* and *2649*. The third set is reproduced below. For the last set see *3728*.

It is not possible to date this set with precision. The inclusion of items up until the end of March 1947 on the last page, and a date, 1947, on the first page, suggest that the notes were prepared some time in or after the summer of 1947, but possibly even in early 1948, when Orwell was in Hairmyres Hospital. 'How the Poor Die' was initially marked 'Never printed,' with the note 'Perhaps filed in my papers,' and the instruction, 'passage marked between brackets' (as being appropriate for publication); these words are crossed through and '"Now" 1946' added. This suggests that 'How the Poor Die' was first listed before October 1946 and the listing amended after publication in November 1946. Perhaps in listing 'How the Poor Die' Orwell automatically copied much of what he had included in his early 1945 list (where it appears as unpublished) and then realised that the essay had been published. That would suggest that the list was made up some time after November 1946 (when the publication of the essay would be fresh in his mind); it might even suggest that he made up the list when he was not well. One other factor to be considered is Orwell's note that 'Lear, Tolstoy and the Fool' was to be reprinted, abridged, in *Politics*. Dwight

Macdonald did not reprint it, and Orwell compiled this list whilst still expecting the article to appear. (The last number of *Politics* was for Winter 1948–49.) It is likely, therefore, that this list was completed late in 1947 or early in 1948.

The list is written on three openings of a notebook measuring $8\frac{5}{8} \times 6\frac{1}{8}$ inches. The entries are written in three columns (with some overlap) of recto pages and there are a number of notes on the facing versos. In printing the list, the disposition of the entries has not been precisely maintained; the facing-page notes have been placed immediately after the entries to which they refer, using Orwell's superscript references, except for two facing-page notes stipulating what should *not* be published: these are placed after all the other entries. Words crossed out by Orwell have been set within half square brackets. Editorial notes are indicated by superscript letters to avoid confusion with Orwell's references.

Title	*Source etc.*	*Remarks*
"Shooting an Elephant"	"New Writing" 1936	Reprinted rather often already.
"Marrakech"	"New Writing" 1939	Doubtful
"My Country Right or Left"	'New Writing" 1940	..
"Looking Back on the Spanish War"	"New Road" 1943	Should be reprinted[1]

1 Some of this v. topical but [first] part should be worth reprinting, esp. part V.

"As One Non-Combatant to Another" (verse)	"Tribune" 1943	Among press cuttings. Might be reprinted together with Alex Comfort's poem.
"Memories of the Blitz" (verse)	"Tribune" 1943	Among press cuttings.
"London Letters" (about 15)	"Partisan Review" 1941–1945	Extracts from these could be formed together to make a short book.
"As I Please" (about 50)	"Tribune" 1944–5, 1946–7	
"Notes on Nationalism"	"Polemic" 1945	Should be reprinted

French German & Italian translations & Finnish

"How the Poor Die" ⌈(passage marked between brackets)⌉	⌈Never printed⌉ "Now" 1946	⌈Perhaps filed in papers⌉
"The Story of an Experiment"	["Scope" 1945] Not printed[a]	Doubtful
"Poetry & the Microphone	"New Saxon Pamphlets" 1945	

"Gandhi in Mayfair" Fielden's Beggar my Neighbour	"Horizon" 1943	Reprinted once.
Antisemitism in Britain"	"Contemporary Jewish Record" (New York) 1945.	Doubtful
"Propaganda & Demotic Speech"	"Persuasion" 1944	Doubtful
"The British General Election"	"Commentary" 1945	Doubtful
"Grandeur et Décadence du Roman Policier Anglais"	"Fontaine" 1945 Russian translation[b]	V. Doubtful
"Jack London" (introduction to collection of short stories)	Paul Elek 1946	Possible
"The Prevention of[1] Literature"	"Polemic" 1945 (Also reply by Randall Swingler & my comments.)	Should be reprinted Reprinted in German[c] trans. [Finnish]

1   Reprinted (abridged version) in "Atlantic Monthly." NB. that the latter version is inadequate. Ditto various versions of "Politics & the English Language" (eg. in "New Republic.") Only the "Horizon" version is complete.

"Herbert Read"	"Poetry Quarterly" 1945 "Horizon"	
"Politics & the English Language"*	[Contact] 1946	[Should be reprinted]
	Reprinted a number of times.[d] (sometimes abridged)	

*NB. The reprintings included an edition privately printed by the "News of the World" for circulation among the staff. This is a rarity of which it might be worth securing a copy.

"A Hanging"	"Adelphi" 1931 Under name of Eric Blair Reprinted in the "Savoy" 1946	
"Second Thoughts on James Burnham"	"Polemic" 1946	Reprinted as pamphlet
"Why I write"°	"Gangrel" 1946	?
"Leonard Merrick"	Introduction to Eyre & Spottiswoode edition of "Peggy Harper."	Possible

"The Intellectual Revolt" (not my title).	4 articles in "Manchester Evening News", reprinted with summing-up article by M.O.I. (in translation). 1946	Just possible.
"Politics vs. Literature: an° Examination of Gulliver's Travels."	"Polemic" 1946 German translation (?)	Should be reprinted.
Editorial (unsigned)	"Polemic", May 1946	?
"Lear, Tolstoy & the Fool"[1]	"Polemic" 1947 "Politics" (much abridged) 1947.	Should be reprinted. (unabridged)

1   Reprinted much abridged in "Politics."
NB. that this version is inadequate.[e]

Article (5000) on James Burnhams° "The Struggle for the World"	"New Leader" (New York) 1947	Would go with the other one.

. . . .

NB. *Not* to be reprinted: an essay called "Culture & Democracy" in "Victory or Vested Interest?" This was transcribed from shorthand notes of a lecture, & was grossly altered without my knowledge.
Also *not* to be reprinted: introduction to collection of old pamphlets.

a. Not traced.
b. See *2828*.
c. After 'German' Orwell wrote 'trans' and repeated it on the next line.
d. Orwell inserted a superscript reference here referring again to note 1 following 'The Prevention of Literature.'
e. Macdonald did not reprint any of this essay, but when Orwell compiled this list he still expected its publication; see headnote and *3160, n. 1*.

1948

3324. To Gwen O'Shaughnessy

1 January 1948   Handwritten

Ward 3
Hairmyres Hospital
East Kilbride
Nr. Glasgow

Dear Gwen,[1]

I thought you'd like to hear how I was getting on. I believe Mr Dick[2] sent you a line about my case. As soon as he listened to me he said I had a fairly extensive cavity in the left lung, & also a small patch at the top of the other lung—this, I think, the old one I had before. The X-ray confirms this, he says. I have now been here nearly a fortnight, & the treatment they are giving me is to put the left lung out of action, apparently for about 6 months, which is supposed to give it a better chance to heal.[3] They first crushed the phrenic nerve, which I gather is what makes the lung expand & contract, & then pumped air into the diaphragm, which I understand is to push the lung into a different position & get it away from some kind of movement which occurs automatically. I have to have "refills" of air in the diaphragm every few days, but I think later it gets down to once a week or less. For the rest, I am still really very ill & weak, & on getting here I found I had lost 1½ stone, but I have felt better since being here, don't sweat at night like I used & have more appetite. They make me eat a tremendous lot. At present I am not allowed out of bed because apparently one has to get adjusted to having the extra air inside. It is a nice hospital & everyone is extremely kind to me. I have also got a room to myself, but I don't know whether that will be permanent. I have of course done no work for 2–3 months, but I think I may be equal to some light work soon & I am arranging to do a little book-reviewing.

Richard was tremendously well when I came away. After I was certain what was wrong with me I tried to keep him out of my room, but of course couldn't do so entirely. When Avril goes up to London in Jan. or Feb. to do some shopping I am going to take the opportunity of having Richard thoroughly examined to make sure he is O.K. We boiled his milk ever since you warned us, but of course one can forget sometimes. I am trying to buy a T.B.-tested cow, & I think we are on the track of one now. With Bill Dunn[4] in the house it is easier about animals, as he is going to pay part of his board by looking after our cows, which means that at need we can go away. I must say Richard doesn't look very T.B, but I would like to be sure. I think they had quite a good Christmas at Barnhill. There were 4 of them including Richard,

& there was a nice goose we bought off the Kopps.[5] I was glad to get away before Xmas so as not to be a death's head. I am afraid I didn't write any Xmas letters or anything & it's now a bit late even for New Year wishes. I hope by the summer I shall be well enough to go back to Barnhill for a bit & you & the kids will come again. Maybe there'll be a pony to ride this time—we have got one at present but he is only borrowed. They had a New Year party for the patients here, all the beds dragged into one ward & there were singers & a conjuror. I hope you had a good Christmas. Love to the kids.

Yours
George

1. Dr. Gwen O'Shaughnessy, widow of Eileen Blair's brother, Laurence ('Eric') O'Shaughnessy, killed tending the wounded at Dunkirk, 1940.
2. Dr. Bruce Dick, specialist in charge of the Thoracic Unit at Hairmyres Hospital. David Astor recalled that Orwell discovered that Dick 'had been on the opposite side to him on the Spanish civil war, and he decided not to engage in political talk. He was half amused that he'd fallen into the hands of a doctor who was completely disapproving of him' (*Remembering Orwell*, 199). This might be construed as indicating that Dick had served in Spain but in a letter to Ian Angus, 10 September 1996, Dr. James Williamson (see *n. 3*) thought that 'bunkum. . . . I have never heard of this nor do I think it at all likely . . . I cannot see him dashing off to Franco's side . . . I never heard him mention politics, Spain or Franco let alone the Civil War.'
3. In *Remembering Orwell*, Professor James Williamson, who was a junior doctor in the Thoracic Unit at Hairmyres Hospital when Orwell was a patient, describes Orwell's condition and treatment, and the technique of paralysing the phrenic nerve, which controls the expansion and contraction of the lung:

   It was a fairly trivial operation: you could do it in five minutes. You just pull the muscle aside, expose the nerve, and tweak it with a pair of forceps. The patient would get one sudden pain, and the diaphragm would jump, and that was the diaphragm paralysed for three to six months, until the nerve recovered again. Then we pumped air into his abdomen. The diaphragm was pushed up by this, and the lungs were collapsed. You put anything from four hundred to seven hundred cc of air in, under low pressure, with a special machine, through a needle which was a fairly elephantine-looking thing, a hollow needle about three inches long, actually. The first time you did it, you used a local anesthetic,° because you had to go very cautiously and advance it very slowly. But after that you just stuck it in, because patients agreed that if it was done expertly, one sharp jab was better than all this fiddling about with anesthetics and things.

   I remember he used to dread each 'refill' and couldn't relax at all when he was on the table. But he never complained. In fact we all noticed how much self-control he had. There was never a gasp, or any kind of noise from him when we did this.

   I don't think he would ever have been terribly infectious. The person who is highly infectious is the person who is coughing a lot, whose sputum has a lot of TB bacilli in it. He wasn't coughing a lot, nor was his sputum, as I remember it, terribly strongly positive. But he would still be a potential danger to other people, particularly to young people like his son.

   Most patients made much use of sputum mugs but Orwell's tuberculosis was not of that kind, and Williamson did not recall his having a sputum mug on his bedside locker: 'Mind you, I don't think there was any room for anything on his bedside locker because there were always books everywhere' (197–98). See also *3376, n. 1*.
4. For Bill Dunn, see *3235, n. 2*.
5. Georges Kopp had been Commandant of the POUM militia in which Orwell served in the Spanish civil war. They had remained friends and Kopp had married Gwen O'Shaughnessy's half-sister, Doreen. At this time the Kopps were running a farm at Biggar outside Edinburgh; see *2999, n. 1*.

3325. To Julian Symons

2 January 1948   Handwritten

Ward 3
Hairmyres Hospital
East Kilbride
Lanarkshire

Dear Julian,

Thanks ever so for sending the pen, which as you see I'm using. Of course it'll do just as well as a Biro & I prefer the colour of the ink. My other was just on its last legs & you can't use ink in bed.

I think I'm getting a bit better. I don't feel quite so deathlike & am eating a lot more. They stuff food into me all the time here. I don't know whether my weight is going up, because I'm kept strictly in bed at this stage of the treatment. They have put the affected lung out of action, which involves pumping air into one's diaphragm. I have this done every few days. It's a nice hospital & everyone is very kind to me. I was recommended to come here by my London chest specialist, & did so rather than go to London simply to avoid the long journey. It wasn't much fun coming even here in that state, but I could do most of it by car. It's funny you always think Scotland must be cold. The west part isn't colder than England, & the islands I should think decidedly warmer on average, though probably the summer isn't so hot. When I'm well enough to leave hospital I shall have to continue with this air-pumping business, so shall stay either in Glasgow or London for some months & just dodge up to Jura when I can. I have arranged things fairly well there. We, ie. my sister & I, have the house, & a young chap who lost a foot in the war[1] & is taking up farming lives with us & farms the croft. Another friend of mine acts as a sort of sleeping partner,[2] financing the croft & coming to help at the busy times. So I don't have bad conscience about living in a farmhouse & keeping someone else off the land, & at the same time can go away whenever I want to as our animals will be looked after in our absence. I'm just going to embark on cows, just one or two, because I'm in terror of Richard getting this disease & the safest thing is to have a T.T cow. I'm also going to get him thoroughly examined when my sister goes up to London. Of course I kept him off me once I was certain what was wrong with me, but he has certainly been exposed to infection. He has got such a splendid physique & I don't want him to wreck it.

About book reviewing. I had no thoughts of going back to the M.E. News. I am merely arranging to do a review once a fortnight for the Observer, & I think I shall try & fix one once a fortnight for someone else, as I'm probably up to doing one article a week now. I think that shows I'm better, as I couldn't have contemplated that a few weeks ago. I can't do any serious work—I never can do in bed, even when I feel well. I can't show you the part-finished novel. I never show them to anybody, because they are just a mess & don't have much relationship to the final draft. I always say a book doesn't exist until it is finished. I am glad you finished the life of your

249

brother.[3] It is such a ghastly effort ever to finish a book nowadays.

I agree with you about Tribune, though I think it's probably Fyvel rather than Kimche[4] who is responsible for the over-emphasis on Zionism. They would have done better when Labour got in to label themselves frankly a government organ, a. because in all major matters they *are* in agreement with the government, b. because Labour has no weekly paper definitely faithful to it & is in fact on the defensive so far as the press goes. The evil genius of the paper has I think been Crossman,[5] who influences it through Foot[6] & Fyvel. Crossman & the rest of that gang thought they saw an opening for themselves in squealing about foreign policy, which in the circumstances was bound to go badly, & so Tribune has been in the position of coming down on the side of the government whenever there is a major issue, eg. conscription, & at the same time trying to look fearfully left by raising an outcry about Greece etc. I really think I prefer the Zilliacus lot, since after all they do have a policy, ie. to appease Russia. I started writing an open letter to Tribune about this, but was taken ill before I finished it.[7] I particularly hate that trick of sucking up to the left cliques by perpetually attacking America while relying on America to feed & protect us. I even get letters from American university students asking why Tribune is always going for the USA & in such an ignorant way.

Well, this is quite a long letter. So my thanks again for sending the pen. I'll send my old Biro sometime when I've got a bit of paper & perhaps you'd be kind enough to get it refilled. My best respects to your wife.

Yours
George

1. Bill Dunn.
2. Sir Richard Rees, who is also described by Bill Dunn as a sleeping partner in *Remembering Orwell*, 183, and *Orwell Remembered*, 232. Rees put in £1,000, about half of which was spent on a lorry, at Rees's suggestion (*Orwell Remembered*, 234).
3. *A. J. A. Symons: His Life and Speculations* (1950). A. J. A. Symons (1900–1941), scholar and bibliophile (he edited *Book-Collector's Quarterly* with Desmond Flower, 1930–34), was a well-known personality of the London literary scene. He is now best known for *The Quest for Corvo: An Experiment in Biography* (1934).
4. Tosco Fyvel (1907–1985), writer, editor, journalist, and broadcaster, met Orwell in January 1940 and they became good friends; he was said to have known and understood Orwell better than anyone; see *2654, n. 1*. Fyvel was the son of an early Zionist leader who was associated with Theodor Herzl, the founder of Zionism. Unsurprisingly, Fyvel was actively pro-Zionist, especially in the years immediately after World War II, and on this subject he and Orwell disagreed sharply. Fyvel records that Orwell astonished the editorial board of *Tribune* by calling Zionists 'a bunch of Wardour Street Jews who have a controlling influence over the British press' (Wardour Street being 'a somewhat pejorative shorthand term for the ailing British film industry'). Kimche found it impossible to convince Orwell how wrong he was about 'Wardour Street Jews,' how little they represented Anglo-Jewry, and how few were Zionists. Later, Fyvel conceded 'that in 1946 [Orwell] foresaw more clearly than I how Zionism would lead to Israeli militarism' (Tosco Fyvel, *George Orwell: A Personal Memoir*, 1982, 96, 140, and 204). Jon Kimche (1909–1994), author and journalist, was acting editor of *Tribune*, 1942–46, editor, 1946–1948; and editor of the *Jewish Observer*, 1952–67. He and Orwell worked together at Booklovers' Corner, 1934–35. He contributes several reminiscences to *Remembering Orwell*. See also *212, n. 8*.
5. R. H. S. Crossman (1907–1974), scholar, journalist, and left-wing politician (Labour M.P., 1945–55); assistant editor of *The New Statesman*, 1938–55. Strenuous efforts were made to stop the publication of his political diaries (4 vols., 1975–81). See also *639, n. 7*.

6. Michael Foot (1913–), left-wing politician, writer, and journalist; M.P., 1945–55 and 1960–92. He was appointed managing director of *Tribune* in 1945, when Aneurin Bevan became a member of the post-war Labour Cabinet, and served as editor 1948–52 and 1955–60. Fyvel described him as 'a superb journalist, but I would not in 1945 have guessed at his future rise to political eminence': he became Leader of the Labour Party, in Opposition, in 1980, but resigned when the party was defeated at the General Election in 1983. See also *2955, n. 2*. Fyvel commented on this letter: 'Flattered though I should have been to be coupled with the future leader of the Labour Party, this was fantasy . . . by 1948, I had opted out of the political side of *Tribune* and . . . [was] as strongly pro-American and opposed to Left-wing anti-Americanism as Orwell was' (Fyvel, *George Orwell*, 139, 158).

7. 'In Defence of Comrade Zilliacus'; see *3254*.

3326. To Humphrey Dakin

3 January 1948   Handwritten

> Ward 3
> Hairmyres Hospital
> East Kilbride
> Lanarkshire

Dear Humphrey,

Have you killed another pig or are you planning to kill one? If you have any bacon to sell I am in the market.

I have been ill for about 2 months & was removed to this hospital about a fortnight ago. It's T.B., the left lung. Of course I've had this coming to me for years. I imagine I'll be here several months, as it's a slow treatment, & in any case I am fearfully pulled down. I hope I'll be back in Jura in the good part of the summer & perhaps the kids will come & get shipwrecked again, then perhaps I'll go somewhere warm next winter if I can fix it. Richard was blooming when I came away, but I'm going to have him thoroughly examined as he has undoubtedly been exposed to infection.

> Yours
> Eric

3327. To Leonard Moore

3 January 1948[1]   Handwritten

> Ward 3
> Hairmyres Hospital
> East Kilbride
> Lanarkshire

Dear Moore,

Perhaps you can be kind enough to answer this[2] for me. I don't feel I can cope with it. You could tell him I'm not answering letters much at present, perhaps.

I wrote to my sister to look out the number of "Polemic" containing the essay on Swift,[3] & she says she can't find it. I am afraid it is either lost or in London. I don't know if another would be procurable. The magazine has stopped & is already rather a rarity.

Yours sincerely
Eric Blair

1. Dated '3.1.47' in error.
2. Unidentified.
3. 'Politics vs. Literature: An Examination of *Gulliver's Travels*,' *Polemic*, 5, September–October 1946; see *3089*.

3328. To Edmund Wilson

3 January 1948   Handwritten

Ward 3
Hairmyres Hospital
East Kilbride
Lanarkshire

Dear Mr Wilson,[1]
You'll remember me, I dare say. I am writing to ask if you could be kind enough to help me to get a couple of books, unprocurable here. One is your own book "The Triple Thinkers". I've been trying for some time to get it—I particularly want to read your essay on "The Turn of the Screw." The other was a book I've searched for intermittently for years & was reminded of by your mentioning it recently in the New Yorker, Van Wyck Brooks's "The Ordeal of Mark Twain" (wasn't it "The Tragedy of M.T." by the way?)[2] One simply can't get books in this country. It is infuriating. Nothing has been reprinted for years. If one wants anything in the least bit out of the common one has to go to the British Museum, & they put every difficulty in your way even then. In this place I can't ever get books sent from the libraries because they won't send them to infectious places. I would be awfully obliged if you could get me those two books, & if you let me know what it costs I'll see you're paid. Of course if your own book is out of print I don't want to rob you of a copy.

I've been very ill for several months & am likely to be in this hospital several months more. It is T.B., very unpleasant, but they seem confident of patching me up all right. I took the liberty of writing to you because apart from frequently reviewing one another[3] I remember we did have lunch together once about 1944.[4]

Yours sincerely
Geo. Orwell

Wilson replied on 10 January. He sent Orwell Brooks's book on Mark Twain and also *The World of Washington Irving*, 'the best volume of his literary history of the United States.' Both books were in Orwell's library at his death, as were several by Wilson: *Axel's Castle, To the Finland Station,* and *The Triple Thinkers.* In his letter, Wilson does not mention that he is sending any of his books, but it is plain that at least one of his letters is lost, for, according to Orwell's letter of 12 February (see *3343*), Wilson had said he was sending a carbon copy of an essay on Henry James, but that is not mentioned in the letter of 10 January. See also Orwell's letter of 14 February, *3345*, which takes up Wilson's 10 January request for *Keep the Aspidistra Flying.* Probably the letters from Wilson arrived out of chronological order. Wilson remonstrated mildly with Orwell about his assumption in *The English People* that all insects in America 'are indiscriminately known as "bugs." ' He said he had tried to disabuse Orwell of that misunderstanding when they had met in London. Orwell replies to this on 14 February. Wilson also comments on the use of 'womanize,' which he has seen in highbrow English journalism, seemingly as a derogatory word used of 'men who have a sexual interest in women' (Edmund Wilson, *Letters on Literature and Politics, 1912–72,* edited by Elena Wilson, New York, 1977, 450–51).

1. Edmund Wilson (1895–1972), critic, essayist, novelist, short-story writer, and poet of individualistic Marxist persuasion. Among his most important critical books are *Axel's Castle* (1931), on Symbolist poets; *To the Finland Station* (1940), on the intellectuals who paved the way for the Russian Revolution; *The Triple Thinkers* (1938), on multiple meanings in the work of certain writers; *The Wound and the Bow* (1941), on art and neuroses; *The Boys in the Back Room* (1941), on contemporary American novelists; *Patriotic Gore* (1962), on the literature of the American Civil War; and *O Canada: An American's Notes on Canadian Culture* (1965). Several volumes of his short essays were collected; he edited some of F. Scott Fitzgerald's work and wrote a sharp attack on the methods employed in the editing of American literature (*The Fruits of the M.L.A.,* 1968); a number of his plays were published and also several volumes of poetry. Probably his best-remembered non-critical work is the collection of short stories *Memoirs of Hecate County* (1946). He reviewed for *The New Yorker* (care of which Orwell addressed this letter), 1944–48. See also Orwell's later letters to Wilson, *3343* and *3345*.
2. Van Wyck Brooks (1886–1963), American critic and biographer, winner of the Pulitzer Prize for *The Flowering of New England* (1936). As early as January 1931, Orwell had expressed interest in Mark Twain when writing to Max Plowman; see *102*. The book he refers to here was *The Ordeal of Mark Twain* (1920).
3. Perhaps 'frequently' is a slight exaggeration. Orwell mentions Wilson's essay on Kipling (later collected in *The Wound and the Bow*) in his own essay on Kipling, *Horizon,* February 1942 (see *948*) and reviewed *The Wound and the Bow* in *The Observer,* 10 May 1942 (see *1151*). Wilson had reviewed *Dickens, Dali & Others* in *The New Yorker,* 25 May 1946, and *Animal Farm,* 7 September 1946, also in *The New Yorker.* Wilson acutely recognises Orwell's contradictory gifts in the first of these reviews. He said that he had heard that in England Orwell was described as 'a combination of Leftism and Blimpism': that was perfectly true, he said, and with his talent as essayist, journalist, and novelist, made Orwell 'a unique figure among the radical intellectuals of the turbid thirties and forties. It has also made him sometimes slightly ridiculous, but his not fearing to appear ridiculous is one of the good things about him,' for he is not like so many who have 'mastered all the right sets of answers' and have thus slipped easily 'into all the right attitudes.' Though 'one frequently finds him quite unintelligent about matters that are better understood by less interesting and able critics,' yet he has those good English qualities, now coming to seem old-fashioned: 'readiness to think for himself, courage to speak his mind, the tendency to deal with concrete realities rather than theoretical positions, and a prose style that is both downright and disciplined'; what he does and does not like 'make, in their own way, a fairly reliable guide, for they suggest an ideal of the man of good will.'
4. They met in the summer of 1945.

3329. To George Woodcock

4 January 1948   Handwritten

Ward 3
Hairmyres Hospital
East Kilbride
Lanarkshire

Dear George,

I'd been meaning to write for some time to explain I wouldn't be coming down to London after all. As I feared, I am seriously ill, T.B. in the left lung. I've only been in the hospital about a fortnight, but before that I was in bed at home for about 2 months. I'm likely to be here for some time, because the treatment, which involves putting the lung out of action, is a slow one, & in any case I'm so pulled down & weak that I wouldn't be able to get out of bed for a couple of months or so. However, they seem confident they can patch me up all right, & I have felt a bit less like death since being here. It's a nice hospital & everyone is very kind. With luck I may be out for the summer & then I think I'll try & get a correspondent's job somewhere warm next winter. I have [had] this disease before, but not so badly, & I'm pretty sure it was the cold of last winter that started me off.

I hope the F.D.C.[1] is doing something about these constant demands to outlaw Mosley & Co. Tribune's attitude I think has been shameful, & when the other week Zilliacus wrote in demanding what amounts to Fascist legislation & creation of 2nd-class citizens, nobody seems to have replied. The whole thing is simply a thinly-disguised desire to persecute someone who can't hit back, as obviously the Mosley lot don't matter a damn & can't get a real mass following. I think it's a case for a pamphlet, & I only wish I felt well enough to write one. The central thing one has comes[2] to terms with is the argument, always advanced by those advocating repressive legislation, that "you cannot allow democracy to be used to overthrow democracy—you cannot allow freedom to those who merely use it in order to destroy freedom". This of course is true, & both Fascists & Communists do aim at making use of democracy in order to destroy it. But if you carry this to its conclusion, there can be no case for allowing any political or intellectual freedom whatever. Evidently therefore it is a matter of distinguishing between a real & a merely theoretical threat to democracy, & no one should be persecuted for expressing his opinions, however anti-social, & no political organisation suppressed, unless it can be shown that there is *a substantial threat to the stability of the state.* That is the main point I should make any way. Of course there are many others.

I've done no work whatever for 2–3 months. In this place I couldn't do serious work even if I felt well, but I intend shortly to start doing an occasional book review, as I think I'm equal to that & I might as well earn some money. Richard was blooming when I came away, but I'm going to have him thoroughly examined, as he has of course been subjected to infection. All the best to Inge.

Yours
George

1. The Freedom Defence Committee, of which Orwell was Vice-Chairman; George Wood-cock, Secretary; and Herbert Read, Chairman. The FDC's Bulletins for Spring and Autumn 1948 (Nos. 6 and 7), though reporting efforts to help other unpopular causes—deserters, Polish 'recalcitrants' (its quotes), Dr. Alan Nunn May, and Norman Baillie-Stewart—surprisingly make no mention of 'Mosley & Co.'
2. comes] to come

3330. To Helmut Klöse

12 January 1948   Handwritten

Ward 3
Hairmyres Hospital
East Kilbride
Lanarkshire

Dear Klöse,

I am ashamed I have not written earlier to thank you for those apples you sent, also for your long letter of advice about the tractors. But as I dare say you know I have been seriously ill for about 3 months. It is TB of the left lung. I was brought to this hospital some weeks ago, & I am glad to say I am feeling definitely better. Of course I'm frightfully weak & have lost a great deal of weight, but I don't feel sick & giddy all the time as I did at first, & have got some appetite back. I imagine I shall be under treatment for a long time, as it is a slow cure which involves disabling the defective lung so as to let it heal without having to work. However they seem quite confident of being able to patch me up, & they say this disease is not so dangerous at my age as if I was younger. Of course I've done not a stroke of work for months past, but I am going to start doing a little book-reviewing soon.

In your letter you were inclined to think the BMB was the best light tractor. However, after getting all the specifications from a firm which deals in these tractors, I finally decided on the one you told me of first, the Iron Horse. From the photographs I thought it was a bit more solidly constructed than the other, which would be an advantage in a place like Jura, & also you can hitch horse-drawn implements on to it, which would be a great help because one could then use it for cutting the hay & even the oats. It also has a 5-cwt trailer which would be useful for potatoes, manure & so on. I am getting a circular saw, but I believe at present it's almost impossible to get blades. I will take your advice & not try to run a dynamo off the tractor. Actually we find we can light the house quite satisfactorily with paraffin lamps. We use the Tilly incandescent lamps which are very powerful & don't use much oil.

255

Karl[1] & David Astor came & visited me here yesterday, bringing loads of food with them. It was very kind of them to make the long uncomfortable journey. The weather has turned absolutely filthy, snow & fog alternating, making me quite glad to be in bed. There was marvellous weather in Jura all the time before I came away, brilliant sunshine on the snow & the sea as blue & smooth as the Mediterranean. The average winter temperature there is very mild & the grass seems to be quite nourishing up till about Christmas. The blackfaced sheep remain out all the winter without being fed, & the highland cattle can get through the winter without feeding, though of course it's better to feed them.

My little boy, now 3½, is getting enormous. We are trying to get hold of an attested cow so as to make sure that he doesn't get this disease of mine. I hope I shall see you again some time.

Yours
Geo. Orwell

1. Karl Schnetzler; see *534A, headnote* and *2893*.

3331. To Mary Fyvel

16 January 1948   Handwritten

Ward 3
Hairmyres Hospital
East Kilbride
Lanarkshire

Dear Mary,

You really oughtn't to have sent me all that stuff—but any way, thanks awfully for it. I do hope you could spare it.[1] I think I am getting better. It's a slow process, but I feel somewhat better & they seem to think the X rays show signs of improvement. I have air pumped into my diaphragm once a week, & later shall have it pumped between the ribs as well. Richard was blooming when I came away. He is now 3½ or a little over. He is still backward about talking, partly I think because he doesn't see enough of other children, but very bright & self-reliant in other ways. He is out helping with the farm work all day long, getting himself covered with mud from head to foot. He has had measles & whooping cough this year, but they made very little impression on him, & I am sorry to say he also fell down & cut his forehead & had to have stitches put in. However I think the scar will disappear in a year or two. Shortly my sister is going up to London to do shopping, & then we will take the opportunity to have Richard thoroughly examined. I must say he doesn't look like a TB case, but it's as well to be sure as he has been exposed to infection. We're also negotiating for a TT cow as the milk in Scotland is a bit suspect. It's a shame I shan't be able to see him for some months, not till I am non-infectious.

I hope you like your new house. Tosco gave me the impression it was somewhere near Amersham, but I don't think it can be if it's in Bucks?[2] I hope you're O.K. for fuel this winter. That's one advantage in Jura, we can wangle almost all the coal & oil we want, & of course there is wood & peat if one can be bothered. I believe that what started me off this time was that awful cold last winter. Love to Tosco & the kids, & thank you so much again.

Yours
George

1. Although the war had ended 2½ years earlier, food was still strictly rationed; see *3017, n. 3* and *3332, n. 3.*
2. Amersham is in Buckinghamshire.

3332. To Celia Kirwan

20 January 1948   Handwritten

Ward 3
Hairmyres Hospital
East Kilbride
Lanarkshire

Dearest Celia,

How delightful to get your nice long letter. I've been here about a month after being ill for about two months at home. I thought I'd told you what was wrong with me. It is TB, which of course was bound to get me sooner or later, in fact I've had it before, though not so badly. However I don't think it is very serious, & I seeming° to be getting better slowly. I don't feel so death like as I did a month ago, & I now eat quite a lot & have started to gain weight slowly, after losing nearly 2 stone. Today when I was X-rayed the doctor said he could see definite improvement. But I'm likely to be here a long time, as it's a slow treatment, & I don't think I shall even be fit to get out of bed for about 2 months. Richard is tremendously well & growing enormous. Of course I'm going to have him thoroughly examined when Avril takes him up to London shortly, but by the look of him I don't think he's caught this disease. I was very glad to be able to get away just before Christmas, so as not to be a death's head. There were 4 of them at Barnhill & a nice fat goose & plenty to drink, so I expect they had quite a good Christmas. This is the second Christmas I've spent in hospital.[1] It's always rather harrowing, with the "parties" they have—all the beds dragged into one ward, & then a concert & a Christmas tree. This is a very nice hospital & everyone is most kind to me, & I have a room to myself. I'm starting to attempt a very little work, ie. an occasional book review, after doing nothing for 3 months.

Yes, I remember the Deux Magots.[2] I think I saw James Joyce there in 1928, but I've never quite been able to swear to that because J. was not of very distinctive appearance. I also went there to meet Camus who was supposed to have lunch with me, but he was ill & didn't come. I suppose Paris has cheered up a bit since I was there at the beginning of 1945. It was too gloomy for words then, & of course it was almost impossible to get anything to eat & drink, & everybody was so shabby & pale. But I can't believe it is what it used to be. It's lucky for you you're too young to have seen it in the 'twenties, it always seemed a bit ghostlike after that, even before the war. I don't know when I'll see France again, as at present one can't travel because of this currency business,[3] but if one of my books *did* strike it lucky I'd get them to keep some of the francs in France so that I could go & spend them. If I'm cured & about by then as I assume I shall be, I am going to try & wangle a correspondent's job this winter so as to winter in a warm place. The winter of 1946–7 in London was really a bit too thick, & I think it was probably what started me on this show. In Jura it's a bit better, because it isn't quite so cold & we get more coal, also more food, but it's a bit awkward if one needs medical attention at a time when one can't get to the mainland. Early last year my sister dislocated her arm & was nearly drowned going across to the doctor in a tiny motor boat. Inez[4] exaggerated our later adventure a bit, but we did have a very nasty accident in the famous whirlpool of Corrievrechan (which comes into a film called "I know where I'm going") & were lucky not to be drowned. The awful thing was having Richard with us, however he loved every moment of it except when we were in the water. I think Jura is doing him good except that he doesn't see enough of other children & therefore is still very backward in talking. Otherwise he is most enterprising & full of energy, & is out working on the farm all day long. It's nice to be able to let him roam about with no traffic to be afraid of. Write again if you get time. I love getting letters.

With much love
George

1. The first time was when Orwell went into Uxbridge Cottage Hospital just before Christmas 1933 with pneumonia.
2. The Café aux Deux Magots, much frequented by writers, on the Boulevard Saint-Germain in Paris.
3. At the end of August 1947, because of the grave financial crisis, the Labour government reduced food rations, and banned pleasure motoring and holidays abroad. Clement Attlee, the Prime Minister, said, 'I have no easy words for the nation. I cannot say when we shall emerge into easier times.' On 29 September, the Midlands was deprived of power for one day a week to cut fuel costs. On 9 October 1947, the government cut the bacon ration to one ounce a week. The following month the potato ration was cut to 3 pounds per week. These were among the steps taken to reduce foreign indebtedness, especially in dollars.
4. Inez Holden; see Orwell's letter to Celia Kirwan, 7 December 1947, *3312*.

3333. To Anthony Powell
25 January 1948   Handwritten

Ward 3
Hairmyres Hosp.
East Kilbride
Lanarkshire

Dear Tony,
Thanks so much for your letter. It doesn't matter about the saddle.[1] We're supposed to have one coming, but if you do chance to run across another I'll always buy it because it wouldn't hurt to have two. The petrol situation is so calamitous that one has to use horses for certain purposes, & also the chap who lives with us & farms the croft lost a foot in Italy[2] & it's easier for him to round up cattle etc. on horseback. No, I don't think one could use a side saddle. It would be like shooting a fox sitting or something. I must say in the days when I used to ride I sometimes secretly thought I'd like to try a side saddle, because I believe it's almost impossible to fall off.

I've been here 5 or 6 weeks & I think I'm getting better. I don't feel nearly so deathlike & they say the X rays are beginning to show progress, though very slight. I'd done about half my novel & shan't touch it again till I'm well, but I'm starting to do a very little light work, ie. book reviews. I've just done one[3] & feel I've broken a spell as I hadn't even contemplated working for 3 months. My handwriting is so bad because my right arm is half crippled. I've had trouble in it for some time & it's probably of a tuberculous nature, which it seems doesn't matter much but is hellish painful for the time being. I'd like to do something for the TLS, but if I do it'll have to be handwritten, because even if I had a typewriter here I can't at present get my hand into that position. Did I tell you I was starting a uniform edition, as everyone seems to be doing, a sign of approaching senility I think. I am starting off with one called "Coming Up for Air" which was published in 1939. This is a very nice hospital & everyone is very good to me. I imagine I'll be in bed for months yet, & even when I get out will have to go on being an out-patient, as the treatment lasts about 6 months. In that case I'll have to stay in Glasgow & get down to London or up to Jura for a few days when I can. Of course I can't see Richard till I'm non-infectious. He's growing into a real tough. I'm going to have him examined for TB when my sister goes up to London shortly, but I can't believe there's anything wrong with him.

All the best to Violet. I hope to see you within a few months anyway.
Yours
George

1. Orwell had asked Powell if he could find a saddle, 29 November 1947; see *3308*.
2. Bill Dunn.
3. A review of *India Called Them* by Lord Beveridge; see *3336*.

3334. BBC Copyright Department to Orwell

26 January 1948

Miss B. H. Alexander, of the BBC Copyright Department, wrote to Orwell on 26 January 1948 (to his London address) saying she had not had a reply from him to her letter of 23 December 1947 asking for retroactive authority for quoting from *The English People* in a European Service broadcast; see *3316*. She repeated details of the fee offered and also asked if he would 'give us blanket authority to broadcast your works subject to payment of the appropriate fee under the Standard Terms Agreement.' The carbon copy of this letter in the BBC Archive is marked: '16 Feb   Still no reply.'

3335. To Eugene Reynal

28 January 1948   Handwritten; copy

> Ward 3
> Hairmyres Hospital
> East Kilbride
> Lanarkshire, Scotland

Dear Mr. Reynal,[1]
I must thank you very kindly for the food parcel which you so kindly sent me & which reached me here about a week ago. It was a very pleasant surprise. I was particularly thrilled to find in it a tin of olive oil, a thing we have not seen for years.

I expect Leonard Moore told you I was ill, as I asked him to let anyone in the USA with whom I had any connections know I should be out of action for some months. It is TB of the left lung. I have been ill for three months or more, but actually I think ever since that vile winter of 1946–47. I feel better & I think I have just about turned the corner, but the cure is a slow one at best. Of course I can't do any serious work till I'm in good health, but I am beginning to do just a little journalism. After months of idleness, I'm afraid my handwriting is getting a bit funny, but that is because I have my right arm in plaster & haven't got used to this yet.

Thank you so much again.

> Yours sincerely,
> George Orwell

1. Of Reynal & Hitchcock, New York, publishers of *Dickens, Dali & Others* (1946), the U.S. edition of *Critical Essays*.

3336. Review of *India Called Them* by Lord Beveridge
The Observer, 1 February 1948

Lord Beveridge's biography of his parents is primarily, as he says, a study of their characters, but most readers will probably value it more as a picture of British India in the forgotten decades between the Mutiny and Kipling's *Plain Tales from the Hills*.

Both the Beveridges, Henry and Annette, came from a commercial middle-class background, Scottish in the one case, Yorkshire in the other. They went out to India with an intense interest in Oriental affairs but with no imperialist traditions or connections. Henry had passed top into the Indian Civil Service in 1857, one of the very first batch of "competition wallahs."[1] He was the best type of Scottish intellectual, agnostic, mildly but obstinately radical, ambitious, but not supple enough to succeed in an official career. Throughout life he never seems to have budged from an opinion because of outside pressure, and his views on India were exactly the wrong ones to hold at that date. He knew that India could not yet be independent, but he held that the aim of British rule should be "to prepare for its own extinction," and that the first step towards this—the Indianisation of the services—should be greatly accelerated.

A generation earlier these views would have seemed reasonable to Macaulay: a generation later, much of what Henry Beveridge advocated was within sight of happening. But the period covered by his career, 1858–1893, was a bad period in Indian-British relations. Among the British, imperialist sentiment was stiffening and an arrogant attitude towards "natives" was becoming obligatory. The greatest single cause was probably the cutting of the Suez Canal. As soon as the journey from England became quick and easy the number of Englishwomen in India greatly increased, and for the first time the Europeans were able to form themselves into an exclusive "all white" society. On the other side the Nationalist movement was beginning to gather bitterness. Henry Beveridge supported unpopular reforms, wrote indiscreet magazine articles, and in general stamped himself as a man of dangerous views. As a result he was repeatedly passed over for promotion and spent most of his career in subordinate jobs on fever-stricken islands of the Ganges delta.

Annette, his wife, was first and foremost his intellectual companion, but her development was very different. Coming out to India under Indian sponsorship to run a school for Bengali girls, she started out with much more vehemently pro-Indian views than her husband, but in the end swung round to a position that could almost be called Conservative. Part of the reason was that she was repelled by the Indian attitude towards women. In her old age, in England, she was to be a local secretary of the National Women's League for Opposing Woman Suffrage.

After retirement the two of them had what almost amounted to a second lifetime of thirty-five years, filled up with heavy literary labours. Annette translated Persian fairy tales and learned Turki at 60: Henry spent twenty years in translating the Persian history of Akbar. Toward the end Annette grew so deaf that they could only communicate in writing. They died in 1929, within a few months of each other. Besides some good photographs, the book contains a fascinating table setting forth the exact composition of an Anglo-Indian household in the 'eighties. From this one learns just why it was necessary for the Beveridges—a couple with three children, living very modestly by European standards—to have thirty-nine servants.

1. 'Competition wallah' was the term applied to those who were admitted to the Indian Civil Service by competitive examination, introduced in 1856, instead of through influence; properly, a competitioner, 'wallah' being the Urdu equivalent of the suffix –er, though usually understood by British people to mean a person or fellow.

3337. To David Astor

1 February 1948   Handwritten

> Ward 3
> Hairmyres Hospital
> East Kilbride
> Lanarkshire

Dear David,

Thanks so much for your letter. Before anything else I must tell you of something Dr Dick has just said to me.

He says I am getting on quite well, but slowly, & it would speed recovery if one[1] had some streptomycin (STREPTOMYCIN).[2] This is only obtainable in the USA, & because of dollars the B.O.T.[3] (or whoever it is) won't normally grant a licence. One can however buy it there if one has some dollars. He suggested that you with your American connections might arrange to buy it & I could pay you. He wants 70 grammes, & it costs about £1 a gramme. I would be awfully obliged if you could put this transaction through for me, as no doubt you can do it quicker than I could myself. There is no twist or illegality about this, Dr Dick says, & the stuff is not difficult to send. I suppose it will mean paying out about 300 dollars. If you want to be repaid in dollars, I think I have enough, as I had started building up a reserve of dollars in the US, otherwise I can pay you in sterling. I must in either case pay you, as it is a considerable sum & of course the hospital can't pay it.

I received from McIntyre[4] a parcel of butter & eggs, & he told me you had instructed him to send this weekly. It is awfully kind, but I am going to ask him not to send the eggs, as I can't use them in those numbers & I expect the hens aren't laying too well now. I know ours at Barnhill are still doing very badly. I feel we ought to pay for Bob[5] if we have him 10 months of the year—however. He only gets hay in the winter—of course he'd get oats if he were doing harder work—but he was in excellent condition when I came away. Our new cow has just arrived & my sister can't leave until it has calved. I'm afraid my writing is awful, but I have my arm in plaster. It's much better that way, as it doesn't hurt but it is awkward for certain purposes such as writing & eating. I also have to shave left-handed. Dr Dick says he will write to you. I suppose it will be best to have the drug sent to him. His correct designation is Mr Bruce Dick.

Yours
George

1. 'one' may be 'we.'
2. Streptomycin was discovered in the United States in 1944 and was at this time being tested in Britain by the Medical Research Council.
3. Board of Trade, which controlled imports, and at this time refused to allow as many as it could, especially if payment was in dollars.
4. Presumably one of the Astor estate staff on Jura.
5. A horse loaned by the Astors to Orwell.

3338. To Philip Rahv

4 February 1948   Handwritten

Ward 3
Hairmyres Hospital
East Kilbride
Lanarkshire
Scotland

Dear Rahv,
As you see the writer of the enclosed[1] asks me to take up his affair with you, & I'm sending the letter on as I really don't remember what it's all about. I imagine he asked me if he could translate some of my P.R. articles, in which case I will have told him that it was all right so far as I was concerned but that he must ask you. Do let him if you can. They're simply starved of reading matter & of course they can't pay anything for serial rights.

As you see I'm in hospital. It's T.B. of the left lung, & at the moment I've also got my right arm in plaster. I've been in bed 3 months or more & haven't really been well since the beginning of 1947. I think it was really that awful winter of 1946–47 that started it off. However the cure is going on all right & I'm going to have some new drug called streptomycin. I suppose I'll be out & about by the summer—about a year wasted in all. Of course I can't do any serious work when I am like this.

Till recently you've still been very kindly sending me P.R. I meant to tell you please don't, as I've had a subscription to the English edition for some time. A friend of mine[2] has just written you a furious letter about Arthur Koestler's London Letters. I must say I rather agree with him & was meaning to take it up with Arthur when next I see him. It's disgraceful to keep on squealing about petty discomforts like petrol rationing that don't touch the mass of the people.

Please remember me to the others.

Yours
Geo. Orwell

1. This was a letter of 16 January 1948 from Dr. Fritz Eberhard, Leiter des Deutschen Büros für Friedensfragen (Chief of the German Office for Problems Arising from the Peace) concerning a translation of 'Toward European Unity' which he had published in the *Stuttgarter Rundschau*. *Partisan Review*, which had published the article in its July–August 1947 issue, wrote to him because he had not first obtained permission. This seems either to have been a genuine oversight—because Eberhard had sent *Partisan Review* sample copies, which was what had drawn their attention to this translation—or a misunderstanding of Orwell's co-operation as tacit approval to go ahead. Eberhard was anxious to have the matter cleared up and asked Orwell to intercede because of the wish to publish translations of Koestler's London Letters also. He concluded his letter to Orwell by saying he hoped to meet him in London in February or March if their friend Marjorie Springe could arrange this.
2. Unidentified.

3339. To Fredric Warburg

4 February 1948   Handwritten

> Ward 3
> Hairmyres Hospital
> East Kilbride
> Lanarkshire

Dear Fred,

Thanks so much for your letter.[1] As you inferred, my beginning to do articles in the Observer is a sign of partial revival, though even that is an effort, especially as I now have my right arm in plaster. I can't attempt any serious work while I am like this (1½ stone under weight) but I like to do a little to keep my hand in & incidentally earn some money. I've been definitely ill since about October, & really, I think, since the beginning of 1947. I believe that frightful winter in London started it off. I didn't really feel well all last year except during that hot period in the summer. Before taking to my bed I had finished the rough draft of my novel all save the last few hundred words, & if I had been well I might have finished it by about May. If I'm well & out of here by June, I might finish it by the end of the year—I don't know. It is just a ghastly mess as it stands, but the idea is so good that I could not possibly abandon it. If anything should happen to me I've instructed Richard Rees, my literary executor, to destroy the MS. without showing it to anybody, but it's unlikely that anything like that would happen. This disease isn't dangerous at my age, & they say the cure is going on quite well, though slowly. Part of the cure is to put the affected lung out of action for six months, which gives it a better chance to heal. We are now sending for some new American drug called streptomycin which they say will speed up the cure.

Richard is getting enormous & is very forward in everything except talking. I'm going to have him thoroughly examined when my sister goes up to town, but I really don't think he's T.B. to judge by the look of him. It's sad that I can't see him again till I'm non-infectious. Please remember me to Pamela and Roger.

> Yours
> George

1. Warburg wrote to Orwell on 2 February 1948 saying that Orwell's review of *India Called Them* by Lord Beveridge in *The Observer*, 1 February (see *3336*), 'gave me heart to write and enquire how you are getting on.' He said there was nothing they needed to consult about but he would be greatly cheered by 'a line, however brief, as to how you are and how soon you hope to come out of that wretched hospital.'

3340. To Fredric Warburg

4 February 1948

PLEASE DO STOP   DELIGHTED TO SEE YOU[1]   GEORGE

1. This was, presumably, in response to a telegram from Warburg and sent by Orwell after he had posted his letter of 4 February.

3341. To Leonard Moore

5 February 1948   Handwritten

Ward 3

Dear Moore,

Thanks for your letter. Yes, I've started to do a few book reviews, but that's about all I can do. I am still very weak, & I don't imagine I shall get up for some months. However I'm going to have a new drug called streptomycin, when we can get it from the USA, which they say will speed up the cure.

I'll remember about the MS. of the novel,[1] when it gets done. I can't touch it till I am well, & I generally look on the revision as taking about 5 months.

Yours sincerely
Eric Blair

1. *Nineteen Eighty-Four.*

3342. To David Astor

Monday, [9 February 1948][1]   Handwritten

Dear David,

Just a hurried note to say thanks awfully your seeing about the streptomycin. Meanwhile you'll have had a telegram[2] which crossed your letter & which I hope you didn't bother to answer. Just having heard I got time to ring up last night, & as you were down in the country I then wired, as I did think it conceivable my original letter hadn't gone off. We get them posted in a rather sketchy way here.

Of course I must pay you for the stuff. But I'll try & think of something else you'd like, or your little girl.

I've just heard the Darrochs[3] are "definitely leaving" Kinuachdrach, but I still can't find out what the row was about. It's a sad business after D.D. has broken his back reclaiming the farm, & awkward for the Fletchers[4] too. However, they'll have to get another tenant if only to look after their cattle.

All well here. They pump me so full of air once a week that I feel like a balloon for two days afterwards.

Yours,
George

1. The letter is dated only 'Monday.' There is an annotation, not in Orwell's hand, at its top left corner, '5.40–7.26   WES 3316' and below that telephone number, another, 'SLO.5613.'
2. Not traced.
3. Donald and Katie Darroch; see *3003, n. 2.*
4. Robin and Margaret Fletcher; see *3025, n. 2.*

3343. To Edmund Wilson

12 February 1948   Handwritten

Ward 3
Hairmyres Hospital
East Kilbride
Lanark. Scotland

Dear Wilson,
Many thanks for your letter received a week or two back. What I am really writing to say is:[1] you said you would send a carbon of the Henry James essay, but if you have not already done so, don't bother, because I have just got hold of the essay in an anthology called "American harvest."

I'd love it if you could find me a copy of the Van Wyck Brooks book,[2] ie. the early version—I didn't know he had dolled it up later. I'll send you a copy of a novel I am having reprinted this year.[3] It came out in 1939 & was rather killed by the war, & has been very thoroughly out of print because the stocks were blitzed. It's not much good but bits of it might interest you.

I am getting on O.K. but rather slowly. I am going to have something called streptomycin which it seems is wonderful. Please excuse handwriting, my arm is in plaster.

Yours sincerely
Geo. Orwell

1. See Orwell's letter, 3 January 1948 and notes to it, *3328.*
2. *The Ordeal of Mark Twain*, first published in 1920.
3. *Coming Up for Air*, in the Uniform Edition, published 13 May 1948.

3344. To David Astor

Saturday, [14 February 1948][1]   Handwritten

Dear David,
Did you really not want the pens? They're very useful, as my Biro was out of action & also lost, & my Rollball not functioning very well. This is yours I'm writing with.

The Van Gogh exhibition apparently begins on the 21st.

I'd certainly love to come down to your Abingdon place in the summer for a weekend, if I'm about by then. It would be lovely having the river at your door. Probably in June or July there'd be good fishing, dace & chub. The Thames fishing can be quite good. I caught some good fish at Eton, but hardly anybody outside College knew the place, as it was in the backwater joining on College field.

I still haven't got to the bottom of the row at Kinuachdrach, but I gather it was between Bill & Donald. I assume Donald won't leave immediately. The Fletchers are advertising for another tenant. They'll have to have someone to look after their herd of Highlands.

By the way, I think you said poor old Niel° Darroch might want to sell his boat—do you remember whether it was petrol or paraffin?

Yours
George

1. Dated only 'Sat.' The Van Gogh Exhibition opened at the Tate Gallery, London, on 10 December 1947 and ran to 14 January 1948; it visited Birmingham, 24 January to 14 February 1948, and Glasgow—near where Orwell was in hospital—20 February to 14 March 1948. This letter is so fresh with hope that it must surely have been written before the course of streptomycin began: that, he wrote to Middleton Murry on 20 February 1948, had 'just started'; and contrast the tone of this letter and that to Murry. Saturday, 14 February, is, therefore, the most likely date for this letter. That also must place the letter here dated 16 February 1948 to that particular Monday; see *3349*.

3345. To Edmund Wilson

14 February 1948[1]   Handwritten

Ward 3
Hairmyres Hospital
East Kilbride
Lanark. Scotland

Dear Wilson,
Thanks so much for your letter of Jan 10th, which must have crossed one of mine. I've told you I'll send you a copy of "Coming Up for Air" when reprinted,[2] & if there are still copies I'll get Warburg to send you a copy of "Homage to Catalonia" my Spanish war war° book. Of course everyone is long ago fed up with that subject, but actually the book has some historical value, I think. "Keep the Aspidistra Flying" is one of several books that I have

suppressed. I didn't let it be reprinted, & it is pretty thoroughly out of print. That dreadful little "English People" book was written before I had that conversation with you about the American vocabulary.[3] It was meant as a piece of war propaganda which I was almost physically bullied into writing by W. J. Turner, the poet, now dead.[4] The publishers held it up for years because they thought it bad propaganda, then produced it in 1947 with a few sentences stuck in to show that the war had ended in the mean time.

Thanks so much for sending the books. I read your essay on James with great interest, but I must say I think you're wrong about "The Turn of the Screw". Please excuse handwriting. I have to write at such an awkward angle.

Yours sincerely
Geo. Orwell

1. Addressed to Wilson at *The New Yorker*, in New York City, and readdressed to him at Hotel Vendome, 160 Commonwealth Avenue, Boston. The letter shows, in addition to the repetition of 'war,' two false starts, both scored through (and not transcribed here).
2. See Orwell's letter to Wilson, 12 February 1948, *3343* and *3328, n. 3*.
3. See *3328, endnote*.
4. For *The English People*, see *2475*; for W. J. Turner, *1743, n. 1*.

3346. 'Marx and Russia'
The Observer, 15 February 1948

This essay was prompted by the publication of *What is Communism?* by John Petrov Plamenatz (1912–1975), published by *National News-Letter*, associated with Commander Stephen King-Hall's *News-Letter Service* (founded in 1936). King-Hall (1893–1966) contributed an introduction. Plamenatz had his first book, *Consent, Freedom and Political Obligation*, published by Oxford University Press in 1938. Also published by him in Orwell's lifetime were *The Case for General Mihailovic* (privately printed, 1944), *What is Communism?*, 1947, and *Mill's Utilitarianism* (with *The English Utilitarians*), 1949. Notes made in the preparation of this review and for several other articles published in 1948 are in Orwell's Second Literary Notebook; see *3515*. Relevant notes have been abstracted and placed directly following the review or essay to which they refer. Notes concerning Orwell's stay at Hairmyres, found in this Notebook as well, have also been abstracted and placed at appropriate points in the chronological arrangement. All such notes are indicated as being from the Second Literary Notebook.

The word "Communism," unlike "Fascism," has never degenerated into a meaningless term of abuse. Nevertheless, a certain ambiguity does cling to it, and at the least it means two different things, only rather tenuously connected: a political theory, and a political movement which is not in any noticeable way putting the theory into practice. On the face of it, the deeds of the Cominform might seem more important than the prophecies of Marx, but, as Mr. John Plamenatz reminds us in his recently-published booklet, the original vision of Communism must never be forgotten, since it is still the dynamo which supplies millions of adherents with faith and hence with the power to act.

Originally, "Communism" meant a free and just society based on the principle of "to each according to his needs." Marx gave this vision probability by making it part of a seemingly inevitable historical process. Society was to dwindle down to a tiny class of possessors and an enormous class of dispossessed, and one day, almost automatically, the dispossessed were to take over. Only a few decades after Marx's death the Russian Revolution broke out, and the men who guided its course proclaimed themselves, and believed themselves, to be Marx's most faithful disciples. But their success really depended on throwing a good deal of their master's teaching overboard.

Marx had foretold that revolution would happen first in the highly industrialised countries. It is now clear that this was an error, but he was right in this sense, that the kind of revolution that he foresaw could not happen in a backward country like Russia, where the industrial workers were a minority. Marx had envisaged an overwhelmingly powerful proletariat sweeping aside a small group of opponents, and then governing democratically, through elected representatives. What actually happened, in Russia, was the seizure of power by a small body of classless professional revolutionaries, who claimed to represent the common people but were not chosen by them nor genuinely answerable to them.

From Lenin's point of view this was unavoidable. He and his group had to stay in power, since they alone were the true inheritors of the Marxist doctrine, and it was obvious that they could not stay in power democratically. The "dictatorship of the proletariat" had to mean the dictatorship of a handful of intellectuals, ruling through terrorism. The Revolution was saved, but from then onwards the Russian Communist party developed in a direction of which Lenin would probably have disapproved if he had lived longer.

Placed as they were, the Russian Communists necessarily developed into a permanent ruling caste, or oligarchy, recruited not by birth but by adoption. Since they could not risk the growth of opposition they could not permit genuine criticism, and since they silenced criticism they often made avoidable mistakes: then, because they could not admit that the mistakes were their own they had to find scapegoats, sometimes on an enormous scale.

The upshot is that the dictatorship has grown tighter as the regime has grown more secure, and that Russia is perhaps farther from egalitarian Socialism to-day than she was 30 years ago. But, as Mr. Plamenatz rightly warns us, never for one moment should we imagine that the original fervour has faded. The Communists may have perverted their aims, but they have not lost their mystique. The belief that they and they alone are the saviours of humanity is as unquestioning as ever. In the years 1935–39 and 1941–44 it was easy to believe that the U.S.S.R. had abandoned the idea of world revolution, but it is now clear that this was not the case. The idea has never been dropped: it has merely been modified, "revolution" tending more and more to mean "conquest."

No doubt unavoidably in so short a book, Mr. Plamenatz confines himself to one facet of his subject, and says very little about the role and character of the Communist parties outside the U.S.S.R. He also barely touches on the question of whether the Russian regime will, or indeed can, grow more liberal of its own accord. This last question is all-important, but for lack of precedents one can only guess at the answer.

Meanwhile, we are faced with a world-wide political movement which threatens the very existence of Western civilisation, and which has lost none of its vigour because it has become in a sense corrupt. Mr. Plamenatz concludes bleakly that though the U.S.S.R. will not necessarily precipitate an aggressive war against the West, its rulers regard a struggle to the death as inevitable, and will never come to any real agreement with those whom they regard as their natural enemies. Evidently, as Commander Stephen King-Hall says in his Introduction, if we want to combat Communism we must start by understanding it. But beyond understanding there lies the yet more difficult task of being understood, and—a problem that few people seem to have seriously considered as yet—of finding some way of making our point of view known to the Russian people.

3347. Notes for 'Marx and Russia'

Second Literary Notebook

"What is Communism?"[1]

C. unlike "Fascism", means something.

Nevertheless—significant Mr L.[2] *can only discuss one*[3] *aspect in short volume.*

3 aspects—historical, role of C.P. in USSR, ditto in foreign countries (put less loosely).

Mr L. chooses chiefly historical—at first sight least urgent, but really important because original dream always present as motive force.

Kingdom of heaven—Marx's schematization—fully accepted by Russian Bolsheviks—thrown over board° completely in revolution—(had to be because Marx wrong & Lenin right—Lenin saw opportunity)—dictatorship over proletariat—party's greatest aim always to cling to power—resulting structure & methods—tendency to be self-perpetuating.

But—dream & self-justification always there. Fanaticism not affected by inconsistency.

Other important questions. i. Is there any mechanism by which the Russian régime can become more liberal? ii. Would the character of the foreign C. parties change if they became real mass parties?
Mr L. barely touches—but useful reminder—unchanged mentality when real objectives changed.

1. "What is Communism?" is the title of J. P. Plamenatz's book, discussed by Orwell in 'Marx and Russia'; see *3346*.

2. The contexts in which this abbreviation is used show clearly by comparison with the completed article that Orwell is referring to Plamenatz—'Mr P.'
3. Words underlined in the manuscript in the Second Literary Notebook are set in roman here and elsewhere.

3348. To Helmut Klöse

15 February 1948   Handwritten

> Ward 3
> Hairmyres Hospital
> East Kilbride
> Lanarkshire

Dear Klöse,
Thanks ever so much for the apples, which arrived yesterday. It's wonderful to have apples in such fine condition as late as this. I have been here 2 months & am getting on quite well. They say I am only improving rather slowly, but we are sending to America for a new drug called streptomycin which they say will speed things up. We have got our T.T. cow & she is due to calve about this week. I quite agree with you about goats. My wife & I kept them for years & found them most productive. Only, as we have almost unlimited grazing & it doesn't cost much to feed an animal, we might as well have cows, as it [is] nice to be able to make butter. I think we shall be able to keep the milch cows free from infection, as they will have a stall (or byre as it is called in Scotland) to themselves & won't mix much with the other cattle. The beef cattle are generally kept out of doors the whole year round. The light tractor we ordered is supposed to arrive soon, but I imagine there will be all sorts of delays about various of the attachments. I hope it isn't too difficult to get spare parts. Provided we can keep the tractor in running order it should be most useful. I ordered among other things a disc harrow, which is almost unheard of in these parts but which should be useful in cutting up the clods. Everything in Jura, & even on the mainland in the Highlands, is done in the most primitive way. Oats are always broadcast, mowing is largely done with the scythe, & the sheaves are nearly always bound up by hand, which is a miserable wet job & very tiring. Turnips are thinned out by hand & potatoes lifted with the fork. However we're getting a potato lifter with the tractor.

My sister is going up to London shortly & will then have my little boy medically examined, but I've no doubt he is all right. There can't be much wrong with him by the speed with which he grows out of his clothes, & the amount of noise he makes.

Thanks so much again,

> Yours
> Geo. Orwell

3349. To David Astor

Monday [16 February 1948][1]   Handwritten

Dear David,

I've had 2 letters from you today. I'll take the business one first. I'm perfectly willing to do the reviews for the U.S., in fact I'd like it, as they will probably want them rather longer than yours, & I prefer that. I presume that they will be for papers more or less on a level with the Observer & similar in tone. The only caveat is, that I might have a relapse or something, & any way I can only do about 2 hours work each day. They will be starting with the streptomycin soon, & though I don't suppose so, it *may* have unpleasant effects, like M. & B.[2] But anyway, up to capacity I'll certainly do the reviews.

As to the streptomycin. Thanks awfully for getting it on the wing so quickly.[3] I suppose it will get here in only a few days. If you really don't want to be paid for it O.[K.],[4] I won't press it. But I really could easily have paid, not only in £s but even in dollars, because I remember now, I have at least 500 lying by in New York. I don't need tell you I am grateful. Let's hope it does its stuff. I gather they aren't very satisfied with my case at present. I haven't gained weight for 2 weeks, & I have a feeling I am getting weaker, though mentally I am more alert. Dr Dick seems anxious to start in with the strepto as early as possible.

I'm sorry A.K.[5] has blown up. He's a bit temperamental. I thought his fi[rst] despatch from France was very good. The London Letters he has been doing in P.R. are shocking & I have been meaning to have a row with him about them—just one long squeal about basic petrol[6] etc.

I'll let you know how the strepto goes.

Yours
George

1. For dating, see *3344, n. 1.*
2. May and Baker, manufacturers of pharmaceuticals; their initials were a shorthand means of referring to sulphonamides. See *3223, n. 2.*
3. David Astor wrote to Dr. Dick on 19 February 1948 thanking him for encouraging Orwell— he referred to him as 'Blair'—to get the streptomycin and offering to help in getting anything else that would aid Orwell's recovery. He made it clear that he wished to pay for any drugs that would help and said he was 'in communication with Blair on this' and trying to convince him to accept help. He asked Dick not to discuss payment with Orwell, 'as I think the only possibility of persuading him to be reasonable is that it should be a very private matter between him and me.' He could make another visit to Hairmyres Hospital, he said, 'this coming Sunday [22 February] or on Sunday, 7th March,' the latter being slightly more convenient. Was Orwell doing too much work, he asked; he could either increase or decrease it as would prove desirable. A letter from Henry R. Whitney, in New York, 11 February 1948, informed Astor that 70 grams of streptomycin had been sent to Dr. Dick 'by Air Mail via separate planes' on that day. He had also arranged for three shipments of CARE parcels to be sent and various food parcels and parcels of clothing, shoes, and vitamins to various people in Britain and on the Continent. One CARE parcel had been sent to Orwell on 19 December 1947.
4. There is a punch-hole in the letter which takes out what is evidently a 'K' here and 'rst' of 'first,' below.
5. Arthur Koestler; see *3338.*
6. 'Basic' petrol was the amount allowed before supplements for special purposes were added. See *3360* for petrol allowance and miles per gallon.

3350. To John Middleton Murry

20 February 1948   Handwritten

> Ward 3
> Hairmyres Hospital
> East Kilbride
> Lanarkshire

Dear Murry,

I know I have treated you badly by promising an article & not doing it, but I don't know if you have heard I have been ill for a long time—in bed since about last November, but really, I think, I have been ill since the beginning of 1947. It is T.B., the disease which was bound to claim me sooner or later, & I think that horrible winter of 1946–7 started me off. This is a nice hospital & everyone is very kind to me, & they seem fairly confident of being able to patch me up. I've just started on a new drug called streptomycin which works wonders in some cases & may do so in mine. But in any case I don't suppose I'll be out & about before June. I can't do any real work now, I am too weak & pulled down, but I do a little light work such as book reviews. Please do send me a copy of the book.[1] I'm sure to read it with interest, though whether I'd get round to writing about it is a different question.

> Yours sincerely
> Geo. Orwell

1. *The Free Society* (1948), in which Murry came close to approving war against the Soviet Union, contrary to his long-held pacifist views and hence E. L. Allen's *Pacifism and the Free Society: A Reply to John Middleton Murry* (1948). See Orwell's letter to Murry, 5 March 1948, *3358*, and the final paragraph of his letter to Dwight Macdonald, 7 March 1948, *3359*.

3351. To Fredric Warburg

20 February 1948   Handwritten

> Ward 3
> Hairmyres Hospital
> East Kilbride
> Lanarkshire

Dear Fred,

I'd love it if you came to see me[1]—don't put yourself out of course. Visiting hours are: Wed.s, Saturdays & Sundays, any time after 2 pm, Tuesdays any time after 4 pm. Actually they aren't at all strict about the hours. I've started having the streptomycin—impossible to tell for some weeks whether it is doing its stuff.

Please remember me to everyone.

> Yours
> George

1. Warburg wrote on 25 February 1948 to say that he had virtually completed arrangements to come to Glasgow on the night of 9 March and he expected to be at the hospital soon after 2:00 P.M. on the 10th. He enclosed a copy of *The Edge of Darkness* by John Prebble (1915–), which Secker & Warburg was publishing on 8 April 1948 and which he described as 'one of the best war novels to come out of the late war.'

3351A. Letter to Ivor Brown, 20 February 1948: see Vol. XX, Appendix 15

3352. Hairmyres Hospital Timetable[1]
Secondary Literary Notebook

Time table at this hospital (times all approximate)

★12 midnight—injection
  5.30 am—noise (people going to & fro, water being drawn, etc.) begins.
  6.30 am—called, with hot water.
  7 am—temperature taken
  7.30 am—breakfast
★8 am—injection
  8.15 am—cleaning begins (continues on & off for about 2 hours)
  9 am—bed made
  ..   medicine
  10 am—temperature taken
  10.30 am—doctors come round
  11–12 noon—during this time, though of course not every day, one goes to be X-rayed, "refilled", etc.
  12 noon—lunch
  2 pm—temperature taken
  3 pm—tea
★4 pm—injection
  6 pm—temperature taken
  6.30 pm—supper
  10 pm—temperature taken
       lights out

NB. that the injections are a temporary feature.

1. It is not possible to date this timetable precisely, but it must have been written after Orwell began his course of streptomycin injections on 19 or 20 February 1948. This is therefore a convenient, rather than a precise, position to place it.

3353. To Fredric Warburg

22 February 1948   Handwritten

> Ward 3
> Hairmyres Hospital
> East Kilbride
> Lanarkshire

Dear Fred,
I forgot to say, if we have any copies left, could you please send a copy of "Homage to Catalonia" to Edmund Wilson (care of the New Yorker, I suppose) with my compliments.

I've started on the streptomycin, but of course we can't tell for some weeks[1] whether it's doing its stuff. Any way it doesn't seem to have any side-effects.

> Yours
> George

1. 'weeks' substituted for 'months,' which has been crossed out.

3353A. To Lydia Jackson

25 February 1948   Handwritten

> Ward 3
> Hairmyres Hospital
> East Kilbride
> Lanarkshire

Dear Lydia,
Thanks so much for 2 letters which reached me simultaneously. I shan't be out of here by Easter, but do go up to Barnhill if you feel like it. Quite likely it will be nice weather by then. Only give Avril plenty of notice because of meeting you.

I don't expect to be out of here much before the summer. I've really been very ill since about November, & in fact I wasn't really well all last year. I think it was that beastly winter of 1946–7 that started me off. I've been in this hospital 2 months, & for some time I didn't seem to get better, but I'm now having the new drug streptomycin, & I think it's already doing me good, though they can't judge for about a month whether it's really doing its stuff. Even when I get out of here I imagine I'll have to stay in Glasgow for a bit to continue treatment as an out-patient, but I shall be able to run up to Jura or down to London for short periods. Of course I can't do any serious work. I did nothing for about 3 months, but latterly I've started doing a few book reviews, to keep my hand in & earn a little money.

Avril is in London this week to do some shopping, & Richard is going to stay with Gwen.[1] I believe you kindly got some honey for us from Titley,[2] & I asked A. to pick it up & pay you for it.

Please remember me to Pat.[3]

With love
Eric

1. Gwen O'Shaughnessy, Eileen's sister-in-law and widow of her brother, Laurence. She lived at Greenwich.
2. Titley was one of Orwell's neighbours at Wallington; he is referred to by Orwell in his Domestic Diary, *518, 6.4.40*. It is unlikely that they had met for several years.
3. Pat Donahue was a friend of Lydia Jackson's; they rented Orwell's cottage at Wallington; see *2666*. She is described by Lydia Jackson in her autobiography (written under her pen-name, Elisaveta Fen), *A Russian England*, 398–99, 421–27, and 446–48.

3354. To Gleb Struve

25 February 1948   Handwritten

Ward 3
Hairmyres Hospital
East Kilbride
Lanarkshire
Scotland

Dear Struve,[1]

I'm sorry to say that I haven't been able to do anything with these sketches[2]—a pity, but as you know we're not well off for magazines in England now, & also I'm incapacitated by being tied to my bed. I've been ill since about last November. It is T.B., not, I imagine, very dangerous, but enough to keep me very sick & helpless for a long time. I'm now having the new drug streptomycin, which it appears is marvellous for this disease, so I hope I may be out & about again by the summer. Of course I have done almost no work for 3 months or more.

You asked about "Burmese Days". If obtainable at all, it would be in the Penguin edition.[3] I can never get hold of a copy myself, but the Penguin people occasionally send me an account, so I suppose the book is in print. It's not being reissued in England till 1949, but I believe Harcourt Brace are going to reissue it in the USA, when, I'm not quite certain.[4] They were asses not to do so immediately after I'd had that bit of luck with "Animal Farm" but American publishers don't seem to like doing reprints.

If I can manage to get hold of "We"[5] when it comes out I'll try to do a long review of it for somebody.

The above address will find me for the time being, but my permanent addresses are the London one & Barnhill, Isle of Jura, Argyllshire.

Yours sincerely
Geo Orwell

1. Gleb Struve (1898–1985) had in 1947 been appointed Professor of Slavic Languages and Literature at the University of California, Berkeley. See *2421, n. 1*.

2. Presumably the Mandelstam sketches referred to in Orwell's letter to Struve of 21 April 1948; see *3387*.
3. 60,000 copies were published in May 1944. It was out of print by March 1953 (Willison).
4. The Uniform Edition was published by Secker & Warburg in January 1949. Harcourt, Brace published 3,000 copies of a 'new' American edition by photolitho-offset from the Uniform Edition, 19 January 1950; a second impression of 2,000 copies was published on 5 April 1951 (Willison).
5. Publication of this English translation of Yevgeny Zamyatin's *We* (written in 1920) fell through, so Orwell did not review an English edition. See *3387, n. 3*.

3355. To Hermon Ould

28 February 1948   Handwritten

> Ward 3
> Hairmyres Hospital
> East Kilbride
> Lanarkshire

Dear Mr Ould,[1]
Herewith the banker's order for my subscription etc. to the P.E.N.

> Yours truly
> Geo Orwell

1. Hermon Leonard Ould (1885 or 86–1951), playwright and translator, was General Secretary of the International P.E.N. Club from 1926. Desmond MacCarthy, President, International P.E.N. Club (P.E.N. = Poets, Playwrights, Editors, Essayists and Novelists), wrote to Orwell on 15 January 1948 asking him to become a member. He had asked Orwell to join two years earlier; see Orwell's letter to Arthur Koestler, 13 April 1946, *2973*. Orwell must have replied about 24 January 1948, agreeing to join, for on 26 January Ould wrote to Orwell saying he was sure MacCarthy would be glad Orwell would join even though he could take no part in celebrations or organisational work. On 16 February 1948, Ould wrote again to say that the Executive Committee had elected him and asked him for the entrance fee of £1.1s and annual subscription of £2.12.6, if possible by banker's order form. Orwell's application form has survived (at the Harry Ransom Humanities Research Center, University of Texas at Austin). He gave his address as Barnhill and his qualifications as 'Writer, journalist (publishers Secker & Warburg).' Ould acknowledged Orwell's banker's order on 2 March 1948 and sent him his membership card.

3356. Review of *The Atlantic Islands* by Kenneth Williamson

The Observer, 29 February 1948

The Faeroe Islands, to judge by Mr. Kenneth Williamson's photographs, are almost completely treeless. They are volcanic islands rising in perpendicular cliffs out of cloudy, stormy seas, with their cultivable soil distributed in such narrow pockets that the farmer cannot even use a plough, but has to do everything with a clumsy handleless spade. They have no natural wealth except their fisheries. Nevertheless, whereas most of the island groups fringing Britain are being rapidly depopulated, these others, even poorer and barer, have quadrupled their population in the last hundred years.

Perhaps this is partly because the Faeroese have succeeded in remaining owner-peasants, with no landlord class and no very great differences of wealth. Most of the land is cultivated on the primitive strip system, and the grazing grounds are owned communally. Mr. Williamson, who was stationed in the Faeroes for several years during the war, found the Faeroese a tough, simple, rustic people, but by no means uncultivated, for the local schools are fairly good and a proportion of the children are sent to Denmark to finish their education. They are of pure Viking stock and still speak their ancient Norwegian dialect, only rather unwillingly using Danish for official purposes. Except perhaps in the folk-lore (there is a story of a seal-wife which seems to have an Irish sound) the original Celtic inhabitants have left hardly any traces.

How essentially poor the islands are can be seen from the local diet, which consists quite largely of whale meat and sea birds. With scanty soil and rather chilly summers it is not worth growing grain, and the chief crops are hay and potatoes, which means that not many sheep or cattle can be kept through the winter. Apart from mutton dried in the wind like biltong, the people's animal food has to come out of the sea. The annual massacre of the whales—schools of them are driven into the harbour of Thorshavn, the capital, and there slaughtered with bill-hooks, turning the sea crimson in their death-struggles—is an important event; the hunting of the sea birds is even more so. The Faeroese eat not only gannets, which are eaten in some other places, but guillemots, gulls, cormorants, and above all, puffins. Mr. Williamson is an enthusiast for Faeroese cookery, but most of the dishes he describes are slightly horrible to read about. Their key-note seems to be the combination of fishy and greasy meat with sweet sauces.

The Faeroese are exceedingly hospitable. Any stranger arriving at a farm-house, Mr. Williamson says, is assumed to be dying of starvation, and has to act accordingly. It must be a little difficult to respond when one is offered boiled puffins with strawberry jam.

Nationalism is not yet strong in The Faeroes,[1] and only a very few of the inhabitants objected to the islands being occupied by Britain during the war. Moreover, The Faeroes were our most reliable source of fish throughout the war, and at one time were responsible for three-quarters of the British supply. All through the dark days of 1940 and 1941, when the Iceland boats refused to sail without air escorts which Britain could not provide, the tiny Faeroese boats plied to and fro, their sole armament one Bren gun each. They were bombed, machine-gunned, blown up by mines and even torpedoed. But they also made a good deal of money, which has been employed in bringing the fishing fleet up to date, on the assumption that the trade with Britain will continue. One would like to learn for certain, from some authoritative source, that this hope is not being disappointed.

1. A plebiscite voted for independence, but the Lagting (a combined parliament and jury) overturned that result, and in 1948 The Faroes became self-governing within Danish jurisdiction. The population has continued to increase.

3357. To Emilio Cecchi

3 March 1948   Handwritten

Ward 3
Hairmyres Hospital
East Kilbride
Lanarkshire
Scotland

Dear Mr Cecchi,[1]
Thanks so much for your letter of the 15th February, which I have just received (my flat in London has been empty for six months). As you see by the above address, I am in hospital. I have been ill with tubercolosis° since about November last—actually, I think, since earlier. However, I [am][2] getting better, & hope I may be up & about again by the summer. Of course this has upset all my plans & work. I would have liked very much to have met you if I had been in London. I had planned to spend part of the winter there.

Thank you so much for writing me up in the Corriere della Sera. I have just been trying to puzzle out what you said. I think Italian must be less like Latin than Spanish, which I can generally manage to read.

I am afraid I shall probably be here till about June, but I may not be in bed all that time. Any way, if you are in England any time, please drop me a line, just in case it should be possible to meet. The above address will find me for some time, but my most permanent address is Barnhill, Isle of Jura, Argyllshire.

Yours sincerely
Geo. Orwell

1. For Emilio Cecchi, see *3178, n. 1.* He annotated Orwell's letter, 'sped[ito] art[icolo] 24 novem. 1949' (sent article 24 November 1949).
2. A punch-hole has removed these letters.

3358. To John Middleton Murry

5 March 1948   Handwritten

Ward 3
Hairmyres Hospital
East Kilbride
Lanarkshire

Dear Murry,
Thanks very much for the book,[1] which I read with interest. I agree with your general thesis, but I think that in assessing the world situation it is very rash to assume that the rest of the world would combine against Russia. We have a fearful handicap in the attitude towards us of the coloured races, & the under-privileged peoples generally (eg. in S. America), which we possibly don't deserve any longer but which we have inherited from our imperial past.

I also think it is rash to assume that most orientals, or indeed any except a few westernised ones, would prefer democracy to totalitarianism. It seems to me that the great difficulty of our position is that in the coming show-down we must have the peoples of Africa & the Middle East—if possible of Asia too, of course—on our side, & they will all look towards Russia unless there is a radical change of attitude, especially in the USA. I doubt whether we can put things right in Africa, at least in some parts of it, without quite definitely siding with the blacks against the whites. The latter will then look [to] the USA for support, & they will get it. It can easily turn out that we & America are alone, with all the coloured peoples siding with Russia. Perhaps even then we could win a war against Russia, but only by laying the world in ruins, especially this country.

I'm sorry to hear about your illness. My own seems to be getting better rapidly. They can't say yet whether the streptomycin is doing its stuff, but I certainly have been a lot better the last week or so. I imagine however that I shall be in bed for another month or two, & under treatment at any rate until the summer. The lung has been collapsed, which is supposed to give it a better chance to heal, but of course it takes a long time, & meanwhile they have to keep on pumping air into one's diaphragm. Fortunately this is a very nice hospital & very well run. Everyone is extraordinarily kind to me. It is sad I cannot see my little boy until I am non-infectious, however he will be able to come & visit me when I am allowed out of doors. He is getting on for 4 & growing enormously, though he is a bit backward about talking, because we live in such a solitary spot that he doesn't see enough of other children. I have got our place in Jura running pretty well now. I myself couldn't farm the land that went with the house, but a young chap who was wounded in the war lives with us & farms it. We are pretty well found there, & better off for fuel & food than one is in London. The winters also are not quite so cold, funnily enough. The chief difficulties are that in bad weather one is sometimes cut off from the mainland, & that one is chronically short of petrol. However one can use a horse if one is obliged to. Of course I have to go up to London occasionally, but the journey only takes 24 hours, less if one flies. I was half way through a novel when I took to my bed. It ought to have been finished by May—possibly I might finish it by the end of 1948 if I get out of here by the summer.

Please remember me to your wife.

Yours sincerely
Geo. Orwell

1. *The Free Society*; see *3350, n. 1*.

3359. To Dwight Macdonald

7 March 1948   Handwritten

> Ward 3
> Hairmyres Hospital
> East Kilbride
> Lanarkshire
> Scotland

Dear Dwight,

Thanks so much for sending me your book on Wallace, which I have read with the greatest interest. Have you done anything about finding an English publisher? In case you haven't, I am writing to Victor Gollancz bringing the book to his attention.[1] If you're not already in touch with some other publisher, I would write to Gollancz & send him a copy. In spite of the awful paper shortage etc., the book should find a publisher here, as people are naturally interested in Wallace, as the man who is likely to cause "our" candidate to lose the election.[2] (It's difficult to keep up with American politics here, but it does look as though Wallace is making great strides lately. I'm afraid he may get the whole anti-war vote, as Chamberlain did before the war.) And I think Gollancz is your man, as he is politically sympathetic & is able to bring a book out quickly, as Warburg, for instance, can't. I suppose you know his address—17 Henrietta St.   Covent Garden, London WC.2. The book might do with some minor modifications for the English public, but you could fix all that with G.

There's another instance of Wallace's habit of issuing garbled versions of his speeches, which might be worth putting in. When he was over here, Wallace of course played down the Palestine issue, or at least didn't make mischief about it. He was no sooner in France than he referred to the Jewish terrorists as a "maquis" fighting against a British occupation. This appeared in French reports of his speech, but not in any English-language paper (except one, I think the Christian Science Monitor, which somehow got hold of it), presumably having been cut out from versions issued to them. The "Manchester Guardian" documented the facts at the time.

As you see I'm in hospital. It's T.B., a disease I've had hanging over me all my life, but I think that damnable winter of 1946–7 in London started me off. I've been in bed since about November. However they've got the thing well in hand & I expect to be out & about by the summer. I'm having streptomycin, which is an almost complete novelty in this country. It's all a great bore—nearly a year's work lost. I did nothing at all for 3 months, & even now can only do light jobs like book reviews. I can't touch anything serious till I'm out of bed & a great deal stronger. However, I'm starting my uniform edition this year & shall start off by reprinting a novel which was published in 1939 & rather killed by the war.[3] I believe Harcourt Brace are going to reprint my Burma novel.[4] They were BFs not to do so immediately after having that bit of luck with "Animal Farm."

What's happened to "Politics?" I haven't seen it for months. I told my agent in New York to take out a subscription for me, but she seemed rather reluctant to do so, evidently thinking I ought to get all the American papers free.

Isn't it funny how surprised everyone seems over this Czechoslovakia business?[5] Many people seem really angry with Russia, as though at some time there had been reason to expect different behaviour on the Russians' part. Middleton Murry has just renounced his pacifism & written a book (practically) demanding a preventive war against the USSR![6] This after writing less than 10 years ago that "Russia is the only inherently peaceful country."

Excuse bad handwriting

Yours
Geo. Orwell

1. Letter not traced; Orwell also drew Warburg's attention to Macdonald's book, *Henry Wallace: The Man and the Myth* (New York, 1948); see *3362, n. 1*.
2. Henry Wallace (1888–1965), who had been Vice-President, was superseded by Harry S Truman for that office. In the 1948 election he became the candidate of the left-wing Progressive Party, which received over one million popular votes. Thomas E. Dewey was expected to win the election (and a famous headline prematurely showed him as doing so), but Truman won with a two-million majority of the popular vote. See also *3215, n. 1.*
3. *Coming Up for Air*, published in May 1948.
4. *Burmese Days*; see *3354, n. 4.*
5. On 27 February 1948, Klement Gottwald (1896–1953), Communist Prime Minister of Czechoslovakia, announced that the resignation of twelve centre and right-wing ministers had been accepted by President Edvard Beneš (although a week earlier Beneš had stated that there would be no Communist takeover of Czechoslovakia). Jan Masaryk (son of Czechoslovakia's 'founding father') remained Foreign Minister, and attention (and hopes) were focused on him as the means whereby a total victory for the Communists might be averted. However, on 10 March 1948 he was found dead in the courtyard beneath his flat in Prague. The Communist line was that Masaryk had committed suicide in 'a moment of nervous breakdown.' Those who opposed the Communist takeover, which had become complete, regarded his death as murder.
6. *The Free Society*; see *3350, n. 1.*

3360. To Anthony Powell
8 March 1948   Handwritten

Ward 3
Hairmyres Hospital
East Kilbride
Lanarkshire

Dear Tony,

Thanks so much for your letter. I'm already doing another book for the TLS (a rather dreadful anthology of recent American stuff called "Spearhead"),[1] & I've put in for a novel which I know is coming along some time, so I don't suppose they'd send me the Mark Twain book.[2] (By the way, after many years of trying I have at last got hold of a very rare book, Van Wyck Brooks's

"The Tragedy of Mark Twain",[3] which he afterwards called in & re-issued in a garbled version.) I am a lot better. I am having a drug called streptomycin, which is a novelty in this country but is thought to be very good. It appears to be doing its stuff, though it's too early for them to say for certain. The doctor says that my lung is healing up fast & that I ought to be out & about by the summer. Of course I should probably have to continue having treatment, but in that case I could take rooms in Glasgow & get up to Jura or down to London for a week at a time.

Richard has been down to London recently, & I had him X rayed—nothing wrong with him, as I had known beforehand, but one likes to be sure. I'm keeping on my flat as a pied a terre,° but I have sent most of the furniture up to Jura. We've got the Jura place running pretty well now, the only snag is transport, as at present they're giving us 6 gallons a month for a car that, on a highland road, only does 10 miles to the gallon. However, one can use a horse (I got a saddle by the way, but I'm always in the market for another), & I'm trying to get a motor boat that runs off paraffin.

I've arranged to bring out my uniform edition at the rate of 1 volume a year, & at present I have got six books to go in it, as I have suppressed several.[4] I hope there'll be others later. Of course this is a lousy time to start, because the whole idea is to have all the books uniform in format & price, & at present you have to charge 10/6 for a book that just makes you ashamed to look at it. I had always wanted to have something very sort of chaste but solid in blue buckram for about 5/–. I notice both Evelyn Waugh's & Graham Greene's uniform editions are very cheap-looking. They don't seem to be able to make a book now with covers that don't bend. It makes one very envious to see American books.

Please give everyone my love.

Yours
George

1. Reviewed 17 April 1948; see *3380*.
2. Orwell does not appear to have reviewed a novel or the book on Mark Twain for the *TLS*.
3. *The Ordeal of Mark Twain*, 1920 edition; see *3328*.
4. In his Notes for My Literary Executor, 31 March 1945, Orwell said he did not wish *A Clergyman's Daughter*, *Keep the Aspidistra Flying*, *The Lion and the Unicorn*, and *The English People* reprinted in the Uniform Edition then being discussed. He also stated, 'Of course, after I am dead I do not object to cheap editions of any book which may bring in a few pounds for my heirs'; see *2648*.

3361. Review of *My Caves* by Norbert Casteret, translated by R. L. G. Irving

The Observer, 14 March 1948

How many people in Great Britain would know without consulting a dictionary that spelaeology has something to do with caves? Probably not many, for though "pot-holing" has its Pennine enthusiasts, cave-exploration has never ranked as a widely popular pastime. Even the vocabulary of the full-time spelaeologist is full of words like "*siphon*" and "*chatière*," which have no exact equivalent in English.

It is otherwise in France, which is exceptionally rich in caves, especially in the Pyrenees and the Dordogne. Some of them extend for stupendous distances underground, though France does not contain any single cavern as large as the one near Trieste, into which it would be possible to put the Roman church of St. Peter's, dome and all. Before one can even start exploring some of the larger caves, it is often necessary to climb, or be lowered, down a perpendicular pothole which may descend as much as 1,000 or 2,000 feet. Once at the bottom one may find an underground stream on which it is possible to travel for miles at a stretch in a rubber boat, but often one has to crawl—much use is made of the technical term "reptation," meaning a worm-like movement—down galleries barely wider than one's body, with slimy mud or sharp stalagmites underneath one.

Much of the travelling has to be done in complete darkness, for all kinds of lighting apparatus are awkward to carry and liable to be damaged by water. Often a promising exploration is cut short by a "siphon," that is, a point at which the roof of a cave descends below the surface of the stream that flows through it. There is no way of passing a "siphon" except by diving underneath it, without knowing in advance whether the ledge of rock extends for a few feet or 50 yards.

Mr. Casteret, a lifelong spelaeologist, naturally insists on the scientific and practical value of his chosen pastime. It has led to the discovery of important new reserves of water, it has taught us much of what we know about palaeolithic man, and it has also increased our knowledge of the habits of bats. But it is clear enough from his descriptions of his adventures that the true spelaeologist is not moved by any utilitarian consideration, but by a mysterious urge to get as deep under ground as possible and to penetrate to places where no human being has ever been before. Some of these places, with their monstrous stalactites like cathedral pillars, are astonishingly beautiful, as the photographs in Mr. Casteret's book show. In some of the more accessible caves, on the other hand, life is made horrible by evil-smelling clouds of bats, creatures which it is difficult to love, though Mr. Casteret defends them warmly.

The equipment used in exploring caves is extremely elaborate and ingenious. Ladders are made of steel wire so delicate that a yard of ladder weighs only about three ounces. Rubber boats which will support a man can be carried, when deflated, in a rucksack. For very deep descents the spelaeologist is strapped into parachute harness and lowered on a wire to which a telephone is attached. The kind of clothes that are worn are also important, not only because it is desirable to keep dry but even more because it is important not to get stuck. More than one spelaeologist has died of starvation because his coat rucked up when he was trying to force his way through a narrow "cat run." There are, of course, other dangers, not to mention such discomforts as having to swim across underground rivers whose temperature is only a degree or two above freezing. However, human beings vary in their notion of what constitutes pleasure, and spelaeology is no more dangerous and uncomfortable than mountaineering, and is perhaps more useful. The photographs in this book, all of them taken by magnesium flash in circumstances of the utmost difficulty, are excellent.

3362. To Leonard Moore

19 March 1948   Handwritten

> Ward 3
> Hairmyres Hospital
> East Kilbride
> Lanarkshire

Dear Moore,

Thank you for your letter. I didn't object to the jacket, & it had "Uniform Edition" on it, which I wanted to make sure of. But I did think the light green cover was unsuitable & asked Warburg whether he could manage to change the cloth for something darker.[1] I favour dark blue, or any dark colour except red, which always seems to come off on one's fingers. I thought the format was all right. Of course the price is fearful for a reprint, but I suppose subsequent volumes need not be so expensive.

I see that "Burmese Days" is supposed to come out in the same edition only a few months later. I believe the Penguin edition is still in print, as you sent me an account of sales recently. I suppose the Penguin people won't print many more, otherwise it may damage the Warburg edition.

Warburg suggested that I should bring out another volume of essays in the fairly near future. I think it would be better not to do this for another 2–3 years, as people feel rather cheated if they buy a book & finds° it contains things which they have read in magazines only a year or so earlier.

> Yours sincerely
> Eric Blair

1. Fredric Warburg had visited Orwell, presumably on 10 March, as arranged (see *3351, n. 1*), bringing a specimen binding case (or cloth) for the Uniform Edition. Orwell was evidently dismayed to find that a light-green colour had been chosen (see his letter to Julian Symons, *3363*). Warburg took note of Orwell's wish that a darker colour be selected. Orwell had some of his own books rebound in dark blue; these included a presentation copy of *Animal Farm* for his son, Richard (see George Orwell's Books, *3734, n. 1*). Orwell's own preference for a dark blue binding has been chosen for this edition of the collected works. Warburg wrote to Orwell on 15 March, expressing 'real pleasure' at finding him 'in better shape and better spirits than I had anticipated.' He realised that Orwell would require all his patience and control 'to overcome the obstacles to a complete restoration of health,' but he did not doubt that Orwell could do that 'since you still have many books you still wish to write.' With this letter, Warburg returned Dwight Macdonald's 'story' of Henry Wallace (see *3359*), 'a grim and horrifying portrait which reminds one so very, very much of a certain editor of a Leftist weekly known to both of us.' He offered to send Orwell 'books, magazines or any other commodity' he would like and gave him the address of Robert Giroux, at Harcourt, Brace (who would later prepare the U.S. edition of *Nineteen Eighty-Four* for the press). He reported that he had spent a couple of pleasant days in Edinburgh with Richard Rees after leaving Orwell, and commented on 'how much politer the Scots are than the English, and particularly

the Londoners!' In his reference to 'a certain editor of a Leftist weekly,' Warburg presumably had Kingsley Martin in mind; see *2105, n. 1* and Bernard Crick's Introduction to *Unwelcome Guerrilla: George Orwell and the New Statesman—An Anthology*, edited by Alan George (1984).

3363. To Julian Symons

21 March 1948   Handwritten

Ward 3
Hairmyres Hospital
East Kilbride
Lanarkshire

Dear Julian,

I've at last found a box to put this pen in, so I'd be much obliged if you could get me a refill. No hurry, of course. Herewith also postal order for 3/6 which I found among my papers. I forget what the refills cost.

I thought you'd like to hear that I am getting a lot better. I have been having the streptomycin for about a month, & evidently it is doing its stuff. I haven't gained much weight, but I am much better in every other way, & longing to get up, which of course they won't let me do for ages yet. I can really only do light work still, ie. book reviews. I did write two longer articles,[1] but I find my fingers are all thumbs as soon as I attempt anything serious. However, the doctor is very pleased with the way I am going on & says I should be up & about by the summer. I may have to continue with periodical treatment for some months after that, but in that case I shall get a room in Glasgow & run up to Jura or down to London between treatments. Apparently even after they have killed off the germs they often keep the lung collapsed until they consider it is healed.

Richard is very well, &, so far as I can judge from photographs, growing rapidly. I can't see him till I am non-infectious, which is rather annoying. Various people have been to see me, including Fred Warburg who brought a blank of my uniform edition which we are starting this year. I was rather dismayed to find he had chosen a light green cover, but maybe he'll be able to get hold of some darker stuff. I think a uniform edition should always be very chaste looking & preferably dark blue.[2] I read your article on George Eliot in the Windmill[3] with interest, but I must say I've never been able to read G. E. herself. No doubt I'll get round to it someday. Recently I read one or two of the minor novels of Charlotte Bronte which I hadn't read before—was astounded by how sexy they were. I've just read Mauriac's "Thérèse", not so good as "A Woman of the Pharisees", I thought, but it started me thinking about Catholic novelists, & after reading Heppenstall's article in P[artisan] R[eview] I am trying to get hold of Léon Bloy whom I have never read.[4] The "Politics & Letters"[5] people sent me a copy of their magazine & I wrote a piece for the "Critic & Leviathan" series, though, as I say, I really can't write long articles now. I was quite well impressed by the magazine, which I hadn't seen before, & maybe it will develop into the sort of thing we need so badly.

The trouble always is that you must have an angel or you can't keep the magazine alive. "Politics" is evidently already tottering—it's become a quarterly which is usually a very bad symptom. Dwight Macdonald sent me a copy of a little book on Wallace which he has just published—very good, & I am urging Gollancz to publish it over here. I am afraid W. may well cause "our" man to lose the election, & then Lord knows what may happen. However, whichever way one looks the news is really too depressing to talk about.

Write if you get time, & please remember me to your wife. I do hope I'll be about in the summer & will be able to see everybody again.

Yours
George

1. It is not clear which are these two articles and which are the two referred to by Orwell in his letter to George Woodcock, 24 May 1948, *3403*. The tenses may help: here Orwell says 'I did write' and on 24 May he says 'I have two long articles on hand.' Some jottings on the inside back cover of Orwell's Second Literary Notebook (see *3515*) may also be a guide. These notes indicate that he had three articles to write for *The Observer*, one of 800 words and two of 600 words; he gives no dates by when these were to be written, and because he contributed six pieces to *The Observer* between 1 February and 6 June, these are not identifiable. He noted that he had an article of 800 to 1,000 words to write for the *TLS*. This might be the review of *Spearhead*, 17 April 1948 (see *3380*), which is of article length (and much longer than the number of words allotted), or his review of *The Novelist as Thinker*, 7 August 1948 (see *3436*), which is of the right length and in the right chronological position in Orwell's list; see *3515, n. 58*. Three other articles are listed, each with dates by when they must be completed: for *Politics and Letters* (2,000?) by June 20; for *Progressive* (2,000), also by June 20; and for *Commentary* (3,000?) by July 20. These are almost certainly 'Writers and Leviathan,' published Summer 1948 (see *3364*), which S. N. Levitas had read by 25 May 1948 (see *3410, n. 1*); 'Britain's Left-Wing Press,' published (in Madison, Wisconsin) June 1948 (see *3366*); and 'The Labour Government After Three Years,' published October 1948 (see *3462*). It is probable that the two articles referred to in the letter to Symons are 'Writers and Leviathan' and 'Britain's Left-Wing Press.' In the letter to Woodcock in May, Orwell may be referring to 'The Labour Government After Three Years' and either 'George Gissing' (see *3406*), intended for *Politics and Letters*, either No. 4 or 5, but not published (issue 5 did not appear), or 'Such, Such Were the Joys' (see *3409*). However, Orwell certainly did not expect 'Such, Such Were the Joys' to be published in his lifetime, and he may well have thought of it as being more than a sketch. Thus, 'George Gissing' is the more likely article referred to.
2. See *3362, n. 1*.
3. 'George Eliot and the Crisis of the Novel,' *The Windmill*, 1947 [No. 3.; n.d.]. This issue is bound in one volume, dated 1947, in the British Library and it follows two earlier 1947 numbers; the date stamp is '22 Dec 47.' *The Windmill* was edited by Reginald Moore and Edward Lane (pseudonym of Kay Dick); twelve numbers were published from 1944 to 1948.
4. Rayner Heppenstall's article was 'Léon Bloy and the Religious Novel' according to the cover of *Partisan Review*, February 1948, but the list of contents and the article itself have the title 'Two Novels by Léon Bloy.' The novels were *La Femme Pauvre* and *Le Désespéré*. For Bloy, see *3420, n. 4*.
5. *Politics and Letters, a Review of Literature and Society*, was edited by Clifford Collins, Raymond Williams, and Wolf Mankowitz. It incorporated *The Critic* (produced by the same editors), which ran for only two issues, both in 1947. 'Writers and Leviathan' appeared in issue 4, Summer 1948; Orwell's essay 'George Gissing' (see *3406*) should have been published in the next issue but that failed to appear.

3364. 'Writers and Leviathan'
Politics and Letters, Summer 1948[1]

The preparatory notes Orwell made for this article are reproduced as *3365*.

The position of the writer in an age of State control is a subject that has already been fairly largely discussed, although most of the evidence that might be relevant is not yet available. In this place I do not want to express an opinion either for or against State patronage of the arts, but merely to point out that *what kind* of State rules over us must depend partly on the prevailing intellectual atmosphere: meaning, in this context, partly on the attitude of writers and artists themselves, and on their willingness or otherwise to keep the spirit of Liberalism alive. If we find ourselves in ten years' time cringing before somebody like Zhdanov, it will probably be because that is what we have deserved. Obviously there are strong tendencies towards totalitarianism at work within the English literary intelligentsia already. But here I am not concerned with any organised and conscious movement such as Communism, but merely with the effect, on people of good will, of political thinking and the need to take sides politically.

This is a political age. War, Fascism, concentration camps, rubber truncheons, atomic bombs, etc., are what we daily think about, and therefore to a great extent what we write about, even when we do not name them openly. We cannot help this. When you are on a sinking ship, your thoughts will be about sinking ships. But not only is our subject-matter narrowed, but our whole attitude towards literature is coloured by loyalties which we at least intermittently realise to be non-literary. I often have the feeling that even at the best of times literary criticism is fraudulent, since in the absence of any accepted standards whatever—any *external* reference which can give meaning to the statement that such and such a book is 'good' or 'bad'—every literary judgement consists in trumping up a set of rules to justify an instinctive preference. One's real reaction to a book, when one has a reaction at all, is usually 'I like this book' or 'I don't like it', and what follows is a rationalisation. But 'I like this book' is not, I think, a non-literary reaction; the non-literary reaction is 'This book is on my side, and therefore I must discover merits in it'. Of course, when one praises a book for political reasons one may be emotionally sincere, in the sense that one does feel strong approval of it, but also it often happens that party solidarity demands a plain lie. Anyone used to reviewing books for political periodicals is well aware of this. In general, if you are writing for a paper that you are in agreement with, you sin by commission, and if for a paper of the opposite stamp, by omission. At any rate, innumerable controversial books—books for or against Soviet Russia, for or against Zionism, for or against the Catholic Church, etc.—are judged before they are read, and in effect before they are written. One knows in advance what reception they will get in what papers. And yet, with a dishonesty that sometimes is not even quarter-conscious, the pretence is kept up that genuinely literary standards are being applied.

Of course, the invasion of literature by politics was bound to happen. It must have happened, even if the special problem of totalitarianism had never arisen, because we have developed a sort of compunction which our grandparents did not have, an awareness of the enormous injustice and misery of the world, and a guilt-stricken feeling that one ought to be doing something about it, which makes a purely aesthetic attitude towards life impossible. No one, now, could devote himself to literature as single-mindedly as Joyce or Henry James. But unfortunately, to accept political responsibility now means yielding oneself over to orthodoxies and 'party lines', with all the timidity and dishonesty that that implies. As against the Victorian writers, we have the disadvantage of living among clear-cut political ideologies and of usually knowing at a glance what thoughts are heretical. A modern literary intellectual lives and writes in constant dread—not, indeed, of public opinion in the wider sense, but of public opinion within his own group. As a rule, luckily, there is more than one group, but also at any given moment there is a dominant orthodoxy, to offend against which needs a thick skin and sometimes means cutting one's income in half for years on end. Obviously, for about fifteen years past, the dominant orthodoxy, especially among the young, has been 'left'. The key words are 'progressive', 'democratic' and 'revolutionary', while the labels which you must at all costs avoid having gummed upon you are 'bourgeois', 'reactionary' and 'Fascist'. Almost everyone nowadays, even the majority of Catholics and Conservatives, is 'progressive', or at least wishes to be thought so. No one, so far as I know, ever describes himself as a 'bourgeois', just as no one literate enough to have heard the word ever admits to being guilty of anti-semitism. We are all of us good democrats, anti-Fascist, anti-imperialist, contemptuous of class distinctions, impervious to colour prejudice, and so on and so forth. Nor is there much doubt that the present-day 'left' orthodoxy is better than the rather snobbish, pietistic Conservative orthodoxy which prevailed twenty years ago, when the *Criterion* and (on a lower level) the *London Mercury* were the dominant literary magazines. For at the least its implied objective is a viable form of society which large numbers of people actually want. But it also has its own falsities which, because they cannot be admitted, make it impossible for certain questions to be seriously discussed.

The whole left-wing ideology, scientific and utopian, was evolved by people who had no immediate prospect of attaining power. It was, therefore, an extremist ideology, utterly contemptuous of kings, governments, laws, prisons, police forces, armies, flags, frontiers, patriotism, religion, conventional morality, and, in fact, the whole existing scheme of things. Until well within living memory the forces of the left in all countries were fighting against a tyranny which appeared to be invincible, and it was easy to assume that if only *that* particular tyranny—capitalism—could be overthrown, Socialism would follow. Moreover, the left had inherited from Liberalism certain distinctly questionable beliefs, such as the belief that the truth will prevail and persecution defeats itself, or that man is naturally good and is only corrupted by his environment. This perfectionist ideology has persisted in nearly all of us, and it is in the name of it that we protest when (for instance) a Labour government votes huge incomes to the King's daughters or shows hesitation about nationalising steel. But we have also accumulated in our minds a whole series of unadmitted contradictions, as a result of successive bumps against reality.

The first big bump was the Russian Revolution. For somewhat complex reasons, nearly the whole of the English left has been driven to accept the Russian régime as 'Socialist', while silently recognising that its spirit and practice are quite alien to anything that is meant by 'Socialism' in this country. Hence there has arisen a sort of schizophrenic manner of thinking, in which words like 'democracy' can bear two irreconcilable meanings, and such things as concentration camps and mass deportations can be right and wrong simultaneously. The next blow to the left-wing ideology was the rise of Fascism, which shook the pacifism and internationalism of the left without bringing about a definite restatement of doctrine. The experience of German occupation taught the European peoples something that the colonial peoples knew already, namely, that class antagonisms are not all-important and that there is such a thing as national interest. After Hitler it was difficult to maintain seriously that 'the enemy is in your own country' and that national independence is of no value. But though we all know this and act upon it when necessary, we still feel that to say it aloud would be a kind of treachery. And finally, the greatest difficulty of all, there is the fact that the left is now in power and is obliged to take responsibility and make genuine decisions.

Left governments almost invariably disappoint their supporters because, even when the prosperity which they have promised is achievable, there is always need of an uncomfortable transition period about which little has been said beforehand. At this moment we see our own government, in its desperate economic straits, fighting in effect against its own past propaganda. The crisis that we are now in is not a sudden unexpected calamity, like an earthquake, and it was not caused by the war, but merely hastened by it. Decades ago it could be foreseen that something of this kind was going to happen. Ever since the nineteenth century our national income, dependent partly on interest from foreign investments, and on assured markets and cheap raw materials in colonial countries, had been extremely precarious. It was certain that, sooner or later, something would go wrong and we should be forced to make our exports balance our imports: and when that happened the British standard of living, including the working-class standard, was bound to fall, at least temporarily. Yet the left-wing parties, even when they were vociferously anti-imperialist, never made these facts clear. On occasion they were ready to admit that the British workers had benefited, to some extent, by the looting of Asia and Africa, but they always allowed it to appear that we could give up our loot and yet in some way contrive to remain prosperous. Quite largely, indeed, the workers were won over to Socialism by being told that they were exploited, whereas the brute truth was that, in world terms, they were exploiters. Now, to all appearances, the point has been reached when the working-class living-standard *cannot* be maintained, let alone raised. Even if we squeeze the rich out of existence, the mass of the people must either consume less or produce more. Or am I exaggerating the mess we are in? I may be, and I should be glad to find myself mistaken. But the point I wish to make is that this question, among people who are faithful to the left ideology, cannot be genuinely discussed. The lowering of wages and raising of working hours are felt to be inherently anti-Socialist measures, and must therefore be dismissed in advance, whatever the economic situation may be. To suggest that they may be unavoidable is merely to risk being plastered with those labels that we are all terrified of. It is far safer to evade the issue and pretend that we can put everything right by redistributing the existing national income.

To accept an orthodoxy is always to inherit unresolved contradictions. Take for instance the fact, which came out in Mr. Winkler's essay in this series, that all sensitive people are revolted by industrialism and its products, and yet are aware that the conquest of poverty and the emancipation of the working class demand not less industrialisation, but more and more. Or take the fact that certain jobs are absolutely necessary and yet are never done except under some kind of coercion. Or take the fact that it is impossible to have a positive foreign policy without having powerful armed forces. One could multiply examples. In every such case there is a conclusion which is perfectly plain but which can only be drawn if one is privately disloyal to the official ideology. The normal response is to push the question, unanswered, into a corner of one's mind, and then continue repeating contradictory catchwords. One does not have to search far through the reviews and magazines to discover the effects of this kind of thinking.

I am not, of course, suggesting that mental dishonesty is peculiar to Socialists and left-wingers generally, or is commonest among them. It is merely that acceptance of *any* political discipline seems to be incompatible with literary integrity. This applies equally to movements like Pacifism and Personalism, which claim to be outside the ordinary political struggle. Indeed, the mere sound of words ending in -ism seems to bring with it the smell of propaganda. Group loyalties are necessary, and yet they are poisonous to literature, so long as literature is the product of individuals. As soon as they are allowed to have any influence, even a negative one, on creative writing, the result is not only falsification, but often the actual drying-up of the inventive faculties.

Well, then, what? Do we have to conclude that it is the duty of every writer to 'keep out of politics'? Certainly not! In any case, as I have said already, no thinking person can or does genuinely keep out of politics, in an age like the present one. I only suggest that we should draw a sharper distinction than we do at present between our political and our literary loyalties, and should recognise that a willingness to *do* certain distasteful but necessary things does not carry with it any obligation to swallow the beliefs that usually go with them. When a writer engages in politics he should do so as a citizen, as a human being, but not *as a writer*. I do not think that he has the right, merely on the score of his sensibilities, to shirk the ordinary dirty work of politics. Just as much as anyone else, he should be prepared to deliver lectures in draughty halls, to chalk pavements, to canvass voters, to distribute leaflets, even to fight in civil wars if it seems necessary. But whatever else he does in the service of his party, he should never write for it. He should make it clear that his writing is a thing apart. And he should be able to act co-operatively while, if he chooses, completely rejecting the official ideology. He should never turn back from a train of thought because it may lead to a heresy, and he should not mind very much if his unorthodoxy is smelt out, as it probably will be. Perhaps it is even a bad sign in a writer if he is not suspected of reactionary tendencies to-day, just as it was a bad sign if he was not suspected of Communist sympathies twenty years ago.

But does all this mean that a writer should not only refuse to be dictated to by political bosses, but also that he should refrain from writing *about* politics? Once again, certainly not! There is no reason why he should not write in the most crudely political way, if he wishes to. Only he should do so as an individual, an outsider, at the most an unwelcome guerrilla on the flank of a regular army. This attitude is quite compatible with ordinary political usefulness. It is reasonable, for example, to be willing to fight in a war because one thinks the war ought to be won, and at the same time to refuse to write war propaganda. Sometimes, if a writer is honest, his writings and his political activities may actually contradict one another. There are occasions when that is plainly undesirable: but then the remedy is not to falsify one's impulses, but to remain silent.

To suggest that a creative writer, in a time of conflict, must split his life into two compartments, may seem defeatist or frivolous: yet in practice I do not see what else he can do. To lock yourself up in the ivory tower is impossible and undesirable. To yield subjectively, not merely to a party machine, but even to a group ideology, is to destroy yourself as writer. We feel this dilemma to be a painful one, because we see the need of engaging in politics while also seeing what a dirty, degrading business it is. And most of us still have a lingering belief that every choice, even every political choice, is between good and evil, and that if a thing is necessary it is also right. We should, I think, get rid of this belief, which belongs to the nursery. In politics one can never do more than decide which of two evils is the less, and there are some situations from which one can only escape by acting like a devil or a lunatic. War, for example, may be necessary, but it is certainly not right or sane. Even a general election is not exactly a pleasant or edifying spectacle. If you have to take part in such things—and I think you do have to, unless you are armoured by old age or stupidity or hypocrisy—then you also have to keep part of yourself inviolate. For most people the problem does not arise in the same form, because their lives are split already. They are truly alive only in their leisure hours, and there is no emotional connection between their work and their political activities. Nor are they generally asked, in the name of political loyalty, to debase themselves as workers. The artist, and especially the writer, is asked just that—in fact, it is the only thing that politicians ever ask of him. If he refuses, that does not mean that he is condemned to inactivity. One half of him, which in a sense is the whole of him, can act as resolutely, even as violently if need be, as anyone else. But his writings, in so far as they have any value, will always be the product of the saner self that stands aside, records the things that are done and admits their necessity, but refuses to be deceived as to their true nature.

1. For the dating of this essay, see *3363, n. 1*; it was No. 5 in a series, Critic and Leviathan. When the essay was reprinted in *The New Leader* (New York), 19 June 1948, this biographical note was added: 'George Orwell, distinguished political analyst and literary critic, is the author of "Animal Farm" which caused a furor° in the U.S. when published last year. His other books include the collection of essays, "Dickens, Dali and Others," and "The Lion and the Unicorn." Formerly literary editor of the London *Tribune*, Orwell has led an active career in which he fought in the Spanish Civil War, worked as a teacher, lived in Paris, spent some years in Burma, and was a member of the staff of the British Broadcasting System°. He is also a novelist. This essay, "Writers and Leviathan," here receives its first American publication; in England, it was printed by "Politics & Letters." '

3365. Preparatory Notes for 'Writers and Leviathan'
Second Literary Notebook

Corruption of aesthetic standards by political motives.[1]

All art purposive (world-view)
Impossibility of enjoying what is dangerously inimical

Does not this concede that only subject & purpose are important?

But: 1. Craftsmanship
2. Not all good books deliver same message
3. Matter of experience (eg. what is the moral of most of Shakespeare's comedies?)
4. Spontaneity must always enter at some point.

Disentangling motives.

Justification for emphasising the propagandist side of literature at this moment, because this is an age in which political feelings are always near the surface of consciousness. The following things have happened to make political feelings crowd out aesthetic ones:

1. Everyone frightened (continuity of liberal culture threatened).
2. Compunction (over economic inequality).
3. "Enlightened" people have passed from opposition to power.

Effects of Russian revolution & rise of Fascism. Sense of responsibility, difficulty of taking irresponsible extremist attitudes.

Above all, always an orthodoxy, incumbent on all within any intellectual group.

(Orthodoxy sometimes entails contradictions—must not be thought out. (eg. all militarism evil—Red Army.))

As soon as orthodoxy accepted, intellectual honesty impossible, (unless clear distinction drawn between political & aesthetic worlds.)

Example: antisemitism. Unsympathetic Jewish character in novel.

Compare the sincere approach. Emphasise intellectual freedom consists in freedom to report truthfully & no essential difference between position of journalist & creative writer (internal reporting).

Quote Soviet directive. Note (against R. W.) [2] *important thing is not tying literature down to a low level but implied command to tell lies. This destroys faculties (subjective truth).*

Conclusion: must engage in politics. Must keep issues separate.
Must not engage in party politics as a writer. Recognition of own prejudices only way of keeping them in check.

1. Words underlined in the manuscript are in roman type. A short rule marks the end of a page in Orwell's Notebook if his notes take more than a single page.
2. Presumably Raymond Williams (1921–1988), one of the three editors of *Politics and Letters*, although Orwell does not refer to Williams in his article. Williams had written an essay in the first number of *Politics and Letters*, Summer 1947, 'The Soviet Literary Controversy.' He was later appointed a Fellow of Jesus College, and Reader in Drama, Cambridge University. His books include several on aspects of drama and also *Culture and Society, 1780–1950* (1958), *The Long Revolution* (1961), and *Orwell* (1971), in the Fontana Modern Masters series.

3366. 'Britain's Left-Wing Press'

Progressive (Madison, Wisconsin), June 1948[1]

The preparatory notes Orwell made for this article are reproduced as *3367*.

The outstanding peculiarity of the British press as a whole is its extreme concentration; there are relatively few papers, and the bulk of them is owned by a small ring of people. This is partly due to the small size of the country, which makes it possible for the London daily papers to be on sale in the early morning as far north as Glasgow.

A few first-class provincial papers, such as the Manchester° *Guardian*, do indeed exist, but none of them has a large circulation, and in effect the whole country up to and beyond the Scottish border is covered by eight London dailies. As for weekly reviews and monthly magazines, nothing of any importance is published outside London.

This special structure of the British press has existed for 30 years. Thus by the time an independent left-wing press became politically possible, it was already financially impossible. To start a new paper that could compete with the existing ones would need a capital of several million pounds, and no new daily or evening paper, apart from the tiny *Daily Worker*, has been launched in London since 1918. The following figures, which are necessarily approximate, will give some idea of how readership is distributed in a country which has recently been voting predominantly Labor.

If one considers only papers with a definite political orientation, and leaves the provincial press out of account, the total weekly circulation of the British press is something over 100 millions. Of this, about 23 millions are accounted for by papers that could be described as "Left."[2] But this includes the Liberal *News-Chronicle*, which is certainly "enlightened," or "progressive," but would not in all circumstances be a reliable supporter of a Labor Government. If one counts only papers having a definite affiliation with a left-wing party, then the figure is about 14 millions, or less than one-seventh of the total. At present there are in Britain only six left-wing papers of any consequence. These six papers are:

THE DAILY HERALD. Circulation over two millions, the third highest among British daily papers. *The Herald* can be regarded as the official Labor Party paper, but it represents essentially the trade-union (and more conservative) end of the party. It was founded in 1914,[3] and for the next 15 years, with a policy and attitude very much more radical than it displays today, it floundered along under a series of editors, always on the verge of bankruptcy. Even when its circulation touched 400,000 it could not be made to pay its way, because at that time commercial advertisers were unwilling to patronize a left-wing paper.

In 1929 *The Herald* was re-organized, its stock divided half-and-half between the Trade Union Congress and Odham's, a big publishing firm which owns several low-class weeklies. In the process *The Herald* was transformed into an ordinary popular paper, so far as tone and make-up go, but it was agreed that Odham's should have no control over its political policy, which should be directed by the Labor Party.

This agreement has been kept. Although it sometimes has good foreign correspondents, *The Herald* is a very dull paper, much inferior as reading matter to several other papers of the same stamp. It has, nevertheless, kept a steady circulation of two millions for more than a dozen years, partly, no doubt, because it gives full information on trade-union affairs. Its public is almost entirely working-class.

REYNOLD'S NEWS. Sunday paper, circulation about 700,000. (This is a small circulation as British Sunday papers go. One of them claims seven millions!) *Reynold's* is sometimes referred to in the American press as "a fellow travelers' paper," but this is not strictly true. Officially it is the paper of the Cooperative Party, which is the political organ of the cooperative movement and is now more or less completely merged with the Labor Party. There is, however, a strong Communist influence in *Reynold's*, affecting even its book reviews. It sometimes gives the impression of being three papers in one—partly Cooperative, partly Communist, and in part an ordinary Sunday paper devoted to sports, crime, and the Royal Family. *Reynold's* sometimes has intelligent articles, but on the whole it is an unsatisfactory paper, combining a sectarian atmosphere with the faults of the gutter press.

THE NEW STATESMAN AND NATION. Weekly review, circulation about 80,000. *The New Statesman* was founded in 1913, and since then has "incorporated" three rival papers of similar stamp: it is now by far the most influential of British political weeklies. Once again, it is usual to describe *The*

New Statesman as "fellow-traveling," and once again this is not strictly true, though in this case I should say that it is substantially true.

On occasion *The New Statesman* has turned definitely against the Communist line, as for instance during the Russo-German pact, and it may perhaps do so again if Russian aggression in Europe goes much further. But over a period of about 20 years *The New Statesman* has probably done more than any one thing—certainly more than any one periodical—to spread an uncritically Russophile attitude among the British intelligentsia, all the more so because it has no connection with the Communist Party and preserves an ostensibly detached attitude towards the U.S.S.R.

Apart from H. Kingsley Martin, its editor, many well-known left-wing publicists are or have at some time been associated with it: Leonard Woolf, H. N. Brailsford, John Strachey, Harold Laski, J. B. Priestley, R. H. S. Crossman, and others.

On technical grounds *The New Statesman* deserves its pre-eminence. Over many years it has remained at a high journalistic level and has preserved, if not a completely consistent policy, at any rate a distinctive attitude. The whole of the "enlightened" pinkish middle class reads it as a matter of habit. Its position corresponds fairly closely to that of *The New Republic* in America, but it is, I should say, a somewhat more adult paper.

TRIBUNE. Weekly review, circulation uncertain, but probably about 20,000. *Tribune* was founded a year or two before the war, and was at that time a rather vociferous paper costing threepence (five cents), with a mainly working-class circulation. It was controlled by Sir Stafford Cripps, who had recently been disciplined by the Labor Party for forming a fractional organization, the Socialist League. The Communists, who were then in their Popular Front phase, regarded *Tribune* with approval and helped to distribute it.

After the Russo-German pact and the outbreak of war this support fell away, and *Tribune*'s circulation, which had never been large, dropped to 2,000. In 1941, when Cripps had joined the Government and had therefore been obliged to sever his connection with the paper, it was taken over by Aneurin Bevan, the present Minister of Health.

Bevan reorganized it as a sixpenny paper of roughly the same stamp as *The New Statesman*, and during the remainder of the war it was probably the best, and certainly by far the most independent, of left-wing periodicals. It was, indeed, the only English paper which, while maintaining a responsible attitude and supporting the war effort, was radically critical of the Churchill Government. It was also the only paper on the Left which made any effort to counter Soviet Russian propaganda.

After the 1945 general election Bevan joined the Government, and *Tribune* became the organ of a group of young Labor MP's of whom Michael Foot is probably the best known. This group (not to be confused with the crypto-Communists) supports the Government's program in the main but is critical of its foreign policy, especially in regard to Greece and Palestine.

Unavoidably, *Tribune* has lost some of its vigor since Labor took office. It suffers from the embarrassment that always besets rebels when their own side has won, and in addition, its attacks on Ernest Bevin's foreign policy have been somewhat unreal, since on the all-important issue of standing up to Russia it is not genuinely in opposition. A few Communists and fellow-travelers occasionally write for *Tribune*, but all of those who have anything to do with determining its policy are extremely anti-Communist. In spite of surface appearances, it is much the most reliable supporter that the present Government has among weekly papers. Its public, most of which it gained during the war, is probably middle-class in the main, since it is generally accepted that the British working class will not pay more than threepence for a weekly paper.

FORWARD. Weekly review of essentially working-class type, published in Glasgow. *Forward* could hardly be called an influential paper, and its circulation is probably small, but it is interesting as an expression of the old-style, rebellious, maximalist version of socialism which still flourishes on the banks of the Clyde. It is almost always in disagreement with the Government, but its policy is extremely erratic: it is pro-Russian wherever possible, but on the other hand it is anti-Communist and is a strong defender of the freedom of speech and press. *Forward* is directed by Emrys Hughes, a rather turbulent back-bench Labor MP. Well-known writers such as Bernard Shaw, Bertrand Russell, and Sean O'Casey write for it occasionally.

THE DAILY WORKER. Circulation uncertain, but probably reaches 100,000 at times. *The Daily Worker* was founded in 1929 and was suppressed for about two years during the war for defeatist activities. Since its early days it has improved considerably, and sometimes has good scientific articles and book reviews, but it has remained a propaganda sheet rather than a newspaper. On the other hand, compared with the continental or even the American Communist press, *The Daily Worker* is not a very scurrilous paper. It is kept going partly by voluntary subscriptions from sympathizers. Recent attempts to finance it by selling shares to the general public were only partially successful.

These six papers that I have enumerated are all that Britain possesses—that is, all that is of the slightest importance—in the way of a left-wing press. Beyond this there are only obscure sheets dealing with trade-union intelligence or purely local affairs, and thin little magazines which hardly pretend to be aimed at the big public, and one or two periodicals devoted to direct Soviet propaganda and not having much bearing on British politics.

Of the small sectarian magazines, the Communist *Labor Monthly* probably has the widest circulation. Considering the smallness of their resources, the Communists are a great deal more enterprising than the Labor Party. They issue innumerable pamphlets, and they even own or control a chain of bookshops in which, naturally, their own publications are to the fore. They also, for some years before and during the war, exercised considerable influence on the Liberal *News-Chronicle* (circulation about one and a half millions).

But of course it is not Communist competition that is really important from the Labor Party's point of view. The essential fact is that the Government which undoubtedly represents the mass of the people is daily attacked and misrepresented by a huge and on the whole efficient Tory press, while not having any asset of its own except a single daily paper. As for the British Broadcasting Company,[4] which is an independent corporation, it is neither a friend nor an enemy. Its foreign services are under government supervision, but in home politics it could fairly be described as neutral.

For more than a year a commission appointed by the Government has been inquiring—rather gingerly, and in the face of some opposition—into the state of the British press. Whatever its findings, they are not likely to lead to any very drastic changes, since the press is not one of the industries marked down for nationalization in the near future. But it is probable that something will be done to limit the multiple ownership of newspapers. At present it can happen—does happen in one or two cases—that a single press lord owns or controls as many as 100 periodicals of one kind or another, and dictates the policy of all of them.

It is also probable that a new London evening paper will be launched in conjunction with *The Daily Herald*.[5] The Left obviously needs better publicity, but in a still mainly capitalist country, with a public that has been used for decades to reading the same papers, it is not easy for a left-wing press to grow up unless it is heavily subsidized.

The whole question has been much discussed during the past two years, without any very definite conclusion being reached. On the one hand, the majority of British journalists would be delighted to see the press lords overthrown: on the other hand, all journalists of whatever color are alarmed at the prospect of a state-controlled or party-controlled press. The Labor Party, with its huge membership and steady flow of funds, could certainly afford to publicize itself a great deal better than it does at present. But whether any political party, having subsidized a press of its own, would then have the imagination to conduct it in a non-totalitarian manner, remains to be seen.

1. Probably written by the time Orwell wrote to Julian Symons, 21 March 1948; see *3363, n. 1. Progressive* included this biographical note about Orwell: 'George Orwell, widely known British critic and author, has had a varied career; at one time or another, he taught school, worked in Burma, lived in Paris, fought in the Spanish Civil War, and served on the staff of the British Broadcasting Company.° He was formerly literary editor of the London Tribune. Orwell is perhaps best known to the U.S. public for his book, "Animal Farm." Among his other books are "The Lion and the Unicorn" and "Dickens, Dali,° and Others."'
2. Orwell's calculations in arriving at these totals can be found in his preparatory notes; see *3367*.
3. The *Daily Herald* was first published on 25 January 1911 and the *Daily Worker* on 1 January 1930.
4. Orwell probably wrote 'BBC' and the American sub-editor, in spelling out these letters, mistakenly took the 'C' to stand for 'Company' instead of 'Corporation.' 'Company' would not be an error that Orwell would make.
5. No such evening paper was launched. Orwell lists the three evening papers then published in his notes (see *3367* and see *3367, n. 2*).

3367. Preparatory Notes for 'Britain's Left-Wing Press'
Second Literary Notebook

British Newspapers

	D. Express	3,000,000	★	D. Worker	100,000	
	Mirror	3,000,000		$\times 6 - 1$	500,000 [4]	
★	Herald	2,000,000				
	Mail	1,500,000	★	New Statesman	80,000	
★	News-Chron	1,500,000		Spectator	30,000	
	Telegraph	1,000,000		Time & Tide	20,000	
	Times	275,000		Economist	25,000	
	Graphic	800,000	★	Tribune	20,000	
					———	
★	M. Guardian	250,000			175,000	
		———				
$\times 6$		$13,325,000 \times 6 = 79,950,000$ [1]				
	E. News	500,000			2,000,000 $\times 6$ [5]	
	Standard	250,000			1,500,000 ··	
	Star	350,000			250,000 ··	
		———				
$\times 6$		$1,100,000 \times 6 = 6,600,000$ [2]				
	News of W.	7,000,000		D H	12,000,000	
	S. Express	3,000,000		N C	9,000,000	
	Dispatch	3,000,000		M G	1,500,000	
	Pictorial	3,000,000			650,000	
	Times	250,000			80,000	
	Observer	300,000			20,000	
					———	
★	Reynold's News	650,000		L W.	23,250,000 $\pm$? [6]	
		———			———	
		17,200,000	17,200,000 [3]			
					103,875,000 +	

Orwell's rough workings on facing verso:

$$13,325$$
$$6$$
———
$$79,950$$
$$80,000,000$$
$$6,000,000$$
$$17,200,000$$
$$500,000$$
$$175,000$$
———
$$103,875,000$$

1. Total of weekday papers originating from London; regional, Scottish, Welsh, and Irish daily papers are not included here or in other totals. The asterisks were added by Orwell; they indicate left-wing papers. The *Daily Worker* is listed separately in the next column.
2. Total of the three London evening papers. Only the *Evening Standard* is now published.
3. Total of the London-based Sunday newspapers. 'News of W.' is *News of the World*.
4. In his article Orwell says the *Daily Worker*'s circulation is uncertain 'but probably reaches 100,000 at times.' Presumably for this reason he multiplies by 6 minus 1 to allow for some overestimate of circulation. See also *n. 6.*
5. This set of three figures comprises the daily circulations of the three left-wing daily newspapers (*Daily Herald, News Chronicle,* and the *Manchester Guardian*), each to be multiplied by six, the products being given immediately below.
6. The circulation of the *Daily Worker* has not been included in the total. 'L. W.' is 'Left Wing' [newspapers and journals]. The newspapers are D H, *Daily Herald*; N C, *News Chronicle*; and M G, *Manchester Guardian*; the first two are no longer published, and the last named is now *The Guardian.* The last three figures are for *Reynold's News, The New Statesman,* and *Tribune.*

3368. To Leonard Moore

23 March 1948   Handwritten

> Ward 3
> Hairmyres Hospital
> East Kilbride
> Lanark

Dear Moore,

Thanks for your letter of the 19th. I don't think I'll do the article for the "Writer," though thanks for the offer. I am doing about one book review a week for one paper or another, & it is about all I can manage. Just tell them I am ill & can't undertake a great deal, could you. It amuses me that they should approach me for an article, as when I was with Tribune I had some very acrimonious correspondence with them when I showed up one of their phoney "schools of Journalism." Perhaps it is a different editor now.[1]

> Yours sincerely
> Eric Blair

1. Orwell is confusing two series of his contributions to *Tribune* and their ensuing correspondence. On 8 September 1944, he discussed problems of literary patronage and the difficulties facing young writers (see 'As I Please,' 41, *2547*). Among many correspondents was the editor of *The Writer.* Orwell attacked schools of journalism on 6 October, 17 November, and 8 December 1944 (see 'As I Please,' 43, 48, and 51; *2560, 2579,* and *2590*) and this led to an acrimonious letter from the director of one such school, Martin Walter; see *2579.*

23 March 1948

3369. To George Woodcock

23 March 1948   Handwritten

Ward 3
Hairmyres Hospital
East Kilbride
Lanarkshire

Dear George,

Thanks so much for the 3 pamphlets, & for your own poems.[1] I intend to write to you at greater length about the latter, but first, two points.

1. There's a slip in your introduction to Tolstoy's pamphlet. He didn't die in 1901. I *think* he died in 1912—any way he was over 80,[2] & I imagine he wrote a good many pamphlets after this one.

2. Is the Freedom Defence Committee taking up any position about this ban on Communists & Fascists?[3] (It's only important at this moment in relation to Communists, & is aimed only at them.) It's not easy to have a clear position, because, if one admits the right of governments to govern, one must admit their right to choose suitable agents, & I think *any* organisation, eg. a political party, has a right to protect itself against infiltration methods. But at the same time, the *way* in which the government seems to be going to work is vaguely disquieting, & the whole phenomenon seems to me part of the general breakdown of the democratic outlook. Only a week or two ago the Communists themselves were shouting for unconstitutional methods to be used against Fascists, now the same methods are to be used against themselves, & in another year or two a pro-Communist government might be using them against us. Meanwhile the general apathy about freedom of speech etc. constantly grows, & that matters much more than what may be in the statute books. It seems to me a case for a pamphlet—but, at any rate, the F.D.C. ought to declare its attitude, I think.[4]

More later. I hope the Canada business comes off.[5] It would be an interesting change. I believe there's incredible fishing in Canada, if you care about that.

Yours
George

1. The three pamphlets were the first, and only, publications in a series, The Porcupine Pamphlets, edited by George Woodcock for the Porcupine Press: *The Soul of Man under Socialism* by Oscar Wilde, *The Slavery of Our Times* by Leo Tolstoy, and *A Defence of Poetry and a Letter to Lord Ellenborough* by Percy Bysshe Shelley. Orwell reviewed *The Soul of Man under Socialism* in *The Observer*, 9 May 1948; see *3395*. The poems for which Orwell also thanks Woodcock were his book of poems, *Imagine the South* (1947).
2. Leo Tolstoy (1828–1910). Woodcock's 1901 was probably caused by a typographic reversal of the last two numbers.
3. The Freedom Defence Committee did do what it could to protest at the way that political records of those in the Civil Service who were alleged to be Communists or Fascists were being investigated. A letter was published in *Freedom Defence Committee Bulletin*, 7 Autumn 1948, Orwell being one of the signatories; see *3441*. This was circulated to the press, but only two low-circulation journals printed it: *Socialist Leader*, 21 August 1948, and *Peace News*, 27 August 1948.

301

4. George Woodcock reprinted almost all this paragraph in his 'Recollections of George Orwell,' *Northern Review*, August–September 1953 (reprinted in *Orwell Remembered*, 199–210), as an example of Orwell's concern for civil liberties despite his illness. A typewritten copy of the whole paragraph has survived in the FDC Archives, annotated by Woodcock: '3 weeks' and 'Davy will write to G.O. later (after review of Wilde's book)'; see *3388* and *3403*. Charles Davy was a sub-editor on *The Observer*.

5. Woodcock left for Canada in the spring of 1949, where he was to become Professor of English at the University of British Columbia. See *2725, n. 3*.

3370. To Celia Kirwan

24 March 1948   Handwritten

Ward 3
Hairmyres Hospital
East Kilbride
Lanarkshire

Dearest Celia,

I was delighted to get your two letters dated the 7th & the 18th. I don't know why the one addressed to the Observer had been unforwarded for so long. The other was probably lying about at Barnhill while my sister was away. She has been down in London shopping while Richard stayed with relatives.[1] I do hope your bronchitis is better. I know what a misery it is & how depressed it leaves one afterwards. Did they give you M & B? I used to have that, & though it's vile to take it certainly did its stuff. I believe the new sorts are not so lethal as M & B 693.[2] I am much better, though it will evidently be a good long time before I am out of bed. I am having streptomycin, the new anti-T.B. drug & am about half way through the course of injections. It has made a wonderful difference, except that I haven't gained much weight yet. But I feel better & have a good appetite, & can even do a little work of sorts, ie. book reviews. The doctor thinks I may be able to get out of hospital some time in the summer. I may have to attend for some time as an out-patient, but in that case I can take a room in Glasgow & go up to Jura or down to London between treatments. They are all flourishing at home. I had Richard Xrayed° & there is nothing wrong with him. I didn't suppose there was, but I liked to make sure as he had been exposed to infection. I can't, unfortunately, see him till I am non-infectious, but I had him photographed recently. He is getting enormous. He is still backward in talking, which, as you say, is probably due to not seeing enough of other children. However, even at Barnhill he does see others about once a week, & sometimes somebody with a child comes to stay. I suppose he'll be going to school about the end of 1949. I have now sent most of my furniture & books to Barnhill & shall keep on the London flat only as a pied à terre. I must, of course, be in London part of the time, but I think I shall make our permanent home in Jura. It's a good place for Richard to grow up in, especially if the bombs start dropping before long. We have got the place running pretty well now, everything except electric light which is impossible while petrol is scarce. A friend lives with us & runs the farm, which means we can go away when we want to & our animals are looked after. The chief headache really is petrol, also tyres, as we have to fetch our stores once a week.

I'm glad you liked "Burmese Days". I'm starting my uniform edition this year & starting off with a novel called "Coming Up for Air" which was published in 1939. I'll send you a copy when it comes out. Fred Warburg was up here the other day & showed me the binding he had chosen for the edition—it was pretty awful, actually, but one can't choose nowadays. The French edition of "Animal Farm" came out recently[3] & I saw one or two reviews, but of course I don't know how it sold. I have never yet had a good sale with a book in France. The translation of "Burmese Days" which came out last year[4] must have fallen quite flat, which it deserved to, as it was a most damnable translation. It's sad to be just reprinting old books instead of getting on with my new one—however, I shan't be in here for ever, & I dare say really this illness may have done me good. I had felt so desperately tired ever since about 1945. I must say that I am now getting a bit fed up with lying in bed, now that spring is starting, & longing to get home & go fishing. I wish I was with you in Paris, I wonder if they have put Marshal Ney's statue back outside the Closerie des Lilas—but I dare say the Germans melted him down to get the bronze.[5]

Write again some time.

With much love
George

1. Probably 23 February to 8 March, a period when Avril's Diary lacks entries.
2. See *3223, n. 2*.
3. *Les Animaux Partout!*, translated by Sophie Dévil (Paris, October 1947); 5,000 copies were printed.
4. *Tragédie Birmane*, translated by Guillot de Saix (Paris, August 1946); 7,800 copies were printed.
5. Marshal Ney's statue stands close by where he was executed in 1815. It was erected in 1853 and described by Rodin as the most beautiful in Paris. The Closerie des Lilas, 171 Boulevard du Montparnasse, Paris 6, had its origins as a dance hall in the nineteenth century. It became a café much frequented by famous writers and artists—Mallarmé, Valéry, Verlaine, Sartre, Gide, Braque, Modigliani, and Hemingway (see his *Moveable Feast*), among others; Lenin and Trotsky played chess there. That era passed after Orwell's death and it became a very expensive restaurant with an adjacent café-bar. In *Down and Out in Paris and London*, Orwell, describing his Russian friend Boris, wrote: 'Boris always talked of the war as the happiest time of his life. . . . Anything to do with soldiers pleased him. His favourite café was the Closerie des Lilas in Montparnasse, simply because the statue of Marshal Ney stands outside it' (*CW*, I, 20). The Closerie des Lilas ('The Lilac Tree Garden') possibly underlies the Chestnut Tree Café of *Nineteen Eighty-Four*, where the former revolutionaries, Jones, Aaronson, and Rutherford while away their last months (*CW*, IX, 78–81) and where chess could be played: Winston 'had a nostalgic vision of his corner table [at the Chestnut Tree Café], with the newspaper and the chessboard and the ever-flowing gin' (306).

3371. To Fredric Warburg

Friday, [26 March; or 2 April 1948][1]   Handwritten

[Hairmyres Hospital]

Dear Fred,

I agree with you,[2] I'm against illustrations for a book of this kind. These illustrations in particular, though they have some very clever touches in them, are too elaborate. Some that appeared in one or two of the foreign translations were better, actually. But I think it's better to leave the whole idea alone.

I read Michael's MS[3] and was rather well impressed by it. Meanwhile I haven't sent it back yet because of not getting a big enough bit of brown paper. But I will soon.

It's lovely weather here & I have just received the first lot of daffodils from Jura.

Yours,
George

1. Warburg wrote to Orwell on 25 March. In the normal course of events in those days, his letter would have been delivered on Friday, 26 March. That Friday was Good Friday, which in Scotland is not a general holiday. It is possible that the letter was delivered on Good Friday and Orwell, who only dated his letter 'Friday,' replied on the same day. Alternatively, the letter may have been written on Friday, 2 April. In favour of the earlier date is the arrival of the first daffodils from Jura. Unfortunately, Avril does not mention when daffodils came out; she records the first snowdrops (9 February), crocus in full bloom (13 March), and the first tulip (14 April). However, she does note that on 24 March Bill Dunn returned to Barnhill from Glasgow. He must have seen Orwell there, and it is likely that that is how Orwell received his first daffodils from Jura.
2. Warburg sent Orwell illustrations for *Animal Farm* by Vera Bock, which had been intended for a shortened version of the book to be published in *Life*. That did not come to fruition, and the illustrations were requested by Warburg with the idea of producing an illustrated edition of *Animal Farm*. Although Warburg and his co-director, Roger Senhouse, admired the illustrations, they decided against using them unless Orwell was particularly keen. 'Every reader,' wrote Warburg, 'has his own view on the appearance of the characters . . . an illustrator, however skillful, could not avoid irritating many.'
3. Almost certainly Michael Felix Kennard's. Born 1924, Austria (as Michael Koessler), he had come to England in 1938 and was cared for by Fredric Warburg. He had shown his manuscript to Orwell, but in 1992 could not be sure that this particular reference was to him. He had served in the same Home Guard platoon as Orwell and Warburg (see *All Authors Are Equal*, 35–39, for Warburg's amusing account of the platoon commanded by Sgt. Orwell, dubbed 'the Foreign Legion' owing to its multi-national composition). Befriended by Orwell, with whom he shared an interest in fishing (see Orwell's letter to him, 7 June 1948, *3412*), he visited Jura two or three times and also visited Orwell in hospital. Orwell wished him to have his fishing rods, and these were given to Kennard by Avril after Orwell's death. Kennard, who worked in advertising, designed a number of dust-jackets for Secker & Warburg, including those for *Animal Farm* and *Nineteen Eighty-Four*. (Information provided by Michael Kennard.)

In 1960, Fredric Warburg recorded reminiscences of Orwell for the BBC Third Programme, broadcast 2 November 1960. Cut from his recording, but surviving in a transcript in the Orwell Archive, is an account of a conversation between the two men at Hairmyres Hospital that began by Orwell asking how Michael Koessler was getting on. Warburg said 'pretty well, but he's not very happy because he really wants to be a farmer.' Orwell was puzzled: 'He's a Jewish boy,' he said. 'I'm surprised he's interested in farming. I should have thought he was more interested in money, making money in a direct way.'

Warburg told him that that was not so and went on to tell the interviewer, Rayner Heppenstall, that this exchange revealed particularly clearly how Orwell's mind worked. Orwell, said Warburg, 'placed people and events and structures in categories—sort of platonic ideas. And to him a Jew was a man who was primarily interested in making money, and a Communist was a man who followed Stalin, and everything—a Frenchman, a Russian, a Jew, a Christian, a Trotskyist—everybody in his mind had a pattern, a rigid pattern, and it was very difficult for him to believe that they could ever depart from this pattern . . . this was the strength and the weakness of Orwell as a thinker and as a writer: that everything in his mind was arranged rather tidily in closely-knit, clearly-defined, ideas.' To Warburg, this anecdote about Koessler was the 'most significant illumination . . . about [Orwell's] way of thinking.'

3372. To Ivor Brown

27 March 1948   Handwritten

Ward 3
Hairmyres Hospital
East Kilbride
Lanarkshire

Dear Ivor Brown,[1]
I have been through the Joad book ("Decadence")[2] & I must say I didn't find it very stimulating. What about my doing a piece on Oscar Wilde's "The Soul of Man under Socialism," which has just been reprinted as a pamphlet? I have a copy here.[3] It raises some quite interesting points.

It was very nice seeing you last week. I think I am going on well, & today I was allowed up for half an hour, for the first time.

Yours sincerely
Geo. Orwell

1. Ivor Brown (1891–1974), editor of *The Observer*; see *1480, n. 2.*
2. C. E. M. Joad (1891–1953), philosopher and polemicist with a gift for giving his subjects a popular appeal, was a long-serving member of the BBC radio programme 'The Brains Trust.' *Decadence: A Philosophical Inquiry* was published in London, 1948, in New York, 1949.
3. One of the pamphlets from George Woodcock that Orwell acknowledged in his letter of 23 March 1948; see *3369* and *3369, n. 1. The Soul of Man Under Socialism* was first published in the *Fortnightly Review*, February 1891.

3373. To Sally McEwan

27 March 1948   Handwritten

Ward 3
Hairmyres Hospital
East Kilbride
Lanarkshire

Dear Sally,[1]
It seems literally years since I have heard from you, or of you? How are things going? I am going to send this to the Nature Clinic, hoping they'll forward it

if you aren't still there. How is your young man? Are you married? And how is little Sally? Excuse this filthy pen. It is all I have, as my other one is being refilled.

I dare say you heard I am suffering from T.B. I have been ill since last November, but really, I think, since the beginning of 1947. It was that vile winter of 1946–7[2] that started me off. Of course we had a lovely summer during which I wrote about half of a novel, but finally I had to take to my bed & when I got a specialist from the mainland to come & see me he at once said that one lung was badly infected. I am going on pretty well & during the past six weeks or so have been very much better. I am now allowed out of bed for ½ an hour a day, which is a great treat. They think I may get out of hospital some time during the summer, but I may have to go on being an out-patient for a while. I am having streptomycin, which is evidently doing its stuff, but I shall come to the end of that in a few weeks' time. The most annoying thing about all this is that it means losing about a year's work. My novel was supposed to be finished this May, but of course I can't touch it until I get out of here & am much stronger.

Richard is in tremendous form. I can't see him again till I am non-infectious, but I had him photographed recently, & could see how he had grown even in 2½ months since I had seen him. He will be 4 in May. He is still rather backward about talking, but quite forward in every other way & terrifyingly energetic. I had him X-rayed to make quite sure he had not caught this disease off me, but of course he was O.K. He had measles & whooping cough during last summer, but they didn't worry him & in fact we were hardly able to keep him in bed. He also cut his forehead very badly & had to have 3 stitches put in it, but I think the scar will disappear after a year or two.

We have got more furniture at Barnhill now, & the place is running quite well. Transport is still the chief difficulty. We have got a car now, but the headache is tyres, apart from the everlasting petrol difficulty. However, we also have a horse which can be used in moments of emergency. A friend now lives with us & farms the croft, which is a good arrangement, because we don't then feel guilty about occupying land & not using it, & also when we like we can go away, because there is someone to look after our animals. We have got a cow now, also of course hens, & am thinking of pigs. We've also got more of a garden now, & have made an end of all those awful rushes. I have planted a lot of fruit trees & bushes, but I am not sure yet whether trees will do much good in such a windy place.

Write some time & let me know how everything is going. The above address will find me for some time, I am afraid.

Yours
George

1. Sally McEwan (d. 1987), at one time a secretary at *Tribune*, stayed at Barnhill with her daughter in 1946; see *3027, n. 1*.
2. Orwell mistakenly wrote 1947–8.

3374. Diary
Second Literary Notebook

<u>30.3.48.</u>   When you are acutely ill, or recovering from acute illness, your brain frankly strikes work & you are only equal to picture papers, easy crossword puzzles etc. But when it is a case of a long illness, where you are weak & without appetite but not actually feverish or in pain, you have the impression that your brain is quite normal. Your thoughts are just as active as ever, you are interested in the same things, you seem to be able to talk normally, & you can read anything that you would read at any other time. It is only when you attempt to write, even to write the simplest & stupidest newspaper article, that you realise what a deterioration has happened inside your skull. [1] At the start[2] it is impossible to get anything on to paper at all. Your mind turns away to any conceivable subject rather than the one you are trying to deal with, & even the physical act of writing is unbearably irksome. Then, perhaps, you begin to be able to write a little, but whatever you write, once it is set down on paper, turns out to be stupid & obvious. You have also no command of language, or rather you can think of nothing except flat, obvious expressions: a good, lively phrase never occurs to you. And even when you begin to re-acquire the habit of writing, you seem to be incapable of preserving continuity. From time to time you may strike out a fairly good sentence, but it is extraordinarily difficult to make consecutive[3] sentences sound as though they had anything to do with one another. The reason for this is that you cannot concentrate for more than a few seconds, & therefore cannot even remember what you said a moment ago. In all this the striking thing is the contrast between the apparent normality of

---

your mind, & its helplessness when you attempt to get anything on to paper. Your thoughts, when you think them, seem to be just like your thoughts at any other time, but as soon as they are reduced to some kind of order they always turn out to be badly-expressed platitudes.

What I would like to know is whether enough is known about the localisation of brain functions to account for this kind of thing. It would seem natural enough if[4] the effect of illness were simply to stop you thinking,[5] but that is not what happens. What happens is that your mind is just as active as usual, perhaps more so,[6] but always to no purpose. You can use words, but always inappropriate words,[7] & you can have ideas, but you cannot fit them together. If mental activity is determined, for instance, by the supply of blood to the brain, it looks as though when you are ill there is enough blood to feed[8] the areas[9] that produce stupid thoughts, but not the ones that produce intelligent thoughts.

1. *skull*] replaces *brain* which was crossed through
2. *At the start*] replaces *To begin with* which was crossed through
3. *consecutive*] interlinear insertion
4. *It would . . . if*] interlinear insertion
5. *thinking*] originally followed by *this would seem natural* which was crossed through

6. *What happens . . . more so*] replaces *You can think, and do think just as intensely as usual* which was crossed through
7. *always inappropriate words*] replaces *you can only use them clumsily* which was crossed through
8. *feed*] replaces *supply* which was crossed through
9. *areas*] replaces *blood vessels* which was crossed through

3375. To David Astor

31 March 1948   Handwritten

Ward 3
Hairmyres Hospital
East Kilbride
Lanarkshire

Dear David,

Do you ever see this paper?[1] It's not wonderful, but deserves encouragement, I think, especially after "Polemic" died an untimely death.

I received last week a parcel containing the incredible gift of a 7 lb. bag of sugar. It came from Jamaica, & it now occurs to me it must have been from your wife. But there was no address on it. It also contained a slab of guava cheese which I sent home because I knew Richard would love it. I'd like to know where I could write & thank your wife for so kindly thinking of me.

I've been rather under the weather the last few days with a beastly sore throat—it isn't important, of course, but very painful & annoying. Otherwise I am getting on O.K. I now get up for half an hour a day, & I expect shortly I shall be wheeled out in the grounds occasionally. I have also got my arm out of the plaster, which is a great treat, though I can't straighten it yet.

Everything is all right at Barnhill. I put enquiries on foot about Neil's boat, but I hear in a roundabout way that he doesn't want to sell it. However, something else will turn up. It appears that Bob[2] doesn't like the new cow & chases her round, however before long he'll have a more congenial companion as Bill is getting another horse. He was reshod again recently, & Bill says he is in very good condition, although he's had nothing but hay through the winter.

I hope your little girl is all right. Richard has grown even since I saw him, to judge by his photographs.

Yours
George

1. Possibly *Politics and Letters*, to which Orwell had contributed 'Writers and Leviathan'; see *3364*. The journal ceased with the issue in which his article was published, Summer 1948.
2. A horse on loan from the Astors.

3376. To Mrs. David Astor
5 April 1948   Handwritten

Ward 3
Hairmyres Hospital
East Kilbride
Lanarkshire

Dear Mrs Astor,
I believe it was you who sent me a 7 lb. bag of sugar from Jamaica, also a tin of pears & some guava jelly. It was extremely kind of you to think of it. I was especially delighted to get the sugar, which my sister will use for making jam. I have been getting on pretty well, but just this last week have been feeling rather bad with a sore throat & various other minor ailments which are probably secondary effects of the streptomycin I am having. I think they are probably going to stop the injections for a few days & then go on again when when° these effects have worn off.[1]

I haven't seen Richard, my little boy, since before Christmas, as I can't see him while I am infectious. However I have had him photographed & can see that he is growing fast & is in good health. My sister says he is learning to talk better. I had been rather worried about that, though he is not backward in any other way.

Please forgive bad handwriting. My writing is bad enough at the best of times, but whatever is wrong with me has affected my fingernails & it is difficult to hold on to the pen. With many thanks again.

Yours sincerely
Geo. Orwell

1. Professor James Williamson, who was a junior doctor at Hairmyres Hospital when Orwell was a patient (see *3324, n. 3*), remembers the arrival of the streptomycin and its effect on Orwell (*Remembering Orwell*, 200).
   I think it was a hundred grams we got, which would have been enough to start him off. He got, I think, one injection a day, an intramuscular injection. Or it may have been half a gram twice a day. Anyway, he seemed to be perking up, but within a short space of time he developed this fearful allergic reaction. He came out in a generalized skin rash; his whole skin became red and inflamed and itching, and his mouth became inflamed, and ulcers appeared and his eyes were all red, and his hair started to come out. But he was very stoical about it. I mean, most people would have been round the bend with that.
   Subsequently we learned that if somebody got an allergic reaction, you could desensitize them by going back and starting with a tiny dose, and giving a slightly larger dose the next day, and so on, just verging on an allergic reaction. But we didn't know that at the time. So his drugs were given to two other patients at the hospital. If it had been two or three years later, it would have been pretty easy to cure his TB. But you see, he might still have died from a hemorrhage because the hemorrhage was really a sort of indirect result of the TB. You can actually die of a hemorrhage although the TB is cured, because if you have an area of the lung where there is an artery crossing, and that area is exposed and eroded because of the damage done by the old TB, then you can bleed to death from that. In the end, when he left us, he was in fact a bit better. We did get his sputum negative, you see.
   In a note for Professor Crick, written many years later, Dr Williamson said that Orwell's TB was 'pretty "chronic" . . . It was not the type that would have largely cleared with effective drug treatment and he would always have been breathless and incapacitated' (Crick, 3rd edition (1992), 602).

3377. To David Astor

Wed., [7 April 1948]   Handwritten

Dear David,
Thanks ever so much for sending the reading rest. It's a most ingenious thing, & ever so light on one's body. I can't write much as I am in a lousy state with this sore throat, rash all over me etc. If they definitely decide it is due to the streptomycin they will knock that off for a few days to let the other symptoms subside. Otherwise am O.K. & put on 3 lb last week. Thanks so much again.

Yours
George

P.S. I've just this moment received your letter. I wouldn't come & see me when I'm like this. I'm just a misery to myself & everyone else. Re *books*. I sent back Gallacher's book & the Joad book[1] (delay owing to difficulty of making up a parcel here). I haven't any other books belonging to the Obs. at present. The arrangement was that I was to do a short piece on O. Wilde's "Soul of Man under Socialism," which I think is an interesting subject & want to do when I am fit for anything again. But I have a copy of my own.

1. William Gallacher, *The Rolling of the Thunder* (published November 1947 and February 1948). C. E. M. Joad, *Decadence: A Philosophical Inquiry*; see *3372, n. 2*. Gallacher (1881–1965) was a Communist Party M.P., 1935–1950. From 1935 to 1945 he was the only Communist M.P.; he was then joined by Phil Piratin (1907–1995). Both lost their seats in 1950.

3378. Diary Entry

This entry is taken from Orwell's last (not his Second) Literary Notebook. Although written a year after the treatment it describes, it is placed here because Orwell started a fifty-day course of treatment with streptomycin on 19 or 20 February 1948; fifty days later would be 8 or 9 April.

24.3.49. *Before I forget them it is worth writing down the secondary symptoms produced by streptomycin when I was treated with it last year. Streptomycin was then almost a new drug & had never been used at that hospital before. The symptoms in my case were quite different from those described in the American medical journal in which we read the subject up beforehand.*
At first, though the streptomycin seemed to produce an almost immediate improvement in my health, there were no secondary symptoms, except that a sort of discoloration appeared at the base of my finger & toe nails. Then my face became noticeably redder & the skin had a tendency to flake off, & a sort of rash appeared all over my body, especially down my back. There was no itching associated with this. After abt 3 weeks I got a severe sore throat, which did not go away & was not affected by sucking penicillin lozenges. It was very painful to swallow & I had to have a special diet for some weeks.

There was now ulceration with blisters in my throat & on the insides of my cheeks, & the blood kept coming up into little blisters on my lips. At night these burst & bled considerably, so that in the morning my lips were always stuck together with blood & I had to bathe them before I could open my mouth. Meanwhile my nails had disintegrated at the roots & the disintegration grew, as it were, up the nail, new nails forming beneath meanwhile. My hair began to come out, & one or two patches of quite white hair appeared at the back (previously it was only speckled with grey.)

After 50 days the streptomycin, which had been injected at the rate of 1 gramme a day, was discontinued. The lips etc. healed almost immediately & the rash went away, though not quite so promptly. My hair stopped coming out & went back to its normal colour, though I think with more grey in it than before. The old nails ended by dropping out altogether, & some months after leaving hospital I had only ragged tips, which kept splitting, to the new nails. Some of the toenails did not drop out. Even now my nails are not normal. They are much more corrugated than before, & a great deal thinner, with a constant tendency to split if I do not keep them very short.

At that time the Board of Trade would not give import permits for streptomycin, except to a few hospitals for experimental purposes. One had to get hold of it by some kind of wire-pulling. It cost £1 a gramme, plus 60% Purchase Tax.

3379. To David Astor

[14 April 1948]¹ Handwritten

Dear David,

I thought you'd like to hear that Bobbie is making himself useful. Part of the field behind the house was too steep a slope for the small tractor, so they harnessed Bobbie into the harrow & he behaved "like a lamb," Bill says. So perhaps now they can use him in the trap, which is as well, as the car needs new wheels as well as tyres.

They've stopped the streptomycin for a few days & the unpleasant symptoms have practically disappeared. Shortly they will continue with the strepto, which has about 3 weeks to go. It's evidently doing its stuff as my last 3 tests were "negative," ie no TB germs. Of course that doesn't necessarily mean they're all dead, but at any rate they must have taken a pretty good beating. I have felt better the last day or two & have nearly finished the article I promised for the Obs.² The weather has at last improved, & I'm longing to go out, which I think they may soon let me do, in a chair, of course.

Yours
George

1. Alternative dates for this undated letter are 14, 21, 28 April 1948. In his letter to Astor, on 4 May 1948 Orwell writes of having had his fourth negative test.
2. Probably his review of Wilde's *The Soul of Man under Socialism*; see *3395*.

3380. Review of *Spearhead: Ten Years' Experimental Writing in America*, edited by James Laughlin

Times Literary Supplement, 17 April 1948[1]

The preparatory notes Orwell made for this review are reproduced as *3381*.

The exchange of literary intelligence between country and country is still far from brisk, even where there is no political obstruction. Only the other day a critic in a French weekly review could remark that, so far as he was aware, the United States had not produced any new writers since 1939. We ourselves, not being dependent on translations, are able to be a little better informed, but even so it is a fact that most of the younger American writers are only known to this country because of stray contributions to magazines. Few of them have yet appeared here in book form. *Spearhead*, Mr. James Laughlin's anthology of recent American prose and verse, is therefore useful, although, as he admits himself, it is not fully representative.

An anthology of this kind is not, of course, intended to give a picture of the American literary scene as a whole. Mr. Laughlin has explicitly confined himself to experimental and "non-commercial" writing, and most of the contents are drawn from such magazines as the *Kenyon Review* and the *Partisan Review*, or from his own annual miscellany, *New Directions*. Even so, the selection is less interesting than it might have been, since it consists almost entirely of "creative" writing—that is, poems and stories—while much of the best and liveliest American writing of the past ten years has been done by literary critics and political essayists. An anthology based mainly on the "little reviews" ought not to leave out Lionel Trilling, Dwight Macdonald, Clement Greenberg and Nicola Chiaramonte: one might also have expected to find Edmund Wilson, Mary McCarthy and Saul Bellow. However, this book does introduce to the English reader a number of young writers who are less known here than they deserve to be—for example, Paul Goodman, Karl Shapiro, Delmore Schwarz and Randall Jarrell. There are also, of course, contributions from various "established" writers (William Carlos Williams, E. E. Cummings, Henry Miller and others), and even from such veterans as Ezra Pound and Gertrude Stein.

One fact this book brings out is that American literary intellectuals are still very much on the defensive. There is evidently much more feeling that the writer is a hunted heretic and that *"avant garde"* literature, as it is rather solemnly called, is totally different from popular literature, than exists in England. But one cannot help noticing, while reading Mr. Laughlin's introduction and then the items that follow it, that this feeling of isolation is largely unjustified. To begin with, the *"avant garde"* and the "commercial" obviously overlap, and are even difficult to distinguish from one another. A number of the stories in this book, notably those of Jack Jones, Robert Lowry and Tennessee Williams, would fit easily into dozens of big-circulation magazines. But in addition, it is doubtful whether American literature has had during the past ten or fifteen years the "experimental" character that Mr. Laughlin claims for it. During that period literature has extended its subject-matter, no doubt, but there has been little or no technical innovation. There has also been surprisingly little interest in prose as such, and an all-round tolerance of ugly and slovenly writing. Even in verse it could probably be shown that there has been no real innovator since Auden, or even since Eliot, to whom Auden and his associates admittedly owed a great deal.

No English prose-writer in the immediate past has played with words as Joyce did, nor on the other hand has anyone made a deliberate attempt to simplify language as Hemingway did. As for the sort of cadenced "poetic" prose that used to be written by, for instance, Conrad, Lawrence or Forster, no one nowadays attempts anything of the kind. The most recent writer of intentionally rhythmical prose is Henry Miller, whose first book was published in 1935, when he was already not a young man. A striking thing about the prose-writers in Mr. Laughlin's collection is how like one another they all are in manner, except when they drop into dialect. The Anarchist Paul Goodman, for instance, certainly has unusual subject-matter for his stories, but his manner of approach is conservative enough. So also with the stories—again, unusual in theme—by H. J. Kaplan and John Berryman. No one to-day could produce a book of parodies corresponding to Max Beerbohm's *A Christmas Garland*: the differences between one writer and another, at any rate the surface differences, are not great enough. It is true, however, that the contemporary lack of interest in the technique of prose has its good side, in that a writer who is not expected to have a "style" is not tempted to practise affectations. This reflection is forced on one by the most noticeably mannered writer in the collection, Djuna Barnes, who seems to have been disastrously influenced by Rabelais, or possibly by Joyce.

The verse in this anthology is very uneven, and a better selection would have been possible. Randall Jarrell, for instance, is represented by five poems, including the excellent "Camp in the Prussian Forest"; but his tiny masterpiece, "The Ball Turret Gunner," which ends with the memorable line, "When I died they washed me out of the turret with a hose," is not there. Perhaps the best poem in the book is by E. E. Cummings. He is an irritating writer, partly because of his largely meaningless typographical tricks, partly because his restless bad temper soon provokes a counter-reaction in the reader, but he has a gift for telling phrases (for instance, his often-quoted description of Soviet Russia—"Vicariously childlike kingdom of slogan"), and, at his best, for neat, rapidly moving verse. In this collection he is at the top of his form in a short poem in praise of Olaf, a conscientious objector, which has slightly the air of being a pastiche of *Struwwelpeter*. Olaf's barely printable punishments at the hands of the military are first described, and then:—

> Our president, being of which
> assertions duly notified
> threw the yellowsonofabitch
> into a dungeon, where he died
>
> Christ (of His mercy infinite)
> i pray to see; and Olaf, too

> preponderatingly because
> unless statistics lie he was
> more brave than me; more blond than you.[2]

Throughout this anthology the best poems, almost without exception, are the ones that rhyme and scan in a more or less regular manner. Much of the "free" verse is simply prose arranged in lines of arbitrary length, or sometimes in highly elaborate patterns, with the initial word moving this way and that across the page, apparently on the theory that a visual effect is the same thing as a musical rhythm. If one takes passages of this so-called verse and rearranges them as prose, it becomes actually indistinguishable from prose, except, in some cases, by its subject-matter. A couple of examples will be enough:

> It was an icy day. We buried the cat, then took her box and set match to it in the back yard. Those fleas that escaped earth and fire died by the cold. (William Carlos Williams.)

> The old guy put down his beer. Son, he said (and a girl came over to the table where we were: asked us by Jack Christ to buy her a drink). Son, I am going to tell you something the like of which nobody ever was told. (Kenneth Patchen.)

Kenneth Rexroth's long poem, "The Phoenix and the Tortoise," which again looks like prose if rearranged as prose, is perhaps in a different category. Such a passage as this, for instance:—

> The institution is a device
> For providing molecular
> Process with delusive credentials.
> "Value is the reflection
> Of satisfied appetite,
> The formal aspect of the tension
> Generated by resolution
> Of fact." Over-specialization,
> Proliferation, gigantism.

is not verse in the ordinary sense, but this is probably due not to sheer slovenliness but to the notion, perhaps derived from Ezra Pound or from translations of Chinese poems, that poetry can consist of lapidary statements without any rhythmical quality. The weakness of this method of writing is that it sacrifices not only the musical appeal of verse but also its mnemonic function. It is precisely the fact of having recognizable rhythms, and usually rhyme as well, that makes it possible for verse, unlike prose, to exist apart from the printed page. An enormous amount of "free" verse has been produced during the past thirty or forty years, but only so much of it has survived, in the sense of being remembered by heart, as contained cadences of a kind impossible in prose. The chief reason, at any rate in England and America, for breaking away from conventional verse-forms was that the

English language is exceptionally poor in rhymes; a deficiency already obvious to the poet of the nineties who wrote:—

> From Austin back to Chaucer,
> My wearied eyes I shove,
> But never came across a
> New word to rhyme with love.

This shortcoming naturally had a cumulative effect, and by the Georgian period it had led to an unbearable staleness and artificiality. The way out was through the total or partial abandonment of rhyme, or through double rhymes and the use of colloquial words which would previously have been considered undignified, but which allowed the stock of available rhymes to be extended. This, however, did not do away with the need for rhythm but, if anything, increased it. Indeed, successful rhymeless poems—for example, Auden's *Spain*, or many passages in Eliot's work—tend to be written in strongly accented, non-iambic metres. Recently, as one can see even in this anthology, there has been a tendency to return to traditional stanza forms, usually with a touch of raggedness that is a legacy from "free" verse. Karl Shapiro, for instance, is very successful in handling what is really an adaptation of the popular ballad, as in his poem "Fireworks":—

> In the garden of pleistoscene flowers we wander like Alice
> Where seed sends a stalk in the heavens and pops from a pod
> A Blue blossom that hangs in the distance and opens its chalice
> And falls in the dust of itself and goes out with a nod.
> How the hairy tarantulas crawl in the soft of the ether
> Where showers of lilies explode in the jungle of creepers;
> How the rockets of sperm hurtle up to the moon and beneath her
> Deploy for the eggs of the astral and sorrowful sleepers!

Of the short stories in this anthology perhaps the best is John Berryman's "The Imaginary Jew"; it describes a young man who goes to a political meeting, full of generous sentiments and disgusted by anti-semitism, and then suddenly gains a much deeper insight into the Jewish problem through the accident of being mistaken for a Jew himself. Paul Goodman's story, "A Ceremonial," which supposedly takes place "not long after the establishment among us of reasonable institutions"—that is, after the Anarchist revolution—is a spirited attempt to describe happiness, a feat which no writer has ever quite accomplished. H. J. Kaplan's longish story, "The Mohammedans," is the kind of which one feels inclined to say that it shows great talent but one is not certain what it is about. Georg Mann's satire on Communism, "Azef Wischmeier, the Bolshevik Bureaucrat," would have been funny if it had been a dozen pages long instead of nearly fifty. There is a long extract from Henry Miller's *Tropic of Capricorn*. Like all of its author's earlier writings, it contains some fine passages, but it would have been better to pick a chapter from the less *exagéré Tropic of Cancer*, which remains Miller's masterpiece, and which is still a very rare book, so successfully has it been hunted down by the police of all countries.

315

Apart from the written pieces, the anthology includes two sets of fairly good but not outstanding photographs. One set, taken by Walker Evans, accompanies a piece of "reportage" on the southern cotton farmers by James Agee.[3] The other set, by Wright Morris, consists of photographs of buildings, mostly ruinous, each accompanied by a long caption in the form of a sort of prose poem. These captions are nothing very much in themselves, but the idea is a good one and might be profitably followed up. The other chief curiosity of the book is a collection, compiled by Mr. Laughlin, of the poems of Samuel Greenberg, a Jewish youth, son of very poor parents, who died about 1918, aged less than twenty. They are queer poems, full of misspellings and neologisms, and sometimes more like growing embryos than completed writings, but they show considerable power. Mr. Laughlin demonstrates by parallel quotations that Hart Crane lifted numerous lines from Greenberg without acknowledgment.

All in all, this book is useful, in that it introduces about forty American writers, of whom more than half are unknown or barely known in England; but it would have been a good deal better if it had been compiled expressly for an English audience. Actually it is a book designed for America, evidently imported into this country in sheets (Henry Miller's favourite verb has been laboriously blacked out by hand, over a stretch of fifty pages), and it is likely to give English readers a somewhat lopsided impression. It should be repeated that where American writing particularly excels at this moment is in literary criticism and in political and sociological essays. This, no doubt, is largely because in the United States there is more money, more paper and more spare time. The magazines are fatter, the "angels" are richer, and, above all, the intelligentsia, in spite of its sense of grievance, is numerous enough to constitute a public in itself. Long, serious controversies, of a kind extinct in England, can still happen; and, for instance, the battles that raged round the question of "supporting" the late war, or round the ideas of James Burnham or Van Wyck Brooks, produced material that would have been better worth reprinting, and more representative, than much of the contents of *Spearhead*. Moreover, the book suffers from the fact that it is neither uncompromisingly "highbrow," nor, on the other hand, is it a cross-section of current American literature. It leaves out several of the best living American writers on the ground that they are not *avant garde*, while at the same time it includes Kay Boyle and William Saroyan. It also—but perhaps this is unavoidable in any bulky anthology compiled from contemporary work—includes one or two pieces of sheer rubbish. The editors of the Falcon Press are to be congratulated for their enterprise, but another time they would do better to choose their material for themselves and to cast the net more widely.

1. This review was published anonymously, as was then the custom of the *TLS*. Orwell had written to James Laughlin (1914–) on 16 July 1940 (see *659*) in response to Laughlin's request that he might publish Orwell's essay on Henry Miller, 'Inside the Whale.' Laughlin was the publisher of New Directions books, and Orwell's essay appeared in *New Directions in Prose and Poetry* (1940).
2. Cummings's lines (*Poems 1923–1954*) should read (closed up as shown):

line 1: our president, being of which
l. 4: into a dungeon, where he died
l. 5: Christ(of His mercy infinite)
l. 6: i pray to see;and Olaf, too
l. 9: more brave than me:more blond than you.
3. From *Let Us Now Praise Famous Men* (Boston, MA, 1941).

3381. Preparatory Notes for Review of *Spearhead*
Second Literary Notebook

"Spearhead"

Cut off from USA—useful reminder—not altogether representative.

Short survey of contents—(NB. position of US intelligentsia—multiplication of "little reviews".)[1]

Not altogether representative—critical writing.

On the defensive. McL. on "experimental" writing. NB. no real experimentation in prose in past dozen years (partial exception Henry Miller.) Cf. Paul Goodman. Note also disappearance of "style" (good thing on the whole.) Max Beerbohm's parodies. Verse? Doubtful if real development after Eliot. Eliot (Pound) partly re-introduced European outlook, but partly driven in that direction by lack of rhymes in English. One way out double rhymes (Hopkins—grotesqueness—Karl Shapiro). No rhyme. But E. always rhythmical (if set up as prose—example K. Rexroth[2] *merely clipped form of prose.) Meanwhile slight tendency to return to traditional forms—in USA, pastiche of popular ballad.*
More about contents.

1. Orwell has marked these two lines to be transferred to the start of the fourth note, before 'On the defensive.'
2. Orwell spelt this 'Rexwroth.'

3382. To Leonard Moore
17 April 1948   Handwritten

Ward 3
Hairmyres Hospital
East Kilbride
Lanarkshire

Dear Moore,
Many thanks for your letter of the other day. It was kind of Miss Otis,[1] but, if you are writing to her, you might tell her that there honestly isn't anything I need. I am quite well cared for here.

I wonder if you could get me a copy of a book called L'UNIVERS CONCENTRATIONNAIRE, by David ROUSSET[2] (at any rate that is the author's name, but I am not completely sure of the book). It's published in Paris, but I don't know what publisher. I would have written to somebody to get it for me, but I don't know what is the correct manner of paying, when one isn't supposed to send currency out of the country.[3] Could we do it for instance through one of the publishers who are doing translations of various books of mine?

I am a lot better. I have had a bad time with the secondary effects of the streptomycin, but the TB. seems definitely better, & I begin to hope I shall be out of hospital some time in the summer. They tell me, however, that I shall have to go very slow for about a year, so far as physical exertion goes.

Yours sincerely
Eric Blair

1. Elizabeth R. Otis, Orwell's U.S. agent for contributions to journals.
2. For Orwell's reaction to Rousset's book and Roger Senhouse's translation, see *3393*.
3. Owing to the financial crisis, paying for goods from abroad sought by individuals was difficult if not impossible.

3383. To Philip Rahv

17 April 1948   Handwritten

Ward 3
Hairmyres Hospital
East Kilbride
Lanarkshire

Dear Rahv,

Many thanks for your letter.[1] I think Slater[2] would undertake the London Letter readily enough. If he won't, or isn't satisfactory, it is not very easy to suggest suitable people. Perhaps Mark Benney,[3] whose work you perhaps know, might suit you.

I'll write you something when I can. I am still pretty sorry for myself, especially as I have just finished a course of streptomycin. I hope I may get out of hospital some time during the summer, but they tell me I shall have to go very slowly for about a year. I was about half way through a novel when I was taken ill, & expected to finish it this spring. As it is I can't touch it till I get out of bed & am a lot stronger. Even now I am more than a stone below weight, & very weak. I do book reviews etc., but that's about all I'm equal to. Please remember me to everyone.

Yours sincerely
Geo. Orwell

1. Rahv had written on 29 March 1948. He imagined 'England' a very poor place for sick people at the present time. Arthur Koestler was in America, he said, and enjoying himself so much he thought he might stay permanently [which he did not], but that meant the London Letter was

not being written, and he wondered whether Humphrey Slater would be an appropriate person to take it over. He asked whether Orwell had thought of visiting America—there was every kind of climate available and many people in America who would very much like to meet him. He asked how Orwell's novel was getting on and whether he had anything he could publish in *Partisan Review*. Koestler's last London Letter appeared in January 1948. Rahv followed Orwell's recommendation, and Slater contributed the next London Letter to *Partisan Review*, in the July 1948 issue.

2. Hugh (Humphrey) Slater (1906–1958) edited *Polemic*, 1945–47. See *731, n. 1*.
3. Mark Benney, pseudonym for Henry Ernest Degras (1910–) became famous with his book *Low Company: Describing the Evolution of a Burglar* (1936), which he had written in prison. He became a figure on the London literary scene for a time. Shortly after the war he became a professor of social science in the United States.

3384. Diary
Second Literary Notebook

<u>18.4.48.</u>   *How memory works, or doesn't.*[1] *Last night, as I was settling down after the lights had been turned out, I suddenly, for no apparent[2] reason remembered something that had happened during the war. This was that at some time or other[3]—when, I did not know, but it was evidently a good long time back—I was shown a document which was so secret that the Minister concerned, or his secretary (I think it was his secretary), apparently had orders not to let it pass out of his own hand. I therefore had to come round to his side of the desk & read it over his shoulder. It was a short*

---

pamphlet or memorandum printed on good quality white paper & bound with green silk thread. But the point is that though I remembered the scene vividly—especially the secretive way in which he held the page for me to read it, as though there were danger of some[4] other unauthorised person getting a glimpse of it—I had no memory whatever as to what the document was.

This morning I thought it over, & was able to make some inferences. The only Minister I was in touch with during the war was Cripps, in 1942 & 1943, after his mission to India. The document must have had something to do with India or Burma, because it was in this connection (when I was working in the Indian Section at the BBC) that I occasionally saw Cripps. The person who showed me the document must have been David Owen, Cripps's secretary. I then remembered that after reading it I made some such comment as, "I should think you would keep a thing like that secret," which made it all the more likely that the document had something to do with India. In the afternoon I mentioned the matter to Richard Rees, & then later I remembered a little more, but in a doubtful way. I think—but I remember this much less well than I remember the style of print & paper—that the document was a memorandum on our post-war treatment of Burma, then occupied by the Japanese, saying that Burma would have to revert to "direct rule" (meaning martial law) for several years before civil government was restored. This, of course was a very

———————

different tale from what we were giving out in our propaganda. *And I think (but any memory I have of this is very vague indeed) that on the strength of it I may have dropped a hint to one of the Burmese in London, warning him not to trust the British government too far.*

If I did drop any such hint, this would have amounted to a breach of trust, & perhaps that was why I had preferred to forget the whole[5] incident. But then why did I suddenly remember it again? What impresses me even more than my having remembered[6] the scene without remembering what the document was about, is[7] that it was, so to speak, quite a new memory.[8] The moment the episode came back to me, I was aware that it had never crossed my mind for years past. It had suddenly[9] popped up to the surface, after lying forgotten for—I think—quite five[10] years.

1. *How . . . doesn't*] replaces *Astonishing vagaries of memory* which was crossed through
2. *apparent*] replaces *particular* which was crossed through
3. *or other*] replaces *during the war* which was crossed through
4. *there were danger of some*] interlinear insertion
5. *whole*] interlinear insertion
6. *my having remembered*] replaces *the fact that I remembered* which was crossed through
7. *is*] originally followed by *the sudden reappearance of this episode in my mind after it had been forgotten for years* which was crossed through
8. *memory*] originally followed by *I was aware that it had never crossed my mind for years past.* which was crossed through
9. *suddenly*] replaces *simply* which was crossed through
10. *five*] replaces *four* which was crossed through

3385. To Roger Senhouse

19 April 1948   Handwritten

Ward 3
Hairmyres Hospital
East Kilbride
Lanarkshire

Dear Roger,

Thanks so much for your letter. I'll duly correct & send back the proofs.[1] I'm glad you followed the Penguin edition—I didn't know you were going to print so soon & was going to write & say to use the Penguin version, which is the best.

I've been having a lousy time with the secondary effects of the streptomycin. However, it's all over now & evidently the drug has done its stuff. It's rather like sinking the ship to get rid of the rats, but worth it if it works. The doctor is pleased with my case, & seems to think I shall get out some time in the summer, but I shall have to go very quietly for about a year, & for some months I may have to attend for periodical treatment. In that case I suppose I'll have to stay most of the time in Glasgow, or perhaps Edinburgh, which is pleasanter & not far away. I'll have to go up to Jura & down to London occasionally, but they tell me to avoid travel as much as possible. I was about half way through my novel when I was taken ill. I might have finished it by May—as it is, I don't know. If I get out of here in the summer, I suppose I might finish it by the end of the year. Fred wanted me to publish another book of reprinted essays, but I think it would be a mistake. It's much better to let them lie a few years.

Richard Rees was here to see me yesterday. He's got lots of room in his flat, he says, & indeed I may go & stay with him when I come out. I hardly know Edinburgh, but he says it's very nice.

By the way, when in Paris could you get me a copy of a book called (I think) L'UNIVERS CONCENTRATIONNAIRE by David ROUSSET? I asked Moore to get me one,[2] but I dare say he'll get it wrong somehow. I don't know what it costs, but you can let me know afterwards. I am glad the Prebble book[3] is going well.

Yours sincerely
George

1. Of *Burmese Days*. The Penguin edition of 1944 followed the first, U.S., edition of 1934, in the main; the Gollancz edition of 1935 was modified for fear of libel actions and therefore 'garbled,' to use Orwell's description. However, it did include genuine revisions by Orwell. The Secker & Warburg edition introduced a number of errors. See Textual Note to *CW*, II.
2. See *3382* and, for Senhouse's response, *3393, n. 1*.
3. *The Edge of Darkness*, published by Secker & Warburg, 8 April 1948; see *3351, n. 1*.

3386. To Julian Symons

20 April 1948   Handwritten

Ward 3
Hairmyres Hospital
East Kilbride
Lanark.

Dear Julian,

Thanks so much for sending the pen, & prospectively for some chocolate[1] you mentioned. I am so glad to hear you are going to have a baby. They're awful fun in spite of the nuisance, & as they develop one has one's own childhood over again. I suppose one thing one has to guard against is imposing one's own childhood on the child, but I do think it is relatively easy to give a child a decent time nowadays & allow it to escape the quite unnecessary torments that I for instance went through. I'm not sure either that one ought to trouble too much about bringing a child into a world of atomic bombs, because those born now will never have known anything except wars, rationing etc., & can probably be quite happy against that background if they've had a good psychological start.

I am a lot better, but I had a bad fortnight with the secondary effects of the streptomycin. I suppose with all these drugs it's rather a case of sinking the ship to get rid of the rats. However they've stopped the strepto now & evidently it has done its stuff. I am still fearfully weak & thin, but they seem pleased with my case & I think I may get out some time during the summer. If I do, I imagine I shall have to stay in Glasgow, or at any rate somewhere near, so as to come in about once a fortnight & be examined & "refilled" (with air). No doubt I shall be able between times to get down to London & up to Jura, though they tell me I shall have to travel as little as possible, & in any case to take things easy for about a year. It's better to keep on with the treatment at this hospital, as its a very good hospital & they know my case. I am longing to get up to Jura at any rate for a few days, to see Richard & see how the farm work is going, but I should have to be careful not to do much. I'm afraid that even when completely cured I shall be not much good physically for the rest of my life—I never was strong or athletic, but I don't like an altogether sedentary life, & I shall have to readjust my habits so that I can get about without making too much muscular effort, no more digging or chopping wood, for instance.

It's funny you should have mentioned Gissing. I am a great fan of his (though I've never read "Born in Exile", which some say is his masterpiece, because I can't get hold of a copy), & was just in the act of re-reading two reprints, which I promised to review for Politics & Letters.[2] I think I shall do a long article on him, for them or someone else. I think "The Odd Women" is one of the best novels in English. You asked about my uniform edition. They're starting with a novel called "Coming Up for Air", which was published in 1939 & rather killed by the war, & doing "Burmese Days" later in the year. I just° corrected the proofs of the latter, which I wrote more than 15 years ago & probably hadn't looked at for 10 years.[3] It was a queer experience—almost like reading a book by somebody else. I'm also going to try & get Harcourt Brace to reprint these two books in the USA but even if they do so they'll probably only take "sheets", which never does one much good. It's funny what BFs American publishers are about re-prints. Harcourt Brace have been nagging me for 2 years for a manuscript, any kind of manuscript, & are now havering with the idea of doing a series of reprints, but when I urged them to reprint "Burmese Days" immediately after they had cleaned up on "Animal Farm", they wouldn't do so. Nor would the original publishers of "B.D", though they too were trying to get something out of me. Apparently reprints in the USA are done mostly by special firms which only take them on if they are safe for an enormous sale.

Yes, I thought the last number of "Politics" quite good, but I must say that in spite of all their elegies I retain dark suspicions about Gandhi,[4] based only on gossip, but such a lot of gossip that I think there must be something in it.

Please remember me to your wife.

Yours
George

1. Chocolate and sweets were then severely rationed. Their rationing ended on 24 April 1949, but soon after, on 14 July, it was re-imposed at four ounces a week.
2. See *3292*, *n. 2* regarding Orwell's writing on Gissing, and headnote to *3406*.

3. Orwell read the proofs for the Penguin edition of *Burmese Days* in December 1943; see *CW*, II, Textual Note, 309.
4. Mahatma (Mohandas Karamchand) Gandhi (1869–1948), a major figure in the struggle for Indian independence and a continuing force in Indian life after his death. He was fatally shot on 30 January 1948 by a Hindu fanatic. See Orwell's 'Reflections on Gandhi,' *Partisan Review*, January 1949, *3516*.

3387. To Gleb Struve

21 April 1948   Handwritten

Ward 3
Hairmyres Hospital
East Kilbride
Lanarkshire (Scotland)

Dear Struve,

I'm awfully sorry to have to send this[1] back, after such a long delay, having finally failed to find a home for it. But as you see by the above, I am in hospital (tuberculosis), & at the time of receiving your letter I wasn't able to do very much. I am better now, & hope to get out of here some time during the summer, but of course the treatment of this disease is always a slow job.

I have arranged to review "We" for the Times Lit. Supp., when the English translation comes out.[2] Did you tell me that Zamyatin's widow is still alive & in Paris? If so, & she can be contacted, it might be worth doing so, as there may be others of his books which some English publisher might be induced to take, if "We" is a success. You told me that his satire on England, "The Islanders," had never been translated, & perhaps it might be suitable.[3]

I hope you will forgive me for my failure to find an editor for Mandelstam's sketches. There are so few magazines in England[4] now. "Polemic" died of the usual disease, & the other possible one "Politics & Letters," was no good.

You asked about my novel, "Burmese Days." I think it is still in print as a Penguin, but there won't be many copies left. It is being reprinted about the end of this year, as I am beginning a uniform edition, & that is second on the list. I *may* succeed in getting some of these books reprinted in the USA as well.

Yours sincerely
Geo. Orwell

P.S. This address will find me for some months, I'm afraid.[5]

1. Presumably the Mandelstam sketches mentioned later in the letter.
2. An English translation, by Gregory Zilboorg, was, in fact, published in New York by E. P. Dutton in 1924 and reprinted the following year. It was republished in 1952 with an introduction by Peter Rudy and a preface by Marc Slonim. Although Orwell knew of the U.S. edition, he had not seen it. The French translation, *Nous autres*, which Orwell reviewed in *Tribune*, 4 January 1946 (see *2841*), was published in Paris in 1929. The first 'book edition' in Russian was not published until 1952, and then in New York, but it did appear in an émigré journal in 1927. See Orwell's letters to Fredric Warburg and Gleb Struve, 22 November 1948, *3495* and *3496*.

3. Yevgeny Zamyatin (see *2841, n. 1*) came to England in 1916 to supervise the building of Russian icebreakers in the northeast of England and Scotland. He wrote two satires on English life, *The Islanders*, written in England in 1917, and *The Fisher of Men*, written in 1918 on his return to Russia. The first is set in Jesmond, near Newcastle upon Tyne and the second in Chiswick. A translation by Sophie Fuller and Julian Sacchi was published in 1984. In their introduction, the translators refer to Zamyatin's having written several articles on H. G. Wells, 'whose visions of the future were echoed in Zamyatin's *We*. In its turn, *We* was to influence . . . *1984*'; and '*Islanders* was in many ways a starting point for *We*.'
4. Struve had gone to California in 1947 to take up a university appointment; see *3354, n. 1*.
5. The postscript is written at the head of this letter.

3388. To George Woodcock

24 April 1948   Handwritten

Ward 3
Hairmyres Hospital
East Kilbride
Lanark.

Dear George,
I haven't written earlier because I've been having a bad time for a fortnight or so with the secondary effects of the streptomycin. I have read your poems with attention. I liked best the long poem at the end, "Waterloo Bridge", & after that I think "Ancestral Tablet", "The Agitator", & "The Island". I think you get your best effects with 10-syllable lines whch are a bit irregular so as to give a sort of broken-backed movement, like "And again, I am thinking of the angels & William Blake" or "This is the preposterous hour when Caesars rise". But, I think you need to make up your mind a bit better on the subject of rhyme. Part of the time you use ordinary rhymes, but a good deal of the time assonances[1] like thought-white, hours-fears, etc. I must say I am against this kind of rhyme, which seems to me only, as it were, an intellectual rhyme, existing on the paper because we can see that the final consonant is the same. The lack of rhymes in English is a very serious difficulty & gets more serious all the time, as familiar rhymes get more & more hackneyed, but I have always felt that if one is to use imperfect rhymes, it would be better to make the vowel sound & not the consonant the same. Eg. open-broken, fate-shape, sound to me more like rhymes than eyes-voice, town-again, & so forth. However, I'm no judge of such things.

I did a short article—not actually a review but one of those articles they have on the leader page—for the Observer on Wilde's "Soul of Man under Socialism", which may help it a little. Charles Davy, one of the sub-eds, asked me if I could do a short article, when they have a pretext for it, on the Freedom Defence Committee, its aims & scope. I will do so, of course,[2] & no doubt it would bring in a few contributions. I suppose I should be correct in saying that there is not now any other organisation having just those aims (except of course the N.C.C.L.,[3] which I might be able to give a quiet kick at in passing.)?

I am a lot better. The streptomycin had in the end some very nasty effects, however it's all over now, & the drug has I think done its stuff. I don't know if it's killed all the germs, but it must have given them a nasty knock, as they haven't been able to find any in me lately. I hope I may get out of hospital some time during the summer, but even when I do I shall have to stay most of the time within reach of this hospital, perhaps in Edinburgh, which is fairly near & pleasanter than Glasgow. No doubt I can get up to Jura or down to London for short periods, but if I have to come here once a fortnight or so for treatment, I must be in the neighbourhood most of the time, otherwise it means too much travelling. I shall evidently have to avoid all physical effort for about a year. Actually they are anxious to prevent me from going up to Jura at all, as they think I should immediately start chopping wood, etc., but I really don't think I should when I am as short of breath as at present. I am very anxious when I am up to go there for at any rate a week, not only to see Richard but to see how the farm work is getting on. Richard is getting enormous to judge by his photos. Of course when I am out I can have him to stay with me, but he can't come & see me here in the infectious part of the hospital.

I wonder how your plan of going to Canada is working out. I think it's the sort of country that could be quite fun for a bit, especially if you like fishing! Please give all the best to Inge.

Yours
George

P.S. I've lost your new address—I'm going to send this care of the F.D.C.[4]

1. Assonance, or vocalic rhyme, is, properly speaking, the like sound of vowels in pairs or groups of syllables whose consonants differ—i.e., the kind of rhyme Orwell prefers: fate-shape. The open-broken example is one of the very rare examples of such rhyme in the *Sonnets* of Shakespeare (No. 61, lines 1 and 3).
2. Charles Davy wrote again to Orwell on 19 May 1948 noting that E. M. Forster had resigned from the National Council for Civil Liberties and wondering whether Orwell could use this in his article about the Freedom Defence Committee, about which he had recently written to him. He suggested Orwell say that the purge of the Civil Service was compelling people concerned with civil liberties to re-think their attitude; that the NCCL had been infiltrated by Communists; and also might give some account of the work of the Freedom Defence Committee. Davy had not spoken to the editor about this particular idea (this outline, presumably), but he had mentioned it, and the editor would accept a short article. See letters to Woodcock, *3369*, *3369, n. 4*, and *3403*.
3. The National Council for Civil Liberties 'had become virtually a Communist Front organization, certainly reluctant to defend the critics of the comrades.' This led to the foundation of the Freedom Defence Committee, which survived until 1949, when 'counter-purges had been successful in the NCCL' (Crick, 497).
4. The postscript is written at the head of this letter.

3389. To Leonard Moore

26 April 1948   Handwritten

Ward 3
Hairmyres Hospital
East Kilbride
Lanarkshire

Dear Moore,

Many thanks for your letter & the account. Warburg's statements are herewith. As to the copies of "Coming Up for Air." Do you think you could send me one here,[1] & one to my sister at Barnhill, Jura & in addition send off some presentation copies for me with a slip saying "with the author's compliments", or words to that effect? I suppose I shall want some extra copies as usual. I ought really to sign some of these, but it's such a fag sending off books from here, as I can't get hold of brown paper etc. so I'd rather you did it for me, if you don't mind. The people I want them sent to are:—

Edmund Wilson, care of the New Yorker.
Dwight Macdonald, care of "Politics", 45 Astor Place, New York 3, N.Y.
R. G. Fletcher, Ardlussa, Isle of Jura, Argyllshire.
Anthony Powell, 1 Chester Gate, London N.W.1
Sir Osbert Sitwell, care of Macmillans, publishers.
Mrs Celia Kirwan, Hotel Crystal, Rue St. Benoît, Paris 6eme
    I think that makes 2 extra copies to date.

Yours sincerely
Eric Blair

1. Orwell's letter has been annotated in Moore's office indicating that copies were sent to him, his sister, and those listed below, on 3 May 1948. See *3433*.

3390. To John Middleton Murry

28 April 1948   Handwritten

Ward 3
Hairmyres Hospital
East Kilbride
Lanarkshire

Dear Murry,

Thank you for your letter. I'm very sorry to hear the Adelphi is coming to an end.[1] At any rate it's had a long run for its money, longer than most magazines. I could do you a review, but I'm not keen on doing the Joad book. I looked at it recently, & it didn't seem to me to be *about* anything. How about the third volume of Osbert Sitwell's autobiography,[2] which has come out recently & which I think is very good in a way? You wouldn't need send a copy, as I have one already. It would be better to do more than 1000 words if you have the space. I note that you want the copy by May 15, but perhaps you could let me know whether you think this a suitable book.

I am a lot better. The streptomycin had some very unpleasant secondary effects, but they have mostly disappeared, & I think it has done its stuff. I hope to get out some time this summer, but I gather that I shall have to go very slowly for about a year, & shall have to continue periodical treatment as an out-patient for some time. In that case I shall stay in Glasgow or Edinburgh & go up to Jura for short trips when I can. They are very busy on the farm now, ploughing up land which has not been touched since 1915, & will be stocking up with cattle soon. Of course I don't actually have to be there, but I would like to see what is going on, also to see my little boy, whom I haven't seen since Christmas for fear of infection. I get photographs of him, & he is evidently growing enormous.

Yours
Geo. Orwell

1. It survived until 1955.
2. Orwell reviewed Sitwell's *Great Morning* in the July–September 1948 issue of *The Adelphi*; see *3418*.

3391. To Leonard Moore

     1 May 1948   Handwritten

Ward 3
Hairmyres Hospital
East Kilbride
Lanarkshire

Dear Moore,
Many thanks for sending the book,[1] & for managing to get hold of a copy so promptly.

I don't think it's worth bothering about signatures, really.[2] Most of them are only complimentary copies to people I hardly know. But I wonder if you could be kind enough to procure & send one more copy to someone I forgot. This is Julian Symons, 16 St John's Park, Blackheath S.E.3.

Yours sincerely
Eric Blair

1. Presumably *L'Univers Concentrationnaire* by David Rousset; for Orwell's response to this book and its translation, see *3393*.
2. For complimentary copies of the Uniform Edition of *Coming Up for Air*. The letter is annotated to indicate that Moore's office sent Symons his copy on 3 May 1948.

3392. To Dwight Macdonald
2 May 1948   Typewritten

Until this letter, all Orwell's letters that have survived since that to Leonard Moore of 31 October 1947 had been handwritten, owing to his being ill in bed. On 10 May, Orwell told Julian Symons he had 'organised a typewriter at last'; see *3397*.

Ward 3
Hairmyres Hosp.
East Kilbride
Lanarkshire

Dear Dwight,

Thanks so much for your letter, and prospectively for sending the books.[1] Yes, I got Politics, as a matter of fact 2 copies, as you sent one to me direct here. It set me thinking again about Gandhi, whom I never met but whom I know a certain amount about. The funny thing is that though he was almost certainly used by the British for their own ends over a long period, I'm not certain that in the long run he failed. He was not able to stop the fight[ing] between Moslems and Hindus, but his major aim of getting the British out of India peacefully did finally come off. I personally would never have predicted this even five years ago, and I am not sure that a good deal of the credit should not go to Gandhi. Of course a Conservative government would never have got out without a fight, but the fact that a Labour government did so might indirectly be due to Gandhi's influence. One might say that they only agreed to dominion status because they knew they couldn't hold on to India much longer, but this doesn't apply for instance to Burma, a country which was extremely profitable to us and easy enough to hold down. I think, pace tua, that Gandhi behaved abominably, or at any rate stupidly, in 1942 when he thought the Axis had won the war, but I think also that his prolonged effort to keep the Indian struggle on a decent plane may have gradually modified the British attitude.

Incidentally, this business of assassinating important individuals[2] is something one has to take account of. In the same number I see you note regretfully that Walter Reuther[3] has a bodyguard, but I also see that he has just been seriously wounded—the second attempt, I believe. I notice also that you speak more or less approvingly of the Esprit[4] crowd. I don't know if you know that some at any rate of these people are fellow travellers of a peculiarly slimy religious brand, like Macmurray[5] in England. Their line is that Communism and Christianity are compatible, and latterly that there is no choice except Communism or Fascism and one must therefore regretfully choose the former. But this is all right, because Communism will presently shed certain unfortunate characteristics such as bumping off its opponents, and if Socialists join up with the CP they can persuade it into better ways. It's funny that when I met Mounier[6] for only about 10 minutes in 1945 I thought to myself, that man's a fellow traveller. I can smell them. I believe Sartre has been latterly taking the same line.

I'm sorry Gollancz fell through.[7] I don't know if it's any use trying Warburg. He read the book and was impressed by it, but of course he is chronically short of paper and takes years to get a book out. The binding is the real trouble here. I must say I feel envious when I see American books now, their solidity and so on. The way British books are printed now makes one ashamed to be associated with them. I asked them to send you a copy of the first book in my uniform edition, coming out in a fortnight or so. I must say I wish I could have started this edition at a time when one could get hold of decent bindings. I feel that a uniform edition which in any case is a sign of approaching senility ought to be very chaste-looking in buckram covers. Have you got an agent over here, or an agent with connections here? It's worth while I think.

Yes, I think Lanarkshire was where Owen[8] flourished. It's rather an unpleasant industrial county with a lot of coal mines, and its chief ornament is Glasgow. Out here it's quite pleasant though. I am longing to go out of doors, having barely done so for six months. They now let me up an hour a day and I think they would let me out a little if it were warmer. It's been a horrible spring, however not so bad as last year.

I'm in sympathy with the Europe-America leaflet you sent,[9] but I don't know if there's anything I personally can do about it. Thanks for your query, but there is honestly not anything I want. We are well cared for here and people have been very kind about sending me food etc.

Yours
George

1. Macdonald had written on 23 April 1948 and he sent a parcel of books by separate mail. He mentions two of these in his letter: Joseph Wood Krutch, *Samuel Johnson* (1944) and T. Polner, *Tolstoy and His Wife*, translated by N. Wreden (1945). These, he wrote, 'are two of the best modern biographies I know,' especially the first. He asked Orwell if he shared his 'private enthusiasm for Dr. Johnson.' Orwell did not respond to this in his reply. Krutch (1893–1970) was drama critic to *The Nation*, 1924–51. Polner's book was among those owned by Orwell at his death.
2. Gandhi had been assassinated on 30 January 1948; see *3386, n. 4*.
3. Walter Philip Reuther (1907–1970), President of the United Automobile Workers of America, 1946–70; President of the Congress of Industrial Organizations, 1952–55. He was one of those instrumental in the merger of the CIO with the American Federation of Labor in 1955 and served as Vice-President of the AFL–CIO until, in disagreement with the President of the organization, he took the UAW out. He had worked in a Soviet car factory for two years in the 1930s, but later was critical of the Soviets. He was killed when his plane crashed in fog.
4. *Esprit* was a periodical launched in 1932 by Emmanuel Mounier (see *n. 6*) 'to close the gap between communist and non-communist Frenchmen.' At the same time, Mounier inaugurated 'the Personalist movement, a non-party philosophy between Marxism and Existentialism' (J. F. Falvey, *The Penguin Companion to Literature* (1969), II, 553).
5. John Macmurray (1891–1976), Grote Professor of the Philosophy of Mind and Logic, University of London, 1929–44; Professor of Moral Philosophy, University of Edinburgh, 1944–58. His many books include *The Philosophy of Communism* (1933), *The Structure of Religious Experience* (1936), *Challenge to the Churches* (1941), and *Constructive Democracy* (1943). In Orwell's pamphlet collection is a copy of his Peace Aims Pamphlet *Foundations of Economic Reconstruction* (1942).
6. Emmanuel Mounier (1905–1950), writer, literary critic, intellectual leader in the French Resistance, was a Roman Catholic and Marxist sympathiser and the founder of the journal *Esprit* (see *n. 4*). He was influenced by Bergson and Péguy (see *3420, n. 5*), and, with others,

published *La Pensée de Charles Péguy* (1931), several books on Personalism, and some 170 articles. He advocated economic revolution, a new socialist system, respect for the individual, and an active Roman Catholic Church in order to implement ethical values appropriate to the age. He particularly addressed the needs of apathetic and disorientated post-war youth (J. F. Falvey, see *n. 4*).

7. Orwell had suggested to Gollancz that he publish Macdonald's *Henry Wallace: The Man and the Myth* (see *3359*; for Wallace, see *3359, n. 2*). Macdonald told Orwell that, though Gollancz was at first enthusiastic, he had written later saying he could not get the book out in time. 'God knows why he couldn't have figured that out first, but publishers don't seem, as a class, overly intelligent.' The book was doing badly in the United States, having sold only 3,500 copies in two months despite good reviews. However, Macdonald was having 'a lot of fun' speaking at colleges on Wallace 'to expose the man's lies and demagogy, and the almost 100% Commie entourage which writes his speeches.'

8. The text of Macdonald's letter that has survived is a carbon copy. It contains no reference to Owen, so that may well have been in a postscript added only to the top copy, perhaps prompted by Macdonald's writing out the address of Hairmyres Hospital. Robert Owen (1771–1858), born and died in Wales, a successful Lancashire cotton manufacturer, established the model industrial town of New Lanark in Scotland, with good living conditions for the employees complete with non-profitmaking shops. He was a pioneer of the co-operative movement and an early socialist. He took over the town of Harmonie in Indiana in 1825, renamed it New Harmony, and for three years endeavoured to establish a co-operative community there. It was beset with quarrels and, having lost much money, he returned to Britain in 1828.

9. A leaflet issued in connection with a proposed series of meetings—the first had by then been held—'on the Russian culture purge. Speakers: Nicolas Nabokov, Meyer Schapiro, Lionel Trilling, and myself. It was a success—about 400 people, $300 profit, and solid speeches.'

3393. To Roger Senhouse

3 May 1948   Typewritten

[No address]

Dear Roger,

I had managed to get a copy of L'Univers Concentrationnaire from another source and have read it in conjunction with your translation.[1] I'm not sure whether your approach is right. I don't know French well enough to judge, but Rousset's style doesn't seem to be a particularly unusual or lyrical one—at any rate, not beyond the first chapter. In many cases I would have used a simpler phrase than you do, and often more literal. For instance I would translate the first sentence of the book as "The great lonely city of Buchenwald." A little further down, "Squalid sheds squatting in a semi-circle" etc. I don't see any alliteration in the French to correspond to squalid-squatting, and you seem to me to alter the sense of some words, eg. "haute" translated gaunt. I would have translated the first part of the sentence: Helmstedt: sheds grouped in a circle and camouflaged by the seeping of their own filth, uncovered stacks of cases containing bombs and torpedoes, fields of wheat and mustard, and, across the plain, the tall black silhouettes of pit shafts. (I take it from you that "puits" means that. It sounds as if it ought to mean the actual hole in the ground, but it can't in the context, and I suppose it must mean the winding gear above the shaft.) I may be wrong, but my instinct is simplicity every time. The "dramatic present" is a great difficulty. Personally I am against it except when it is used for generalisation, ie. describes something typical. I think in genuine narration one should avoid it. One great difficulty also is that there is no proper English equivalent for "concentrationnaire." Obviously one can't say "concentrationary." One can use "concentration-camp" as an adjective, but it is very cumbersome. In the extracts in an American magazine in which I first came across this book, the expression used was "K.Z." which I think stands for something or other in German.[2] In the title, if you try to translate the original, I think I'd avoid "universe" if possible and use "world."

I rather think I missed out one correction in that list I sent you with the proof of "Burmese Days." Page 97, line 13 from top: "of blue rings of hills." Should be "by blue rings of hills." Perhaps you could add this?[3]

I am getting up for an hour a day now and beginning to put on a few clothes. They haven't let me out yet, but I think they would if it was warmer. I'll send back the MS separately, because I must get hold of a bit of string. Please give all the best to Fred.[4]

Yours
George

1. Senhouse had written to Orwell on 26 April 1948 saying how extraordinary it was that Orwell should ask him to bring a copy of David Rousset's *L'Univers Concentrationnaire* from Paris (see *3385*), because he had just finished translating it. He wanted advice and was sending Orwell a copy of the translation, which not even his co-translator of the Simone de Beauvoir novels (Y. Moyse) had seen. It was 'vilely difficult,' for the book was 'a prose dirge, magnificent in French at times when he loses himself in word patterns and makes use of vowel sounds impossible in English. So the 1st Chapter—a general survey of the concentrationary universe—has had to receive adaptation, in trying to create an equivalent rhythm and occasional harsh vowel sequence'; he gives examples. 'Rather it is modern free verse,' W. R. Rodgers with an overtone of Gerard Manley Hopkins. What was really required was a translator who had experienced some of the horrors of the camps—'the *sound*, the *smell*.' Rousset, he wrote, was 'the great cataloguer, the final chronicler of the camps. I feel inept. The whole thing is in his bones, poor fellow, inexorably.'
2. Konzentrationslager (Concentration Camp).
3. The correction was made; see *CW*, II, Textual Note, 99/18.
4. Senhouse thanked Orwell for his 'valid and useful criticism' on 7 May 1948. He knew the first chapter 'was shamefully over-treated' and he was in agreement with Orwell on the need for simplicity throughout. He described Rousset to Orwell, though he had not dug out many personal details. 'Rousset has a pad over his left eye, and several teeth missing; a round, fat face, benign, so far as the twinkle in one eye can give him full expression; and robust, though small—dumpy, almost—with maybe something wrong with one of his legs, for he did not walk very quickly.' He asked him if he were a Communist, and he replied, 'No—a Marxist.' Senhouse mentioned 'the extraordinary changes and *volte-face* taking place' in France then. Thus, Malraux (suggested as someone who might write an introduction to the French edition of *Homage to Catalonia*; see Orwell's letter, 7 April 1947, *3209*), was 'very hard at work helping de Gaulle.' Senhouse's translation of Rousset's book, made with Y. Moyse, was published in 1951 as *A World Apart*.

3394. To David Astor

4 May 1948   Typewritten

Ward 3
Hairmyres Hosp.

Dear David,

I wonder how you are getting on. I was a bit under the weather last time I wrote because of the secondary effects of the streptomycin. My skin is still peeling off in places and my hair coming out, but otherwise it's all gone and I am a lot better. They let me up for an hour a day now and let me put a few clothes on, and I think they might let me out if only it was a bit warmer. I suppose it's too early to say whether the streptomycin has done its stuff but any way they've had 4 negative reactions running, so the germs must have taken a pretty good knock. Mr Dick has made no definite pronouncement yet, but I gather I shall get out some time in the summer and then have to continue with "refills" once a week for a long time. In that case I'll stay in Edinburgh where I can share Richard Rees's flat, and get up to Jura or down to London when I can. I must stay somewhere near the hospital, otherwise I should be travelling the whole time.

They seem to be very busy at Barnhill. They'v[e] broken about 4 acres of new land and sown the oats and potatoes. The new miniature tractor is evidently a success and Bob has been working well. It's funny that if he doesn't mind harrowing he doesn't like going in the trap, but possibly they have been trying him without blinkers in which case he may be frightened of the shafts. However Bill is getting another horse, an Irish one I think, of about the same size as Bob, to pull the cart. I think I told you I looked at the photos in the livestock book and Bob is definitely a "garron,"[1] with the points very well marked. According to the book the breed was originally produced by crossing a percheron with a Shetland pony, which must have been a shocking sight. The Darrochs are leaving about now and a Pole[2] is coming to Kinuachdrach. I didn't gather from Robin Fletcher's letter whether he is married or not. Richard is evidently flourishing. He will be 4 shortly. Another year and I suppose I shall have to start thinking about his schooling. I suppose it is almost time to direct his attention towards the alphabet, but I'm not going to hurry him, because I do not think he will ever be what they call "a one for book learning," and I remember the miseries I went through because of the then-prevalent idea that you were half-witted if you couldn't read before you were six.

It's foully cold here and raining most of the time. We were having snow and frosts a day or two ago. Apparently in Jura they've had good weather. The parcels you so kindly arranged have evidently arrived at Barnhill, and my sister says one of them included a piece of cloth large enough to make an overcoat, which I'll be very glad of.

Yours
George

1. A small and inferior kind of horse bred and chiefly used in Ireland and Scotland (*OED*).
2. Tony Rozga and his wife, Jeannie, from Midlothian. For their reminiscences of Orwell, see *Remembering Orwell*, 185–87. These indicate clearly Orwell's natural generosity, his enjoyment of life on Jura, and how very ill he was. See also *3432, n. 1.*

3395. Review of *The Soul of Man under Socialism* by Oscar Wilde
The Observer, 9 May 1948

The preparatory notes Orwell made for this review are reproduced as *3396*.

Oscar Wilde's work is being much revived now on stage and screen, and it is well to be reminded that Salome and Lady Windermere were not his only creations. Wilde's "The Soul of Man under Socialism," for example, first published nearly 60 years ago,[1] has worn remarkably well. Its author was not in any active sense a Socialist himself, but he was a sympathetic and intelligent observer; although his prophecies have not been fulfilled, they have not been made simply irrelevant by the passage of time.

Wilde's vision of Socialism, which at that date was probably shared by many people less articulate than himself, is Utopian and anarchistic. The abolition of private property, he says, will make possible the full development of the individual and set us free from "the sordid necessity of living for others." In the Socialist future there will not only be no want and no insecurity, there will also be no drudgery, no disease, no ugliness, no wastage of the human spirit in futile enmities and rivalries.

Pain will cease to be important: indeed, for the first time in his history, Man will be able to realise his personality through joy instead of through suffering. Crime will disappear, since there will be no economic reason for it. The State will cease to govern and will survive merely as an agency for the distribution of necessary commodities. All the disagreeable jobs will be done by machinery, and everyone will be completely free to choose his own work and his own manner of life. In effect, the world will be populated by artists, each striving after perfection in the way that seems best to him.

To-day, these optimistic forecasts make rather painful reading. Wilde realised, of course, that there were authoritarian tendencies in the Socialist movement, but he did not believe they would prevail, and with a sort of prophetic irony he wrote: "I hardly think that any Socialist, nowadays, would seriously propose that an inspector should call every morning at each house to see that each citizen rose up and did manual labour for eight hours"—which, unfortunately, is just the kind of thing that countless modern Socialists would propose. Evidently something has gone wrong. Socialism, in the sense of economic collectivism, is conquering the earth at a speed that would hardly have seemed possible 60 years ago, and yet Utopia, at any rate Wilde's Utopia is no nearer. Where, then, does the fallacy lie? If one looks more closely one sees that Wilde makes two common but

333

unjustified assumptions. One is that the world is immensely rich and is suffering chiefly from maldistribution. Even things out between the millionaire and the crossing-sweeper, he seems to say, and there will be plenty of everything for everybody. Until the Russian Revolution, this belief was very widely held—"starving in the midst of plenty" was a favourite phrase—but it was quite false, and it survived only because Socialists thought always of the highly developed Western countries and ignored the fearful poverty of Asia and Africa. Actually, the problem for the world as a whole is not how to distribute such wealth as exists but how to increase production, without which economic equality merely means common misery.

Secondly, Wilde assumes that it is a simple matter to arrange that all the unpleasant kinds of work shall be done by machinery. The machines, he says, are our new race of slaves: a tempting metaphor, but a misleading one, since there is a vast range of jobs—roughly speaking, any job needing great flexibility—that no machine is able to do. In practice, even in the most highly-mechanised countries, an enormous amount of dull and exhausting work has to be done by unwilling human muscles. But this at once implies direction of labour, fixed working hours, differential wage rates, and all the regimentation that Wilde abhors. Wilde's version of Socialism could only be realised in a world not only far richer but also technically far more advanced than the present one. The abolition of private property does not of itself put food into anyone's mouth. It is merely the first step in a transitional period that is bound to be laborious, uncomfortable, and long.

But that is not to say that Wilde is altogether wrong. The trouble with transitional periods is that the harsh outlook which they generate tends to become permanent. To all appearances this is what has happened in Soviet Russia. A dictatorship supposedly established for a limited purpose has dug itself in, and Socialism comes to be thought of as meaning concentration camps and secret police forces. Wilde's pamphlet and other kindred writings—"News from Nowhere,"[2] for instance—consequently have their value. They may demand the impossible, and they may—since a Utopia necessarily reflects the aesthetic ideas of its own period—sometimes seem "dated" and ridiculous; but they do at least look beyond the era of food queues and party squabbles, and remind the Socialist movement of its original, half-forgotten objective of human brotherhood.

1. The *Soul of Man under Socialism* was first published in *The Fortnightly Review*, February 1891, and was included in *Sebastian Melmoth*, 1891, with the title 'The Soul of Man.' This edition was published as a Porcupine Pamphlet; see *3369, n. 1*.
2. *News from Nowhere, or An Epoch of Rest: being some chapters from a Utopian romance*, by William Morris; first published as a serial in *The Commonweal* during 1890, and then as a book in an unauthorised edition, Boston, MA, 1890; then London, 1891.

3396. Preparatory Notes for Review of *The Soul of Man under Socialism*

Second Literary Notebook

Wilde (Soul of Man under Socialism) (1891)

"Every man must be left quite free to choose his own work."

"There is only one class in the community that thinks more about money than the rich, & that is the poor."

"With the abolition of private property, marriage in its present form must disappear." (Prec. sentence: *"Socialism annihilates family life, for instance."*)

"Individualism, then, is what through Socialism we are to attain to."

"When private property is abolished there will be no necessity for crime, no demand for it; it will cease to exist." (Above: *"The less punishment, the less crime."*)

"All work of that [degrading][1] *kind should be done by a machine."* (*"And I have no doubt that it will be so."*) (*"On mechanical slavery, the slavery of the machine, the future of the world depends."*)

[Socialism would relieve us of the] *"sordid necessity of living for others."*

1. The square brackets here and in the next quotation are Orwell's.

3397. To Julian Symons

10 May 1948   Typewritten

Ward 3
Hairmyres Hospital
East Kilbride   Lanark

Dear Julian,

Thanks ever so much to yourself and your wife for the chocolate and the tea and rice, which got here last week. I'd been meaning to write. You see I've organised a typewriter at last. It's a bit awkward to use in bed, but it saves hideous misprints in reviews etc. caused by my handwriting. As you say, the ball-bearing pen is the last stage in the decay of handwriting, but I've given mine up years ago. At one time I used to spend hours with script pens and squared paper, trying to re-teach myself to write, but it was no use after being taught copperplate and on top of that encouraged to write a "scholarly" hand. The writing of children nowadays is even worse than ours used to be, because they will teach them this disconnected script which is very slow to write. Evidently the first thing is to get a good simple cursive script, but on top of that you have to teach hand control, in fact learning to write involves learning to draw. Evidently it can be done, as in countries like China and Japan anyone who can write at all writes more or less gracefully.

I am glad E and S[1] are pleased with the biography, but don't let them get away with "The Quest for AJA Symons" as a title. It is true that if a book is going to sell no title can kill it, but I am sure that is a bad one. Of course I can't make suggestions without seeing the book, but if they insist on having the name, something like "A.J.A. Symons: a Memoir" is always inoffensive.[2]

"Coming Up for Air" isn't much, but I thought it worth reprinting because it was rather killed by the outbreak of war and then blitzed out of existence, so thoroughly that in order to get a copy from which to reset it we had to steal one from a public library.[3] Of course you are perfectly right about my own character constantly intruding on that of the narrator. I am not a real novelist anyway, and that particular vice is inherent in writing a novel in the first person, which one should never do. One difficulty I have never solved is that one has masses of experience which one passionately wants to write about, eg. the part about fishing in that book, and no way of using them up except by disguising them as a novel. Of course the book was bound to suggest Wells watered down. I have a great admiration for Wells, ie. as a writer, and he was a very early influence on me. I think I was ten or eleven when Cyril Connolly and I got hold of a copy of Wells's "The Country of the Blind" (short stories) and were so fascinated by it that we kept stealing it from one another. I can still remember at 4 o'clock on a midsummer morning, with the school fast asleep and the sun slanting through the window, creeping down a passage to Connolly's dormitory where I knew the book would be beside his bed. We also got into severe trouble (and I think a caning—I forget) for having a copy of Compton Mackenzie's "Sinister Street."[4]

They now tell me that I shall have to stay here till about August. The germs are evidently liquidated, but the actual healing of the lung and build-up of strength takes a long time. I'm still terribly short of breath and I suppose shall continue to be as long as they keep the lung collapsed, which might be a year or more. However it's worth it to get a good mend. They now let me out of doors for a little each day, and I feel so much better that I think I shall be able to do a little serious work again. What chiefly worries me is Richard, whom I haven't seen for 4 or 5 months. However I may be able to arrange for him to have a short stay in Glasgow, and then he can come and visit me. I don't know who put that par in the Standard[5]—someone who knew me, though there were the usual mistakes. I don't think they ought to have given my real name.

Please remember me to your wife.

Yours
George

1. Eyre and Spottiswoode, the publishers of the biography; see *n. 2*.
2. Julian Symons's biography of his brother was called *A. J. A. Symons: His Life and Speculations* (1950). Orwell refers to A. J. A. Symons's *The Quest for Corvo: An Experiment in Biography* (1934).
3. See *3155, n. 2* for Miss Murtough's offer to borrow a copy from her local public library. Whether or not the copy was 'permanently stolen' is not known.

4. Cyril Connolly recalls the incident less painfully. He and Orwell alternately won a prize given by Mrs. Wilkes, the headmaster's wife, for the best list of books borrowed from the school library. However, 'we were both caught at last with two volumes of *Sinister Street* and our favour sank to zero' (*Enemies of Promise*, 1948, chapter 19).
5. On 5 May 1948, in the 'Londoner's Diary,' a gossip column in the *Evening Standard*, there was a paragraph about Orwell which referred to his wife's death.

3398. To Leonard Moore

12 May 1948   Typewritten

Ward 3
Hairmyres Hospital
East Kilbride
Lanarkshire

Dear Moore,
On going through my books I see that I wrote an introduction for a book of collected pamphlets for Allan Wingate more than a year ago. I don't know why the book hasn't come out,[1] but I think it is time they paid me for the introduction. If I remember rightly, I was promised £50 and was paid £10 in advance: or it may have been that I was promised £40—anyway, I think £40 is the sum involved. Perhaps you could communicate with them about it.

I am a lot better and the infection has evidently been quelled, but the doctors think I should remain here till about August. However, I feel so much better that I think I can get back to a little serious work and am starting on the second draft of my novel.[2] I don't know how far I shall [get] as it is awkward working in bed, but if I can get well started before leaving hospital I should get the book done before the end of the year.

Yours sincerely
Eric Blair

1. *British Pamphleteers*, edited with Reginald Reynolds. The letter has been annotated in Moore's office: 'autumn.' Volume 1 was published 15 November 1948. The second volume, in which Orwell was not involved, appeared in 1951.
2. *Nineteen Eighty-Four*.

3399. To Roger Senhouse

Thursday, [13 or 20 May 1948][1]   Handwritten

[No address]

Dear Roger,
I'm awfully sorry about the delay in sending this back. I trust it will arrive all right.

I've already got Rousset's "Les Jours de Notre Mort",[2] but haven't read it yet. The trouble with this concentration-camp literature is that there is such a

lot of it. I wanted to read Rousset because from extracts I had seen I thought he had more grasp than most of the people who have written on the subjects.°
The point is that these forced-labour camps are part of the pattern of our time, & are a very interesting though horrible phenomenon. What is wanted now is for someone to write a scholarly work on concentration & forced-labour camps, drawing on Rousset & all the others.

I've started revising the novel,[3] but I do only a very little, perhaps an hour's work each day. However at that rate I should get through several chapters before leaving hospital. I am still not certain when this will happen, nor whether I shall have to continue out-patient treatment after leaving. Richard Rees is up at Jura, or has been for the weekend. I imagine they must have had lovely weather. Please remember me to Fred.

Yours
George

1. *CEJL* dated this 6? May 1948. However, Orwell had written on 3 May, and it is now known that Senhouse replied on 7 May (see *3393, n. 4*). Orwell here writes as if the delay in returning 'this' (Senhouse's translation of *L'Univers Concentrationnaire* probably) was excessive, and the implication may be that Senhouse had sent him a reminder; thus either 13 or 20 May seems more likely.
2. A novel, published 1947, with the subtitle 'La vie clandestine dans les camps.'
3. *Nineteen Eighty-Four.*

3400. To Leonard Moore
     15 May 1948   Typewritten

Ward 3
Hairmyres Hospital
East Kilbride
Lanarkshire

Dear Moore,
I wonder whether you could be kind enough to send a copy of "Coming Up for Air" to Evelyn Waugh, care of Chapman & Hall, with my compliments.[1]

Yours sincerely
[Signed] Eric Blair
Eric Blair

1. Annotated in Moore's office: 'done.'

3401. To Evelyn Waugh

16 May 1948   Typewritten

Ward 3
Hairmyres Hospital
East Kilbride
Lanarkshire

Dear Mr Waugh,
Very many thanks for sending the copies of "Black Mischief" and "A Handful of Dust." I was particularly glad to get the latter book, as for some reason I have never read it. I am starting a uniform edition myself, and I have told my agents to send you a copy of a novel of mine called "Coming Up for Air."

I am indebted to you for a very good and sympathetic review in the "Tablet" of my book of essays.[1] In discussing the one on P. G. Wodehouse, you mentioned the "pacifist strain" in his writings. This started me thinking about him again, and on looking up a rare early book called "The Gold Bat"[2] I found passages which suggested that Wodehouse had had some kind of connection with the Liberal Party, about 1908, when it was the anti-militarist party. I will add a footnote to this affect if I ever reprint the essays.[3]

I am here being treated for tuberculosis, but they seem to have made a good job of my case, and I hope to get out some time during the summer.

Yours sincerely
[Signed] Geo. Orwell
George Orwell

1. Waugh reviewed *Critical Essays* in the *Tablet*, 6 April 1946; it was reprinted in *The Essays, Articles and Reviews of Evelyn Waugh*, edited by Donat Gallagher (1983).
2. *The Gold Bat*, a school story (1904). Orwell refers to this book in his essay 'In Defence of P. G. Wodehouse'; see *2624* and *2624, n. 18*.
3. *Critical Essays* was not reprinted until after Orwell's death. It was published in the Uniform Edition, 22 February 1951, but no note was added.

3402. Diary

Second Literary Notebook

21.5.48.   9.45 am. *The following noises now happening simultaneously. A radio. A gramaphone.° Vacuum cleaner running intermittently. Orderly singing intermittently. Noise of hammering from outside. Usual clatter of boots & trolleys, whistling, cries of rooks & gulls, cackling of hens in the distance, taps running, doors opening & shutting, intermittent coughing.*

Immediately below on the same page is written:

Things not foreseen in youth as part of middle age.

Perpetual tired weak feeling in legs, aching knees. Stiffness amounting to pain in small of back & down loins. Discomfort in gums. Chest more or less always constricted. Feeling in the morning of being almost unable to stand up. Sensation of cold whenever the sun is not shining. Wind on the stomach (making it difficult to think). Eyes always watering.

As painful as a grapestone under a dental plate
As noisy as a mouse in a packet of macaroni
As haughty as a fishmonger

3402A. To Lydia Jackson

24 May 1948   Handwritten

> Ward 3
> Hairmyres Hospital
> East Kilbride
> Lanarkshire

Dear Lydia,

Thanks so much for your letter. I am so glad to hear that you have handed in your thesis & expect to get your doctorate all right.[1] I know so well that feeling that one *must* accomplish something which perhaps has not much material value but has become an end in itself.

I am ever so much better & now get up for 2 hours a day, & go out in the grounds for short walks when it is fine. I can only walk at a snail's pace, because I am still extremely short of breath, but that will improve. They still haven't told me definitely when I shall get out, probably in August, but there is good news in so much that when I do get out I may not have to continue with treatment, at any rate weekly treatment. Hitherto they have been pumping air into my diaphragm once a week, but they have now stopped & will probably not start again. If they don't, I can go back to Barnhill when I come out. If I do have to attend for treatment, I am arranging to stay in Edinburgh, which is not far away & very much more civilized than Glasgow.[2]

They're evidently all well at Barnhill & very busy. We have got another cow & Bill has started buying his own cattle. Everyone says Richard is coming on fast, & that he has not forgotten me. I am trying to arrange for him to be brought here some time next month, so that I can at least see him for one afternoon. I haven't seen him since before Christmas – it was impossible to bring him here, because of the danger of infection. However, I don't think I'm infectious any longer, & in any case I can go out of doors now. From his photographs he is evidently growing enormous. Avril says that he is now frightened of boats. I hope this won't last, but it is an interesting development. Previously he wasn't at all frightened in a boat, indeed not enough so, & liked to hang over the side in the most dangerous way. When we were nearly drowned in Corrievrechan,[3] he seemed to take the whole experience in his stride, but I think his present fear may be a delayed reaction to that.

I hope the Chekhov plays go all right. I suppose, as always nowadays, it will be years before the book appears.[4] My uniform edition has at last started, & the first book was reprinted, I mean appeared, last week. In bed I can't do much, but I generally get in one or two hours' work a day & have begun to tinker with the novel[5] a little again. I hope to get it finished by the end of this year, but in that case it wouldn't appear much before the end of 1949, such are the bottlenecks nowadays. Otherwise all I do is a few book reviews to bring in a bit of money. I tried to get a copy of "The Possessed"[6] to replace your copy that I seem to have lost, but haven't secured one yet.

I don't know when I'll be in London, though after I get out I shall have to go down at least once. Do you think you could even come up here for a week-end, or at any rate a day or two? Now that I could get out we could go for a little stroll together, & in June, at any rate, the weather ought to be decent. There are places near here where you could stay, & if it isn't too delicate a suggestion to make, I could pay your expenses. I would love to see you again. The other night I was wishing very much that you were with me. At any rate, tell me what you think. And please remember me to Pat.

With love
George[7]

1. Lydia Jackson was a psychologist and her D.Phil was awarded by the University of Oxford in 1949.
2. Orwell might also have been attracted to Edinburgh because Sir Richard Rees was living there.
3. For this incident, see Diary, *3257*, 19.8.47, and *3257, n. 3.*
4. The individual plays were published between 1951 and 1954; they appeared in a single Penguin in 1959.
5. *Nineteen Eighty-Four.*
6. A novel by Dostoievski (1871–72), also known as *The Devils.* Among Orwell's books at his death was a copy of the second of the two volumes of the translation by C. Garnett, 1931; see *3734.*
7. Of the twenty-nine surviving letters Orwell wrote to Lydia Jackson, eighteen are signed Eric and eleven are signed George. There is no apparent pattern of use but he began with Eric in 1939 and ended with that name in 1949. He used George and Eric in 1944 and 1945, George in 1947, and Eric in 1948 and 1949 except for this letter.

3403. To George Woodcock
24 May 1948   Typewritten

[No address]

Dear George,
I received another letter from Charles Davey,[1] drawing my attention to the fact that E. M. Forster has resigned from the NCCL. I then sat down, or sat

up rather, with the idea of writing that article on the F.D.C., but on second thoughts I really don't think I can do it. To begin with I have two long articles on hand[2] and I can't do much yet, but what is more to the point, I don't know enough factually about the FDC for the purpose. Do you think you could do the article? I think you said Davey had written to you. Perhaps you could ring him up. I don't know if you know him—he is a very nice chap. I don't know exactly what they want, but I assume they would want an account of the Committee and its activities, in general terms, with some remarks on the threat to individual liberty contained in the modern centralised state. I don't like shoving this off on to you, on the other hand if they are willing for you to write the article they'll pay you quite well for it.[3]

I hadn't yet thanked you for the copy of the book of essays. Of course I was delighted to see the one on myself appearing in book form.[4] I liked the one on Bates[5] whose book I read years ago. All nineteenth-century books about S. America have a wonderful Arcadian atmosphere, though I think I was always more attracted by the pampas than by the forest. I suppose you've read "The Purple Land." And the one on hymns, which I'd always been meaning to write something about myself. I think you're wrong in saying that people respond to a hymn like Abide with me (by the way shouldn't it be "the darkness deepens," not "gathers")[6] chiefly because of wars, unemployment etc. There is a great deal of inherent sadness and loneliness in human life that would be the same whatever the external circumstances. You don't mention two of the best hymns, "praise° to the holiest" and "Jerusalem my happy home"—this one, I think, however, must be a great deal earlier than the other groups you were studying. In Ancient and Modern[7] if I remember rightly it's heavily expurgated to get the Catholic imagery out.

I am much better and now get up for two hours a day, and even go out a little when it is warm. They haven't told me definitely when I can leave hospital, but probably about August. They now seem to think that I won't have to continue with treatment when I leave, which would be a great blessing as it would mean I could go back to Jura instead of having to hang about in Glasgow or Edinburgh. Richard is by all accounts extremely well and growing enormous. Of course I haven't seen him for months, but I am trying to arrange for him to be brought here for at any rate an afternoon, now that I can go out of doors and can see him in the grounds.

Please give all the best to Inge. I've gone and lost your new address, but I will think of someone to send this care of. I will write to Charles Davey about the article.

Yours
George

1. Charles Davy; see 3388, n. 2.
2. 'on hand' meaning not completed. When writing to Julian Symons on 21 March 1948 (see 3363), he said, 'I did write two longer articles.' Those were most probably 'Writers and Leviathan' and 'Britain's Left-Wing Press' (see 3363, n. 1). The two long articles on hand are probably 'George Gissing,' intended for Politics and Letters, and 'The Labour Government After Three Years,' published in Commentary, October 1948, but, according to Orwell's Second Literary Notebook, due by 20 July (see 3515). The essay on Gissing was not published; Politics and Letters did not survive after issue 4. See 3363, n. 1 for fuller details.

3. At least until 3 October 1948 there is no article or letter in *The Observer* about the Freedom Defence Committee.
4. In *The Writer and Politics* by George Woodcock (1947); the chapter was first published in *Politics*, December 1946, as 'George Orwell, Nineteenth Century Liberal'; for a brief summary, see *3160, n. 3*.
5. Henry Walter Bates (1825–1892), who visited South America in 1848. He was the author of *The Naturalist on the River Amazons,*° 2 vols. (1863).
6. Orwell is correct.
7. The first of several editions of *Hymns Ancient and Modern* 'for use in the Services of the Church [of England]' was published in 1861. Orwell would have been familiar with the Standard Edition of 1916, containing 779 hymns. The hymns Orwell mentions are 27, 172, and 236 respectively. Ironically, in the light of his comments here and elsewhere on Roman Catholicism, 'Praise to the Holiest in the height' is by Cardinal John Henry Newman.

3404. To Michael Kennard

25 May 1948   Handwritten

Ward 3
Hairmyres Hospital
East Kilbride
Lanarkshire

Dear Michael,[1]
The boats to Jura run on Mondays, Wednesdays & Fridays, so your best plan is to travel to Glasgow on Sunday & take the Monday boat. The itinerary is:
8 am leave Glasgow Central Station for GOUROCK
Join boat at Gourock
About 1 pm reach EAST TARBERT
Take bus to WEST TARBERT
Join boat at West Tarbert
About 4 pm reach CRAIGHOUSE (Jura)
Take hired car to ARDLUSSA, where we meet you.
My sister knows you are coming some time, & all you have to do is to send her a line letting her know *well in advance* when you are coming, so that she can arrange about meeting you & about the hired car to meet you at Craighouse. You must write a fortnight or so before the date, because the posts are slow. Her address is Miss Blair, Barnhill, Isle of Jura, Argyllshire. If there's any calamity such as the car being out of order, you might have to travel the last few miles on a pony or something like that, but we generally manage the journey all right. I hope you get decent weather. I should take either some gum boots or other thick boots with you, as it's often muddy if the weather isn't dry. I'm afraid I shall not be back by then, as I'm not likely to get out of here till about August, though I am a great deal better. But the others expect you & will like having you there. Please give everyone my love.

Yours
George

1. See *3371, n. 3*.

3405. To Celia Kirwan

27 May 1948   Handwritten

Ward 3
Hairmyres Hospital
East Kilbride
Lanarkshire

Dearest Celia,

Thanks ever so much for your letter. I must say, anything to do with UNESCO sounds pretty discouraging. Any way, I should knock all the money you can out of them, as I don't suppose they'll last much longer.

I am ever so much better & for some time past they have not been able to find any germs in me. They are now having a last try, & if they don't find any this time we can presumably regard the germs as quelled, though of course the healing-up process takes a long time. I am still frightfully weak & thin, but I get up for 2 hours every day & go outside a little. I still can't write a great deal, but I get a little done each day. They haven't said definitely when I shall leave hospital, but probably about August, & what is very good news, they now seem to think I shan't have to continue with out-patient treatment, which means I can go back to Jura instead of having to hang about in Glasgow or Edinburgh. They seem to have been having marvellous weather in Jura & are very busy with the farm work, Richard included. I haven't seen him since before Christmas, for fear of infection, but I could see him now if I can fix for him to be brought here for a day or two. He is getting enormous & is evidently learning to talk more. He had his fourth birthday this month.

How I wish I were with you in Paris, now that spring is there. Do you ever go to the Jardin des Plantes? I used to love it, though there was really nothing of interest except the rats, which at one time overran it & were so tame that they would almost eat out of your hand. In the end they got to be such a nuisance that they introduced cats & more or less wiped them out. The plane trees are so beautiful in Paris, because the bark isn't blackened by smoke the way it is in London. I suppose the food & so on is still pretty grisly, but that will improve if the Marshall plan[1] gets working. I see you have to put a 10 franc stamp[2] on your letter, which gives one an idea of what meals must cost now.

I can't help feeling that it's a bit treacherous on Arthur's part if he does settle down in the USA.[3] He was talking about doing it before. I suppose he is furious about what is happening in Palestine, though what else was to be expected I don't know. His lecture tour seems to have been quite a success. I wonder if he has got back yet, & what he will do about his place in Wales. It seems a pity to start sending roots down somewhere & then tear them up again, & I can imagine Mamaine not liking it.

It seems years since I have seen you, & in fact it must be 15 months. It's funny to think I haven't been out of Scotland for over a year, though I could have been if I had stayed well. This business has put my work back frightfully. The book I am at work on was to be finished at the beginning of this year—now it can't be finished before the end of the year, which means not coming out till the end of 1949. However it's something to be capable of working again. Last year before they brought me here I really felt as though I were finished. Thank Heaven Richard looks as if he is going to have good health. We have got 2 tested cows now, so at any rate he won't get this disease through milk, which is the usual way with children. Take care of yourself & write to me again some time.

With love
George

1. The Marshall Plan, properly the European Recovery Program, was the outcome of the Paris Economic Conference, July 1947, to aid post-war recovery in a number of European countries. It was financed by the United States ($17 billion in grants and loans over four years) and was named after U.S. Secretary of State George C. Marshall (1880–1959), whose advocacy of such aid was instrumental in bringing the scheme to fruition. In 1953 General Marshall was awarded the Nobel Peace Prize in recognition of his work in this field.
2. Ten francs was about 1p or 3½¢ in mid-1948.
3. Arthur Koestler, who had been living with his wife, Mamaine, in Wales, decided he would like to move to the United States. The Koestlers lived there for a short time.

3405A. To Lydia Jackson
31 May 1948   Handwritten

Ward 3
Hairmyres Hospital
East Kilbride
Lanarkshire

Dear Lydia,

Thanks so much for your letter. If you come on the 3rd July that will be fine. I hope by then I may be getting up a bit more (at present 2 hours a day) & it may be better weather. I don't know if I can book accommodation, but could you try writing to the Torrance Hotel, East Kilbride, which I believe is bearable, or else Mathieson's Cafe, Eaglesham. And let me know what all this is going to cost. Don't bother to bring anything with you. I am honestly very well off for food, as people keep sending me stuff from America.

It's nasty weather most of the time at present. I go out for a little each day when it's not too cold, & can now walk a fair distance, but I have to go at a snail's pace & rest frequently, as my breathing is still very bad. On Jura they've been having a heat wave & a severe drought, & Avril says the water supply was dried up, which is an awful bore, though of course it doesn't last for ever. They have got another cow, besides some bullocks, & a pig, or else they are going to get a pig shortly. I hope Richard grows up liking animals. At any rate at present he doesn't show signs of being frightened of them. I remember the geese we had when he was only 2, and the way he stood up to them & drove them off with a stick, though they were taller than he was.

Please remember me to Pat.

With love
Eric.

345

3406. 'George Gissing'

May–June 1948?

The preparatory notes Orwell made for this article are reproduced as *3407*.

Orwell's essay on George Gissing was intended for *Politics and Letters*, but that journal did not survive long enough to publish it. The typescript was discovered by one of the editors, Clifford Collins, in the summer of 1959 and published for the first time in the *London Magazine*, June 1960.

Collins, on 1 August 1959, in a letter to Orwell's widow, Sonia, at that time married to Michael Pitt-Rivers, said that in 1947 he had asked Orwell to write a review article on Gissing for *Politics and Letters*. Giving a precise date for its completion (and for that of 'Such, Such Were the Joys') is probably impossible. In his letter to Julian Symons, 21 March 1948 (see *3363*), Orwell says he had written 'two longer articles.' It has been suggested that these are almost certainly 'Writers and Leviathan,' *3364*, and 'Britain's Left-Wing Press,' *3366*; see *3363*, n. 1. Writing to George Woodcock, on 24 May 1948, Orwell says, 'I have two long articles on hand'; see *3403*. Although it is argued here (see *3408*) that 'Such, Such Were the Joys' was completed whilst Orwell was at Hairmyres, it is more probable that the two articles Orwell had in mind when writing to Woodcock were those on Gissing and 'The Labour Government After Three Years,' due according to Orwell's Second Literary Notebook by 20 July (though not published in *Commentary* until October 1948; see *3462*), precisely one month after he recorded that the Gissing article and 'Britain's Left-Wing Press' were due. When Orwell wrote to Julian Symons on 20 April 1948 (see *3386*), he said he was 'just in the act of re-reading two reprints [of books of Gissing], which I promised to review for Politics and Letters.° I think I shall do a long article on him, for them or someone else.' Orwell may have had, for a time, two articles in mind, a review of the two reprints and a longer essay. What he wrote was an amalgam of the two, though leaning in the direction of an essay.

The typescript that survives of the Gissing essay has at its head Orwell's address at Hairmyres Hospital. Orwell did not begin typing letters—so far as the extant evidence shows—until 2 May 1948. The machine on which the essay was typed is not that which Orwell had at Barnhill. The Hairmyres machine has, for example, a wide 'W,' a light comma, a tiny dot over the 'i,' and a small top serif to figure one, all in contradistinction to the Barnhill typewriter. The letters typed at Hairmyres seem to have been done on this same machine (as would be expected). It is difficult to be certain, but the typing seems to have characteristics associated with Orwell's work. There is some x-ing through (with capital X's), a little over-typing, but no slippage. Whereas Orwell may not have felt well enough to retype forty-six pages of 'Such, Such Were the Joys' (see *3408–9*), he may have felt up to nine pages of 'George Gissing.' Too much weight should not be placed on typewriter-identification, however; it would not have been impossible for machines at Barnhill and Hairmyres to be exchanged.

There is a final clue to the dating of this essay. At the top of the first page is written (not in Orwell's hand), 'P&L 4 5 10pt. Plantin.' This indicates that the essay was intended for either issue 4 or 5 of *Politics and Letters* and was to be set in 10 point Plantin (that journal's type-face). The '4' might have been an error: Orwell already had 'Writers and Leviathan' in that issue. Issue 5 never appeared.

The typescript is reproduced with the few significant alterations listed in the notes.

In the shadow of the atomic bomb it is not easy to talk confidently about progress. However, if it can be assumed that we are *not* going to be blown to pieces in about ten years' time, there are many reasons, and George Gissing's novels are among them, for thinking that the present age is a good deal better than the last one. If Gissing were still alive he would be younger than Bernard Shaw, and yet already the London of which he wrote seems almost as distant as that of Dickens. It is the fog-bound, gas-lit London of the 'eighties, a city of drunken puritans, where clothes, architecture and furniture had reached their rock-bottom of ugliness, and where it was almost normal for a working-class family of ten persons to inhabit a single room. On the whole Gissing does not write of the worst depths of poverty, but one can hardly read his descriptions of lower-middle class life, so obviously truthful in their dreariness, without feeling that we have improved perceptibly on that black-coated, money-ruled world of only sixty years ago.

Everything of Gissing's—except perhaps one or two books written towards the end of his life—contains memorable passages, and anyone who is making his acquaintance for the first time might do worse than start with *In the Year of the Jubilee*. It was rather a pity, however, to use up paper in reprinting two of his minor works* when the books by which he ought to be remembered are and have been for years completely unprocurable. *The Odd Women*, for instance, is about as thoroughly out of print as a book can be. I possess a copy myself, in one of those nasty little red-covered cheap editions that flourished before the 1914 war, but that is the only copy I have ever seen or heard of. *New Grub Street*, Gissing's masterpiece, I have never succeeded in buying. When I have read it, it has been in soup-stained copies borrowed from public lending libraries: so also with *Demos*, *The Nether World* and one or two others. So far as I know, only *The Private Papers of Henry Ryecroft*, the book on Dickens, and *A Life's Morning*, have been in print at all recently. However, the two now reprinted are well worth reading, especially *In the Year of the Jubilee*, which is the more sordid and therefore the more characteristic.

In his introduction Mr William Plomer remarks that "generally speaking, Gissing's novels are about money and women," and Miss Myfanwy Evans says something very similar in introducing *The Whirlpool*. One might, I think, widen the definition and say that Gissing's novels are a protest against the form of self-torture that goes by the name of respectability. Gissing was a bookish, perhaps over-civilized man, in love with classical antiquity, who found himself trapped in a cold, smoky, Protestant country where it was impossible to be comfortable without a thick padding of money between yourself and the outer world. Behind his rage and querulousness there lay a perception that the horrors of life in late-Victorian England were largely unnecessary. The grime, the stupidity, the ugliness, the sex-starvation, the furtive debauchery, the vulgarity, the bad manners, the censoriousness— these things were unnecessary, since the puritanism of which they were a relic

* *In the Year of the Jubilee* and *The Whirlpool*. By George Gissing. (Watergate Classics. 12/6 each.) [Orwell's footnote.]

no longer upheld the structure of society. People who might, without becoming less efficient, have been reasonably happy chose instead to be miserable, inventing senseless tabus with which to terrify themselves. Money was a nuisance not merely because without it you starved; what was more important was that unless you had quite a lot of it—£300 a year, say—society would not allow you to live gracefully or even peacefully. Women were a nuisance because even more than men they were the believers in tabus, still enslaved to respectability even when they had offended against it. Money and women° were therefore the two instruments through which society avenged itself on the courageous and the intelligent. Gissing would have liked a little more money for himself and some others, but he was not much interested in what we should now call social justice. He did not admire the working class as such, and he did not believe in democracy. He wanted to speak not for the multitude, but for the exceptional man, the sensitive man, isolated among barbarians.

In *The Odd Women* there is not a single major character whose life is not ruined either by having too little money, or by getting it too late in life, or by the pressure of social conventions which are obviously absurd but which cannot be questioned. An elderly spinster crowns a useless life by taking to drink; a young pretty girl marries a man old enough to be her father; a struggling schoolmaster puts off marrying his sweetheart until both of them are middle-aged and withered; a good-natured man is nagged to death by his wife; an exceptionally intelligent, spirited man misses his chance to make an adventurous marriage and relapses into futility: in each case the ultimate reason for the disaster lies in obeying the accepted social code, or in not having enough money to circumvent it. In *A Life's Morning* an honest and gifted man meets with ruin and death because it is impossible to walk about a big town with no hat on. His hat is blown out of the window when he is travelling in the train, and as he has not enough money to buy another, he misappropriates some money belonging to his employer, which sets going a series of disasters. This is an interesting example of the changes in outlook that can suddenly make an all-powerful tabu seem ridiculous. Today, if you had somehow contrived to lose your trousers, you would probably embezzle money rather than walk about in your under-pants. In the 'eighties the necessity would have seemed equally strong in the case of a hat. Even thirty or forty years ago, indeed, bareheaded men were booed at in the street. Then, for no very clear reason, hatlessness became respectable, and today the particular tragedy described by Gissing—entirely plausible in its context—would be quite impossible.

The most impressive of Gissing's books is *New Grub Street*. To a professional writer it is also an upsetting and demoralising book, because it deals among other things with that much-dreaded occupational disease, sterility. No doubt the number of writers who suddenly lose the power to write is not large, but it is a calamity that *might* happen to anybody at any moment, like sexual impotence. Gissing, of course, links it up with his habitual themes—money, the pressure of the social code, and the stupidity of women.

Edwin Reardon, a young novelist—he has just deserted a clerkship after having a fluky success with a single novel—marries a charming and apparently intelligent young woman, with a small income of her own. Here, and in one or two other places, Gissing makes what now[1] seems the curious remark that it is difficult for an educated man who is not rich to get married. Reardon brings it off, but his less successful friend, who lives in an attic and supports himself by ill-paid tutoring jobs, has to accept celibacy as a matter of course. If he did succeed in finding himself a wife, we are told, it could only be an uneducated girl from the slums. Women of refinement and sensibility will not face poverty. And here one notices again the deep difference between that day and our own. Doubtless Gissing is right[2] in implying all through his books that intelligent women are very rare animals; and if one wants to marry a woman who is intelligent *and* pretty, then the choice is still further restricted, according to a well-known arithmetical rule. It is like being allowed to choose only among albinos, and left-handed albinos at that. But what comes out in Gissing's treatment of his odious heroine, and of certain others among his women, is that at that date the idea of delicacy, refinement, even intelligence, in the case of a woman, was hardly separable from the idea of superior social status and expensive physical surroundings. The sort of woman whom a writer would want to marry was also the sort of woman who would shrink from living in an attic. When Gissing wrote *New Grub Street* that was probably true, and it could, I think, be justly claimed that it is not true today.

Almost as soon as Reardon is married it becomes apparent that his wife is merely a silly snob, the kind of woman in whom "artistic tastes" are no more than a cover for social competitiveness. In marrying a novelist she has thought to marry someone who will rapidly become famous and shed reflected glory upon herself. Reardon is a studious, retiring, ineffectual man, a typical Gissing hero. He has been caught up into an expensive, pretentious world in which he knows he will never be able to maintain himself, and his nerve fails almost immediately. His wife, of course, has not the faintest understanding of what is meant by literary creation. There is a terrible passage—terrible, at least, to anyone who earns his living by writing—in which she calculates the number of pages that it would be possible to write in a day, and hence the number of novels that her husband may be expected to produce in a year—with the reflection that really it is not a very laborious profession. Meanwhile Reardon has been stricken dumb. Day after day he sits at his desk: nothing happens, nothing comes! Finally, in panic, he manufactures a piece of rubbish; his publisher, because Reardon's previous book had been successful, dubiously accepts it. Thereafter he is unable to produce anything that even looks as if it might be printable. He is finished.

The desolating thing is that if only he could get back to his clerkship and his bachelorhood, he would be all right. The hardboiled journalist who finally marries Reardon's widow sums him up accurately by saying that he is the kind of man who, if left to himself, would write a fairly good book every two years. But, of course, he is not left to himself. He cannot revert to his old profession, and he cannot simply settle down to live on his wife's money:

public opinion, operating through his wife, harries him into impotence and finally into the grave. Most of the other literary characters in the book are not much more fortunate, and the troubles that beset them are still very much the same today. But at least it is unlikely that the book's central disaster would now happen in quite that way or for quite those reasons. The chances are that Reardon's wife would be less of a fool, and that he would have fewer scruples about walking out on her if she made life intolerable for him. A woman of rather similar type turns up in *The Whirlpool* in the person of Alma Frothingham. By contrast there are the three Miss Frenches in *In the Year of the Jubilee*, who represent the emerging lower-middle class—a class which, according to Gissing, was getting hold of money and power which it was not fitted to use—and who are quite surprisingly coarse, rowdy, shrewish and unmoral. At first sight Gissing's "ladylike" and "unladylike" women seem to be very different and even opposite kinds of animal, and this seems to invalidate his implied condemnation of the female sex in general. The connecting link between them, however, is that all of them are miserably limited in outlook. Even the clever and spirited ones, like Rhoda in *The Odd Women* (an interesting early specimen of the New Woman), cannot think in terms of generalities, and cannot get away from readymade standards. In his heart Gissing seems to feel that women are natural inferiors. He wants them to be better educated, but, on the other hand, he does not want them to have freedom, which they are certain to misuse. On the whole the best women in his books are the self-effacing, home-keeping ones.

It is very much to be hoped that a complete edition of Gissing's works will be published when paper becomes more plentiful. There are several of his books that I have never read, because I have never been able to get hold of them, and these unfortunately include *Born in Exile*, which is said by some people to be his best book. But merely on the strength of *New Grub Street*, *Demos* and *The Odd Women* I am ready to maintain that England has produced very few better novelists. This perhaps sounds like a rash statement until one stops to consider what is meant by a novel. The word "novel" is commonly used to cover almost any kind of story—*The Golden Asse*, *Anna Karenina*, *Don Quixote*, *The Improvisatore*, *Madame Bovary*, *King Solomon's Mines* or anything else you like—but it also has a narrower sense in which it means something hardly existing before the nineteenth century and flourishing chiefly in Russia and France. A novel, in this sense, is a story which attempts to describe credible human beings, and—without necessarily using the technique of naturalism—to show them acting on everyday motives and not merely undergoing strings of improbable adventures. A true novel, sticking to this definition, will also contain at least two characters, probably more, who are described from the inside and on the same level of probability— which, in effect, rules out novels written in the first person. If one accepts this definition, it becomes apparent that the novel is not an art-form in which England has excelled. The writers commonly paraded as "great English novelists" have a way of turning out either to be not true novelists, or not to be Englishmen. Gissing was not a writer of picaresque tales, or burlesques, or comedies, or political tracts: he was interested in individual human beings, and the fact that he can deal sympathetically with several different sets of motives, and make a credible story out of the collision between them, makes him exceptional among English writers.

Certainly there is not much of what is usually called beauty, not much lyricism, in the situations and characters that he chooses to imagine, and still less in the texture of his writing. His prose, indeed, is often disgusting. Here are a couple of samples:

> Not with impunity could her thought accustom itself to stray in regions forbidden, how firm soever her resolve to hold bodily aloof. (*The Whirlpool*).

> The ineptitude of uneducated English women in all that relates to their attire is a fact that it boots not to enlarge upon. (*In the Year of the Jubilee.*)

However, he does not commit the faults that really matter. It is always clear what he means, he never "writes for effect," he knows how to keep the balance between récit and dialogue and how to make dialogue sound probable while not contrasting too sharply with the prose that surrounds it. A much more serious fault than his inelegant manner of writing is the smallness of his range of experience. He is only acquainted with a few strata of society, and, in spite of his vivid understanding of the pressure of circumstance on character, does not seem to have much grasp of political or economic forces. In a mild way his outlook is reactionary, from lack of foresight rather than from ill-will. Having been obliged to live among them, he regarded the working class as savages, and in saying so he was merely being intellectually honest; he did not see that they were capable of becoming civilized if given slightly better opportunities. But, after all, what one demands from a novelist is not prophesy, and part of the charm of Gissing is that he belongs so unmistakeably to his own time, although his time treated him badly.

The English writer nearest to Gissing always seems to me to be his contemporary, or near-contemporary, Mark Rutherford. If one simply tabulates their outstanding qualities, the two men appear to be very different. Mark Rutherford was a less prolific writer than Gissing, he was less definitely a novelist, he wrote much better prose, his books belong less recognizably to any particular time, and he was in outlook a social reformer and, above all, a puritan. Yet there is a sort of haunting resemblance, probably explained by the fact that both men lack that curse of English writers, a "sense of humour." A certain low-spiritedness, an air of loneliness, is common to both of them. There are, of course, funny passages in Gissing's books,[3] but he is not chiefly concerned with getting a laugh—above all, he has no impulse towards burlesque. He treats all his major characters more or less seriously, and with at least an attempt at sympathy. Any novel will inevitably contain minor characters who are mere grotesques or who are observed in a purely hostile spirit, but there is such a thing as impartiality, and Gissing is more capable of it than the great majority of English writers. It is a point in his favour that he had no very strong moral purpose. He had, of course, a deep loathing of the ugliness, emptiness and cruelty of the society he lived in, but he was concerned to describe it rather than to change it. There is usually no one in his books who can be pointed to as the villain, and even when there is a villain he is not punished.[4] In his treatment of sexual matters Gissing is surprisingly frank, considering the time at which he was writing. It is not that he writes pornography or expresses approval of sexual promiscuity, but simply that he is willing to face the facts. The unwritten law of English fiction, the law that the hero as well as the heroine of a novel should be virgin when married, is disregarded in his books, almost for the first time since Fielding.

Like most English writers subsequent to the mid-nineteenth century, Gissing could not imagine any desirable destiny other than being a writer or a gentleman of leisure.[5] The dichotomy between the intellectual and the lowbrow already existed, and a person capable of writing a serious novel could no longer picture himself as fully satisfied with the life of a business-man, or a soldier, or a politician, or what-not. Gissing did not, at least consciously, even want to be the kind of writer that he was. His ideal, a rather melancholy one, was to have a moderate private income and live in a small comfortable house in the country, preferably unmarried, where he could wallow in books, especially the Greek and Latin classics. He might perhaps have realised this ideal if he had not managed to get himself into prison immediately after winning an Oxford scholarship: as it was he spent his life in[6] what appeared to him to be hackwork, and when he had at last reached the point where he could stop writing against the clock, he died almost immediately, aged only about forty-five. His death, described by H. G. Wells in his *Experiment in Autobiography*, was of a piece with his life. The twenty novels, or thereabouts, that he produced between 1880 and 1900 were, so to speak, sweated out of him during his struggle towards a leisure which he never enjoyed and which he might not have used to good advantage if he had had it: for it is difficult to believe that his temperament really fitted him for a life of scholarly research. Perhaps the natural pull of his gifts would in any case have drawn him towards novel-writing sooner or later. If not, we must be thankful for the piece of youthful folly which turned him aside from a comfortable middle-class career and forced him to become the chronicler of vulgarity, squalor and failure.

1. now] *interlinear insertion; originally typed before* makes *and X-ed through*
2. right] *first typed as* write, *X-ed through and immediately corrected*
3. Gissing's books,] *originally followed by* and he is not even altogether lacking in the spirit of comedy, *but X-ed through later (after the paper had been taken out of the machine and re-inserted)*
4. he is not punished] *originally followed* pointed to as the villain, *but X-ed through*
5. leisure] *typed as* liesure *and corrected by hand in bright-blue Biro*
6. in] *originally typed before* his life *but X-ed through*

3407. Preparatory Notes for 'George Gissing'
Second Literary Notebook

Geo. Gissing[1]

Gissing's novels are among the things that make one feel the world has improved (emphasise gloom.)
These particular books—note out of print condition of G.
Indicate plots—point out that they contain G's habitual subjects—money, disagreeable women, squalor.
Always something interesting in G's books (except some later ones). Always something squalid. Redefine preoccupations named by Plomer etc.—not so much money & women, as unnecessary dreariness caused by anachronistic puritanism.
"Men & women who could" etc. Note it is less money that° an attitude towards money, which goes with an attitude towards life in general. "The Odd Women"—lives of all major character's° ruined. "A Life's Morning"—loss of a hat. Best of all, "New Grub Street." Difficulty of marriage. Reardon & his wife. Almost literally done to death. Would not need to be the same nowadays. (Perhaps the hat here.)

Gissing's place. A high one, because true novelists rare in Eng. lit.

Great virtue, no sense of humour. Not an elegant writer (bad period), but has the basic literary qualities a novelist has to have. Not much social vision, & the characteristic modern writer's fault of not being able to imagine a worth-while life, except as a writer. Rather dreary ideal—£500 a year & Greek scholarship. But truthful. Sex. Compare with contemporaries, Meredith, Stevenson. (?)

1. A heading above *George Gissing* has been crossed through: *The Problem of Crypto-Communism.*

3408. Background to 'Such, Such Were the Joys'

It is well-nigh impossible to assign a date—or dates—to the composition and completion of Orwell's essay on his time at St Cyprian's preparatory school. Its position here is dictated by the belief that the essay was finally revised by about midsummer 1948. The facts and the consequential conjectures are as follows.

Orwell attended St Cyprian's, Eastbourne, from September 1911 to December 1916. The essay refers to 'All this' being 'thirty years ago or more,' suggesting that he was writing between 1941 and 1946, or later. Since his statement comes immediately after his reference to having left St Cyprian's, his 'thirty years ago or more' might reasonably imply 1946 to 1948. It could also— and probably did—refer only to the final revision of the essay.

Orwell must have written the essay after 1938, the year Cyril Connolly's *Enemies of Promise* was published, and to which, he told Fredric Warburg, it was 'a sort of pendant'; see *3232*. When Orwell wrote that, on 31 May 1947, a version of the essay had been completed, but the surviving typescript shows that it was subjected to further revision.

Orwell described the typescript he sent to Fredric Warburg as very bad commercial typing, much emended. Warburg wrote on 6 June 1947: 'I have read the autobiographical sketch about your prep. school and passed it to Roger [Senhouse].' Orwell's next extant letter to Warburg, 1 September 1947, does not mention the essay.

In 1946 and 1947, whilst Orwell was in Jura, Mrs. Miranda Wood (then Mrs. Miranda Christen) stayed in Orwell's London flat (see 3735). Anthony Powell had introduced Mrs. Wood to Orwell; she was technically a German citizen who had spent the war years in Java and was awaiting a divorce and a passage to Singapore—both long-drawn-out processes. She has left a private memoir of her association with Orwell; see 3735. In the summer of 1947 she undertook to do some typing for Orwell, using the machine she found in Orwell's flat. In the main she typed a draft of *Nineteen Eighty-Four*, of which a single page, numbered 239, has survived (see Facsimile, 183), but she also typed a fair copy of 'Such, Such Were the Joys.' She has described the copy from which she was to type as 'a bleary typescript' that 'looked as if it had been lying around for a considerable time.' This could have been the top copy of the carbon sent to Warburg; or it may have been the actual copy sent to Warburg if Warburg returned that to Orwell in, say, June 1947. What is plain is that the typescript sent to Mrs. Wood had been around for some time and that what she typed could not have been the bad commercial typing sent to Warburg. Orwell expected to 'get down to some work' only about 19 April 1947 (see 3212), and it is inconceivable that 'Such, Such Were the Joys' would have taken precedence over *Nineteen Eighty-Four*. Further, it was some little time after taking up residence in Orwell's flat that batches of the manuscript of *Nineteen Eighty-Four* started to arrive at fortnightly intervals and it was later on that the typescript of 'Such, Such Were the Joys' was included as 'a separate sheaf of papers in the package' of *Nineteen Eighty-Four* material.

A typescript of 'Such, Such Were the Joys' survives. This has a number of emendations in Orwell's hand; a very few literals and an omitted word are written in another hand. This typescript is not of a piece: it is made up of two different typings. Pages 1–17 are typed on a different machine from pages 18–63 (contrast 'i,' 'r,' 't' and fount size). Mrs. Wood positively identified page 239 in the Facsimile of *Nineteen Eighty-Four* as her work of that summer of 1947 (and she was able to examine the original when the Facsimile Edition was being prepared). Pages 1–17 correspond to the typewriter-face *and style* of that page (239). Pages 18–63 correspond to the typewriter-face, *but not the style* of the typed section of the drafts of *Nineteen Eighty-Four* comprising Facsimile pages 196–209 (Goldstein's Testament). Those *Nineteen Eighty-Four* pages are typical of Orwell's typing: there are x-ings through, overtypings, and four of the eleven pages show the last line of the page running away as the sheet slips out of the grip of the roller (a fault typical of the non-professional typist and never found in the work of a professional). The typing of pages 18–63 of 'Such, Such Were the Joys' does show an occasional overtyping, some erasure, one or two x-ings through, but no last lines running off the page. Its particular characteristic is the omission of spaces between words, something which Orwell does (as do most typists) occasionally, but nothing like in the quantity found here. Although the page has a reasonably professional look, it would seem that the typist was either not too experienced or that he/she found the space-bar sluggish to the touch. (The characteristics associated with Orwell's typing mentioned here are also those found in the typing of his letters over many years.) Its seems, therefore, that pages 1–17 are all that remain of Mrs. Wood's typing of 'Such, Such Were the

Joys' and that 18–63 were typed by someone else on Orwell's machine at Jura but not by Orwell himself. Did a visitor to Jura in the autumn of 1947 or at some time in 1948 type those pages for Orwell? It is impossible to show conclusively who might have done this. Dr. Gwen O'Shaughnessy and Lucy and Jane Dakin visited Barnhill in 1947, and there were many other visitors. One, Richard Rees, had run a magazine and written books and he was the kind of person who would have helped out. Perhaps the most likely person to come to Orwell's aid was Lydia Jackson (the writer Elisaveta Fen). In his letter to her of 31 May 1948 (*3405A*) Orwell writes of her coming to see him on 3 July; his letter of 30 June (*3416A*) suggests she comes 'after lunch on Sunday,' presumably 4 July. Earlier in the year, Avril's Diary (*3514*) records that she arrived at Barnhill on 26 March 1948 and left on 2 April having ridden Bill Dunn's horse hard and 'played chamber music on the battery wireless set'—perhaps as she typed? It is inconceivable that she passed through Glasgow on the way to Jura earlier in the year without calling to see Orwell, and she probably visited him also on the return journey. No correspondence survives to show she then visited Hairmyres. However, it is suggested that she did call to see Orwell; that he gave her an amended typescript of 'Such, Such Were the Joys'—the typescript Mrs. Wood had made—and that she retyped pages 18–63 at Jura, using Orwell's machine, and either bringing the completed text back to him on her way through Glasgow or posting it to him. Orwell then made a few manuscript amendments. Most of Orwell's emendations are in his usual firm, clear hand. Two, possibly three—'draughty,' 'tines,' and perhaps 'Hastings'—are noticeably shakier. It would be unwise to make too much of this, but they are consonant with someone writing in bed. A number of the corrections—for example, 'draughty' for 'dreadful' and 'servile' for 'senile'—are consonant with the typist's misreading of Orwell's handwriting.

Although it cannot be proved, it looks as if 'Such, Such Were the Joys' was not completed until May or June 1948.

So much for facts and conjectures. They do nothing to indicate when the work was written though they take its completion to a little later in Orwell's life. The most likely time for the writing of a first draft must be 1939–40, when the motivation to write his 'pendant' to *Enemies of Promise* would be strongest, and especially the empty months of 1940. Professor Crick adduces a number of references which suggest such a period (587–88). As he suggests, Orwell's reference in 'As I Please,' 77, 14 March 1947 (*3190*) to having 'The other day . . . had occasion to write something about the teaching of history in private schools' is compatible with revision and does not need to imply that the essay was being put down in writing for the first time.

Orwell described the typescript he sent Warburg as commercially typed and badly done (see *3232*). This could not be Mrs. Wood's typing on chronological grounds and because she was far too experienced a typist to produce work of that description. She had been a secretary to Duckworth, the publishers, before the war and then worked at the Oxford University Press in India. Orwell was too poor to pay for commercial typing in 1939–40, when, in any case, he had time to do his own typing. He did engage a typist to do some of his work in 1945–46, when the amount of work he was doing at least allowed him the luxury of paying someone to type for him (see *2689, endnote*). It is possible, then, that the poor-quality typescript sent to Warburg was produced in 1945 or 1946, time enough, coupled with the move to Jura, for the typescript to become 'bleary.'

There are few certainties here, but it seems possible that 'Such, Such Were the Joys' was drafted in 1939–40; revised and typed commercially in 1945–46, perhaps with an eye to publication, but put aside because of the risk of causing too much personal offence; dug out again in the spring of 1947 (hence the reference in 'As I Please,' 77), and taken up to Jura; sent to Warburg, 31 May 1947 (see *3232*), and then, probably later in the summer, to Mrs. Wood for retyping; further revised, necessitating the retyping of pages 18–63 on the machine Orwell had at Barnhill, possibly by Lydia Jackson at the end of March 1948; and, finally, subjected to a few handwritten corrections, made by Orwell at Hairmyres Hospital, bringing the completion of the essay to May or June 1948. The text here (*3409*) is reproduced from this typescript. The essay was first published in *Partisan Review*, September–October 1952. *Partisan Review* omitted the last five sentences, from 'But it is a fact that. . . .'

This degree of revision, especially at a time when Orwell was much preoccupied with writing *Nineteen Eighty-Four*, given that he was well aware that 'it is really too libellous to print' (see *3232*) indicates how important this essay was to him. He realised it could not be published until some of those most concerned were dead. It would seem that 'Such, Such Were the Joys' had for Orwell comparable importance to *Nineteen Eighty-Four*—which is *not* to say (as have some critics) that the two works are related in content and attitude.

Earlier printings of 'Such, Such Were the Joys' have shown changes of names to avoid giving offence to those then living. The text given here is that revised by Orwell but with the original names. It is hoped that, after all this time, no hurt will be sustained by anyone mentioned.

See Crick, 58–80; Shelden, 26–53, 58–62, U.S.: 25–49, 53–57; Stansky and Abrahams, I, 38–83; and three essays by Robert Pearce: 'Truth and Falsehood: George Orwell's Prep School Woes,' *Review of English Studies*, n.s., XLIII (1992), 367–86; 'The Prep School and Imperialism: The Example of Orwell's St. Cyprian's,' *Journal of Educational Administration and History* (January 1991), 42–53; 'Orwell and the Harrow History Prize,' *Notes & Queries*, 235 (ns 37) (December 1990), 442–43. For reminiscences, see Cyril Connolly, *Enemies of Promise*, chapter 19, 'White Samite'; *Orwell Remembered*, 32–36 (which includes an excerpt from Connolly); *Remembering Orwell*, 4–11 (which includes John Wilkes, the headmaster).

3409. 'Such, Such Were the Joys'

1939?—June 1948?

Soon after I arrived at St. Cyprian's (not immediately, but after a week or two, just when I seemed to be settling into the routine of school life) I began wetting my bed. I was now aged eight, so that this was a reversion to a habit which I must have grown out of at least four years earlier.

Nowadays, I believe, bed-wetting in such circumstances is taken for granted. It is a normal reaction in children who have been removed from their homes to a strange place. In those days, however, it was looked on as a disgusting crime which the child committed on purpose and for which the proper cure was a beating. For my part I did not need to be told it was a crime. Night after night I prayed, with a fervour never previously attained in my prayers, "Please God, do not let me wet my bed! Oh, please God, do not let me wet my bed!", but it made remarkably little difference. Some nights the

thing happened, others not. There was no volition about it, no consciousness. You did not properly speaking *do* the deed: you merely woke up in the
morning and found that the sheets were wringing wet.

After the second or third offence I was warned that I should be beaten next
time, but I received the warning in a curiously roundabout way. One
afternoon, as we were filing out from tea, Mrs Wilkes, the headmaster's wife,
was sitting at the head of one of the tables, chatting with a lady of whom I
know nothing, except that she was on an afternoon's visit to the school. She
was an intimidating, masculine-looking person wearing a riding habit, or
something that I took to be a riding habit. I was just leaving the room when
Mrs Wilkes called me back, as though to introduce me to the visitor.

Mrs Wilkes was nicknamed Flip, and I shall call her by that name, for I
seldom think of her by any other. (Officially, however, she was addressed as
Mum, probably a corruption of the "Ma'am" used by public schoolboys to
their housemasters' wives.) She was a stocky square-built woman with hard
red cheeks, a flat top to her head, prominent brows and deepset, suspicious
eyes. Although a great deal of the time she was full of false heartiness, jollying
one along with mannish slang ("*Buck* up, old chap!" and so forth), and even
using one's Christian name, her eyes never lost their anxious, accusing look.
It was very difficult to look her in the face without feeling guilty, even at
moments when one was not guilty of anything in particular.

"Here is a little boy," said Flip, indicating me to the strange lady, "who
wets his bed every night. Do you know what I am going to do if you wet
your bed again?" she added, turning to me. "I am going to get the Sixth Form
to beat you."

The strange lady put on an air of being inexpressibly shocked, and
exclaimed "I-should-*think*-so!" And here there occurred one of those wild,
almost lunatic misunderstandings which are part of the daily experience of
childhood. The Sixth Form was a group of older boys who were selected as
having "character" and were empowered to beat smaller boys. I had not yet
learned of their existence, and I mis-heard the phrase "the Sixth Form" as
"Mrs Form". I took it as referring to the strange lady—I thought, that is, that
her name was Mrs Form. It was an improbable name, but a child has no
judgement in such matters. I imagined, therefore, that it was *she* who was to
be deputed to beat me. It did not strike me as strange that this job should be
turned over to a casual visitor in no way connected with the school. I merely
assumed that "Mrs Form" was a stern disciplinarian who enjoyed beating
people (somehow her appearance seemed to bear this out) and I had an
immediate terrifying vision of her arriving for the occasion in full riding kit
and armed with a hunting whip. To this day I can feel myself almost
swooning with shame as I stood, a very small, round-faced boy in short
corduroy knickers, before the two women. I could not speak. I felt that I
should die if "Mrs Form" were to beat me. But my dominant feeling was not
fear or even resentment: it was simply shame because one more person, and
that a woman, had been told of my disgusting offence.

A little later, I forget how, I learned that it was not after all "Mrs Form"
who would do the beating. I cannot remember whether it was that very night

357

that I wetted my bed again, but at any rate I did wet it again quite soon, Oh, the despair, the feeling of cruel injustice, after all my prayers and resolutions, at once again waking between the clammy sheets! There was no chance of hiding what I had done. The grim statuesque matron, Margaret by name, arrived in the dormitory specially to inspect my bed. She pulled back the clothes, then drew herself up, and the dreaded words seemed to come rolling out of her like a peal of thunder:

"REPORT YOURSELF to the headmaster after breakfast!"

I put REPORT YOURSELF in capitals because that was how it appeared in my mind. I do not know how many times I heard that phrase during my early years at St. Cyprian's. It was only very rarely that it did not mean a beating. The words always had a portentous sound in my ears, like muffled drums or the words of the death sentence.

When I arrived to report myself, Flip was doing something or other at the long shiny table in the ante-room to the study. Her uneasy eyes searched me as I went past. In the study Mr Wilkes, nicknamed Sambo, was waiting. Sambo was a round-shouldered, curiously oafish-looking man, not large but shambling in gait, with a chubby face which was like that of an overgrown baby, and which was capable of good-humour. He knew, of course, why I had been sent to him, and had already taken a bone-handled riding-crop out of the cupboard, but it was part of the punishment of reporting yourself that you had to proclaim your offence with your own lips. When I had said my say, he read me a short but pompous lecture, then seized me by the scruff of the neck, twisted me over and began beating me with the riding crop. He had a habit of continuing his lecture while he flogged you, and I remember the words "you dir-ty lit-tle boy" keeping time with the blows. The beating did not hurt (perhaps, as it was the first time, he was not hitting me very hard), and I walked out feeling very much better. The fact that the beating had not hurt was a sort of victory and partially wiped out the shame of the bed-wetting. Perhaps[1] I was even incautious enough to wear a grin on my face. Some small boys were hanging about in the passage outside the door of the ante-room.

"D'you get the cane?"

"It didn't hurt," I said proudly.

Flip had heard everything. Instantly her voice came screaming after me:

"Come here! Come here this instant! What was that you said?'

"I said it didn't hurt," I faltered out.

"How dare you say a thing like that? Do you think that is a proper thing to say? Go in and REPORT YOURSELF AGAIN!"

This time Sambo laid on in real earnest. He continued for a length of time that frightened and astonished me—about five minutes, it seemed—ending up by breaking the riding crop. The bone handle went flying across the room.

"Look what you've made me do!" he said furiously, holding up the broken crop.

I had fallen into a chair, weakly snivelling. I remember that this was the only time throughout my boyhood when a beating actually reduced me to tears, and curiously enough I was not even now crying because of the pain.

The second beating had not hurt very much either. Fright and shame seemed to have anaesthetised me. I was crying partly because I felt that this was expected of me, partly from genuine repentance, but partly also because of a deeper grief which is peculiar to childhood and not easy to convey: a sense of desolate loneliness and helplessness, of being locked up not only in a hostile world but in a world of good and evil where the rules were such that it was actually not possible for me to keep them.

I knew that the bed-wetting was (a) wicked and (b) outside my control. The second fact I was personally aware of, and the first I did not question. It was possible, therefore, to commit a sin without knowing that you committed it, without wanting to commit it, and without being able to avoid it. Sin was not necessarily something that you did: it might be something that happened to you. I do not want to claim that this idea flashed into my mind as a complete novelty at this very moment, under the blows of Sambo's cane: I must have had glimpses of it even before I left home, for my early childhood had not been altogether happy. But at any rate this was the great, abiding lesson of my boyhood: that I was in a world where it was *not possible* for me to be good. And the double beating was a turning-point, for it brought home to me for the first time the harshness of the environment into which I had been flung. Life was more terrible, and I was more wicked, than I had imagined. At any rate, as I sat snivelling on the edge of a chair in Sambo's study, with not even the self-possession to stand up while he stormed at me, I had a conviction of sin and folly and weakness, such as I do not remember to have felt before.

In general, one's memories of any period must necessarily weaken as one moves away from it. One is constantly learning new facts, and old ones have to drop out to make way for them. At twenty I could have written the history of my schooldays with an accuracy which would be quite impossible now. But it can also happen that one's memories grow sharper after a long lapse of time, because one is looking at the past with fresh eyes and can isolate and, as it were, notice facts which previously existed undifferentiated among a mass of others. Here are two things which in a sense I remembered, but which did not strike me as strange or interesting until quite recently. One is that the second beating seemed to me a just and reasonable punishment. To get one beating, and then to get another and far fiercer one on top of it, for being so unwise as to show that the first had not hurt—that was quite natural. The gods are jealous, and when you have good fortune you should conceal it. The other is that I accepted the broken riding crop as my own crime. I can still recall my feeling as I saw the handle lying on the carpet—the feeling of having done an ill-bred clumsy thing, and ruined an expensive object. *I* had broken it: so Sambo told me, and so I believed. This acceptance of guilt lay unnoticed in my memory for twenty or thirty years.

So much for the episode of the bed-wetting. But there is one more thing to be remarked. This is that I did not wet my bed again—at least, I did wet it once again, and received another beating, after which the trouble stopped. So perhaps this barbarous remedy does work, though at a heavy price, I have no doubt.

ii.

St. Cyprian's was an expensive and snobbish school which was in process of becoming more snobbish, and, I imagine, more expensive. The public school with which it had special connections was Harrow, but during my time an increasing proportion of the boys went on to Eton. Most of them were the children of rich parents, but on the whole they were the un-aristocratic rich, the sort of people who live in huge shrubberied houses in Bournemouth or Richmond, and who have cars and butlers but not country estates. There were a few exotics among them—some South American boys, sons of Argentine beef barons, one or two Russians, and even a Siamese prince, or someone who was described as a prince.

Sambo[2] had two great ambitions. One was to attract titled boys to the school, and the other was to train up pupils to win scholarships at public schools, above all at Eton. He did, towards the end of my time, succeed in getting hold of two boys with real English titles. One of them, I remember, was a wretched, drivelling little creature, almost an albino, peering upwards out of weak eyes, with a long nose at the end of which a dewdrop always seemed to be trembling.[3] Sambo always gave these boys their titles when mentioning them to a third person, and for their first few days he actually addressed them to their faces as "Lord So-and-so." Needless to say he found ways of drawing attention to them when any visitor was being shown round the school. Once, I remember, the little fair-haired boy had a choking fit at dinner, and a stream of snot ran out of his nose onto his plate in a way horrible to see. Any lesser person would have been called a dirty little beast and ordered out of the room instantly: but Sambo and Flip laughed it off in a "boys will be boys" spirit.

All the very rich boys were more or less undisguisedly favoured. The school still had a faint suggestion of the Victorian "private academy" with its "parlour boarders", and when I later read about that kind of school in Thackeray I immediately saw the resemblance. The rich boys had milk and biscuits in the middle of the morning, they were given riding lessons once or twice a week,[4] Flip mothered them and called them by their Christian names, and above all they were never caned. Apart from the South Americans, whose parents were safely distant, I doubt whether Sambo ever caned any boy whose father's income was much above £2,000 a year. But he was sometimes willing to sacrifice financial profit to scholastic prestige. Occasionally, by special arrangement, he would take at greatly reduced fees some boy who seemed likely to win scholarships and thus bring credit on the school. It was on these terms that I was at St. Cyprian's myself: otherwise my parents could not have afforded to send me to so expensive a school.

I did not at first understand that I was being taken at reduced fees; it was only when I was about eleven that Flip and Sambo began throwing the fact in my teeth. For my first two or three years I went through the ordinary educational mill: then, soon after I had started Greek (one started Latin at eight, Greek at ten), I moved into the scholarship class, which was taught, so far as classics went, largely by Sambo himself. Over a period of two or three years the scholarship boys were crammed with learning as cynically as a goose is crammed for Christmas. And with what learning! This business of making a gifted boy's career depend on a competitive examination, taken when he is only twelve or thirteen, is an evil thing at best, but there do appear to be preparatory schools which send scholars to Eton, Winchester, etc. without teaching them to see everything in terms of marks. At St. Cyprian's the whole process was frankly a preparation for a sort of confidence trick. Your job was to learn exactly those things that would give an examiner the impression that you knew more than you did know, and as far as possible to avoid burdening your brain with anything else. Subjects which lacked examination-value, such as geography, were almost completely neglected, mathematics was also neglected if you were a "classical", science was not taught in any form—indeed it was so despised that even an interest in natural history was discouraged—and even the books you were encouraged to read in your spare time were chosen with one eye on the "English paper." Latin and Greek, the main scholarship subjects, were what counted, but even these were deliberately taught in a flashy, unsound way. We never, for example, read right through even a single book of a Greek or Latin author: we merely read short passages which were picked out because they were the kind of thing likely to be set as an "unseen translation." During the last year or so before we went up for our scholarships, most of our time was spent in simply working our way through the scholarship papers of previous years. Sambo had sheaves of these in his possession from every one of the major public schools. But the greatest outrage of all was the teaching of history.

There was in those days a piece of nonsense called the Harrow History Prize, an annual competition for which many preparatory schools entered. It was a tradition for St. Cyprian's to win it every year, as well we might, for we had mugged up every paper that had been set since the competition started, and the supply of possible questions was not inexhaustible. They were the kind of stupid question that is answered by rapping out a name or a quotation. Who plundered the Begums?[5] Who was beheaded in an open boat? Who caught the Whigs bathing and ran away with their clothes? Almost all our historical teaching was on this level. History was a series of unrelated, unintelligible but—in some[6] way that was never explained to us—important facts with resounding phrases tied to them. Disraeli brought peace with honour. Hastings[7] was astonished at his moderation. Pitt called in the New World to redress the balance of the Old. And the dates, and the[8] mnemonic devices! (Did you know, for example, that the initial letters of "A black Negress was my aunt: there's her house behind the barn" are also the initial letters of the battles in the Wars of the Roses?) Flip, who "took" the higher forms in history, revelled in this kind of thing. I recall positive orgies of dates, with the keener boys leaping up and down in their places in their eagerness to shout out the right answers, and at the same time not feeling the faintest interest in the meaning of the mysterious events they were naming.

"1587?"

"Massacre of St. Bartholomew!"

"1707?"

"Death of Aurangzeeb!"

"1713?"

"Treaty of Utrecht!"

"1773?"

"Boston Tea Party!"[9]

"1520?"

"Oo, Mum, please, Mum—"

"Please, Mum, please, Mum! Let me tell him, Mum!"

"Well! 1520?"

"Field of the Cloth of Gold!"

And so on.

But history and such secondary subjects were not bad fun. It was in "classics" that the real strain came. Looking back, I realise that I then worked harder than I have ever done since, and yet at the time it never seemed possible to make quite the effort that was demanded of one. We would sit round the long shiny table, made of some very pale-coloured, hard wood, with Sambo goading, threatening, exhorting, sometimes joking, very occasionally praising, but always prodding, prodding away at one's mind to keep it up to the right pitch of concentration, as one might keep a sleepy person awake by sticking pins into him.

"Go on, you little slacker! Go on, you idle, worthless little boy! The whole trouble with you is that you're bone and horn idle. You eat too much, that's why. You wolf down enormous meals, and then when you come here you're half asleep. Go on, now, put your back into it. You're not *thinking*. Your brain doesn't sweat."

He would tap away at one's skull with his silver pencil, which, in my memory, seems to have been about the size of a banana, and which certainly was heavy enough to raise a bump: or he would pull the short hairs round one's ears, or, occasionally, reach out under the table and kick one's shin. On some days nothing seemed to go right, and then it would be: "All right, then, I know what you want. You've been asking for it the whole morning. Come along, you useless little slacker. Come into the study." And then whack, whack, whack, whack, and back one would come, red-wealed and smarting—in later years Sambo had abandoned his riding crop in favour of a thin rattan cane which hurt very much more—to settle down to work again. This did not happen very often, but I do remember, more than once, being led out of the room in the middle of a Latin sentence, receiving a beating and then going straight ahead with the same sentence, just like that. It is a mistake to think such methods do not work. They work very well for their special purpose. Indeed, I doubt whether classical education ever has been or can be successfully carried on without corporal punishment.[10] The boys themselves believed in its efficacy. There was a boy named Hardcastle, with no brains to speak of, but evidently in acute need of a scholarship. Sambo was flogging him towards the goal as one might do with a foundered horse. He went up for a scholarship at Uppingham, came back with a consciousness of having done badly, and a day or two later received a severe beating for idleness. "I wish I'd had that caning before I went up for the exam," he said sadly—a remark which I felt to be contemptible, but which I perfectly well understood.

The boys of the scholarship class were not all treated alike. If a boy were the son of rich parents to whom the saving of fees was not all-important, Sambo would goad him along in a comparatively fatherly way, with jokes and digs in the ribs and perhaps an occasional tap with the pencil, but no hair-pulling and no caning. It was the poor but "clever" boys who suffered. Our brains were a gold-mine in which he had sunk money, and the dividends must be squeezed out of us. Long before I had grasped the nature of my financial relationship with Sambo, I had been made to understand that I was not on the same footing as most of the other boys. In effect there were three castes in the school. There was the minority with an aristocratic or millionaire background, there were the children of the ordinary suburban rich, who made up the bulk of the school, and there were a few underlings like myself, the sons of clergymen, Indian civil servants, struggling widows and the like. These poorer ones were discouraged from going in for "extras" such as shooting and carpentery,° and were humiliated over clothes and petty possessions. I never, for instance, succeeded in getting a cricket bat of my own, because "Your parents wouldn't be able to afford it." This phrase pursued me throughout my schooldays. At St. Cyprian's we were not allowed to keep the money we brought back with us, but had to "give it in" on the first day of term, and then from time to time were allowed to spend it under supervision. I and similarly-placed boys were always choked off from buying expensive toys like model aeroplanes, even if the necessary money stood to our credit. Flip, in particular, seemed to aim consciously at inculcating a humble outlook in the poorer boys. "Do you think that's the sort of thing a boy like you should buy?" I remember her saying to somebody—and she said this in front of the whole school; "You know you're not going to grow up with money, don't you? Your people aren't rich. You must learn to be sensible. Don't get above yourself!" There was also the weekly pocket-money, which we took out in sweets, dispersed by Flip from a large table. The millionaires had sixpence a week, but the normal sum was threepence. I and one or two others were only allowed twopence. My parents had not given instructions to this effect, and the saving of a penny a week could not conceivably have made any difference to them: it was a mark of status. Worse yet was the detail of the birthday cakes. It was usual for each boy, on his birthday, to have a large iced cake with candles, which was shared out at tea between the whole school. It was provided as a matter of routine and went on his parents' bill. I never had such a cake, though my parents would have paid for it readily enough. Year after year, never daring to ask, I would miserably hope that this year a cake would appear. Once or twice I even rashly pretended to my companions that this time I *was* going to have a cake. Then came teatime, and no cake, which did not make me more popular.

Very early it was impressed upon me that I had no chance of a decent future unless I won a scholarship at a public school. Either I won my scholarship, or I must leave school at fourteen and become, in Sambo's favourite phrase "a little office boy at forty pounds a year." In my circumstances it was natural that I should believe this. Indeed, it was universally taken for granted at St. Cyprian's that unless you went to a "good" public school (and only about fifteen schools came under this heading) you were ruined for life. It is not easy to convey to a grown-up person the sense of strain, of nerving oneself for some terrible, all-deciding combat, as the date of the examination crept nearer—eleven years old, twelve years old, then thirteen, the fatal year itself! Over a period of about two years, I do not think there was ever a day when "the exam", as I called it, was quite out of my waking thoughts. In my prayers it figured invariably: and whenever I got the bigger portion of a wishbone, or picked up a horse-shoe, or bowed seven times to the new moon, or succeeded in passing through a wishing-gate without touching the sides, then the wish I earned by doing so went on "the exam" as a matter of course. And yet curiously enough I was also tormented by an almost irresistible impulse *not* to work. There were days when my heart sickened at the labours ahead of me, and I stood stupid as an animal before the most elementary difficulties. In the holidays, also, I could not work. Some of the scholarship boys received extra tuition from a certain Mr Knowles,[11] a likeable,[12] very hairy man who wore shaggy suits and lived in a typical bachelor's "den"—booklined walls, overwhelming stench of tobacco—somewhere in the town. During the holidays Mr Knowles used to send us extracts from Latin authors to translate, and we were supposed to send back a wad of work once a week. Somehow I could not do it. The empty paper and the black Latin dictionary lying on the table, the consciousness of a plain duty shirked, poisoned my leisure, but somehow I could not start, and by the end of the holidays I would only have sent Mr Knowles fifty or a hundred lines. Undoubtedly part of the reason was that Sambo and his cane were far away. But in term-time, also, I would go through periods of idleness and stupidity when I would sink deeper and deeper into disgrace and even achieve a sort of feeble, snivelling defiance, fully conscious of my guilt and yet unable or unwilling—I could not be sure which—to do any better. Then Sambo or Flip would send for me, and this time it would not even be a caning.

Flip would search me with her baleful eyes. (What colour were those eyes, I wonder? I remember them as green, but actually no human being has green eyes. Perhaps they were hazel.) She would start off in her peculiar, wheedling, bullying style, which never failed to get right through one's guard and score a hit on one's better nature.

"I don't think it's awfully decent of you to behave like this, is it? Do you think it's quite playing the game by your mother and father to go on idling your time away, week after week, month after month? Do you *want*[13] to throw all your chances away? You know your people aren't rich, don't you? You know they can't afford the same things as other boys' parents. How are they to send you to a public school if you don't win a scholarship? I know how proud your mother is of you. Do you *want* to let her down?"

"I don't think he wants to go to a public school any longer," Sambo would say, addressing himself to Flip[14] with a pretence that I was not there. "I think he's given up that idea. He wants to be a little office boy at forty pounds a year."

The horrible sensation of tears—a swelling in the breast, a tickling behind the nose—would already have assailed me. Flip would bring out her ace of trumps:

"And do you think it's quite fair to *us*, the way you're behaving? After all we've done for you? You *do* know what we've done for you, don't you?" Her eyes would pierce deep into me, and though she never said it straight out, I did know. "We've had you here all these years—we even had you here for a week in the holidays so that Mr Knowles could coach you. We don't *want* to have to send you away, you know, but we can't keep a boy here just to eat up our food, term after term. *I* don't think it's very straight, the way you're behaving. Do you?'

I never had any answer except a miserable "No, Mum," or "Yes, Mum," as the case might be. Evidently it was *not* straight, the way I was behaving. And at some point or other the unwanted tear would always force its way out of the corner of my eye, roll down my nose, and splash.

Flip never said in plain words that I was a non-paying pupil, no doubt because vague phrases like "all we've done for you" had a deeper emotional appeal. Sambo, who did not aspire to be loved by his pupils, put it more brutally, though, as was usual with him, in pompous language. "You are living on my bounty" was his favourite phrase in this context. At least once I listened to these words between blows of the cane. I must say that these scenes were not frequent, and except on one occasion they did not take place in the presence of other boys. In public I was reminded that I was poor and that my parents "wouldn't be able to afford" this or that, but I was not actually reminded of my dependent position. It was a final unanswerable argument, to be brought forth like an instrument of torture when my work became exceptionally bad.

To grasp the effect of this kind of thing on a child of ten or twelve, one has to remember that the child has little sense of proportion or probability. A child may be a mass of egoism and rebelliousness, but it has no accumulated experience to give it confidence in its own judgements. On the whole it will accept what it is told, and it will believe in the most fantastic way in the knowledge and powers of the adults surrounding it. Here is an example.

I have said that at St. Cyprian's we were not allowed to keep our own money. However, it was possible to hold back a shilling or two, and sometimes I used furtively to buy sweets which I kept hidden in the loose ivy on the playing-field wall. One day when I had been sent on an errand I went into a sweetshop a mile or more from the school and bought some chocolates. As I came out of the shop I saw on the opposite pavement a small sharp-faced man who seemed to be staring very hard at my school cap. Instantly a horrible fear went through me. There could be no doubt as to who the man was. He was a spy placed there by Sambo! I turned away unconcernedly, and then, as though my legs were doing it of their own accord, broke into a clumsy run. But when I got round the next corner I forced myself to walk again, for to run was a sign of guilt, and obviously there would be other spies posted here and there about the town. All that day and the next I waited for the summons to the study, and was surprised when it did not come. It did not seem to me strange that the headmaster of a private school should dispose of an army of informers, and I did not even imagine that he would have to pay them. I assumed that any adult, inside the school or outside, would collaborate voluntarily in preventing us from breaking the rules. Sambo was all-powerful, and[15] it was natural that his agents should be everywhere. When this episode happened I do not think I can have been less than twelve years old.

I hated Sambo and Flip, with a sort of shamefaced, remorseful hatred, but it did not occur to me to doubt their judgement. When they told me that I must either win a public-school scholarship or become an office-boy at fourteen, I believed that those were the unavoidable alternatives before me. And above all, I believed Sambo and Flip when they told me they were my benefactors. I see now, of course, that from Sambo's point of view I was a good speculation. He sank money in me, and he looked to get it back in the form of prestige. If I had "gone off," as promising boys sometimes do, I imagine that he would have got rid of me swiftly. As it was I won him two scholarships when the time came, and no doubt he made full use of them in his prospectuses. But it is difficult for a child to realise that a school is primarily a commercial venture. A child believes that the school exists to educate and that the schoolmaster disciplines him either for his own good, or from a love of bullying. Flip and Sambo had chosen to befriend me, and their friendship included canings, reproaches and humiliations, which were good for me and saved me from an office stool. That was their version, and I believed in it. It was therefore clear that I owed them a vast debt of gratitude. But I was *not* grateful, as I very well knew. On the contrary, I hated both of them. I could not control my subjective feelings, and I could not conceal them from myself. But it is wicked, is it not, to hate your benefactors? So I was taught, and so I believed. A child accepts the codes of behaviour that are presented to it, even when it breaks them. From the age of eight, or even earlier, the consciousness of sin was never far away from me. If I contrived to seem callous and defiant, it was only a thin cover over a mass of shame and dismay. All through my boyhood I had a profound conviction that I was no good, that I was wasting my time, wrecking my talents, behaving with monstrous folly and wickedness and ingratitude—and all this, it seemed, was inescapable, because I lived among laws which were absolute, like the law of gravity, but which it was not possible for me to keep.

iii

No one can look back on his schooldays and say with truth that they were altogether unhappy.

I have good memories of St. Cyprian's, among a horde of bad ones. Sometimes on summer afternoons there were wonderful expeditions across the Downs to a village[16] called Birling Gap, or to Beachy Head, where one bathed dangerously among the chalk boulders and came home covered with cuts. And there were still more wonderful midsummer evenings when, as a special treat, we were not driven off to bed as usual but allowed to wander about the grounds in the long twilight, ending up with a plunge into the swimming bath at about nine o'clock. There was the joy of waking early on summer mornings and getting in an hour's undisturbed reading (Ian Hay, Thackeray, Kipling and H. G. Wells were the favourite authors of my boyhood) in the sunlit, sleeping dormitory. There was also cricket, which I was no good at but with which I conducted a sort of hopeless love affair up to the age of about eighteen. And there was the pleasure of keeping caterpillars—the silky green and purple puss-moth, the ghostly green poplar-hawk, the privet hawk, large as one's third finger, specimens of which could be illicitly purchased for sixpence at a shop in the town—and, when one could escape long enough from the master who was "taking the walk," there was the excitement of dredging the dew-ponds on the Downs for enormous newts with orange-coloured bellies. This business of being out for a walk, coming across something of fascinating interest and then being dragged away from it by a yell from the master, like a dog jerked onwards by the leash, is an important feature of school life, and helps to build up the conviction, so strong in many children, that the things you most want to do are always unattainable.

Very occasionally, perhaps once during each summer, it was possible to escape altogether from the barrack-like atmosphere of school, when Siller,[17] the second master, was permitted to take one or two boys for an afternoon of butterfly hunting on a common a few miles away. Siller was a man with white hair and a red face like a strawberry, who was good at natural history, making models and plaster casts, operating magic lanterns, and things of that kind. He and Mr Knowles were the only adults in any way connected with the school whom I did not either dislike or fear. Once he took me into his room and showed me in confidence a plated, pearl-handled revolver—his "six-shooter", he called it—which he kept in a box under his bed. And oh, the joy of those occasional expeditions! The ride of two or three miles on a lonely little branch line, the afternoon of charging to and fro with large green nets, the beauty of the enormous dragon flies which hovered over the tops of the grasses, the sinister killing-bottle with its sickly smell, and then tea in the parlour of a pub with large slices of pale-coloured cake! The essence of it was in the railway journey, which seemed to put magic distances between yourself and school.

Flip, characteristically, disapproved of these expeditions, though not actually forbidding them. "And have you been catching *little butterflies*?" she would say with a vicious sneer when one got back, making her voice as babyish as possible. From her point of view, natural history ("bug-hunting" she would probably have called it) was a babyish pursuit which a boy should be laughed out of as early as possible. Moreover it was somehow faintly plebeian, it was traditionally associated with boys who wore spectacles and were no good at games, it did not help you to pass exams, and above all it smelt of science and therefore seemed to menace classical education. It needed a considerable moral effort to accept Siller's invitation. How I dreaded that sneer of *little butterflies*! Siller, however, who had been at the school since its early days, had built up a certain independence for himself: he seemed able to handle Sambo, and ignored Flip a good deal. If it ever happened that both of them were away, Siller acted as deputy headmaster, and on those occasions, instead of reading the appointed lesson for the day at morning chapel, he would read us stories from the Apocrypha.

Most of the good memories of my childhood, and up to the age of about twenty, are in some way connected with animals. So far as St. Cyprian's goes, it also seems, when I look back, that all my good memories are of summer. In winter your nose ran continually, your fingers were too numb to button your shirt (this was an especial misery on Sundays, when we wore Eton collars), and there was the daily nightmare of football—the cold, the mud, the hideous greasy ball that came whizzing at one's face, the gouging knees and trampling boots of the bigger boys. Part of the trouble was that in winter, after the age of about ten, I was seldom in good health, at any rate during term time. I had defective bronchial tubes and a lesion in one lung which was not discovered till many years later. Hence I not only had a chronic cough, but running was a torment to me. In those days however, "wheeziness," or "chestiness," as it was called, was either diagnosed as imagination or was looked on as essentially a moral disorder, caused by over-eating. "You wheeze like a concertina," Sambo would say disapprovingly as he stood behind my chair; "You're perpetually stuffing yourself with food, that's why." My cough was referred to as a "stomach cough", which made it sound both disgusting and reprehensible. The cure for it was hard running, which, if you kept it up long enough, ultimately "cleared your chest."

It is curious, the degree—I will not say of actual hardship, but of squalor and neglect, that was taken for granted in upper-class schools of that period. Almost as in the days of Thackeray, it seemed natural that a little boy of eight or ten should be a miserable, snotty-nosed creature, his face almost permanently dirty, his hands chapped, his nails bitten, his handkerchief a sodden horror, his bottom frequently blue with bruises. It was partly the prospect of actual physical discomfort that made the thought of going back to school lie in one's breast like a lump of lead during the last few days of the holidays.

A characteristic memory of St. Cyprian's is the astonishing hardness of one's bed on the first night of term. Since this was an expensive school, I took a social step upwards by attending it, and yet the standard of comfort was in every way far lower than in my own home, or, indeed, than it would have been in a prosperous working-class home. One only had a hot bath once a week, for instance. The food was not only bad, it was also insufficient. Never before or since have I seen butter or jam scraped on bread so thinly. I do not think I can be imagining the fact that we were underfed, when I remember the lengths we would go in order to steal food. On a number of occasions I remember creeping down at two or three o'clock in the morning through what seemed like miles of pitch-dark stairways and passages—barefooted, stopping to listen after each step, paralysed with about equal fear of Sambo, ghosts and burglars—to steal stale bread from the pantry. The assistant masters had their meals with us, but they had somewhat better food, and if one got half a chance it was usual to steal left-over scraps of bacon rind or fried potato when their plates were removed.

As usual, I did not see the sound commercial reason for this under-feeding. On the whole I accepted Sambo's view that a boy's appetite is a sort of morbid growth which should be kept in check as much as possible. A maxim often repeated to us at St. Cyprian's was that it is healthy to get up from a meal feeling as hungry as when you sat down. Only a generation earlier than this it had been common for school dinners to start off with a slab of unsweetened suet pudding, which, it was frankly said, "broke the boys' appetites." But the underfeeding was probably less flagrant at preparatory schools, where a boy was wholly dependent on the official diet, than at public schools, where he was allowed—indeed, expected—to buy extra food for himself. At some schools,[18] he would literally not have had enough to eat unless he had bought regular supplies of eggs, sausages, sardines, etc.; and his parents had to allow him money for this purpose. At Eton, for instance, at any rate in College, a boy was given no solid meal after mid-day dinner. For his afternoon tea he was given only tea and bread and butter, and at eight o'clock he was given a miserable supper of soup or fried fish, or more often bread and cheese, with water to drink. Sambo went down to see his eldest son at Eton and came back in snobbish ecstasies over the luxury in which the boys lived. "They give them fried fish for supper!" he exclaimed, beaming all over his chubby face. "There's no school like it in the world." Fried fish! The habitual supper of the poorest of the working class! At very cheap boarding-schools it was no doubt worse. A very early memory of mine is of seeing the boarders at a grammar school—the sons, probably, of farmers and shop-keepers—being fed on boiled lights.

Whoever writes about his childhood must beware of exaggeration and self-pity. I do not want to claim that I was a martyr or that St. Cyprian's was a sort of Dotheboys Hall. But I should be falsifying my own memories if I did not record that they are largely memories of disgust. The overcrowded, underfed, underwashed life that we led *was* disgusting, as I recall it. If I shut my eyes and say "school," it is of course the physical surroundings that first come back to me: the flat playing-field with its cricket pavilion and the little shed by the rifle range, the draughty[19] dormitories, the dusty splintery passages, the square of asphalt in front of the gymnasium, the raw-looking pinewood chapel at the back. And at almost every point some filthy detail obtrudes itself. For example, there were the pewter bowls out of which we had our porridge. They had overhanging rims, and under the rims there were accumulations of sour porridge, which could be flaked off in long strips. The porridge itself, too, contained more lumps, hair and unexplained black things than one would have thought possible, unless someone were putting them there on purpose. It was never safe to start on that porridge without investigating it first. And there was the slimy water of the plunge bath—it was twelve or fifteen feet long, the whole school was supposed to go into it every morning, and I doubt whether the water was changed at all frequently—and the always-damp towels with their cheesy smell; and, on occasional visits in the winter, the murky sea-water of the Devonshire Baths, which came straight in from the beach and on which I once saw floating a human turd. And the sweaty smell of the changing-room with its greasy basins, and, giving on this, the row of filthy, dilapidated lavatories, which had no fastenings of any kind on the doors, so that whenever you were sitting there someone was sure to come crashing in. It is not easy for me to think of my schooldays without seeming to breathe in a whiff of something cold and evil-smelling—a sort of compound of sweaty stockings, dirty towels, faecal smells blowing along corridors, forks with old food between the prongs,[20] neck-of-mutton stew, and the banging doors of the[21] lavatories and the echoing chamberpots in[22] the dormitories.

It is true that I am by nature not gregarious, and the W.C. and dirty-handkerchief side of life is necessarily more obtrusive when great numbers of human beings are crushed together in [a] small space. It is just as bad in an army, and worse, no doubt, in a prison. Besides, boyhood is the[23] age of disgust. After one has learned to differentiate, and before one has become hardened—between seven and eighteen, say—one seems always to be walking the tightrope over a cesspool. Yet I do not think I exaggerate the squalor of school life, when I remember how health and cleanliness were neglected, in spite of the hoo-ha about fresh air and cold water and keeping in hard training. It was common to remain constipated for days together. Indeed, one was hardly encouraged to keep one's bowels open, since the only aperients tolerated were Castor Oil or another almost equally horrible drink called Liquorice Powder. One was supposed to go into the plunge bath every morning, but some boys shirked it for days on end, simply making themselves scarce when the bell sounded, or else slipping along the edge of the bath among the crowd, and then wetting their hair with a little dirty water off the floor. A little boy of eight or nine will not necessarily keep himself clean unless there is someone to see that he does it. There was a new boy named Bachelor, a pretty, mother's darling of a boy, who came a little while before I left. The first thing I noticed about him was the beautiful pearly whiteness of his teeth. By the end of that term his teeth were an extraordinary shade of green. During all that time, apparently, no one had taken sufficient interest in him to see that he brushed them.

But of course the differences between home and school were more than physical. That bump on the hard mattress, on the first night of term, used to give me a feeling of abrupt awakening, a feeling of: "This is reality, this is what you are up against." Your home might be far from perfect, but at least it was a place ruled by love rather than by fear, where you did not have to be perpetually on your guard against the people surrounding you. At eight years old you were suddenly taken out of this warm nest and flung into a world of force and fraud and secrecy, like a goldfish into a tank full of pike. Against no matter what degree of bullying you had no redress. You could only have defended yourself by sneaking, which, except in a few rigidly defined circumstances, was the unforgivable sin. To write home and ask your parents to take you away would have been even less thinkable, since to do so would have been to admit yourself unhappy and unpopular, which a boy will never do. Boys are Erewhonians: they think that misfortune is disgraceful and must be concealed at all costs. It might perhaps have been considered permissible to complain to your parents about bad food, or an unjustified caning, or some other ill-treatment inflicted by masters and not by boys. The fact that Sambo never beat the richer boys suggests that such complaints were made occasionally. But in my own peculiar circumstances I could never have asked my parents to intervene on my behalf. Even before I understood about the reduced fees, I grasped that they were in some way under an obligation to Sambo, and therefore could not protect me against him. I have mentioned already that throughout my time at St. Cyprian's I never had a cricket bat of my own. I had been told this was because "your parents couldn't afford it." One day in the holidays, by some casual remark, it came out that they had provided ten shillings to buy me one: yet no cricket bat appeared. I did not protest to my parents, let alone raise the subject with Sambo. How could I? I was dependent on him, and the ten shillings was merely a fragment of what I owed him. I realise now of course, that it is immensely unlikely that Sambo had simply stuck to the money. No doubt the matter had slipped his memory. But the point is that I assumed that he had stuck to it, and that he had a right to do so if he chose.

How difficult it is for a child to have any real independence of attitude could be seen in our behaviour towards Flip. I think it would be true to say that every boy in the school hated and feared her. Yet we all fawned on her in the most abject way, and the top layer of our feelings towards her was a sort of guilt-stricken loyalty. Flip, although the discipline of the school depended more on her than on Sambo, hardly pretended to dispense strict justice. She was frankly capricious. An act which might get you a caning one day, might next day be laughed off as a boyish prank, or even commended because it "showed you had guts." There were days when everyone cowered before those deepset, accusing eyes, and there were days when she was like a flirtatious queen surrounded by courtier-lovers, laughing and joking, scattering largesse, or the promise of largesse ("And if you win the Harrow History Prize I'll give you a new case for your camera!"), and occasionally even packing three or four favoured boys into her Ford car and carrying them off to a teashop in town, where they were allowed to buy coffee and cakes. Flip was inextricably mixed up in my mind with Queen Elizabeth, whose relations with Leicester and Essex and Raleigh were intelligible to me from a very early age. A word we all constantly used in speaking of Flip was "favour." "I'm in good favour," we would say, or "I'm in bad favour." Except for the handful of wealthy or titled boys, no one was permanently in good favour, but on the other hand even the outcasts had patches of it from time to time. Thus, although my memories of Flip are mostly hostile, I also remember considerable periods when I basked under her smiles, when she called me "old chap" and used my Christian name, and allowed me to frequent her private library, where I first made acquaintance with "Vanity Fair." The high-water mark of good favour was to be invited to serve at table on Sunday nights when Flip and Sambo had guests to dinner. In clearing away, of course, one had a chance to finish off the scraps, but one also got a servile[24] pleasure from standing behind the seated guests and darting deferentially forward when something was wanted. Whenever one had the chance to suck up, one did suck up, and at the first smile one's hatred turned into a sort of cringing love. I was always tremendously proud when I succeeded in making Flip laugh. I have even, at her command, written vers d'occasion, comic verses to celebrate memorable events in the life of the school.

I am anxious to make it clear that I was not a rebel, except by force of circumstances. I accepted the codes that I found in being. Once, towards the end of my time, I even sneaked to Siller about a suspected case of homosexuality. I did not know very well what homosexuality was, but I knew that it happened and was bad, and that this was one of the contexts in which it was proper to sneak. Siller told me I was "a good fellow," which made me feel horribly ashamed. Before Flip one seemed as helpless as a snake before the snake-charmer. She had a hardly-varying vocabulary of praise and abuse, a whole series of set phrases, each of which promptly called forth the appropriate response. There was "*Buck* up, old chap!", which inspired one to paroxysms of energy; there was "Don't *be* such a fool!" (or, "It's path*e*tic, isn't it?"), which made one feel a born idiot; and there was "It isn't very straight of you, is it?", which always brought one to the brink of tears. And yet all the while, at the middle of one's heart, there seemed to stand an incorruptible inner self who knew that whatever one did—whether one laughed or snivelled or went into frenzies of gratitude for small favours— one's only true feeling was hatred.

iv.

I had learned early in my career that one can do wrong against one's will, and before long I also learned that one can do wrong without ever discovering what one has done or why it was wrong. There were sins that were too subtle to be explained, and there were others that were too terrible to be clearly mentioned. For example, there was sex, which was always smouldering just under the surface and which suddenly blew up into a tremendous row when I was about twelve.

At some[25] preparatory schools homosexuality is not a problem, but I think that St. Cyprian's may have acquired a "bad tone" thanks to the presence of the South American boys, who would perhaps mature a year or two earlier than an English boy.[26] At that age I was not interested, so I do not actually know what went on, but I imagine it was group masturbation. At any rate, one day the storm suddenly burst over our heads. There were summonses, interrogations, confessions, floggings, repentances, solemn lectures of which one understood nothing except that some irredeemable sin known as "swinishness" or "beastliness" had been committed. One of the ringleaders, a boy named Cross,[27] was flogged, according to eyewitnesses, for a quarter of an hour continuously before being expelled. His yells rang through the house. But we were all implicated, more or less, or felt ourselves to be implicated. Guilt seemed to hang in the air like a pall of smoke. A solemn, blackhaired imbecile of an assistant master, who was later to be a Member of Parliament, took the older boys to a secluded room and delivered a talk on the Temple of the Body.[28]

"Don't you realise what a wonderful thing your body is?" he said gravely. "You talk of your[29] motor-car engines, your Rolls-Royces and Daimlers and so on. Don't you understand that no engine ever made is fit to be compared with your body? And then you go and wreck it, ruin it—for life!"

He turned his cavernous black eyes on me and added sadly:

"And you, whom I'd always [believed][30] to be quite a decent person after your fashion—you, I hear, are one of the very worst."

A feeling of doom descended upon me. So I was guilty too. I too had done the dreadful thing, whatever it was, that wrecked you for life, body and soul, and ended in suicide or the lunatic asylum. Till then I had hoped that I was innocent, and the conviction of sin which now took possession of me was perhaps all the stronger because I did not know what I had done. I was not among those who were interrogated and flogged, and it was not until after the row was well over that I even learned about the trivial accident which had connected my name with it. Even then I understood nothing. It was not till about two years later that I fully grasped what that lecture on the Temple of the Body had referred to.

At this time I was in an almost sexless state, which is normal, or at any rate common, in boys of that age; I was therefore in the position of simultaneously knowing and not knowing what used to be called the Facts of Life. At five or six, like many children, I had passed through a phase of sexuality. My friends were the plumber's children up the road, and we used sometimes to play games of a vaguely erotic kind. One was called "playing at doctors," and I remember getting a faint but definitely pleasant thrill from holding a toy trumpet, which was supposed to be a stethoscope, against a little girl's belly. About the same time I fell deeply in love, a far more worshipping kind of love than I have ever felt for anyone since, with a girl named Elsie at the convent school which I attended. She seemed to me grown up, so I suppose she must have been fifteen. After that, as so often happens, all sexual feeling seemed to go out of me for many years. At twelve I knew more than I had known as a young child, but I understood less, because I no longer knew the essential fact that there is something pleasant in sexual activity. Between roughly seven and fourteen, the whole subject seemed to me uninteresting and, when for some reason I was forced to think of it, disgusting. My knowledge of the so-called Facts of Life was derived from animals, and was therefore distorted, and in any case was only intermittent. I knew that animals copulated and that human beings had bodies resembling those of animals: but that human beings also copulated I only knew, as it were, reluctantly, when something, a phrase in the Bible, perhaps, compelled me to remember it. Not having desire, I had no curiosity, and was willing to leave many questions unanswered. Thus, I knew in principle how the baby gets into the woman, but I did not know how it gets out again, because I had never followed the subject up. I knew all the dirty words, and in my bad moments I would repeat them to myself, but I did not know what the worst of them meant, nor want to know. They were abstractly wicked, a sort of verbal charm. While I remained in this state, it was easy for me to remain ignorant of any sexual misdeeds that went on about me, and to be hardly wiser even when the row broke. At most, through the veiled and terrible warnings of Flip, Sambo and all the rest of them, I grasped that the crime of which we were all guilty was somehow connected with the sexual organs. I had noticed, without feeling much interest, that one's penis sometimes stands up of its own accord (this starts happening to a boy long before he has any conscious sexual desires), and I was inclined to believe, or half-believe, that *that* must be the crime. At any rate, it was something to do with the penis—so much I understood. Many other boys, I have no doubt, were equally in the dark.

After the talk on the Temple of the Body (days later, it seems in retrospect: the row seemed to continue for days), a dozen of us were seated at the long shiny table which Sambo used for the scholarship class, under Flip's lowering eye. A long, desolate wail rang out from a room somewhere above. A very small boy named Duncan, aged no more than about ten, who was implicated in some way, was being flogged, or was recovering from a flogging. At the sound, Flip's eyes searched our faces, and settled upon me.

"*You see,*" she said.

I will not swear that she said, "You see what you have done," but that was the sense of it. We were all bowed down with shame. It was *our* fault. Somehow or other we had led poor Duncan astray: *we* were responsible for his agony and his ruin. Then Flip turned upon another boy named Clapham. It is thirty years ago, and I cannot remember for certain whether she merely quoted a verse from the Bible, or whether she actually brought out a Bible and made Clapham read it; but at any rate the text indicated was:

"Whoso shall offend one of these little ones that believe in me, it were better for him that a millstone were hanged about his neck, and that he were drowned in the depth of the sea."

That, too, was terrible. Duncan was one of these little ones;[31] we had offended him; it were better that a millstone were hanged about our necks and that we were drowned in the depth of the sea.

"Have you thought about that, Clapham—have you thought what it means?" Flip said. And Clapham broke down into snivelling tears.

Another boy, Hardcastle, whom I have mentioned already, was similarly overwhelmed with shame by the accusation that he "had black rings round his eyes."

"Have you looked in the glass lately, Hardcastle?" said Flip. "Aren't you ashamed to go about with a face like that? Do you think everyone doesn't know what it means when a boy has black rings round his eyes?"

Once again the load of guilt and fear seemed to settle down upon me. Had *I* got black rings round my eyes? A couple of years later I realised that these were supposed to be a symptom by which masturbators could be detected. But already, without knowing this, I accepted the black rings as a sure sign of depravity, *some* kind of depravity. And many times, even before I grasped the supposed meaning, I have gazed anxiously into the glass, looking for the first hint of that dreaded stigma, the confession which the secret sinner writes upon his own face.

These terrors wore off, or became merely intermittent, without affecting what one might call my official beliefs. It was still true about the madhouse and the suicide's grave, but it was no longer acutely frightening. Some months later it happened that I once again saw Cross, the ringleader who had been flogged and expelled. Cross was one of the outcasts, the son of poor middle-class parents, which was no doubt part of the reason why Sambo had handled him so roughly. The term after his expulsion he went on to

Eastbourne College, the small local public school, which was hideously despised at St. Cyprian's and looked on as "not really" a public school at all. Only a very few boys from St. Cyprian's went there, and Sambo always spoke of them with a sort of contemptuous pity. You had no chance if you went to a school like that: at the best your destiny would be a clerkship. I thought of Cross as a person who at thirteen had already forfeited all hope of any decent future. Physically, morally and socially he was finished. Moreover I assumed that his parents had only sent him to Eastbourne College because after his disgrace no "good" school would have him.

During the following term, when we were out for a walk, we passed Cross in the street. He looked completely normal. He was a strongly-built, rather good-looking boy with black hair. I immediately noticed that he looked better than when I had last seen him—his complexion, previously rather pale, was pinker—and that he did not seem embarrassed at meeting us. Apparently he was not ashamed either of having been expelled, or of being at Eastbourne College. If one could gather anything from the way he looked at us as we filed past, it was that he was glad to have escaped from St. Cyprian's. But the encounter made very little impression on[32] me. I drew no inference from the fact that Cross, ruined in body and soul, appeared to be happy and in good health. I still believed in the sexual mythology that had been taught me by Sambo and Flip. The mysterious, terrible dangers were still there. Any morning the black rings might appear round your eyes and you would know that you too were among the lost ones. Only it no longer seemed to matter very much. These contradictions can exist easily in the mind of a child, because of its own[33] vitality. It accepts—how can it do otherwise?—the nonsense that its elders tell it, but its youthful body, and the sweetness of the physical world, tell it another story. It was the same with Hell, which up to the age of about fourteen I officially believed in. Almost certainly Hell existed, and there were occasions when a vivid sermon could scare you into fits. But somehow it never lasted. The fire that waited for you was real fire, it would hurt in the same way as when you burnt your finger, and *for ever*, but most of the time you could contemplate it without bothering.

v.

The various codes which were presented to you at St. Cyprian's—religious, moral, social and intellectual—contradicted one another if you worked out their implications. The essential conflict was between the tradition of nineteenth-century asceticism[34] and the actually existing luxury and snobbery of the pre-1914 age. On the one side were low-church Bible Christianity, sex puritanism, insistence on hard work, respect for academic distinction, disapproval of self-indulgence: on the other, contempt for "braininess" and worship of games, contempt for foreigners and the working class, an almost neurotic dread of poverty, and, above all, the assumption not only that money and privilege are the things that matter, but that it is better to inherit them than to have to work for them. Broadly, you were bidden to be at once a Christian and a social success, which is impossible. At the time I did not perceive that the various ideals which were set before us cancelled out. I merely saw that they were all, or nearly all, unattainable, so far as I was concerned, since they all depended not only on what you did but on what you *were*.

Very early, at the age of only ten or eleven, I reached the conclusion—no one told me this, but on the other hand I did not simply make it up out of my own head: somehow it was in the air I breathed—that you were no good unless you had £100,000. I had perhaps fixed on this particular sum as a result of reading Thackeray. The interest on £100,000 would be £4,000 a year (I was in favour of a safe 4 percent), and this seemed to me the minimum income that you must possess if you were to belong to the real top crust, the people in the country houses. But it was clear that I could never find my way into that paradise, to which you did not really belong unless you were born into it. You could only *make* money, if at all, by a mysterious operation called "going into the City," and when you came out of the City, having won your £100,000, you were fat and old. But the truly enviable thing about the top-notchers was that they were rich while young. For people like me, the ambitious middle-class, the examination passers, only a bleak, laborious kind of success was possible. You clambered upwards on a ladder of scholarships into the Home[35] Civil Service or the Indian Civil Service, or possibly you became a barrister. And if at any point you "slacked" or "went off" and missed one of the rungs in the ladder, you became "a little office boy at forty pounds a year." But even if you climbed to the highest niche that was open to you, you could still only be an underling, a hanger-on of the people who really counted.

Even if I had not learned this from Sambo and Flip, I would have learned it from the other boys. Looking back, it is astonishing how intimately, intelligently snobbish we all were, how knowledgeable about names and addresses, how swift to detect small differences in accents and manners and the cut of clothes. There were some boys who seemed to drip money from their pores even in the bleak misery of the middle of a winter term. At the beginning and end of the term, especially, there was naively snobbish chatter about Switzerland, and Scotland with its ghillies and grouse moors, and "my uncle's yacht," and "our place in the country," and "my pony" and "my pater's touring car." There never was, I suppose, in the history of the world a time when the sheer vulgar fatness of wealth, without any kind of aristocratic elegance to redeem it, was so obtrusive as in those years before 1914. It was the age when crazy millionaires in curly top hats and lavender waistcoats gave champagne parties in rococo houseboats on the Thames, the age of diabolo and hobble skirts, the age of the "knut" in his grey bowler and cutaway coat, the age of *The Merry Widow*, Saki's novels, *Peter Pan* and *Where the Rainbow Ends*, the age when people talked about chocs and cigs and ripping and topping and heavenly, when they went for divvy weekends at Brighton and had scrumptious teas at the Troc. From the whole decade before 1914 there seems to breathe forth a smell of the more vulgar, un-grown-up kinds of luxury, a smell of brilliantine and crème de menthe and soft-centre chocolates, —an atmosphere, as it were, of eating everlasting strawberry ices on green lawns to the tune of the Eton Boating Song. The extraordinary thing was the way in which everyone took it for granted that this oozing, bulging wealth of the English upper and upper-middle classes would last for ever, and was part of the order of things. After 1918 it was never quite the same again. Snobbishness and expensive habits came back, certainly, but they were self-conscious and on the defensive. Before the war the worship of money was entirely unreflecting and untroubled by any pang of conscience. The goodness of money was as unmistakeable as the goodness of health or beauty, and a glittering car, a title or a horde of servants was mixed up in people's minds with the idea of actual moral virtue.

At St. Cyprian's, in term time, the general bareness[36] of life enforced a certain democracy, but any mention of the holidays, and the consequent competitive swanking about cars and butlers and country houses, promptly called class distinctions into being. The school was pervaded by a curious cult of Scotland, which brought out the fundamental contradiction in our standard of values. Flip claimed Scottish ancestry, and she favoured the Scottish boys, encouraging them to wear kilts in their ancestral tartan instead of the school uniform,[37] and even christened her youngest child by a Gaelic name. Ostensibly we were supposed to admire the Scots because they were "grim" and "dour" ("stern" was perhaps the key word), and irresistible on the field of battle. In the big schoolroom there was a steel engraving of the charge of the Scots Greys at Waterloo, all looking as though they enjoyed every moment of it. Our picture of Scotland was made up of burns, braes, kilts, sporrans, claymores, bagpipes[38] and the like, all somehow mixed up with the invigorating effects of porridge, Protestantism and a cold climate. But underlying this was something quite different. The real reason for the cult of Scotland was that only very rich people could spend their summers there. And the pretended belief in Scottish superiority was a cover for the bad conscience of the occupying English, who had pushed the Highland peasantry off their farms to make way for the deer forests, and then compensated them by turning them into servants. Flip's face always beamed with innocent snobbishness when she spoke of Scotland. Occasionally she even attempted a trace of Scottish accent. Scotland was a private paradise which a few initiates could talk about and make outsiders feel small.

"You going to Scotland this hols?"

"Rather! We go every year."

"My pater's got three miles of river."

"My pater's giving me a new gun for the twelfth. There's jolly good black game where we go. Get out, Smith! What are you listening for? You've never been in Scotland. I bet you don't know what a black-cock[39] looks like."

Following on this, imitations of the cry of a black-cock, of the roaring of a stag, of the accent of "our ghillies," etc., etc.

And the questionings that new boys of doubtful social origin were sometimes put through—questionings quite surprising in their mean-minded particularity, when one reflects that the inquisitors were only twelve or thirteen!

"How much a year has your pater got? What part of London do you live in? Is that Knightsbridge or Kensington? How many bathrooms has your house got? How many servants do your people keep? Have you got a butler? Well, then, have you got a cook? Where do you get your clothes made? How many shows did you go to in the hols? How much money did you bring back with you?" etc., etc.

I have seen a little new boy, hardly older than eight, desperately lying his way through such a catechism:

"Have your people got a car?"

"Yes."

"What sort of car?"

"Daimler."

"How many horse-power?"

(Pause, and leap in the dark.) "Fifteen."

"What kind of lights?"

The little boy is bewildered.

"What kind of lights? Electric or acetylene?"

(A longer pause, and another leap in the dark.) "Acetylene."

"Coo! He says his pater's car's got acetylene lamps. They went out years ago. It must be as old as the hills."

"Rot! He's making it up. He hasn't got a car. He's just a navvy. Your pater's a navvy."

And so on.

By the social standards that prevailed about me, I was no good, and could not be any good. But all the different kinds of virtue seemed to be mysteriously interconnected and to belong to much the same people. It was not only money that mattered: there were also strength, beauty, charm, athleticism and something called "guts" or "character," which in reality meant the power to[40] impose your will on others. I did not possess any of these qualities. At games, for instance, I was hopeless. I was a fairly good swimmer and not altogether contemptible at cricket, but these had no prestige value, because boys only attach importance to a game if it requires strength and courage. What counted was football, at which I was a funk. I loathed the game, and since I could see no pleasure or usefulness in it, it was very difficult for me to show courage at it. Football, it seemed to me, is not really played for the pleasure of kicking a ball about, but is a species of fighting. The lovers of football are large, boisterous, nobbly boys who are good at knocking down and trampling on slightly smaller boys. That was the pattern of school life—a continuous triumph of the strong over the weak. Virtue consisted in winning: it consisted in being bigger, stronger, handsomer,[41] richer, more popular, more elegant, more unscrupulous than other people—in dominating them, bullying them, making them suffer pain, making them look foolish, getting the better of them in every way. Life was hierarchical and whatever happened was right. There were the strong, who deserved to win and always did win, and there were the weak, who deserved to lose and always did lose, everlastingly.

I did not question the prevailing standards, because so far as I could see there were no others. How could the rich, the strong, the elegant, the fashionable, the powerful, be in the wrong? It was their world, and the rules they made for it must be the right ones. And yet from a very early age I was aware of the impossibility of any *subjective* conformity. Always at the centre of my heart the inner self seemed to be awake, pointing out the difference between the moral obligation and the psychological *fact*. It was the same in all matters, worldly or other-worldly. Take religion, for instance. You were supposed to love God and I did not question this. Till the age of about fourteen I believed in God, and believed that the accounts given of him were true. But I was well aware that I did not love him. On the contrary, I hated him, just as I hated Jesus and the Hebrew patriarchs. If I had sympathetic feelings towards any character in the Old Testament, it was towards such people as Cain, Jezebel, Haman, Agag, Sisera: in the New Testament my friends, if any, were Ananias, Caiaphas, Judas and Pontius Pilate. But the whole business of religion seemed to be strewn with psychological impossibilities. The Prayer Book told you, for example, to love God and fear him: but how could you love someone whom you feared? With your private affections it was the same. What you *ought* to feel was usually clear enough, but the appropriate emotion could not be commanded. Obviously it was my duty to feel grateful towards Flip and Sambo; but I was not grateful. It was equally clear that one ought to love one's father, but I knew very well that I merely disliked my own father, whom I had barely seen before I was eight and who appeared to me simply as a gruff-voiced elderly man forever saying "Don't." It was not that one did not want to possess the right qualities or feel the correct emotions, but that one could not. The good and the possible never seemed to coincide.

There was a line of verse that I came across not actually while I was at St. Cyprian's, but a year or two later, and which seemed to strike a sort of leaden echo in my heart. It was: "The armies of unalterable law."[41a] I understood to perfection what it meant to be Lucifer, defeated and justly defeated, with no possibility of revenge. The schoolmasters with their canes, the millionaires with their Scottish castles, the athletes with their curly hair—these were the armies of the unalterable law. It was not easy, at that date, to realise that in fact it *was* alterable. And according to that law I was damned. I had no money, I was weak, I was ugly, I was unpopular, I had a chronic cough, I was cowardly, I smelt. This picture, I should add, was not altogether fanciful. I was an unattractive boy. St. Cyprian's soon made me so, even if I had not been so before. But a child's belief in its own shortcomings is not much influenced by facts. I believed, for example, that I "smelt," but this was based simply on general probability. It was notorious that disagreeable people smelt, and therefore presumably I did so too. Again, until after I had left school for good I continued to believe that I was preternaturally ugly. It was what my schoolfellows had told me, and I had no other authority to refer to. The conviction that it was *not possible* for me to be a success went deep enough to influence my actions till far into adult life. Until I was about thirty I always planned my life on the assumption not only that any major undertaking was bound to fail, but that I could only expect to live a few years longer.

But this sense of guilt and inevitable failure was balanced by something else: that is, the instinct to survive. Even a creature that is weak, ugly, cowardly, smelly and in no way justifiable still wants to stay alive and be happy after its own fashion. I could not invert the existing scale of values, or turn myself into a success, but I could accept my failure and make the best of it. I could resign myself to being what I was, and then endeavour to survive on those terms.

To survive, or at least to preserve any kind of independence, was essentially criminal, since it meant breaking rules which you yourself recognized. There was a boy named Cliffy Burton[42] who for some months oppressed me horribly. He was a big, powerful, coarsely handsome boy with a very red face and curly black hair, who was forever twisting somebody's arm, wringing somebody's ear, flogging somebody with a riding crop (he was a member of Sixth Form), or performing prodigies of activity on the football field. Flip loved him (hence the fact that he was habitually called by his Christian name), and Sambo commended him as a boy who "had character" and "could keep order." He was followed about by a group of toadies who nicknamed him Strong Man.[43]

One day, when we were taking off our overcoats in the changing-room, Burton picked on me for some reason. I "answered him back," whereupon he gripped my wrist, twisted it round and bent my forearm back upon itself in a hideously painful way. I remember his handsome, jeering red face bearing down upon mine. He was, I think, older than I, besides being enormously stronger. As he let go of me a terrible, wicked resolve formed itself in my heart. I would get back on him by hitting him when he did not expect it. It was a strategic moment, for the master who had been "taking" the walk would be coming back almost immediately, and then there could be no fight. I let perhaps a minute go by, walked up to Burton with the most harmless air I could assume, and then, getting the weight of my body behind it, smashed my fist into his face. He was flung backwards by the blow, and some blood ran out of his mouth. His always sanguine face turned almost black with rage. Then he turned away to rinse his mouth at the washing-basins.

"*All right!*" he said to me between his teeth as the master led us away.

For days after this he followed me about, challenging me to fight. Although terrified out of my wits, I steadily refused to fight. I said that the blow in the face had served him right, and there was an end of it. Curiously enough he did not simply fall upon me there and then, which public opinion would probably have supported him in doing. So gradually the matter tailed off, and there was no fight.

Now, I had behaved wrongly, by my own code no less than his. To hit him unawares was wrong. But to refuse afterwards to fight, knowing that if we fought he would beat me—that was far worse: it was cowardly. If I had refused because I disapproved of fighting, or because I genuinely felt the matter to be closed, it would have been all right; but I had refused merely because I was afraid. Even my revenge was made empty by that fact. I had struck the blow in a moment of mindless violence, deliberately not looking far ahead and merely determined to get my own back for once and damn the consequences. I had had time to realise that what I did was wrong, but it was the kind of crime from which you could get some satisfaction. Now all was nullified. There had been a sort of courage in the first act, but my subsequent cowardice had wiped it out.

The fact I hardly noticed was that though Burton formally challenged me to fight, he did not actually attack me. Indeed, after receiving that one blow he never oppressed me again. It was perhaps twenty years before I saw the significance of this. At the time I could not see beyond the moral dilemma that is presented to the weak in a world governed by the strong: Break the rules, or perish. I did not see that in that case the weak have the right to make a different set of rules for themselves; because, even if such an idea had occurred to me, there was no one in my environment who could have confirmed me in it. I lived in a world of boys, gregarious animals, questioning nothing, accepting the law of the stronger and avenging their own humiliations by passing them down to someone smaller. My situation was that of countless other boys, and if potentially I was more of a rebel than most, it was only because, by boyish standards, I was a poorer specimen. But I never did rebel intellectually, only emotionally. I had nothing to help me except my dumb selfishness, my inability—not, indeed, to despise myself, but to *dislike* myself—my instinct to survive.

It was about a year after I hit Cliffy Burton in the face that I left St. Cyprian's for ever. It was the end of a winter term. With a sense of coming out from darkness into sunlight I put on my Old Boy's tie as we dressed for the journey. I well remember the feeling of that brand-new silk tie round my neck, a feeling of emancipation, as though the tie had been at once a badge of manhood and an amulet against Flip's voice and Sambo's cane. I was escaping from bondage. It was not that I expected, or even intended, to be any more successful at a public school than I had been at St. Cyprian's. But still, I was escaping. I knew that at a public school there would be more privacy, more neglect, more chance to be idle and self-indulgent and degenerate. For years past I had been resolved—unconsciously at first, but consciously later on—that when once my scholarship was won I would "slack off" and cram no longer. This resolve, by the way, was so fully carried out that between the ages of thirteen and twenty-two or three I hardly ever did a stroke of avoidable work.

Flip shook hands to say good-bye. She even gave me my Christian name for the occasion. But there was a sort of patronage, almost a sneer, in her face and in her voice. The tone in which she said good-bye was nearly the tone in which she had been used to say *little butterflies*. I had won two scholarships, but I was a failure, because success was measured not by what you did but by what you *were*. I was "not a good type of boy" and could bring no credit on the school. I did not possess character or courage or health or strength or money, or even good manners, the power to look like a gentleman.

"Good-bye," Flip's parting smile seemed to say; "it's not worth quarrelling now. You haven't made much of a success of your time at St. Cyprian's, have you? And I don't suppose you'll get on awfully well at a public school either. We made a mistake, really, in wasting our time and money on you. This kind of education hasn't much to offer to a boy with your background and your outlook. Oh, don't think we don't understand you! We know all about those ideas you have at the back of your head, we know you disbelieve in everything we've taught you, and we know you aren't in the least grateful for all we've done for you. But there's no use in bringing it all up now. We aren't responsible for you any longer, and we shan't be seeing you again. Let's just admit that you're one of our failures and part without ill-feeling. And so, good-bye."

That at least was what I read into her face. And yet how happy I was, that winter morning, as the train bore me away with the gleaming new silk tie (dark green, pale blue and black, if I remember rightly) round my neck! The world was opening before me, just a little, like a grey sky which exhibits a narrow crack of blue. A public school would be better fun than St. Cyprian's, but at bottom equally alien. In a world where the prime necessities were money, titled relatives, athleticism, tailor-made clothes, neatly-brushed hair, a charming smile, I was no good. All I had gained was a breathing-space. A little quietude, a little self-indulgence, a little respite from cramming—and then, ruin. What kind of ruin I did not know: perhaps the colonies or an office stool, perhaps prison or an early death. But first a year or two in which one could "slack off" and get the benefit of one's sins, like Doctor Faustus. I believed firmly in my evil destiny, and yet I was acutely happy. It is the advantage of being thirteen that you can not only live in the moment, but do so with full consciousness, foreseeing the future and yet not caring about it. Next term I was going to Wellington. I had also won a scholarship at Eton, but it was uncertain whether there would be a vacancy, and I was going to Wellington first. At Eton you had a room to yourself—a room which might even have a fire in it. At Wellington you had your own cubicle, and could make yourself cocoa in the evenings. The privacy of it, the grown-upness! And there would be libraries to hang about in, and summer afternoons when you could shirk games and mooch about the countryside alone, with no master driving you along. Meanwhile there were the holidays. There was the .22 rifle that I had bought the previous holidays (the Crackshot, it was called, costing twenty-two and sixpence), and Christmas was coming next week. There were also the pleasures of over-eating. I thought of some particularly voluptuous cream buns with could be bought for twopence each at a shop in our town. (This was 1916, and food-rationing had not yet started.) Even the detail that my journey-money had been slightly miscalculated, leaving about a shilling over—enough for an unforeseen cup of coffee and a cake or two somewhere on the way—was enough to fill me with bliss. There was time for a bit of happiness before the future closed in upon me. But I did know that the future was dark. Failure, failure, failure—failure behind me, failure ahead of me—that was by far the deepest conviction that I carried away.

vi.

All this was thirty years ago and more. The question is: Does a child at school go through the same kind of experiences nowadays?

The only honest answer, I believe, is that we do not with certainty know. Of course it is obvious that the present-day *attitude* towards education is enormously more humane and sensible than that of the past. The snobbish-ness that was an integral part of my own education would be almost unthinkable today, because the society that nourished it is dead. I recall a conversation that must have taken place about a year before I left St. Cyprian's. A Russian boy, large and fair-haired, a year older than myself, was questioning me.

"How much a-year° has your father got?"

I told him what I thought it was, adding a few hundreds to make it sound better. The Russian boy, neat in his habits, produced a pencil and a small notebook and made a calculation.

"My father has over two hundred times as much money as yours," he announced with a sort of amused contempt.

That was in[44] 1915. What happened to that money a couple of years later, I wonder? And still more I wonder, do conversations of that kind happen at preparatory schools now?

Clearly[45] there has been a vast change of outlook, a general growth of "enlightenment," even among ordinary, unthinking middle-class people. Religious belief, for instance, has largely vanished, dragging other kinds of nonsense after it. I imagine that very few people nowadays would tell a child that if it masturbates it will end in the lunatic asylum. Beating, too, has become discredited, and has even been abandoned at many schools. Nor is the underfeeding of children looked on as a normal, almost meritorious act. No one now would openly set out to give his pupils as little food as they could do with, or tell them that it is healthy to get up from a meal as hungry as you sat down. The whole status of children has improved, partly because they have grown relatively less numerous. And the diffusion of even a little psychological knowledge has made it harder for parents and schoolteachers to indulge their aberrations in the name of discipline. Here is a case, not known to me personally, but known to someone I can vouch for, and happening within my own lifetime. A small girl, daughter of a clergyman, continued wetting her bed at an age when she should have grown out of it. In order to punish her for this dreadful deed, her father took her to a large garden party and there introduced her to the whole company as a little girl who wetted her bed: and to underline her wickedness he had previously painted her face black. I do not suggest that Flip and Sambo would actually have done a thing like this, but I doubt whether it would have much surprised them. After all, things do change. And yet—!

The question is not whether boys are still buckled into Eton collars on Sunday, or told that babies are dug up under gooseberry bushes. That kind of thing is at an end, admittedly. The real question is whether it is still normal for a schoolchild to live for years amid irrational terrors and lunatic misunderstandings. And here one is up against the very great difficulty of knowing what a child really feels and thinks. A child which appears reasonably happy may actually be suffering horrors which it cannot or will not reveal. It lives in a sort of alien under-water world which we can only penetrate by memory or divination. Our chief clue is the fact that we were once children ourselves, and many people appear to forget the atmosphere of their own childhood almost entirely. Think for instance of the unnecessary torments that people will inflict by sending a child back to school with clothes of the wrong pattern, and refusing to see that this matters![46] Over things of this kind a child will sometimes utter a protest, but a great deal of the time its attitude is one of simple concealment. Not to expose your true feelings to an adult seems to be instinctive from the age of seven or eight onwards. Even the affection that one feels for a child, the desire to protect and cherish it, is a cause of misunderstandings. One can love a child, perhaps, more deeply than one can love another adult, but it is rash to assume that the child feels any love in return. Looking back on my childhood, after the infant years were over, I do not believe that I ever felt love for any mature person except my mother, and even her I did not trust, in the sense that shyness made me conceal most of my real feelings from her. Love, the spontaneous, unqualified emotion of love, was something I could only feel for people who were young. Towards people who were old—and remember that "old" to a child means over thirty, or even over twenty-five—I could feel reverence, respect, admiration or compunction, but I seemed cut off from them by a veil of fear and shyness mixed up with physical distaste. People are too ready to forget the child's *physical* shrinking from the adult. The enormous size of grown-ups, their ungainly, rigid bodies, their coarse, wrinkled skins, their great relaxed eyelids, their yellow teeth, and the whiffs of musty clothes and beer and sweat and tobacco that disengage from them at every movement! Part of the reason for the ugliness of adults, in a child's eyes, is that the child is usually looking upwards, and few faces are at their best when seen from below. Besides, being fresh and unmarked itself, the child has impossibly high standards in the matter of skin and teeth and complexion. But the greatest barrier of all is the child's misconception about age. A child can hardly envisage life beyond thirty, and in judging people's ages it will make fantastic mistakes. It will think that a person of twenty-five is forty, that a person of forty is sixty-five, and so on. Thus, when I fell in love with Elsie I took her to be grown-up. I met her again, when I was thirteen and she, I think, must have been twenty-three; she now seemed to me a middle-aged woman, somewhat past her best. And the child thinks of growing old as an almost obscene calamity, which for some[47] mysterious reason will never happen to itself. All who have passed the age of thirty are joyless grotesques, endlessly fussing about things of no importance and staying alive without, so far as the child can see, having anything to live for. Only child life is real life. The schoolmaster who imagines that he is loved and trusted by his boys is in fact mimicked and laughed at behind his back. An adult who does not seem dangerous nearly always seems ridiculous.

I base these generalisations on what I can recall of my own childhood outlook. Treacherous though memory is, it seems to me the chief means we have of discovering how a child's mind works. Only by resurrecting our own memories can we realise how incredibly distorted is the child's vision of the world. Consider this, for example. How would St. Cyprian's appear to me now, if I could go back, at my present age, and see it as it was in 1915? What should I think of Sambo and Flip, those terrible, all-powerful monsters? I should see them as a couple of silly, shallow, ineffectual people, eagerly clambering up a social ladder which any thinking person could see to be on the point of collapse. I would no more be frightened of them than I would be frightened of a dormouse. Moreover, in those days they seemed to me fantastically old, whereas—though of this I am not certain—I imagine they must have been somewhat younger than I am now. And how would Cliffy Burton appear, with his blacksmith's arms and his red, jeering face? Merely a scruffy little boy, barely distinguishable from hundreds of other scruffy little boys. The two sets of facts can lie side by side in my mind, because those happen to be my own memories. But it would be very difficult for me to see with the eyes of any other child, except by an effort of the imagination which might lead me completely astray. The child and the adult live in different worlds. If that is so, we cannot be certain that school, at any rate boarding school, is not still for many children as dreadful an experience as it used to be. Take away God, Latin, the cane, class distinctions and sexual taboos, and the fear, the hatred, the snobbery and the misunderstanding might still all be there. It will have been seen that my own main trouble was an utter lack of any sense of proportion or probability. This led me to accept outrages and believe absurdities, and to suffer torments over things which were in fact of no importance. It is not enough to say that I was "silly" and "ought to have known better." Look back into your own childhood and think of the nonsense you used to believe and the trivialities which could[48] make you suffer. Of course my own case had its individual variations, but essentially it was that of countless other boys. The weakness of the child is that it starts with a blank sheet. It neither understands nor questions the society in which it lives, and because of its credulity other people can work upon it, infecting it with the sense of inferiority and the dread of offending against mysterious, terrible laws. It may be that everything that happened to me at St. Cyprian's could happen in the most "enlightened" school, though perhaps in subtler forms. Of one thing, however, I do feel fairly sure, and that is that boarding schools are worse than day schools. A child has a better chance with the sanctuary of its home near at hand. And I think the characteristic faults of the English upper and middle classes may be partly due to the practice, general until recently, of sending children away from home as young as nine, eight or even seven.

I have never been back to St. Cyprian's. Reunions, old boys' dinners and such-like leave me something more than cold, even when my memories are friendly. I have never even been down to Eton, where I was relatively happy, though I did once pass through it in 1933 and noted with interest that nothing seemed to have changed, except that the shops now sold radios. As for St. Cyprian's, for years I loathed its very name so deeply that I could not view it with enough detachment to see the significance of the things that happened to me there. In a way, it is only within the last decade that I have really thought over my schooldays, vividly though their memory has always haunted me. Nowadays, I believe, it would make very little impression on me to see the place again, if it still exists. (I remember hearing a rumour some years ago that it had been burnt down.) If I had to pass through Eastbourne I would not make a detour to avoid the school: and if I happened to pass the school itself I might even stop for a moment by the low brick wall, with the steep bank running down from it, and look across the flat playing field at the ugly building with the square of asphalt in front of it. And if I went inside and smelt again the inky, dusty smell of the big schoolroom, the rosiny smell of the chapel, the stagnant smell of the swimming bath and the cold reek of the lavatories, I think I should only feel what one invariably feels in revisiting any scene of childhood: How small everything has grown, and how terrible is the deterioration in myself! But it is a fact that for many years I could hardly have borne to look at it again. Except upon dire necessity I would not have set foot in Eastbourne. I even conceived a prejudice against Sussex, as the county that contained St. Cyprian's, and as an adult I have only once been in Sussex, on a short visit. Now, however, the place is out of my system for good. Its magic works no longer, and I have not even enough animosity left to make me hope that Flip and Sambo are dead or that the story of the school being burnt down was true.[49]

Cyril Connolly annotated his copies of the essay when it was printed in *The Orwell Reader* (1956) and *The Collected Essays Journalism and Letters* (1968). His verbal annotations are here denoted by 'CC'; the two books by 'OR' and 'CEJL.'

1. Perhaps] *handwritten insert*
2. Sambo] *OR has* Sim; *CCOR,* Sambo
3. Lord Poolington° (Savile) in *CCOR;* Ld Polington° / Savile / (Mexborough), *CCCEJL.* This was John Raphael Wentworth Savile, Viscount Pollington (1906–1980), succeeded his father as 7th Earl of Mexborough, 1945. His education continued at Downside and Cambridge. He served in the Intelligence Corps and was in India 1941–45.
4. Against this sentence, *CCOR* has: 'This was an "extra" for which they paid, including myself. Milk & biscuits were "medical." '
5. Begums] *typed* 'Bagams'; 'e' *written over first* 'a'; 'u' *written above second* 'a', *but not in Orwell's hand; OR and CEJL set as* 'Begams'; *CC altered second* 'a' *of OR to* 'u'
6. some] the *in typescript; crossed through and Orwell has written in* some
7. Hastings] Clive *in typescript; Orwell has crossed through this name and written in* Hastings. *OR and CEJL both print* Clive, *CCOR has written* Warren Hastings *in margin.*
8. the] *handwritten insertion by Orwell*
9. "1773 . . . Party!"] *interlinear insertion in Orwell's hand*
10. *In margin, CCOR has see* Dr J—Dr Samuel Johnson.
11. *Typescript has* Knowles, *but OR and CEJL have* Batchelor; *CC annotates both texts* Knowles. *Knowles was a part-time teacher of Latin and Greek; see Shelden,* 47; U.S.: 43.
12. *Typed as* likable; *insertion of* e *probably not by Orwell*
13. *want] handwritten underlining*
14. *to Flip] handwritten insertion by Orwell*
15. *and] handwritten insertion by Orwell*
16. to a village called Birling Gap] *OR omits; CCCEJL has broken underlining to* village. *Birling Gap is very close to the shore on a minor road west of Eastbourne, a little to the south of Eastdean.*
17. Siller] *OR and CEJL have* Brown; *CCCEJL annotates* Siller. This was Robert L. Sillar (spelt with an 'a'). He taught geography and drawing and enthusiastically led the boys in nature-study field-trips, which Orwell greatly enjoyed. See Shelden, 47–48; U.S.: 43–44.
18. some schools] *typed as one school; emendation in Orwell's hand*
19. draughty] *typed as* dreadful; *the emendation is Orwell's but in a rather wavering hand*
20. prongs] *in the margin, in Orwell's hand (but not very firmly) is* tines?
21. the] *handwritten insertion by Orwell*
22. in] *typed as* of; *emended in Orwell's hand*
23. the] *typed as* an; *emended in Orwell's hand*
24. servile] *typed as* senile; *emended in Orwell's hand*

25. some] *handwritten insertion by Orwell*
26. *Marginal annotation, CCCEJL:* Pacheco
27. Cross] *OR and CEJL substitute* Horne; *CCCEJL annotates* Hardcastle
28. *CCOR and CCCEJL annotate* Loseby. Captain Charles Edgar Loseby, M.P. (1881–1970), schoolmaster, then barrister-at-law, wounded Cambrai and awarded MC, 1917; Coalition National Democratic and Labour M.P., 1918–22; barrister in Hong Kong, 1945 to retirement.
29. your] *interlinear insertion in Orwell's hand*
30. [believed]] *interlinear insertion in a hand other than Orwell's*
31. ones;] ones *in original*
32. on] *typed as* one
33. own] physical *inserted after* own *in Orwell's hand, then heavily scored through*
34. asceticism] *typed as* ascetism; *corrected in Orwell's hand*
35. Home] *interlinear insertion in Orwell's hand*
36. bareness] *typed as* barness; *the handwritten correction does not seem to be Orwell's*
37. *CCCEJL has against this line,* Kirkpatricks
38. bagpipes] *typed as* babpipes, *with* g *written over* b *in uncertain hand*
39. *Hyphenated by Sonia Orwell*
40. to] of *typed; editorial emendation*
41. handsomer] d *omitted in typescript; inserted by (Orwell's?) hand*
41a. From George Meredith, 'The Woods of Westermain'.
42. Cliffy Burton] *OR and CEJL print* Johnny Hale; *CCCEJL annotates* Clifford Burton
43. *CCOR annotates?* Burton / ? Bhuna
44. in] *interlinear insertion in Orwell's hand*
45. Clearly] *typescript runs on; manuscript marking for break of paragraph*
46. matters!] *ends paragraph in typescript;* Orwell *marks to run on*
47. some] *typescript has* one; *emended in Orwell's hand*
48. could] *typescript has* one could; one *is heavily scored through*
49. But it is a fact that for many years . . . was true.] *last five sentences omitted when* 'Such, Such Were the Joys' *was first published* (Partisan Review, *Sept.–Oct. 1952). The school burnt down in May 1939. There was one casualty, a sixteen-year-old servant, Winifred Higgs. The school was not rebuilt (Shelden, 62; U.S.: 57).*

3410. To S. M. Levitas

4 June 1948 Handwritten

Ward 3
Hairmyres Hospital
East Kilbride
Lanarkshire, Scotland

Dear Mr Levitas,

Many thanks for your letter of May 25th.[1] I would like very much to write something for you later, but I am not able to do very much at present. I have been ill (tuberculosis) since last autumn & in hospital since before Christmas. It is still on my conscience that last November[2] you sent me a proof of an article by James Burnham & asked me to write a commentary on it. I did not even reply, because I was really very ill at the time & unequal to writing letters. I am now a good deal better, & hope to get out of here about August, though I suppose I shall have to go rather slowly for about a year after that. Meanwhile I am not doing very much work & have rather too much on hand already. But later on I should be delighted to write for the "New Leader" a few times a year, as you suggest.

Yours sincerely
Geo. Orwell

1. S. M. Levitas, Executive Editor of *The New Leader*, New York, had written on 25 May 1948 to say he had seen Orwell's essay 'Writer and Leviathan' in *Politics and Letters*, Summer 1948 (see *3364*). He had asked that journal for permission to reprint the article in *The New Leader* (and it was reprinted, 19 June 1948). He reminded Orwell of his promise of 'about a year ago' (see *3288*) to contribute 'an original piece' for *The New Leader* and said he hoped for three or four articles a year from Orwell. He hoped Orwell was aware that *The New Leader* was 'the only publication of the "left" in this great, big country of ours which had combatted totalitarianism for the last 25 years' and it could boast of the best contributors in America in 'this life and death struggle for decency and democracy.'
2. Levitas had written on 21 October 1947; see *3288*.

3411. Review of *Heyday of a Wizard* by Jean Burton

The Observer, 6 June 1948

Daniel Dunglas Home,[1] the original of Browning's "Mr. Sludge," has the curious distinction of being the only spiritualist medium—at any rate, the only "physical" medium—who was never caught out. His life was lived in a blaze of publicity, and a considerable literature has accumulated round it. The Czar Alexander II, the Empress Eugénie, the King of Prussia and a respectable section of the British aristocracy devoutly believed in him; so did writers and scientists like Ruskin, Bulwer Lytton, Thackeray, Sir William Crookes, Elizabeth Browning and Harriet Beecher Stowe. On countless occasions Home floated through the air, usually in a horizontal position, materialised spirit hands out of nothing, extracted tunes from musical instruments without touching them, and caused heavy pieces of furniture with which he was not in contact to skip about the room like ballet dancers. And in only one very doubtful instance was any evidence of trickery produced against him.

Moreover, nothing that is known of Home's private life suggests that he was a conscious fraud. He was something of a social climber, and made two wealthy marriages, partly as a result of his spiritualistic activities, but he was not venal. He would accept expensive presents such as jewellery, but he refused money payments, and he would not "perform" to order. He dismayed his fellow-mediums by deriding "dark séances" and exposing some of the tricks by which "manifestations" are normally produced. And though he had some bitter enemies, such as Robert Browning, his relationships with other people and his general manner of life make it very difficult to believe that he was a vulgar impostor.

And yet—a point that Miss Jean Burton fails to emphasise—there must have been imposture of some kind. Many of the stories that are told of Home are flatly incredible, all the more so because everything has the appearance of being above-board. Unlike all other "physical" mediums,

Home accomplished some of his most astonishing feats in daylight or strong artificial light, and very often they were tricks of a kind that could not be reproduced by a conjurer, except on prepared ground. For example, William Howitt, author of "The History of the Supernatural," deposes to having seen a table rise off the ground and turn over until its top was perpendicular, a flower pot which was standing on it remaining in place "as if screwed to the surface." The table then sailed into the next room and took up a position above another table, where it remained suspended in the air. It is clear that things of this kind cannot actually have happened. One could begin to believe in them only if there were other recorded instances, and no similar claims have been successfully made for any medium since Home. But one does not solve the problem by writing off the accounts of Home's séances as "all lies" or "all imagination." For, after all, why should reputable and intelligent people conspire to tell stories which were bound to get them laughed at? One must conclude that Home, whether he was conscious of it or not, had some kind of hypnotic power which enabled him to induce delusions in whole groups of people.[2]

Miss Burton hardly discusses this question. Her book is essentially a biography, and she simply relates the facts of Home's life with very little comment, not even definitely rejecting the suggestion that he was an ordinary fraud. The late Mr. Harry Price's introduction does not take the matter much further, though he throws out what is probably a useful hint by classifying Home as a "poltergeist medium." Home, whose heyday was in the 'sixties and 'seventies, did not work under what would now be considered test conditions, and the people who attended his séances are long since dead, but it might be possible to learn more about the nature of his powers by closely examining the records that remain.

His most celebrated feat—and very justly celebrated if it really happened—was to float out of one window and in at the next, three stories above street level. This was very minutely described by two witnesses, but their accounts have been analysed in Mr. Bechhofer Roberts's book on spiritualism, and elsewhere, and shown to be full of inconsistencies. Miss Burton's book makes amusing reading, and it is useful in that it assembles a great deal of information and indicates other sources, but what is most needed is a critical examination of the evidence on which Home's reputation rests. For the phenomena of spiritualism, like the pranks of the poltergeist, are not interesting in themselves. What is interesting is the question of how people can be induced to believe in them: and there, perhaps, this paragon among mediums could be made to yield us a little more information.

1. Daniel Dunglas Home (1833–1886), American spiritualist medium who proved triumphantly successful in the United States and Europe. Browning saw him perform at a séance in Ealing, West London, 23 July 1855. Browning was convinced he was a fraud, but Mrs. Browning, at least initially, thought him genuine. For the poem and useful notes (on which this information draws) see *Robert Browning: The Poems*, edited by John Pettigrew and Thomas J. Collins (1981), I, 821–60, 1162–68; for general background, see K. H. Porter, *Through a Glass Darkly: Spiritualism in the Browning Circle* (1958).
2. On 20 June 1948, *The Observer* published the following letter from Martin Herne:

Mr. George Orwell uses one rather odd argument in his review of Miss Burton's biography of David Home, the celebrated medium. He could "begin to believe" in some of the reported phenomena, he says, "only if there were other recorded instances, and no similar claims have been successfully made". He concludes that Home "had some kind of hypnotic power which enabled him to induce delusions in whole groups of people".

But why should it be easier to believe in this remarkable "hypnotic power?" If there are any "other recorded instances" of it, Mr. Orwell should cite them—remembering that Home seems to have employed none of the usual hypnotic techniques.

There is a great deal of scattered evidence that unexplained movements of objects occur in the neighbourhood of certain persons; some "poltergeist" phenomena may belong to this category. It seems to me, on the whole, easier to suppose that Home had this capacity (whatever its nature) developed to an abnormal degree, than to credit him with a "hypnotic power" which appears to be otherwise unknown.

This would not exclude elements of trickery from his displays. The question is whether the tables *etc.* ever did move, if only sometimes, without trickery. If so, it would be of great scientific interest.

3412. To Michael Kennard

7 June 1948   Handwritten

> Ward 3
> Hairmyres Hospital
> East Kilbride
> Lanarkshire

Dear Michael,

I am not sure what date you are going to Jura, but at any rate, let my sister know in advance, won't you.

About the fishing. I don't know if you've got a rod, but if not, my rod is there, & there is a book with a fair number of flies, & some spare casts. The landing net (not a very good one) screws on to the case which holds the spare top of my rod. If you've got a creel, take it, because we haven't one.

The people who own the land say, will you keep a record of what you catch, because those lochs are hardly ever fished & they want to know whether they are worth restocking.

You'll find that to fish any of these lochs is a day's expedition. Probably my sister can take you in the car to the nearest place on the road, but you still have to walk 3–4 miles over bad going. You can find your way by the map fairly easily. I want to give you some information about the various lochs, otherwise you can waste your time by going to the wrong ones. You might make a note of what I tell you, & you can identify the places by the maps we have at Barnhill.

LOCH GLAS. No fish in this.

LOCH na CONAIRE. Said to be fish in this, but I don't think anyone knows for certain.

GLENGARRISDALE LOCH (nearest to Glengarrisdale bay°). I haven't fished this, but there are fish in it.

LOCH ABURAH.[1] Full of small fish. I didn't get anything bigger than about 5 ounces.

LOCH nan EILEAN. This has a lot of trout, bigger than in Loch Aburah. I haven't caught anything much over ½ lb, but I feel pretty sure there are bigger fish there. Without a boat one can't get into the deepest water, but there is a place where there is pretty deep water close in shore. On the east or north-east side (side nearest Barnhill) you will find a place where the bank makes a steep face, & here there is a deep pool. If there are big fish there, they won't rise to the surface, but if you tried with a spinner (which I haven't got by the way) or even a worm, you might have some luck.

You have to wade a bit. If it is reasonably warm weather, the loch water gets very warm, & I found the best thing is to take a pair of shorts & if possible a pair of gym shoes, & then you can wade almost up to your waste° without having to be wet all the way home.

By the way there are no fish there except trout, ie. brown trout. There are no coarse fish, & the sea trout can't get up there because the streams are too small. If you want to fish in the sea, my sister says our dinghy is leaking so badly that it is almost unseaworthy, but that is probably only because it has got too dry & the boards have shrunk. There is also another old boat at another beach which should be more or less usable.

I hope you will have decent weather at Jura & have some sport. I wish very much I could come with you, but I don't expect to get out of here till about August, & even then it will be months before I can walk far enough to go fishing. Please give my love to Fred & Pamela, & can you tell Fred that I am doing just a very little work.[2]

Yours
George

1. Loch Aburah: properly Loch a Bhùrra (see *3258, n. 7*).
2. See *3426* for Warburg's gratitude to Orwell for enabling Kennard to enjoy 'so delightful a holiday.'

3413. To Leonard Moore
8 June 1948　　Handwritten

Barnhill
Isle of Jura[1]
Argyllshire

Dear Moore,

Yes, I authorised Mrs Jelenska[2] to ask you for copies of "Burmese Days" & "Coming Up for Air." I had not got copies myself, but I thought you probably would have. If you have it, could you be sure to give her either the American edition of "Burmese Days" or the Penguin edition, not the one done by Gollancz, which is slightly different. And I should tell her you want back any copies you lend her, because both of these books are very difficult to get. Someone recently had my very last copy of "Burmese Days," & I have not seen a copy of the other for years.

I did not want any fee for "Animal Farm" from the Poles or any other Slavs,[3] but I don't see why they should not pay a small fee (they wouldn't offer much in any case) if they decide to do one of the other books.

Yours sincerely
Eric Blair

1. There is no known reason for Orwell writing as from Barnhill, Jura. All his other letters about this time, including several to Moore, are addressed from Hairmyres. He did not expect to leave hospital until August (see *3410* and *3415*) and, in the event, left on 25 July (see *3423*). It is possible that his long letter to Michael Kennard dated 7 June (see *3412*) was not completed until the 8th, and, when writing to Moore, his mind was full of thoughts of Jura, which he so longingly describes in his letter to Kennard.
2. Mrs. Teresa Jeleńska translated *Animal Farm* for the League of Poles Abroad, London, as *Folwark Zwierzęcy* (December 1946). The letter has been annotated 'No' in Moore's office against *Coming Up for Air*.
3. 'I did not . . . other Slavs' has been heavily underscored in Moore's office. K. A. G. S. Lane, of Christy & Moore (see *3081, n. 1*) told Ian Angus (18 August 1981) that Leonard Moore 'allowed Blair a great deal of liberty in who° he gave translation permission to . . . he rather played ducks & drakes very badly with Moore in regard to publication in Dictator countries.' Lane remembered 'L.P.M. blowing his top' because Orwell wished Yvonne Davet's translation to be published by Gallimard, without royalty, even though Moore had it on offer with Hachette. For publication without royalty, Christy & Moore were involved in much work and received no fee.

3414. To Leonard Moore

12 June 1948   Handwritten

Ward 3
Hairmyres Hospital
East Kilbride
Lanarkshire

Dear Moore,

Thanks for your letter of the 10th. Yes, I could do the review on the Graham Greene book,[1] so perhaps you could cable to the New Yorker to that effect? I will airmail the article not later than June 25th. It doesn't matter about a copy of the book, as I have one already.

Yours sincerely
Eric Blair

1. *The Heart of the Matter*; the review appeared in *The New Yorker*, 17 July 1948; see *3424*.

3415. To Leonard Moore

25 June 1948   Handwritten

> Ward 3
> Hairmyres Hospital
> East Kilbride
> Lanarkshire

Dear Moore,

I have air-mailed my review to the New Yorker. Could you please charge your usual commision to me & then get Miss Otis[1] to keep the money for me, as before. I like to keep some dollars over there.

I am much better & now get up for three hours daily. Probably I shall leave hospital about August, but it depends on when my lung goes back to its normal shape after the collapse therapy has worn off. I have begun doing a little work on my novel again,[2] so no doubt I shall finish it this year all right. I wonder if "Coming Up for Air" got any notices—I suppose it would get a few, although only a reprint. Perhaps you could send me on any press cuttings that have piled up.

> Yours sincerely
> Eric Blair

1. Elizabeth R. Otis, of Orwell's U.S. agents for his journalism, McIntosh & Otis, New York.
2. *Nineteen Eighty-Four.*

3416. To Anthony Powell

25 June 1948   Typewritten

> Ward 3
> Hairmyres Hospital
> East Kilbride
> Lanarkshire

Dear Tony,

I received a letter from your friend Cecil Roberts[1] asking me if he could have my flat. I had to write and tell him it was impossible. I am awfully sorry about this, but they have already been riding me like the nightmare for lending it to Mrs Christen, and threatening to let the Borough take it away from me. I don't want this to happen because I must have *a* pied à terre in London, and also I have a little furniture still there and a lot of papers which it's awkward to store elsewhere. Even if I gave up the flat they won't let you transfer the lease, and of course they have their own candidates ready many deep, with bribes in their hands.[2]

If you happen to see Graham Greene, could you break the news to him that I have written a very bad review of his novel[3] for the New Yorker. I couldn't do otherwise—I thought the book awful, though of course don't put it as crudely as that. I am going to review Kingsmill's book[4] for the Obs. as soon as possible, but I still have another book to get out of the way first.[5] I seem to be getting quite back into the journalistic mill, however I do tinker a little at my novel and no doubt shall get it done by the end of the year.

I am a lot better and now get up for three hours a day. I have been playing a lot of croquet, which seems quite a tough game when you've been on your back for 6 months. In the ward below me the editor of the Hotspur[6] is a patient. He tells me their circulation is 300,000. He says they don't pay very good rates per thou, but they can give people regular work and also give them the plots so that they only have to do the actual writing. In this way a man can turn out 40,000 words a week. They had one man who used to do 70,000, but his stuff was "rather stereotyped." I hope to get out in August, but the date isn't fixed because it depends on when my lung resumes its normal shape after the collapse therapy has worn off. Richard is coming to see me early in July. He couldn't before because of infection. I suppose I shall hardly know him after six months.

It's my birthday to day—45, isn't it awful. I've also got some more false teeth, and, since being here, a lot more grey in my hair. Please remember me to Violet.

Yours
George

1. Cecil A. ("Bobby") Roberts, sometime manager of Sadler's Wells Theatre, had recently been demobilised from the Royal Air Force.
2. Accommodation was very difficult to find in the years immediately after the war. Premiums, often illegal, were charged. Most leases included a clause forbidding the lessee to sub-let or 'part with possession' in whole or in part, whether or not money changed hands. That restriction is still common though almost impossible to enforce.
3. *The Heart of the Matter*; see *3414* and *3424*.
4. *The Dawn's Delay*; see *3425*.
5. Probably *Mr. Attlee: An Interim Biography*; see *3419*.
6. A weekly paper for boys published from 1933 to 1959. In a letter to Ian Angus, 17.9.96, Professor Williamson said this man shared a room with Orwell for a while and that Professor Dick was interested to see how they got on. 'In the event they got on well together (as I think almost anyone would have . . .).'

3416A. To Lydia Jackson

30 June 1948   Handwritten

Ward 3
Hairmyres Hospital
East Kilbride
Lanarkshire

Dear Lydia,
Thanks so much for your letter. I couldn't work out exactly what I owe you – anyway, here is £5 to go on with. I hope the hotel will be bearable. I think it must be quite near here, & there is a bus that runs to the hospital. I am getting up for 3 hours a day now, but actually I can stay up for a bit longer. Can you

look in after lunch on Sunday? They generally give me my tea about 3 or half past, & I will get them to give us both a cup & then we can go out for a nice stroll. I hope the weather will keep up. It's been filthy here, but has cheered up a little today & yesterday. There are some quite nice walks here if it doesn't rain. I can walk about a couple of miles now. When you get here, ask for me at Ward 3 & they will show you in. So looking forward to seeing you.[1]

With love
Eric.

1. The letter is annotated (in what is probably Lydia Jackson's hand): 'Killermont St. / top of Buchanan St. / No 70 / or 71 / no 2 Bus Platform.

3417. To the Secretary, Freedom Defence Committee (George Woodcock)

30 June 1948   Handwritten

Ward 3
Hairmyres Hospital
East Kilbride
Lanarkshire

Dear Sir,
Ref: your letter dated June 16th, with draft of the F.D.C.'s statement on the purge of civil servants. I am in agreement & you may quote me as a supporter.[1]

Yours faithfully
Geo. Orwell

1. The statement was published in the FDC *Bulletin*, 7, Autumn 1948, and in two journals: see *3441*.

3418. Review of *Great Morning* by Osbert Sitwell

The Adelphi, July–September 1948

As the successive wars, like ranges of hills, rear their bulk between ourselves and the past, autobiography becomes a sort of antiquarianism. One need only be a little over forty to remember things that are as remote from the present age as chain armour or girdles of chastity. Many people have remarked nostalgically on the fact that before 1914 you could travel to any country in the world, except perhaps Russia, without a passport. But what strikes me in retrospect as even more startling is that in those days you could walk into a bicycle shop—an ordinary bicycle shop, not even a gunsmith's—and buy a revolver and cartridges, with no questions asked. Clearly, that is not the kind of social atmosphere that we shall ever see again, and when Sir Osbert Sitwell writes of "before 1914" with open regret, his emotion can hardly be called reactionary. Reaction implies an effort to restore the past, and though the world might conceivably be pushed back to the pattern of 1938, there can be no more question of restoring the Edwardian age than of reviving Albigensianism.

Not that Sir Osbert's early years were altogether carefree, as readers of the first two volumes of his autobiography will have noticed. His father, Sir George Sitwell, was a trying man to have any dealings with: an architectural genius gone astray, who squandered fantastic sums in megalomaniac building schemes, which extended even to altering the landscape and constructing artificial lakes whose water seeped into the coalmines below and caused endless lawsuits—all this while considering a shilling a week sufficient pocket-money for a boy of nineteen, and even refusing to rescue his wife from the clutches of a money-lender. Architecture apart, his main purpose in life—not, perhaps, from downright malice but as a sort of prolonged practical joke—was to force everyone connected with him into doing whatever he or she most disliked. Osbert, whose antipathy to horses was well known, was driven into a cavalry regiment, then escaped into the Grenadier Guards, then, when he seemed too happy in the Guards, was found a job in the Town Clerk's office in Scarborough, after receiving lessons in pot-hooks (to improve his handwriting) at the age of twenty. The war rescued him from this, but his brother and sister were similarly treated. Nevertheless the last few years before the war were happy ones, and, making all allowance for his abnormal position as a rich man's son, he is probably right in feeling that English life then had a gaiety that has never been recovered.

Life in the Guards was pleasant because it meant being stationed in London, which in its turn meant theatres, music and picture galleries. Osbert's brother officers were civilized and tolerant, and his colonel even excused him for sitting in a café with Jacob Epstein,[1] who was in private's uniform. It was the age of Chaliapin and the Russian Ballet, and of the revival in England of a serious interest in music and painting. It was also the age of ragtime and the tango, of the k-nuts[2] in their grey top hats, of house-boats and hobble skirts, and of a splashing to and fro of wealth such as the world had not seen since the early Roman empire. The Victorian puritanism had at last broken down, money was pouring in from all directions, and the sense of guilt which is now inseparable from a privileged position had not yet developed. Barney Barnato and Sir William Whiteley[3] were held up as models to emulate, and it was meritorious not merely to be rich, but to look rich. Life in London was a ceaseless round of entertainment, on a scale unheard-of before and barely imaginable now:

> One band in a house was no longer enough, there must be two, even three. Electric fans whirled on the top of enormous blocks of ice, buried in banks of hydrangeas, like the shores from which the barque departs for Cythera. Never had there been such displays of flowers. . . . Never had Europe seen such mounds of peaches, figs, nectarines and strawberries at all seasons, brought from their steamy tents of glass. Champagne bottles stood stacked on the sideboards. . . . As guests, only the poor of every race were barred. Even foreigners could enter, if they were rich.

There was also the life of the country houses, with their platoons of servants. Osbert, inimical to horses, was no hunting man, but he enjoyed his shooting expeditions in spite of, or perhaps because of the fact that he never succeeded in killing anything, and his talks with the crabbed old gamekeeper, a type of man now extinct—the type that accepts a position of vassalage, and within that framework is able to enjoy a considerable independence.

Of course, if you happened not to belong to the world of champagne and hothouse strawberries, life before 1914 had serious disadvantages. Even today, after two murderous wars, the manual workers throughout most of the world are probably better off, in a physical sense, than they were then. In Britain they are unquestionably better off. But will this still be true after a third world war, this time conducted with atom bombs? Or even after another fifty years of soil erosion and squandering of the world's fuel resources? Before 1914, moreover, people had the inestimable advantage of not knowing that war was coming, or, if they did know it, of not foreseeing what it would be like. Sir Osbert does not claim much more than that life in those days was fun for a privileged minority, and, as anyone who has read *Before the Bombardment*[4] will know, he is perfectly alive to the vulgarity and grotesqueness of the whole epoch. His political outlook, in so far as this book implies one at all, seems to be a mild liberalism. "In those days," he says, "the rich were as much and unjustly revered as they are now reviled." But in the golden summer of 1914 he greatly enjoyed being rich, and he is honest enough to say so.

There is now a widespread idea that nostalgic feelings about the past are inherently vicious. One ought, apparently, to live in a continuous present, a minute-to-minute cancellation of memory, and if one thinks of the past at all it should merely be in order to thank God that we are so much better than we used to be. This seems to me a sort of intellectual face-lifting, the motive behind which is a snobbish terror of growing old. One ought to realise that a human being cannot continue developing indefinitely, and that a writer, in particular, is throwing away his heritage if he repudiates the experience of his early life. In many ways it is a grave handicap to remember that lost paradise "before the war"—that is, before the other war. In other ways it is an advantage. Each generation has its own experience and its own wisdom, and though there is such a thing as intellectual progress, so that the ideas of one age are sometimes demonstrably less silly than those of the last—still, one is likelier to make a good book by sticking to one's early-acquired vision than by a futile effort to "keep up." The great thing is to be your age, which includes being honest about your social origins. In the nineteen-thirties we saw a whole literary generation, or at least the most prominent members of a generation, either pretending to be proletarians or indulging in public orgies of self-hatred because they were not proletarians. Even if they could have kept up this attitude (today, a surprising number of them have either fled to America or found themselves jobs in the B.B.C. or the British Council), it was a stupid one, because their bourgeois origin was not a thing that could be altered. It is to Sir Osbert Sitwell's credit that he has never pretended to be other than he is: a member of the upper classes, with an amused and leisurely attitude which comes out in his manner of writing, and which could only be the product of an expensive upbringing. Probably, so far as his memory serves him, he records his likes and dislikes accurately, which always needs moral courage. How easy it would have been to write of Eton or the Grenadier Guards in a spirit of sneering superiority, with the implication that from earliest youth he was the holder of enlightened sentiments which, in fact, no comfortably-placed person did hold a generation ago. Or how easy, on the other hand, to stand on the defensive and try to argue away the injustice and inequality of the world in which he grew up. He has done neither, with the result that these three volumes (*Left Hand, Right Hand, The Scarlet Tree* and *Great Morning*), although the range they cover is narrow, must be among the best autobiographies of our time.[5]

1. Jacob Epstein (1880–1959; Kt., 1954), sculptor. He was born in New York but settled in England when he was about twenty-five.
2. A k-nut was a fashionable young man; the 'k' was usually pronounced, the hyphenation used here indicating that. The *OED* records its first use in 1911, in the Cambridge University journal *Granta*. Orwell discusses knuts (unhyphenated) in 'In Defence of P. G. Wodehouse,' 20 February 1945; see *2624*.
3. Barnett Barnato (originally Barney Isaacs) (1852–1897), a financier who became wealthy through exploiting diamond mines in South Africa. No Sir William Whiteley is recorded in Burke's Peerage for this period, nor in *Who's Who* in the twentieth century. Orwell may have erroneously given the originator of Whiteley's department store in Bayswater, London, a knighthood, as he had Gordon Comstock do for John Drinkwater in *Keep the Aspidistra Flying* (see Textual Note, *CW*, IV, 287, 138/5–6). William Whiteley (1821–1907) developed a huge store, 'The Universal Provider,' where one could buy 'Everything from a Pin to an Elephant,' as his slogans put it. He was murdered by a man claiming to be an illegitimate son. The store was sold in 1927; closed in 1981; then developed as a shopping mall.
4. *Before the Bombardment*, a novel by Osbert Sitwell, was published in 1926.
5. This was Orwell's last contribution to *The Adelphi*. The first, a review of Lewis Mumford's *Herman Melville*, was published in *The New Adelphi*, March–May, 1930; see *96*.

3419. Review of *Mr. Attlee: An Interim Biography* by Roy Jenkins[1]

The Observer, 4 July 1948

When one is writing of a living person, and especially of a statesman whose leadership one accepts, it is not easy to preserve a critical attitude. However, this unofficial or semi-official biography remains well on the right side of hero-worship, while at the same time it brings out the unspectacular qualities which have enabled Mr. Attlee to keep his feet through very difficult times and to out-stay many more brilliant men.

Mr. Attlee first won his Limehouse seat in 1922, but his personal connection with the constituency started over 40 years ago and has been almost unbroken ever since. He went there in the first place to become a part-time helper at a public-school mission. In those days he was still a strong Conservative: at Oxford, he tells us, he had "admired strong ruthless rulers" and "professed ultra-Tory opinions." Within a year, however, as a result of what he saw in the East End, he was a member of the I.L.P. and the Fabian Society, and he soon became active as a pamphleteer and street-corner speaker.

It was partly because of this long connection with a single constituency that he was one of the few Labour M.P.s who kept their seats in the calamity of 1931, and the thinning of the ranks gave him a chance of showing his talents which he might not otherwise have had. But, as Mr. Jenkins rightly emphasises, his accession to the leadership of the Parliamentary Labour Party was not simply an accident brought about by Lansbury's resignation. It had to be confirmed by the Party, and it was the result of Mr. Attlee's proved abilities. Even when he was Leader of the Opposition he was not generally looked on as the likeliest man to become Prime Minister if Labour won the next election. During the war years, however, his reputation grew steadily, in spite of his somewhat embarrassing position as second-in-command to a Conservative Premier, which naturally caused murmurings from time to time within his own party.

Mr. Jenkins usually, though not invariably, defends Mr. Attlee's political judgments. Certainly he was very right in resisting the pre-war clamour for a Popular Front, which would simply have weakened the Labour Party without bringing any electoral advantage. On the other hand, he must share some of the blame for the contradictory policy of simultaneously demanding a firm stand against Germany and opposing rearmament, which created a bad impression all over Europe. It is unfortunate that Mr. Jenkins has chosen to take his narrative no further than the 1945 General Election. This is not so definite a turning-point as it appears, since the difficulties which the Labour Government now has to contend with were partly created in the two or three years before it took office. Probably it was an error on the part of the Labour Party not to get out of the coalition when it became clear that the war was definitely won. Had it done so, it would have avoided inheriting the Yalta and Potsdam agreements and would have had time to make clear its position on certain issues which were afterwards obscured or falsified in the election campaign.

The book contains a fairly full account of Mr. Attlee's early days as a boy at Haileybury and an undergraduate at Oxford. One learns with a certain feeling of appropriateness that as a cricketer he was a poor batsman and bowler, but a good fielder. The photographs are undistinguished, but curiously enough they confirm the "Daily Mail's" statement—made at the time of his becoming Leader of the Opposition—that Mr. Attlee's head is the same shape as Lenin's.

1. Roy Harris Jenkins (1920–; Life Peer as Lord Jenkins of Hillhead, 1987), politician and writer, was Labour M.P. from 1948; a member of the Executive Committee of the Fabian Society, 1949–61; Chancellor of the Exchequer, 1967–70; Deputy Leader of the Labour Party, 1970–72, and President of the European Community Commission, 1977–81. He broke with the party and stood as the first candidate for the Social Democratic Party in 1981, but lost the by-election. He then was SDP M.P., 1982–87.

3420. To Julian Symons

10 July 1948   Handwritten

Ward 3
Hairmyres Hospital
East Kilbride
Lanarkshire

Dear Julian,
I must thank you for a very kind review in the M.E. News[1] which I have just had a cutting of. I hope your wife is well and that everything is going all right. I thought you would like to hear that I am leaving here on the 25th. They seem to think I am pretty well all right now, though I shall have to take things very quietly for a long time, perhaps a year or so. I am only to get up for six hours a day, but I don't know that it makes much difference as I have got quite used to working in bed. My sister brought Richard over to see me this week, the first time I had seen him since Christmas. He is tremendously well and almost frighteningly energetic. His talking still seems backward, but in other ways I should say he was forward. Farm life seems to suit him, though I am pretty sure he is one for machines rather than animals. I get up for three hours a day at present, and go for short walks and play croquet, but I'm getting rather bored here and looking forward to getting home. I don't think I shall be in London until the winter, by which time I hope I'll have finished this blasted novel which should have been finished this spring. Also I'm afraid that if I go up to London I shan't stay in bed etc. There is no one much to talk to here. In the ward below this the editor of the Hotspur is a patient, but he's rather dull. He tells me their circulation is 300,000. I recently wrote a long essay on Gissing for Politics and Letters, but I had to do it almost without books as you simply can't get Gissing's books now. As far as I can discover there is no biography of Gissing, except that silly one in the form of a novel by Morley Roberts.[2] It is a job that is crying out to be done. A year or two back Home and Van Thal[3] asked me if I would do one, but of course I couldn't do all the research that would be needed. I recently read Graham Greene's new novel and thought it was just awful. I also wasn't so up in the air as most people about Evelyn Waugh's The Loved One, though of course it was amusing. Unlike a lot of people I thought Brideshead Revisited was very good, in spite of hideous faults on the surface. I have been trying to read a book of extracts from Leon Bloy,[4] whose novels I have never succeeded in getting hold of. He irritates me rather, and Peguy,[o5] whom I also tried recently, made me feel unwell. I think it's about time to do a new counterattack against these Catholic writers.[6] I also recently read Farrell's Studs Lonigan[7] for the first time, and was very disappointed by it. I don't know that I've read much else.

The weather here was filthy all June but now it's turned at last and they are getting the hay in with great speed. I am longing to go fishing, but I suppose I shan't be able to this year, not because fishing in itself is much of an exertion, but because you always have to walk five or ten miles and end up by getting soaked to the skin. Please remember me to your wife. After the 25th my address will be as before, ie. Barnhill, Isle of Jura, Argyllshire.

Yours
George

1. Symons had reviewed the reprint of *Coming Up for Air* in the *Manchester Evening News*, 19 May 1948.
2. *The Private Life of Henry Maitland* (1912).
3. The publishing house.
4. Léon Marie Bloy (1846–1917), French novelist whose work attacks the bourgeois conformism of his time. He expected the collapse of that society and became increasingly influenced by Roman Catholic mysticism, expressed particularly in his Journal, 1892–1917. Orwell had among his books at the end of his life, Bloy's *Pilgrim of the Absolute* (selections), translated by J. Coleman and H. L. Binsse, with an introduction by Jacques Maritain (1947). For Orwell's intention to read Bloy, see his letter to Julian Symons, 21 March 1948, *3363*. See also N. Braybrooke, 'The Two Poverties: Léon Bloy and Orwell,' *Tablet*, 7 April 1951.
5. Charles Péguy (1874–1914; killed at the Battle of the Marne), poet and essayist. As an old republican and socialist, he founded *Cahiers de la Quinzaine* (1900–14). This set out 'To tell the truth, the whole truth, nothing but the truth, to tell flat truth flatly, dull truth dully, sad truth sadly'—that was its doctrine and method, and, above all, its action (Péguy, quoted by Daniel Halévy, *Peguy and 'Les Cahiers de la Quinzaine,'* 1946, 52). In the course of his editing, his Roman Catholicism and his patriotism were intensified. He reacted against the 'new sociology' (which he insisted on terming 'sociagogy') and pursued the relationship of daily life to the spiritual world. He saw the division of France into opposing factions—republicans and conservatives, free-thinkers and Catholics, and so on—as false. To him there were only 'two parties in France, separated not, as Clemenceau said, by a barricade . . . but in mean and modern style, by a ticket-office. On one side, the tape-measure, papers and figures functioned; on the other, production and paying. . . . On either side of the ticket-office there were Catholics, free-thinkers and Jews' and Péguy sided with the Catholics, free-thinkers and Jews who did the paying and against those 'who took up the payments' (Halévy, 94). Péguy published *Le Mystère de la Charité de Jeanne d'Arc* in 1909. Orwell owned Péguy's *Men and Saints*, translated by A. and J. Green (1947). A favourite story of Orwell's, which he dramatised for the BBC, was Anatole France's *L'Affaire Crainquebille* (11 August 1943; see *2230*); this was first published by Péguy in *Cahiers de la Quinzaine*.
6. See his review of Graham Greene's *The Heart of the Matter*, especially after the references to Bloy and Péguy, *3424, n. 1*.
7. James Thomas Farrell (1904–1979), prolific and successful U.S. novelist and a forthright social and literary critic (for example, *The League of Frightened Philistines*, 1945). His range is considerably wider than is exemplified by the trilogy for which he is best known, *Young Lonigan* (1932), *The Young Manhood of Studs Lonigan* (1934), and *Judgment Day* (1935). Orwell had a copy of *Studs Lonigan*, published in 1943 by Constable.

3421. To George Woodcock
12 July 1948   Handwritten

Ward 3
Hairmyres Hospital
East Kilbride
Lanarkshire

Dear George,

I don't know the first thing about Jack London's copyrights. London died, I think in 1915,[1] & I had always understood that copyright in an author's works lapsed 25 years after his death.[2] But one does seem to read of publishing firms "acquiring" the copyright of Dickens, etc., so perhaps it is only that they stop paying royalties after 25 years. Elek didn't say anything about it to me when they published those short stories.[3] Any lawyer or literary agent could let you know. Did you by the way make any agreement with Christy & Moore?[4] They would know all about copyright.

I am leaving here on the 25th & my address will be Barnhill as before. Of course I've got to go on living an invalid life, only getting up for half the day, for some months, perhaps for as long as a year, but they seem to think I am pretty well cured & will end up perfectly O.K. so long as I don't relapse during the next few months. It will be rather a bore not being able to go fishing etc., but it's worth it & I don't mind being in bed as I have got used to writing there.

Richard came to see me last week. He is now 4 & is terrifically well & strong, & almost frighteningly full of energy. We have got two cows in production now so he is getting well dosed with cream. I think he is still backward in talking but otherwise rather forward if anything.

I wish the Porcupine Press[5] would reprint some of Gissing's novels. I was writing an essay on him recently & I find that it is now impossible to get hold of his books, at least the ones I wanted, even from the London Library. If they would reprint "New Grub Street" & "The Odd Woman" I would gladly write introductions for them if that would help. It's possible that Someone° else is doing it however, as 3 of his books have been reprinted recently.

Please give my love to Inge. My address will be as before. I don't suppose I'll be down to London before the winter, as I must take this invalid business seriously.

Yours
George

1. Jack London died in 1916.
2. Copyright law is too complex to summarise here, but at the time Orwell was writing, it ran for 28 years from its formal registration in the United States and could be renewed for a second term of 28 years. In England it ran for fifty years after the author's death, but has now, under European Community law, been extended to seventy years.
3. Elek published Jack London, *Love of Life and Other Stories*, with an introduction by Orwell, in November 1946 (see *2781*).
4. On 25 October 1947 Orwell recommended his own literary agent, Christy & Moore, to Woodcock and had also written to them for Woodcock; see *3294* and *3296*.
5. The Porcupine Press did not publish anything of Gissing's; see *3369, n. 1.*

3422. To Dwight Macdonald

15 July 1948   Handwritten postcard

Dear Dwight,
Thanks ever so for those books you sent.[1] As from July 25th[2] my address will be as before, ie. Barnhill, Isle of Jura, Argyllshire. I'm a lot better, though of course I'll have to continue living a semi-invalid life for some months, perhaps a year.

Yours
Geo. Orwell

1. See *3392, n. 1.*
2. 'As from July 25th' is underlined; typed at the bottom left-hand corner of the postcard is 'change noted jm.'

3423. To Leonard Moore

15 July 1948   Typewritten

Ward 3
Hairmyres Hospital
East Kilbride
Lanarkshire

Dear Moore,
Thanks for your last letter. I had of course no objection to the broadcast of "Animal Farm" in German.

Someone has just written saying a friend of hers in Budapest wants to translate A.F. into Hungarian. I should think it very unlikely indeed that it would be allowed publication there, and I also couldn't remember offhand whether anyone has made a Hungarian translation already. Any way, the name and address of the would-be translator are: Gencsy Ferencne (a woman, apparently), Lepke Utca 21, Budapest.[1] Do you think you could send her a line telling her one way or the other how it stands about translation, and not making any reference to the political colour of the book. I imagine one has to be very discreet in writing to these countries, otherwise one either gets the letter stopped or gets the person at the other end into trouble.

I am leaving here on July 25th, so my address after that will be Barnhill. Of course I have got to go on living a semi-invalid life for a long time, perhaps as long as a year, but I don't mind as I have got quite used to working in bed.

Yours sincerely
Eric Blair

1. Orwell's letter has been annotated in Moore's office to indicate that a letter was sent on 20 July 1948. No Hungarian translation was published in Orwell's lifetime.

3424. Review of *The Heart of the Matter* by Graham Greene

The New Yorker, 17 July 1948

A fairly large proportion of the distinguished novels of the last few decades have been written by Catholics and have even been describable as Catholic novels. One reason for this is that the conflict not only between this world and the next world but between sanctity and goodness is a fruitful theme of which the ordinary, unbelieving writer cannot make use. Graham Greene used it once successfully, in "The Power and the Glory," and once, with very much more doubtful success, in "Brighton Rock." His latest book, "The Heart of the Matter" (Viking), is, to put it as politely as possible, not one of his best, and gives the impression of having been mechanically constructed, the familiar conflict being set out like an algebraic equation, with no attempt at psychological probability.

Here is the outline of the story: The time is 1942 and the place is a West African British colony, unnamed but probably the Gold Coast. A certain Major Scobie, Deputy Commissioner of Police and a Catholic convert, finds a letter bearing a German address hidden in the cabin of the captain of a Portuguese ship. The letter turns out to be a private one and completely harmless, but it is, of course, Scobie's duty to hand it over to higher authority. However, the pity he feels for the Portuguese captain is too much for him, and he destroys the letter and says nothing about it. Scobie, it is explained to us, is a man of almost excessive conscientiousness. He does not drink, take bribes, keep Negro mistresses, or indulge in bureaucratic intrigue, and he is, in fact, disliked on all sides because of his uprightness, like Aristides the Just. His leniency toward the Portuguese captain is his first lapse. After it, his life becomes a sort of fable on the theme of "Oh, what a tangled web we weave,"[a] and in every single instance it is the goodness of his heart that leads him astray. Actuated at the start by pity, he has a love affair with a girl who has been rescued from a torpedoed ship. He continues with the affair largely out of a sense of duty, since the girl will go to pieces morally if abandoned; he also lies about her to his wife, so as to spare her the pangs of jealousy. Since he intends to persist in his adultery, he does not go to confession, and in order to lull his wife's suspicions he tells her that he has gone. This involves him in the truly fearful act of taking the Sacrament while in a state of mortal sin. By this time, there are other complications, all caused in the same manner, and Scobie finally decides that the only way out is through the unforgivable sin of suicide. Nobody else must be allowed to suffer through his death; it will be so arranged as to look like an accident. As it happens, he bungles one detail, and the fact that he has committed suicide becomes known. The book ends with a Catholic priest's hinting, with doubtful orthodoxy, that Scobie is perhaps not damned. Scobie, however, had not entertained any such hope. White all through, with a stiff upper lip, he had gone to what he believed to be certain damnation out of pure gentlemanliness.

I have not parodied the plot of the book. Even when dressed up in realistic details, it is just as ridiculous as I have indicated. The thing most obviously wrong with it is that Scobie's motives, assuming one could believe in them, do not adequately explain his actions. Another question that comes up is: Why should this novel have its setting in West Africa? Except that one of the characters is a Syrian trader, the whole thing might as well be happening in a London suburb. The Africans exist only as an occasionally mentioned background, and the thing that would actually be in Scobie's mind the whole time—the hostility between black and white, and the struggle against the local nationalist movement—is not mentioned at all. Indeed, although we are shown his thoughts in considerable detail, he seldom appears to think about his work, and then only of trivial aspects of it, and never about the war, although the date is 1942. All he is interested in is his own progress toward damnation. The improbability of this shows up against the colonial setting, but it is an improbability that is present in "Brighton Rock" as well, and that is bound to result from foisting theological preoccupations upon simple people anywhere.

The central idea of the book is that it is better, spiritually higher, to be an erring Catholic than a virtuous pagan. Graham Greene would probably subscribe to the statement of Maritain, made apropos of Léon Bloy, that "there is but one sadness—not to be a saint,"[1] A saying of Péguy's is quoted on the title page of the book to the effect that the sinner is "at the very heart of Christianity" and knows more of Christianity than anyone else does, except the saint. All such sayings contain or can be made to contain, the fairly sinister suggestion that ordinary human decency is of no value and that any one sin is no worse than any other sin. In addition, it is impossible not to feel a sort of snobbishness in Mr. Greene's attitude, both here and in his other books written from an explicitly Catholic standpoint. He appears to share the idea, which has been floating around ever since Baudelaire, that there is something rather distingué in being damned; Hell is a sort of high-class night club, entry to which is reserved for Catholics only, since the others, the non-Catholics, are too ignorant to be held guilty, like the beasts that perish. We are carefully informed that Catholics are no better than anybody else; they even, perhaps, have a tendency to be worse, since their temptations are greater. In modern Catholic novels, in both France and England, it is, indeed, the fashion to include bad priests, or at least inadequate priests, as a change from Father Brown. (I imagine that one major objective of young English Catholic writers is not to resemble Chesterton.) But all the while—drunken, lecherous, criminal, or damned outright—the Catholics retain their superiority, since they alone know the meaning of good and evil. Incidentally, it is assumed in "The Heart of the Matter," and in most of Mr. Green's other books, that no one outside the Catholic Church has the most elementary knowledge of Christian doctrine.

This cult of the sanctified sinner seems to me to be frivolous, and underneath it there probably lies a weakening of belief, for when people really believed in Hell, they were not so fond of striking graceful attitudes on its brink. More to the point, by trying to clothe theological speculations in flesh and blood, it produces psychological absurdities. In "The Power and the

Glory," the struggle between this-worldly and other-worldly values is convincing because it is not occurring inside one person. On the one side, there is the priest, a poor creature in some ways but made heroic by his belief in his own thaumaturgic powers; on the other side, there is the lieutenant, representing human justice and material progress, and also a heroic figure after his fashion. They can respect each other, perhaps, but not understand each other. The priest, at any rate, is not credited with any very complex thoughts. In "Brighton Rock," on the other hand, the central situation is incredible, since it presupposes that the most brutishly stupid person can, merely by having been brought up a Catholic, be capable of great intellectual subtlety. Pinkie, the racecourse gangster, is a species of satanist, while his still more limited girl friend understands and even states the difference between the categories "right and wrong" and "good and evil." In, for example, Mauriac's "Thérèse" sequence,[2] the spiritual conflict does not outrage probability, because it is not pretended that Thérèse is a normal person. She is a chosen spirit, pursuing her salvation over a long period and by a difficult route, like a patient stretched out on the psychiatrist's sofa. To take an opposite instance, Evelyn Waugh's "Brideshead Revisited," in spite of improbabilities, which are traceable partly to the book's being written in the first person, succeeds because the situation is itself a normal one. The Catholic characters bump up against problems they would meet with in real life; they do not suddenly move onto a different intellectual plane as soon as their religious beliefs are involved. Scobie is incredible because the two halves of him do not fit together. If he were capable of getting into the kind of mess that is described, he would have got into it years earlier. If he really felt that adultery is mortal sin, he would stop committing it; if he persisted in it, his sense of sin would weaken. If he believed in Hell, he would not risk going there merely to spare the feelings of a couple of neurotic women. And one might add that if he were the kind of man we are told he is—that is, a man whose chief characteristic is a horror of causing pain—he would not be an officer in a colonial police force.

There are other improbabilities, some of which arise out of Mr. Greene's method of handling a love affair. Every novelist has his own conventions, and, just as in an E.M. Forster novel there is a strong tendency for the characters to die suddenly without sufficient cause, so in a Graham Greene novel there is a tendency for people to go to bed together almost at sight and with no apparent pleasure to either party. Often this is credible enough, but in "The Heart of the Matter" its effect is to weaken a motive that, for the purposes of the story, ought to be a very strong one. Again, there is the usual, perhaps unavoidable, mistake of making everyone too highbrow. It is not only that Major Scobie is a theologian. His wife, who is represented as an almost complete fool, reads poetry, while the detective who is sent by the Field Security Corps to spy on Scobie even writes poetry. Here one is up against the fact that it is not easy for most modern writers to imagine the mental processes of anyone who is not a writer.

It seems a pity, when one remembers how admirably he has written of Africa elsewhere, that Mr. Greene should have made just this book out of his wartime African experiences. The fact that the book is set in Africa while the action takes place almost entirely inside a tiny white community gives it an air of triviality. However, one must not carp too much. It is pleasant to see Mr. Greene starting up again after so long a silence, and in postwar England it is a remarkable feat for a novelist to write a novel at all. At any rate, Mr. Greene has not been permanently demoralized by the habits acquired during the war, like so many others. But one may hope that his next book will have a different theme,[3] or, if not, that he will at least remember that a perception of the vanity of earthly things, though it may be enough to get one into Heaven, is not sufficient equipment for the writing of a novel.[4]

a. From Sir Walter Scott's *Marmion*, VI, xvii. It continues: 'When first we practise to deceive!'
1. Orwell had recently been reading Bloy and Péguy, Bloy in an edition with an introduction by Maritain; see letter to Julian Symons, 10 July 1948, *3420, ns. 4, 5, 6.*
2. In his letter to Julian Symons, 21 March 1948 (see *3363*), Orwell said he had just read *Thérèse* and 'it started me thinking about Catholic novelists.'
3. Greene's next book was one of his 'entertainments,' *The Third Man* (1950); that was followed by *The End of the Affair* (1951).
4. In his letter to Orwell of 22 July 1948 (see *3426*), Fredric Warburg said his review of *The Heart of the Matter* was 'fluttering the dovecots.' Warburg's copy of *The New Yorker* had not yet arrived, so he had not read the review but he had just seen a director of Viking Press, Greene's New York publisher, who had shown the review to Graham Greene. On 11 August 1948, D. F. Boyd, Chief Producer, Talks Department, BBC, wrote to Orwell to say that he and Norman Luker, Head of the Talks Department, had read his review of *The Heart of the Matter* with much interest, and they were reminded that they wanted to find out whether he could undertake some broadcasting for them. They were running two book-review programmes in the Third Programme, and 'even more important in a sense is the weekly Critics programme which resumes in September in the Home Service.' No answer has been traced, but Orwell did not broadcast again.

3425. Review of *The Dawn's Delay* by Hugh Kingsmill
The Observer, 18 July 1948

These four tales, which Mr. Hugh Kingsmill first published in 1924, are all essentially fantasies, and two of them are cast in the future. One of them, indeed, is imagined as happening just about now. There is no particular reason for this timing, but it is interesting to notice that the public events which make up the background are not much more ludicrous or catastrophic than what has actually happened.

Two of the tales are only squibs, though one of them—"The End of the World," which describes an all-destroying comet that failed to arrive on time—is a very amusing one. The more considerable pieces are "W.J." and "The Return of William Shakespeare." "W.J." is a character study, ultimately rather touching in spite of its farcical approach, of a neurotic genius, one of those people who are going to write the world's greatest book but never actually get to the point of starting. "The Return of William Shakespeare," on the other hand, although it is built round a complicated and almost-credible plot, is mainly a pretext for some detailed Shakespearean criticism.

A scientist, we are told, has discovered a method of resuscitating the dead, and Shakespeare is brought to life for a period of about six weeks in the year 1943. He never makes any public appearances, and in fact spends the whole of his second lifetime in hiding in order to escape two rival newspaper proprietors who are hoping to exploit him for their own ends. In his seclusion he reads what the critics have said about him and delivers a long exposition of the meaning of his works—which, of course, gives Mr. Kingsmill his opportunity.

At this point it is difficult not to remember the late Logan Pearsall Smith's remark that everyone who writes about Shakespeare ultimately goes mad. With however open a mind one starts out, it is seemingly almost impossible not to emerge with some all-explaining theory into which Shakespeare's most careless utterance has to be fitted. This tendency is seen at its worst, of course, in "interpretations" of Hamlet. Hamlet, for example, had seduced Ophelia before the play started, he had a neurotic fixation upon his mother, he was a woman in disguise, he was a lunatic, he was Shakespeare's son, he was the Earl of Essex.

Mr. Kingsmill does not indulge in anything so extravagant as this, but one does have the feeling that Shakespeare is being slightly distorted in accordance with a preconceived plan. All through Shakespeare's writings, Mr. Kingsmill thinks, there runs a struggle between the principle of love and the principle of power, or success, which can be traced in the plays of the various periods, and which was related to the ups and downs of Shakespeare's own life. The theory is ingeniously worked out, but Mr. Kingsmill is sometimes a little high-handed in his treatment of words. To give one example, the Dark Lady (identified with Mary Fitton) is credited with a melancholy disposition on the strength of her "mourning eyes," although in its context in the Sonnets "mourning" only means black. On the other hand, the discussion of Falstaff, and of the difficult question of Shakespeare's attitude towards him (does he want us to side with Falstaff or with the odious Prince Hal?), is excellent.

One thing that these stories, especially "The End of the World," bring out is the comparative light-heartedness of the world of twenty years ago. It is to be hoped that his publishers will reprint some more of Mr. Kingsmill's earlier works.

3426. Fredric Warburg to Orwell

19 and 22 July 1948

On 19 July 1948, Warburg wrote to Orwell saying he had heard from Michael Kennard that Orwell was looking very much better; he had also mentioned Orwell's interest in getting more of Gissing's novels back into print. He thanked Orwell for enabling 'Michael to have so delightful a holiday—the best I think he has had in this country—but it is not necessary for me to tell you how he enjoyed it, since you have seen him yourself and it was written all over his face.' See *3412*. The main burden of the letter concerned *Nineteen Eighty-Four*:

I was of course specially pleased to know that you have done quite a substantial amount of revision on the new novel. From our point of view, and I should say also from your point of view, a revision of this is far and away the most important single undertaking to which you could apply yourself when the vitality is there. It should not be put aside for reviews or miscellaneous work, however tempting, and will I am certain sooner rather than later bring in more money than you could expect from any other activity. If you do succeed in finishing the revision by the end of the year this would be pretty satisfactory, and we should publish in the autumn of 1949, but it really is rather important from the point of view of your literary career to get it done by the end of the year, and indeed earlier if at all possible.

On 22 July, he wrote to tell Orwell of the great interest aroused in Japan by *Animal Farm*. The Americans had submitted fifty to seventy-five titles of Western books to Japanese publishers and invited them to make bids for them. *Animal Farm* received the most bids; forty-eight Japanese publishers were anxious to publish it. It was 'finally knocked down to an Osaka firm who are paying 20 cents or 20 yens° per copy, I am not sure which.' It would not make Orwell wealthy, and the yen could be spent only in Japan: 'Perhaps a trip one Spring in cherry time might be practicable for you, if and when the world clears up a bit.'

Orwell evidently did not respond to either letter, for when Warburg wrote to him on 1 September 1948 he said he had not heard from him for many weeks. For Orwell's response to the publication of *Animal Farm* in Japan and the blocked yen, see *3437*. The Japanese translation, Dōbutsu Nōjō, was published by Ōsaka Kyōiku Tosho, 15 May 1949.

3427. To Dr. Tergit

21 July 1948   Typewritten

> Ward 3
> Hairmyres Hospital
> East Kilbride
> Lanarkshire

Dear Dr Tergit,
Many thanks for your letter dated the 15th.
"Animal Farm" has been translated into German. The translation was made first in Switzerland, but they are now producing a cheaper edition for Germany. It has also been broadcast by the BBC in German, and (I think) by the American radio as well. But very many thanks for your offer.

> Yours truly
> [Signed] Geo. Orwell
> George Orwell

3428. To George Woodcock

23 July 1948   Handwritten

Dear George,
I'm leaving hospital at last, so my address will be as before, ie. Barnhill, Isle of Jura, Argyllshire. Of course I've got to go on living an invalid life for 6 months or so, perhaps more, but at any rate I'm much better. I've got your book to review for the Obs.,[1] but I haven't done it yet. Please remember me to Inge.

Yours
George

1. *The Writer and Politics*; reviewed 22 August 1948 in *The Observer*, see *3443*.

3429. Avril Blair to Michael Kennard

29 July 1948   Handwritten

Barnhill
Isle of Jura
Argyll.

Dear Michael
Thanks very much for your letter & cigs for which I enclose cheque for 17/6.
    Everything going on well here. Most of the hay is cut & in ricks. We have more or less fixed up the tractor to pull the reaper. A lot of swearing bursts out occasionaly° when the knife sticks. Bill is just off to sail in a yacht race at Tarbert leaving me to the tender mercies of the cows.
    We have been doing awfully well with the creels & one day got 3 lobsters in the one pot! The fishing is also pretty good & I have·been trying to fix up a kiln to smoke some mackerel.
    The car wheels turned up, so the poor old thing is running again, but missing badly on about three cylinders. Its misery to drive her for long.
    Eric returned yesterday & looks much better. He has got to take it very easy but is interested in how things are going & has been going round the estate today; practically everything is new or different since he was[1] last at home. Richard Rees is also here for a day or two & we all (not E) bravely went down & had a bathe this afternoon. The water was icy despite the fact that we are in the midst of a terrific heat wave.
    We have just been erecting a large tent in the garden for the overflow of visitors who start arriving tomorrow.
    Terrific Sports,° Land° & water,° are taking place in Ardlussa on Aug 7th. I am on the Committee! I should think the whole Island will turn up. Last year there were 150 present & it ended up with a tremendous Tug-of-war, & the rope broke!

So glad you enjoyed your holiday. Do come up again if you ever have any more time off.

Yours
Avril

1. This word appears to be written as 'has.'

3430. Domestic Diary

31 July–24 December 1948   Handwritten

<u>31.7.48.</u> *Re-opening this diary[1] after seven months absence in hospital. Returned here on 28.7.48. Weather at present extremely hot & dry, no wind. Oats very short in the straw, presumably owing to drought in spring. Hay mostly cut & in ricks. Roses, poppies, sweet williams[,] marigolds full out, lupins still with some flowers, candytuft about over, clarkia coming on. Fruit bushes, other than raspberries, have not done very well & I shall move most of them. Trees fairly good. A lot of apples on some of the 1946 trees, but not much growth. Strawberries superlatively good. A. says they have had about 20 lb. (50 plants), & there are more coming on, though of course getting small now. First lot of peas almost ready to pick. Lettuces good, turnips ditto, runner beans not so good. The things that always seem to fail here are anything of the onion family. Two lots of chicks coming on, 5 10-week & 10 6-week, R.I.R. × Leghorn,[2] good chicks & very even size. Pig, born about March, very good specimen. Has been fed almost entirely on potatoes & milk, the young chicks on oatmeal & milk. Both cows still in milk. The first (Rosie) calved about February, now supposed to be in calf again (to the Highland bull.) Grass pretty good, & thistles not nearly so bad as they used to be.*

Cannot for some time to come do anything in garden, except very light jobs such as pruning.

Fishing has been good. One night recently they caught 80 fish, & also 8 lobsters in a week.

Lamps in bad condition & want spare parts. Many tools missing.

At the bottom of the facing page, Orwell has written this list. All are ticked except the hammer; the third line is crossed through and ticked.

Order Tilly mantles & vapourisers.
  ,,   *hammer*
  ,,   *washers (for taps)*
  ,,   *plug for bathroom basin.*
  ,,   *lamp chimneys.*

1. This diary is Orwell's fifth, started on 12 September 1947. Words underlined by Orwell are set in Roman.
2. Rhode Island Red crossed with Leghorn.

3431. Review of *Eton Medley* by B. J. W. Hill

The Observer, 1 August 1948

It is hard to disentangle admiration from dismay when one learns that Eton in 1948 is almost exactly what it was in 1918. If any change at all can be inferred from the photographs in Mr. Hill's book, it is that the boys now go about bareheaded, owing to the lamentable shortage of top hats. Otherwise their clothes are just the same, and so is everything else. The procession of boats, lighted by fireworks, still glides down the river on the Fourth of June, the Wall Game is still played amid seas of mud, the flogging block is still there, a bit chipped by the bomb which hit Upper School, but doubtless still serviceable.

Mr. Hill says that a New Zealand Air Force officer, in England during the war, wrote asking him for an account of Eton and its educational system. The subject was too large to be dealt with in a letter, and Mr. Hill embarked instead on a careful description of Etonian daily life, with many photographs and a few reproductions of old engravings. His book is pleasantly written as well as informative, but it is unavoidably—and, indeed, almost unconsciously—an apology for a form of education that is hardly likely to last much longer.

At the end Mr. Hill remarks mildly that Eton will no doubt change as the years go on, but that he hopes that the changes will be self-imposed and not too rapid. And he points out, as a mark of vitality, that since the war more people than ever have been willing to pay the very large fees that are demanded. But unfortunately more is involved than the attitude of parents. Whatever may happen to the great public schools when our educational system is reorganised, it is almost impossible that Eton should survive in anything like its present form, because the training it offers was originally intended for a landowning aristocracy and had become an anachronism long before 1939. The top hats and tail coats, the pack of beagles, the many-coloured blazers, the desks still notched with the names of Prime Ministers had charm and function so long as they represented the kind of elegance that everyone looked up to. In a shabby and democratic country they are merely rather a nuisance, like Napoleon's baggage wagons, full of chefs and hairdressers, blocking up the roads in the disaster of Sedan.

On the other hand, Eton will presumably remain a school, which it is physically well suited to be. It has magnificent buildings and playing-fields, and, unless it is finally swallowed by Slough, beautiful surroundings. It also has one great virtue which is fairly well brought out in Mr. Hill's book, and that is a tolerant and civilised atmosphere which gives each boy a fair chance of developing his own individuality. The reason is perhaps that, being a very rich school, it can afford a large staff, which means that the masters are not overworked; and also that Eton partly escaped the reform of the public schools set on foot by Dr. Arnold and retained certain characteristics belonging to the eighteenth century and even to the Middle Ages. At any rate, whatever its future history, some of its traditions deserve to be remembered. The price of this book is surely hard to justify.[1]

1. The book cost £1.10s.

3431A. Domestic Diary

<u>1.8.48.</u> *A very little rain yesterday evening & in the night. Today overcast, & cooler. Sea like a sheet of lead. Midges very bad.*
<u>2.8.48.</u> *Fine but not very hot most of day. This evening mist & rain. Sea calm.*
   A. started new cylinder of Calor Gas yesterday.
   Bob removed to Tarbert today. To be returned first week in October.

On the facing page opposite 2.8.48, Orwell has written, and ticked:

Order Calor Gas
Order broccoli plants

3432. To Michael Meyer

   3 August 1948   Typewritten

> Barnhill
> Isle of Jura
> Argyllshire

Dear Michael,
I received your letter this morning. I'm awfully sorry, but the date you name is impossible. At the moment we have 4 adults and 3 children in a house with 5 bedrooms, and prospectively 8 adults and 3 children (some people are coming to help with the harvest.) Some of them are overflowing into tents,[1] but there's also the food difficulty. If you can possibly manage any time in September I'd be delighted to see you. It's generally quite pleasant then. I don't suppose by the way this letter will go off till the 7th, so I'll address it to Clackmannanshire.
   I have spent since last November in hospital (T.B.), and only came out 10 days ago. I was really ill most of last year, having I think started off in that horrible cold winter of 1946–7. I'm much better now, but I've still got to live an invalid life probably till some time next year. I only get up for half the day and can't manage any kind of exertion. However it's a great pleasure to be home again, and I am getting on with some work. I have got quite used to working in bed. I hope you are liking it in Sweden.[2] I should think it might be rather like this in some ways. Richard is enormous and in marvellous health. He's still a bit backward about talking, but otherwise very bright. The illness has put my work back fearfully. I was supposed to finish a novel by the beginning of this year, but as it is I shan't finish it till about Christmas. However I've started reprinting others in a uniform edition. I shall probably be in London for a short time in the winter, so if we don't manage to meet before, ring me up when you are over here again. I'm so sorry about August.
> Yours
> George

413

1. 'The Rozgas remember (and a photograph confirms) that there was a tent that summer, but [Orwell] slept in it himself, on a camp-bed, wanting all the fresh air he could get' (Crick, 544). Avril's letter to Humphrey Dakin, 14 December 1948 (see *3507*), says they were 'full up at Barnhill all summer & at one point were eleven strong & overflowing into a tent.' For Jeannie Rozga's account of the tent in the garden, see *Remembering Orwell*, 187; for an illustration of Barnhill showing the tent, see Crick, plate 30.
2. From 1947 to 1950, Michael Meyer was a lecturer in English at the University of Uppsala, Sweden.

3433. To Leonard Moore

3 August 1948   Typewritten

Barnhill
Isle of Jura
Argyllshire

Dear Moore,

Edmund Wilson tells me he didn't receive a copy of "Coming Up for Air." My impression was that we sent him one, but do you think you could arrange for another to be sent to him.[1] I see he gives his address as Wellfleet, Mass., but perhaps care of the New Yorker might be safer. As he is literary editor he probably gets flooded with books, so it might be wise to put "from George Orwell" on the outside of the packet. Also, do you know whether one was sent to Dwight Macdonald, (Care of "Politics," 45 Astor Place, New York 3)? I thought we sent one at the same time as the one to Wilson, but if not could you send him one too.

I left hospital 10 days ago and am very glad to get home. I am only getting up for half the day, but it is very nice weather at last and very pleasant to sit about out of doors.

Yours sincerely
[Signed] Eric Blair
Eric Blair

1. Annotated in Moore's office against this paragraph, 'done,' and, below the text of the letter, '8 copies dispatched on 3rd May. 1 to his sister.' Orwell had asked Moore to send copies to Wilson and Macdonald on 26 April 1948; see *3389*.

3434. To Edmund Wilson

3 August 1948   Typewritten

Barnhill
Isle of Jura
Argyllshire

Dear Wilson,

Many thanks for your letter. I am so sorry they didn't send you a copy of "Coming Up for Air." I thought I had told them to. At any rate, I've told them to send one now.

I much enjoyed "The Ordeal of Mark Twain"[1] which you kindly sent me, but I still think someone ought to write a proper biography to replace that awful Paine book.[2]

I got out of hospital 10 days ago, and am much better, but I have got to continue living an invalid life at any rate for some months. However it is a great treat to be at home again, and I have got so used to working in bed that I don't mind it.

Yours sincerely
[Signed] Geo. Orwell
George Orwell

P.S. If you get round to reading "Coming Up" you may notice that it has not got a semi-colon in it.[3] I should think there are very few modern books of which one could say that.

1. By Van Wyck Brooks (1920).
2. The authorised biography, *Mark Twain, a Biography: The Personal and Literary Life of Samuel Langhorne Clemens* by Albert B. Paine (3 vols., 1912).
3. This was Orwell's intention, as he explained to Roger Senhouse, 22 October 1947 (see *3290*, but nevertheless three crept in; see *CW*, VII, Textual Note, 249–50.

3435. Domestic Diary

<u>3.8.48.</u> *A little rain during the night. Today very still, overcast, fairly warm, but chilly after about 8 pm. Sea very smooth & reflection of lighthouse[1] visible (supposed to be sign of rain.)*

One of the R.I.R. hens is ill—comb a good colour, & eats all right, but legs as if partially paralysed.

<u>4.8.48.</u> *Most of day very still, misty, reasonably warm. A little rain the° evening. B.[2] finished cutting the other patch of hay.*

Tractor does this quite satisfactorily, although it is not meant to have the reaper attached to it & has to be guided in a rather awkward manner.

Some sweet peas coming out, but not good. Forgot to mention, Yesterday° 3 eagles over the field in front (I think 3, though I only saw 2 at any one time). Onc attacked another, made it drop its prey, which looked like a rat or rabbit, & then swooped down & got it. They make a screaming noise, which I thought only the buzzards made.

415

5.8.48.   *Still & overcast, sea less calm. Some rain during the night, I think. A & B.*[3] *took up the creels this morning & got 3 crabs. Angus*[4] *yesterday brought some dabs, which had been got by spearing them, I think at Midge bay.*[5]

Montbretia flowers appearing. A few red hot pokers budding. A few flower buds on the gladioli (not good.)

On the facing page opposite 5.8.48, Orwell has written, and ticked:

Order wick for hanging lamp.
  ditto Valor[6]

1. This must be the lighthouse at Crinan, six miles east-southeast of Barnhill. From the ridge to the east of Barnhill, the coast of the mainland is easily visible; see Shelden, plate facing 373, and, for a grander perspective, the fine colour illustration in *Die Stern, Kultur Journal*, 1983, 'Die Insel des Grossen Bruders (wo George Orwell "1984" schrieb),' 192–202, by Dorothee Kruse; photographs by Klaus Meyer-Andersen.
2. Bill Dunn.
3. Avril and Bill.
4. Angus M'Kechnie, a lobster fisherman who lived at Ardlussa (but was not on the Astors' payroll). It is not always clear whether Orwell writes McKechnie or M'Kechnie; the latter is used in this edition.
5. Presumably a family name for one of the local bays.
6. An oil-stove made by the Calor Oil Company.

3436. Review of *The Novelist as Thinker*, edited by B. Rajan

Times Literary Supplement, 7 August 1948   Published anonymously

It seems doubtful whether a book ought to be entitled *The Novelist as Thinker* unless it has been written with the definite intention of studying the novel as a vehicle for thought. Actually, more than one-third of this "symposium" (it is the fourth number of *Focus*,[1] which is not exactly a periodical, but a book that appears about once a year) consists of matter unconnected with the title: in the main section there are six essays on contemporary English and French novelists, contributed by four writers, and not apparently selected according to any kind of plan. In these six essays, Mr. D. S. Savage deals with Mr. Aldous Huxley and Mr. Evelyn Waugh, Mr. G. H. Bantock with Mr. Christopher Isherwood and L. H. Myers, Mr. Thomas Good with M. Jean-Paul Sartre, and Mr. Wallace Fowlie with M. François Mauriac. One other item in the book, though it is not concerned with novels or novelists, has an indirect bearing on some of the problems that have been raised earlier. This is a long essay on criticism by Mr. Harry Levin, author of the well-known book on James Joyce.

Mr. Savage's two contributions are of very unequal value. The first is a fairly well balanced study of Mr. Aldous Huxley's work from *Crome Yellow* onwards (for some reason the brilliant early short stories of *Limbo* are not mentioned), leading to the probably correct conclusion that Mr. Huxley's mystical pacifism is simply a kind of death wish based on a sense of futility. As Mr. Savage points out, Mr. Huxley's final position was implicit in his earliest work, and the teachings of D. H. Lawrence had no permanent effect upon him. The essay on Mr. Evelyn Waugh, on the other hand, is lopsided, and would give a misleading impression to anyone who had not read the books which are supposedly being discussed. Mr. Savage begins by comparing Mr. Waugh, perhaps justly, with that traditional figure, the clown with the aching heart, but having said this he decides that his author's outstanding characteristic is "immaturity," and refuses to discuss him from any other angle. He does not even mention Mr. Waugh's conversion to Catholicism, which obviously cannot be left out of account in any serious study of his work. In *Brideshead Revisited* Mr. Savage can see only nostalgia for adolescence, and does not seem to have noticed that the essential theme of the book is the collision between ordinary decent behaviour and the Catholic concept of good and evil.

Mr. Wallace Fowlie's study of M. Mauriac also suffers from incompleteness, since it is concerned entirely with Mauriac's early work, and does not mention *Thérèse Desqueroux* or *A Woman of the Pharisees*. However, it rightly emphasizes the fact that M. Mauriac is essentially a Catholic novelist—that is, a novelist whose themes would not occur to a Protestant—and the perhaps allied fact that "he always fails in the depiction of virtuous characters." Mr. Thomas Good's essay on M. Sartre is not so much criticism as popularization of an author who, at least in this country, is still talked about rather than read. As an exponent of Existentialism, M. Sartre must, of course, be judged by his fellow-philosophers; but as a novelist and political essayist he gives the impression—it is not dispelled by Mr. Good—of being one of those writers who set on paper the process instead of the results of thought, and, after many pages of feverish cerebration, end by stating the obvious. Of Mr. G. H. Bantock's two essays, the one on L. H. Myers is the more sympathetic—perhaps too sympathetic. Myers was a lovable man[2] and a delicate and scrupulous writer, but he lacked vitality, and it is stretching loyalty rather far to compare him favourably with Mr. E. M. Forster, as Mr. Bantock seems disposed to do. In the other essay, Mr. Bantock disposes of Mr. Isherwood "as thinker" by saying, in effect, that he is not a thinker: he admits, but seems to undervalue, his author's readability, which, after all, is not a quality with which any writer is born.

In the middle section of the book are a number of not very distinguished poems by Mr. E. E. Cummings, Mr. Clifford Collins and others. The last three contributions are all written by Americans. Mr. Harry Levin, writing of "Literature as an Institution," examines the "sociological" theory of criticism, formulated by Taine and developed by the Marxists, according to which literature is a product of environment: he urges the equal importance of tradition and apprenticeship, which enable literature to develop along its own lines without necessarily acting as a mirror for contemporary social conditions. Mr. Andrews Wanning contributes a rapid survey of present-day literary activities in the United States, from the *Partisan Review* to the comic strips, and finally, there is a rather pointless short story by Mr. Arthur

417

Mizener, "You Never Go Back to Sleep," about a novelist who was underrated.

1. *Focus*, 1–5, 1945–50, edited by B. Rajan and Andrew Pearse. No. 6 was advertised but not published.
2. It was L. H. Myers (1881–1944) who advanced £300 to enable the Orwells to spend some months in North Africa for the sake of Orwell's health. Orwell never learned that Myers was the donor.

3437. To Leonard Moore

7 August 1948   Typewritten

Barnhill
Isle of Jura
Argyllshire

Dear Moore,
Many thanks for your letter of the 4th. Of course I am very pleased to hear about the Japanese translation of A.F. I suppose if the sales amounted to anything one could always buy kimonos or something with the blocked yen. I should like it if I could have one or two copies of the translation when printed.[1]

Yours sincerely
[Signed] Eric Blair
Eric Blair

1. The letter has been annotated in Moore's office: 'Audrey note'—presumably referring to Orwell's request for copies of the translation, not the purchase of kimonos, and ticked through. For this translation, see *3426*.

3438. Domestic Diary

7.8.48. *Overcast with sunny intervals. Windy & rather cold. B. put the hay in the back field into coils.*

On the facing page opposite 7.8.48, Orwell has written, and ticked:

Order methylated (from Glasgow)

8.8.48. *Fine, rather cold. Wind in north. Sea calm. Some clarkia now out. One plum tree sending out long shoots from low down, which I presume must be cut out. A great many young rabbits about, but difficult to get a shot. Wrote to two addresses about boats.*[1]
9.8.48. *Fine, not very warm. One fancies a fire in the evening nowadays. Dahlias budding well. Red hot poker shoots coming up very fast.*

They seem to shoot up a foot or more in 3 or 4 days. Very many rabbits about.
<u>10.8.48.</u> *Fine, not very warm. Wind tends to be northerly. Mainland looked closer than I have ever seen it. B. & his friends put the hay in the back field into ricks. Took the runners out of the strawberries, ie. the worst ones.*
<u>11.8.48.</u> *Still, overcast, fairly warm. A very few drops of rain in the afternoon. Midges very bad. Sea calm.*
<u>12.8.48.</u> *Still. Fine in morning, clouding over in afternoon, & a little rain in the evening & at night. Sea calm. Some hay brought in. Rick lifter very successful. A. & B.D. fished & got 13 saythe.*
<u>13.8.48.</u> *Beautiful hot day. Sea calm, & glassy-smooth in afternoon. Several more ricks brought in. A. cut grass in front. B. & the others fished in the evening & caught 70 saythe.*
<u>14.8.48.</u> *Less warm, & sea somewhat rougher. A few drops of rain in the evening. When B. & the others went down to fish, the calf followed them down & even began to swim after them.*
<u>15.8.48.</u> *Overcast, still, not very warm. Light rain part of day. Sea less calm. A. planted out broccoli. With the journey, & lying about after arrival, the plants have been out of the ground at least a week. Chaffinches seem to be flocking already.*

1. Not traced.

3439. To Celia Kirwan

16 August 1948   Typewritten

Barnhill
Isle of Jura
Argyllshire

Dear Celia,[1]
How nice to hear from you. I got out of hospital about 3 weeks ago and am very much better, though of course I still have to live an invalid life and only get up half the day. Next year I trust I shall be more active. The house is very full now with four people staying here, including Inez,[2] and they are very busy getting the hay in, which of course I can't help with. Richard is tremendously well and energetic, and helps with everything. The weather hasn't been very good, but better than it was in the earlier part of the summer. What I really wanted to say was that if you'd like to come and stay here any time we'd love to have you. At present the house is crammed to bursting, in fact two people have overflowed into tents, but in September it won't be, and it is often very nice here then. If you do like to come any time, you must let me know the date well in advance, because of the slowness of posts here, and I'll give you the full instructions about the journey, which looks formidable on paper but isn't really.

Please remember me to Diana.[3] Inez sends love. I shall probably be in London for a bit in the winter but I think not before then.

With love
George

1. Celia Kirwan, twin sister of Mamaine Koestler; see Orwell's letter to her of 27 October 1947, *3298*.
2. Inez Holden (1906–1974), writer; Celia's cousin; see *1325, n. 1*.
3. Diana Cooke (the poet Diana Witherby).

3440. Domestic Diary

<u>16.8.48.</u> *Dull & damp. Sea fairly calm.*

<u>17.8.48.</u> *Overcast in morning, some sun in afternoon. Very large lobster (4½ lb.) caught this morning. Cylinder of Calor Gas gave out. Must have been leaking.*

<u>18.8.48.</u> *Fine sunny day, not much wind. Sea calm. B.D. brought in some more hay, & put some more in the back field into ricks. The barn is now full & a stack will have to be built. Tied back cherry trees & cut out dead branches. Began weeding border. Killed first queen wasp.*

<u>19.8.48.</u> *Beautiful sunny day, with a little breeze. Sea fairly calm. B. & R.[1] made small stack, covering with tarpaulin. Only one rick now to be brought in. Pig now put outside the gate, but does not go far afield yet. Weeded some more of the border.*

Methylated running very short.

On the facing page opposite 18 and 19.8.48, Orwell has written, and ticked all but michaelmas daisies:

> *Order daffodil bulbs*
> ‥ *crocus* ‥
> ‥ *scilla* ‥
>   *peony roots*
>   *quince trees* [crossed through]
>   *lupins*
>   *michaelmas daisies*
>   *1 cwt lime*
>   *phloxes*

<u>20.8.48.</u> *Beautiful sunny day. Little wind. Sea calm. B. & R. clearing up last of hay. Weeded some more.*

1. Almost certainly Sir Richard Rees, but Tony Rozga, Orwell's Polish neighbour, and even his son Richard are possible (see his letter to Michael Meyer, 22 August 1948, *3444*). In his Diary entry for 31.8.48 he refers to Rozga as 'Tony.' Avril, in her letter to Michael Kennard, 29 July 1948 (see *3429*), said: 'Richard Rees is also here for a day or two'; his visit might have been extended or repeated.

3441. Civil Service Purge

Freedom Defence Committee Statement, 21 August 1948

The Freedom Defence Committee's *Bulletin* 7, Autumn 1948, published a statement about the way in which the records of members of the Civil Service were being investigated. Orwell had raised this with George Woodcock in his letter of 23 March 1948 (see *3369*; and also *3388 ns. 2* and *3*). The statement was also published in the *Socialist Leader*, 21 August 1948, and in *Peace News*, 27 August 1948. The version in *Peace News*, reproduced here, was preceded by a statement (given here in italics, as in the original) which made a distinction between the FDC and the Communist-dominated National Council for Civil Liberties. Orwell agreed to sign the statement on 30 June 1948; see *3417*.

The Freedom Defence Committee has called for a reform of the secret method by which Civil Servants and other persons are being discharged from Government employment because of alleged Communism or Fascism.

Unlike the National Council for Civil Liberties, which has called for the suppression of all Fascists and unlimited freedom for all Communists, the Freedom Defence Committee has recognised that a government's actions must be dictated by its political and social responsibilities.

The following statement has been issued:—

The Freedom Defence Committee, having observed the manner in which the investigation of the political records of members of the Civil Service accused of Communist or Fascist affinities is being carried out, believes that additional safeguards are essential if the risk of injustice is to be reduced to a minimum.

We would emphasise that we do not consider it our function to make any criticism of the actual dismissal or transference of employees whom the Government thinks undesirable. Unless one is prepared to deny the principle of government, it is impossible to contest the right of the administration to choose its employees and reject those whose activities seem to endanger it. For this reason we consider that the general issue is a political one which this Committee, under its constitution, cannot discuss.

AMENDMENTS

We advocate the following amendments to the method of procedure:
(a) The individual whose record is being investigated should be permitted to call a trade union or other representative to speak on his behalf.
(b) All allegations should be required to be substantiated by corroborative evidence, this being particularly essential in the case of allegations made by representatives of MI5 or the Special Branch of Scotland Yard, when the sources of information are not revealed.
(c) The Civil Servant concerned, or his representative, should be allowed to cross-examine those giving evidence against him.

The statement bears the following signatures:

Gerald Brenan   J. Middleton Murry
Fenner Brockway   George Orwell
Alex Comfort   S. Vere Pearson
Rhys J. Davies   R. S. W. Pollard
E. M. Forster   D. S. Savage
Victor Gollancz   Osbert Sitwell
B. H. Liddell Hart   Dinah Stock
C. E. M. Joad   Julian Symons
Augustus John   Michael Tippett
Harold J. Laski   Wilfred Wellock
Henry Moore   J. Allen Skinner
Stuart Morris   Herbert Read

3442. Domestic Diary

21.8.48. Horrible day, with driving rain & violent wind, from E. part of the time. Flowers in garden much blown about. B. & A. caught 9 mackerel last night.

3443. Review of *The Writer and Politics* by George Woodcock

The Observer, 22 August 1948

"Any honest artist," writes Mr. George Woodcock, "is an agitator, an anarchist, an incendiary," and this bold statement can be taken as the keynote of his book. It is a book of collected essays, rather heterogeneous in character and dealing more with individuals than with generalities, but always coming back to that painful and—as it seems to-day—almost insoluble problem, the relationship between literature and society.

In the opening essay the problem is stated directly. In our own age a serious writer cannot ignore politics as he could in the nineteenth century. Political events affect him too nearly, and he is too much aware of the fact that his seemingly individual thoughts are the product of his social environment. He therefore attempts, as so many writers of the past 20 years have done, to take a direct part in politics, only to find that he has entered a world in which intellectual honesty is regarded as a crime. If he toes the line he destroys himself as a writer, while if he refuses to do so he is denounced as a renegade. This drives him to take refuge in dilettantism, or, perhaps even worse, to alternate between one attitude and the other. Only by embracing libertarian anarchism, Mr. Woodcock maintains, can the writer make himself politically effective without losing his integrity: and he at any rate demonstrates successfully that anarchism is not the same thing as woolly-minded Utopianism. He does not, however, fully meet the objection that anarchism is simply another -ism and that all movements involving large groups of people tend to be alike in their intellectual atmosphere.

This essay is followed by another on political myth-making, and then by three studies of revolutionary thinkers whose writings are less known in Britain than they might be: Proudhon, one of the founders of the French Socialist movement; Herzen, the friend and financial supporter of Bakunin; and Kropotkin, the biologist and sociologist, whose inventive and pragmatical outlook makes him one of the most persuasive of anarchist writers. After this there are essays on a series of contemporary writers—Silone, Koestler, Graham Greene, and others[1]—most of whom are alike in combining a "left" outlook with hostility to orthodox Communism. Silone comes nearest to winning Mr. Woodcock's complete approval, but he treats Graham Greene with marked friendliness—Greene, it seems, though a Catholic, is *anima naturaliter anarchistica*. Koestler is condemned because of the change of front which he makes, or seems to make, in "Thieves in the Night," a book which condones the totalitarian methods that he had previously attacked in "Darkness at Noon."

Among the other essays there is one on the sociology of hymns—an excellent subject, but too shortly treated, since Mr. Woodcock is interested almost exclusively in the revivalist hymns and does not discuss the medieval Latin hymns and their translations, nor, on the other hand, the occasional modern specimens (such as those of Henry Newman), which possess literary value.

1. Chapter 7 is devoted to Orwell.

3444. To Michael Meyer
22 August 1948   Typewritten

Barnhill
Isle of Jura
Argyllshire

Dear Michael,
I'm awfully sorry, but I can't manage such dates as you mention. I don't think there'll be any room *in* the house till towards the end of September. Recently two people overflowed into a tent, but we shall have to take that down soon because of the winds. It's also not possible to come here for as short a time as two or three days. There are only boats three days a week, and it's always more or less a day's journey, because one has to get up this end of the island after landing. I'm awfully sorry about all this and do hope I don't seem to be putting you off. I would so have liked to see you. Any way, come next year if you can, and let me know a good time in advance, so that I can make sure there is room in the house and arrange about meeting you. The posts by the way can only be depended on to reach here once a week, usually on a Saturday.

I am much better but can't do anything involving exertion. I don't even milk the cows, which, as you say, is hard work. I potter about a little in the garden, but I can't lift or carry anything heavy, or walk far. Next year I trust I shall be more or less normal. Richard is tremendously well and helps quite a lot round the farm. This year we are keeping a pig, the first time I have ever tried one. It seems to be quite easy to bring up, and grows very fast. I think I shall be in London in the winter, probably in December or January, according to when I finish the book I am writing.

Yours
George

3445. Domestic Diary

<u>22.8.48.</u> *Very slightly better day. Strong wind in morning, but sunny. Some driving rainstorms in afternoon, but a few bright intervals. Wind still strong, mostly from W., sometimes from S. Sea rough. Much white water round the lighthouse.[1] B. brought down sheep & put them in the field with a view to dipping them.*
<u>23.8.48.</u> *Horrible day. Raging wind from all directions. Sunny in morning, driving rain showers in afternoon. Tent blown down. Some apples blown off. Sea rough, much white water. B. & R. successfully dipped the sheep in the small iron tank used for rainwater. Wind dropped somewhat towards evening.*

On the facing page opposite 23.8.48, Orwell has written, and ticked:

Order paraffin.

<u>24.8.48.</u> *Better day. Some showers about mid-day, otherwise fine & sunny, not much wind. Sea calmer. Sticked[2] a few dahlias.*
<u>25.8.48.</u> *Misty during last night. Today mostly dry, blowy, overcast & intermittent rain. Sea less rough.*
<u>26.8.48.</u> *Fine, still, sunny day. B. is putting-up wires, parallel with the ground, to lean corn sheaves against instead of stooking them. New methylated came, ie. 1 gallon, but we also got a bottle of it from McKechnie, so we have 9 pints in hand. NB. to note how long it lasts. Removed seed pods from wallflowers, which we are going to leave in the ground. People always grow them as biennials, but I think in fact they are perennials, & they might do one more fairly good flowering after the first year.[3] A. cut grass.*

On the facing page opposite 26.8.48, Orwell has written, but not ticked:

Order tarpaulin

<u>27.8.48.</u> *Beautiful warm day. No wind. Sea very calm. B. & R.[4] started cutting corn. Very difficult because stalks are so short.*

424

<u>28.8.48.</u> *Fine till evening, more wind than yesterday. Sea less calm. B. & R. continued mowing the field. They have got some of the sheaves against wires today instead of stooking them. Put the young cockerel in pen to fatten. Fine about 6 pm onwards some light rain.*°

<u>29.8.48.</u> *Some heavy rain in the night, & strong wind. Today damp, overcast, rather blowy, but warm. It appears the sheaves had stood up in spite of the rain in the night, so this method is justified. Retied the new fruit trees, which were becoming chafed owing to being tied with string.*

Some gladioli out. They are not so good this year. The roses are really admirable. Godetias now about at their best.

On the facing page opposite 29.8.48, Orwell has written, and ticked:

Write about boat

<u>30.8.48.</u> *Filthy day. Too wet to do anything out of doors. Sea less rough. Appears to be clearing a bit this evening.*

1. Presumably Crinan Lighthouse, about six miles away; see *3435*, n. 1 and *3457*, 19.9.48.
2. Orwell quite clearly writes 'Sticked,' not 'Staked.'
3. Wallflowers, if left in the ground, will usually flower a second year, though they are inclined to become leggy.
4. Again, it cannot be quite certain who is cutting corn, Richard Rees or Tony Rozga see *3440*, n. 1, though perhaps Rozga is more likely here. 'R' can sometimes be Orwell's son; he might be more likely to confuse a snake and a slow worm (see *3449*) than Rees or Rozga.

3446. To Melvin Lasky

31 August 1948   Typewritten; copy

Barnhill
Isle of Jura
Argyllshire
Scotland

Dear Mr Lasky,[1]
Many thanks for your letter of the 14th (only just arrived—the posts are rather infrequent here.) So long as it is all right with "Commentary" of course I am delighted to have any of my articles reprinted and to get paid for them as well.

If I have anything further that seems at all suitable I will suggest it to you. I am not doing very much, because as you know I have been under treatment for tuberculosis for a long time, and it has set my work back almost a year. I am struggling with a book which was to have been finished by the beginning of this year and actually won't get finished much before Christmas, so I can't do any serious journalism at present. I don't of course know whether your review is literary as well as political, but a month or two back I wrote an essay on George Gissing which might possibly interest you. It was for a paper called "Politics and Letters" which is so much behind time with its current issue that I am afraid it may have died[2] as these little reviews so often do.

It must be ghastly being in Berlin now.[3] I trust you won't all have to fly with the MVD[4] on your heels.

Yours sincerely
[Signed] Geo. Orwell
George Orwell

1. Melvin Jonah Lasky (1920–), literary editor of *The New Leader* (N.Y.), 1942–43; U.S. Combat Historian, 1944–45; editor of *Der Monat* (Berlin; sponsored by the American Military Government; see 3470 and 3479), 1948–58; co-editor, *Encounter* (London), from 1958. The article mentioned was 'Armut und Hoffnung Grossbritanniens,' ('The Labour Government After Three Years,' *Commentary*, October 1948; see 3462), published in *Der Monat*, No. 3, December 1948. *Der Monat* serialised *Animal Farm*, reworking Scarpi's translation (*Farm der Tiere*) as *Der Hofstaat der Tiere*, February–April 1949; and *Nineteen Eighty-Four* in Wagenseil's translation, *Neunzehnhundertvierundachtzig*, November 1949–March 1950.
2. *Politics and Letters* had ceased publication; see 3406, headnote.
3. The Russians began strict road checks of vehicles entering Berlin on 1 April 1948 and this was stepped up to a total blockade at the end of June. A huge airlift, of upwards of 1,000 British and American planes a day, kept the city supplied until the Russians lifted the blockade on 12 May 1949.
4. The MVD was the Soviet secret police. The sequence began with CHEKA (initials, standing, in English, for 'extraordinary commission'), followed by OGPU, NKVD, MVD, and KGB.

3447. To Leonard Moore

31 August 1948   Typewritten

Barnhill
Isle of Jura
Argyllshire

Dear Moore,

Thank you for two letters. Unless I get ill again or something of that kind, the novel[1] should be finished by about the beginning of December, so you should have it before Christmas.

I don't seem to have a copy of "Down and Out" of any description. Would it not be possible to get hold of a Penguin copy? If not we shall have to get one by the same rather devious means as with "Coming Up for Air."

Did you by any chance have a copy of "Polemic" of about the end of 1946, containing an essay of mine called "Lear, Tolstoy and the Fool?" I don't seem to have a copy of this, and as the magazine has come to an end it may not be possible to get back numbers.

Yours sincerely
[Signed] Eric Blair
Eric Blair

1. *Nineteen Eighty-Four.*

3448. To William Phillips

31 August 1948   Typewritten

Barnhill
Isle of Jura
Argyllshire
Scotland

Dear Phillips,[1]

Many thanks for your letter of the 24th. Yes, I'd like very much to review Gandhi's Autobiography.[2] You didn't say what length?° But I suppose the length of one of the longer reviews in PR?

I came out of hospital at the end of July and am much better, but I have to go on being a semi-invalid for at any rate some months. Next year I trust I may be more or less normal again. At present of course I am trying to catch up lost time, in particular to finish a book which should have been done about the beginning of this year, but won't I am afraid be finished much before Christmas.

Yours sincerely
[Signed] Geo. Orwell
George Orwell

1. William Phillips, with Philip Rahv, edited *Partisan Review*.
2. *The Story of My Experiment with Truth*; the review appeared in *Partisan Review*, January 1949; see *3516*. An annotation on Phillips's letter indicates that the book was mailed on 7 September 1948.

3449. Domestic Diary

31.8.48.   *Filthy day. Rain more or less continuous up to about 5 pm, then fine for two hours, then more rain. Mostly light, but quite a downpour during the night. Sea fairly calm. Tony[1] saw some kind of shark or grampus in Kinuachdrach harbour, which, according to him, jumped out of the water & caught a seagull.*

Peony roots now 6/– each!

On a separate page following 31.8.48, Orwell tabulates details for spraying fruit trees, etc.:

Spraying of fruit trees etc.

Apples.		Remarks.
1. Dec–mid–Feb.	Tar oil (3½–50)	
2. Early May (pink kind)	Lime sulphur (1–50)	Not in hot sun
3. Late May (petal fall)	Bordeaux Mixture	

Plums.
1. Dec. to Mid–Jan.   *Tar oil (3½–50)*
  Mid–May (post blossom) *Derris (1 lb.–50 galls)*

Cherries.
  Dec. to Jan.   *Tar oil (3½–50)*
  Mid–June   *Derris (1 lb.–50)*

Black Currants.
1. Dec.–Feb.   *Tar oil (3½–50)*
  Early April   *Lime sulphur (1–50)*
  July–August   *Bordeaux Mixture (?)*
  (after fruit picked)

Red Currants.
1. Dec–Feb.   *Tar oil (3½–50)*

Gooseberries.
1. Dec.–Feb.   *Tar oil (3½–50)*
  June   *Derris (weaker than for*
           plums & cherries)

NB. Tar Oil. *Mix with own volume of water, stir well & then add bulk of water.*
Lime sulphur. *All apples can stand it* before *blossoming*.

1.9.48. *Slightly better day. Some showers in morning & afternoon, also some light drizzle, but most of day fine & still. Sea calm. B. & R. cut some more corn, with difficulty, as the knife gets clogged with mud in this weather. Large slow-worm living in the peat, apparently as a permanency, as I have several times seen it. Probably this is the "snake" R. saw there. Retied cherry trees.*

3450. From S. M. Levitas

   2 September 1948

Orwell had written to S. M. Levitas, executive editor of *The New Leader*, New York, on 4 June 1948 in answer to a reminder from Levitas that he had promised to contribute to his magazine (see *3410*); he had explained that he was ill with tuberculosis and unable to contribute anything for the time being. Levitas wrote again on 2 September. He hoped Orwell was 'completely recovered . . . and . . . back in harness,' that his health was 'O.K. and that you will come through,' but *The New Leader* needed 'pieces' from him on any subject and of any length, because they had 'a terrific job proselytizing thousands and thousands of people' and Orwell's help and co-operation were really needed. No reply from Orwell has been traced.

3451. Domestic Diary

2.9.48. Filthy day till afternoon, when clearing up somewhat. Sea rougher, with some breakers. The second calf (2 months old) is to be bought in by the farm for £10. Apparently this is an equitable price, as it is pure-bred (a heifer) & has had about 60 galls of milk.

Rain during night.

3.9.48. Better day. A shower in the afternoon & a slight one in the morning, otherwise fine & still. Sea fairly calm. B. & R. continued cutting corn.

4.9.48. Beautiful, still, warm day. A very little breeze. Sea calm. B. & R. continued cutting. Started weeding the border under house.

5.9.48. Filthy day, wet & blowy, up to about 4 pm. After that a few showers, but finer on the whole. Sea roughish, Weeded gooseberry patch. Gooseberry bushes are still very small & poor, but do not seem diseased.

3452. To Fredric Warburg

6 September 1948   Typewritten

Barnhill
Isle of Jura
Argyllshire

Dear Fred,

Thanks so much for your letter.[1] I am about half way through the revision of my novel and unless I get ill again or something of that kind I should have it done in time to let you have it early in December. My health seems to be getting much better, though of course I am still living an invalid life, more or less. I am going up to Glasgow next week to be X-rayed again, and perhaps after that they will let me get up a bit more. I feel a great deal better and don't get out of breath so much, but I can't walk far or do anything requiring the smallest physical strength. Unfortunately the weather has been very poor. Last month it was better, but now it has turned filthy. They got the hay in all right but are having an awful business with the corn. Of course I can't help with anything like that. Richard is tremendously well and active. He helps me in the garden and is really quite useful. I am sorry to say he took to smoking recently, however it didn't last long as he made himself most horribly sick and has been off it ever since, almost like the advertisement which says "tobacco habit conquered in three days."

Moore told me you wanted a copy of "Down and Out" for the uniform edition. I haven't got one, not even a Penguin. I suppose at worst we can pinch one from a public library, as before.

Please remember me to everybody.

Yours
George

1. Warburg had written to Orwell on 1 September 1948 saying he was seeing Orwell's U.S. publisher (Harcourt, Brace) on 8 September and wished to give him the latest possible information on the progress of his novel (*Nineteen Eighty-Four*). He would be glad of a note from Orwell's 'remote fastness.' Since he had not heard from Orwell for many weeks, he hoped that meant he was making steady progress.

3453. Domestic Diary

<u>6.9.48</u>. *Filthy day, clearing partially in afternoon. Began weeding currant patch. Have now decided not to move these bushes, as they have made better growth than I had thought.*

Pig keeps getting through the fence into the yard, & might find his way into the garden, which must not be allowed.

Finished the bottle of methylated started on 26.8.48. This means one bottle lasts 10–12 days, so a gallon (6 bottles?) should last at best 2 months.

On the facing page opposite 6.9.48, Orwell has written, and ticked the first two items:

Plant tulips about 20th October.
Write about petrol
    ..   *ashes*[1]
    ..   *rubber tubing*
Order garden forks (2)
    .. *lamp washers (pump)*
    .. *tools for boat*

1. 'ashes' is slightly uncertain; Orwell may have wanted to obtain a supply to lay on the paths. See *3459*, 21.9.48.

3454. Appeal by Freedom Defence Committee

7 September 1948

Issue 7 of the Freedom Defence Committee's *Bulletin*, Autumn 1948, draws to its readers' attention a letter sent to the press for publication 'early in September.' A copy of the actual letter sent to *The New Statesman and Nation* has survived. This is dated 7 September 1948. At its foot is a note: 'The original signatures are available for inspection at this office.' The letter was also published, sometimes differently paragraphed, in *Northern Echo*, Darlington, 16 September (abridged); *Tribune*, 17 September; *Peace News*, 17 September (abridged); and *Socialist Leader*, 18 September; it was not published by *The New Statesman and Nation*, nor by any of the longer-run papers. This is the version as published by *Tribune*; the text is complete but the first, long, paragraph of the Committee's letter has been split into three.

The British people accept freedom as a matter of course, and tend to forget that its price is "eternal vigilance." Even if they remember that famous saying, they do not seem to realise that vigilance is an activity involving time, energy and money.

The Freedom Defence Committee was set up in 1945 "to uphold the essential liberty of individuals and organisations, and to defend those who are persecuted for exercising their rights to freedom of speech, writing and action."

Our Bulletin, which is available to anyone who applies to the Secretary, shows to what an extent our existence has been justified. Cases of unjust imprisonment, excessive sentences and racial discrimination are frequent. Threats to freedom of speech, writing and action, though often trivial in isolation, are cumulative in their effect and, unless checked, lead to a general disrespect for the rights of the citizen.

The Committee gives aid to individuals or organisations irrespective of their political views, the nature of the attack on their freedom being the sole criterion on which it is determined whether or not action should be taken. The Committee is opposed in principle to all forms of military and industrial conscription, and works for the abolition of the Emergency Powers Act, Defence Regulations and all existing statutes restricting the freedom of political action.

We need a regular income of at least £1,000 if we are to carry on efficiently.[1] This has not been forthcoming in the past year and our accounts now show a deficit of over £145. To enable our work to go forward, therefore, we need an immediate sum of at least £500. Our basic requirements are modest enough—a thousand regular subscribers at a guinea a year; but we are also in desperate need of lump-sum donations to enable us to pay our debts and keep our office open.

Subscriptions and donations should be sent to Herbert Read, Chairman, Freedom Defence Committee, 8, Endsleigh Gardens, London, W.C.1.

(*Signed*) Benjamin Britten, E. M. Forster,
Augustus John, George Orwell,
Herbert Read, Osbert Sitwell.

1. *Bulletin* 6, Spring 1948, describing the Committee's financial difficulties, said that they could not even afford a duplicating machine.

3455. Domestic Diary

7.9.48. *Filthy day, sea rough. Did nothing out of doors.*
8.9.48. *Much better day, sunny & fairly warm, sea calmer. B. & R. finished cutting corn. Weeded rest of the currants.*
9.9.48. *Fine but not very warm. Not much wind in day-time, & sea fairly calm. Wind sprang up about 8 pm & became very violent during the night, with some rain. Weeded raspberries. A good many suckers, which can be used to fill up gaps. Some lupins still flowering.*

10.9.48. *Sunny, strong wind. Sea rough. Corn too wet to be stacked, so they are throwing it down on the ground again.*
Started weeding the other lot of currants.
11.9.48. *Vile day in the morning, blowy & rainy. Sea rough. Afternoon somewhat better, but with showers. Sea calming down.*
12.9.48. *Heavy rain & much wind in the night, clearing in the morning. Some showers, & not very warm, but the day fine on the whole. Sea calm. B. & R. brought the new boat back from Colonsay.*[1] *It appears it was rough in the Atlantic, though quite calm in the Sound. In the afternoon put wire netting along the fence to keep the pig out. He still gets in, but probably cannot do so if it is well tied down at the bottom.*
13.9.48. *Filthy day, sea rough. Cleared up somewhat in the evening. B. & R. could not get the boat's engine to start, probably owing to dirty plugs. Ordered some young turkeys (3–4 months). (Unobtainable).*
14.9.48. *(Hairmyres).*[2] *Much better day, quite warm part of the time. Sea fairly smooth. Just a little bumpiness before reaching Gigha.*[3] *One child sick. Comparatively little of the hay on the mainland is gathered in.*
15.9.48. *Tremendous rain in the night, with some thunder.*
16.9.48. *(Glasgow). Dull overcast day, but little or no rain. Evidently the tremendous rain of the other night happened all over the country. Some fields near Hairmyres were completely flooded. Very unwell, temperature about 101° each evening.*
17.9.48. *(Barnhill). Fairly fine day, but windy. Roughish crossing, but not quite enough so to be sick. Lime has arrived.*

On the facing page opposite 17.9.48, Orwell has written, and ticked:

Plant peonies
Prune raspberries

1. Colonsay is a much smaller island than Jura, lying some fifteen miles to its west; the journey by boat would have been about twice that distance.
2. Orwell had returned to Hairmyres Hospital for an examination by Mr. Dick; see letter to David Astor, 9 October 1948, *3467*.
3. Gigha is a small island lying southwest of Jura.

3456. To Leonard Moore

18 September 1948   Typewritten

Barnhill
Isle of Jura
Argyllshire

Dear Moore,
This is in answer to three letters of yours, or from your office.
I don't remember that I actually gave Mr Madejski[1] permission to translate anything of mine. I think I merely told him that in principle I was always glad

to have anything translated, and referred him to you. Of course make any stipulations you think proper. The only thing I want to make sure of is that where it is a case of a foreign country where one can't expect to make much money, such as Germany at this moment, or any oriental country, I don't want a translation to fall through merely because adequate payment is not offered. Even from a financial point of view I imagine it is worth putting oneself on the map in Germany, which is likely to become a good market again within a few years.

I am quite agreeable to the proposed broadcasting of "Shooting an Elephant,"[2] and to the Danish offer for the serial rights in "A Hanging."[3]

Yours sincerely
[Signed] Eric Blair
Eric Blair

1. Not identified. An annotation to Orwell's letter shows that Moore replied on 4 October, but his letter has not been traced and Orwell's next letters to Moore throw no light on this proposal.
2. Broadcast on the BBC Home Service, 12 October 1948.
3. The Danish rights were bought by the magazine *Magazinet*.

3457. Domestic Diary

<u>18.9.48.</u> *Fine clear day, not very warm, in the morning, some rain & wind in afternoon & evening. B. & R. stacking corn, which apparently has dried up in the last two days. A. picked blackberries (first this year.)*
<u>19.9.48.</u> *Alternately sunny & overcast, a few light showers, not very warm. Sea calm close in. Breakers over towards Crinan.[1] Tried boat. Very easy to steer. Planted peonies (six, red). Very roughly planted. Pruned raspberries. Not certain whether I did it correctly.*

1. See *3445, n. 1.*

3458. To Anthony Powell

[20 September 1948][1]   Picture postcard, handwritten; copy

Thanks so much for your postcard. I expect to be in London either in December or January (probably Jan.) according to when I get my book finished. I'm much better but still have to go very slowly & spend half the day in bed. Please remember me to Violet.   George.

1. The card shows Inverlussa, Isle of Jura; the message is undated, but the card is postmarked 20 September 1948.

3459. Domestic Diary

<u>20.9.48.</u>   *One sharp shower, otherwise fine, clear & rather cold. Some wind from W. B. & R. have about finished the stack, which is to be covered with a tarpaulin. Find one of the blackcurrants (ie. those planted last year) has already sent up a small plant, presumably by layering.*

<u>21.9.48.</u>   *Clear, fine day, rather cold. Little wind. Sea calm inshore. Started burning rubbish to get wood ash. A. planted sweet williams in nursery bed.*

<u>22.9.48.</u>   *Heavy rain in the night. From about 10 am onwards a beautiful, clear, sunny day, reasonably warm. Took boat down to the nearest bay to collect firewood. A. sowed winter spinach.*

<u>23.9.48.</u>   *A few small showers, but most of day simply overcast & rather cold. Wind from E. in the morning. A. & B. went over to Tarbert via Crinan for the cattle market. Boat ran well. B. bought 48 lambs for 24/– each. Last year's price was about 43/–. Felt very unwell, did not go out of doors.*

<u>24.9.48.</u>   *Filthy day, all day, Sea rough. Unwell, stayed in bed. B's sheep arrived.*

<u>25.9.48.</u>   *Filthy night & morning, clearing slightly in the afternoon. Not much wind. Sea calmer. Got up for a little. The cats keep catching young rats, ie. what I think are young rats & not field mice. Did not know they bred so late in the year as this.*

<u>26.9.48.</u>   *Horrible day. Very heavy rain in the night, & rain almost continuous throughout the day. Strong wind in the morning, mostly from S. The boat will have to be covered with a tarpaulin, as rain of this strength is liable to fill it up & sink it. Ground everywhere is a morass.*

<u>27.9.48.</u>   *Rain in night, but a much better day, sunny & windy. Sea rough. Some more rain in evening.*

<u>28.9.48.</u>   *Vile morning, pelting with rain, violent wind from south, sea very rough. Not cold. A few fine patches during afternoon.*

<u>29.9.48.</u>   *Better day, sunny & windy. One short shower in the morning. Sea fairly calm.*

3460. To Herbert Read

30 September 1948   Handwritten

Barnhill
I. of Jura
Argyllshire

Dear Read,
Herewith cheque for £1 for the F.D.C.[1] which was sent to me as the person could not remember the address.[2]

Yours
Geo. Orwell

1. Freedom Defence Committee; see *2725*, *n. 2*.
2. Annotated by Read: 'Ackngd 13/10/48. (Asked if he knows Mr Sitmetzler's address).' No reply from Orwell traced. 'Sitmetzler' must be Karl Schnetzler, for whom see *2893*.

3461. Domestic Diary

<u>30.9.48.</u> *Still, sunny & fairly warm in morning, still & overcast in afternoon. Sea calm in morning, growing slightly more choppy. Leaves beginning to fall.*

3462. 'The Labour Government After Three Years'

Commentary October 1948

This article was published by *Commentary*[1] under the title 'Britain's Struggle for Survival: The Labor[2] Government After Three Years.' Orwell states in his Notes for My Literary Executor, mid-1949, that the title was not his; see *3727*. In his Second Literary Notebook he wrote preparatory notes for this article (see *3463*); these have the title 'The Labour Gov.t after three years.' This, clearly, is Orwell's title and it has been restored here. That Notebook also states that the article was to be completed by 20 July, almost exactly three years to the day (26 July 1945) when the Labour Government took office. From Melvyn Lasky's wish to print a German version of the article in *Der Monat* (see Orwell's letter of 31 August 1948, *3446*), it would seem that the article had been completed by mid-August at the latest, as might be expected. The fact that the Labour Government's fourth year of office was well under way by the time the article appeared in *Commentary* may explain the non-Orwell title. The German translation, 'Armut und Hoffnung Grossbritanniens,' is drawn from the *Commentary* title; Orwell's title is dropped.

Der Monat (1 Jahrgang, Nummer 3, Dezember 1948) took liberties with the article's arrangement. The English original has 28 paragraphs. The German version transfers English paragraphs 21–24 to the end of the article; thus the German order of the English paragraphs is 25–28, 21–24. The German also makes slight verbal changes, which clarify and amplify the original. In English paragraph 25, 'It is noticeable that people' becomes (when translated back into English): 'It is noticeable that these people'; in the next sentence, 'there is not a weekly or monthly paper of standing which is a reliable supporter of the government' has had added, after 'paper of standing,' 'with perhaps the exception of *Tribune*.' This second addition smacks of Orwell himself, and so these amendments in *Der Monat* have been accepted into this version. *Der Monat* also omits the third sentence of paragraph 11, 'The housing situation . . . unbearably dull,' and the last two sentences of paragraph 13, 'It is true . . . inflationary.' The final sentence of paragraph 8 omits the reference to the Tories and reads (translated back into English): 'becoming a sleeping partner in an Anglo-Saxon conglomerate.' These cuts and especially the omission of the reference to the Tories seem designed for a German audience, and therefore these passages have not been altered here. The editor is grateful to Elizabeth Oliver for collating the German and English texts.

It is characteristic of our age that at the time of the 1945 General Election one could see fairly clearly what problems the Labor government was facing, and that it is just as difficult today as it was then to predict either success or failure. This is the age of the unresolved dilemma, of the struggle which never slows down and never leads to a decision. It is as though the world were suffering from a disease which is simultaneously acute, chronic, and not fatal.

In Britain we have lived for three years in a state of almost continuous crisis, like one of those radio serials in which the hero falls over a precipice at the end of each instalment. The supreme calamity is, of course, always averted, but the end of the story never seems to be any nearer. Bankruptcy has been put off and put off by American loans, by "austerity," and by the spending of reserves, and when those expedients cease to work it may be put off still further, possibly for decades, by a successful drive for exports: but the fundamental problem of making Britain genuinely solvent without sinking the standard of living to an unbearably low level remains untouched.

It is, I think, important to realize that in Britain the struggle between collectivism and laissez-faire is secondary. The main objective is national survival. Looking on from the outside and reading the British press, one might easily get the idea that the country is groaning beneath bureaucratic misrule and would be only too glad to return to the good old days of free enterprise; but this merely appears to be so because the big capitalists and the middling entrepreneur class are disproportionately vocal.

Britain is in many ways a conservative country, but it is also a country without a peasantry, one in which the desire for economic liberty is not strong or widespread. Property, in Britain, means a house, furniture, and a few hundred pounds' worth of savings; freedom means freedom of thought and speech, or the power to do what you choose in your spare time. The great majority of people take it for granted that they will live on wages or salaries rather than profits, welcome the idea of birth-to-death social insurance, and do not feel strongly one way or the other about the nationalization of industry. Rationing and controls generally are, of course, in a sense unpopular, but this is only important in that it increases the exhaustion and boredom resulting from eight years of overwork.

We are handicapped, in fact, not by any positive desire to return to capitalism but by the habits of mind acquired during prosperity (including the ideology of the socialist movement itself).

Even today, and even in left-wing circles, it is not fully grasped that Britain's economic position is an inherently bad one. A small overpopulated country, importing its food and paying for it with exports, can only keep going so long as the rest of the world is not industrialized. If the present world-wide development of industry continues, there will in the long run be no reason for international trade, except in raw materials, a few tropical products, and possibly a few luxury goods. All the advantage will lie—does already lie—with large autarchic countries like Russia or the United States. Britain, therefore, can only survive as an "advanced" and populous country if it is integrated into a much larger area.

At present, this may happen in one of four ways. One is by the formation of a union of Western Europe plus Africa; another is by tightening the links of the Commonwealth and transferring perhaps half the population of Britain to the English-speaking dominions; a third is by allowing Britain, with the rest of Europe, to become part of the Russian system; and the final possibility is by the accession of Britain to the United States. The objection in every case is obvious.

The first alternative, the most canvassed at present and perhaps the most hopeful, faces enormous difficulties and dangers, of which Russian hostility is only the most immediate. The second, even supposing the dominions to be prepared for it, could probably not be carried out except by a despotic government which was accustomed to transporting human beings like shiploads of cattle. The third, though it may happen as a result of defeat in war, can be ruled out as a possibility, since no one except a handful of Communists desires it. The fourth is quite likely to happen, but it is unacceptable from a British point of view, since it would mean becoming very definitely a junior partner and being tied to a country which everyone except a few Tories regards as politically backward.

Even if any of these possibilities, or some combination of them, comes to pass, it will only do so after a long delay, whereas the need for solvency is immediate. The leaders of the Labor government, therefore, can only make their plans on the assumption that Britain has got to be self-sufficient in the near future. They are endeavoring to bring a European union into being, they hope and believe that when it exists the dominions will adhere to it, and they are determined—indeed, they are obliged—to remain on good terms with the United States; but their immediate aim must be to make Britain's exports balance her imports. And they have to do this with worn-out industrial equipment, with foreign preoccupations which demand large armed forces and are therefore a heavy drain on man-power, and with a working class which is tired and not too well fed, and which fought the war and voted at the General Election in the expectation of something quite different.

In 1945, approximately half the electorate voted Labor. I believe it would be an exaggeration to say that the majority of these people voted for Socialism. They voted for full employment, bigger old-age pensions, the raising of the school-leaving age, more social and economic equality, and more democracy all round; and for nationalization of industry as a way of bringing these things about. The government, even if it wants to, cannot afford to disappoint its supporters altogether, and therefore has to combine basic reconstruction with immediate reforms that make the reconstruction more difficult. It would have been almost impossible, for instance, for a Labor government not to give re-housing first priority; but, necessary though the houses are, this means reducing the labor and materials that can be allotted to industrial building. The change-over to national ownership is not in itself an inspiring process, and in the popular regard the Labor party is the party that stands for shorter working hours, a free health service, day nurseries, free milk for school children, and the like, rather than the party that stands for Socialism.

Unfortunately, given the desperate shortage of nearly everything, it is not easy to improve the lives of the people in any material way. Physically, the average British citizen is probably somewhat worse off than he was three years ago.[3] The housing situation is extremely bad; food, though not actually insufficient, is unbearably dull. The prices of cigarettes, beer, and unrationed food such as vegetables are fantastic. And clothes rationing is an increasing hardship since its effects are cumulative. We are in the transition period which awaits all left-wing parties when they attain to power, and which always comes as a painful surprise because so little has been said about it beforehand. In general, left-wing parties gain their following by promising better material conditions, but when the test comes it always turns out that those conditions are not attainable immediately, but only after a long, self-denying struggle during which the average man is actually worse off than he was before he started. And precisely because he is worse off he refuses, or is unable, to make the effort demanded of him. One sees a perfect illustration of this in the struggle over the British coal mines.

The coal mines had to be nationalized, because in no other way was it possible to recapitalize them to the extent needed to bring them up to date. At the same time nationalization makes no immediate difference. The basic fact about the British mines is that they are old and neglected, and working conditions in them are so intolerable that without direct coercion, or the threat of unemployment, it is almost impossible to recruit sufficient labor to keep them going. Ever since the war ended we have had about fifty thousand less miners than we need, with the result that we can only with the greatest difficulty produce enough coal for our own needs, while an extra fifteen million tons for export seems an almost impossible objective. Of course the mines can be and probably will be modernized, but the process will take several years, and in the meantime, in order to make or buy the necessary machinery, our need of coal will be all the greater.

The same situation reproduces itself in less acute forms throughout the whole of industry. Nor is it easy, when people are tired already, to get them to work harder by direct economic inducements. If wages are evened out, labor drifts away from the more disagreeable jobs: if especially high rates are paid for those jobs, absenteeism increases, because it is then possible to earn enough to live on by working only three or four shifts a week. Not only individual absenteeism, but the innumerable stoppages and unofficial strikes of the past few years have probably been due to sheer exhaustion quite as much as to any economic grievance. It is true that the amount of time lost by industrial disputes has been small compared with what it was in the years immediately following the 1914–18 war, but there is the important difference that the strikes of that period, when successful, brought concrete benefits to the working class. Today, when the main problem is how to produce a bare sufficiency of goods, a strike is in effect a blow against the community as a whole, including the strikers themselves, and its net effect is inflationary.[4]

Underneath our present difficulties there lie two facts which the Socialist movement has always tended to ignore. One is that certain jobs which are vitally necessary are never done except under some kind of compulsion. As soon as you have full employment, therefore, you have to make use of forced labor for the dirtier kinds of work. (You can call it by some more soothing name, of course.) The other fact I have already alluded to: the radical impoverishment of Britain—the impossibility, at this stage, of raising the working-class standard of living, or even, probably, of maintaining it at its present level.

I do not profess to know whether our immediate economic problem will be solved. Putting aside the danger of war with the Soviet Union, it depends in the short run on the success of the Marshall Plan, and in the somewhat longer run on the formation of a Western Union or on the ability of Britain to keep ahead in the scramble for markets. But what is certain is that we can never return to the favored position that we held in the 19th and early 20th centuries. Until they found themselves in power and therefore up against hard facts, British Socialists would not readily admit that our national income, which they wanted to divide more equitably, was in part the product of colonial exploitation. Over a long period we not only produced less than we consumed (our exports have not balanced our imports since 1913), but we had the benefit of cheap raw materials and assured markets in countries which we held as colonies or could overawe by military force.

There were many reasons why this state of affairs could not last forever, and one reason was the decay of imperialist sentiment in the British people themselves. One sees here the still unsolved contradiction that dwells at the heart of the Socialist movement. Socialism, a creed which grew up in the industrialized Western countries, means better material conditions for the white proletariat; it also means liberation for the exploited colored peoples. But the two aims, at least temporarily, are incompatible. The leaders of the Socialist movement have never said this, or never said it loudly enough, and they are now paying for their timidity. Because the basic economic situation is not understood, hardships which are in fact unavoidable have the appearance of being due to the persistence of social inequality. The country houses and the smart hotels are still full of rich people, and it is tempting to imagine that if only they were wiped out there would be enough of everything for everybody. The fact that we are poorer than we were, that for a long time we shall go on being poorer, and that no redistribution of income can substantially alter this, is not clearly grasped, and morale suffers accordingly.

It is a commonplace that the Labor government has failed badly in its publicity. There has been a good deal of exhortation, especially in the last few months, but the day-to-day process of telling the public what is happening, and why, has not been systematically undertaken, nor had the need for it been realized beforehand. It was typical of the government's way of doing things to let people imagine for a year or more that things were going fairly well, and then suddenly to plaster the walls with posters bearing the almost threatening slogan "Work or Want". The housing shortage, the fuel shortage, bread rationing, and Polish immigration have all caused more resentment than they need have done if the underlying facts had been properly explained. Nor has the government been very successful in "selling" Britain abroad, as one can see from the fact that we are execrated all over the world, to a great extent unjustly, for our actions in Palestine, while the enormously more important settlement with India passes almost unnoticed.

So far as publicity inside Britain is concerned, the government has two great difficulties to contend with. One is its lack of vehicles of expression. With the exception of a single daily paper, the *Herald*, all that matters of the British press is controlled either by Tories, or, in a very few cases, by left-wing factions not reliably sympathetic to a Labor government. The BBC on the other hand is a semi-autonomous corporation which is neutral in home politics and can only be used to a limited extent for official announcements. The other difficulty the government suffers from is that almost up to the moment of the general election it was in coalition with its opponents and therefore had no chance to make its own position clear.

Before the war, years of steady propaganda had won over to the Labor party the bulk of the manual workers and part of the middle class: but this was old-fashioned Socialist propaganda, largely irrelevant to a postwar world in which Britain is weakened and impoverished, Germany and Japan prostrate, Russia in effect an enemy, and the United States an active world power. During the more desperate period of the war the Labor party was not in a position to declare an independent policy, though in my opinion it made a serious mistake in not getting out of the coalition as soon as it became clear that the war was won. Then came the general election, at extremely short notice. The Labor party went to the country, as it was bound to do in the circumstances, promising peace abroad and prosperity at home.

If it had been truthful it would have explained that there were very hard times ahead, all the harder because the first steps towards socialism now had to be taken, and that the ending of the hot war with the Axis merely meant the beginning of a cold war with the Soviet Union. To say, as every Labor candidate did, "A Labor government will get along better with Russia" was about equivalent to saying "A Protestant government will get along better with the Vatican." But the average voter did not grasp the fact, obvious since 1943, that Russia was hostile, nor the fact that Communism and Social Democracy are irreconcilable enemies; and meanwhile the election had to be won. The Labor party won it partly by irredeemable promises. It could hardly be blamed for doing this, but the confusion in the public mind between a Left policy and a pro-Russian policy had ugly possibilities, and it is owing to good luck rather than good management that they have not been realized. If the pro-Russian enthusiasm that grew up during the war had persisted, the spectacle of Britain engaging in a seemingly meaningless quarrel with the USSR, and keeping up large and expensive armed forces in consequence, might have split the Labor movement from top to bottom. For it could then have been plausibly said that our hardships were due to an anti-Communist policy forced upon us by America. This, of course, is what the Communists and crypto-Communists do say, but with less success than they might legitimately have expected, because of the cooling-off of Russophile feeling. This cooling-off has not been due to Labor party propaganda but to the behavior of the Russian government itself. Of course there is always the possibility of a sudden revulsion in popular feeling if, for example, we appeared to be on the verge of war for some frivolous reason.

With all the difficulties that I have enumerated—the threatening and perhaps desperate economic situation, the tug-of-war between pre-election promises and essential reconstruction, the exhaustion and disappointment which express themselves in absenteeism and unjustified strikes, the resentment of small business men and middle-class people generally who are more and more fed up with controls and heavy taxation—in spite of all this, the government is still in a very strong position. The next general election is two years away, and before then something calamitous may happen, but given anything like a continuance of present conditions, I do not believe that the Labor party can be turned out of office. At present, although it has enemies, it has no ideological rival. There is only the Conservative party, which is bankrupt of ideas and can only squeal about grievances which are essentially middle-class or upper-class, and the opposition on the Left, the Communists and "cryptos" and the disgruntled Labor supporters who might follow them. These people have failed to bring about the split they were trying for, because they have identified themselves with a threatening foreign power, while in home affairs they have no program radically different from that of the Labor party itself.

One must remember that between them the Labor party and the Conservative party adequately represent the bulk of the population, and unless they disintegrate it is difficult for any other mass party to arise. The Communists are able to exert considerable influence by using "infiltration" methods, but in any open contest their position is hopeless, and that of the Fascist groups is even more so. Mosley[5] is again active, and anti-Semitism has increased over the past year or two, but the growth of a serious Fascist movement is not to be feared at present, because without the break-up of the old parties the potential membership for it does not exist. Electorally, it is only the Conservatives that the Labor party has to fear, and there is no sign that they are making much headway. It is true that they made large gains in the local-government elections, probably because people who do not as a rule bother to vote, especially women, wanted to register their exasperation with unpopular controls such as potato rationing. But in parliamentary by-elections the Labor party has not lost a single seat that it won in 1945; this is quite unprecedented for a party that has been in power for three years. The Conservatives could only win the next general election by swinging over both the "floating vote" (middle class and white-collar workers), and, in addition, the two million votes which were cast for the Liberals in 1945. The mass of the manual workers are not likely ever again to vote for the Conservative party, which is identified in their minds with class privilege and, above all, with unemployment.

If the Conservatives returned to power it would be a disaster, because they would have to follow much the same policy as a Labor government, but without possessing the confidence of the people who matter most. With Labor securely in power, perhaps for several successive terms, we have at least the chance of effecting the necessary changes peacefully. No doubt

441

Britain will survive, at some level or another, in the sense that there will not actually be mass starvation; the question is whether we can survive as a democratic country with a certain decency of social atmosphere and political behavior. For a long time to come, unless there is breakdown and mass unemployment, the main problem will be to induce people to work harder; can we do it without forced labor, terrorism, and a secret police force? So far, in spite of the cries of agony from the Beaverbrook press,[6] the government has encroached very little upon individual liberty. It has barely used its powers, and has not indulged in anything that could reasonably be called political persecution. But then the decisive moment has not yet come.

Other countries, notably France, are in a position essentially similar to that of Britain, and perhaps the same problem faces all countries sooner or later. Left-wing governments only come to power in periods of calamity, and their first task is always to get more work out of exhausted and disappointed people. So far as Britain is concerned, all one can say is that the British people are very patient, very disciplined, and will put up with almost anything so long as they see a reason for it. The most urgent need is for the government to enter, more intelligently than it has done hitherto, upon the job of basic explanation, so that the average man, who endured the war in the vague hope that it would lead to something better, may understand *why* he has got to endure overwork and discomfort for years more, with no immediate recompense except an increase in social equality.

As yet, the advent of a Labor government has made no marked difference in the intellectual atmosphere of Britain, and it has affected the position of people in the liberal professions (other than doctors) less than it has affected business men and manual workers. The habitually discontented and mistrustful attitude of the left-wing intelligentsia has hardly been modified at all. The outlook of these people is adequately represented by the *New Statesman*, and perhaps also by *Tribune*, and by such publicists as Laski, Cole, and Crossman.[7] All of them, of course, support the Labor party—some of them, indeed, are organizationally connected with it—but they always regard it with impatience, and they are usually in disagreement with its foreign policy. The fashionable attitude has always been to look on the Labor party as a machine which will not move faster than it is pushed, and to suspect its leaders of wanting, not actually to sell out to the enemy, but to slow down the rate of change and keep the social structure as nearly intact as possible. It is noticeable that these people still habitually talk about "British imperialism" and "the British ruling class" as though nothing had happened, and with the apparent implication that Churchill and Company are still in some way ruling the country. A symptom of the Labor party's low prestige is the fact that there is not a weekly or monthly paper of standing with perhaps the exception of *Tribune*[8] which is a reliable supporter of the government.

To account for this attitude, and its failure to change when Labor came to power, one has to remember several things. One is the sell-out of Macdonald[9] and his group in 1931, which left behind it a sort of traumatic shock and a half-conscious feeling that a Labor government is of its nature weak and potentially treacherous. Another is the fact that the Labor party is essentially a working-class party, the organ of the unionized industrial workers, while the theoreticians of Socialism are mostly middle-class. The Labor party has a policy, but has no clearcut ideology which can compete with Marxism. It exists primarily to win better conditions for the wage-earners, and at the same time it has an ethical, quasi-religious tradition, deriving ultimately from evangelical Protestantism and not acceptable to middle-class intellectuals who have been subjected to Continental influences. The difference of outlook is generally over things happening outside Britain. In the years before the war it was, with few exceptions, only the middle-class supporters of the Labor party who were interested in the struggle against fascism abroad, and there is a similar division over Palestine now. The workers, in so far as they bother about the matter at all, are not anti-Bevin on the Palestine issue, whereas nearly all left-wing intellectuals are violently so. This is less a difference of policy than of subjective feeling. Few people could tell you what our Palestine policy is or was (assuming that we ever had one), and fewer still could tell you what it ought to be. But the reaction to the plight of the Jewish DP's, to the achievements of the Zionist settlers, and perhaps also to the spectacle of British soldiers being blown up by terrorists, varies according to class background.

During and since the war there has appeared a new generation of intellectuals whose more vocal members are anti-Socialist in outlook—or, at any rate, are opposed to centralism, planning, direction of labor, and compulsory military service, and, in general, to the interference of the state with the individual. This outlook expresses itself in movements variously called anarchism, pacifism, and personalism; there are also the minor nationalist movements (Welsh and Scottish), which have gained ground in recent years and which have the same anti-centralist tendency. Most younger writers seem to have hostility to the government, which they accuse almost in the same breath of being reactionary and *dirigiste*.

There has been considerable outcry about the waning of intellectual liberty and the tendency of writers, artists, and scientists to degenerate into official hacks. This is partly justified, but the blame does not lie with the Labor party. What has happened is that for about a dozen years past the economic status of writers, if not of all artists, has been deteriorating, and they have had to look more and more to the state and to semi-official bodies such as the BBC to give them a livelihood. The war accelerated the process, and the present government has merely carried on a tradition which it inherited from its predecessor. The Labor party does not, as such, have any literary or artistic policy. It is headed by practical men who are not much inclined either to befriend the artist or to "coordinate" him in the totalitarian fashion. The recent tightening-up of employment regulations does contain a potential threat to all intellectuals, because it makes it possible, in theory, to classify any unsuccessful writer or artist as a non-worker and direct him into "gainful employment." However, this does not happen in practice. The right to starve, so important to those who genuinely care about literature or the arts, seems to be almost as well guaranteed as it was under pure capitalism.[10]

1. *Commentary* was originally *The Contemporary Jewish Record*; Orwell wrote 'Anti-Semitism in Britain' for it, April 1945; see *2626*.
2. Orwell's preparatory notes for this article show that he spelt Labour with a 'u' and doubtless his typescript did the same. However, 'Labor' has been retained in line with the practice adopted of following the house-styles of printed material.
3. This sentence was cut from *Der Monat*; see *headnote*.
4. The last two sentences of this paragraph were cut from *Der Monat*; see *headnote*.
5. Sir Oswald Mosley (1896–1980), successively Conservative, Independent, and Labour M.P. He founded his New Party in 1931, and became a devoted advocate of Hitler; his party became the British Union of Fascists.
6. Right-wing newspapers, including the *Daily Express*, the London *Evening Standard*, and the *Sunday Express*, owned by Lord Beaverbrook (1879–1964).
7. Harold J. Laski (1893–1950), political theorist, Marxist, author, and journalist; Professor of Political Science, University of London, from 1926; member of the Executive Committee of the Labour Party, 1936–49. G. D. H. Cole (1889–1959), Chichele Professor of Social and Political Theory, University of Oxford, and Fellow of All Souls; socialist and prolific writer. An influential book about this time was his *The Intelligent Man's Guide to the Post-War World* (1947), referred to by Orwell as 'Mr G. D. H. Cole's last 1143-page compilation' in his article 'In Defence of Comrade Zilliacus'; see *3254*. Richard Crossman; see *3325, n. 5.*
8. For changes made to this paragraph in *Der Monat* and accepted in this edition, see *headnote*.
9. Ramsay MacDonald (1866–1937), first Labour Prime Minister, in a minority government in 1924 supported by Liberals, and then in 1929–31. He was not alone in being overcome by the world depression of this period; after he offered his resignation, on 24 August 1931, he remained in office, to the astonishment of his colleagues, as head of a coalition government with Conservatives and Liberals. In 1935 he exchanged roles with Stanley Baldwin (who had, in effect, become prime minister), and served as Lord President of the Council, resigning that office six months before his death. He has, fairly or not, ever since been reviled by the Labour Party for what it considers an act of betrayal.
10. This editorial note appears on the first page of the article in *Commentary*:
    For many of the democratic peoples throughout the world, Great Britain's socialist experiment represents a crucial hope for the development of a workable alternative to both capitalism and Communism; and from any point of view, the success or failure of Britain's Labor government must be recognized as immensely important to the final outcome of the present struggle between East and West. GEORGE ORWELL, one of the most acute political observers in England, here examines the record of the Labor government in terms of the fundamental question: is socialism compatible with democracy? Mr. Orwell, at once an intellectual and a man of action, fought in the POUM militia during the Spanish Civil War, served with the British Home Guard during the recent conflict, and has been literary editor of the London *Tribune*. He is the author of a number of books, of which the latest is *Animal Farm*, a satire on Communism. He was born in Bengal, India, in 1903.

3463. Preparatory Notes for 'The Labour Government After Three Years'

Second Literary Notebook

"The Labour Gov.t after three years."

The real crisis has not come yet. (Resources have not run out).
Have to be discussed in terms of underlying factors.

i.. *Britain's fundamentally bad economic position, not entirely remediable even by change-over to Socialism.*

Population too large for food-output—must import[1] food etc.
To pay for food—exports.
Have not done this since about 1914—industry antiquated, high standard of living. Colonial exploitation (loss of colonies inevitably means at least <u>*temporary*</u> *impoverishment).*
Paid for with interest on loans etc—now running out.
Reconstruction of industry—but scramble for exports precarious way of living when (a) others doing the same, (b) primary-prod. countries becoming more industrialised.
Solutions:—
(a) European federation + Africa. Difficulties of.
(b) Commonwealth as autarkic area. Difficulties of.
(c) To become part of USA. Difficulties of.

<u>ii.</u> *At present, policy followed is to try & make G.B. solvent while introducing Socialism, or at least public ownership of major industries, all-round social insurance, etc.*
Difficult reconstruction period, not foreseen by average man. (Instance coal mines).
Nationalisation makes no difference in itself—merely makes solution possible.

Fatigue after war years. Full employment—no incentive to do unpleasant jobs (difficulties of arranging money incentives).
Impossibility of envisaging life without luxuries.
Possible unwillingness when the pinch comes to cut down our standard of living for the benefit of the coloured races.
Persistence of class-distinction—bad effect on morale.
Freeze wages—cut profits—a morale issue.
Foreign policy. Unpopularity of service in armed forces. Need to safeguard raw materials & strategic routes—expensiveness of commitments.
Food. Since 1946 (bread rationing) poorest workers, esp. women, probably underfed.
Black market. Basic petrol. Spivs. Gambling.
Unofficial strikes. Absenteeism. Go slow.
Health service. Popular.
Housing—calamitous but good progress rel. to other countries.
Education—failure to democratise.
Unpopularity of controls—mainly middle-class.

<u>iii.</u> *Foreign policy.*
Largely dominated by geography.
G.B. too exhausted for adventuring—foreign policy essentially defensive.
Since 1945 (earlier) conditioned by Russian hostility & absolute necessity for hanging on to strategic spots.

Spain? Palestine? (Greece different issue).

Crisis of the foreign policy always danger of sudden drop in govern-ment's°popularity, esp. if somehow connected with added discomforts at home.
Dropping-off of popularity of USSR. But war with USSR morally impossible unless it appeared purely defensive.
Anti-Americanism. Now fashionable, but not much substance.
Anti-semitism? Probably increased (but danger of revival of Fascism exaggerated). Must affect reactions to Palestine issue.

iv. *General issue of liberty vs. security.*
Left-wing theory—workers not interested in liberty, only in security. (But without some liberty, no security.)
True so far as conscious thinking goes. No hostility to controls.
But disappointment. Standard of living hardly higher, freedom of movement less.
In the long run, possibly unemployment might lose its terrors? (By being forgotten.)
Chief sensation of most people—overwork, dull life.
All-round regulation sought in name of security, then resisted in name of liberty.
Fight against the boss—State becomes the boss.

v. *Strikes—antisocial nature of in time of scarcity.*
Only effective weapon when against private capitalist in competition with other capitalists: Otherwise is essentially a blow against commun-ity as a whole & inconveniences chiefly the working class. General effect inflationary.

---

vi. *The government's failure in publicity.*
Lack of a left-wing press—radio more or less neutral.
Falsifications of election campaign (we are going to be better off—a Labour Gov.t will get on better with Russia).
By staying in coalition till last moment, Labour inherited Conservative policy.
Stupid failure to publicise—constant fulmination against "Commu-nism", no attempt to explain.
Issues like Polish labour misunderstood.

vii. *Electoral prospects.*
Labour record unprec. good.
But local elections—increased poll—women voting against controls.
Floating vote. Anomalies of Brit. electoral system.
Possibility of Conservative victory—unlikely.
In any case a calamity, as Conservative Gov.t would never have support of manual workers.

viii. Disadvantages of democracy vs. dictatorship.
Only advantage on the other side—look at the countries that do not have democracy.

Order.

The real clash not socialism vs. private enterprise.
The real strain not yet.
Special bad economic situation of G.B. (prospectively the same for all industrialised nations.)
Point reached—impossibility (?) of maintaining living standards.
Just this moment introduction of Socialism.
Everyone tired, bored, disappointed.
Strikes.
Inherent difficulty of a transition period (instance coal mines)
Left gov.ts always take power in moments of disaster.

Bad economic situation coincides with bad international situation.
Note potential danger of this (less food because more troops because hostility towards USSR).
If not come to a head, Russian gov.t to thank for this.
Could always happen that way if definite embroilment abroad.
N.B. African difficulty.
Gov.t's failure in publicity.
N.B. this partly due to nature of Socialist propaganda over many years.
Partly to coalition—general election.
Public failure to understand.

Electoral situation.

Advantages/disadvantages of democracy.

1. *'pay' crossed out before 'import.'*

3464. Domestic Diary

1.10.48.[1]   *Filthy day, all day. Boat gets a lot of water in it, evidently taking some in through the seams.*

1. This entry and those for 2, 3, and 4 October were initially entered as for August ('8' instead of '10'); the error was corrected by Orwell when he got to the last entry for the page, that for 4 October. These entries were probably all made at the same time; see *3466* and *3466, n. 1* for incorrect item under 2.10.48.

3465. Review of *The Novel and the World's Dilemma* by Edwin Berry Burgum

The Times Literary Supplement, 2 October 1948   Published anonymously

At the beginning of this fairly comprehensive survey of contemporary novelists Mr. Burgum claims that "the significance of fiction in the modern world can hardly be overestimated," and adds that prose and not poetry must be the dominant literary form in an age such as our own. The reason is that there is no longer a common culture in which a large range of words can be assumed to have more or less the same associations for everybody, so that the sort of shorthand which poetry necessarily employs is only intelligible to small groups of people. All writing has to consist partly of explanation, which is permissible in a novel, but which, if it were attempted in verse, would simply cause it to break down into prose. Only in the form of fiction, therefore, can good literature reach a large public. This is probably truer in the United States than in more homogeneous countries such as France or Britain, but at any rate it is true that the quantity of good verse published during the present century has been very small, while there have been many novelists who must be regarded as serious thinkers, and who have also been popular enough to be influential. Even a purely sociological study of them, with literary qualities as far as possible ignored, could be valuable.

Unfortunately Mr. Burgum's approach is not only sociological but political. What he demands of a novelist is, in effect, "socialist realism," though he is broadminded enough to allow that novels written according to other prescriptions can have at any rate symptomatic value. He considers in all some fifteen writers, of whom roughly half are Europeans. The Europeans include Proust, Joyce, Kafka and three or four others; the Americans are Gertrude Stein, Mr. Hemingway, Mr. Faulkner, Mr. Saroyan, Mr. Steinbeck, Dreiser, Thomas Wolfe and Mr. Richard Wright. The chapter headings—"Franz Kafka and the Bankruptcy of Faith," "The Promise of Democracy in Richard Wright's *Native Son*," and the like— sufficiently indicate Mr. Burgum's attitude. Writers like Proust or Joyce are admitted to be accomplished artists, but they are are chiefly valuable as examples of bourgeois decadence: the best writers are the "progressive" ones.

This sounds more plausible in general terms than when Mr. Burgum descends to particulars. He gives his warmest praise to Mr. Steinbeck's *The Grapes of Wrath* and to the Negro novelist, Mr. Richard Wright. Mr. Wright is certainly a gifted and vigorous writer, but not more so than some dozens of others among his contemporaries, and it is clear that Mr. Burgum singles him out primarily because he is a Negro and sympathetic to Communism.[1] The peculiar excellence of *The Grapes of Wrath* is explained as being due to the fact that Mr. Steinbeck was stimulated into optimism by the reforms of the New Deal, of which the book was a sort of by-product. In some of the essays the fact seems to have been wrenched, or mis-remembered, to fit the theory. The essay on Mr. Aldous Huxley contains several errors, and Mr. Burgum's interpretation of *Point Counter Point* is based partly on an incident in the plot

448

which he has remembered wrongly. All in all, a reader is left with the feeling that, though many of the best writers of this century certainly have been in some sense decadent, more is needed by a novelist, or a critic, than a belief in progress and democracy.

1. Richard Wright (1908–1960), novelist and short-story writer, is best known for his *Native Son* (1940), was given a laudatory review by Orwell, *Tribune*, 26 April 1940; see *616*. That novel not only abandoned the mask of docile acceptance then demanded of blacks but proved a best-seller and, in 1941, was dramatised and produced on Broadway with Wright playing the lead role of Bigger Thomas. He joined the Communist Party in 1932 and was executive secretary of the Chicago branch of the John Reed Club (of left-wing writers and artists). He left the Communist Party in 1944 and later settled in Paris (where he died), shifting from Marxism to Existentialism. He wrote a distinguished autobiography, *Black Boy* (1945).

3466. Domestic Diary

2.10.48. Nice, sunny, still day, fairly warm till evening. Sea calm. A. & B. took the boat down to Ardlussa to get the stores. The run from Barnhill to Ardlussa evidently takes about an hour. Started clearing strawberries. A curlew has adopted the fruit field & is there most of the time. Swallows seem to have flown. Bracken now brown everywhere.[1]
3.10.48. Beautiful day, except for 1 short shower in the morning. Planted crocuses (200, yellow).
4.10.48. Beautiful day. A. picked a lot of blackberries. Planted scillas (100). A lamb died yesterday, the one that was lame. Probable reason, getting onto its back, or into a rut it could not get out of. As it was only just dead when found, the others ate it, which I did not fancy. The large calf is thought to have ringworm. Some lupins still flowering, & even new buds forming. Tremendous roaring of stags every night.
5.10.48. A little rain in the night, I think. Today a very still, overcast day, not very warm. Sea glassy. Flapping of cormorant's wings audible from the sea-shore (about 400 yards away). Today a hind & fawn got into the field, & when chased out by Bob the hind ran into the wire & broke its leg, so B. had to shoot it. Transplanted a few raspberry suckers to fill up gaps in rows; the book says you should not do this.
6.10.48. Very still day, sunny in afternoon. Sea calm. A. & I.[2] *made new house for the pig, making the walls of hay stuffed between two sheets of wire netting. Seems fairly wind-tight. Berries now at best on rowans. A lot of blackberries, very large.*

On the facing page opposite 5 and 6.10.48, Orwell wrote, ticking the last three of the four items, and underlining 'Order hay' and 'parrafin'°:

Order Aladdin[3] chimney
Order hay.
··   parrafin.°
··   other tractor

7.10.48.   Beautiful, still day, quite warm till evening. Finished clearing the strawberries. Runners not so bad as last year. The others went out in the boat & took the creels round to the other bay. Some trouble with the petrol feed, but the engine was firing on all 4 cylinders, for almost the first time. Felt very unwell in evening (temperature 101°).
8.10.48.   Strong wind all day. Sea rough. Rain in late evening. Unwell, stayed in bed (temperature 99°).

1. After 'everywhere' Orwell wrote, then crossed out, 'Planted crocuses (200, yellow)'; this item then appears under 3 October. Orwell may have written several entries at the same time: see *3464, 1.10.48, n. 1.*
2. Avril and, presumably, Ian M'Kechnie, an estate worker at Ardlussa who lived at Inverlussa. The 'I.' cannot be Orwell himself: the full point is quite clear; see *3471, 11.10.48.*
3. Trade name for a room heater fuelled by paraffin.

3467. To David Astor

9 October 1948   Typewritten, handwritten postscript

Barnhill

Dear David,

Thanks so much for your letter. A little before getting it I had written to Mr Rose,[1] sending him a short review of one book and making suggestions for some others. I think I had put on the list of books I should like to have one called "Boys will be Boys"[2] (about thrillers etc.), of which the publishers have now sent me a copy: so even if he would like to have me review it, there is no need to send it to me.

You were right about my being not very well. I am a bit better now but felt very poorly for about a fortnight. It started funnily enough with my going back to Hairmyres to be examined,[3] which they had told me to do in September. Mr Dick seemed to be quite pleased with the results of his examination, but the journey upset me. Any kind of journey seems to do this. He told me to go on as at present, ie. spending half the day in bed, which I quite gladly do as I simply can't manage any kind of exertion. To walk a mile or pick up anything in the least heavy, or above all to get cold, promptly upsets me. Even if I go out in the evening to fetch the cows in it gives me a temperature. On the other hand so long as I live a senile sort of life I feel all right, and I seem to be able to work much as usual. I have got so used to writing in bed that I think I prefer it, though of course it's awkward to type there. I am just struggling with the last stages of this bloody book, which is supposed to be done by early December, and will be if I don't get ill again. It would have been done by the spring if it had not been for this illness.

Richard is tremendously well and is out of doors in all weathers. I am sorry to say he took to smoking recently, but he made himself horribly sick and that has put him off it. He also swears. I don't stop him of course, but I am trying to improve my own language a bit. The weather has been absolutely filthy, except for three or four days just recently. Bill Dunn managed to get all his hay and corn in early, but a lot must have been spoiled elsewhere. The farm is building up. He has now got about 50 sheep and about 10 head of cattle, some of which are my property. We have also got a pig which will go to be baconed shortly. I had never kept one before and shan't be sorry to see the last of this one. They are most annoying destructive animals, and hard to keep out of anywhere because they are so strong and cunning. We have built up a bit of a garden here now. Of course a lot of it has gone back owing to my not being able to do anything, but I hope to get an Irish labourer[4] to do some digging this winter and even this year we had quite a few flowers and lashings of strawberries. Richard seems interested in farm and garden operations, and he helps me in the garden and is sometimes quite useful. I would like him to be a farmer when he grows up, in fact I shouldn't wonder if anyone who survives will have to be that, but of course I'm not going to force him.

I don't know when I'm coming up to London. First I must finish this book, and I'm not keen on London just before Xmas. I had thought of coming in January, but I must wait till I feel up to travelling. I'm a bit out of touch with the news, partly because the battery of my wireless is getting weak, but everything looks pretty black. I don't personally believe an all-out shooting war could happen now, only perhaps "incidents" such as used to occur all the time between Russia and Japan, but I suppose the atomic war is now a certainty within not very many years. This book I am writing is about the possible state of affairs if the atomic war *isn't* conclusive. I think you were right after all about de Gaulle being a serious figure. I suppose at need we shall have to back the swine up rather than have a Communist France, but I must say I think this backing-up of Franco, which now appears to be the policy is a mistake. In France there doesn't seem to be an alternative between de Gaulle and the Communists, because apart from the CP there has never been a mass working-class movement and everyone appears to be either pro-CP or bien pensant. But I shouldn't have said from what little knowledge I have that things were the same in Spain. No doubt it is the American Catholics who saved Franco from being turfed out in 1945. I am still worried about our policies in Africa and South Asia. Is Crankshaw[5] still going to Africa for you, I wonder? It's all most depressing. I keep thinking, shall I get such and such a book done before the rockets begin to fly and we go back to clay tablets.

There is an eagle flying over the field in front. They always come here in windy weather.

Yours
George

[Written at head of first side of letter:]
P.S. Do you happen to know anyone who restores pictures. A picture of mine has been damaged (a slit in the canvas) & though it isn't worth anything I should like to have it repaired.

1. Jim Rose, a member of the literary editor's staff of *The Observer*; see *3493*.
2. *Boys Will be Boys: The Story of Sweeney Todd, Deadwood Dick, Sexton Blake, et al.*, by E. S. Turner (1948; revised, 1957). Orwell did not review this book.
3. See *3455*, *14.9.48* and *16.9.48*.
4. Francis (Francey) Boyle, a road-worker; see Crick, 525.

5. Edward Crankshaw (1909–1984), novelist and critic, member of diplomatic staff on *The Observer* from 1947; British Military Mission to Moscow, 1941–43. In *David Astor and 'The Observer,'* Richard Cockett states: 'Orwell was instrumental in making David aware of the post-war problem of decolonization in Africa. Orwell had always taken an interest in Indian independence—the subject of his first "Forum" [22 February 1942; see *981*]—and towards the end of the war he persuaded David that the next great challenge to British post-imperialism would come in Africa, a continent which then excited little interest, apart from the fighting in the desert. Orwell argued that Africa would become the greatest challenge for decolonization, and it was there that Britain could avoid the mistakes made during the course of the struggle for Indian independence. *The Observer* was thus the first, and for a long time the only, British paper to focus on the problems of decolonization in Africa and in particular the plight of Africans on their own continent' (126). See Orwell's letter to Astor of 19 November 1948, *3490*, for Orwell's pleasure that *The Observer* 'is taking up Africa.'

3468. Domestic Diary

<u>9.10.48.</u> *Dreadful day, all day. Sea rough. Impossible to fetch stores etc.*

3469. Review of *Gandhi and Stalin* by Louis Fischer

The Observer, 10 October 1948

"Given a shelf of freedom on which to stand," writes Mr. Louis Fischer, "and using the crowbar of individual power, Gandhi undertakes to move the earth." It sounds splendid, of course. But, since it is apparently offered as the basis for a political programme, one feels inclined to ask: What would Gandhi do if he *wasn't* given a shelf to stand on?

The fact that this question is never clearly answered vitiates the whole book. In outline Mr. Fischer's argument is simple enough. Russia is a danger to world peace and must be resisted: we, the Western nations, can resist successfully only if we make our own democracy work: the way to do this is to follow the teachings of Gandhi. As to the first two propositions, they can hardly be disputed, and Mr. Fischer does useful work in setting them forth. He puts the case against the Stalin regime in a vigorous journalistic style, backed up by his long personal experience of Russian conditions, and he rightly emphasises, what is still not sufficiently grasped in this country, that the struggle between Russia and the West may be decided by the attitude of the coloured peoples. At present we are losing the battle for Asia and Africa, and to win it will mean a change of attitude which is not yet within sight of happening. But the invocation of Gandhi in support of a merely "progressive," anti-totalitarian programme is a *non sequitur*.

The fact is that Gandhi's political methods were almost irrelevant to the present situation, because they depended on publicity. As Mr. Fischer admits, Gandhi never had to deal with a totalitarian Power. He was dealing with an old-fashioned and rather shaky despotism which treated him in a fairly chivalrous way and allowed him to appeal to world opinion at every step.

It is difficult to see how his strategy of fasting and civil disobedience could be applied in a country where political opponents simply disappear and the public never hears anything that the Government does not want it to hear. Moreover, it appears that when Mr. Fischer tells us that we should follow Gandhi's teaching, he does not actually mean that we should follow Gandhi's teaching. He wants to prevent the expansion of Russian imperialism, non-violently if we can, but violently if we must: whereas Gandhi's central tenet was that you must not use violence even if the alternative is defeat. Asked to give an opinion on the German Jews, Gandhi apparently answered that they should have committed mass suicide, and thus "aroused the world"—an answer which seems to embarrass even Mr. Fischer. Most of Mr. Fischer's political conclusions are such as any person of good will can agree with heartily: but the attempt to derive them from Gandhi seems to be founded on personal admiration rather than genuine agreement.

3470. **To Leonard Moore**

10 October 1948   Typewritten

Barnhill
Isle of Jura
Argyllshire

Dear Moore,
Thank you for your letter. I am glad you managed to fix the Danish broadcast of "Animal Farm." I enclose the contract for the Italian version of "Coming Up",[1] signed.

I also enclose two other letters. One is a document from some magazine run by American M.G.[2] in Germany. I suppose I agreed to their reprinting some article, but I'm not certain what article it was.[3] Any way, could you please collect the fee for me, which apparently is £25. There doesn't seem to be anywhere on it where I have to sign it. The other letter is from somebody called Frank Taylor.[4] Is that by any chance the representative of Reynall° & Hitchcock whom I met very briefly a year or two ago in London? Anyway I assume I don't have to do anything about it.[5]

Yours sincerely
[Signed] Eric Blair
Eric Blair

1. Mondadori, who published several Italian translations of Orwell's work, issued its edition of *Coming Up for Air* in June 1966.
2. American Military Government, Berlin. It sponsored *Der Monat*.
3. Presumably this was 'Armut und Hoffnung Grossbritanniens' ('The Labour Government After Three Years'), *Der Monat*, No. 3, December 1948; see *3446, n. 1* and *3462*. Orwell acknowledged receipt of £25 on 29 October 1948; see *3479*.
4. Not specifically identified, but presumably a representative of Reynal & Hitchcock, which had published *Dickens, Dali & Others*.
5. It is not known what 'it' was. The letter has been annotated in Moore's office: 'E.M.B. Enter in rough day book,' initialled 'EMB'; and, illegibly, '[all] books.'

3471. Domestic Diary

10.10.48. *Very heavy rain in night. Pools everywhere this morning. Today overcast, thick mist, very still, & raining lightly all morning. Rain stopped in afternoon & mist grew thicker. B. & Ian[1] went over to Crinan, rather dangerous in this mist as they had no compass. Pig's new house gets very wet inside, but this is due to water trickling down the hillside & could be dealt with by a small trench round the wall.*
11.10.48. *Thick mist last night, & some rain, I think. Today blowy & overcast, but no rain till evening. Sea rough. Ian & B. had some difficulty getting to Crinan, because there was so much water in the boat that it had got into the engine. All right on return journey. Ian has taken the boat to Ardlussa for Malcolm[2] to see whether there is a board loose. Eagle over the field today & yesterday. The cats keep catching shrews, which apparently are in the haystack. Yesterday we ate the first cockerel (May hatched). Quite good & made a sufficient meal for 6 people. 3 more coming on. New consignment of drink today (12 bottles). Bill's new puppy arrived (bitch). A. dug trench round pig-sty.*

1. Ian M'Kechnie.
2. Malcolm M'Kechnie, Ian's father.

3472. Radio Broadcast of 'Shooting an Elephant'
12 October 1948

Orwell's account of 'Shooting an Elephant,' first published in *New Writing*, No. 2, Autumn 1936, was broadcast in its entirety in the BBC Home Service, 3:40 to 4:00 P.M, 12 October 1948. It was read by Arthur Bush. The text was taken from *Penguin New Writing*, No. 1, November 1940, in which the essay had been reprinted. There are one or two very slight changes from the Penguin version.

3473. Domestic Diary

12.10.48. *Very blowy all day. Only a few drops of rain. Sea rough, breakers outside. Sty seems all right now that A. has dug trench. Apples not quite ripe yet. Borders about due for clearing.*
13.10.48. *Sunny day with a number of sharp showers. A. & I. began clearing the larger borders. Pain in side very bad. Sea calm.*

3474. To Leonard Moore

15 October 1948   Typewritten

Barnhill
Isle of Jura
Argyllshire

Dear Moore,

Many thanks for your letter. Reynall° & Hitchcock's terms sound very good to me. I am particularly glad you managed to arrange the reprints.[1]

Unless something happens I shall finish my novel[2] early in December—actually earlier than that, but there is the typing to be done, and it is unfortunately very long. I will send one copy direct to Warburg. Do I understand that you want two copies *in addition* to this?

Yours sincerely
[Signed] Eric Blair
Eric Blair

1. Reynal & Hitchcock published only one edition of *Dickens, Dali & Others*, and no reprints of any of Orwell's other books. However, the company was later taken over by Harcourt, Brace, and this might refer to the reprints the latter brought out: *Burmese Days* (first published in the United States by Harper, 1934) and *Coming Up for Air*, issued in January 1950, with *Down and Out in Paris and London* (first published in the United States by Harper, 1933).
2. *Nineteen Eighty-Four.*

3475. Domestic Diary

16.10.48. (Some days missed out, apparently.)[1] Sunny day, with some showers. Rather chilly. Sea calm. Continued clearing the borders. Paraffin is running low. 40 gall barrel only seems to last about 6 weeks at this time of year. Picked the Golden Spire apples, three large ones. A very good-flavoured apple, though I think it is really a cooker.

Pain in side very bad on & off. Temperature (night) 100°.

17.10.48. Sunny day with a few showers. Rather chilly. Sea calm. Did not go out of doors.

18.10.48. Clear, sunny, rather cold day. No rain till night. Sea calm. A. continued clearing borders.

19.10.48. Overcast day. No rain till night. Sea fairly calm, but B., who returned from Crinan, said it was choppy in the middle of the Sound.

20.10.48. Overcast day, rainy in afternoon. Water supply suddenly stopped, & B. & A. had to go & unblock the pipe leading from the burn to the tank, which had got a lump of mud in it. A lot of potatoes are rotting this year because of the waterlogged state of the ground. We are said to have had 20'[2] of rain in the last two months. Not so bad here, but a lot lost at Ardlussa, it seems. Paraffin situation now desperate.

21.10.48. Overcast day, with occasional drizzle. Sea calm. A. & B. went down to Ardlussa in the boat to bring back 5 galls paraffin. Boat ran well but there is still one unlocated leak.

1. This is Orwell's own entry.
2. Twenty feet: Orwell must mean twenty inches (20″).

3476. To Leonard Moore

22 October 1948   Typewritten

Barnhill
Isle of Jura
Argyllshire

Dear Moore,

Many thanks for your letter. I am very glad to hear about the interlinear Swedish translation of A.F.[1]

I have almost finished the novel and shall have it ready for typing early in November, so it should be all finished by the time I promised, ie. beginning of December. It is extremely long, I should say 100,000 or even 125,000 words. I have not definitely decided on the title. I am inclined to call it either NINETEEN EIGHTY-FOUR or THE LAST MAN IN EUROPE, but I might just possibly think of something else in the next week or two.

Yours sincerely
[Signed] Eric Blair
Eric Blair

1. This has not been identified. A Swedish edition of *Animal Farm, Djurfarmer Saga*, was published by Albert Bonniers Forlag in 1946, but it is not interlinear. In 1952 the Swedish Polyglot Club published *Animal Farm* as Vol. 4 in 'The Polyglot's Choice Series,' Stockholm. This was edited by N. R. Roberts 'with sense stress by J. D. O'Connor.'

3477. To Fredric Warburg

22 October 1948   Typewritten

Barnhill
Isle of Jura
Argyllshire

Dear Fred,

You will have had my wire by now, and if anything crossed your mind I dare say I shall have had a return wire from you by the time this goes off. I shall finish the book, D.V.,[1] early in November, and I am rather flinching from the job of typing it, because it is a very awkward thing to do in bed, where I still have to spend half the time. Also there will have to be carbon copies, a thing which always fidgets me, and the book is fearfully long, I should think well over 100,000 words, possibly 125,000. I can't send it away because it is an unbelievably bad MS and no one could make head or tail of it without explanation. On the other hand a skilled typist under my eye could do it easily enough. If you can think of anybody who would be willing to come, I will send money for the journey and full instructions. I think we could make her quite comfortable. There is always plenty to eat and I will see that she has a comfortable warm place to work in.

I am not pleased with the book but I am not absolutely dissatisfied. I first thought of it in 1943. I think it is a good idea but the execution would have been better if I had not written it under the influence of TB. I haven't definitely fixed on the title but I am hesitating between NINETEEN EIGHTY-FOUR and THE LAST MAN IN EUROPE.

I have just had Sartre's book on antisemitism, which you published, to review. I think Sartre is a bag of wind and I am going to give him a good boot.[2]

Please give everyone my love.

Yours
George

1. D.V.: *Deo Volente* (God willing).
2. *Portrait of the Anti-Semite*; reviewed in *The Observer*, 7 November 1948; see *3485*.

3478. Domestic Diary

<u>22.10.48.</u>   *Clear, windy day, cold. Picked the apples, 4½ lb, ie. about 5½ with the others.*

<u>23.10.48.</u>   *Nasty day, drizzling a good deal of the time. Sea calm till about 5 pm. The others went down in the boat to Ardlussa to fetch the stores, getting back just before the sea got up. Boat ran well but still takes in water. New drum of paraffin arrived, also Calor gas.*

<u>24.10.48.</u>   *Filthy day, about the worst we have had. Rain incessant, considerable wind, sea rough. Not very cold, however. A. & B. baled boat, which was full of water. Leaks in roof very bad (2 places).*

NB. to get Robert Shaw to deal with the tiles.

Started new Calor Gas. Ditto new drum of paraffin, which should last about 6 weeks.

On the facing page opposite 24.10.48, Orwell has written, and underlined 15.11.48:

See Robert Shaw[1] about roof.
Order paraffin about 15.11.48

<u>25.10.48.</u>   *Better day, sunny but very cold. Wind in north. Sea fairly calm. Rabbits sitting along the bank sunning themselves.*

<u>26.10.48.</u>   *Frost last night. Some short showers of hail & sleet this morning, & one short rain shower in afternoon. Otherwise clear, sunny & cold. Sea*

very calm. B. thinks he has found the leak in the boat, which is in the shaft.
Has plugged it up with grease, which is possibly all it needs. Pruned red
currants (very lightly.)
<u>27.10.48.</u>   *Frost again last night, after rain in the earlier part of the night.*
Today a beautiful, sunny, still day, but cold. Sea less calm. A. finished
clearing border. Some of the leaves on the fruit trees going, after the frost.
Pruned raspberries some more, cutting out all that had fruited. Deer keep
getting into the field.
<u>28.10.48.</u>   *Fine, clear, sunny day, decidedly cold. There is still water in the*
boat, so evidently there is another leak somewhere.

1. Robert Shaw was a building contractor who lived at Lagg, which lies on the coast road about fifteen miles south of Barnhill.

3479. To Melvin Lasky

29 October 1948   Typewritten, copy

Barnhill
Isle of Jura
Argyllshire
Scotland

Dear Mr. Lasky,
Very many thanks for your letter and the copy of Der Monat.[1] I can't read a
word of German, except the words everyone knows, but it looks most
impressive and I do hope it will be a success. Thank you also for the cheque
for £25 which I received earlier and should have acknowledged.

As to writing. I am too unwell and too busy to undertake anything new. As
you know I have been under treatment for TB and am still far from well, in
fact I may have to go into a sanatorium again for part of the winter, and I am
also struggling to finish a book, besides book reviews etc. I will get my agent
to send you a copy of my book on the Spanish civil war and if you wish to
extract any passage you can do so, but I don't honestly think I can write any
more about it.[2] With Koestler it is rather different. I can't rework the essay,
but if you cared I could write an additional piece mentioning "The Yogi and
the Commissar" and discussing "Thieves in the Night." Actually there is
much in this book that is interesting, but it all revolves round the fact that
Koestler feels himself to be first and foremost a Jew. My experience is that if,
nowadays, you write about any Jewish problem in a grown-up manner you
are accused of antisemitism; and of course one doesn't want, for publication
in Germany, to write anything that could even be called antisemitic. But if
you would like me to do anything about this I will, and in that case could you
indicate what length. I am sorry not to be more helpful, but I am really not at
my best. I can do just so much, and don't like to undertake what I can't carry
out.

I am not sure what the position is about "Animal Farm." But I *think* some
kind of cheap edition is in process of being made for Germany, and

presumably whoever is doing it has all the rights.[3] Yes, I saw a radio version of it had been done, in fact they sent me a copy of the text, which of course I couldn't read.

I am glad to see you have Borkenau[4] writing for you, and I would like to have his address. I think he was at Marburg university when I last heard from him. If you are seeing him, could you tell him from me that I made two attemts° to send him a copy of the German version of Animal Farm when it first appeared, but in each case they came back to me as one wasn't then allowed to send books into Germany.

Yours sincerely
George Orwell

1. Presumably a specimen copy of Der Monat, not one containing anything by Orwell; see 3470, n. 3.
2. Homage to Catalonia. Nothing seems to have been extracted—indeed, Leonard Moore wrote that he had no copy available for Lasky; see 3480, n. 1.
3. Der Monat serialised a translation of Animal Farm; see 3446, n. 1 and 3480.
4. Orwell had admired Dr. Franz Borkenau since he reviewed his book The Spanish Cockpit, Time and Tide, 31 July 1937; see 379. Borkenau had been a member of the Communist Party for eight years and an official of the Comintern, but 'reverted to a belief in liberalism and democracy,' as Orwell put it in his review of Borkenau's The Communist International, New English Weekly, 22 September 1938; see 485. He also reviewed his book The Totalitarian Enemy, Time and Tide, 4 May 1940; see 620. No letters from Orwell to Borkenau have survived, but one from Borkenau, 14 September 1949, is summarised at 3690. On 25 May 1964, Mrs. Hilde Borkenau wrote to Ian Angus that her husband's books and papers had been lost in transit from England to Germany; Orwell's letters were included in this consignment.

3480. To Leonard Moore

29 October 1948   Typewritten

Barnhill
Isle of Jura
Argyllshire

Dear Moore,

Could you please be kind enough to procure a copy of "Homage to Catalonia"[1] and send it to Melvin J. Lasky, editor of "Der Monat." The address apparently is Berlin Dahlen, Saargemünder Str. 25 (Information Services Divn. APO 742). This is the American army magazine that recently sent me a cheque for a reprint. They may want to extract and translate passages from the book.

They also want to serialise "Animal Farm." My impression is that some kind of cheap edition is in process of being made for Germany, and I suppose whoever is doing it has all the rights?[2]

I wired a week ago to ask Warburg if he could find me a good stenog. to come here and type my book. It's a tiresome job when one is too weak to sit up at a table for long periods, and in any case can't be done in bed, where I have to be half the day. On the other hand I can't send the MS away because it is in too much of a mess to be intelligible unless I was there to help decipher it.

I haven't heard from Warburg yet, but if he can't find anyone possibly you might be able to help me?[3] Of course it's awkward nowadays to find people to take on a job for a fortnight, with two goes of seasickness thrown in.

Yours sincerely
[Signed] Eric Blair
Eric Blair

1. Two annotations made in Moore's office (in different hands) read: 'we haven't a copy' and 'wrote 8.11.48.'
2. Two annotations were made in Moore's office: 'no, they are free' (available) and 'Amstutz [Swiss publishers of *Animal Farm*] still trying to make some arrangement for edit to be pub in Ger.' For dates of the serialisation of *Animal Farm* in *Der Monat*, see 3446, n. 1.
3. Annotations made in Moore's office read: 'How get there? Pay expenses & £7 a week'; 'Has he a typewriter'; 'Miss E. Keddie, 47 Barkeston Gdns S.W.5.'

3481. To Julian Symons

29 October 1948   Typewritten

Barnhill
Isle of Jura
Argyllshire

Dear Julian,
I can't thank you enough for the tea, which I do hope you could spare. My sister, who keeps house for me, was enchanted to see it and asked me to say she will pack up a little butter for you next churning day. I am so glad to hear that all is well with your wife and daughter and that you enjoy having a baby. They're really great fun, so much so that I find myself wishing at each stage that they could stay like that. I suppose you are on the steady grind of 5 bottles and 15 nappies a day. It's funny that they are so insatiably greedy when they are small babies and then between about 2 and 6 it is such a fight to get them to eat, except between meals. I wonder which milk you are using. We brought up Richard on Ostermilk, which seemed to be better than National Dried.[1] His cousin was brought up on Cow and Gate and became grossly fat on it. You've got a big battle ahead when it comes to weaning time.

I was very well for some time after leaving hospital but have been very poorly again for the last month. Ironically it started with my going back to the hospital to be re-examined and being upset by the journey. We had a filthy summer, which doesn't help one to recover. Latterly the weather has been quite nice but I have been too sick and sorry to go out of the house much. I can work, but that is about all I can do. Even to walk half a mile upsets me. I was going to come down to London in January, but I am consulting with my doctor and if he thinks it best I shall go into a private sanatorium, if I can find one, for the worst of the winter, ie. Jan–Feb. I could go abroad perhaps, but the journey might be the death of me, so perhaps a sanatorium would be best. I think I am going to give up my London flat, as I never use it at present and it costs me about £100 a year and a lot of nuisance. Of course I shall have to get another London place later. I shall finish my book, D.V., in a week or ten days, but I am rather flinching from typing it, which is a tiring job and in any case can't be done in bed where I have to be half the day. So I am trying to get a good stenog. to come here for a fortnight. I can't send the MS away because it is in too much of a mess to be intelligible unless I am there to explain. The trouble is it's not easy to get typists for short periods nowadays, at least good ones, and some might funk the journey. It's only a two-hour crossing, but one can be very sick in two hours, as I well know.

I am rather surprised to hear of John Davenport associating himself with a CP or near-CP paper.[2] He used not to be that way inclined, that I knew of. "Politics & Letters" I am sorry to say has disappeared and is supposed to be reappearing next year as a monthly, rather to my annoyance as they had an article of mine. It is nonsense what Fyvel said about Eliot being antisemitic. Of course you can find what would now be called antisemitic remarks in his early work, but who didn't say such things at that time? One has to draw a distinction between what was said before and what after 1934. Of course all these nationalistic prejudices are ridiculous, but disliking Jews isn't intrinsically worse than disliking Negroes or Americans or any other block of people. In the early twenties, Eliot's antisemitic remarks were about on a par with the automatic sneer one casts at Anglo-Indian colonels in boarding houses. On the other hand if they had been written after the persecutions began they would have meant something quite different. Look for instance at the Anglophobia in the USA, which is shared even by people like Edmund Wilson. It doesn't matter, because we are not being persecuted. But if 6 million Englishmen had recently been killed in gas vans, I imagine I should feel insecure if I even saw a joke in a French comic paper about English-women's teeth sticking out. Some people go round smelling after antisemitism all the time. I have no doubt Fyvel thinks I am antisemitic.[3] More rubbish is written about this subject than any other I can think of. I have just had Sartre's book on the subject for review, and I doubt whether it would be possible to pack more nonsense into so short a space. I have maintained from the start that Sartre is a bag of wind, though possibly when it comes to Existentialism, which I don't profess to understand, it may not be so.

Richard is blooming. He is still I think backward about talking, but lively enough in other ways and really almost helpful about the farm and garden. Something tells me he won't be one for book-learning and that his bent is for mechanics. I shan't try to influence him, but if he grew up with the ambition of being a farmer I should be pleased. Of course that may be the only job left after the atom bombs. If the show does start and is as bad as one fears, it would be fairly easy to be self-supporting on these islands provided one wasn't looted. The winters are a good deal milder than in England, which means that at a pinch one can keep animals through the winter without fodder, and in fact the sheep are very rarely fed in a normal winter. For the first time in my life I have tried the experiment of keeping a pig. They really are disgusting brutes and we are all longing for the day when he goes to the butcher, but I am glad to see they do well here. He has grown to a stupendous size purely on milk and potatoes, without our buying any food for him from outside. In another year or so I shall have to be thinking about Richard's schooling, but I am not making any plans because one can't see far ahead now. I am not going to let him go to a boarding school before he is ten, and I would like him to start off at the elementary school. If one could find a good one. It's a difficult question. Obviously it is democratic for everyone to go to the same schools, or at least start off there but when you see what the elementary schools are like, and the results, you feel that any child that has the chance should be rescued from them. It is quite easy, for instance, to leave those schools at 14 without having learned to read. I heard on the wireless lately that 10 percent° of army recruits, aged 19, have to be taught to read after they join the army. I remember in 1936 meeting John Strachey[4] in the street—then a CP member or at least on the staff of the Worker—and him telling me he had just had a son and was putting him down for Eton. I said "How can you do that?" and he said that given our existing society it was the best education. Actually I doubt whether it is the best, but in principle I don't feel sure that he was wrong. However I am taking no decisions about Richard one way or the other. Of course we may all have been blown to hell before it becomes urgent, but personally I don't expect a major shooting war for 5 or 10 years. After the Russians have fully recovered and have atomic bombs,[5] I suppose it isn't avoidable. And even if it is avoided, there are a lot of other unpleasantnesses blowing up.

Please remember me to your wife and give my best regards to your daughter.

Yours
George

1. National Dried was a milk powder, akin to proprietary brands such as Ostermilk, made available by the government to mothers of young babies through Baby Clinics.
2. John Davenport (1906–1966), critic and man of letters, a friend of many writers and painters. The paper was probably *Our Time*, to which he was a contributor. In the autumn of 1948 it was edited by Frank Jellinek and in 1949 by Randall Swingler.
3. Tosco Fyvel, a long-standing friend of Orwell's, comments on Orwell's remark that he, Fyvel, doubtless thought him anti-Semitic in *George Orwell: A Personal Memoir*, 178–82: 'I would never have said that,' though he reported that Malcolm Muggeridge thought Orwell 'at heart strongly anti-Semitic.' Fyvel went on, 'Put baldly like that, I would not agree. . . . It was unthinkable that he should ever have been openly anti-Semitic. But his ideological views concerning the assimilation into British culture of a strong Jewish ethnic minority were a different matter.' He analyses Orwell's reactions with care and quotes with approval Koestler's remark that 'Orwell's imagination was limited as the imagination of each of us is limited'; he was referring to Orwell's understanding of the fate of the Jews in Europe. Koestler went on, 'We can all produce only a limited amount of calories of indignation.' Orwell, concludes Fyvel, 'had more than sufficient calories of indignation to make him the great writer he was'; further, 'as if to show that he knew more about such things than one might think, he did call his last rebel in *Nineteen Eighty-Four* Emmanuel Goldstein and modelled him on Trotsky.'
4. John Strachey (1901–1963), politician and political theorist; Labour M.P., 1929–31, 1945–63. In 1946 he became a prominent member of the Labour government. See *304, n. 2*.
5. Soviet Russia tested its first atomic bomb in September 1949.

3482. Domestic Diary

<u>29.10.48.</u>   *Fine, but windy & cold. Hay arrived (1 ton, 25 bales). If possible the boat will be dragged up tomorrow, as it still takes in water. A. forked the other border. Sea rough.*
<u>30.10.48.</u>   *Heavy rain in the night. Today fine, and cold. The others dragged the boat up & propped it so that the stern can perhaps be caulked at low tide. B. shot a rabbit which the dogs stole off the kitchen table the moment it had been skinned. Clocks go back tonight.*
<u>31.10.48.</u>   *Rain in night. Violent wind all day, but not cold. Sea rough.*
<u>1.11.48.</u>   *Fine & cold.*

3483. From Roger Senhouse

2 November 1948   First two paragraphs of carbon copy

My dear George,
On receipt of your telegram we had a copy made, which I sent up to my niece in Scotland, an efficient girl who knows most people in Edinburgh, or at any rate how to get hold of the right person for the purpose in hand. She rang up her friend, Herd, to put in orders to find the right stenographer for your purpose. I did not regard it as excessively urgent, despite the fact that you telegraphed your request, since the date line was some way into this month. So far, I have had no good result but she promised to write me again yesterday as to her progress. Since the letter is not to hand I feel that I must report. I conceived the immediate idea that a Scots lassie would be the most appropriate and adequate to fulfil your requirements; after all, it is a tremendous trek up from London, and there is also the question of climate—I dare say more clement than here, at the moment—and the general way of life on an island in the far north. If Edinburgh fails, I think Glasgow will provide. Give me three more days and you will know the result. Certainly we won't let you down, whatever happens.

It is excellent news that you have found time to revise the novel. The tinge of disappointment is apparent in your letter when you state that the stress and uncertainty of the threat of your wretched disease comes through in the writing, and perhaps cannot be expunged to your liking. The astonishing feat of putting "finis" to the work is surely a triumph. . . .

3484. Domestic Diary

<u>2.11.48.</u>   *Filthy day, rain almost continuous. Roof dripping badly. Biro pen gave out, after only about 6 weeks.[1] Sea rough. Eagles overhead.*
<u>3.11.48.</u>   *Day partly sunny, with some showers. Very heavy rain in the*

evening. Sea rough. Cows' yield has gone up a bit, no doubt thanks to the new hay. B. has seen several more of the light-coloured rabbits.
4.11.48.   *Finer, but cold. A. planted garden spirea, & phloxes.*
5.11.48.   *Cold. Some fine patches & some drizzle. A little hail in the morning. Sea calm. Wind in north. A. planted polyanthi.*
6.11.48.   *Beautiful, still, windless day, warm in the sun, cold out of it. Sea calm. A. & I.[2] planted tulips, about 100. A. started clearing bed under window. Felt very bad in afternoon & evening, no doubt as a result of going out.[3]*

1. Orwell asked Julian Symons to obtain a Biro for him on 26 December 1947 (see *3318*), enclosing £3 to pay for it. There is no record of Biros being bought in 1948.
2. Ian M'Kechnie.
3. It is clear from the past entries that Orwell has been able to do virtually no physical work in the garden; on 15 November (see *3488*), he tells Anthony Powell he cannot so much as pull up a weed and that to walk even a few hundred yards upsets him. Thus, his feeling very bad is a result of simply going outside, not going out to help with the garden. This is the period when he is typing the final version of *Nineteen Eighty-Four*, and, from the way his Biro has run out so quickly, revising heavily as well.

3485. Review of *Portrait of the Anti-Semite* by Jean-Paul Sartre; translated by Erik de Mauny
The Observer, 7 November 1948

Anti-Semitism is obviously a subject that needs serious study, but it seems unlikely that it will get it in the near future. The trouble is that so long as anti-Semitism is regarded simply as a disgraceful aberration, almost a crime, anyone literate enough to have heard the word will naturally claim to be immune from it; with the result that books on anti-Semitism tend to be mere exercises in casting motes out of other people's eyes. M. Sartre's book is no exception, and it is probably no better for having been written in 1944, in the uneasy, self-justifying, quisling-hunting period that followed on the Liberation.[1]

At the beginning, M. Sartre informs us that anti-Semitism has no rational basis: at the end, that it will not exist in a classless society, and that in the meantime it can perhaps be combated to some extent by education and propaganda. These conclusions would hardly be worth stating for their own sake, and in between them there is, in spite of much cerebration, little real discussion of the subject, and no factual evidence worth mentioning.

We are solemnly informed that anti-Semitism is almost unknown among the working class. It is a malady of the bourgeoisie, and, above all, of that goat upon whom all our sins are laid, the "petty bourgeois." Within the bourgeoisie it is seldom found among scientists and engineers. It is a peculiarity of people who think of nationality in terms of inherited culture and of property in terms of land.

Why these people should pick on Jews rather than some other victim M. Sartre does not discuss, except, in one place, by putting forward the ancient and very dubious theory that the Jews are hated because they are supposed to have been responsible for the Crucifixion. He makes no attempt to relate anti-Semitism to such obviously allied phenomena as, for instance, colour prejudice.

Part of what is wrong with M. Sartre's approach is indicated by his title. "The" anti-Semite, he seems to imply all through the book, is always the same kind of person, recognisable at a glance and, so to speak, in action the whole time. Actually one has only to use a little observation to see that anti-Semitism is extremely widespread, is not confined to any one class, and, above all, in any but the worst cases, is intermittent.

But these facts would not square with M. Sartre's atomised vision of society. There is, he comes near to saying, no such thing as a human being, there are only different categories of men, such as "the" worker and "the" bourgeois, all classifiable in much the same way as insects. Another of these insectlike creatures is "the" Jew, who, it seems, can usually be distinguished by his physical appearance. It is true that there are two kinds of Jew, the "Authentic Jew," who wants to remain Jewish, and the "Inauthentic Jew," who would like to be assimilated; but a Jew, of whichever variety, is not just another human being. He is wrong, at this stage of history, if he tries to assimilate himself, and we are wrong if we try to ignore his racial origin. He should be accepted into the national community, not as an ordinary Englishman, Frenchman, or whatever it may be, but as a Jew.

It will be seen that this position is itself dangerously close to anti-Semitism. Race-prejudice of any kind is a neurosis, and it is doubtful whether argument can either increase or diminish it, but the net effect of books of this kind, if they have an effect, is probably to make anti-Semitism slightly more prevalent than it was before. The first step towards serious study of anti-Semitism is to stop regarding it as a crime. Meanwhile, the less talk there is about "the" Jew or "the" anti-Semite, as a species of animal different from ourselves, the better.

1. For a note on the huge number of French people killed by the French themselves after the Liberation of France, see *2631, n. 1.*

3486. Domestic Diary

<u>7.11.48.</u> *Beautiful, still, sunny day. Coldish. Sea less calm.*
<u>8.11.48.</u> *Frost in night. Clear, still, sunny day. Coldish. Sea fairly calm. B. took the younger milch cow to the bull (Khilachrain). Should calve in August. A. continued clearing border under house. Pruned the blackcurrants (a very little). Scillas showing. Qy. whether one should cover them up. Trouble with cable of tractor. Drink running low. NB. to order. Saw some blackbirds today. They are rare enough here to make one wonder what they are. A. saw a flight of thrushes, possibly migrants, ie. fieldfares or redwings.*

One oar belonging to the dinghy in this bay has been washed away. Gladioli & dahlias over. New buds still coming on the roses.

On the facing page opposite 8.11.48, Orwell has written, and ticked:

Order gin etc.

<u>9.11.48.</u> *Heavy wind in night. Very heavy sea. A little rain in the afternoon, after which the sea subsided somewhat.*
<u>10.11.48.</u> *Still, overcast day, mild. Sea slightly choppy.*
<u>11.11.48.</u> *Still, overcast, warm. Rain in night. Sea not very calm. The others fished in Barnhill bay & got 15. The oar which was washed away has come back. Polyanthi planted recently trying to flower.*

3487. Publication of *British Pamphleteers*, Vol. 1

15 November 1948

Volume 1 of this two-volume work stated on its title-page that it had been edited by George Orwell and Reginald Reynolds. As Orwell makes clear in the Introduction, which he wrote, the book was 'compiled and arranged' by Reynolds. The first volume included pamphlets from the sixteenth to the eighteenth centuries. It was published by Allan Wingate. Orwell did not live to see the second volume. Orwell's introduction is reproduced at about the time it was completed, in the spring of 1947; see *3206*. See also his review of Pamphlet Literature, *The New Statesman and Nation*, 9 January 1943, *1807*; and 'As I Please,' 51, *Tribune*, 8 December 1944, *2590*.

3488. To Anthony Powell

15 November 1948   Typewritten

> Barnhill
> Isle of Jura
> Argyllshire

Dear Tony,
Please excuse bad typing, but I am in bed and this is a very decrepit typewriter. Thanks so much for your letter. Yes, *do* send the Barry Pain[1] etc. books. I love anything like that. Maybe some of them would be worth binding. There are people in Edinburgh who bind books. I came out of hospital in July very much better, but have been in lousy health for the last month or more and am trying to arrange to spend the worst of the winter in a sanatorium. I suppose it's a step up over last winter, ie. a sanatorium not a hospital—perhaps in 1949 I might manage to spend the winter at home. I could go abroad perhaps, but I am afraid the journey would literally be the

death of me. I can work, but that is about all I can do. To walk even a few hundred yards promptly upsets me. It's annoying that after a filthy summer we've been having nice autumn weather but I can't so much as pull a weed up in the garden. I am just on the grisly job of typing out my novel. I can't type much because it tires me too much to sit up at table, and I asked Roger Senhouse to try and send me a stenog. for a fortnight, but of course it's not so easy to get people for short periods like that. It's awful to think I've been mucking about with this book since June of 1947, and it's a ghastly mess now, a good idea ruined, but of course I was seriously ill for 7 or 8 months of the time. Richard is blooming, and getting enormous. I don't think somehow he'll be much of a one for booklearning. He is rather backward in talking and shows no interest in learning his letters (age 4½), but on the other hand is good with machinery and likes working on the farm, fishing and things like that. I'm not going to influence him, but would like it if he went in for farming, perhaps the only job there will be left after the atom bombs. Another year and I suppose he will be going to school. I just re-read "From a View to a Death"[2] and enjoyed it immensely. I put in for the Aubrey book[3] with the Observer but don't know whether I shall get it. If you see Malcolm,[4] tell him from me that I recently read his book on Samuel Butler[5] and that though I enjoyed it I consider it quite shameful. Please remember me to Violet. I hope the family are well.

Yours
George

1. Barry Pain (1864–1928), humorous novelist, author of the *Eliza* books, very popular in the Edwardian era. Orwell, in his list of books read in 1949, records that he [re-]read them in January 1949.
2. A novel by Anthony Powell, 1933.
3. *John Aubrey and His Friends* by Anthony Powell.
4. Malcolm Muggeridge (1903–1990), novelist, critic, journalist, and television personality. In the late '30s he had corresponded with Orwell about the Spanish civil war. During the war Anthony Powell introduced them, and they remained friends until Orwell's death.
5. *Samuel Butler* by Malcolm Muggeridge.

3489. Domestic Diary

16.11.48. *Diary not filled up for some days. The last two days wet & windy, before that still & overcast. Not cold. Sea today pretty heavy. A. has finished clearing the bed under the window & replanted the forget-me-nots. Pig has been lame, & one day would not even take any food. Now better, but still somewhat lame. Probably rheumatism, due to damp sty. He has been moved into the garage temporarily. B. has got lumbago. The crossbred pullets (May hatched) look about ready to lay, but have not started yet. NB. to order paraffin & methylated.*

On the facing page opposite 16.11.48, Orwell has written, and ticked the first item:

Order paraffin
Order methylated.

<u>17.11.48.</u> *Damp & overcast, some rain. Very heavy rain in the evening. Sea rough. The new bull arrived, a young white shorthorn (beef.) Has been 5 days on the boat & is thin & in poor condition generally.*
<u>18.11.48.</u> *Beautiful day, quite warm. Sea calm. A. has put up wires for the climbing roses. Pruned the plum trees. These are mostly very poor trees. Some roses still in bloom. Also a flower or two on the wallflowers which have been left in position.*

3490. To David Astor

    19 November 1948   Typewritten

Barnhill
Isle of Jura
Argyllshire

Dear David,
Thanks so much for your letter. If you'd really like to give Richard something for Christmas, I wonder whether one can still get Meccano sets?[1] I should think he is about ripe for one of the lower grades. Of course he'll lose all the bolts, but still that is the kind of thing he likes. He is tremendously active about the farm and household, has to take part in all operations such as chopping firewood, filling lamps etc., and even insists on pouring out my ration of gin for me every evening. He goes fishing with the others and caught several fish the other day. I am so glad your little girl is going on well. I suppose at 20 months she will be talking a bit, as well as walking. Julian Symons, whom I think you met at lunch once, has just got a baby and seems very absorbed in it. Margie Fletcher[2] is over on the mainland having her fourth.

It's very kind of Charoux[3] to help about restoring the picture. When I can get round to doing so I'll make a crate and send it to him direct. I never can remember his address but I expect I have a letter of his somewhere. It's only a very small picture, about 20″ by 16″, so it won't be difficult to pack. In sending it here those bloody fools Pickfords succeeded in making a slit in the canvas and also chipping it in two places, but I don't imagine it would be difficult to mend. It's of no value, but it has sentimental associations and I think is quite a good painting. There was also that picture which you gave me and which got blitzed.[4] I was going to have that restored, but it's a more extensive job as it got scratched all over. It was thrown right across the room by the blast.

I am on the grisly job of typing out my book which I have at last finished after messing about with it ever since the summer of 1947. I tried to get a stenog. to come here and do it for me, but it's awkward to get anyone for such a short period so I am doing it myself. I feel somewhat better now, but I was in absolutely lousy health for about a month and I have decided if I can arrange it to go into a private sanatorium for Jan–Feb, which is the worst of the winter. Dr. Dick thinks it would be a good idea. I seem to be all right so long as I stay in bed till lunch time and then spend the rest of the day on a sofa, but if I walk even a few hundred yards or pull up a few weeds in the garden I promptly get a temperature. Otherwise everything is going well here and the farm has had quite a good first year in spite of the vile weather. There is now a bull, which is very good and quiet and I trust will remain so, as I can't run very fast these days. Bobbie, your pony, is still at Tarbert, and I am not sure whether McIntyre° wants us to winter him or not. I had a talk with your brother about it when I met him at the sports about August, but subsequently there was some mix-up and nobody from here has been down as far as Tarbert for some months. Anyway, if they would like us to winter Bobbie, we are pleased to do so, as he is useful to us in several ways and also makes a companion for the other horse. I do not know whether I shall be in London at any time in the near future—I suppose some time next year, but I must try and get my health right.

I am so glad the Obs. is taking up Africa so to speak. Also that O'Donovan[5] is going on reporting Asia for you. He is really a great acquisition. Your friend de Gaulle seems to be bent on making mischief all round. However it rather looks now as if there won't be war for some years.

Yours
George

1. Trade name for a metal construction kit, very popular in the 1930s. During the war, card substitute had been used to reduce the all-metal content of the original sets. As with almost everything at this time, sets were in short supply. 'Meccano sets' is underlined and an annotation, 'Miss Brockhole For' is linked to these words; she was David Astor's secretary.
2. Margaret Fletcher, Orwell's landlord's wife; see *2638*, *n. 13*.
3. A picture-framer and restorer; his address is given in Orwell's address book as 65 Holland Park Road, [London], W. 14.
4. A flying bomb fell close by the Orwells' flat in Mortimer Crescent on 28 June 1944, and considerable damage was caused; as well as the picture, the manuscript of *Animal Farm* was affected. The Orwells had to move out—to Inez Holden's flat.
5. Patrick O'Donovan, who had joined *The Observer* in 1946 and worked with distinction as a roving correspondent abroad.

3491. To Leonard Moore

19 November 1948   Typewritten

Barnhill
Isle of Jura
Argyllshire

Dear Moore,

Yes, do let the Curacoa people[1] translate A.F. free of charge. I think they might send me a bottle of their liqueur, but as a matter of fact I don't like it.

I don't think I'll trouble you about the typist. It is all rather a muddle. I asked Warburg to get someone for me, and Roger Senhouse set his niece who lives in Edinburgh on to the job. I still haven't heard from her, but she might at some moment produce a typist and it would then be rather awkward if I had meanwhile engaged somebody from London. Meanwhile I am getting on with the job myself and should finish it before the end of the month, or not much later than that. I am in better health, but I am trying to arrange to go into a private sanatorium for the worst of the winter, ie. January and February. I might go abroad, but I don't care about journeys at present.

Yours sincerely
Eric Blair

1. The Caribbean island of Curaçao can be spelt with either ending. A translation of *Animal Farm* was made into Papiamento, as *Pastorie Otrabanda*. It was serialised in a Catholic Workers' paper, according to Orwell's Notes on Translations prepared for his literary executor, 1949. The Orwell Archive does not possess a copy, but one, described by K.A.G.S. Lane, of Christy & Moore, as like a comic newspaper, was in his possession. The language is a Spanish-based creole.

3492. Domestic Diary

_19.11.48._ *Filthy day, rainy & very blowy. Sea rough. The first pullet started laying (May hatched). Pig active again. There are rats in the corn stack. B's lumbago better. R.[1] caught several fish yesterday.*

1. Presumably Orwell's son, Richard; see letter to David Astor, 19 November 1948, *3490*.

3493. Jim Rose to Orwell
20 November 1948

Rose (who signed his name over 'Literary Editor' (of *The Observer*), which had been crossed through) sent Orwell two of the books he had picked out from the lists Rose had sent him and suggested reviews of up to 600 words of either or both of them. A slip for Richard Aldington's *Four English Portraits* is with the letter, and from the context of the letter it would seem that the second book was *The English Comic Album*, by Leonard Russell and Nicolas Bentley. If Orwell thought a review would be improved by an illustration from the book, he was asked to suggest one.

Rose also asked Orwell when he could expect reviews of any of the books he was working on, 'for example, the T. S. Eliot and Eric Partridge books.' He was also asked whether he was 'going to do a short note on Mr. Crump'[1] or whether he had decided against that. The book by T. S. Eliot was his *Notes towards the Definition of Culture*; Orwell's review was published on 28 November 1948; see *3498*. His review of *The English Comic Album* appeared on 2 January 1949; see *3517*. Orwell's only other review for *The Observer*, and his last, was of *The Great Tradition* by F. R. Leavis, published 6 February 1949; see *3543*. The book by Partridge was probably *A Dictionary of Forces' Slang, 1939–45* (November 1948), or, but less likely, his *A World of Words* (October 1948).

1. Unidentified. Possibilities include Leslie Maurice Crump, a former Indian civil servant who wrote historical prose; Geoffrey Crump, whose *A Manual of English Speech* was published in January 1948—a book that might have interested Orwell in the course of writing *Nineteen Eighty-Four*; and H. Highfield, *The Crump Family*, August 1947. The books left by Orwell at his death provide no clues. No note by Orwell has been traced.

3494. Domestic Diary

20.11.48. *Some sharp showers, with hail, but mostly fine. A. & B. brought the new van home (Chevrolet). Another pullet laying (I think). Pruned gooseberries.*
21.11.48. *One shower, otherwise beautiful day. Sea very calm & a wonderful colour. B. trying to clean the mud from the back yard. Needs hose. Pruned the apple trees (not very hard). With the exception of one espalier tree, these have made very little growth. Qy. whether they need more manure & were grassed down too early.*

On the facing page opposite 21.11.48, Orwell has written, and ticked:

Order hose (60' ¾")

3495. To Fredric Warburg

22 November 1948   Typewritten

Barnhill
Isle of Jura
Argyllshire

Dear Fred,
I have just heard from Gleb Struve that the firm of John Westhouse has gone bankrupt. It was they who were bringing out an English translation of Zamyatin's "We," a book I think I have talked to you about. In case you don't remember, Zamyatin was a Russian writer who died in Paris in 1937. "We" was written about 1923 and was refused publication by the Soviet authorities, and I believe has never been published in Russian.[1] There was I think an English (American) translation years ago, but I have never seen it and the book in effect existed only in a French translation which was itself a rarity. It is quite a remarkable book. It was no doubt suppressed by the Russian authorities because they thought it was a satire on themselves, but I should say it was more a satire on Utopianism generally, and incidentally I think Aldous Huxley's "Brave New World" was partly plagiarised from it. I should think it is the kind of book it might interest you to take over. Struve says the translation was already made, though he himself hadn't seen it, and that he had written an introduction for the book. If interested, do you think you could get in touch either with the receivers or what ever they are called

who are handling Westhouse's affairs,[2] or with Struve, whose address is 2851 BuenaVista Way, Berkeley 8, California.

I haven't heard anything from Roger's niece in Edinburgh, so I am typing my book myself. I can't do an awful lot each day, because it tires me too much to sit up for long periods, but I have done nearly half and will let you have the completed job early in December.[3]

Yours
George

1. An English translation was published in New York in 1924; the French translation in Paris in 1929. *We* was published in Russian in an émigré journal in 1927, but not in book form in Russian until 1952. For fuller details, see *3387, n. 2.*
2. The letter has been annotated in Warburg's office: 'R. Granville White Receiver & Manager c/o John Westhouse 49 Chancery Lane WC 2.
3. Warburg replied on 26 November. He said he had written to Westhouse's receiver but imagined that the matter would not be settled for some weeks. He was 'bitterly disappointed' that Secker's had failed to find Orwell a typist. George Malcolm Thomson, of the *Evening Standard*, had suggested a likely candidate only the day before, but, when asked, she could not spare the necessary time. He said that 'there is no book in preparation . . . which arouses the interest of Roger and myself to a greater extent than "1984" '—originally typed as "1948."

3496. To Gleb Struve

22 November 1948   Typewritten

Barnhill
Isle of Jura
Argyllshire

Dear Struve,

Thanks so much for your letter of November 6th (only just got here.) I have written to Warburg, explaining the circumstances about "We," and suggesting that if interested he should write either to you or to the people handling Westhouse's affairs. Of course if Warburg isn't interested there are plenty of others.

Yes, of course it's all right about the Russian translation of "Animal Farm."[1] Naturally I don't want any money from D.Ps, but if they ever do produce it in book form I should like a copy or two of that. Did I tell you it was done into Ukrainian by the D.Ps in the American Zone about a year ago? I understand that the American authorities seized about half the copies printed and handed them over to the Soviet repatriation people, but that about 3000 copies got distributed.

I'll look out for your Turgenev translation in "Politics."[2] I am better in health but not very grand. I think I am going to spend the worst of the winter, ie. January and February, in a sanatorium somewhere. I am just busy typing out a book I have been messing about with ever since some time in 1947—it should have been finished nearly a year ago if it had not been for this illness.

Yours sincerely
Geo. Orwell

1. The Russian translation of *Animal Farm*, *Skotskii Khutor*, was made by M. Kriger and Gleb Struve, and appeared in *Possev*, a weekly social and political review, Nos. 7–25, 1949; it was published as a book (by *Possev*) in 1950; see *3659* and *3662, n. 1. Possev*, which means the sowing of seed, outlasted the Soviet Union. It had its offices in London and Frankfurt (the latter bombed by the KGB in 1962); it was 'unashamedly anti-Soviet' and gave away books to Soviet citizens who would agitate at home 'for the Christian-Democratic cause.' In 1990 it was allowed to open a bookshop in Moscow and to circulate its magazine, *Grani*, in the Soviet Union (*Independent*, 18 February 1990).
2. *Politics* ceased publication before Struve's article on Turgenev could be published.

3497. Domestic Diary

22.11.48. Fine clear day. Sea calm. One pullet died (the one that had previously injured its breast in some way.)
23.11.48. Very dull, overcast day. Cold, but misty. Mainland invisible. Three eggs. The RIRs[1] are still moulting badly.
24.11.48. Cold during the night. Today fine & sunny, but cold. Wind in East. Wallflowers keep trying to flower.
25.11.48. Cold. Wind E. or S.E.
26.11.48. Fairly fine, but very cold. Wind E. or S.E. Sea moderately calm. One RIR. has begun laying.
27.11.48. Still & chilly.

1. Rhode Island Reds.

3498. Review of *Notes towards the Definition of Culture* by T. S. Eliot

The Observer, 28 November 1948

In his new book, "Notes towards the Definition of Culture," Mr. T. S. Eliot argues that a truly civilised society needs a class system as part of its basis. He is, of course, only speaking negatively. He does not claim that there is any method by which a high civilisation can be created. He maintains merely that such a civilisation is not likely to flourish in the absence of certain conditions, of which class distinctions are one.

This opens up a gloomy prospect, for on the one hand it is almost certain that class distinctions of the old kind are moribund, and on the other hand Mr. Eliot has at the least a strong *prima facie* case.

The essence of his argument is that the highest levels of culture have been attained only by small groups of people—either social groups or regional groups—who have been able to perfect their traditions over long periods of time. The most important of all cultural influences is the family, and family loyalty is strongest when the majority of people take it for granted to go through life at the social level at which they were born. Moreover, not having

473

any precedents to go upon, we do not know what a classless society would be like. We know only that, since functions would still have to be diversified, classes would have to be replaced by "élites," a term Mr. Eliot borrows with evident distaste from the late Karl Mannheim.[1] The élites will plan, organise and administer: whether they can become the guardians and transmitters of culture, as certain social classes have been in the past, Mr. Eliot doubts, perhaps justifiably.

As always, Mr. Eliot insists that tradition does not mean worship of the past; on the contrary, a tradition is alive only while it is growing. A class can preserve a culture because it is itself an organic and changing thing. But here, curiously enough, Mr. Eliot misses what might have been the strongest argument in his case. This is, that a classless society directed by élites may ossify very rapidly, simply because its rulers are able to choose their successors, and will always tend to choose people resembling themselves.

Hereditary institutions—as Mr. Eliot might have argued—have the virtue of being unstable. They must be so, because power is constantly devolving on people who are either incapable of holding it, or use it for purposes not intended by their forefathers. It is impossible to imagine any hereditary body lasting so long, and with so little change, as an adoptive organisation like the Catholic Church. And it is at least thinkable that another adoptive and authoritarian organisation, the Russian Communist Party, will have a similar history. If it hardens into a class, as some observers believe it is already doing, then it will change and develop as classes always do. But if it continues to co-opt its members from all strata of society, and then train them into the desired mentality, it might keep its shape almost unaltered from generation to generation. In aristocratic societies the eccentric aristocrat is a familiar figure, but the eccentric commissar is almost a contradiction in terms.

Although Mr. Eliot does not make use of this argument, he does argue that even the antagonism between classes can have fruitful results for society as a whole. This again is probably true. Yet one continues to have, throughout his book, the feeling that there is something wrong, and that he himself is aware of it. The fact is that class privilege, like slavery, has somehow ceased to be defensible. It conflicts with certain moral assumptions which Mr Eliot appears to share, although intellectually he may be in disagreement with them.

All through the book his attitude is noticeably defensive. When class distinctions were vigorously believed in, it was not thought necessary to reconcile them either with social justice or with efficiency. The superiority of the ruling classes was held to be self-evident, and in any case the existing order was what God had ordained. The mute inglorious Milton[2] was a sad case, but not remediable on this side of the grave.

This, however, is by no means what Mr. Eliot is saying. He would like, he says, to see in existence both classes *and* élites. It should be normal for the average human being to go through life at his predestined social level, but on the other hand the right man must be able to find his way into the right job. In saying this he seems almost to give away his whole case. For if class distinctions are desirable in themselves, then wastage of talent, or inefficiency in high places, are comparatively unimportant. The social misfit, instead of being directed upwards or downwards, should learn to be contented in his own station.

Mr. Eliot does not say this: indeed, very few people in our time would say it. It would seem morally offensive. Probably, therefore, Mr. Eliot does not believe in class distinctions as our grandfathers believed in them. His approval of them is only negative. That is to say, he cannot see how any civilisation worth having can survive in a society where the differences arising from social background or geographical origin have been ironed out.

It is difficult to make any positive answer to this. To all appearances the old social distinctions are everywhere disappearing, because their economic basis is being destroyed. Possibly new classes are appearing, or possibly we are within sight of a genuinely classless society, which Mr. Eliot assumes would be a cultureless society. He may be right, but at some points his pessimism seems to be exaggerated. "We can assert with some confidence," he says, "that our own period is one of decline; that the standards of culture are lower than they were 50 years ago; and that the evidence of this decline is visible in every department of human activity."

This seems true when one thinks of Hollywood films or the atomic bomb, but less true if one thinks of the clothes and architecture of 1898, or what life was like at that date for an unemployed labourer in the East End of London. In any case, as Mr. Eliot himself admits at the start, we cannot reverse the present trend by conscious action. Cultures are not manufactured, they grow of their own accord. Is it too much to hope that the classless society will secrete a culture of its own? And before writing off our own age as irrevocably damned, is it not worth remembering that Matthew Arnold and Swift and Shakespeare—to carry the story back only three centuries—were all equally certain that they lived in a period of decline?

1. Karl Mannheim (1883–1947), Austro-Hungarian sociologist who, after teaching in Germany, went to England and taught at the University of London. Orwell might have had in mind his *Ideology and Utopia* (1929), but the concept of the élite owes more in its origination to Vilfredo Pareto (1848–1923), Italian sociologist and economist.
2. In Thomas Gray's 'Elegy Written in a Country Churchyard', st. 15: 'Some mute inglorious Milton here may rest.'

3499. To Gwen O'Shaughnessy

28 November 1948   Typewritten

Barnhill
Isle of Jura
Argyllshire

Dear Gwen,[1]
I wonder whether you know of a private sanatorium where they would be likely to have room for me. I have not felt really well since September, and sometimes felt very bad, and I thought it would be a good idea to go into a sanatorium for the worst of the winter, ie. January and February and perhaps

part of March. Dr Dick agreed with me and recommended me to a place called the Grampian Sanatorium at Kingussie,[2] which is the only private sanatorium in Scotland. However, they are full up. I have no doubt there are many more in England, however. It must be a private place, because the public ones will all have waiting lists, and also I must have a room to myself, otherwise I can't work. I can't of course pay things like 30 guineas a week, but can pay anything reasonable. Do you know of anywhere?

I hope the kids are well. All is well here and Richard is bursting with energy. He goes out fishing with the others now, and sometimes catches quite a lot of fish. The weather just lately has been very nice, beautiful still sunny days and not at all cold, but I hardly ever go out of doors because the smallest exertion upsets me. The pig has grown to a stupendous size and goes to the butcher next week. We are all longing to get rid of him, as he is so destructive and greedy, even gets into the kitchen sometimes. Bill has got a young bull which seems a nice quiet beast and I trust will remain so. Avril is going up to London for a week or so in December to do some shopping and to see about giving up the Islington flat, which I don't want to keep on as it is simply an expense. I have finished my book, which I had been messing about with since some time in 1947. I am busy typing it out now, a ghastly job as it tires me to sit up much and I have to do most of it in° a sofa. I tried to get a stenog. to come here for a fortnight and do it for me, but the arrangements went wrong. Avril sends love.

Yours
George

1. Gwen O'Shaughnessy, wife of Eileen Blair's brother, Laurence O'Shaughnessy, was, like her husband (who had been killed at Dunkirk), a doctor.
2. Kingussie lies about thirty miles due south (over the mountains) of Inverness; about thirty-eight miles by road. See Dr. Bruce Dick's letter to David Astor, 5 January 1949, 3518, for something of Orwell's search for a sanatorium in the south.

3500. Domestic Diary

28.11.48. *Beautiful, windless day, sea like glass. A faint mist. Mainland invisible.*
29.11.48. *Still, overcast day, not cold. Sea less calm. Bobbie brought back today. Rather unkempt, but seems in fairly good condition. A double egg today, apparently from one of the pullets.*

3501. To Leonard Moore

30 November 1948   Typewritten

> Barnhill
> Isle of Jura
> Argyllshire

Dear Moore,
I am afraid there has been a mix-up about this typing business and that you and perhaps the typing agencies you applied [to] have been put to unnecessary trouble. What happened was this. I wrote first to Warburg, asking him to engage a typist in London, but he and Senhouse apparently decided that it would be easier to arrange it in Edinburgh, because of the journey, although, of course, the tiresome part of the journey is not between London and Scotland but between Jura and the mainland. I waited for a bit, and then Roger Senhouse said he was putting his niece in Edinburgh on to the job of finding a typist. Meanwhile in case nothing materialised I had started doing it myself. Then apparently Warburg rang you up and I got two letters from you, suggesting the names of two people in London, but I couldn't close with this in case Senhouse's niece suddenly produced somebody. I have never heard from her, and now I hear from Senhouse that in fact she couldn't get anybody. Meanwhile I have almost finished the typing and shall send it off probably on the 7th December, so you should get it in about a week. I do hope the two women whose names you suggested have not been inconvenienced or put off other engagements or anything like that. It really wasn't worth all this fuss. It's merely that as it tires me to sit upright for any length of time I can't type very neatly and can't do many pages a day.
    These copies I am sending you are only carbons, and not first-class typing. If you think bad typing might prejudice the MS. with the American publishers, it would be worth having it redone by a commercial agency. But if you do decide on that, can you see that they don't make mistakes. I know what these agencies are like. As the thing is typed already, and I don't *think* I have left any errors in it, it should be easy enough, but it is wonderful what mistakes a professional typist will make, and in this book there is the difficulty that it contains a lot of neologisms.

> Yours sincerely
> Eric Blair

3502. Domestic Diary

30.11.48. *Fine, blowy day, coldish. Sea rough. Apparently two RIRs are laying now.*
1.12.48. *Fine & blowy, sea rough. Some rain in the late evening. 3 or 4 eggs most days now.*
2.12.48. *Very violent wind in the night & throughout today. A good deal*

of rain. Very heavy seas. The pram dinghy[1] smashed to pieces, as the sea came up onto what is normally dry land. Trouble with the feed pipe of the lorry, the carburetter apparently not filling of its own accord.
<u>3.12.48.</u> *Overcast day, some rain. Wind dropped during the course of the day. Sea still roughish, but nothing like yesterday. Most of the cattle now coming down to the byre of their own accord. Paraffin almost at an end. Lorry now apparently O.K.*

1. A pram (or, more properly, praam) is a flat-bottomed dinghy with squared-off bow; in the phrase Orwell used, 'dinghy' is tautological.

3503. To Leonard Moore

4 December 1948   Typewritten

Barnhill
Isle of Jura
Argyllshire

Dear Moore,
Thanks for your letter. The cheque I received from Allan Wingate was for £15.[1] I can't remember for certain whether I was paid something in advance when I gave them the manuscript, but my impression is that I received £10. I can't find any record of it in my account book, however. I believe the understanding was that two thirds of the royalties should go to Reginald Reynolds and one third to me. I should be obliged if you would collect them when and if any become due, and no doubt Allan Wingate would know just how much I have received in advance.

I have sent off two copies of the MS of my book to you and one to Warburg. Perhaps you could acknowledge them when received, because there is always a slight possibility of a mishap in the post.

Yours sincerely
Eric Blair

1. For *British Pamphleteers*, Vol. 1, published 15 November 1948; see letter to Moore, 12 May 1948, *3398*.

3504. Domestic Diary

<u>4.12.48.</u> *Beautiful, still, sunny day, with a short shower in the afternoon. Two rainbows parallel to one another, one of them much fainter than the other. Qy. why this sometimes happens when there are rain & sun together. Sea calm. It appears that the bull is about 16 months old, having been born in July 1947, so he is fairly well advanced for his age, though in poor condition. Applied lime (a little) to fruit bushes.*
<u>5.12.48.</u> *Wind got up strongly in the night. Today almost incessant rain &*

strong wind. Sea rough. Feeling very unwell. Calor Gas cylinder about at an end. (Started 29.10.48, ie. has run 5 weeks.) Put on new cylinder.
<u>6.12.48.</u> *Wind dropped during night. Beautiful, still, sunny day. Sea very calm. Did not feel well enough to go outside. Pig went to be slaughtered today. The others went on down to Craighouse to get paraffin, but could get only 1 gallon. Situation almost desperate till new supply reaches the island. New ram arrived today. Wireless batteries about finished (forget when put in).*
<u>7.12.48.</u> *Still, fairly sunny day. A little rain in the morning. Sea less calm. A. brought back the internal fat etc. of the pig. Huge chunks of fat & meat on the cheeks. Paid for slaughtering & butchering the pig £1, & the trotters. Feeling very unwell.*

No entries until 19.12.48, which follows immediately after 7.12.48 on the same page.

3505. Fredric Warburg's Report on *Nineteen Eighty-Four*

13 December 1948   Typewritten

<u>Strictly Confidential</u>
This is amongst the most terrifying books I have ever read. The savagery of Swift has passed to a successor who looks upon life and finds it becoming ever more intolerable. Orwell must acknowledge a debt to Jack London's "IRON HEEL", but in verisimilitude and horror he surpasses this not inconsiderable author. Orwell has no hope, or at least he allows his reader no hope, no tiny flickering candlelight of hope. Here is a study in pessimism unrelieved, except perhaps by the thought that, if a man can conceive "1984", he can also will to avoid it. It is a fact that, so far as I can see, there is only one weak link in Orwell's construction; <u>he nowhere indicates the way in which man, English man, becomes bereft of his humanity.</u>
"1984" is "Animal Farm" writ large and in purely anthropomorphic terms. One hopes (against hope?) that its successor will supply the other side of the picture. For what is "1984" but a picture of man unmanned, of humanity without a heart, of a people without tolerance or civilization, of a government whose <u>sole</u> object is the maintenance of its power, of its absolute totalitarian power, by every contrivance of cruelty. Here is the Soviet Union to the nth degree, a Stalin who never dies, a secret police with every device of modern technology.
<u>Part One sets the scene.</u> It puts Orwell's hero, Winston Smith, on the stage. It gives a detailed and terrifying picture of the community in which he lives. It introduces the handful of characters who serve the plot, including Julia with whom Winston falls in love. Here we are given the telescreen, installed in every living-room, through which the secret police <u>perpetually</u> supervise the words, gestures, expressions, and thoughts of all

members of the Party; newspeak, the language devised by the Party to prevent thought; the big brother (B.B.) whose face a metre wide is to be seen everywhere on placards etc; doublethink, the formula for 100% political hypocrisy; the copiously flowing synthetic gin, which alone lubricates the misery of the inhabitants; the Ministry of Truth, with its three slogans—War Is Peace, Freedom Is Slavery, Ignorance Is Strength— and its methods of obliterating past events in the interests of the Party.

The political system which prevails is Ingsoc = English Socialism. This I take to be a deliberate and sadistic attack on Socialism and socialist parties generally. It seems to indicate a final breach between Orwell and Socialism, not the socialism of equality and human brotherhood which clearly Orwell no longer expects from socialist parties, but the socialism of marxism and the managerial revolution. "1984" is among other things an attack on Burnham's managerialism; and it is worth a cool million votes to the conservative party; it might well be the choice of "Daily Mail" and "Evening Standard"; it is imaginable that it might have a preface by Winston Churchill after whom its hero is named. "1984" should be published as soon as possible, in June 1949.

Part Two contains the plot, a very simple one. Winston falls in love with a black-haired girl, Julia. This in itself is to be considered heretical and illegal. See Part I, sec. 6 for a discussion of sex and love, but in any case "the sexual act, successfully performed, was rebellion. Desire was thought-crime. . . . . ." A description of their lovemaking follows, and these few passages alone contain a lyrical sensuous quality utterly lacking elsewhere in the book. These passages have the effect of intensifying the horrors which follow.

Julia and Winston, already rebels, start to plot; contact O'Brien, a fellow rebel as they think; are given "the book" of Emmanuel Goldstein, the Trotsky of his community; and Winston reads it. It is a typical Orwellism that Julia falls asleep while Winston reads part of the book to her. (Women aren't intelligent, in Orwell's world.)

Goldstein's book as we may call it (though it turns out later to have been written by the secret police) is called "The Principles of Oligarchical Collectivism" and we are given many pages of quotations from it. It outlines in a logical and coherent form the world situation as Orwell expects it to develop in the next generation. (Or does it?) It would take a long essay to discuss the implications of the astounding political philosophy embodied in this imagined work, which attempts to show that the class system, which was inevitable until circa 1930, is now in process of being fastened irrevocably on the whole world at the very moment when an approach to equality and liberty is for the first time possible. The book is quoted in Part 2, sec. 9, which can almost be read as an independent work.

Before passing to Part 3, I wish to call attention to the use made by Orwell of the old nursery rhyme, Oranges and Lemons, said the bells of St. Clements. This rhyme plays a largish part in the plot and is worth study. It ends, it will be remembered, with the words "And here comes the chopper to chop off your head." This use of a simple rhyme to achieve in due course an effect of extreme horror is a brilliant and typical Orwellism which places him as a craftsman in the front rank of terror novelists.

"1984" by the way might well be described as a horror novel, and would make a horror film which, if licensed, might secure all countries threatened by communism for 1000 years to come.

Part Three contains the torture, breakdown, and re-education of Winston Smith, following immediately upon his arrest in bed with Julia by the secret police. In form it reminds one of Arthur Koestler's "Darkness at Noon", but is to my mind more brutal, completely English, and overwhelming in its picture of a thorough extermination of all human feeling in a human being. In this part Orwell gives full rein to his sadism and its attendant masochism, rising (or falling) to the limits of expression in the scene where Winston, threatened by hungry rats which will eat into his face,[1] implores his torturer to throw Julia to the rats in his place. This final betrayal of all that is noble in man leaves Winston broken and ready for re-education as a willing adherent of Ingsoc, the necessary prelude in this society to being shot for his "thoughtcrime", for in Ingsoc there are no martyrs but only broken men wishing to die for the good of their country.

"We shall meet in the place where there's no darkness." This phrase, which recurs through the book, turns out to be in the end the brilliantly lit passage and torture chambers of the Ministry of Love. Light, for Orwell, symbolizes (I think) a horrible logical clarity which leads to death and destruction. Darkness, as in the womb and perhaps beside a woman in the night, stands for the vital processes of sex and physical strength, the virtues of the proles, that 80% of the population of Ingsoc who do the work and do not think, the "Boxers"[2] of "1984", the pawns, the raw material without which the Party could not function.

In Part III Orwell is concerned to obliterate hope; there will be no rebellion, there cannot be any liberation. Man cannot stand against Pain, and the Party commands Pain. It is almost intolerable to read Part III which, more even than the rest of the book, smells of death, decay, dirt, diabolism and despair. Here Orwell goes down to the depths in a way which reminds me of Dostoievsky. O'Brien is his grand inquisitor, and he leaves Winston, and the reader, without hope. I cannot but think that this book could have been written only by a man who himself, however temporarily, had lost hope, and for physical reasons which are sufficiently apparent.

These comments, lengthy as they are, give little idea of the giant movement of thought which Orwell has set in motion in "1984". It is a great book, but I pray I may be spared from reading another like it for years to come.

[Initialled by Warburg]

1. Typed as 'fact'.
2. 'Boxers' probably refers to the revolutionary animals inspired by Boxer of *Animal Farm*; but this might be a reference to the Boxers of the Boxer Rebellion against Western infiltration into China, 1899–1900, although the proles are (as Warburg puts it) pawns rather than revolutionaries. Their Chinese name translates as 'fists of righteous harmony'.

3506. David Farrer's[1] Report on *Nineteen Eighty-Four*
15 December 1948

My reaction to a book which has been highly praised by someone else in this office is liable to be highly critical. It was in a fault-finding mood, in consequence, that I approached the new Orwell, which perhaps lends additional force to my statement that if we can't sell fifteen to twenty thousand copies of this book we ought to be shot.

In emotive power and craftsmanship this novel towers above the average. Orwell has done what Wells never did, created a fantasy world which yet is horribly real so that you *mind* what happens to the characters which inhabit it. He also has written political passages which will set everyone talking and an extremely exciting story—the arrest is superbly done; the mounting suspense in Part II is perhaps more nerve-racking even than the horrors of Part III; as for those horrors, I believe they are so well-written that, far from being put off, the public will gobble them up. In fact the only people likely to dislike "1984" are a narrow clique of highbrows!

"1984" might well do for Orwell what 'The Heart of the Matter' did for Graham Greene (it's a much better book)[2]—establish him as a real best-seller. I know that Heinemann went all out on the latter, appealing to booksellers and critics alike to back up their 50,000 printing. We obviously can't print 50,000, but I think we ought in the next month or so to consider whether 15,000 ought not to be a minimum printing,[3] for not only do I believe in Orwell's book, I feel that with Orwell's name and *our* recently won fresh prestige in the fiction field we *can* achieve a very large subscription and a spate of publication-week reviews.

1. David Farrer joined Secker & Warburg in November 1946 and was described by Fredric Warburg as 'a key executive,' shrewd and practical. See Warburg's *All Authors Are Equal*, 72–78.
2. See Orwell's review of Greene's novel, *The New Yorker*, 17 July 1948, *3424*.
3. In fact, Secker & Warburg printed 26,575 copies on 8 June 1949 and a further 15,695 copies in that year.

3507. Avril Blair to Humphrey Dakin
14 December 1948   Handwritten

Barnhill
Isle of Jura

Dear Humph
Thanks for your letter & Henry's[1] which I return. I believe I really owed you a letter as I never wrote to condole your mother's death.

I am writing as from Barnhill though actually in London for a few days as E has decided to give up the Canonbury flat. It was becoming a liability & hasn't been used hardly at all for the past two years. So I am clearing up & purging a lot of junk & doing frantic Xmas shopping in between.

E is still far from well & is going to take some more treatment in Jan & Feb. I think they really pushed him out of hospital too soon, in the usual manner, & they made him go back for a further X-ray (which proved satisfactory) in September; a most tiring journey if you dont° feel well. He has just finished his book which he has been working at for the last eighteen months, so I think that is a relief to his mind. Otherwise we are all very fit & the farm progressing & expanding by leaps & bounds, the latest addition is a white shorthorn bull, a most docile animal—at present! Our pig was slaughtered last week & I was delighted to see the last of him as his appetite in the last few months has been more than colossal & I seemed to spend my life boiling potatoes & skimming milk for him. However he was a credit to the diet & although most of the carcase went to be baconed, we have been eating at him the whole week.

Richard Rees is keeping house while I am away so I expect hell reigns. They have so much meat on the premises that they will all be smelling like blood hounds when I get back. What happened was, that a gimmer[2] fell into a ditch & got drowned & Bill found her only just dead, so he hastily skinned & butchered her & they have, I suppose, been living on roast mutton.

Richard Rees has just bought an enormous ex-Army truck for the farm, which rather terrifies me to drive on these roads; they are so narrow that there is no room for mistakes or else one is in the ditch. However nothing untoward has happened yet.

Little Rick is very fit. He still has a strong tendency to engineering coupled with boundless energy & physical violence. I think he is bound to be a future scrum half for Scotland, especially as he is encouraged by Bill who was a terrific rugger player before he lost his leg.

Glad the family are all getting on so well. I enclose a few whatnots. I don't suppose the apron or slippers will fit Charlotte so she better have the toffee.

I had the most excruciating meeting with Aunt Nellie[3] yesterday. She steadfastly refused to eat or drink anything all day, so I couldn't, as the restaurants are too full to allow one person to sit having nothing while the other eats; so we pushed our way half fainting through crowds of shoppers while she told me that she was saving up to pay her landlord more rent because she thought she wasn't paying him enough!

We have been full up at Barnhill all summer[4] & at one point were eleven strong & overflowing into a tent. Mostly men, so dead sea fruit[5] as far as any help to me went. I am quite enjoying my few days° holiday.

Sorry that the bottom has dropped out of the pig market. Eric is very keen to have a sow next year, so I expect that my potatoe-boiling° activities will be increased ten fold.

Love to all
Avril

1. Henry Dakin, Humphrey's son and Orwell's nephew.
2. A young ewe (Scots).

3. Nellie Limouzin, Avril and Orwell's aunt.
4. See letters to Michael Meyer, 3 August 1948, and to Celia Kirwan, 16 August 1948, *3432, n. 1* and *3439*.
5. Dead Sea Fruit, or Apples of Sodom, are disappointing in that though they look attractive, 'within are full of ashes.'

3508. To Tosco Fyvel

18 December 1948   Handwritten

Barnhill
Isle of Jura
Argyllshire

Dear Tosco,
Thanks for your letter. I can't write anything. I am really very ill. I am going into a sanatorium (I think at Cranham, in Glostershire,° but it isn't completely settled yet) early in January. I should have done so two months ago, but I simply had to finish the book I was writing & which, thanks to this illness, I had been messing about with for 18 months. I am now trying to polish off the odds & ends of journalism I am committed to, & then shall drop everything for at least two months. I suppose they will have to give me more streptomycin, at any rate I hope they do, as it seems to work & is much less unpleasant than the other treatments.

Everything is going well here except me. Richard is blooming. The weather also has been beautiful for much of the autumn, but I've barely been out of the house for two months. I've given up my London flat, which was simply becoming a nuisance, but I'll have to get another one later. Please remember me to Mary & to everyone at the office.[1]

Yours,
George

1. The office of *Tribune*; Fyvel had taken over from Orwell as its literary editor.

3509. Domestic Diary

<u>19.12.48.</u>   *Have not been well enough to enter up diary. Weather for the most part has been very still, overcast, not cold, sometimes almost twilight all day. Sea mostly calm. Violent wind once or twice, but little rain. A scilla trying to flower. B. says grass has also grown in the last fortnight. Goose (for Xmas) brought back today. Also a young wild goat (female). Pig after removal of head & trotters weighed 2 cwt. (age about 9 months).*

Started new drum of paraffin. We owe about 10 galls., so that in reality we only have about 30 galls in hand.

NB. to order more almost immediately. Cylinder of Calor gas began to give out today. There must be a leak, probably in the transformer. Started new cylinder (NB. we have only 1 this time).

On the facing page opposite 19.12.48, Orwell has written, and ticked the final item:

> *Order paraffin.*
> *Order Calor gas.*
> *Get insurance stamps.*[1]
> *Order hay (1 ton)*

1. National insurance stamps, required by law, presumably for himself as a self-employed person or for Bill Dunn as Orwell's and Richard Rees's employee.

3510. To David Astor

21 December 1948   Handwritten

Barnhill

Dear David,

I am really very unwell indeed, & have been since about September, & I am arranging to go into a private sanatorium early in January & stay there at least 2 months. I was going to go to a place called Kingussie, reccommended° by Dr. Dick, but they were full up & I have made arrangements to go to a place in Glostershire.° I suppose there might be some slip-up, but if not my address as from 7th Jan. will be The Cotswold Sanatorium, CRANHAM, GLOS.

I tell you this chiefly because I feel I simply must stop working, or rather trying to work, for at least a month or two. I would have gone to a sanatorium two months ago if I hadn't wanted to finish that bloody book off, which thank God I have done. I had been messing about with it for 18 months thanks to this bloody disease. I have polished off all the reviews I promised for the Observer except two, one on Eric Partridge's book and the other on Richard Aldington's book.[1] The latter I will do & send off within the next few days, but the other I just can't in my present state. If you are seeing Mr. Rose,[2] will you please tell him that I am sorry to let him down but am really very ill. I'm afraid I.B.[3] will mark this as another black mark against me, but I just must have a good rest for a month or two. I just must try & stay alive for a while because apart from other considerations I have a good idea for a novel.[4]

Everything is flourishing here except me. The weather has been marvellous, wonderful, still, warm days with the sea an extraordinary luminous green & the bracken almost red. Spring flowers have been trying to flower in the garden. Richard is offensively well, & is out all day helping on the farm. He doesn't seem to know the meaning of ill-health or fatigue. Thank you so much for sending him the present which I expect is a Meccano. I have got him a *stationary* engine which runs by steam, & so he will be able to build a machine & run it off the engine, the same as we do with the tractor. Bobbie is here & in good form. He is bigger than the other horse, Bill's mare, & oppresses her a good deal, but she likes being with him, which I suppose shows that women like that kind of thing really. We sent our pig to be

485

slaughtered a week or two ago. He was only nine months old & weighed 2 cwt. *after* removal of the head & trotters.

I hope your little girl is well. Margie Fletcher's new baby had something wrong intestinally, but it seems to be better now. It's another boy.

Yours
George

1. These books were probably: Eric Partridge, *A Dictionary of Forces' Slang, 1939–1945,* published November 1948 (or *A World of Words,* published October 1948); Richard Aldington, *Four English Portraits,* published November 1948. See letter from Jim Rose, 20 November 1948, *3493.* It is doubtful whether Orwell was fit enough to write these reviews; certainly they did not appear in *The Observer.*
2. Jim Rose, who was arranging with Orwell what he would review for *The Observer.*
3. Ivor Brown, editor of *The Observer;* see *2520, n. 1.*
4. Probably 'A Smoking-Room Story'; see *3723–4.*

3511. To Fredric Warburg

21 December 1948   Handwritten

Barnhill

Dear Fred,
Thanks for two letters. I am really very unwell indeed & am arranging to go into a sanatorium early in January. I suppose there *may* be some slip-up, but if not my address as from 7.1.49 will be The Cotswold Sanatorium, CRANHAM, GLOS. But better consider Barnhill my address till I confirm the other. I ought to have done this 2 months ago but I wanted to get that bloody book finished.

About photos. I have none here, but I'm pretty certain I had a number at my flat, which my sister has just been closing up & dismantling. The photos will have been in a file which will be coming up here, but I suppose not for ages, as anything sent by rail takes months. I'll send you any photos I can when they arrive, but meanwhile could you try first Moore, who I *think* has one or two, & then Vernon & Marie-Louise Richards[1] who took a lot 3 years ago & should have a lot of prints if they haven't chucked them away. You could get their address from that little Anarchist bookshop near you, or from Herbert Read or others. They'd want copyright of course, but not much. They took a number, some very good, some bad—don't pick out the awful ones, will you. At need we could bring a photographer to the sanatorium, but I am really a deathshead at present, & I imagine shall be in bed for a month or so.

I'm glad you liked the book. It isn't a book I would gamble on for a big sale, but I suppose one could be sure of 10,000 any way. It's still beautiful weather here, but I never stir out of doors & seldom off the sofa. Richard is offensively well, & everything else flourishing except me. I am trying to finish off my scraps of book-reviewing etc. & must then just strike work for a month or so. I can't go on as at present. I have a stunning idea for a very short novel which has been in my head for years,[2] but I can't start anything until I am free from high temperatures etc.

Love to all.
George

1. Vernon and Marie-Louise Richards were active in the Anarchist movement; for biographical notes see *3042, n. 1* and *n. 4* respectively. They both took photographs of Orwell at his request for use in newspapers and magazines and, in 1946, photographed him with his adopted son, Richard.
2. Probably 'A Smoking-Room Story'; see *3723–4*.

3512. Domestic Diary

<u>22.12.48.</u> *Very clear, still, coldish weather the last two days. Sea very calm. One now has to light the lamps at about 3 or 3–30 pm. Today curious white streaks on the sea, presumably caused by fry milling round, but no birds taking any interest.*

8½ bales of hay left, out of 25, received nearly 2 months ago. So at this time of year 1 ton (25 bales) should last nearly 3 months, ie. for 2 milch cows & a calf.

<u>24.12.48.</u> *Sharp frosts the last two nights. The days sunny & still, sea calm. A. has very bad cold. The goose for Xmas disappeared, then was found swimming in the sea round at the anchorage, about a mile from our own beach. B. thinks it must have swum round. He had to follow it in a dinghy & shoot it. Weight before drawing & plucking, 10½ lbs.*

Snowdrops up all over the place. A few tulips showing. Some wallflowers still trying to flower.

This concludes Orwell's Domestic Diary.

3513. To Roger Senhouse

26 December 1948   Handwritten; printed heading[1]

BARNHILL,
ISLE OF JURA,
ARGYLL.

Dear Roger,

Thanks so much for your letter. As to the blurb.[2] I really don't think the approach in the draft you sent me is the right one. It makes the book sound as though it were a thriller mixed up with a love story, & I didn't intend it to be primarily that. What it is really meant to do is to discuss the implications of dividing the world up into "Zones of influence" (I thought of it in 1944 as a result of the Teheran Conference), & in addition to indicate by parodying them the intellectual implications of totalitarianism. It has always seemed to me that people have not faced up to these & that, eg., the persecution of scientists in Russia is simply part of a logical process which should have been foreseeable 10–20 years ago. When you get to the proof stage, how would it be to get some eminent person who might be interested, eg. Bertrand Russell[3] or Lancelot Hogben,[4] to give his opinions about the book, & (if he consented) use a piece of that as the blurb? There are a number of people one might choose from.

I am going into a sanatorium as from 6th Jan., & unless there is some last-minute slip-up my address will be, The Cotswold Sanatorium, CRANHAM, GLOS.

Love to all,
George

1. The printed heading is in small sans serif type and quite distinct from the large-fount italic used for many earlier letters, see 3241. In this edition they can be distinguished because the earlier heading has 'Argyllshire,' and this one, 'Argyll.'
2. For *Nineteen Eighty-Four*.
3. Bertrand Russell (1872–1970; 3rd Earl Russell), philosopher, mathematician, lecturer, and writer. Among the many causes for which he fought perhaps the most important was that for nuclear disarmament. See 3089, n. 5. See also Russell's 'George Orwell,' *World Review*, new series 16, June 1950.
4. Lancelot Hogben (1895–1975), scientist and author, first achieved distinction as a geneticist and endocrinologist but later became known to a very wide public for a series of books that introduced science and language to the general reader, especially *Mathematics for the Million* (1936), *Science for the Citizen* (1938), *The Loom of Language* (1943) by F. Bodmer but edited and arranged by Hogben in his series, Primers for the Age of Plenty; and *From Cave Painting to Comic Strip: A Kaleidoscope of Human Communication* (1949). Orwell reviewed his *Interglossa* in the *Manchester Evening News*, 23 December 1943; see 2395.

APPENDIX 1

3514. Avril Blair's Barnhill Diary

Avril Blair kept up Volume V of Orwell's Domestic Diary from 27 December 1947 to 10 May 1948, whilst her brother was in hospital. The five entries for the last days of 1947 are grouped together at 27 December 1947; see 3319. Her entries are brief and in the main restricted to the weather and the minutiae of life at Barnhill. There are occasional notes about visitors (the arrival of one, Lydia Jackson, on 26 March, may have important implications), and the hardship and inconvenience of life on Jura (for instance, the very frequent punctures) are made plain.

__1.1.48.__   *Showers of rain & high wind all day. Sea roughish.*
   1 egg (510)
__2.1.48.__   *Pouring rain all day. Wind rising at night. Very warm for the time of year.*
   2 eggs (512)
__3.1.48.__   *Showery & high wind in the morning. Calm at night. Mild.*

1 egg (513)
<u>4.1.48.</u> *Mild & calm all day. Practically no wind.*
3 eggs (516)
<u>5.1.48.</u> *Strong North wind. Periodic very heavy hail storms. Cold.*
1 egg (517)
<u>6.1.48.</u> *Bright sun & cold wind in the morning. Dull but dry in the afternoon. Sent 4 eggs to Eric.*
1 egg (518)
<u>7.1.48.</u> *Dull with cold north wind. No rain.*
1 egg (519)
<u>8.1.48.</u> *Hail stones & cold wind. Sea roughish. Cleaned the hen house in afternoon.*
2 eggs (521)
<u>9.1.48.</u> *Overcast sky & slight showers of rain. Rather cold. Started to prepare new herbaceous border.*
2 eggs (523)
<u>10.1.48.</u> *Heavy showers. High wind & torrential rain at night. George[1] overhauled the car. One headlight failed on the way home.*
1 egg (524)
<u>11.1.48.</u> *Raining on & off all day. Dark very early.*
No eggs.
<u>12.1.48.</u> *Raining & dark at first but clearing up to quite a fine day. Did all the washing.*
No eggs.
<u>13.1.48.</u> *Pouring rain all day. Mild.*
Bill & I got the byre ready for the cow. Found an almost fossilized rat among the rubbish.
1 egg (525)
<u>14.1.48.</u> *Pouring rain all day. Not cold.*
Went to Ardlussa for mail. Had a puncture.[2]
No eggs
<u>15.1.48.</u> *Beautiful day. Bright sun but cold north wind.*
Planted 100 Lilies of the valley.
1 egg (526)
<u>16.1.48.</u> *Hard frost all day. Ground like iron. Nice & fine but very cold. Sea calm.*
Gathered a sackful of firewood.
Trees arrived from Dobbie[3] also Tarpaulins etc.
No eggs
<u>17.1.48.</u> *Blowing a gale & storms of rain all day. No frost however.*
Planted the four espalier cherry trees in the morning & six fruit trees in herbaceous border in afternoon.
1 egg (527)
<u>18.1.48.</u> *Hail storms with bright sun in between. Very cold & sea rough.*
Planted remainder of trees & bushes.
Started new sack of potatoes.
No eggs

19.1.48. Hail & sleet storms. High wind & rough sea. Very cold.
 1 egg (528)   Bill shot a whitey rabbit.[4]
20.1.48. High wind & rain all day. Rough sea.
 No eggs
21.1.48. Fine day, not very cold.
 Fletchers[5] came up & shot a rabbit.
 No eggs
22.1.48. Lovely day. Bright sun with touch of frost early. Calm sea.
 Transplanted some of the flowers from Nursery bed.
 No eggs. Ian[6] brought some coal.
23.1.48. Beautiful fine day. Slightly frosty. Calm sea.
 Started to clear the yard with Bill.
 1 egg (529)
24.1.48. Lovely fine day. Rather frosty.
 Ground too hard to continue the yard.
 Fletchers came with some coal.
 2 eggs (531)
25.1.48. Fine most of the day but turning to rain at night.
 Started new cylinder of Calor Gas.
 1 egg (532)
26.1.48. Pouring rain all day.
 Did all the washing.
 1 egg (533)
27.1.48. Fine dry day with cold wind. Rough sea.
 1 egg (534)
28.1.48. Beautiful fine day. Quite mild with calm sea.
 Bill & I cleaned the barn & got rid of a lot of rubbish.
 1 egg (535). Cow arrived.
29.1.48. Beautiful day. Bright sun & no wind. Very mild.
 2 eggs (537)
30.1.48. Tearing South East Wind. Occasional showers. Very rough sea.
 1 egg (538)
31.1.48. Fine day with rather high S. W wind. Rough Sea.
 1 egg (539)
1.2.48. Fine morning but wind rising to gale in afternoon & evening.
Pouring with rain at night.
 No eggs
2.2.48. Terrific gale all day. Very rough sea.
 1 egg (540)
3.2.48. Gale still blowing. Very high wind all day & rough sea.
 No eggs
4.2.48. Much better day. Wind still high but fine periods & not so much
rain.
 Went to Ardlussa for mail. 4 galls of petrol from Fletchers.
 1 egg (541)
5.2.48. Raining most of the day with high wind. Not very cold.
 Bill & I put up the calf stall.

2 eggs (543)
6.2.48. Hail & snow storms & high wind. Rather cold.
Bill made the gate for the calf stall.
1 egg (544)
7.2.48. Occasional showers but fine on the whole. Wind rising at night.
Took Rick[7] to childrens° party at Ardlussa & saw a white mountain hare on way home.
1 egg (545)
8.2.48. Raining & misty all day with terrific gale at night.
1 egg (546)
9.2.48. Beautiful fine day with cold N.W. wind. Rather rough sea.
First snowdrops are out. Did all the washing & ironing.
A splendid drying day.
No eggs.
10.2.48. Beautiful day with bright sun. Almost warm. Calm sea.
Went to Ardlussa for mails.
1 egg (547)
11.2.48. Rather showery with high wind.
1 egg (548)
12.2.48. Fine day with a few showers. Quite mild.
Finished planting out flowers from nursery bed.
Manured the rhubarb which is showing.
3 eggs (551)
13.2.48. Fine day. Overcast but very mild.
Staked & wired the loganberries. Cleaned out the hen house & started to dig the side garden. A terrific labour as it is filled with boulders.
2 eggs (553)
14.2.48. Drizzling rain all day.
1 egg (554)
15.2.48. Fine day. Overcast but mild.
Fetched up a sack of wood from the beach & found a perfectly good hairbrush. Dug a bit more garden.
1 egg (555). Started new bag of potatoes.
16.2.48. Nice fine day. Rather cold wind.
Potatoes arrived from Robert Shaw,[8] 6 cwt. Dougie & Ronnie[9] mended the barn roof.
2 eggs (557)
17.2.48. Fine day. Calm sea. Slight frost.
Seed Potatoes & tractor wheels arrived.
No eggs
18.2.48. Lovely day with bright sun & slight frost.
Tried to start the car but found that the battery has run out completely.
1 egg (558). Put down poison for rats. Only one visibly affected.
19.2.48. Calm fine day but very cold, getting milder in the afternoon.
Bill rode the horse into Ardlussa.
2 eggs (560)

<u>20.2.48.</u> *Fine with cold North wind. Slight frost.*
  1 egg (561)
<u>21.2.48.</u> *Slight snow in the morning. Fine & cold in afternoon getting milder towards evening.*
  1 egg (562)
<u>22.2.48.</u> *A beautiful day with bright sun & quite warm. The first time this year that I have heard the birds singing.*
  1 egg (563)

No further entries until 9 March 1948 whilst Avril was in London; see Orwell's letter to Celia Kirwan, 24 March 1948, *3370.*

<u>9.3.48.</u> *Fine with very cold S. West wind. Sea rough.*
  3 eggs
<u>10.3.48.</u> *Fine but overcast. Warmer. Calm Sea.*
  Got the tractor going.
  4 eggs. Started new sack of oatmeal.
<u>11.3.48.</u> *Fine sunny day, but very cold wind. Calm sea.*
  3 eggs
<u>12.3.48.</u> *Fine calm day but still a cold wind.*
  Moved the hens.
  5 eggs
<u>13.3.48.</u> *Fine day with rather cold wind. Calm sea.*
  Crocus in full bloom. McDonalds[10] gave us a kid.
  2 eggs. Cockerel arrived.
<u>14.3.48.</u> *Beautiful day with bright sun & strong wind.*
  Bill ploughed up the patch where the hens had been, with the Iron Horse.
  3 eggs
<u>15.3.48.</u> *Stormy day with rough sea & cold wind.*
  5 eggs.
<u>16.3.48.</u> *High wind with frequent sleet showers. Cold with roughish sea.*
  Took Bill into Ardlussa & had a puncture.
  3 eggs
<u>17.3.48.</u> *Fine day with rather strong wind.*
  Ian & Malcolm arrived by boat in the evening to fetch Bill.
  4 eggs
<u>18.3.48.</u> *Strong S. W. wind rising to a gale in the evening.*
  Started the calf on bruised oats.
  6 eggs. Kid strayed away.
<u>19.3.48.</u> *Fine day with strong S. W. wind but sunny intervals.*
  Spread a little dung & dug & weeded some of the garden. Mannured° the rhubarb.
  Started new cylinder of Calor Gas.
  5 eggs (one broken)
<u>20.3.48.</u> *High wind & frequent showers of rain.*
  Malcolm & George[11] came up with the rations also my new mangle.
  6 eggs

21.3.48. *Fine day with a few showers now & then. A little warmer but wind still rather high.*
Continued the weeding.
6 eggs
22.3.48. *Nice day with fairly strong wind.*
Finished all the washing with the help of the mangle. Started to clear the yard.
7 eggs
23.3.48. *Fine with occasional showers. Wind still high & chilly.*
Still clearing the yard.
5 eggs.
24.3.48. *Beautiful day. Fine & warm.*
Finished clearing the yard. Bill returned from Glasgow.
5 eggs
25.3.48. *Wonderful day. Bright sun, no wind & quite warm.*
Planted the shallots & cleared a bit more ground.
7 eggs.
26.3.48. *Another beautiful day.*
Lydia arrived.[12] Bill & I mended a puncture & had two more on the way back from Ardlussa.
4 eggs.
27.3.48. *Beautiful day with strong wind. Sea rather rough.*
Lydia rode into Ardlussa for the mail.[13]
3 eggs
28.3.48. *Fine but wind rising towards evening.*
Still digging in the garden.
3 eggs.
29.3.48. *Rather stormy with showers of rain.*
Nearly finished the bed for the broad beans.
4 eggs
30.3.48. *Stormy day with bright intervals. Wind rising to gale force at night.*
Planted the broad beans.
5 eggs
31.3.48. *Raging gale all day with pouring rain & very rough sea.*
6 eggs
1.4.48. *Still very stormy & cold. Sea not quite so rough.*
Ian is ploughing the back field.
7 eggs
2.4.48. *Fairly fine, with intervals of bright sun But° still a strong cold wind.*
Lydia went away today.
6 eggs
3.4.48. *Frequent showers of hail & snow with high wind. Cold.*
Hay rake & harrow arrived.
6 eggs
4.4.48. *Fine day with bright sun. High wind but fairly warm.*
Cut the grass for the first time.

6 eggs.

<u>5.4.48.</u> *Very fine with again a high wind.*

3 eggs

<u>6.4.48.</u> *Wet & cold. Stormy sea.*

4 eggs

<u>7.4.48.</u> *Still beastly weather. Very cold.*

3 eggs

<u>8.4.48.</u> *A terrible day. Pouring with rain & very cold.*
Ian & George came up to mend the road & Tom McDonald for some sheep.

7 eggs

<u>9.4.48.</u> *Nice fine day. Quite warm out of the wind.*
Did a lot of gardening. Hoeing etc also some more digging.

4 eggs

<u>10.4.48.</u> *Fairly fine with several showers.*
Went to Ardlussa & had a puncture as usual.

5 eggs.

<u>11.4.48.</u> *Very fine & sunny morning, clouding over in the afternoon.*
Bill & I started to plant the potatoes, a backbreaking job.

6 eggs (1 broken)

<u>12.4.48.</u> *Misty morning change° to fine but sunless day. Very wet in the evening.*
Continued planting the potatoes & got them nearly all done.

5 eggs

<u>13.4.48.</u> *Pouring rain all the morning. A little better in afternoon but still showery. Not cold.*
Primroses have been out for some days & wild cherry tree is just starting. Too wet to finish the potatoes but did all the washing.

5 eggs.

<u>14.4.48.</u> *A really fine day. Beautiful sun & no wind. Quite warm.*
The first tulip is out.[14]
Sowed early peas & cos lettuce. Manured strawberries & raspberries. Pruned the roses.

5 eggs

<u>15.4.48.</u>[15] *Very wet misty morning clearing up in the afternoon. Finished the potatoes at last & planted Dwarf French beans in afternoon; also manured currants & gooseberries. Picked first Rhubarb.*

3 eggs

<u>16.4.48.</u> *Lovely day with quite hot sun & calm sea. Bill & I sowed the back field in the morning & harrowed it with horse & tractor in the afternoon.*

4 eggs

<u>17.4.48.</u> *Another lovely day.*
Boat arrived from Ardlussa.
Dug a trench for the sweet peas in the afternoon & started preparing herbaceous border for seeds.
Went fishing in the evening.

8 eggs 4 laid out.

<u>18.4.48.</u> *Rather wet miserable day clearing up in the evening when we went fishing but caught nothing. Bill shot a rabbit.*

  6 eggs

<u>19.4.48.</u> *Lovely fine day & quite warm.*

  Sowed the new herbaceous border with cornflowers, poppies, clarkia, godetia, sweet sultan, candytuft & saponaria.

  5 eggs

<u>20.4.48.</u> *Another fine day but a little cooler.*

  Bill went down to Lealt to do the ploughing & heard the cuckoo.

  Sowed the house bed with poppies, godetia, Escholschzia° & love-in-the-mist. Sowed the sweet peas. Broad beans sowed 30.3.48 & cos lettuce sowed 14.4.48 are up.

  6 eggs

<u>21.4.48.</u> *Lovely fine day & very warm.*

  Planted the gladioli & a border of escholchzia° & love-in-the-mist. Cut the grass.

  6 eggs. [16]

<u>25.4.48.</u> *Lovely sunny day, as hot as midsummer.*

  Peas showing. Did quite a lot of digging & weeding.

  Carted up the stobs [17] *with horse in the afternoon.*

<u>26.4.48.</u> *Miserable drizzling day.*

  Prepared nesting box & run for broody hen.

  Started new cylinder of Calor Gas.

<u>27.4.48.</u> *Raining & dark all day.*

  Set broody hen.

<u>29.4.48.</u> *Sunny day but cold North wind.*

  Went to cattle sale in Islay. Puncture on way home & had to leave the car at Lagg. [18]

<u>30.4.48.</u> *Fine day but still cold.*

  Sowed turnips & carrots & prepared bed for beetroot, trenching with sea-weed.

  Bill's father came to stay.

<u>1.5.48.</u> *Fine cold day. Sea very calm & blue.*

  Started to prepare final bed for potatoes.

  Walked over to Kinuachdrach with Bill & his father to collect the creels. Two in very bad condition.

<u>2.5.48.</u> *Lovely day but still cold North wind.*

  Everything is very dry.

  Finished bed for potatoes & planted them with some special manure. Also cut the grass.

  Bill shot a rabbit.

<u>4.5.48.</u> *Miserable wet day.*

  Furniture arrived. Made 2¼ lbs butter.

<u>7.5.48.</u> *Fine sunny day.*

  Sowed the beetroot.

<u>9.5.48.</u> *Beautiful day.*

  Cut all the grass, & made a little silo.

> *French beans just showing, also sweet peas.*
> <u>10.5.48.</u>   *Put second sitting of eggs under broody hen. New cow arrived.*

This concludes Avril's diary entries. Orwell makes the first entries in his next diary on 31 July 1948 (see *3430*).

1. George Mackay, a tractorman at Ardlussa.
2. Avril often omits the punctuation at the ends of lines, as here; full-points have been added silently where required, though not in the record of egg production, where the omission is very frequent—almost systematic.
3. Firm of nurserymen in Edinburgh.
4. A rabbit in its white winter coat.
5. Robin Fletcher and his wife (later Margaret Nelson) were Orwell's landlords. He had been a housemaster at Eton but had inherited the Ardlussa Estate, of which Barnhill was part. Mrs. Nelson's account of Orwell and life on Jura is printed in *Orwell Remembered*, 225–29. See *3025, n. 2*.
6. Ian M'Kechnie was an estate worker at Ardlussa who lived at Inverlussa. His father, Malcolm M'Kechnie, who is also referred to, had ten children and was the headman at Ardlussa.
7. Rick was the name Avril called Richard, Orwell's son.
8. A contractor who lived at Lagg, about fifteen miles south of Barnhill.
9. Dougie Clark, an estate worker for the Astors at Tarbert; Ronnie M'Kinnon, a lorry driver who worked for Robert Shaw.
10. Tom McDonald, his wife, and adopted son; Tom was a shepherd and lived at Lealt, about five miles south of Barnhill.
11. Malcolm M'Kechnie (see *n. 6*) and George Mackay (see *n. 1*).
12. Lydia Jackson (Elisaveta Fen; 1899–1983) had met Eileen Blair in 1934, when they were post-graduate students; they had remained friends, and she had lived in Orwell's cottage at Wallington in his absence. See *534A, headnote*. She stayed at Barnhill until 2 April, and it is possible that while there she typed the latter part of a revised version of 'Such, Such Were the Joys'; see *3408*. It is also possible that on her way to or from Jura, or both, she visited Orwell at Hairmyres Hospital, because that retyped version, done on the Jura machine, has some further manuscript changes in Orwell's hand. Avril, in the notes on her Diary which she prepared for Ian Angus, said that at Barnhill Lydia 'played chamber music on the battery wireless set'; she does not say whether she typed anything for Orwell.
13. In her notes on her Diary, Avril complained that Lydia Jackson 'sweated Bill's horse into a lather.'
14. Followed by 'Finished the potatoes,' which is crossed out; see *15.4.48* and *n. 15*.
15. Initially began with the first two sentences of the entry for *16.4.48*; the entry for *15.4.48* includes the item incorrectly entered at *14.4.48* (see *n. 14*). Evidently two or three days were entered at the same time and their events were confused.
16. This is the last entry in Avril's Diary which notes the number of eggs collected. She did not keep up the running total after being away from 23 February to 8 March, perhaps because she did not know how many eggs had been collected then. Those eggs apart, the running total to 21 April (including breakages) would have been 777.
17. Stake or stump (Scots).
18. Islay is the island immediately to the south of Jura; Lagg, a hamlet some fifteen miles south of Barnhill.

APPENDIX 2

3515. Orwell's Second Literary Notebook

1948

Orwell's Second Literary Notebook was written mainly or entirely in 1948 and probably during his time at Hairmyres Hospital. Six entries are notes for essays and reviews published between February and October 1948, though the last of these was marked as due by 20 July and was certainly completed within a week or two of that date. There are diary entries for March, April, and May 1948 and notes for *Nineteen Eighty-Four* which refer to that book in a near-final state. It is possible that the notes for his last book were being made about the time he was writing to friends to say he was well enough to do a little work on his novel; see letter to Leonard Moore, 12 May 1948, *3398*. The notes on language cannot be dated even approximately. The draft poem has in common with 'Such, Such Were the Joys' (*3409*) 'playing doctors' with the plumber's children (early in section iv of the essay), and 'the plumber's daughter, who might be seven, / She showed me all she'd got', when according to the poem, the speaker would have been six years old.

Diary entries and notes made in the preparation of articles and reviews have been abstracted and placed in the chronological sequence for 1948, the notes following the items to which they refer. The balance of the Notebook is reproduced here. The book measures $10\frac{1}{4} \times 8$ inches and is ruled 26 lines to a page. Orwell seems to have worked from both ends of the book simultaneously. Leaves 1–21^r include the notes for articles and reviews and also some diary entries; leaves 21^v–54^r are blank; 54^v–74^r contain notes for three sections of *Nineteen Eighty-Four* and on aspects of language; there are also three names, perhaps for a list he was to prepare in 1949 of those he suspected of being unduly sympathetic to communism (see *3732*). The inside front and back covers are also used. The list below gives the contents of the Notebook in the order in which the items occur. Items abstracted have been annotated within square brackets indicating where they are to be found in the chronological sequence. The contents descriptions below are not necessarily Orwell's.

Rough and inaccurate sketch map of Europe [inside front cover]
Sinclair Lewis—dates
Nationalist leaders and romantics of foreign origin
Continental nationalist leaders and nationalist romantics of non-foreign origin
Corruption of aesthetic standards by political motives [notes for 'Writers and Leviathan,' *3365*]
What is Communism? [notes for a review of Plamenatz's book, *3347*]
Draft of a poem
Spearhead [notes for a review of this anthology, *3381*]
British newspapers [notes for 'Britain's Left-Wing Press,' *3367*]
Diary entry, 30.3.48 [*3374*]
Hairmyres Hospital timetable [*3352*]
Diary entry, 18.4.48 [*3384*]
The Soul of Man under Socialism [notes for a review, *3396*]

George Gissing [notes for essay-review, *3407*]
Popular song titles
Diary entry, 21.5.48 [*3402*]
Things not foreseen in youth . . . [*3402*]
'The Labour Government After Three Years' [notes for this article, *3463*]
[Blank pages]
Archaic and unusual words
Examples of critical English
Borderline expressions and words
Use of foreign words
Universal sayings
Notes for *Nineteen Eighty-Four*, Part 3, Section 6
Latin, French, and other foreign-language words and phrases used in English
Notes for *Nineteen Eighty-Four*, Part 1, Section 7
Notes for *Nineteen Eighty-Four*, Part 1, Section 6
Names of two M.P.s and a journalist
Articles in preparation; Arrangements in USA [inside back cover]

Most of the people mentioned in this Notebook are well known or easily looked up, but for a few who might be less familiar brief notes are given. Orwell sometimes spelt names incorrectly; his spellings have been retained in his text but corrections are given in the notes.

The general layout of the Notebook has been preserved, but this is not a facsimile reprint and Orwell's lineation (where it is fortuitous) has not been followed slavishly. Anything within square brackets is an editorial addition; the one occasion when Orwell uses square brackets is specifically identified. Items abstracted and placed in the chronological sequence are noted, within square brackets, in their position in the Notebook. The rules from the left-hand side of the page mark the end of a page in the Notebook. The rules Orwell drew to separate the columns of foreign-language words and phrases have not been reproduced. In the main, alterations to the original (for example, moving the song-titles to a different section, as marked by Orwell) are noted, and the vagaries of Orwell's punctuation are reproduced, since these are notes, not a finished text. However, correction of insignificant errors and consequential changes of punctuation have been made silently (for example, the omission of full points from 'F.T.' when it is expanded).

It is apparent from variations in ink colour and type of pen that Orwell made entries intermittently and added to earlier entries from time to time. No attempt has been made here to describe the different colours of ink.

[Rough (and inaccurate) sketch map of eastern and southern Europe, from Italy northwards to the North Sea, eastwards to the borders of the USSR, and south to include the Mediterranean Sea. Several countries are shown misplaced and disproportionate in size: Yugoslavia is very large, Poland very small and elongated east-west, and the Black Sea much enlarged.]

<u>Sinclair Lewis—dates</u>

Free Air	— 1919
Main Street	— 1920
Babbit°	— 1922
Arrowsmith	— 1925
E. Gantry	— 1927
Dodsworth	— 1929
Ann Vickers	— 1933
It can't happen here	— 1936?
The Prodigal Parents	
Bethel Merriday	
Cass Timberlaine	— 1945?

<u>Nationalist leaders & romantics of foreign origin.</u>

Name	Object of devotion	Origin	Remarks
Napoleon	France	Corsican	Changed spelling of name.
Hitler	Germany	Austrian	Doubt about name. Un-German appearance. changed name.
Stalin	Russia	Georgian	
Parnell[1]	Ireland	English (extraction)	
Houston Chamberlain[2]	Germany	English	
Lafcadio Hearne[3]	Japan	American	
Carlyle	Germany	Scottish	?
Beaverbrook	Brit. Empire	Canadian	?
De Valera	Ireland	Portuguese? Jewish?	?
Disraeli	England	Jewish (Spanish)	?
R. Kipling	Brit. Empire England	English	Un-English appearance. Unusual origin.
M. Arlen[4]	British upper classes	Armenian	
Poincaré[5]	France	Alsatian?	?
G. Lowes-Dickenson[6] (spelling)	China	English	Little knowledge of China

Baroness von Hutten[7]	English upper classes	German?	
Little Lord Fauntleroy (authoress of)[8]	English aristocracy	American	
G. K. Chesterton	France Catholic Church	English Protestant origin	
Gobineau[9]	Germany, Nordic race?	French	?
W. Churchill	Brit. Empire England	Half-American	?
H. Belloc	France	Half English	?
J. Conrad	British Empire	Polish	v. anti-Russia
L. Trotsky	Russia	Jewish	? changed name[10]
E. M. Forster	India	English	?
Ouida?[11]	?	French?	

Anything is untrue when said by a parrot.

Cont. Nationalist leaders & nationalist romantics of non-foreign origin.

Remarks

Mazzini
Whitman
Gandhi, Nehru etc.
Mustapha Kemal
Lenin   ?
Trotsky (Jewish)   ?
Bakunin   ?

[Corruption of aesthetic standards by political motives—notes for 'Writers and Leviathan,' *3365*]
["What is Communism?"—notes for a review of Plamenatz's book, *3347*]

[Draft of a Poem]

'Twas on a Tuesday morning,
When the pants hung on the line,
The month was April or it might be May,
And the year was nineteen-nine

That
When

2
3
4

Sweet, sweet was the linewash smell,
And sweet the /April/ air,
3

                & there

We played the games that all have played,
Though most remember not,
And the plumber's daughter, who might be seven,
She showed me all she'd got.

And was it that day or another day
2
3
4

———————————

And there was also the reedy stream
2
3
4

             (several stanzas)   Round as a pudding
                                     was my face worn
But how long did that idyll last?   That now is lean
Not even so long as Spring.   & sad
I think the May was still in bloom
When I did the deathly thing.

I met those children on the road
2
3
4

But I said it, yes, I said it,
                 Russian (?)
"I mustn't play with you any more,
"My mother says you're common."

1
2
3
4

———————————

                still as uncommon (?)
As any in the land;
As solid as Gibraltar Rock

My aitches still do stand.

But since that day I never loved
Save those who loved me not (?)
3
4

Now what is the moral of this tale?
2
3
4

(Several stanzas:
I would not swing the great wheel back
My finger has not   The enemy in the looking glass
Nor faltered on the trigger
But let it be written
The world's decline
That skies were bluer & seas were greener
The stickleback had a rosier breast[12]
A bluer egg than now
               a sharper joy
When good King Edward ruled the land
And I was a chubby boy.)

["Spearhead"—notes for the review, *3381*]
[British newspapers—notes for 'Britain's Left-Wing Press,' *3367*]
[Diary entry, 30.3.48, *3374*]
[Timetable at Hairmyres Hospital, *3352*]
[Diary entry, 18.4.48, *3384*]
[Wilde (*The Soul of Man under Socialism*, 1891)—notes for review, *3396*]
[George Gissing—notes for essay-review, *3407*]

Popular Songs

[These lists are arranged in two columns on a single page; for convenience this arrangement has not been followed. Orwell's indications that three titles should be shifted to later periods have been followed; the notes give the original locations. The question-marks are Orwell's. See also 'Songs We Used to Sing,' *2868*]

<u>1900–1912.</u> Chase me, Charlie (?) Oh, do stop your tickling, Jock. Every nice girl loves a sailor. Anybody here seen Kelly (?) Little grey home in the west (?) Let's all go down the Strand. Sailing, sailing, up in an aeroplane. Who were you with last night?

<u>1912–14.</u> Yip-i-yaddy.[13] Killarney. Tipperary. Alexander's ragtime band. Everybody's doing it. Gilbert the Filbert. Burlington Bertie (?)

<u>War Years.</u> We don't want to lose you. Keep the home fires burning. Pack

up your troubles. The watch on the Rhine (when we've wound up). If you were the only girl in the world. The Yanks are coming. K-k-k-Katie. Another little drink. I don't want to get well.

Immediate post-war. The wild, wild women (?)[14] How you gonna keep 'em down on the farm. Pensylvania.° Where do the flies go? I'm getting tired of playing second fiddle. Whose baby are you, dear? Abie my boy. Ours is a nice house, ours is. Coal-black mammie (?) There's nothing sure but— I'm forever blowing bubbles. We won the war.

1920's.   I want to be happy. Yes, we have no bananas. It ain't gonna rain no more. Show me the way to go home. When it's night time in Italy. I wonder where my baby is tonight. Bye-bye, blackbird. Yes, sir, that's my baby. Maggie, yes Ma. Why did I kiss that

dates   girl? Ma, he's kissing me. I'm gonna take a water-melon. I ain't nobody's darling. Horsie, keep your tail up.

[End of first column]

1920's.   Chick, chick, chick, chick, chicken. Sonnie boy. Oh Rose Marie I love you. Tea for two.

1930–35.   I'm dancing with tears in my eyes. Danny boy. Wheezy Anna. There they go, in their joy (?) The bells are ringing for Sally (?)[15] Seven years with the wrong woman.

1935–40.   You can't do that there 'ere. I've got a feeling I've found her.
War years.   Boomps-a-daisy. Roll out the barrel.[16] There'll always be an England. Lili Marlene. Maizy doats. Oh, Johnnie, oh Johnnie. Roll me over in the clover (?)

Soldiers' songs of 1914–18.   Mademoiselle from Armentières. I don't want to join the bloody army. If you want to find the sergeant major (?) The quartermaster's store (?) So we laid down the bucket.[17]

[Diary entry, 21.5.48, *3402*]
[Things not foreseen in youth as part of middle age, *3402*]
["The Labour Gov.t after three years," *3463*]

[The notebook from folio 22ʳ to 54ʳ is blank. In the main it seems to have been entered from the centre towards the back. The four pages of phrases and words to be kept, scrapped, or substituted are all marked as being continuation pages and were presumably written up after the main section on Latin. They are in more or less alphabetical order, so were probably copied from another source.]

Archaic or unusual words used only in one cliché phrase.
Fraught (with)
(Good) trencherman
Wreak (vengeance)

Wrought
Hue (& cry)
High dudgeon

_____

Examples of Critical English

i.   Here it is asserted that at bottom "no one believes in his own death, or to put the same thing in another way, in the unconscious every one of us is convinced of his own immortality." One wonders what students of Existentialism, & particularly of Martin Heidegger's "phenomenology of death", would make of this plain denial of our human readiness to confront death, not as an idea, but as a certainty contributing to our effort to make life authentic here & now?
(Partisan Review. Review of Freud's "On War, Sex & Neurosis".)
Q. To what does the clause "not as an idea" refer?

ii   Turning, for a last comment, to the various followers either of Sutherland or of Piper, one must search in their exhibited work for the signs of lyricism *and* intelligent self-knowledge, richly pigmented self & conscientious skill within the subservience to the leading modes. It is the younger painters giving these signs who may become explicit & individual, finding real & not apparent ends. Among these, I believe that I can detect two, or even four . . . in whom love & growth may be more powerful than hate or death, who obviously disrelish the nostalgic, the art of association, & disrelish even more the art of naivety. (Geoffrey Grigson. Article on "The New 'Romanticism'",

_____

Horizon, March 1948. NB. "Pigmented" has back-reference, & the other jargon ditto to some extent. Note ambiguity of "art of naivete".)

Jargon words & phrases: Avant-garde. Kitsch. Alienated.
Disorientated (ation). Naive. Values. Rationale. Arbitrary(?)
Total values. Atonality. Ideational.

[iii]   This subordination of overt action to the amplification of intrinsic perception is a fundamental feature of the negative side of the aesthetic experience, & its explicit recognition is required, along with putting at a distance nonaesthetic interests, in any adequate description even of this side of the picture.
[Quoted in Partisan Review (in a review) from "Art & the Social Order" by D.W. Gotshalk.)

God, shod, trod, nod, rod, pod, cod, hod, wad, prod, sod, odd[,] plod

Borderline expressions & words

Ennui (pr.)[18]
Sabotage (pr.)
Propaganda (s-p)
Data (s-p)
Prestige (pr.)
Genus (pl.)
Ultimatum (pl.)
Nuance (pr.)
Impresario (pr.)

A foreign *word* (not phrase) is unassimilated, or imperfectly assimilated, when—
i.   It is still pronounced in foreign fashion, or tends to be so,
ii. When there is doubt about its plural,
iii. When it retains an accent or tends to be printed in italics.

Single words taken into English are usually nouns (cliché, démarche, dénouement, etc.), so that anglicising them amounts to anglicising plural-formation & pronunciation.

Never any case for foreign *phrases*.

Foreign *words* admissable when:
i. Already in effect part of language & merely retain traces of foreign pronunciation (prestige, sabotage, vendor, status) or plural (genus). (Merely question of regularising). (Data, propaganda—treat as singular).[19]
ii. Scientific words (plurals to be anglicised in common speech).
iii. Express some new meaning which is needed immediately & would otherwise require a circumlocution (sabotage, putsch). In this case to be taken over & anglicised at once.
iv. Useful abbreviations. i.e., Eg., etc., sic, stet.

Universal sayings.

The thing I can never understand about dust is where it all comes from.
I can remember faces, but I can't remember names.
Dogs (& kiddies) always love me.
I have long narrow feet.
I have high cheekbones.
When I sew a button on, it stays on.
(I have a keen sense of humour.)
(I can be led but I can't be driven).

[Notes for *Nineteen Eighty-Four*, Part III, Section vi]

Lay-out.

General.

Establish W. in café.
Burnt out. Meeting with J.
His life now.
Last memory of his mother.
Salvation.
W. in café. Gin. Picture of BB.
Uneasy about war news.
Drinks gin. Memory of the ——.[20] Unable to live without gin. Physical appearance.
Waiter brings chess problem.
Picture of BB. More war news. (Mental picture of map.)
White always mates.
They can't get inside you—but they can.
The meeting with J.
The telescreen.
Gin. His life now. The sinecure.
More war news?
Sudden memory of his mother. False memory.
The war news. Trumpet call. Crowds cheering.
He loved BB.

Interpolate.

Picture of BB.
Gin.
War news—telescreen

Chap. VI (to be brought in).

The war, & the Eurasian advance in W. Africa, 3 times (4?)
Chessboard. The chess problem. White always mates.
We will destroy your old self (they can't get inside you.) Burnt out: cauterised out.
He had seen her (nobody cared now).
By accident. The Park. Cold, bitter spring day. Grey earth, no birds, the tattered crocuses. Almost not greeting each other. Wandered across grass—bare-looking bushes. Microphones. Arm round waist (didn't matter now). Thickened, rigid, like a corpse. Gooseflesh. On the chairs. Her clumsy shoe—feet had grown broader. "I betrayed you." "One doesn't feel the same." Walking towards Tube station—sudden violent hallucination of his corner in the cafe. Telescreen. Tears.
Gin (3 times at least).
His life. Gin at early morning. The committee (sinecure). No suggestions ever adopted.
His physical appearance—reddened, thickened.
Two or three refs. to the —— (never named)?
$2 + 2 = 5$ (in the dust).

Picture of B.B. (3 or 4 times, & introduce early).
False memories. (Memory of his mother & the Snakes & Ladders?)
The war news. Crowds cheering outside, Too (drunk) to follow.
Feet running in imagination. Relief. (Picture of BB.) What smile under the
moustache. He loved B.B.

Latin (phrases) contd.[21]

Word	Keep or Scrap	Substitute	Remarks
Reductio ad absurdam	Scrap	Context	
Rara avis	Scrap	Rarity	
Sine qua non	Scrap	Indispensible necessity	
Sub judice	Scrap	Under judgement	
Sub rosa	Scrap	Under the rose	
Sine die	Scrap	Indefinitely	
Status quo	Scrap	Context	
Terra firma	Scrap	Solid ground	
Terra incognita	Scrap	Strange ground	
Tertius gaudens	Scrap	Context	
Via (prep.)	Scrap	By way of	
Vae victis	Scrap	Woe to the vanquished	
Vice versa	Scrap	The other way about	
Vox populi (vox dei)	Scrap	Context	
Vis inertiae	Scrap		
Ultra vires	Scrap		
Transit (noun)	Scrap		
Ex parte	Scrap		
Bona fides	Scrap	Good faith	
Bona fide (adj.)	Scrap	Genuinely	
Prima facie			

Inter alia	Scrap	Among other things	
Lapsus linguae	Scrap	Slip of the tongue	
Locum tenens	Scrap	Substitute	
Lingua franca	Scrap	Common tongue	
Magnum opus	Scrap	Masterpiece	

Word	Keep or Scrap	Substitute	Remarks
Modus operandi	Scrap	context	
Modus vivendi	Scrap	context	
Mutatis mutandis	Scrap	[22]	Meaningless
Memento mori	Scrap	Death's head	
Ne plus ultra	Scrap		
Obiter dicta	Scrap	Table talk	
Optimum (adj.)	Scrap	Best	
Pace	Scrap	Context	
Pax (Britannica etc.)	Scrap	Context	
Par (at)	Scrap[23]	Parity	
Pari passu	Scrap	In step	
Per capita	Scrap	[24]	
Pro forma	Scrap	formally (?)	
Post hoc (propter hoc)	Scrap	Context	
Persona grata		Favourably regarded	
Per se	Scrap	In itself	
Quid pro quo	Scrap	Something in return	
Nem. con.	Scrap	Unanimously	

Latin (words)			
Animus	Scrap	feeling	
Agenda	Scrap	business (?)	
Crux	Scrap	key point	
Data	Keep		treat as singular
Dictum	Scrap	saying	
(The) Ego	Scrap	context	
Forte (noun)	Scrap	Strong point	
Genus	Keep		Plural 'uses.
Gratis	Scrap	Free	
Honorarium	Scrap	fee	
Interregnum	Scrap		
Maximum	Keep		Substantive, plural 'ums
Minimum	Keep		..
Minus	Keep		
Nexus	Scrap		
Plebs	Scrap	Common people	
Plus	Keep		
Nil	Keep		

Word	Keep or Scrap	Substitute	Remarks
Plenum	Scrap		
Quietus	Keep[25]		
Quorum	Scrap		
Referendum			
Sanctum			
Sic	Keep		
Super (adj.)	Scrap	Context	
Propaganda	Keep		Treat as singular

	Latin (phrases)		
A fortiori	Scrap	All the more	
A priori	Scrap		
Ab initio	Scrap	From the start	
Ad hoc	Scrap		
Ad infinitum	Scrap	Indefinitely[26]	
Ad nauseam	Scrap	Context	
Advocatus diaboli	Scrap	Devil's advocate	
Casus belli	Scrap		
Corpus vile	Scrap	Guinea pig	
Cui bono	Scrap	Who stands to gain?	
Deus ex machina	Scrap	Fairy godmother	
Et hoc genus (omne)	Scrap	And all others like them	
Ex cathedra	Keep[27]		Papal pronouncements only
Ex officio	Scrap	In virtue of his office	
Exit (noun)	Scrap	Way out	
Exit/exeunt (verbs)	Keep[28]		As stage directions only
Dies irae	Scrap	Day of reckoning	
Contra mundum	Scrap	Against the world	
Fons et origo	Scrap	Source	
In toto	Scrap	Completely	
In vacuo	Scrap	In the void	
Ipso facto	Scrap		
(In) re	Scrap	Concerning	
Ignis fatuus	Scrap	Will o' the wisp	

Foreign words & phrases unnecessarily used in English.
N.B. that this list is not exhaustive but is intended to include only those words & phrases which would be used by people who would agree in principle that the importation of foreign words is undesirable.

LATIN.

i. Phrases & single words used in the manner of phrases.

Mutatis mutandis
Cui bono?
Fons et origo
Et hoc genus (omne)
Modus vivendi
Ad infinitum
Status quo (ante)
Exit/exeunt
Sub judice
Sub rosa
Terra firma
Terra incognita
Persona grata
Sine qua non
Ne plus ultra

Reductio ad absurdum
In toto
Sine die
Contra mundum
Ex officio
Pace
Dies irae
Via   (at)
[31]

Quid pro quo
[32]

Tertius gaudens
[29]
(In) re
[30]

In vacuo
Pax (Britannica etc.)
Vae victis
Par
Vice versa
Obiter dicta
Vox populi (vox dei)
Deus ex machina
Memento mori
Pari passu
Corpus vile
Nem. con.

Magnum opus
Transit (as noun)
Optimum (adj.)
Vis inertiae
Advocatus diaboli
Ipso facto
Pro forma
Rara avis
Ignis fatuus
Per capita
Locum (tenens)
Ad nauseam
Casus belli
Ultra vires
Inter alia
Post hoc, (ergo)
    propter hoc

Lingua franca
Ex cathedra
Ab initio
Bona fides (bonâ fide)
Prima facie

A fortiori
Lapsus linguae
A priori
Ad hoc
Modus operandi
Per se

<u>ii</u>. Single words not assimilated.

? Genus (plural)[33]
? Vortex (··)
? Apex (··)
Vacuum (··)
Plenum[36]
Quorum
  (derivation?)
Nil
Status (plural?)
Versus (v.)
Sic
Maximum (plural?)
Minimum (··)
Quietus
Sanctum
  (sanctorum)
Gratis
Honorarium
  (plural?)
Animus (··)
Interregnum
Nexus (plural?)
(The) ego
Crux
Super (adj.)

[34]
Dictum [35]
Plus
Minus
Forte ("not his forte"
  etc.)
Verbatim (?) (phrase?)
Plebs
Stratum (plural)
Referendum
Agenda
Variorum (edition)
Credo
Data

Propaganda
(Ultimatum)

87[37]

<u>iii</u>. Abbreviations:

I.E.
E.G.
Etc.
Vide
Viz.
N.B.
Pro. tem.

Infra. dig.
Verb. sap. (phrase?)
Non compos (··)
Non est
Q.E.D.
Op. cit.
Nem. con.
Stet
   (dele)
Ad lib(itum)
Sic
Ibid

---

iv. Affixes:

Anti -
Ante -
Pro -
Non -
- cum -
Trans -
Supra -
Super -
Sub -
Extra -
Infra -
Contra -
Ex - (& adj.)
Multi -
Semi -
Post -

FRENCH

i. Phrases & single words used in the manner of phrases.

Ancien régime [38]	[39]	Faute de mieux
Tête à tête	Parti pris	De haut en bas (?)
Pas seul	Pour encourager les	Double entendre
Cul de sac	autres	(phr)?
Nom de plume (N.F.)	Carte blanche	Force majeure
Nom de guerre	Chef d'oeuvre	Idée fixe
Raison d'être	Piece de résistance	Bon mot (phrase?)
Joie de vivre	Sauve qui peut (noun)	En route
Mal de mer	or phrase	Qui vive
Malade imaginaire	Belles lettres	Au fait

à la
40

avante-garde
41

Espirit de corps
42

Pied-à-terre
De luxe

Embarras de richesse
Fait accompli
Petit bourgeois
Enfant terrible
Enfant terrible
Tour de force
Roi fainéant
Noblese oblige
Hors de combat
Lèse majesté
Par excellence
Pis aller
Par excellance
De rigueur
43

Coup de Grace
Bête noire
Reculer pour mieux
  sauter
En masse
Agent provocateur

Volt-face
Impasse
Emigré
Faux pas
(Chauvinism(e))
Sabotage (?)
45

Débutante
Fiancé
Enceinte
Façade
Mystique
Métier
Parvenu
Milieu
(Nuance)

Ultimatum
44

Political words

Agent provocateur
Attaché
Démarche
Entente
Coup
Coup d'état
Fait accompli
Rapprochement
Démenti
Chargé d'affaires
Bloc
Sabotage
Mystique
Bourgeois
Putsch
Lumpenproletariat
(Chauvinism)

Military words

Aide de camp
Échelon

---

ii. Single words not assimilated:

Entrée (into)
Première
Démarche

Fracas
Aplomb
Abandon

Gaffe
Protegé
Liaison

Chassis	Pensée	Début
Chauffeur	Eclat	Char-a-banc(s)
Café	? Restaurant	(N F)
Echelon	Doyen	X Piquant
Bourgeois (ie)	Entr'acte	Savant
Massif	(spelling?).	Ennui
entente	Camouflage	Gamin
Entente	Habitué	Régime
? Entendu	Encore	Ménage
Cliché	X Blasé	Chargé d'affaires
Garage	X Distingué	X Gauche
Attaché	Roué	Aide-de-camp
Embonpoint	Poseur	Purée
46	Rapprochement	Entrepreneur
Déshabille	Démenti	Rapportage
Longueur	X Appropos (de/of)	Grande finale
Cadre	Communiqué	Penchant
Genre	Laissez(r)-faire	Bloc
Chic		X Naif (naïve)
Clientêle	Dénouement	47

OTHER LANGUAGES

Gauleiter
Panzer (division)
Zeitgeist
Kitsch
Putsch
? Flak
Lumpenproletariat
{ Kudos
{ Stasis
? { Kinesis
Dilettante
Hoi polloi
Sotto voce
Shiboleth°
Incognito
Impresario

Attachments

Establish a modus vivendi. *On the basis of the/defence of the* status quo.
Serve as the corpus vile.
Execute a pas seul. *Present with a* fait accompli. *Issue a* démenti.

[Notes for *Nineteen Eighty-Four*, Part I, Section vii]

Chap. vii

If there is hope.
Inaccessibility of the proles (81–84) (p. 116)
Lack of standards of comparison.
Extract from history book.
Greyness of most of life.
The photograph. (95–100)
Contradiction of evidence of senses.
The women shouting about the saucepans (pp. 80–81)
Why should proles revolt?
I understand *how*, not *why*.
Two & two make four.
Party's claims that all getting better & better.

Order.

If there is hope.
And yet—why shd. they revolt? Perfectly satisfied. Treatment of. (81–84, 116)
The women shouting (80–81).
Material progress—standards of comparison. *Extract from history book.*
Musings on—Greyness of life (69)—statistics.
Just once concrete evidence. The photo (95–100).
Complete fading-out of past.
Doubt of the existence of objective reality. Alone? *How—why.* Evidence of senses.[48]
No! 2 + 2 = 4.

[Notes for *Nineteen Eighty-Four*, Part I, Section vi]

Chap. vi.

The woman—2–3 times.
Katharine—stupidity of—relations with—still W's wife.
Party's attitude towards prostitution.
    ditto   sex
W's feelings—impossibility of affair with a Party woman.
Neurotic self-hatred—tendency to shout aloud—talking in sleep—the man seen in the street.

Order:

W. writing in diary—refer to woman.
Impulse to shout aloud.   Ref. Katharine here (just mention W. married).

The man seen in the street—danger of talking in your sleep.
Back to the woman.

Party's attitude to prostitution.
Katharine.
Party's attitude to sex generally. (Sex puritanism—reason for?)
W's longing for a woman of his own—(connection in his mind between
    sexuality & rebellion ?)
End up about woman.
NB. writing it down turns out not to be a relief after all.

SHORT

Tom Braddock (M.P.)[49]
Emrys Hughes (M.P.) ??[50]
Ralph Parker (journalist—News. Chron.?)[51]

Articles.

Observer (800) by[52]
P. & Letters (2000?) by June 20th[53]
Progressive (2000) by June 20th[54]

Moore's statement:
With New Yorker (including G.G. article)[55] 510 dollars   (NB. less?)
With McI. & O.[56]   475 dollars   (less abt 100).

Articles.

Commentary (3000? more?)   by July 20th[57]
Observer (600)
T.L.S. (800–1000?)[58]
Observer (600)

1. Charles Stewart Parnell (1846–1891), Irish nationalist and M.P. who, whilst successfully agitating for Home Rule for Ireland, was named as a co-respondent in a divorce suit and was disgraced, fatally damaging his political activities.
2. Houston Stewart Chamberlain (1855–1927), writer; his *Foundations of the Nineteenth Century* (1899; English trans., 1910) was a precursor of the racial doctrine adopted by the Nazis. He was Richard Wagner's son-in-law. See *2597, n. 7.*
3. Lafcadio Hearn (1850–1904), writer, translator, university teacher, was born at Levkás in the Ionian islands of Irish-Maltese parents. He lived in the United States, 1869–90, and then in Japan, where he became a citizen. He served with distinction as Professor of English at the Imperial University, Tokyo, and wrote several books on Japanese life, culture, and customs; three of his ghost stories were made into a Japanese film, *Kwaidon*, in 1965. A series of lectures he intended to give at Harvard in 1904, *Japan: An Attempt at an Interpretation*, was published in that year; he died before he could deliver them. There is no final 'e' to Hearn.
4. Michael Arlen (1895–1956), novelist and scriptwriter (in Hollywood), was born in Bulgaria as Dikrän Kuyumjian; he changed his name by deed-poll, was educated in England, and became a British citizen in 1928. His best-remembered novel, *The Green Hat* (1924), was filmed starring Greta Garbo.
5. Raymond Poincaré (1860–1934), politician; Premier of France, 1912, 1922–24, and 1926–29; President, 1913–20. He urged severe punishment of Germany after World War I; in 1923 he ordered the occupation of the Ruhr.

6. G. Lowes Dickinson (1862–1932), author and pacifist. Orwell doubtless has in mind his *Letters from John Chinaman: Being an Eastern View of Western Civilization* (London, 1901, published anonymously; New York, 1903). The 1946 edition (with other essays) had an introduction by E. M. Forster. He wrote several books on international anarchy and the causes and cure of war. As Orwell suspected, he had spelt the name incorrectly.

7. Baroness (Freifrau) Bettina von Hutten (née Riddle) (1874–1957), author, was born in Erie, Pennsylvania and educated in New York. She married Freiherr von Hutten zum Stolzenberg in 1897; was divorced in 1909. She regained her U.S. nationality in 1938 and lived in Europe from 1948. Among her many novels were a series featuring 'Pam' (whose name served as the title of the first of the series).

8. *Little Lord Fauntleroy* (1886) was written by Frances Hodgson Burnett (1849–1924). She was born in Manchester, England, but emigrated to the United States in 1865. Among her other books is *The Secret Garden* (1909).

9. Joseph Arthur, Comte de Gobineau (1816–1882), French author and diplomat. His book *The Inequality of Human Races* (1853–55; English trans., 1915) asserted the supremacy of Nordic peoples.

10. Leon Trotsky (1879–1940) was born Lev Davidovich Bronstein. He was exiled to Siberia, but in 1902 escaped to England with a forged passport in the name of one of his gaolers and was thereafter known as Trotsky. See *675, n. 1.*

11. Ouida, pseudonym of Louise de la Ramée (1839–1908), novelist and story-teller. She was born in England of a French father and an English mother. Her pen-name is a child's version of 'Louise.' She was best known for her romances, often then thought rather daring; the most popular is *Under Two Flags* (1867). From 1875 she lived in Italy.

12. The original manuscript looks very like 'breest.'

13. 'Yip-i-yaddy' originally followed 'Sailing, sailing, up in an aeroplane' in the preceding section.

14. 'The wild, wild women (?)' originally followed 'K-k-k-Katie' in the preceding section.

15. Orwell uses '(But) I'm dancing,' 'There they go,' and 'The bells are ringing' in *A Clergyman's Daughter;* see *CW*, III, 114, 157, 164, for example.

16. 'Boomps-a-daisy. Roll out the barrel.' originally followed 'You can't do that there 'ere' in the preceding section and written within brackets.

17. The final section, 'Soldiers' songs,' is separated by a rule and written across the whole width of the column. Punctuation and capitalisation have been reproduced as in Orwell's manuscript. The dates should not be relied upon. The section giving 1914–18 soldiers' songs is surprisingly thin. F. T. Nettleinghame gave the words, and sometimes the music, for nearly two hundred such songs in his two little volumes, *Tommy's Tunes* (1917) and *More Tommy's Tunes* (1918).

18. The abbreviations in parentheses can probably be explained by reference to the next section: pr. = retains traces of foreign pronunciation; s–p = plural forms in their original language but to be treated in English as singular; the meaning of 'pl.' is less certain but looks, from the example given below (genus), as if the word referred to presents difficulties in making a plural form in English: genera for genus; ultimata for ultimatum.

19. Section one has a large square bracket added later at the beginning and another at the end. The last examples (Data . . . singular) and section *iv* have been added later in paler ink. These are two examples of many indications of these lists being supplemented and modified at a later stage. Variations in ink colour are not otherwise noted. Such changes sometimes require slight consequential changes of punctuation and, if these are not significant, they are made silently.

20. The dash is Orwell's. The passage in the final text reads: 'the smell of gin, which dwelt with him night and day, was inextricably mixed up in his mind with the smell of those——' (there is no final punctuation mark); *CW*, IX, 301.

21. These headings appeared at the top of each of four pages of the manuscript; they have been repeated here only at the head of relevant pages.

22. Originally 'Context,' but crossed out.

23. Originally 'Keep,' but crossed out and 'Scrap' substituted.

24. Originally 'A head', but crossed out.

25. In light of the words and phrases Orwell proposed should be scrapped, it might be expected

that 'Quietus' would have been discarded. That he proposed it should be kept may be because it appears in Hamlet's speech beginning 'To be, or not to be': 'When he himself might his quietus make / With a bare bodkin' (3.1.75–76).

26. Originally 'To infinity,' but crossed out and 'Indefinitely' substituted.
27. Originally '(technical),' was added here but crossed out.
28. Originally '(technical),' was added here but crossed out.
29. Originally 'Nem. con. (abbreviation?),' but crossed out.
30. Originally 'Solus (?),' but crossed out.
31. Originally, one below the other, were 'Stet,' the printer's delete sign followed by '(dele),' 'Op. cit.' and 'Ad lib(itum),' bracketed together as 'Abbreviations'; all were crossed out.
32. Originally, one below the other, were 'Plenum (phrase?)' and '(Quorum (··)'; both were crossed out.
33. The words 'Genus,' 'Vortex' and 'Apex' are lightly crossed through, but the query about their plurality remains, so they have been allowed to stand.
34. Originally 'Extra (adj. & noun),' but crossed out.
35. Originally followed by '(a?),' but crossed out.
36. Originally followed by '(see phrases),' but crossed out.
37. The figure '87' is roughly written about here. It is not clear what it refers to; there are 101 items in this section.
38. 'Ancien' was originally enclosed within parentheses, but these have been crossed out. Orwell sometimes omits accents; these have not been supplied here.
39. Originally '? Femme fatale,' but crossed out.
40. Originally '? table d'hôte' and below it '? wagon lit,' but crossed out.
41. Originally 'Entrée (into)' and below it 'Première,' but crossed out.
42. Originally 'Entr'acte (spelling?)' and below it 'Démarche' and then 'Chassis,' but all crossed out. 'Entr'acte' is correctly spelt. When later Orwell enters it in section *ii*, he also queries its spelling.
43. Originally 'Hors d'oeuvre (?)' and below it 'Mystique,' but crossed out.
44. Originally 'Cadre,' but crossed out.
45. Originally 'Régime,' but crossed out.
46. Originally '? Avoir du poids,' but crossed out.
47. Originally 'Aide-de-camp,' but crossed out.
48. Originally 'objective' was written before 'existence,' but crossed out; 'Alone ? *How—why*' was written above the line and marked for inclusion. The surviving pages of the draft manuscript do not include any of the pages referred to in this section
49. Tom Braddock (1887–1976), M.P. for Mitcham, Surrey. He, and the other two, are in Orwell's List of Crypto-Communists and Fellow-Travellers; see *3732*. Orwell seemed doubtful as to whether Braddock should be included because in his column for remarks he has two question marks. Cf. *ns. 50* and *51* below.
50. Emrys Hughes (1894–1969); in Orwell's list (see *n. 49* above), he notes that Hughes was M.P. for Ayrshire, editor of *Forward*, and that he 'Votes with crypto group.' Under Remarks he wrote '? Probably not. Well-meaning, wrong-headed.'
51. Ralph Parker (1908–1964). In Orwell's list (see *n. 49* above), he queries Parker's first name (it is correct) and notes his work as: 'News-Chronicle (Moscow Correspondent 1947). Also Times. "Moscow Correspondent" (1949). "Plot Against Peace" (pub. Moscow 1949.)' Parker also wrote from Moscow for the *New York Times* in 1942. Under Remarks, Orwell wrote: 'Underground member or close F[ellow] T[raveller] ? Stayed on in Moscow (became Soviet citizen.)' The correct title of the second book Orwell mentions is *Conspiracy Against Peace: Notes of an English Journalist*. Parker published later books in Moscow and *Indonesian Impressions* (New Delhi, 1955). He was actually *The Times's* correspondent 1942–47 and thereafter for the *News Chronicle, Daily Worker, New Statesman*, and *Times of India*. Though a Soviet propagandist, he could be critical of the Soviet Union. His special knowledge of literature and theatre led to his becoming the New York impresario Sol Hurok's representative in Russia. He was accused of spying on British diplomats. Parker died in the small village near Moscow where he lived.
52. It is not possible to identify which articles or reviews were intended for *The Observer*. The first *Observer* entry in the second group has been ticked.

53. 'Writers and Leviathan'; see *3364*. For *ns. 54*, *57*, and *58*, see also *3363*, *n. 1* for the problems of identifying the articles Orwell wrote at this time.
54. 'Britain's Left-Wing Press'; see *3366*.
55. Orwell's review of Graham Greene's *The Heart of the Matter*, 17 July 1948; see *3424*. He had reviewed *Lady Gregory's Journals*, 19 April 1947; see *3218*. The sum of $510 presumably is for both reviews and was calculated before payment for the Greene review; $510 was then about £126.50.
56. McIntosh & Otis, Orwell's agents for his journalism in the United States.
57. 'The Labour Government After Three Years'; see *3462*; this entry has been ticked.
58. Either the review of *Spearhead*, 17 April 1948 (see *3380*)—which fits the dating well but is much longer than the estimated word-length and follows two items listed with it to be completed in June and July—or the review of *The Novelist as Thinker*, 7 August 1948 (see *3436*)—which is the right length (820 words) and follows in the list the items for June and July and precedes a review published on 2 October of 570 words (for which Orwell allowed 600 in his list); see *3465*.

INDEX

Volume XIX

This is an index of names of people, places, and institutions, and of titles of books, periodicals, broadcasts, and articles; it is not (with a very few exceptions) a topical index. However, topics discussed in his column 'As I Please', are listed alphabetically under this title in the Cumulative Index in Volume XX. This index lists titles of books and articles in the text, headnotes and afternotes; incidental references to people and places are unindexed. In general, references to England and Britain are not indexed nor are the names of authors and books significant to an author being reviewed but not necessarily to Orwell. Inhabitants of countries are indexed under their countries (e.g., 'Germans' under 'Germany'). Numbered footnotes are indexed more selectively; for example, books listed by an author who is the subject of a footnote are not themselves indexed unless significant to Orwell.

Orwell's book titles are printed in CAPITALS; his poems, essays, articles, broadcasts, etc., are printed in upper and lower case roman within single quotation marks. Book titles by authors other than Orwell are in italic; if Orwell reviewed the book (in this volume), this is noted by 'Rev:' followed by the pagination and a semi-colon; other references follow. Both books and authors are individually listed unless a reference is insignificant. If Orwell does not give an author's name, when known this is added in parentheses after the title. Preparatory Notes for articles have been abstracted from Orwell's Second Literary Notebook (3515) and placed immediately after the articles to which they refer. Articles and broadcasts by authors other than Orwell are placed within double quotation marks. Page references are in roman except for those to numbered footnotes, which are in italic. The order of roman and italic is related to the order of references on the page. Editorial notes are printed in roman upper and lower without quotation marks. If an editorial note follows a title it is abbreviated to 'ed. note:' and the pagination follows. First and last page numbers are given of articles and these are placed before general references and followed by a semi-colon; specific pages are given for reviews of books reviewed as part of a group. The initial page number is given for letters. Punctuation is placed outside quotation marks to help separate information. Salutations in letters to relatives and friends are not usually indexed. Items in two languages are indexed from the English version. In Orwell's Domestic Diary 'R' may stand for his son, Richard, Richard Rees, Robin Fletcher, or Tony Rozga; 'I' may stand for Inez Holden or Ian M'Kechnie. They are indexed under 'R' and 'I' unless identification is reasonably sure.

Letters by Orwell, and those written on his behalf, are given under the addressee's name and the first letter is preceded by 'L:', which stands for letters, memoranda, letter-cards, and postcards; telegrams are distinguished by 'T:' to draw attention to their urgency. If secretaries sign letters on Orwell's behalf, they are not indexed. Letters from someone to Orwell follow the name of the sender and are indicated by 'L. to O:'. References to letters are given before other references, which are marked off by a semi-colon. Letters in response to Orwell's are indicated by (L) after the respondent's name and/or the page number; if they are summarised this is shown by 'sy'. Letters to journals arising from Orwell's contributions are indexed immediately after the item to which they refer; the name of the correspondent (and first page of the letter) follow the indication 'corr:'. These letters are also indexed under the names of the correspondents and indicated by '(corr.)'. References to Orwell, except in correspondence following his contributions to journals, are listed under 'Orwell, refs to:'.

Items are listed alphabetically by the word or words up to the first comma or bracket, except that Mc and M' are regarded as Mac and precede words starting with 'M'. St and Sainte are regarded as Saint.

Three cautions. First, some names are known only by a surname and it cannot be certain that surnames with the same initials, refer to the same person. If there is doubt, both names are indexed. Secondly, the use of quotation marks in the index differs from that in the text in order to make Orwell's work listed here readily apparent. Thirdly, a few titles and names have been corrected silently and dates of those who have died in 1997 (after the page-proofs of the text were completed) are noted in the index.   P.D.; S.D.

Index

Index

Index

Index

Index

Index

Index